Broken Trilogy

J.L. Drake

Broken Trilogy

Copyright © 2015 by J.L. Drake.
All rights reserved.
Second Print Edition: September 2017

Limitless Publishing, LLC
Kailua, HI 96734
www.limitlesspublishing.com

Formatting: Limitless Publishing

ISBN-13: 978-1-68058-991-7
ISBN-10: 1-68058-991-1

Table of Contents

Broken

"You can always fall
Savannah, because I'll be
the one catching you."
~Cole Logan

broken

BROKEN TRILOGY
BOOK ONE

J.L. DRAKE

Prologue

Deceit
Deception
Dishonest
Distortion
Fiction
Myth
Tale
Fib

…any way you say it, it means the same thing…lies.

Chapter One

I don't know how long I've been here—four months, possibly five. Time passes in strange ways when you have no means to mark it. At first, I counted time by the meals I received, but after a while they became fewer and less dependable. I know for sure I've been here one full season. The men went from wearing long sleeve shirts to t-shirts.

My prison is a small room with a rusty bed that squeaks whenever I shift position. A tiny wooden table with a small stool takes up one corner, and a toilet and sink hide behind a ratty curtain in the other. No windows, no TV, nothing to read but an old copy of *Wiseguy* by Nicolas Pileggi. I wasn't one for reading crime novels in the past, but I can recite every single word by heart now.

I hear the familiar sound of the key retracting the lock, and my stomach sinks. I pull at my ratty sweater, wrapping it around my midsection a little tighter—like that is going to help protect me from them.

I hear his boots scuff on the hardwood, and sweat breaks out along the back of my neck. *Shit, it's him.* My skin crawls when I see his sausage-like fingers holding a tray of food for me. His hairy stomach pushes out below his t-shirt and bulges over the top of his jeans. As soon as he spots me, he gives me his lopsided smile.

"*Hola, chica.* How are you today?" His voice is raspy and his accent thick, but I understand every word. His body language is enough in itself. "I asked you a question," he barks at me.

"Fine," I say through the lump in my throat.

He stands holding the tray above me. Finally, I raise my eyes to meet his, and he smirks, showing me how much he enjoys having this power over me. I've had enough encounters with this man to know he won't leave without wanting something in return. Luckily, up until now, it's never been anything sexual—just more head games. That doesn't mean he's never insinuated it. I tremble, shaky fingers pulling at the hem of my cotton nightgown that reaches mid-thigh. I don't need to give him any ideas. His gaze drops to my legs, and he licks his lips.

"Beg," he orders, drawing out the word.

My mouth goes dry. He loves this part. I am an animal to him. He calls me his *perra*, which means dog in Spanish. My temper rises as I try to tell myself to stop, but I can't help it. I am past caring anymore.

I give him the sweetest smile I can muster. "Screw you." I've never spoken more than I absolutely had to since I got here, and suffice it to say, he is blown away by my choice of words. Normally, I do what I'm told while secretly fantasizing the many ways I'd like to kill this man. I try to behave, never wanting to relive my first few days here. The incredible pain after they beat me to a bloody pulp when I didn't do what was asked made me wise up quickly.

My present adrenaline high is short-lived, however, as I watch his eyes narrow and his jaw tighten. He suddenly tosses the tray across the room, shattering the dishes against the wall.

"No food for you, *lengua de mierda*!" he hisses, taking a step toward me. I cover my ears and tuck my knees up to my chest. This man is large enough to pick me up in one hand and toss me across the room, duplicating the tray's fate. He grabs a handful of my hair and drags me, my knees bouncing along the floor like a rag doll. I barely register the pain—I am more aware that this six foot, three hundred seventy-five pound man is hovering over me, enraged. Why did I have to get smart? The only thing I have going for me is they haven't killed me yet. Maybe I am being held for ransom. It's no secret my father has a lot of money, and everyone knows his name—he is running for a second term as mayor of New York City.

I try to force myself up onto my hands, but his boot crushes down on my back, forcing me down hard. My forehead smacks against the floor, and my ears ring. I let out a whimper as my eyes focus on something just out of reach. I hear the sound of him removing his belt, and my heart quickens. No, no, no! This can't be happening. If I could just move a few feet to the right…I muster up all I have and launch myself forward along the floor.

"Where do you think you're going?" His voice is calm—oh, so calm. My fingers wrap around the broken piece of plate, and I tuck my hand under my chest to hide it. "Come." He bends down, grabbing my feet and flipping me over, and drags me back toward the bed. I scream in protest. I kick and wiggle, but his grip is too tight. "Feisty little thing, aren't ya?" he chuckles.

He leans over me, and I take my opportunity. I shoot upward, driving the sharp piece of glass into his neck. His eyes go wide with shock, and he falls to his side with a loud thud, cursing and digging at the object. I scramble to my feet and head for the open door.

I have no idea what direction to go, but I don't care. For the first time in forever I am free of that room. I move as fast as my feet can take me. I'm low on sugar and my head feels light, but I keep going—this is my chance. Physical activity has not been a part of my world for so long it is hard for my brain to wait while my legs try desperately to keep up.

The hallway is long with lots of doors, the wallpaper is ripped in places, and the lighting is low. It looks like an abandoned hotel, but where are the windows? I keep winding around corners, holding myself upright against the walls as my knees grow weak. I have no sense of direction; every hallway looks the same. I hear voices getting louder, and my heart is in my throat. I try pulling and pushing on the closest door handle, but it doesn't budge. Stinging tears race down my cheeks. Panic is kicking in, and sobs overtake me. I fight them back, but I feel I'm letting myself down. I have a chance to escape, and I can't even open a goddamned door! A heavy click followed by a humming noise makes me freeze. Then the lights flicker and go out.

I cover my mouth to stop the screams as my hands shake violently along with my teeth. I press my back against the door for support. A bright flicker off to the left draws my eye, but it quickly dies, replaced by a dull orange glow. Someone is standing about ten feet from me, smoking a fat cigar. I close my eyes and say a silent prayer. When I open them again, I'm met with a mean set of eyes inches from my face. I am unable to move. I know this man. I've seen him a few times before, and I think he runs this place. He puffs away, filling my nose with the nauseating scent of his Montecristo. I'd know that smell anywhere. My father often had parties, and they seemed to be the most popular cigar among his guests.

My knees weaken as he continues to stare silently at me. I hear his shoulder shift in his jacket as his hand comes up and grips my chin tightly. With casual ease, he flicks open and ignites his Zippo, holding it up to inspect the growing lump above my eye. The light goes out, and

I feel his vise-like grip move to the back of my neck as he pushes me to move forward. He obviously knows the building well, since it is still pitch black and he directs me without hesitation. All I can hear is my hammering heartbeat and my short, ragged breaths.

Finally, we stop at a door, and he pushes it open and tosses me inside. I stumble forward and fall to my knees. Suddenly, the lights come on, and I come face to face with the fat man, whose neck is now wrapped in a white bandage. He holds his belt in his hand, snapping it for more effect. The last thing I remember is being pushed onto a couch and the first crack of the belt along my lower back. This kind of pain I'll never forget; it is permanently embedded in my memory. Thankfully, I slip away into a blissful place, one I welcome with open arms.

I wake to blinding pain, the smallest movement causing me to sob, which in turn hurts even more. My brain is cloudy. I can barely form a thought; even breathing is tricky. It takes me a few moments to realize I am back in my prison lying face down on the squeaky bed. I let go and allow the tears to flow. I need something to think about, something to focus on. I remember the first day I came here. Christ—it seems so long ago.

***

"Hello, my love," I purr to my Keurig as I place my beloved mug, which reads "Don't talk to me till this mug is empty," underneath and push the button. My friend Lynn gets a kick out of the fact that I can't function until I have at least one large cup of coffee in me. She bought this mug for my twenty-sixth birthday. It was tucked inside a basket she had done up along with an airline ticket to Fiji for the two of us to escape my crazy world.

Man, what a trip that was. I hear my front door open.

"You're in for it now, Savi!" Lynn shouts as she comes into my kitchen. She holds up a magazine, showing me the cover. As soon as I read the caption, I know I'm in shit.

"Oh, no!" I snatch it from her fingers.

"Oh, yes," she sighs, passing by and opening a cabinet. "So, I take it he hasn't called you yet?"

I shake my head as I study the picture in horror. Us Weekly *has a picture of me at a bar last night, leaning over a table and showing off my behind. The caption reads "Mayor's Daughter Reveals All."*

"I was reaching for my purse!" I shout. "It isn't even my butt—this has been Photoshopped."

"I know that, but will Daddy dearest believe you?" She sips her coffee, eyeing me with concern. "Maybe you should call him first. It might look better if you do."

Lynn and I have been friends forever. We met in middle school the day we got stuck in detention for running our mouths and have been fast friends ever since. She rode the wave of fame and publicity right alongside me. She is my rock as I am hers, and we both consider ourselves the sisters we never had. Perhaps she has a point. I toss the magazine aside, reach for my purse, and pull out my cell. Three rings later, I hear his voice.

"Dad. How are you this morning?" Silence grows on the other end of the line. "You there?"

"Any reason why I'm staring at my daughter on the front cover of yet another popular magazine?"

Shit! Shit! Shit!

"Dad, look, you know I haven't been out much. I've been so careful after what happened last year. But this isn't what it looks like—"

"Save it, Savannah. Do you have any idea what kind of damage you cause me? I have three people working

on this, wasting their time on this crap!"

"Dad, please let me explain—"

"No, Savi, we'll discuss it tomorrow night at dinner."
The line goes dead.

I toss the phone on the counter and rub my face with both hands. Lynn touches my back gently, giving me a few moments to process everything. I sigh and run my hands through my hair. Lynn moves in front of me, getting me to look at her.

"Come on, Savi, let's get out of here."

After a hot shower, I start to come around a little. I pull on my favorite navy blue dress with black boots and a black pea coat.

"Okay, okay, stop fussing," Lynn groans from my door. "You look fine."

"If I end up looking like I have a hangover and the media finds me, you know they'll have a ball with the story."

She grabs my shoulders and looks at me in the mirror. "Who cares what anyone thinks, Savi? Anyone who knows the real you knows you have a heart of gold...and a quick tongue to put people in their place." She grins. "What's not to love?"

"I am pretty great," I joke.

We link arms as we walk out the door. We have to sidestep two painters outside in the hall, and as I push the button on the elevator, I glance at one of the men. He's wearing a massive belt buckle that reads 'Texas' with a longhorn head sticking out of the center.

"He's a long way from home," I mutter.

Lynn shakes her head. "Oh, please." She laughs, noting the direction of my gaze. "They're a dime a dozen at any market." She hustles us into the elevator. I sigh, not eager to face the outdoors.

"Ready?" She slips on her sunglasses.

"I guess so."

"Stop worrying, Savannah," Lynn says through a bite of her bagel. "Your dad will get over this. You know how he is."

"I know. I just hate disappointing him, especially over something like this, and I've been so careful." I think about the last time I made it on the cover of a magazine. I tripped over some drunk and fell flat on my face. It made a great story for the tabloids, and made an even bigger stink with my father. Everything is about image in the public eye, and I am just plain sick of it all. The idea of another four years is enough for me to run screaming for the hills.

"You got plans tonight?" Lynn asks as she tosses her napkin on her plate.

"Yeah, I have a dinner thing for work I have to attend. We're trying to win over another new client."

She makes a sour face. "Sounds...fun." Lucky for Lynn, she works her own hours as an artist in her own studio, while I work for a big marketing corporation. Even though I worked my butt off in school for years, I still feel like they use me for my connection to the mayor to gain clients.

When my mother passed away six years ago after a long battle with cancer, I was mentally and physically exhausted. I changed my last name to her maiden name when my father got more involved in politics. I didn't want people knowing who I was right off the bat. My father didn't understand at first, but now I'm sure he's fine with it. I just needed time and privacy to get on with my life and to get over my grief.

Later that evening, I find myself lost in thought instead of paying attention to the conversation around me. Here I am at another fancy dinner with beyond boring executives, who are talking about nothing remotely interesting. They hardly engage me in conversation and never ask for my opinion. I sit there *and try not to show what I'm thinking. Like how Mr. Roth's tie keeps dipping into his soup, and how his wife pretends not to notice. She keeps trying to hide her smirk—I take it they don't get along very well at home. At least this is a tad amusing. I shift my gaze out the window to Central Park. Oh, what I wouldn't do to go for a run through the snowy paths right about now.*

"*Wherever you are, can I join you?*" *Joe Might asks, leaning over so only I can hear him.*

"*I'm sorry?*"

He smiles. "*You look like you were off somewhere else.*"

Oh. I am embarrassed, caught daydreaming by our hopefully soon-to-be client. This doesn't look good for me.

"*I'm so sorry.*" *I wrinkle my nose, embarrassed to no end.* Nice one, Savi!

"*Don't be.*" *He pulls his hand out from under the table and shows me the phone he's been using to play online poker. I try to hide my laugh; he grins and shrugs.* "*We all know it's a done deal, right?*"

"*I guess so, huh?*" *I say with a sigh.* "*I just wish I could get something stiffer.*" *I point to my glass of Pinot Grigio. I don't drink, as a rule, but this dinner is painful. He winks at me before he clears his throat.*

"*Excuse me, gentlemen, but I need to have a word with Miss Miller.*" *Before I know what is happening, he pulls out my chair and helps me to my feet, walking me through the dining area and out the front door. He hands the valet his ticket, and moments later I'm sitting on the tan, plush seat of his red Corvette.* "*Now.*" *He grins.* "*Let's see about getting you something stiffer—to drink, that is.*" *All I can do is nod like a moron.*

After a few drinks at a Scottish pub, I decide I should get back before I get in any more trouble with the press. There is only the bartender and a lone man in the corner, but Lord knows they'll have a field day if they find me in another pub after what happened last night.

"Let me drive you back to your car, at least," Joe says, standing to shrug on his jacket. He is a handsome man. His gel-styled brown hair and light eyes are a pretty combination. I guess he's in his mid-thirties.

"That's not necessary. I can take a cab."

"Nonsense. I stole you away, so it's only right I return you too." He gestures toward the door. "Is your car at work?"

I shake my head as I slip my purse over my shoulder. "A friend dropped me off this morning."

"Home, then?"

I nod as we walk outside. The ride is nice. He offers more information about his company and asks a few questions about my position.

"So, you'll fax me those samples as soon as you can?" he asks as I duck down to say goodbye through the open window.

"Yes, I will. 'Night, Joe. Thanks for the fun evening— and the ride." I walk toward my condo, deciding to grab the necessary file now rather than tomorrow.

I prop myself against the wall in the elevator, tired and anxious about how my day started. The idea of disappointing Dad again is weighing heavily on me. It seems to be a weekly event. Either it's the media or merely something I say or do around him. God, I really miss my mother! She was so sweet and understanding. She wouldn't have cared if I wore the wrong outfit to lunch or said the wrong thing during a business dinner. Christ, I'm only human. I never wanted to be a part of the public eye in the first place—never once!

I step out to a quiet parking lot. Luckily, my car is parked close by, as my feet are getting sore in my high boots. I open the trunk, reach for my laptop case, and suddenly sense someone is behind me. I start to turn, but a dark cloth is slapped over my face. A hand covers my mouth so I cannot scream. My feet leave the ground as I'm flung over someone's shoulder, and something cold and hard strikes my shin. Fear courses through my veins, and the air is forced out of me as my attacker tosses me roughly into the back of a vehicle. I feel the movement as we speed away. I can't believe this is happening! I am terrified out of my mind.

Someone makes fast work of binding my wrists and ankles. I can make out only shadows around me, and hear male grunts and heavy breathing. Fear has taken over, and I seem to have lost my ability to speak. Someone grips my shoulders, pinning me, while another stretches out over top of me. With all my might, I buck my legs up and nail one of them in the crotch. His screech is ear-piercing as he falls back, then I feel the poke of a needle, and everything gets fuzzy.

That's all I remember from the last day I spoke to my father, my best friend, my coworkers, and since I saw the light of day.

Chapter Two

I attempt to roll off the bed, as I have a horrible case of cotton mouth and desperately need water. My knees buckle as I start the trek to the sink. Normally, my prison room seems so small, but right now it feels like I am a hundred yards from the wall. I must have taken quite a beating; I hurt everywhere.

Finally reaching the sink, I grab the rusty tin container. Water never tasted so good. I wet my lips and let it trickle down my throat before collapsing into a painful ball. I begin to sob, knowing I'll never get out of here. I can only imagine how bad my back looks. It feels wet and burns terribly, my head is throbbing, and my wrists feel tender. He must have tied me up during…my stomach drops. I slowly move my hand down to the hem of my nightgown and pull it up. I let out a small hiss of relief when I see I still have on the same panties as yesterday. My outsides may be damaged, but the rest of me remains, at least for the moment, undefiled. But emotionally, I am spent. My hands cover my face in sudden defeat as I lie on the floor to think. I've been treated like something less than a barnyard animal for way too long. My captors never seem to tire of their sick power trip over me. I'm sure it brings them endless amusement. I get a bath once in a while, during which they take plenty of photos and videos. I have a toothbrush, which has grown disgusting, and a bar of soap, which is down to a small nub. My food, when they decide to feed me, is some kind of soup and crusty bread. The water is always warm, with flakes of dirt in it.

Occasionally, a doctor is brought in to check me over, and twice I had to get IV fluids pumped into me. I was more concerned whether the needle was clean than what they were putting inside me. Once, I tried to ask the doctor for help, but he acted like he didn't understand me. I know he did, because when I mentioned home, he flinched and wouldn't make eye contact. All I got was a jab in the ribs from one of men and shouted admonishments in Spanish for attempting to talk.

My only choice will have to be starvation. I've decided I'm done, and at least my death will be under my control.

I hear footsteps outside my door. At the click of the lock, my body automatically starts to tremble. Sure enough, the fat guy returns with my tray of food. He drops it loudly on the table then glares at me.

"Sore?" he asks with a laugh. I want to lunge at him and jab another piece of plate into his neck. Next time I'll remember to pull it back out and continue until the fat bastard is dead.

"No, you?" I hiss back. Really, what do I have to lose? His face drops and his hand jerks to touch his neck, but he stops himself. He picks up my water glass and pours it out on the floor, and continues to do the same with my soup and bread as he watches me with an insolent smile. A few days ago, I would have been heartbroken, but today it plays right into my decision, and I smile back. *Fuck you.*

A few hours later, I hear the familiar key in the lock. The lights are dim, so I can't see very well. Someone brings a new tray. I hear it scrape on the floor as he puts it down. He moves toward my bed. I smell the familiar aroma of Montecristo and know it is the man with the cigar.

"You need to eat," he says sternly. I don't move. I just lie there, feeling completely defeated. He reaches over and chucks a piece of bread at me. It bounces off my shoulder. "Eat, *perra.*" He leaves, slamming the door behind him.

After some time, I finally move over to the tray and nearly vomit when I see the same meal I've been fed for lunch and dinner for God knows how long—a watery beef stew. Knowing these guys, it's probably rat or possum. It helps reinforce my choice not to eat. I take a sip of the water, and some grit slides down my throat. I cough, choking down the rising bile, and stumble back to bed.

Five more meals are brought to me, five meals that stay untouched. Although my body begs me to eat, my willpower doesn't falter. Needless to say, I feel like shit.

My mother visits me often to whisper words of encouragement. I know it is only my mind's way of coping with starvation, but on some level, it brings me joy to see her again. She is just as I remember—long, dark hair, perfect teeth, and dark eyes. Her touch is so real I can feel the heat from her hand on my face.

"I love you, Savi. You know that, right?" she says. "I'm here for you." She touches my chest right over my heart. "My little angel."

I pull my knees up to my chest and sob as the memory fades.

I wish I were capable of love like that now. Love and trust were things I'd promised myself I would never give away. I've been tested many times, only to be betrayed over and over. It is always a trap. They can have my body, but I will be damned if they will get my soul.

I'm lying in bed, staring at the ceiling, watching it fade in and out of my blurry vision, when I think I hear a popping noise followed by loud shouts. If I were in a clearer frame of mind, I may have understood what was going on, but in my present state, I don't really care.

A series of events seems to happen all at once. There is a loud bang, my door flies open, and a bright light moves all around the room. A man dressed completely in black with a helmet and goggles draws closer. It takes considerable effort, but I roll my head over to face him. The light flashes over my face, making me squint. He pauses for a moment, then shouts something into a radio on his neck. He reaches forward to lift me out of the bed. I groan as his hand grips my back. I don't know if I am dreaming or not, but I don't seem to be able to take it all in. My brain isn't functioning properly.

The man holds me tightly as he carries me down a long hallway. There are a few other men in front of us, dressed in the same black outfit, guns raised and ready to fire. I am so tired, but now I'm wide awake and afraid if I close my eyes I will find myself back in that room again, alone. We travel down a long staircase toward double wooden doors that look to have been blown open. I don't seem to be able to speak; I'm still afraid I'm dreaming.

The air is cold, and it is dark and feels like it might rain. This has to be real. I feel moisture on my face, and the fresh, cold air is so wonderful. I want to cry with the pleasure of it. Three black SUVs are waiting out front. I am placed in the middle vehicle, followed by the man who carried me and three others, including the driver, a man in the front passenger seat, and one in the back facing the opposite direction.

I am quickly fastened in and have a blanket wrapped

around me. The first thing that comes to mind is how clean the blanket smells. We travel away from the building. I have no strength, and my head seems to have a life of its own, bouncing around until it finds a comfortable bump on the blanket. I watch the driver's hands slide over the wheel, perfectly calm. After we are a good distance away from the house, the man who carried me tears off his goggles and helmet. He runs his hand through his black hair and looks over at me. I am surprised to see that he appears to be only a few years older than I am, maybe early thirties.

"Savannah? You're okay now. You're safe," he says quietly in a steady voice.

I just stare at him. I heard what he said, but it doesn't seem to register in my brain. I am still afraid to believe I am really rescued from my prison. Perhaps this is only a nasty trick.

He studies my face for a moment then reaches over. I flinch, closing my eyes momentarily. He pulls his hand back but points at my forehead. "Looks like that hurts. Are you all right? Do you hurt anywhere else?"

I want to tell him about my back, but I am still unable to speak.

"The jet is standing by, sir," the driver says into the rear view mirror.

The man beside me nods. "Good. Tell them we're ten minutes out."

"Yes, sir."

I start to feel dizzy. The lack of food has taken a toll on me. I flop my head against the window and watch as tiny raindrops make paths down the glass. I don't recognize anything. Houses and streets look different, and nothing makes sense. I wonder where I am and where I'm going.

Again, I feel the rush of cool air as I am lifted out of the car. The rain is cold but feels wonderful as my head bobs against my carrier's shoulder. I have no strength left. The raindrops bounce off my face, sweeping away some grime.

If this is a dream, it is the best dream ever.

I am placed on a warm leather couch inside an airplane and watch as ten other men dressed in black board and take their seats. They look like SWAT or something. My vision is getting very fuzzy, and I am so tired.

"Stay with me, Savannah." The voice comes from beside me. I force my eyes open to see my carrier looking down at me. His incredibly dark gaze holds on to me for a moment. A voice sounds over a speaker, and within a matter of minutes, I feel movement, and my carrier is gone from sight. My eyes grow heavy again with the hum of the plane. I have fought sleep for as long as I can. I feel myself sliding down into the void, and my last conscious thought is how I usually hate flying.

***

The calming sound of rustling leaves brings me back to consciousness. I move my head slightly, rubbing my cheek against the softest pillow ever. I smell the faint fragrance of fresh roses. Can this be right? My eyes flutter open, blinking a few times to take in the soft sunlight that fills the room. A wall made up of large windows with three doors that open to a balcony is on one side. An ivory curtain flutters in the breeze, wafting the floral scent of the roses in a glass vase to my eager nostrils. I feel a tug on my arm and realize I have an IV attached to my left wrist. The bag hanging from a pole next to me is almost empty. I take in the queen size sleigh bed with its amazingly red sheets and a duvet that feels like heaven. I am overwhelmed and close my eyes, drifting back to sleep.

***

When I regain consciousness, it's dark, my fluid bag has been changed, and someone has lit a fire in the stone fireplace. The lovely sound of crackling wood almost brings me to tears—it is beyond soothing to my soul. Is this heaven? If so, I'm completely fine with being dead. I hear a creaking sound and freeze.

A door opens off to my right. An older lady, maybe in her fifties, wearing slacks and a blouse, comes in holding a tray. I start to push myself up into a sitting position, but *oh, God, everything hurts.* Sadness washes over her face.

"Oh, no, dear." Her voice is soft. "Please, I'm not here to hurt you. I've been taking care of you for three days."

My mind goes blank. *Three days!* I pull my knees up to my chest and wrap my arms around them, flinching. The pain is another reminder of the hell I've been through.

"Please." She sets the tray down on the table and raises her hands. "My name is Abigail. I didn't mean to scare you. I know you've been through a lot, but you're safe now. I wanted to bring you something to eat, and maybe a few answers." She raises her eyebrow, knowing I am interested. "May I sit?" She points to a rocking chair.

I swallow past the lump in my throat. At least she seems nice enough. I cautiously nod and watch as she pulls the chair over, being careful to not make any sudden movements. I know I should welcome her—and this place—with open arms, but instead I want to curl up in a ball and protect myself. I want so much to believe I'm safe.

"There, that's better." She smiles warmly. "Thank you. Please call me Abigail, or Abby. Everyone else does."

Everyone? Who else is here? I look around, taking in the room again with a more critical eye. It is huge and has a high cathedral ceiling.

"I bet you're wondering where you are," Abby says. I turn back to her. "You're at a safe house. No one here will hurt you. You're extremely dehydrated and malnourished, but you are young, and your body is healing fast. Your back..." She clucks her tongue and looks sadly at me. "Your back must still be very sore, but it will heal soon. It will take some time to get your strength back and feel like your old self again."

I stare at her a moment, then out the window, wondering where exactly I am.

She smiles, sensing my confusion. "You're in North Dakota, Savannah." She pauses a moment while this information sinks in. *Holy shit! Okay, breathe.* "I know it's a lot to take in right now, but once you feel better, I can tell you more. You really need your rest."

Rest, yes, that does sound like a good idea. Suddenly, I'm very tired again.

"But first, Savannah, do you think you could eat for me?"

Oh, God, food. I'm not sure if I am truly safe; eating is out of the question.

"You've lost a lot of weight, and your body is battered. You really need to help it by eating something." She hands me a saltine cracker. "Baby steps."

I slowly reach for it. Holding it in my hand, I look up to see her hopeful eyes. I hold the cracker to my nose, sniffing to see if it is laced with anything. It doesn't smell funny. I take a small, cautious lick. It tastes normal.

The door suddenly flies open, and in strides a huge man. I immediately drop the cracker and pull the blankets up to my chin, turning a terrified look to Abigail. She looks as shocked as I feel at the sudden appearance of our intruder. She stands and shields me from him. "York, what are you doing, coming in here like that? You frightened the life out of us."

He strolls in with a smirk. "Cole told me she arrived, and I wanted to make sure she was adjusting to her new accommodations."

"She's fine. Now, please leave." Her posture tells me she's been up against him before.

He leans to the side to get a better look at me and issues a wolf whistle. "My, she's a pretty one. A real step up from the last, hey?"

The last? Where the hell am I? I feel sick. I see a bowl on the floor and heave over the side, letting my stomach retch and twist, removing anything that may have been in there.

"Oh, no," Abigail moans, coming to my aid. "Here, Savannah, let me help you." She pulls my long hair out of the way. When I finish, she takes a cool cloth to my face. It feels lovely having someone take care of me, though I cannot let my guard down. I am always wary of traps and know better than to let someone get too close. There are many questions firing off in my head. Am I safe? Where the hell is my father?

"Leave. Now," Abigail hisses at York, who doesn't seem to be fazed by my vomit show. "Does Cole know you're here?" she asks, her voice more accusing than anything. That seems to get his attention, and for a moment, concern flickers across his face.

"Fine." He shakes his head then gives me a smile. "See you later, pretty girl."

This man seriously makes me uncomfortable. Abigail seems to have caught my feeling as she pulls the covers around and tucks me in.

"Don't worry about him. He's not around too much, and when he is, Cole watches him carefully." *Cole?* "There isn't a thing that goes on that Cole doesn't know about. That's what makes him so good at what he does."

And what is that, exactly? I want to ask questions, but I can't find my voice…or the strength to stay awake, for that matter. I am spent. I close my eyes and listen to the comforting sound of Abigail's rocking chair.

***

I remain in my bed the next four days, feeling a little better every day. I am helped considerably, I'm sure, by the fluids they are giving me. I haven't had any more unexpected visitors, and Abigail has become a constant, comforting presence as she nurses me back to health. She is kind to me, but so was Maria. I still keep my guard up. *Everyone has their own agenda.* She tries to get me to talk, but I can't; silence is easier for now. She comes and goes throughout the day, opening windows and doors, letting the warm sun find its way to me. The air itself is chilly, but I don't care. It is lovely. Sometimes a bird lands outside the window, its song reminding me how much I miss the outdoors.

I am pleased on the eighth day—wow, I am finally able to keep track of days again—to awaken IV free. I test out my body, limb by limb. My back still hurts like hell, but at least the throbbing headache is gone. I feel like I need to stand and move around, so I slowly slide my legs off the bed. They shake when they begin to bear weight, but they don't let me down. The door opens, and Abigail enters with a beaming smile.

"Well, look at you," she says, both hands to her face. "You're standing!" I feel a small smile tug at my lips but quickly chase it away. I can't let myself be too comfortable. I can trust no one. She comes to my side and wraps my arm carefully around her shoulders. I cry out in pain, and she quickly drops her arm back down. "Your back?"

I don't look at her. I want to cry on her shoulder and let her in, but I can't. I know better. Abigail guides me into the bathroom. I surprise myself with how steady I am by the time we get there. She turns me around and gently pulls my button-up nightgown off my shoulders. I let it fall to just above my bottom while I cover my front with my arms still in the sleeves. She pulls my hair up into a clip. I can see her eye me, but she doesn't say anything.

"Abby, I wanted—" The voice stops suddenly. In the mirror, I see the wide-eyed stare of my rescuer taking in my back. Abigail quickly shields me with a towel.

"Please, Logan, give us a moment." His reflected eyes meet mine, showing sadness, then…anger? He steps back and retreats toward the bedroom door.

"Yes, of course, forgive me," he mutters on his way out. So now I know my carrier's name is Logan.

Abigail runs warm water and helps me into the deep tub. I cry out as the water touches my wounds, and she continues to pour Epsom salts around me.

"Soak, darling. The pain will ease in time." She gently washes my hair, helps scrub my body clean, and empties the tub, refilling it with fresh, warm water. It crosses my mind that in my earlier life I would be very uncomfortable with a stranger washing me. After my experiences in my former prison, I hardly think of it now.

I hold a piece of my hair in front of me, noting how ratty it looks. My nails are dirty, and my feet are in rough shape. All things I took for granted in the past. I wasn't one of those girls who went to the spa monthly, but I did look after myself. But now…I close my eyes and let a few tears slip. I look and feel nothing like my old self. I am someone else now, and I have no idea who that is. I feel completely lost.

Abigail leaves me to my tears, later returning to dry my hair and tuck me back into bed. I notice she has changed the sheets. It feels wonderful to be clean.

She places a bowl of fresh grapes and strawberries next to the bed.

"Only if you feel up to it, dear," she cautions then leaves me to rest.

The next day, Abigail escorts a new visitor in to see me. She is a tall woman wearing thick, green, trendy glasses. She smiles down at me.

"Hello, Savannah. I'm Mel. Someone told me you could use a little pick-me-up." She beams, patting a medium-sized polka-dotted suitcase she pulled behind her. I turn quickly to Abigail, who also grins happily. She moves forward to help me out of bed and slips a cozy bathrobe over my shoulders.

I am settled in a leather chair in the middle of my huge suite, feet propped up on a stool, looking out at the mountains. I let out a comfortable sigh. *Wow, is this really happening?* It still feels like a happy dream.

"Every woman deserves to be pampered now and then," Abigail explains. "It helps us on the inside even more than it shows on the outside, so just relax and let Mel work her magic." I'm nervous to be alone with someone new, but feel better when Abigail pulls up a chair to oversee the proceedings.

Mel treats me like a delicate flower that will crumble if she is too rough. Little does she know I have been treated like someone's *perra* for God knows how long. Her actions calm my nerves, and I soon relax and enjoy the flow of the comb through my freshly washed hair. She snips here and layers there, not asking how I normally wear it. After my hair is blow-dried and styled, she moves to my nails, buffing and polishing. She paints them a deep purple then does the same to my toes. When Mel finishes, Abigail beams at me with delight. She thanks Mel and shows her out.

I sit in the chair and look at my hands and feet. All the dirt and stains are gone, and they look pretty. *Wow, they look normal again.*

"I hope that was all right, Savannah," Abigail says, coming back in the bathroom. "I'm not sure if you're tired or not, but I need to go start lunch. I'll leave you be. If you need anything, just call for me." She points to the intercom. With that, she leaves.

I look in the mirror, and my heart leaps. There I am, the old Savannah, hair cut long to the middle of her back, loose curls halfway up, natural highlights peeking through. I reach up, running my fingers through what feels like silk. If only I felt like the old Savannah on the inside. *No, don't sweat it, this is a start.* I look down, remembering the last time someone washed me and did my hair. I shake my head and force that memory back down. *Okay, I need to get out of this room.*

I find myself heading into the closet, hoping something might fit. To my surprise, everything is my size, even the shoes. I slip on a pink cashmere sweater, which is perfect for my back, and a pair of tan jeggings with flats. I take in how small my waist has become. Christ, how long was I gone? One last look in the mirror, and I think I might be able to face people now that I'm feeling a little more human.

I open the door and step out into a long hallway. My hands grow cold when I realize I have no clue where I am going. I take a deep breath and head to my left. Luckily, after a few minutes, I find a large staircase that spirals around to an entryway. My stomach turns as I hear a low voice. I want to turn around and go back upstairs, but I push on. *Breathe, Savi.*

"Must have been about ten to fifteen slashes across her poor back, and she's such a tiny thing," I hear Abigail say. "I think you're wrong about this one, Logan. She's as innocent as they come."

Wrong?

Both heads turn when I step around the corner into the kitchen. My carrier—I mean, Logan—catches my eye. His jaw drops as he looks at me. I realize he really is a good-looking man with his gelled black hair, dark eyes, and broad shoulders. I instinctively lower my gaze, having learned to avoid eye contact from my prior captors. Sensing my reaction is making them uncomfortable, I force myself to look up.

"Savannah," Abigail says warmly, "you look beautiful. I'm glad you found the clothes."

Logan pulls out a chair for me. "Hello again, Savannah. You look lovely. I see Mel got her hands on you. Please have a seat."

I hesitate for a moment but comply. He sets a prearranged plate in front of me with bacon, eggs, toast, and hash browns, with a glass of orange juice. My stomach twists, but I fight back the nausea. They take a seat on either side of me at the island, sipping coffee and talking about their days. I know they're trying to act normal for me, but it isn't working. Frankly, it is all a bit strange. I can't help wondering what is going on here. What kind of place is this? So many questions fill my head, making it ache. I raise my hand and rub where the bump used to be, but now it is just tender. I see Logan watching me, and his eyes have an odd effect on me. I can't quite place the feeling.

"You really need to eat, dear," Abigail says.

She's right, but somehow, I can't find the will to do so. I just want to cry. Perhaps coming downstairs was a mistake. They continue talking as I pick up a slice of toast and smell it out of habit. It seems fine. The first bite is all right, but the second is quickly rejected. Food and stress do not co-exist in my world anymore.

Abigail sighs as she sets her cup back on its saucer. "Would you like a tour of the grounds now, dear?"

I would, but I also have a ton of questions and don't know where or how to start.

Seeming to understand my dilemma, Logan turns to me with his mug between his hands. "Savannah, I'm sure you must be confused about where you are and what is happening. We'll get together later this afternoon, say around four. Is that all right with you?" I slowly nod, not sure why he can't talk to me right now. "Abigail will show you where my office is." With that, he checks his watch and stands. "Enjoy your day, ladies."

"You too, and I'll be sure to have Savannah there at four," Abigail says. When he leaves, she gathers my dishes. "Come, dear, let's go for that tour." She stops and waves her hand. "First, the kitchen." It is larger than my entire condo, with a view of a lake nestled in front of two mountains. "It's always stocked with food. Please help yourself. If there's something you want that's not here, just let me know, and we'll get it." She opens the huge stainless fridge that is packed with everything imaginable.

"There are always at least eleven people working here, plus those who live here full time, so this is what you'll typically find." I shake my head. I'm just glad I don't have to do the grocery shopping. "There's a wine cellar behind that door if you fancy yourself a glass." She winks.

Wine. Wow. That is something I hadn't thought of for a long time, my general menu being mostly water. Suddenly, I can almost taste my favorite Chateauneuf-du-Pape. Hmm, I will definitely have to check out that wine cellar. I pull my mind back to the room and note that Abigail is leaning against the marble island with a little smile on her face, giving me my moment.

She continues, "I generally do the cooking. It's pretty exhausting, but it is part of my duties, along with making sure you're comfortable here."

That's another comment that makes me realize I'll be here for a while, and my mind once again fills with questions. I really need to start talking, but the wall I have built up for my own protection won't allow me any wiggle room.

"Come, let's move on."

I follow her into a grand living room with a view of miles upon miles of land that weaves throughout the mountains. It is hard to comprehend where I am, but this place is spectacular. I was born and raised in New York City, so all this land is fascinating. The living room has high ceilings with wooden beams and an enormous fireplace. Everything is either dark wood or stone. The couches are red with large black blankets draped over top. A huge, tan rug with black thread woven through in a native pattern sits in the middle of the room, tying together the decor in the sitting area. Despite how massive the room is, it has a cozy feeling. I notice a patch of fluffy white fur on the floor by the couch leg. Someone must have a pet.

We move into the dining room and face the same beautiful view overlooking the lake as the kitchen. A giant wooden table that looks like it seats at least thirty takes up most of the room, with three cast iron chandeliers hanging above. I also notice a security camera tucked near the ceiling, and I quickly look away, not sure who is watching me.

On the top floor, Abigail shows me all the bedrooms, including mine. Next, we head to the bottom floor, down a flight of stairs near the kitchen. There is a game room, indoor pool, workout room, and an entertainment room.

I note how supersized everything is and begin to feel a bit exposed. I want to find a small room and wrap myself up in a blanket.

On our way back to the main part of the house, she points to a shorter hallway and tells me this is where Logan works, his office being at the end of the hall.

"He works a lot, but he's around for dinner and most evenings unless he's traveling. If you're afraid you'll be lonely, don't be. This place is always crawling with people. Some are friendly, and some don't talk that much. You'll learn who's who. When you're in this business, you see a lot of things—things that can change you."

I'm not completely blind to the fact that their job must be high risk and dangerous. I just wish I knew if it was legal.

"So, you take a left out of your bedroom, down the stairs, and another left to the hallway to Logan's office. Remember, your meeting is at four," she prompts, watching for my reaction. I nod, and she smiles. "Well, that's great, then. Are you tired, or would you like to see outside?"

Outside…freedom…I smile and nod toward the door.

She steps outside and continues to talk about the history of the house, but I stand motionless at the doorway. She stops and looks back at me with a sad expression. "Baby steps."

Right, okay.

She hands me a pair of tinted sunglasses. "Put these on, Savannah. Your eyes will need some time to adjust to the light. Thankfully, it's cloudy this time of year."

She gently links arms with me and walks me out onto the stone porch that wraps all around the house. I take a deep breath, filling my lungs with the cleanest air I've ever breathed. A gentle breeze moves my hair around my neck, and I close my eyes, soaking in all the sounds surrounding me. Birds chirping, the rustling of the leaves, water lapping on the shore—it's perfect until I hear the snap of a twig behind me. I jump, gripping Abigail's arm.

"Remember, never far from people," she whispers, pointing to a camouflaged man armed with a semi-automatic assault rifle and blending in seamlessly with the tree beside him. "This is a safe place—one of the best, Savannah—but in order for it to be that way, there has to be constant surveillance. Everyone who works for Cole is top notch. Scout Snipers, Navy SEALs, Green Berets, you name it. If they're Special Forces, we've got them."

Does Cole run this place? And will I ever meet him? I scan the woods, trying to locate more guys, but I can't see any.

"Just because you can't see them doesn't mean they're not here." Abigail takes in my gaze around the property then motions for us to move on. "You'll get used to it, in time."

Time. There's that word again.

"The lake is cooling off fast, but midday some can tolerate the cool water. Not me—too hard on these old bones." She laughs. "There are canoes and kayaks in the boathouse, along with anything else you may want. Don't forget to wear a life preserver!"

We round the house and come up to the front again, and I am growing tired. Walking great distances isn't something I am used to anymore. Abigail senses this and starts pointing to things rather than walking over to them. We stop at the front door. "I can show you the rest later, the stables and the hot tub. All this is yours to use whenever you like. We want you to make yourself at home, Savannah."

We walk back inside and up to "my" room. Before she leaves me to rest, she pauses and sits on my bed.

"I'm sure this is a lot for you to take in after all you've been through, but I promise everything will be fine. The sooner you relax and settle, the easier it will be for you to adjust."

I watch her leave, trying to process everything she said. It doesn't take long for me to drift off to an unsettled sleep.

Chapter Three

I stand in front of the heavy wooden door to Logan's office and admire the doorknob. It looks like a handle from an old sword. Three iron pieces curl around your hand when you grasp it. I know I can't stall any longer and knock gently.

"Come in," I hear him say in a harsh tone, and my hand retreats from the handle. I hate how scared those bastards made me. My mother would be heartbroken to see her once full-of-fire daughter acting like a burned-out wick.

The door bursts open. "York!" he barks, stopping abruptly when he sees me. "Oh, Savannah, I'm sorry. I've been waiting for someone." He steps to the side and glances at his watch. "Is it four already? Please come in, have a seat."

I move inside, taking in his office. His desk stands in front of a floor to ceiling window overlooking the stables and part of the lake. The decor is like most of the rest of the house with its fireplace and couch. Two rifles hang on the wall. I note these almost subconsciously while my attention is drawn at once to the flat screen TV on one wall tuned to a Los Angeles news channel. I feel Logan's gaze on me, but he remains silent. I catch the date from the news anchor—October 26th. I gasp and try to rationalize this date with the day I was taken.

"Yes, they had you a little over seven months, Savannah," he says softly, answering my unspoken question.

I feel the tears welling up. Oh, my God, I've been gone for over half a year! As much as it felt like a lifetime, for some reason, knowing the actual amount of time is soul shattering. It solves the nagging question that's been eating away at me, and now that I know, I am reeling in shock. My hand flies to my chest.

"Please, take a seat." He reaches for my arm and gently guides me over to the couch. He sits across from me, watching me closely. Once I get hold of myself, he begins to speak.

"A lot has gone on since you've been missing, Savannah. I'm sure you have a ton of questions, mainly the one about why you're here and why you were taken."

I nod.

"The men who took you are not just regular kidnappers. They're part of a highly dangerous group called *Los Sirvientes Del Diablos,* which means Servants of the Devil. They are a part of the Cartels and had you hidden well in Tijuana."

Holy shit!

"Your father—"

I sit up straighter when I hear his name. *Is he here? When will I be able to see him?* Again, nothing comes out.

He raises a hand. "Your father has been making a media storm out of your kidnapping."

Great…more unwanted publicity.

"Problem is, Savannah, the two main guys." He holds up a picture. "Rodrigo Heredia." A lump grows in my throat—the Montecristo smoker. He holds up another picture. "and Jose Jorge—"

My stomach lurches violently. I desperately grab the closest trash can and heave stomach bile into it. I sense

Logan behind me as he hands me a napkin and sets a glass of water next to me. I wash out my mouth and sit back on the couch, unable to look him in the eye. I feel embarrassed about my reaction, and his poor office being used like a bathroom.

"I'll take it you recognize Jose?"

I nod again, fighting the urge to scream. *Yes, the bastard made me beg for my meals, whipped my back until it was raw, and took every shred of human dignity away from me!*

Logan hands me a clean napkin—I didn't even notice I had started crying. "What I was going to tell you is both of them managed to elude capture."

My gaze shoots up in horror.

He leans forward, resting his arms on his thighs. "I know, and I'm sorry, but until we know where they are and take them into custody, you need to stay here. Your family, friends, nobody knows you're safe yet. That's the way we have to keep it for now, for their sake as much as yours. It will only be a matter of time before *Los Sirvientes Del Diablos* and the rest of the Cartels find out who rescued you, and when they do, the hunt will resume in earnest. You're worth a lot to them, and I'm sure they're pretty pissed that you're gone."

I stand, shaking my head, not sure what to do with myself. A knock sounds at the door, and York, the ass from last night, comes in, holding up his hands.

"Sorry, sorry, been a busy day—" He catches sight of me. "Hello again, pretty girl." His voice is like velvet.

Screw you, asshole.

"York," Logan spits out. "Take this and deal with it."

York grabs the file from Logan's hand and leaves, but not before giving me a wink.

Logan stands in front of me. He is much taller; I only come up to his chin. "You don't have to stay. It's your right to leave, but if you do, we cannot protect you. I give it one week before you're snatched up again and disappear into thin air. It took us five months to locate you the last time, and we're the best there is." He glances at his watch again, and his jaw tenses. "I have a video conference shortly, but tomorrow you have a meeting at oh eight hundred with Dr. Roberts. He's our resident therapist, and it's mandatory that you attend."

Oh, hell, no! I will not be seeing a shrink!

He crosses his arms, sensing my change in mood. "Mandatory," he repeats. "Abigail will see you make it there on time. For now, if you need anything, go to her. She'll be your aide. Feel free to use anything in the house, and know that the house is under constant watch for everyone's safety. Of course, the bedrooms and bathrooms are not under video surveillance, but the windows and doors all have sensors so we can keep track of who is coming and going. Please understand that the use of phones to call outside of this area is strictly prohibited, as is the use of the internet for communication. We've worked extremely hard to keep this place secret. Only a select few know its location, and they know the consequences if they should ever reveal it. I'll give you a week to decide if you want to stay, and if so, we'll talk more about the rules." He moves to sit behind his desk. "Any questions?"

Yes, about a billion. I shake my head and walk back out the door, closing it behind me. Jesus, there is so much to take in, my mind is reeling. I need to get back to my room and think. Am I really ready to live like this? Trade one prison for another, however posh? Or do I go home and take a chance and risk it all?

***

Dr. Roberts is a tall, skinny man with blond hair, in his mid-fifties. His hazel eyes look warm against his crisp navy suit, the thin tie resting over his belt buckle. He repeatedly taps his right heel against the floor while he thinks.

We are in a small room next to Logan's office. The color scheme is yellow and shades of green. It is quite pretty.

"Not much of a talker?" Dr. Roberts asks, trying to lighten the mood.

We've been staring at one another for the past forty-five minutes. When I first arrived, he asked a few questions, but when I didn't respond, he just watched my behavior, as I did his. I know he is going to go with a shock question to get a response out of me. Oh, here it comes. I can practically smell the smoke from his brain gears turning.

"What's your feeling on Jose Jorge?"

I don't flinch.

He nods and continues scribbling on his tablet. "Savannah, would you like to go home?"

Ah, the follow-up shocker question. Nice one, Doc. I've got to hand it to you. Using family would have cracked me at one time, but not now.

He leans forward, setting his tablet on the table. "Well, I guess we're not going to accomplish anything here today." He removes his thick framed glasses and rubs his eyes, sighing. "If you don't let people in, Savannah, how can we help you? Aren't you tired of being alone?"

Okay, that hit a nerve, almost broke my mask. I am terribly lonely, but when you live with no one to talk to and no one to trust for as long as I have, you almost forget how. People are sneaky creatures.

"Can you at least tell me your favorite color?"

I silently watch him shake his head.

"Okay, fine. I'll see you tomorrow, same time." The door opens, and in walks Abigail.

"Hello, Dr. Roberts. Will you be joining us for lunch?" She smiles at him.

"No, I'm afraid not. Thank you, though. I do love your chicken pot pie." She blushes a little.

Huh. This is interesting. Does soft-spoken Abigail have a crush on the snappy-dresser therapist? I think so.

"Ready, Savannah?" she asks, holding the door open.

***

I wake in a layer of sweat, my heart still wild from my nightmare, and glance at the clock. It's barely past midnight. I can still smell the foul sheets of my prison room. They had been changed only three times during what I now know was over seven months. I bet they never saw any soap even then—probably only rinsed and dried.

Knowing I'll never get back to sleep with the memories of my nightmare still fresh in my mind, I toss my blankets off and grab the robe Abigail left out for me. The cool silk feels amazing against my hot skin.

I make my way downstairs to the bottom floor. The entertainment room window overlooks the lake, and the space is filled with the glow of the lovely, soft moonlight. A black grand piano sits in front of one of the windows. My hands twitch as memories flood over me. I slide onto the cold bench and lift the cover to run my fingers over the keys, feeling how smooth and familiar they are as goose bumps prick along my skin. It has been fourteen years since I've played, fourteen years since I've seen my mother, fourteen years since I promised myself I'd never play again.

"Sweetheart," my father says, coming to my side, "it would really mean a lot if you played for her one last time. Please, play her favorite."

"I—I can't," I whisper through a sob.

"I really need you to do this, sweetie." He nods toward the press that is gathering in the church. Of course, the new up-and-coming politician would have press at his wife's funeral. I look up at him through my tears. It's always a show with him. He stands, pulling me to my feet. "Now." He takes my hands in his. "You can do this, Savi." He gives me a kiss on the cheek and points me toward the front of the room. I shake as I pass by the coffin. My dear mother looks so peaceful. As I sit at the piano, all eyes are on me. I glance at my father, who brushes a tear away and nods at me to start. I feel sick as I look down at the black and white blur. I take a deep breath, not wanting to disappoint. I can't bear to sing, so I only play. Leonard Cohen's oft-covered Hallelujah.

"Thank you," my father whispers.

Still, to this day, I don't know if he was thanking me for doing it for Mom, for him, or for the media.

I shake off the memory and test a key, pushing down, making the first note. I close my eyes and feel the melody. I quietly sing the familiar opening line, hardly recognizing my voice as the tears drop—feeling my mother beside me, playing her part. This was one of our favorites, and she had taught me how to play this same song I would play at her funeral.

"Only play if you want to, Savi," she whispers, glancing over at my father on the phone, pacing the kitchen. *"If it makes you happy, then play. That's why I do."* She kisses my cheek. *"It helps me escape my disease. It sets me free."* She starts to sing again, winking at me, her head swathed with a wrap hiding the fact that she's lost all her pretty dark brown hair that matched my own. Her voice would warm the coldest

38

soul.

I had maybe a quarter of her talent for singing—my skills were in my fingers. I was meant to play the piano.

I open my eyes to the moonlit room, feeling cold. Something catches my eye, and my hands retract off the keys.

"Please, don't stop." Abigail steps out of the shadows. "It's so beautiful."

I close the lid with a snap and swallow a lump in my throat.

"I haven't heard that song in a long time. Your voice is lovely."

I push off the bench, not looking at her, and leave the room. I feel strange hearing Abigail's compliments. I'm not sure what her angle is.

***

The next few days are the same. I go see Dr. Roberts, and we stare at one another for the hour-long session. I walk around the property with Abigail, trying to build up my strength. She never mentions the other night, and I am happy she doesn't. That was a raw moment for me. We have lunch, and I nibble on some fruit and vegetables, but it's something. A nap, followed by watching the horses run around the stables, then dinner. Abigail tells me old folk stories about the mountains, which are really quite interesting, then I head to bed. Sleep isn't something I enjoy, but I know my body needs it, no matter how much I protest. Abigail keeps telling me the small amount of food I eat is why I am always so tired. I know I really need to work on that.

The sun beats down on my face, filling me with all kinds of mixed emotions. I struggle with the idea of staying here. Although it is the most beautiful place in the world, it is not my home. If I do go home, is Logan right about me not making it past a week before I would be kidnapped all over again? My head hurts thinking of all the what-ifs. What if they take me? What if next time they kill me? What if they hurt my father or Lynn?

Abigail takes a seat next to me on the patio. She knows it is one of my favorite places to sit and think. "I love how the water reflects the mountains. Such a pretty display of colors." She's good with me—never tries to force me to talk. She just fills in the silence when it becomes too much for her.

I notice Logan walking with York around the property line.

"Stepping up security," she says as if I asked her the question.

I nod and keep watching.

After a few minutes, she sighs. "He's a good man, Logan. Never married, doesn't date. Claims he doesn't have time. Men," she laughs.

I smile a little too. That does sound like a workaholic male.

"Always an excuse to not let one's guard down."

I know she didn't mean to direct that to me, but I feel a funny sensation in my gut when she says it. Maybe I need to start trusting someone or I'll be lonely the rest of my life, but trusting people…the thought still really scares me.

***

After dinner, I sit on the floor in front of the couch in the living room to soak up the heat from the fireplace. Scoot, the house cat, doesn't seem to mind sharing the warmth with me, I think because he gets a belly scratch from it. He is a fat little thing with an "I don't give a crap about anyone" attitude, which strikes me as quite funny. A lot of the guys wear black, and I swear Scoot rubs up against them just to hear them groan. Now I know exactly where the patches of white fur come from.

None of the guys pay much attention to me. They are always polite but never speak more than they have to. Right now, that works fine for me.

"You should've seen Cole. He flipped his gun around and smoked the guy in the face, breaking his nose, spraying blood all over the place," I hear one guy say to another behind me. "Then he clocks him under the jaw, sending him down the stairs. The rat tried to grab for his gun, but Cole popped three right between his eyes. He never saw it coming."

Holy hell! The mental image I have from that almost makes me gag. Who is this Cole guy?

"I can't believe I missed it," his buddy whines. "So, that's what, number thirty-four for him?"

"Thirty-five," the storyteller corrects. "Not to mention the six he killed with his bare hands. Dude's friggin' Rambo."

A chill runs up my spine. I've never heard anyone talk about killing someone so openly and so casually. Does this Cole come around often? I have no interest in meeting such a stone-cold killer. It frightens me to even think about taking someone's life, let alone...how many times was that?

Scoot paws at my hand. Apparently, I stopped rubbing. "Sorry, kitty." I immediately make up for it by giving his tummy a good once-over.

"I'm going on a guess here, but I'm thinking a 2004 Merlot will make that belly scratch a little more tolerable." A guy grins down at me and hands me a glass of red wine.

I smile with a small nod and take the glass.

He sits in front of me, leaning against the opposite couch and stretching his legs out in front of him. He runs his hand through his brown hair to remove it from his green eyes. It seems like something he has to do often. Scoot doesn't like the interruption, so I make even more of an effort to give him attention. Greedy little cat.

The stranger leans forward. "Mark Lopez." He holds out his hand.

I look at it then move mine into his for a quick shake.

"You're Savannah Miller," he states. "We've already met, but you were kind of out of it."

I look at him, trying to recall his face. He is Latino and tall, although everyone seems tall to me, and I'm 5'6".

"I was sitting in the front passenger seat but never took my mask off, so you're off the hook for not remembering me." He grins playfully.

I look down at my wine. I take a sip, letting it swirl around my tongue. Oh my, it tastes divine.

Logan quietly sits across from us on the stone ledge in front of the fire. He looks tired, and it appears he is nursing a glass of something strong. *Something strong?* Those words bring me back to the restaurant that night with Joe Might. I feel tears coming; my old life seems so far away. Joe probably thought I was a flake for never getting his samples to him.

"Hey," Logan says softly, "you all right?" His sincerity makes me feel a flicker of warmth deep inside.

I quickly nod, not wanting to draw attention to myself.

"Lopez, could you give us a moment?" he asks.

"Sure thing." Mark rises to his feet. "Talk to you later, Savannah." He grins like we are good friends

It makes me feel good. Wow, that's a strange sensation. I really didn't think that feeling was inside of me anymore.

Logan shifts to Mark's spot beside me on the floor. "I see you made friends with the moodiest one in the place." He leans over and fingers Scoot's ear.

The cat purrs into his palm, and his smile grows. I know the two of them have probably spent some quality time together. I take another sip of my wine, not sure what to do.

He is almost painful to look at, he is so attractive. His eyes are so dark they match his black hair, and his shirt stretches over his broad chest, showing just how fit he is.

I run my hand through my hair, not wanting to gawk and needing something to do. "So, tomorrow marks one week since we last spoke. I hear you haven't made any progress with Dr. Roberts. That's disappointing."

My eyes shift away from his.

"You really need to talk to someone, Savannah. Dr. Roberts has done wonders for people in the past. I'm sure if you give him a chance, you'll feel a lot better. That is, if you decide to stay." He pauses and takes a sip of his drink. "It's all right to let people in. You're safe now."

Safe. That's what everyone keeps telling me.

He suddenly turns his head, looking over my shoulder. "Please excuse me." He sighs and hops to his feet.

I sit and think about what Logan said, still keeping up my required efforts with the demanding Scoot. My thoughts are soon interrupted by a conversation between two guys sitting near the window. They are talking about the one named Cole again and how he "popped this rat in the face." The other guy begins to describe another Cole story with so much detail I actually have to get up and walk out of the room. I've decided it's time for bed anyway, and I have heard quite enough.

***

Dr. Roberts glances at me over his glasses. We are

43

forty minutes into our potentially last session. I am having an internal battle with myself, and a side finally wins. I breathe in deeply and decide to take a leap of faith. At this point, I have nothing to lose and maybe something to gain.

"Purple," I whisper. His gaze snaps up from his tablet, his eyes narrowing at me.

"Pardon?"

"My favorite color is purple." My hands twist together; I am feeling uneasy with my decision.

"Well, that's a pretty color." He takes a moment to think. "If you could use three words to describe how you're feeling today, what would they be?"

Only three? I think about it carefully before choosing the words and clear my throat.

"Scared, confused, overwhelmed."

"All normal to be feeling after what you've been through." He nods. "How do you like it here so far?"

I shrug. "Fine."

"What do you like most?"

That's a hard question to answer; there are surprisingly a lot of things. I mean, who wouldn't love the view, the horses, the lake, the air?

"Lots."

He nods again, scribbling on his tablet. "Could you name one thing?"

"Scoot." This makes him laugh.

"Good old Scoot. I swear, that cat runs this house. What is it you like about him?"

I study the doctor for a moment, trying to figure out where this psychobabble might be going.

"He is what he is."

"It's true, animals don't judge like people do. They're trustworthy, loyal companions." He tilts his head. "Were there any animals where you were held?"

The hair on my neck stands up.

"I'm thinking something that might have brought you comfort?"

"No," I shoot back quickly, remembering I desperately want someone to talk to, someone to trust, someone to be my friend. Hell, someone or something to love.

"Okay." Resting his head on his hand, he studies me.

I see his chest rise and fall heavily.

His lips press together before he speaks. "Can you tell me about the night you were taken?"

I hear a door slam shut in my brain.

"Time's up, Doc," I say, jumping to my feet. I can't go there. I don't want to.

He stands too, placing his tablet on his chair.

"Savannah," he says.

I stop mid-step.

"I've been doing this for thirty years. I've seen a lot of patients and heard a lot of stories. You need my help, or this will destroy you. If you leave now, you'll be looking over your shoulder, going mad waiting for those monsters to take you, and that's no way to live. Take Logan's offer. Stay and be safe, and take back your life. Only you can make that choice, but you have to want to fight. Don't let them win."

I wipe my wet cheeks. His words cut me. Everything he says is true, and I know it.

"Just think about it." He opens the door for me.

I walk out and make it to a nearby bathroom where I manage to pull myself together. Looking at my red, glossy eyes in the mirror, I know what I have to do. I fuss with my off-the-shoulder green sweater, making it hang correctly over my leggings. It's funny how my obsessive need to fix myself in case I am being watched by the media comes right back to me. I wonder what else will surface over time.

Chapter Four

Okay, okay, you can do this. I bite my lip and knock on the door, waiting for the command to enter. It comes after a moment, and I slide my hand into the sword handle, squeeze, and push. Logan is sitting on the couch, leaning over the table and looking intently at his laptop. I wait, holding onto the door for support. I'm not sure how to even start this conversation.

"Logan?" I whisper.

He raises his head, and when he sees me, his eyes go wide and soften.

"May I have a word with you?"

His smile runs along his lips as he closes his laptop.

"Of course, Savannah. Come in, take a seat." He points to the couch in front of him. "How was your appointment with Dr. Roberts?"

"Interesting."

"I can see that. Have you made your decision on whether you want to stay or go home?"

I let out a long breath. Okay, here it goes. "I-I think I'd like to stay."

His expression speaks volumes, though I'm not sure why he cares so much. What am I to him but some head case?

"That's a smart idea, Savannah." He moves over to his filing cabinet and pulls out some paperwork, which he places in front of me. "Like I said before, if you wish to stay, you'll need to sign a few waivers, an NDA. That is a non-disclosure agreement."

I nod, glancing at the papers.

"This is a document stating that while you're here and after you leave, you will never give up the location of this house. You'll never discuss why you're here with anyone outside of this house. If you leave the property, you'll have an escort with you at all times. That's for your own protection as well as ours, Savannah. Someone could be following you, and you could lead them right back to us. Know that you can leave at any time, but there's no coming back—we will not protect you a second time. Do you think you can handle all this, being under this much protection? This many rules? You will be totally isolated from your past life."

"I've already lost seven months of my life to those bastards. If this is what it takes to gain it back, then so be it."

I read everything carefully, making sure I understand every word.

"Pen, please." He hands me one from his breast pocket, and I stroke the pen over the black line—Savannah Miller.

He holds out his hand. "Welcome to our house."

I slip my hand in his, noting how small mine is in comparison.

Something flickers over his face, and he pulls away and leans back.

I hop to my feet, not wanting to take up any more of his time. I need to get some air; I feel like I just signed my life away.

I pause at the door. "Thank you, Logan, for saving me."

His smile reaches his eyes. "It was my pleasure, Savannah."

***

I find Abigail waist deep in laundry. She looks beyond stressed, and at the same time has a few of the guys asking her a million and one questions, so I leave her be. She doesn't need to babysit me. I am familiar enough with the house and grounds now to be somewhat comfortable.

I walk down to the lake and around the shore. It is becoming one of my favorite places. Everything is so quiet. Not 'empty' quiet the way my prison was. This is different. It's a comfortable, peaceful place. I don't feel as lonely because of all the wonderful, soft sounds that surround me. It's funny how this kind of quiet isn't really quiet at all. Knowing there are men hidden in trees all around also brings a sense of comfort. I miss my father terribly, and I miss Lynn even more. I even miss my job, but I think living in constant fear would destroy me more than the prison. Yes, the decision to stay is the right choice for me—at least, I hope.

***

Poor Abigail is still pumping out laundry when I return several hours later. She looks exhausted, so I decide to help her out.

I make my way into the kitchen and open the freezer, pulling out a mountain of steaks. I look at the calendar Abigail refers to every night and see there will be fifteen attending tonight's dinner. I set out the meat to thaw while prepping the toppings. I wrap large potatoes in tin foil and chop enough carrots to feed a small army. I cut the bottoms off the asparagus and drizzle it with oil, salt, and pepper. While the oven heats, I peel and chop apples, tossing them into three large casserole dishes with cinnamon, sugar, and a little butter, putting an oat crumble over top.

It shouldn't surprise me that the barbecue is so huge—what isn't huge around here? But nonetheless, it is very intimidating to light. I finally manage to fire it up and start the potatoes without setting the house on fire.

Within an hour, the kitchen starts to smell lovely. I pull out the three apple crisps, setting them aside to cool.

"What is that smell?" I hear someone yell, which is followed by heavy footsteps. "Good God, my mouth is actually watering!" Mark Lopez, the guy from last night, comes around the corner. "Hello, Savi." He grins, looking around. "Are you cooking? Please tell me what that heavenly smell is." He takes a seat on a stool opposite me at the island.

"Apple crisp." I point to the desserts on the counter.

"Well, fuck me sideways...she speaks." He raises a playful eyebrow.

"She does," I shoot back with a smirk. He cracks me up.

"Yes, yes, I'll think of something. Maybe I'll order a pizza—" Abigail stops short when she enters the kitchen and hangs up her cell phone. "Savannah?" She looks shocked.

Oh, no. Maybe I crossed a line doing this. Perhaps I should've stayed away. This is her thing to do.

"I'm sorry."

Her lips turn into a smile.

"Savannah speaks now." Mark grins up at her.

She walks by, giving a playful smack to the back of his head. Taking in the kitchen with a look of amazement at all the food, her eyes dance over at me.

"You did this?" she asks.

"Yes, I'm sorry if I stepped over a line. I was—"

"Sorry? Oh, dear, don't be sorry." Her cheeks flush. "Thank you for doing this. It's so kind of you. You have no idea what a relief it is that someone noticed I need some help around here." She leans in and gives me a huge hug.

I stand stiffly at first, but can't deny the warmth I feel toward her. My arms slowly wrap around her, embracing the affection. I feel a small chip of cement break off around my heart.

"If you guys need a moment, I can leave." Mark laughs. It's such a male thing to joke at an emotional moment.

"Go wash up. I know you boys just came from training." She shoos him out of the kitchen.

Mark sticks his finger in the sauce and pops some in his mouth.

"Yum!"

"Don't make me come after you." She gives him a stern look.

He laughs all the way down the hallway.

I am starting to see she's the mother of the house, and they all respect her.

***

I begin to feel self-conscious when everyone sits down for dinner.

They all compliment me on how great the food is when they find out I made dinner for Abigail. Everything is piled on plates in the center of the table, and they all take turns helping themselves.

Logan enters and takes a seat, apologizing for being late.

Then York comes in and sits a few seats across from me. He winks at me as he takes his seat. Christ, he's unsettling.

Some people make small talk through dinner, mostly about the hockey game that is on tonight. I'm more focused on eating. Baby steps, I keep telling myself. I poke at a piece of potato. I know I have to force myself to eat more, but my stomach seems to be shrunk to the size of a pea.

"Burke wasn't the psychopath," York says in an argument with his buddy across the table. I know what they are talking about right away.

"Who cares? It's just a movie."

"Tommy Desimone was the psychopath," I interject, making the entire table stop and stare.

York gives me a strange look.

Yeah, that's right, creep. I have a voice. "Umm, Tommy was crazy, not Burke." I look at his friend. "And it was actually a book first, called *Wiseguy* by a crime reporter named Nicholas Pileggi, published in January 1985. Five years later, it was made into the movie *Goodfellas.*" I suck in some air. I haven't said this much at once in a very long time. It feels good.

"Oh!" Mark laughs, pointing his knife at York. "You just got schooled!" The entire table bursts out laughing. York watches me while I struggle with the fact I just opened my mouth in front of so many people.

"There was no question. Jimmy could plant you just as fast as shake your hand. It didn't matter to him. At dinner, he could be the nicest guy in the world, but then he could blow you away for dessert." He quotes the book, clearly showing off to me how he already knows all about the novel. I secretly wonder if he is threatening me for embarrassing him.

"Chapter two, paragraph twenty-four," I toss back. "Oh, and we're having apple crisp for dessert. If you could hold off blowing me away until afterward, I'd appreciate it."

Logan breaks into laughter first. The rest of the guys follow.

"She's good," Logan shouts over the roar of the table.

York leans back and folds his arms, watching me. His

eyes make my skin crawl. The noise at the table dies down except for the sound of some of the guys polishing off the last of the food when York pipes up again. Clearly, he had been thinking.

"Savannah, you don't strike me as someone who would read that kind of novel." He stabs his last piece of steak.

I hate that I flinch. I'm sure I'm giving off an uncomfortable vibe. It doesn't go unnoticed, because a smirk appears on his face.

"I'm trying to recall the last time I've seen a copy of that book." He taps his finger against the table dramatically. "Oh, that's right—it was on the little table in your cell."

My hand twitches, my fork bouncing loudly off my plate.

"York." Logan looks up from his meal.

I stare at my hands on my lap as images of that room fight their way to the surface.

"Little wooden table, right, with a stool?" he adds, and my stomach twists painfully.

"Enough, York," Logan warns in a clipped tone.

I rise to my feet, desperate to get away from here, but Logan's warm hand wraps around mine.

"Savannah, please stay."

I stare down at him. I hate all the eyes on me, and I find myself rubbing my uneasy stomach.

He looks at York and nods toward the door. York shakes his head, tosses back his beer, then leaves the table, muttering.

"John," Abigail says, breaking the tension in the room, and the man across from her raises his head. "Are you going into town tomorrow?"

Logan still has my hand. I pull it away. I feel like I don't belong here.

"Sorry, I didn't mean to start anything," I whisper so

only he can hear.

The corners of his mouth turn up. "Are you kidding? It's refreshing seeing someone take on York. He can be an ass sometimes." He reaches for my hand again and tugs. "Please sit."

I sink back down into my chair.

"Abigail, dinner was delicious."

"Thank Savannah—she made it all."

He looks back to me. "You made this?" he asks, surprised.

I nod.

"Don't forget about the apple crisp," Mark adds. "Speaking of…" He leans over to the table against the wall and picks up a bowl then sets the warm dessert in front us before diving right in.

"Impressive. I guess we still have a lot to learn about you." Logan grins and takes a serving for himself.

Yes, something tells me their background checks wouldn't include culinary skills. Despite my little spat with York, I'm feeling happy with myself. I helped Abigail when she needed it, and everyone seems pleased with dinner. The guys all thank me as they leave the table.

***

"Good morning, Savannah." Dr. Roberts catches me in the entryway on my way down to his office for our eight o'clock session. "I was thinking maybe we could have today's session outside?"

"Sure." I follow him across the lawn and down to a covered chair swing. He sits next to me, which feels odd—normally he watches me face on.

We sit in silence, watching an eight-man war canoe race effortlessly across the lake. I wonder who is on it. Mark, Logan, or maybe even York? The morning sun feels warm, but the clouds wrapping themselves around the mountains tell me it won't last long. Perfect weather for Halloween, I guess. I let out an unexpected yawn, and the doctor shifts. I know the silence is about to end.

"How have you been sleeping?"

"Fine," I lie.

He glances over at me and waits.

"Soon as I fall asleep, I'm right back in my prison."

"What happens when you're there?"

I shiver and close my eyes. "I'm alone again. I'm cold. I'm in a dirty, white nightgown and a brown sweater that's way too big for me. I smell mold and rotting food. It's making my stomach turn." I rub my stomach. "Sometimes I wake up vomiting, sometimes I can't wake up at all, but if I do, I feel restless and can't go back to sleep."

"Is it the same dream every night, or does it change?"

"It was the same up until last night. The fat man—"

"Jose Jorge?" he asks, trying to follow me.

"Yes, Jose. He shows up with my tray of food." I pause, pushing my tongue to the roof of my mouth. I want to curse and scream, but I hold back, something I'm used to doing. "He liked the power he had over me. He was a real bully, for lack of a better word."

"Hmm." He shakes his head.

"What?"

"Do you think the change in your dream was because of the situation with York at the dinner table last night?"

I look up at him, confused. How did he know about that?

He shrugs with a chuckle. "You made quite the impression with the guys. They like you."

I look back out over the water. That's kind of nice to hear.

"Perhaps," I agree.

"I can give you something—"

"No, thank you," I cut him off. I don't want anything to alter my newfound feeling of freedom.

"Well, tell me if you change your mind."

The doctor doesn't ask too many more questions about my prison, and I don't offer up any more information. It is quite painful reliving it.

"Tell me about your father, Savannah. What's he like?"

I pull my knees up to my chest, feeling the loss of a parent's comfort. Things weren't always great between us, and I have a lot of mental scars thanks to him, but he is still my dad.

"We're close enough." I swallow past the lump. "We did the typical things together that a working parent could do. When I was younger, we fished and hiked. We didn't get together much when he got deeper into the political world because he became a lot busier and stressed out. I didn't help his stress level back then either."

"What do you mean?"

"I wasn't used to the publicity I had as the mayor's daughter. I hated it. I still do. I was never a party person or a troublemaker, but it seemed whenever I'd go out, somehow the paparazzi found me and would catch me in some compromising pose and spin an embarrassing story. I'd make the front page of some magazine, and my father would have to deal with the repercussions. It happened so often that I stopped going out at all. One time, I tripped over a drunk guy at a pub, and the story read that I was a drunk and needed AA. It nearly killed me when my father started to believe the lies. I just stopped trying to have a life of my own." I stop talking and swallow again. "It was a year since I went to any kind of pub or bar, but one afternoon my friends from work insisted I join them to celebrate landing a new client. I did and had a wonderful time. It felt so good to be out. The next day, the day I was—" I stop, finding it hard to say the word.

"Taken," he says for me.

"Yes. My friend Lynn came by with a copy of *Us Weekly* with me on the front showing off my backside. It had been Photoshopped, of course—my dress wasn't that short. I was so angry that after so long the media would still peg me as a sloppy drunk. I barely drink as it is!" I shake my head. "Of course, my father was furious and told me we'd discuss it over dinner the next night. That never happened." Goosebumps slowly inch up my arms. I take a long breath, trying to rein in my emotions. "I hate that my last conversation with my father was him being disappointed with me again." The doctor hands me a tissue.

"It's hard being in the spotlight when you never asked to be there." He sighs. "Sad that people care more about celebrities than what's going on in their own country. Troops being sent over to fight for our freedom get less media coverage than the Kardashian family." He stands and stretches his legs. "You did well today, Savannah. Try to get some rest tonight. I'll see you tomorrow. Enjoy the sun while it lasts."

"Thanks."

***

My foot is propped against a small table, allowing me to gently rock myself. I lean my head back and smell the oncoming rain. A low rumble echoes over the mountains, warning of the storm that is brewing. It has been a long time since I've watched a good show of force from Mother Nature. In New York, we have the four seasons. I missed them terribly in my prison. My time without so much as a window was terrible.

"May I join you?"

I look up to see Logan standing next to the swing, holding a blanket, a thermos, and two mugs.

"Sure." I sit up to make room for him to join me, surprised and a little pleased that he is being so thoughtful. I know how busy he is all the time.

"I love a good storm," he says as he opens the thermos. "Abby told me you love your coffee. Seems we have something in common." He hands me a mug, and I wrap my chilly fingers around it, seeking its warmth.

"Thank you."

He leans back and drapes the blanket over my lap. "The temperature can drop quickly in Montana this time of year."

Wait, what?

"Montana?"

He shifts, making the seat sway. "Sorry, but you hadn't signed the NDA yet."

"Now that I have, what else can you tell me?" I think I have the right to ask now.

He lets out a long breath. "What do you want to know?"

"Everything," I say without missing a beat. "But first you can tell me who you are." I wave my hand. "Abigail filled me in some. She said you're top of the line trained, and some of you are Special Forces."

He sips his coffee. "We're all Special Forces," he corrects me. "My grandfather was the founder of this group. We're called Shadows. The US government wanted a group of highly trained professionals who could slip in and out of Mexico to gather information on the Cartels, *Los Sirvientes Del Diablos*, and a few other drug and kidnapping rings. At first, that's all we did, and then they started to use us to retrieve hostages and bring them back across the border safely. That's when this place was built. We needed a safe place to bring the kidnapping victims while we tied up the loose ends. We like to call them our 'guests' when they are with us. As soon as it's safe, they go home to live their lives, and we move on to our next job."

"Why Montana? Why not somewhere closer to the border, like Texas or California?"

"Because that's the first place they'd check. Who would think to look in the back mountains of Montana? Plus, we have a pretty good advantage if attacked." He waves at the view. You can see for miles all around us.

I try to remember my journey here, but I still blank out after the cabin of the plane. I think about the other people who were here before me and what it was like for them.

"Were there any who didn't make it? You know, when they got back home."

He nods. "Yes. Some refused our help and went back before it was safe and were taken again or were killed. Some couldn't handle what they had been through and ended it themselves."

Lovely. He must have caught my expression.

"We have a high success rate, Savannah. Eighty-five percent go on to live normal lives."

"Who was the last 'guest' who stayed?"

He looks at me carefully.

"York mentioned something about the last one not being as pretty."

He rolls his eyes.

"York," he mutters to himself. "We haven't had a lot of women here. It's mostly wealthy businessmen. The two women we did have were in their fifties, and they were the wives of some important people. You're the first who's young and, well, pretty."

I blush at his unexpected compliment.

He clears his throat. "Needless to say, the guys were all happy you decided to stay." I don't look up. "Plus, you give York shit, and that's just plain fun to watch."

"Am I the only vic—" *I hate that word*, "person like me here? Are there others?"

"Just you for now."

I nod, thinking about what he said. The clouds start rolling in around us. It is a spectacular show. So many different shades of gray change the color of the lake. I wrap my arms around my middle, feeling my mood shift again.

"He makes me nervous," I confess.

He peers down at me. "Who?"

"York."

"Does he?"

I nod.

"Savannah, look at me, please."

I peel my gaze off the floor and meet his stare.

"If he does or says anything that makes you feel uncomfortable, you tell me right away, okay?"

"I'm sure it's nothing." I shake my head. I feel stupid even saying anything.

"Regardless, you tell me. You tell me if anyone here makes you uncomfortable."

A loud clap of thunder makes me jump, nearly spilling my coffee. I set it down on the table and pull the blanket over me. I bring my knees to my chest, something I've done to protect myself since I learned to fear that terrible click of the key in the lock. The rain comes down like someone turned on a faucet full blast. We both shift toward the middle of the swing, getting out of the way of the splatter. His arm rests behind me and he turns into me, almost like he is shielding me. It must be second nature for him. Although it is a small action, it makes a bubble of warmth grow inside me. *Huh.*

"Can you see them?" I peer into the trees and force the feeling aside.

"I can because I know where to look. That, and I'm

trained to sense their movements."

"So, the whole time you've been sitting here, you can feel them around us?"

He nods, looking off to my right and pointing into a thick wooded area. "One there."

I squint but can't see anything.

"There." He motions to the right a bit with his head. "Two down by the beach."

"Are you playing me?" I ask with a skeptical look.

He smiles and pulls out a small radio and switches the channel. "Beta Seven, come into the clearing." Sure enough, a man off to my right, exactly where Logan first pointed, dressed in camouflage comes walking out. "Back to post." The man turns and disappears into the woods.

"I stand corrected," I say through trembling lips. It is starting to grow very cold.

He stands, offering his hand. "Come, let's get you inside. You're freezing."

***

After a hot shower and some dry clothes, I head down to the living room to my favorite spot in front of the fire. Before I can even sit down, Scoot appears out of nowhere, pouncing on my lap. He walks himself around my waist under my open sweater—apparently, he is cold, or maybe he is marking me with his scent. Either way, it tickles and makes me laugh.

"Now, that's a sweet sound." Logan grins, sitting on the couch across from me. He has changed into a pair of jeans and a black long-sleeve shirt. He looks his age. Thirty-something? His shirt shows off how fit he is. No doubt. These guys always seem to be training for something.

"Feels kind of nice," I admit but don't make eye

contact. Scoot hears Logan's voice and pops his head out by my side. The little bugger made my pink tank top white along the bottom. "Hey," I pat his head, "I thought we had a truce about the fur." He looks up at me and meows. A bright light fills the room, followed by a crack of thunder that shakes the windows. The rain beats hard against the glass, and Scoot runs and hides under a chair. I want to do the same. I stand up, feeling uneasy. It is growing dark even though it is only two in the afternoon. I look out at the woods and think about the men out there. "This place is being monitored by cameras, right?"

"Yes," Logan comes and stands behind me, "twenty-four seven."

"Then why aren't you calling in the guys? It's pouring rain out. It's got be freezing for them. Have they even eaten lunch?" I see a smile grow on his face in the reflection of the window.

"They have huts to protect them from the rain, and proper rain gear. These aren't mall security guards." He chuckles. "A stormy night is a walk in the park for these men. Besides, it's their job, and they do it well."

"But we're not in any danger, right? I mean, you said only a handful of people know where we are, so why do they have to be out there—"

"Just because we can't see danger doesn't mean it doesn't exist," he explains, cutting me off. Folding his arms, he comes to stand next to me. "The men who took you are part of the Cartels, a network that openly kills their own people in broad daylight in the middle of busy streets. The police have no control over them. Shadows has been doing this for almost three generations…just think how many people we've pissed off." He looks down at me over his shoulder. His eyes soften. "Don't worry. I make sure they get fed properly, and their shift ends in two hours."

I nod, feeling a little better about the guys, but not so

much about what he just said. "Abigail mentioned that you're updating the security equipment. Is that just protocol or because I'm here and I bring extra baggage because of who is after me?"

"A bit of both."

I figure since he's on a roll answering my questions, I might as well go for the one that's been eating me alive since I arrived.

"Did my father ask you to come for me?" A crack of thunder makes me stumble over the last word.

"I can't answer that," he says. "I'm sorry."

"When will I be able to speak with him?"

"Soon, when we know it's safe."

"There's that word again," I mutter, jumping at another clap of thunder. Christ, my nerves are shot! I hate feeling so jumpy. I start to grow angry as my emotions twist around. "How much did those bastards ask for my ransom? Tell me—what am I worth?"

"Savannah," he turns to face me, "don't think like that."

I stare him point blank in the eye. Now I know I'm angry.

"Fifty thousand," he murmurs quietly. I feel my stomach drop, tuck, and roll over the hardwood floor.

"Nice to know I missed my life for seven months and I'm only worth fifty thousand! So that's, what—roughly over seven grand a month." I shake my head. "No wonder they barely fed me." I'm bitter, angry, and sad. I try to fight back the tears, but it's no use.

He touches my shoulder, giving it a gentle squeeze. He is struggling with something, I guess about having to tell me my total net worth. Suddenly, it hits me. "If I was only worth fifty grand, why didn't my father pay it? Why did I have to rot away in that cell for almost a year?"

"It's not as simple as handing someone the money,

Savannah. There are always tricks and schemes, and in a lot of cases the victim is killed long before the families even agree to pay to have them returned. They make a fake proof of life video or take pictures before the victim is killed and use them throughout the negotiations."

My blood drains from my face as another flashback plays out in front of me.

He grabs the tops of my arms, holding me steady. "Whoa. You should sit down."

I shake my head, not listening. "W-why was I spared, then? Why not kill me? Then collect. It doesn't make sense."

"That's what we're trying to figure out. When we came for you, we planted evidence setting up Rodrigo's brother. There's been some bad blood between them in the past, and we hoped to throw them off our trail. We knew it wouldn't stand up for long, but it should take the heat off for a while. We need more time to figure out exactly what is going on."

Evidence, fake proof of life, fifty thousand dollars—my head is swimming. Before I know what is happening, I'm placed on the couch and told to put my head between my legs.

"Breathe, Savannah." He runs his strong hand over my back. "You're getting too much information too fast. You've been through a lot, and your body and brain need time to catch up. I promise I'll answer all your questions in time, but that's it for now."

He is right; it is too much. I start to sob.

He pulls me into him, holding me close. His smell engulfs me. It's been years since I had a man hold me, other than my father, and it feels nice…almost safe.

***

I wake to a booming sound that could restart a heart.

I lie on the couch, staring at the fire, and try to catch my breath. Lightning fills the room, followed by another earth-shaking boom. I sit up and look around. I'm alone in this very large house in the middle of a freakin' battle-of-the-gods storm. I make my way slowly toward the kitchen. Abigail must have left the light on for me. The clock reads eleven. I glance outside when the lightning flickers, illuminating the entire lake. I squeeze my eyes and cover my ears, waiting for the next—

"Ahhh," I yelp when it rumbles all around me like a speeding train. It is so unpredictable. I hate it!

I hear voices coming from downstairs and follow them, hoping to find Abigail. I could really use some company right now. They become louder when I reach the entertainment room. The door is partially open. I take a deep breath and step inside. Logan, Mark, York, and three other men I recognize but don't know by name are sitting around a poker table, drinking beer.

"Hey, there, Savi!" Mark gives me a cocky smile. "Did we wake you?" Everyone turns and stares at me.

I shake my head and jump at another boom. "N-no, you didn't."

"You look a little nervous," York chimes in as he sips his beer, glaring at me over his bottle.

"Stop," Logan warns. "Everything okay?"

"Umm, yes." I jump again, heat rushing to my face. "Just looking for Abigail."

"She went to bed a while ago."

"Oh," I whisper, feeling even more anxious about going back to my room, "Thanks."

"Savannah, you want to join us?" Logan asks, giving a flick of the head. I know he is only being nice.

"No, it's okay, you guys enjoy your—" *Boom!* I jerk, closing my eyes for a moment.

Mark stands to make room between him and one of the guys.

I sigh and give in. Who am I kidding? I'd probably sit outside the door just for the comfort of their voices. "Thanks." Mark deals out a new hand and gives me some green chips.

He tells me they play for fun once a week, but once a month they play for money.

"Have you even played before?" York asks as he fiddles with his cards.

"A few times." My grandfather played once in a while. He taught me the basics—mostly how to bluff. I look around the table at the three other guys. "Hi." It felt wrong sitting without introducing myself.

"Savannah, this is the guy who was driving the night we brought you here." Mark points to the man next to me.

"John." He flicks his cigar off to one side as he offers me his hand.

"This was the man in the back, Paul." Mark points, and Paul gives me a wave. "York was in the Escalade in front of us." York smirks. "And this is Keith."

"AKA Beta Seven." Logan winks at me.

"Oh!" I say, remembering him from earlier in the day. Logan got him to come out into the clearing.

Boom! I jump—why does this place have to have so many windows? I stop myself, shocked that I went there. Do I miss my prison walls? No way! Christ, stop!

"Umm, well, I guess this is a little late, but thank you all very much for saving me that night. I owe you."

"It's all in a day's work," John says with a tight nod.

"I know how you can make it up to us." York wiggles his eyebrows. Logan elbows him hard in the side, and he grunts, cursing out loud. "Fuck, sorry! I was only playing."

"Speaking of playing, shall we continue?" Mark asks, tossing a chip into the center.

We play a few hands, and I fold twice, mostly to

watch the body language of the others at the table. Logan and Mark are hard to read, but the others make little slips here and there. By the fifth hand, I think I am ready to stay in, and I chuck two cards and wind up with a pair of twos. Crap! But I go with it; they don't know what I have. Plus, it's fun. Soon it is down to me, Mark, and York.

"Come on, Savi," Mark chuckles, "break that poker face."

I remember what my grandfather said. Grab at something serious that happened in your life and think about it. Pull that hard face from somewhere. So, I do…not like it's hard.

He thinks for a minute then tosses his cards. "Fine! I fold."

Great. One down, one to go. I glance at York, who is studying me. I toss two more chips on the table, raising the bid.

"Hmmm," York mumbles as he stares at me for a few more minutes. "You haven't played a hand yet, so I think you have something." He looks at Mark. "Her face tells a lot. You just have to look for it." York shakes his head in a cocky manner. "Fuck it, I fold."

I couldn't believe it. We had been at this hand for almost thirty minutes, and he's folding. He thinks he's so smart. What an ass. I start looking around the room, behind Mark's chair, then under the table.

"What are you looking for?" York asks, annoyed.

"Oh, um, just your balls." The whole table breaks out in a roar. Paul almost falls out of this chair. Mark turns over York's cards, revealing a pair of tens.

"Well, what did you have?" York barks at me.

I don't have to show him, but it only makes this moment so much better. I flip them over and watch his face fall.

He chews on the inside of his cheek.

I catch Logan watching me. He smiles and seems impressed. I'm impressed, *and* I'm having fun.

"Next Friday, ten p.m., I'm taking you down." Mark points a finger at me as he scoops the chips into a bin. "I will figure you out." He laughs and stands.

I feel myself smiling and really enjoying the company of these guys. I think I may be making friends. The idea thrills yet terrifies me. Can I really be easing back into a normal-feeling life so soon?

"Good night, guys." I wave, and they head off to their bedrooms. Logan walks me to my room and does a quick check for me. I know he is trying to make me feel safer.

"How long until this storm passes?" I glance out the window.

"Forecast says this is a big one. Will you be all right here, or should I get Abigail?"

I turn, shaking my head. "No, I'll be all right." I watch him light my fireplace. "Logan, thanks for tonight. You didn't have to involve me."

He drops the matchstick into the flames and moves to stand in front of me.

"It was fun, and I'm glad you joined us." He waits for a clap of thunder to pass. "Try to get some sleep. Remember, Abigail is just across the hall, and I'm two doors down, on your right."

I nod.

"Safest place you can be is in this house." His eyebrows pinch together like he's thinking as his eyes burn into mine.

I'm very aware of my stomach fluttering.

He moves slowly—making his actions known. "Can I see something?"

I nod, feeling very comfortable with this man.

He brushes my hair away from my face and runs his hot fingers along my temple, stopping at my cheek.

I fight to not close my eyes and bask in the warm feeling that's spreading throughout my body. I let out a small puff of air that I hadn't realized I was holding in.

His eyes close. He looks like he wants to say something, but stops himself. "Good night." He drops his hand and heads for the door, but stops. "Oh, and, Savannah?"

I turn to look at him, still feeling the touch of his hand on my face.

"Please call me Cole."

Wait! What...your name is Cole...Cole Logan?

Chapter Five

I toss and turn all night, now having a face to go with the name I've heard so much about. I find myself dreaming about Cole "popping three" into a sweaty man's forehead. How can such a nice, caring man be a stone-cold killer? I know it's their job to take down bad guys, but the way the guys talk about him, it's as though he doesn't have a soul. Like Cole and Logan are two completely different people. I should have known Logan was his last name—that's how they address everyone here. Abigail does speak fondly of him, and she seems to have a heart of gold. I rub my face roughly.

Why am I so bothered by this? Why do I care about him anyway? All I am is a broken victim worth less than a frigging down payment for a house! It's not like I can even figure out myself anymore. Finally, I give up, kicking off the covers and staring at the ceiling, and wait until morning.

***

I avoid Lo—Cole for the next four days, mainly staying locked in my room. I'm fine with not being around people. Some days I crave it, other times I don't. I love my balcony, and I find that if I sit directly in the right corner near the wall, no one can tell I'm out there. I ask Abigail if she could have Dr. Roberts come to my room for our Monday session. I don't offer an explanation, and she doesn't ask. I can tell she is concerned about me hibernating, but I assure her I just need some time alone to "process." It was, after all, what I had been doing for the past seven months. At least this time it was by choice.

I rub my thumb around my middle finger methodically while a flashback flickers in front of me. Then, suddenly, I am there, reliving it moment by moment.

"Where are you right now, Savannah?"

I hear the doc's words, but they aren't totally registering.

"Where you are? Is it safe?"

Safe? I think, then slowly shake my head.

"Tell me what you're seeing."

"I'm at the place where they took me. I'm so scared. My knee really hurts. It keeps throbbing, and it feels warm and sticky, so I know I'm bleeding." I pause, trembling. "There's an American man here speaking to the others in English." I swallow a growing lump. "Someone throws me to the ground. My knees hit the floor hard—it feels like brick or stone. My hands are tied behind me, and when I fall forward, I hit my face. I keep sucking the cloth bag they put over my head into my mouth when I try to breathe. They yank me back up to my knees, and I can see their shadows moving around in front of me. They keep yelling at each other."

"Okay, you're doing really well, Savannah. Can you make out what they're saying?"

"T-the American is shouting something about proof—needing confirmation." My breathing picks up, and my voice is shaky. "'*Es ella!*' one man shouts. I know what it means. He's saying 'It's her!' The

American man doesn't seem to believe him, then the cloth is pulled off my face." I can tell I'm crying, but I can't stop this flashback...can't help the terror that's ripping through me. "It's dark. I can make out small lights, but my vision is blurry. Someone flashes a bright light in my face. They grab my chin to hold me still."

"Can you see The American?"

"I-I'm so scared, my heart's beating out of my chest. I can barely suck in a breath. The light shifts to the side for a moment, and I see him."

"The American?"

"Y-yes," I choke out. "His face is covered by shadow, but I can feel his eyes glaring down on me. He steps forward and makes the other man let go of my chin. He's standing in front of me. My face is just above his belt. He smells like something familiar, but I can't figure out what it is. He's asking me if I'm Savannah Miller. I look up at him, and I see his cheeks rise—he's smiling at me. I'm begging for him to help me, but he just laughs, and I see at the last minute, he makes a fist. I thought he was going to punch me, but he ends up slapping me across my cheek instead. I fall with no way to protect my face and hit my head on the bricks. His boots flicker in the dim light. They're so distinctive."

"What's distinctive about them?"

My head shakes back and forth, and I break out in a sob. "They leave me on the ground while they continue talking, like I don't exist. I'm crying and pleading for them to let me go, but they ignore me." I'm full-out sobbing now, and hiccupping as I speak. "Who are these people, why have they taken me? Why?"

"Savannah." Dr. Roberts reaches out for me as I heave forward. "Come back to me. You're safe."

I look up at his friendly face.

"You're safe, Savannah. You're not there anymore." He glances over my shoulder and shakes his head at something, but I'm too upset to care.

"Then why does it feel like I am?" I cry. "Every time I close my eyes or let my mind wander, I go back to my personal hell. Those men took so much from me. How do you come back from that? I hate them!" I curl myself into my protective ball. "How can anyone treat a human the way they treated me? I was nothing more than a scrap of human waste to them."

"You're not a scrap of anything, Savannah. You are a strong woman. You survived for those seven months, and you didn't let them beat you down."

"I didn't want to live, though, Doc—I wanted to die," I admit, gripping my chair and sucking in deep breaths. "I just had nothing to do it with, so I decided to starve myself. It was the only thing I—" I point to my chest, "the only thing I could control." I wipe my eyes on my sleeve, trying to calm down. "Tell me, Doc, what does it mean when a person is willing to give up and die? Even now, after a miracle happened and I was saved, I still can't eat. When I do eat, I feel guilty, like I'm betraying myself," I hiss at him.

He takes off his glasses, cleaning the lenses. "What do you think that means?"

I roll my eyes. "A question with a question. Classic, Doc."

He leans back and crosses his legs. "I'd say you hit the lowest point a person can go, so you made a promise to yourself that you intended to keep. Then you got rescued—something you never thought could happen— and when you left that room, perhaps you left a piece of yourself behind." He thinks for a moment. "Savannah, you've only been free for three weeks. Give yourself a chance to heal, a chance for your brain to catch up with what has happened. In time, things will go back to normal. Maybe not exactly the same as it was, but a new normal that will feel right."

I nod through a hiccup.

"You wouldn't believe the things I've heard when I came to work for Shadows. I have helped people see that, yes, they've been through something I'll never understand, but I can still help them find their way back home." He leans forward. "Funny thing is, sometimes going home is going backward for them. Some find starting a new life somewhere else is their ticket to freedom." He raises one hand to rub his jaw. "Let this place protect you and also heal you. You're lucky. Not everyone gets to have this privilege. Just keep telling yourself that you're free, you have a voice, and you have choices."

"All right," I whisper. His words make the ache dull momentarily.

"Now," he stands, picking up his bag, "our session ran a little bit long today." I glance at his watch. We have been talking for two and a half hours. "Have you taken the horses out for a ride yet? If not, you should. There's plenty of countryside to see. Enjoy the rest of your day. I'll see you tomorrow."

***

Cole checks his watch for the fifth time in sixty seconds, waiting impatiently for Dr. Roberts to finish this session with Savannah. He doesn't have time to waste; he needs to know what the good Doc got out of her this morning. Mark Lopez, his best friend and one of his most trusted men, had overheard their conversion from the patio. He said she sounded really upset and thought maybe the doc had made a small breakthrough. Cole wanted to check on her himself and make sure she was okay.

He hasn't seen Savannah since that night in her room when he had wanted to tell her how he felt. As usual, his pride got in the way, and he couldn't. He knew better than to cross a line with a "guest," of course. It was totally unprofessional and not like him at all. He knew she was avoiding him, although Abigail assured him that she just needed some alone time. Kidnap victims tended to take one step forward and two steps back, so he was letting her be, but when Mark came to him, there was nothing he could think of other than making sure she was all right.

He marched right down the hallway and burst into the room. In hindsight, he was glad they were out on the balcony. He felt like a Neanderthal with his lack of courtesy. When Cole moved toward the open doors and heard her sobbing, the doctor caught his eye and shook his head for him not to interrupt. Once he saw she was all right to some degree, he nodded, leaving the room.

What is with this woman? Getting him to drop everything and go find her right in the middle of a conference call? Living with two generations of Special Forces men lends itself to a certain kind of lifestyle. It's a structured, no bullshit, do-your-job-and-do-it-well way of life. He had girlfriends before, but never had much time for them with the family business. A few women never liked the fact he couldn't share much, and how he'd disappear for days at a time. He didn't find he cared enough to let them in. It was easier to hold them at arm's length, especially after the last woman. Yeech!

But with Savannah, it's different. From the moment his eyes met hers, he couldn't shake the protective feeling he had about her. He leans his forehead against the wall with a groan. His father said this could happen one day, but he never believed it. He just wasn't the relationship type; he was married to his job. *Christ, get a grip, man!*

He pushes off the wall—he will not let this ridiculous feeling cloud his judgment. She's just another pretty face who needs help. He lets out a steady, long breath. *Stop thinking about her!* It's just that this damn woman is keeping him up at night. He needs to separate himself from her, and it needs to start now.

Suddenly, her bedroom door opens. He takes a step forward, ready to pounce on the good doctor, when instead she comes out, wiping her eyes with a tissue.

"Oh, hi." Her wide, watery eyes look up at him.

Shit. "Are you all right?" *What was that you were just saying?* He groans internally.

She nods, forcing a smile. Is she nervous? She's acting nervous.

"Yes—mm, I just need some fresh air."

Holy shit, she's nervous; all the signs are there. He holds up his hand to stop her, but Dr. Roberts comes out, scanning his notes. She slides around him and hurries down the hall. Slippery little woman. He shakes his head. She is probably rattled from her session.

"Oh, Cole." Dr. Roberts holds up his recorder. "We should talk."

***

"So, no real description of The American, just that he was there and confirmed she was who they said she was." Cole clicks the audio recorder off, plugging it into the USB cord. He hits a key, uploading the session onto his computer.

"Only that he had flashy boots," the doctor adds. "Honestly, in my professional opinion, she doesn't know anything. You'd have to be one hell of an actress to pull this off."

Cole agrees with the doctor. Not that he thinks Savannah is anything but innocent—it just feels good to have someone confirm it. "Wow." He shakes his head. "This is the third case with this son of a bitch. I wonder what his connection is."

Dr. Roberts rubs his face in thought. "I don't know, but it's still beyond me that they kept her alive all this time. Why not make the exchange? Granted, fifty grand is peanuts, but they've had seven months to up it to a million. It cost them money to keep her fed, not that she ate much."

Cole's stomach turns, remembering what she said about making a promise to herself.

"I don't get it. It's like they kept her on ice. What were they waiting for? I think there's a lot more to this case than what we're seeing." Cole taps his pen on the arm of the chair. "I think you're right. We'll keep her father in the dark. I don't trust it won't go public. There are leaks everywhere. Too many eyes on him."

"Yeah, the man sure loves the media," Dr. Roberts mutters.

"Overall, what are your thoughts on Savannah adjusting here?" Cole has to ask. He needs to know what is making her nervous. Was it today's session or something else?

"I'd say she's doing well. Just the fact that she started talking after fourteen days was impressive. She's an interesting woman. She picks up on a lot more than you'd think. Watch her when you're in a group. She studies people's behavior, then once she feels she understands them, she'll engage. I suspect her trust in people was tested a lot while she was held captive, perhaps even before." He reaches for his bag. "I feel after some time she'll come around, but don't be taken by her feisty behavior. It could be a front. She uses it as a shield to keep people who make her uncomfortable at arm's length. Though if you read her file, she is a bit of a spitfire at times." He stands, fixing his tie. "One thing her physician and I agree on is she was not raped. She shows no signs of any sexual assault."

Cole sinks further into his chair. *Thank fuck!*

"That being said, it sure opens up another whole box of questions."

"Yeah, it sure does." Cole leans forward and shakes his hand. "Okay, Roberts, see you tomorrow."

Cole rises, looking out the floor-to-ceiling window. He tucks his hands into his pockets and watches the clouds float across the mountains. He can't wrap his head around it—no sexual abuse, no million-dollar ransom. They keep her alive for over seven months, and despite her psychological state, she's relatively all right. It just doesn't add up. He needs to start laying out the pieces to this growing puzzle. They're not going to let Savannah get away that easily.

***

I decide to head to the lake in search of a canoe instead of a horseback ride. I don't know how to ride a horse, and I don't feel like learning. I've had way too emotional a day to tumble ass up in a bush somewhere.

I step carefully into the fiberglass boat, balance with my hands on the sides, and gingerly push off from the dock. The paddle glides through the water, sending me away from the house. It's not that I don't want to be here—I do—I just need to get away for a bit to clear my head. I feel emotionally raw from today's session, and I have some things I'd like to mull over and then tuck away so I can make my peace.

The lake is large, and before I know it, the house looks tiny, although I know it is far from it. I was bored the other day and counted sixteen bedrooms, two kitchens—and it has eight barbecues. I would have continued my exploring, but I ran into Keith, who is also known as Seven, getting ready to head out for his shift. He showed me some of his gear and told me the weather in Montana is nothing compared to the heat and sandstorms they've seen in Afghanistan. I wanted to ask about his time there, but the look on his face encouraged me not to.

I tuck the paddle away and lean back, bringing myself to the bottom of the canoe with my feet propped up on the seat. I stare at the clouds, relishing the fact that I can. I drift for a long time. I tune in to every sound. I feel the armor around my chest slowly loosen, and today's stress starts to melt away. I close my eyes. Yes, this is just what I need—me and nature.

***

My eyes flutter open as a new sound finds me. It is almost like something is bobbing repeatedly to the surface. I can hear air bubbles. I pull myself up to a sitting position and take in my surroundings. Six pairs of eyes are staring at me through black goggles, mouths covered with oxygen masks, and six massive rifles resting on top of the water. Holy shit! I open my mouth and let go with one earth-shattering scream, making it bounce off the mountains. One person makes a move toward me, and I jump to my feet. The boat rocks, sending me into the water. The cold water is a shock to my system. It's freezing. My breath is sucked from my lungs in a giant whoosh, and doesn't want to come back. I feel someone wrap their hands around my waist and pull me to the surface. I bat at their arms, kicking with all the strength I have. I scream and clock the nearest with an elbow, causing him to release me. I swim forward and lunge for the overturned boat when I hear my name being yelled.

"Savannah!"

My frozen fingers claw desperately at the wood, but I can't get a grip. My limbs are becoming stiff, and my heartbeat is out of control.

"Savannah, stop, it's us!"

"Get away from me!" I shout. "I won't go back!"

"Savannah, it's Mark."

His voice finally registers. *What?*

He swims up next to me as I'm shaking like a leaf. "It's okay," he whispers, holding his gun and his other hand in the air, showing me he's not a threat. He slowly removes his mask, giving me a glimpse of his face.

I close my eyes and try to calm myself.

"We're sorry. We didn't mean to scare you."

I nod. Being scared doesn't even begin to register how I'm feeling.

"Come on. We have to get you warm."

A speed boat shows up, and Mark and someone else climb aboard with me. Mark wraps a blanket around me while the other guy moves to sit with the driver.

He keeps his goggles on but spits out the air piece.

***

Mark rushes me inside through a door I haven't seen before, meeting Abigail, who already has a bath running for me in my room. I am whisked away before I can say anything else to Mark.

The warm water burns as it thaws my limbs. I'm still reeling with what happened and feel bad, but at the same time, I'm mad at the guys for scaring the shit out of me and ruining my relaxing boat trip.

Abigail tries small talk as I sit buried in bubbles in the tub. She keeps an eye on me as she chats away. "We're having company tonight. It will be nice having someone else for dinner. Why don't you pick something from the left side of the closet tonight?" That means something a little fancier. She prattles on. "You would look lovely in that soft sweater dress. Why don't you try it on?" She fusses about, and I know she's worried about me.

I give her a reassuring smile.

Once out of the tub, I stand staring at the clothes. It's strange having a wardrobe you had no part in buying. The clothes are my style. This would normally shock me, but I guess it was all part of my background check. Plus, you can Google my name and a thousand images will pop up. Google…I haven't thought about using the internet in a long time. I wonder if I can get my hands on a laptop soon.

I blow dry my hair, letting it fall in waves down my back, and apply some light eye makeup that compliments the pinot noir sweater dress that clings to my body, landing a little lower than mid-thigh. It would have been something I'd wear out to dinner with coworkers. It's pretty, with a touch of fun. I ponder the V-neckline. There was a time I wouldn't have, but now I find myself hesitating. It dips a little low, but it is still tasteful. Abigail did say pick something from the left side, and she did mention a sweater dress.

I leave the mirror and head back to the closet to look for shoes. I notice a jewelry box on one of the shelves. I open it and find three beautiful silver bangles. I slip them over my wrist while grabbing a pair of black heels.

Okay, Savi, stop stalling. I shake off my jitters as I walk down the stairs.

***

Cole can't believe what happened this afternoon. He hadn't heard her screams, as he had been on the phone with his father, who was telling Cole that he was going to stop by for dinner tonight. Cole quickly notified Abigail to make his father's favorite meal, honey-glazed ribs, and let the guys know to dress appropriately for dinner. His father is still acting CEO of the company, and is well loved around here. He is a charmer, to say the least. Cole's mother gave him a run for his money, but he landed her in the end. Cole was sad she wasn't coming tonight, but she had a prior engagement—ultimately why his father has some free time. He has a niggling feeling his father has an ulterior motive for showing up tonight. Maybe he has news of a new sighting of The American.

He grabs Mark as he walks by. They are all gathering in the living room, waiting for dinner to be served. His father is in a heavy conversation with Keith, so he takes this time to hear firsthand from Mark what the hell happened on the lake.

"We had just started our drill when we noticed the canoe floating out there. We couldn't see anyone in it, so we swam over to see what it was doing in the middle of the lake. We approached it carefully, since it's always tied up on the dock. Then she suddenly sits up and sees us. I can only imagine what was going through her head. I know how our gear looks. Anyway, she hopped up, looking—" Mark's eyes flicker over Cole's shoulder, "amazing..."

Cole turns and follows his friend's gaze. If his mouth wasn't already open, it sure as hell would be as he takes in the view.

Oh, God, buddy, you're screwed. Fat chance you'll be getting that out of your head tonight.

He watches as the room takes her in, guys sneaking glances here and there. At least they're being respectful.

"You know, there are times when I really enjoy my job," Mark jokes beside him.

Cole catches her gaze as Keith hands her a glass of wine. She still looks nervous. What the hell did he do? Maybe he crossed a line touching her cheek. Oh, God, what a fool he can be. No, it's that stupid magnetic hold she has on him. He takes a large sip of his brandy and turns to see his father grinning at him. Oh, shit. Just what he needs, his father inside his head.

Mark makes a quick exit as he spots Abigail walking by with a tray of stuffed pastries.

Yeah, thanks, man. He walks over to the fireplace, needing something to do. He sneaks a peek at her talking to Paul. This is the first time he's seen her in a dress, and he hopes to hell it will be the last, because his eyes can't help but rake up and down her long, slim legs. The way her dress hugs her body, the way her hair hangs in long waves, all make his stomach flip. Damn this woman!

"Pretty little thing, huh?" his father whispers over his shoulder.

Busted.

"Yeah, she is," he mutters into his glass. His father chuckles, coming to stand in front of him.

"The mayor's daughter," he says, acknowledging who she is. "Her father is making quite the shit storm with the media. When will they learn to keep their mouths shut?"

"I fear we may only have scratched the surface of this case," Cole replies quietly. "Plus, The American is involved with her kidnapping." His father flinches almost imperceptibly at the name. "So, you know what that means."

"Shit, yeah. He won't stop until she's found." He swirls his drink. "Poor girl, her life will never be the same. Have you heard if they'll relocate her?"

Cole's stomach sinks. "I think its best she stays here. She's adjusting well. Witness Protection could send her backward."

"Mmmm." His father coughs as he tries to hide his smile. "Well, I'll see if I can talk to Frank. Maybe after some time passes, we could make a position for her, or she could get a job in town. I'll get her some new paperwork lined up."

***

"Savannah, this is Daniel Logan," Cole says, introducing her to him as they approach.

Her eyes go back and forth as she realizes she is meeting his father.

"Oh-oh." Her smile appears. "It's nice to meet you, Mr. Logan." She holds out her hand for a shake, but he wraps his fingers around hers and kisses the top of her hand. Oh, Lord…

"The pleasure is all mine. Please, call me Daniel."

Her eyes shift to Cole's, then to the floor.

What the hell is that? Christ, he wants to drag her into the corner and demand to know why she's acting strangely around him.

"Dinner is ready," Abigail calls. Mark makes a beeline for the table. "Boys," she mutters, but a grin appears.

"Shall we?" Daniel asks Savannah, holding out his arm. She smiles. Giving in to his charm, she threads her small arm through his and walks toward the dining room.

"Abigail, you outdid yourself again," Daniel compliments her as he holds up a rib. "Delicious."

"Thank you, Daniel. It was my pleasure." Her face warms at all the attention.

A few more stragglers come to the table. Savannah's gasp gets Cole's attention, and his head snaps up to see York sporting a black eye.

"Hello, everyone," York mutters, taking a seat. He makes a dramatic nod. "Savannah." Her hands are over her mouth, and she starts shaking. A moment later, she breaks into full-blown laughter. She reaches over and grabs Mark's arm for support, and he starts laughing too.

Cole's heart skips a beat. He loves her laugh. But what is he missing?

"Something funny?" York raises an eyebrow at them, clearly not impressed.

"I-I'm…" She tries to speak, but she can't form a sentence. Finally, holding her stomach, she manages to get hold of herself. "Excuse me," she says to the group. "I wasn't expecting that." She points to York.

Mark wipes his eyes dry. "I thought this was the best way for you to find out."

"Thanks. I needed it." She grins, her eyes glistening. She looks relaxed. So, is this what Savannah was like before she was taken?

"Is anyone going to explain?" Daniel asks, clearly ready for a good story.

"Well…" Mark's grin speaks volumes. "We had a little encounter with Savi and a canoe today during one of our drills. York was trying to help her when she fell in the water, but she panicked and clocked him good in the eye."

"Lucky hit," York mutters.

"Lucky like winning a game of poker with a pair of twos?" Savannah shoots back.

"Ha!" Daniel laughs. "Oh, Lord, son, I wish you'd told me about her sooner. Seems I've missed out on some good times, hey?"

"I'm sorry, York, truly," Savannah says after the table dies down. "I didn't know who you were, and when you grabbed me, well…" She clears her throat.

"Don't sweat it," York mutters around a rib in his mouth.

"Oh, I would have paid money to have seen that, though." Abigail laughs.

Savannah's mouth drops open before she joins in too. York rolls his eyes. What does he expect when he acts like the house asshole? He has to know he'll be treated like one.

Chapter Six

I sit twirling the stem of my wine glass between my fingers, watching the red wine rise up the sides then bleed back down. I hear the guys joking around while they clean up in the kitchen. Abigail is on the phone with her sister, excited about her coming for a visit soon. I push the sinking feeling away of when I'll see my father next. I long to see him and Lynn.

"How do you like it here, Savannah?" Daniel's question pulls me from my thoughts. He takes a seat next to me at the dinner table.

"It's..." I take a deep breath, "all a little surreal. Don't get me wrong—I'm incredibly thankful. It's just that I went from my old life, to a prison, to this." He nods. "I think I feel like I'm floating with no roots to hold me down. I'm not really sure where I belong."

"Well," he rubs his chin, "you're not the first person to say that." He gives me a reassuring smile. "Have you made any friends yet?"

"Umm, friends? Ah—well, Mark seems friendly enough."

"Yes, Mark has been around for a long time. Good man. Anyone else?"

"I guess Paul, John, and Keith." He nods, agreeing with me. "York is an interesting character."

"Yes, York is something else."

"I love Abigail. She's like mother and sister all rolled into one." I pause, knowing what he is waiting for.

"What about Cole? Has he been friendly?"

Oh, boy. I take a long drink of my wine to stall. Truthfully, I don't really know how I feel about him. I know the stories I've heard scare me to no end, but he's also the first man in twenty-seven years who makes my stomach bubble with warmth. I've had boyfriends in the past, but when my father became mayor, they seemed to enjoy the fame a lot more than I did.

I glance over at Cole in the kitchen. He is such a beautiful man. Once more I take in his tall, lean body, those eyes you could get lost in and never return. Why in the world he hasn't been snatched up still baffles me. I blush when his father clears his throat. Clearly, I just got caught. He lets out a little chuckle.

"Cole's been—" *Caring, kind, respectful, understanding, yummy. Oh, Lord, Savi, get a handle on yourself!* "Great," I say, feeling like an ass. Such a lame answer. "He's been very hospitable." I shake my head as I fumble over my words. "I mean…he makes me feel welcome and secure for the first time in, well, a long time." I shrug, trying to explain better. "I—I don't even know what safe feels like anymore, but whatever he does, it's nice." He grins at me…oh, shit. "But that's his job, so…yeah, I guess he does it well." *Oh, shoot me now!* Why couldn't I have said fine and leave it at that?

He chuckles again, and I close my eyes, mentally slapping my forehead. I'm such a moron!

"Yes, Cole has always been very good at what he does. His mother worries he's a little too dedicated sometimes. She feels he's hiding behind his work. He likes to keep people at arm's length. You know this job can be hard on the head. He was born to be in the Special Forces, but that doesn't mean it doesn't screw with you." He stops himself. "I apologize, forgive me.

My mouth has run away with me."

"No, it's fine. Truthfully, it's refreshing getting a little insight on these guys." Cole, mainly, but I wasn't about to say that.

"So, tell me, Savannah, what did you do for fun back in New York?"

"Fun?" I almost laugh. Fun isn't a word I've used in a long time, even before my prison. "I guess that would be going to listen to live music at local pubs. I'm a sucker for the blues."

"Oh, yeah?" His eyes light up. "You know, there're a few places in town that have live music."

"Town?" I look at him, puzzled. "I wasn't aware we were close to a town."

"Whitestone. It's about fifteen miles from here. You should check it out. One can go a bit stir crazy up here." Huh.

"I guess one would go stir crazy if they were here long enough." I watch his face, waiting for a sign, any indication that I'll be here for a while. He takes a drink, but his face gives nothing away. "I feel like you're telling me to set some roots here, make some friends, and check out the nightlife."

His eyes flicker toward where Cole and Mark are talking.

"I won't be going home for a while, will I, Daniel?"

He doesn't look at me.

"That's a question I can't answer for you right now, Savannah."

My stomach sinks.

"But you just did," I whisper.

***

Cole sits at his desk flipping through footage of the last known sighting of The American crossing the Texas border into Mexico, three days ago. He leans back and rubs his face. *So, this man was stepping back onto Mexican soil while we were all having dinner.* He wonders where he was when Savannah first came here. There's always the possibility they were followed, though it's highly unlikely. They changed cars twice since the airport in North Dakota. Once at the border, and again before they climbed the mountain roads in Montana.

A ping alerting him to an email brings him back from his thoughts. He opens the message from Frank, his main contact within the Army. He clicks the attachment, and it opens to a video of Mayor Doug Fox sending out yet another media message about his daughter. Cole rolls his eyes as he presses play.

"It's another cold New York day that I wake up and do not have my daughter to call. It's been eight months since I've last heard her voice, gave her a hug, or told her I loved her." He pauses for a breath while his chin quivers. "Please, return my sweet Savannah to me." He claps his hand over his mouth. A woman steps up to the microphone, thanking the media for listening. The shaking mayor removes himself from the crowd.

Cole flicks the screen back to The American, deciding something does not add up. The American was normally involved with high profile men, not young women. *Why the mayor's daughter? They'd get more money if they took the mayor. The Cartels normally get more media coverage then, and they love to show their power. However, the mayor is doing a stellar job in that department.* Cole leans into his hands, letting out a long breath.

"Cole?" He looks up to see Savannah standing in his doorway. "Sorry, your door was open." She looks around his office. "Bad time?"

He's barely seen her since the dinner with his father

three days ago.

"No." He drops his hands, trying to shake his stress. "Come in."

She walks toward him, stopping when she gets to the chair. Her small fingers clasp the back of it.

"What can I do for you?"

"May I?" She points to the chair.

"Please."

She sits and crosses her legs, running her hand through her hair and tossing it over to one side. A hint of apples reaches his nose. Focus.

"I think we should talk." She clears her throat, as Cole's stomach twists. "I'm sure you've noticed I've been avoiding you. I thought I should explain myself."

He was not expecting this. He waits for her to go on.

"When I first met you, I called you my carrier because that's what you were to me until I heard Abigail call you Logan. Then one night when I was in the living room, I heard some of the guys talking about this man Cole and how he—" She stops, fumbling with her hands.

"He what?" He wants to know where she is going with this.

"How he killed a rat by popping three between his eyes."

Cole closes his eyes briefly.

"They talked about how many kills this Cole had, as well as the number of barehand kills. I was terrified to meet him. I was starting to let my guard down with you. I like that you did things that—" She blushes, pushing her lips together.

He leans forward in his chair, interested to know more about these things she likes.

"I was caught off guard when you told me your first name. I couldn't believe that Cole was you. After taking some time to think it through, though, I realize I was judging you unfairly, because I don't know you enough to judge you, so for that, I'm sorry."

He watches her carefully, realizing it took a lot for her to come in here and tell him what she has been thinking. He leans back in his chair, a little annoyed at the same time.

"I imagine hearing something like that would frighten you. Sadly, the guys may spill more details as time goes on. I guess you can choose to understand what we do, or you can choose not to. I won't say I'm sorry for killing those people. They were evil. In my line of work, there are the good guys and the bad guys. There can be no blurred lines. It's black and white."

"Okay." Her voice is quiet.

There it is again. This is the problem he has with people. They don't understand his life. They judge and run away. Anger rises in him, but he fights it down. How could she realize what his life is like?

"Now that we have that cleared up, is there anything else?" he asks, letting his temper ease up.

"Yes, actually. I know the rules, but can I get my hands on the internet?"

His back stiffens. The internet always poses problems.

"I'll get Abigail to show you to a study where you can use the computer in private. Remember everything is being monitored."

She stands quickly. "Great. Thank you." Her eyes drift down to his desk and narrow. "Is that me?"

He looks down and sees her file open in front of him. Shit! He snaps it shut, but not before she reaches and pulls out a newspaper article about her disappearance.

"This was snapped the night I was taken." She runs her finger over the picture. "I remember that dress." She squints like she is remembering something. "Hmm."

"What?" He stands and moves to her side to look over her shoulder at the picture. "Do you remember something?"

She flips her hair, and there is that apple smell again.

He pauses, allowing himself to enjoy her scent. After all, he spends basically three hundred and sixty-five days a year with men. Needless to say, Savannah smells amazing. Oh, Lord, there he goes again. He forces himself to concentrate.

"See," she turns to look at him over her small shoulder, "I was having drinks with Joe Might in this little pub. There was the bartender and one old man in the corner. I know because I was on high alert, watching for the damn paparazzi. But this was taken from behind Joe. I would have seen them…wait." She holds the picture closer. "There's a reflection capturing part of a hand. I wish it was clearer. Is there a way to blow it up?"

"Umm, I have the email with the attachment. I could bring it up then blow it up larger." He sits in his chair and opens his email. She follows, standing next to him. He normally would never let anyone see his computer, but he enjoys her not being afraid of him. He quickly opens the attachment and brings the picture up and zooms in on the reflection. The hand becomes a little clearer.

"Look." Savannah leans over him and points at the screen, and her hair brushes over his neck. A jolt runs through him. "It's a silver bracelet with a heart on it."

Cole prints the picture to keep a copy.

She turns and leans against his desk in front of him. She raises her hand, rubbing her forehead. "Something's there, I just know it—like it's sitting on the edge of my memory."

She looks so sweet and serious, trying to remember. Cole can feel his walls starting to crumble, and he wants nothing more than to pull her onto his lap and hold her and tell her everything will be all right. Instead, he reaches for her hand. *Oh, you stupid fool.*

Thankfully, she doesn't pull away, though her eyes travel up from their hands to his eyes. His fingers flex, holding her hand a little tighter. Oh…one little tug and she'd be on his lap, knowing just how much he wants her there.

"Give it time, but it will come. Your mind has a lot to process."

"You sound like Dr. Roberts," she jokes. "Thanks, though." She makes no attempt to pull away, and neither does he.

His stomach is swimming laps with the occasional somersault. *Lord, I'm falling fast. Get a grip!*

York comes busting through the door in the middle of a rant. He stops when he sees Savannah behind the desk. She's crossed Cole's forbidden line. She drops his hand, leaving him feeling a loss. "Hey, Savi, didn't know you made office calls," York mutters sarcastically.

"York." She nods and turns to leave. "How's the eye?"

"Abigail will help you," Cole says to Savannah, "if you remember anything."

"I will, thanks." She smiles, then glares at York. "Be careful out there." She taps her eye on the way out.

God, she is fun to watch. Cole's grin fades as he turns his attention to York, who is shaking his head at him.

"What do you want?"

"No, my friend, I think the question is what is it *you* want?" York nods toward the door as it closes behind her.

***

I try to lose the grin that is tugging at the corners of my mouth, but it's difficult. There is something about Cole Logan that makes all my senses stand at attention. I can't believe I didn't flinch when he held my hand, but it felt right. I put the thought aside. I need to hunt down Abigail.

After Abigail gives me the rundown on what sites were blocked, like email, Skype, and Facebook, I am finally left alone. I bring up Google and type my father's name. There must be a billion links to look up, so I start with the newest one. My stomach twists when I click on the video and watch him pour his heart out about me. I continue watching more news clips until I can't take it anymore. I wipe my eyes dry and Google my name, and pictures and articles come flying at me. I click images and see Lynn and me walking on the beach together. We were laughing after spending the day soaking up some sun. Oh, Lynn. I miss her so much it hurts. I print off the picture.

I search my name and the date I was taken. The *New York Times* has a picture of me on the front cover with a caption 'Mayor's Daughter Disappears—Is This a Cry For Help?' I shake my head, reading on. I follow my story as the newspaper and magazines gathered more information. Lynn even did an interview about our last day together, at the end asking the media to give her some space. My poor Lynn.

I read that I ran off with a biker gang Daddy didn't approve of, that I'm living with a cousin in Canada, and some say I'm in a rehab in California. I start to feel nauseated. The stories make me look like I brought this on myself. Finally, the report was released with a statement from the kidnappers asking for a ransom. However, it didn't seem to make headlines for very long.

"I'll leave this for you, dear." Abigail sets a tray down next to me. "Please try to eat it."

"Thank you, Abigail." I reach over and take a sip of the green smoothie. She smiles, leaving the room.

I go back to the articles on my father and notice he doesn't comment on the ransom so much as just wanting to get me back. Maybe they didn't want to draw attention to it. I flip through a few pictures, wanting one to print one of Dad too. I need some memories to remember who I still am…or was.

I find one of Dad at a fundraiser, smiling at someone who was out of the shot. He was clinking his champagne glass. I press print and something catches my eye. It's a woman's hand holding another glass to his, and there was a silver bracelet with a heart dangling from it on her wrist. Holy crap! I start clicking like mad through the photos to see if I can get a better look at this woman. I realize they were at the annual fundraiser for breast cancer we attend every year to help support the cause. It was something we did for Mom. I shudder at the sudden vision of my mother having to deal with all the chemo. She looked like a different person toward the end of her life.

I guess it was nice to see my father smiling like that four months into my kidnapping, funny as that sounds. It was good to know he wasn't stressed, at least at that moment, but the woman in the picture made my stomach knot. Who the hell was she? I look up the number for the charity organizer and jot it down, hoping I can make a phone call. I'll discuss it with Cole later.

I also search *Los Sirvientes Del Diablos* and Servants of the Devil. I print off their history from Wikipedia, as well as the Cartels. I think I should know what I'm up against. I read about other kidnap victims who got away and lived to tell their stories. They all had one thing mine didn't—a very large ransom. Most were asking for half a million. I start making a list of things that are similar to or different than my kidnapping. I turn on the lamp without a care about how late it's getting. I'm so engulfed in my research.

I was held captive for a lot longer than most. Seems *Los Sirvientes Del Diablos* doesn't like to keep their victims for long. They did a proof of life picture and video on me roughly five times. The stories I'm reading say they only did it twice. So why keep me longer? What purpose did it serve, especially when I was only worth fifty grand? That number still makes my gut churn.

"Savannah?" Abigail says from the doorway. "Will you be joining us for dinner?"

I glance at the time on the computer. I have been at this for nearly five hours.

"Yes, sorry. I lost track of time. I'll be right down." I unfold myself from where I am sitting and gather my things. My brain feels fried. I haven't stared at a computer in a long time. Plus, I had a lot to take in. I drop my stuff in my room and head down the stairs.

I find Abigail hustling about the kitchen. I offer to help, but she says she has it under control, so I go look out the front living room window. The horses are running back and forth along the fence, and a light flickers off in the distance, warning of another flippin' storm coming. Another flicker sends me into a flashback.

***

"Up! Chica apurate!*" the fat man yells at me.*

I hurry to my feet as two women enter with a tub on wheels filled with water. They have a bucket with shampoo, body soap, and a large sponge.

"What's going on?" I ask, feeling my panic rise.

"Picture time," he mutters, standing by the door holding a large, army issue gun. "¡Apúrate!" he screams at the women then disappears out the door. They both approach, and one gives me a small smile.

"We need to remove your clothes," one whispers, "quickly." I'm confused but so happy to see a woman here I don't protest. She helps me into the tub and

proceeds to wash me. She's mostly concentrating on my hands, neck, and face. The other woman won't make eye contact as she starts roughly washing my hair. I want to cry out—it hurts—but I don't, because at least I'm finally getting clean. Before I know it, I'm yanked out of the tub and dried off. When the other woman leaves for a moment, I lean toward the nice one.

"Please, what is your name?" She looks around as her hands fuss with my hair. "Please, I'm so lonely— you're the first person who's been nice to me since I arrived."

"Maria," she barely whispers. "Do as they say! Don't fight them, or they'll kill you."

A hissing noise makes us both jump. The other woman has returned, holding a dress, and looks angrily at Maria. She yanks the dress over my head, letting it fall to my knees. It smells awful, but it looks clean. Someone wraps a blindfold over my eyes, and I start to panic. Is this it? A hand grabs my arm and drags me a few steps out of my room and pushes me to my knees. When the blindfold is removed, I'm staring at a video camera. A bright light is pointed at me, nearly blinding me. I look off to the side and see legs from the thighs down, guns hanging by their sides. I can't see their faces, but there must be ten of them. A newspaper is shoved into my hands.

"Sonria," a man yells from behind a tripod holding a video camera.

"Say your name," the fat man hisses at me. I look over at the video camera and see the red light on. "¡Nombre!"

"S-Savannah Miller," I whisper, then someone snaps the newspaper away. Shit! I want to see the date!

"What's your papa's name, what he do?"

My stomach turns as I lick my dry lips.

"Doug Fox, Mayor of New York."

"Up!" Someone grabs my arm as someone else returns the blindfold. Just as I am being pulled out of the room, I hear the boom of thunder.

***

"Ahh!" I shriek as I am jolted back to the present. I scream again when someone touches my arm and holds me steady. I realize it's Cole, and my hands grip his biceps for support.

"Hey, what's going on? You're white as a ghost," he asks softly.

"Sorry." I shake my head, trying to clear the memory. "I just was remembering something." I take a deep breath and fight the urge to cry.

"Did you eat lunch?"

"No, she didn't." Abigail gives me a shake of her head from the doorway. "I found your sandwich in the trash."

I close my eyes, feeling terrible.

"Sorry, just wasn't hungry."

She sighs, then announces dinner is ready.

"Please don't skip meals, Savi." Cole still has me by my arms.

I look up and see he seems genuinely worried.

"Cole, I need to talk to you about somethi—"

"Whoa, two times in one day, guys. People might talk." York snickers, coming up next to us and cocking one eyebrow inquisitively.

"Perfect timing, as always, York," Cole mutters, watching me. "Let's go eat, shall we?"

I sip my lemonade and manage to eat half of my dinner. I don't engage in the conversation. I am lost in thought about the girl with the bracelet. Who is she? Why is she following me? How does she know my father? Wow, everything tilts. I feel dizzy all of a sudden, and my hand flies out, gripping the edge of the table.

"You don't look so hot, Savi," Mark says from beside me.

"Could you excuse me?" The room spins slightly, but I manage to head outside.

I wrap my sweater around me as I lean over the deck railing. Yes, outside is a good choice. The smell of the storm is thick in the air. It is only a matter of time before the rain will start. The sky looks angry as the dark clouds roll around the mountains. I drop my head, feeling dizzy again.

Maria's face flashes in front of me. She smiled, making me want to cry. She was supposed to be my friend. She used to sneak into my room at night and sit on the floor against the wall, and we'd talk about our families. It only lasted for a few days, but it was something I clung to. I confided in her one night about finding a hunting knife that one of the men dropped while dragging the tub inside my room. I was planning to use it to escape. She asked to see it, and when I showed her, she grabbed it, shoving it in my face and calling out for Jose. She was just using me to find out information, and it crushed my heart. I truly liked Maria, and I thought she liked me. I was badly beaten with a wooden paddle, and my ears rang for two days straight, but I learned an important lesson that night.

Trust no one.

"Gonna be a big one." I jump but don't turn around. My stomach twists like it is battling with my dinner. "Sorry, I didn't mean to scare you."

"I'm sure," I shoot back. York stands by my side, peering down at me through his gray, wolf-like eyes.

"I'm going to give it to you straight, Savannah, now that I finally got you alone." I let out some short breaths, trying to fight the dizzy feeling. "I hear The American was involved in your kidnapping."

"The American?" That's what I called him. "Does he not have a name?"

"We've been watching him for six years, and no one has been able to identify him yet. He's good and runs thick with the Cartels. He's heavily protected. No one has been able to get near him. You need to try to remember every single detail of your encounters with this man. It's crucial."

"I've been try—"

"Not hard enough!" he bites. I turn my head and stare up at him for a moment. I'm seeing double.

"Not hard enough! I'm sorry, but were you held captive for seven months and treated like a dog? No—you weren't. My memories come and go. Sometimes things trigger them, sometimes they don't. I can't force them." I step closer to him. "I'm still trying to process all this. Things are so fucked up, York! So, don't tell me that I'm not trying hard enough." I stagger, feeling ill.

He grips my elbow hard and angrily pulls me out of view of the doors. "I get that you're trying, Savannah, but now that we know The American is involved, it's a game changer. He doesn't lose his prisoners—ever." He lowers his voice. "His name is now linked with you and your disappearance, and now that you're out of the *Los Sirvientes Del Diablos'* hold, you're going to be his number one priority. Do you understand why I'm telling you to use your head and remember everything? This is why. You could fuck this whole place up." He waves his hand over the property. "Fuck, I wish we knew more about you and the situation before we came and got you out. Fucking Cole."

Okay, now everything is spinning. I reach out my hand to a chair for support. "You—you're saying you wouldn't have come for me?"

He makes a pissy face. "What I'm saying is we

should have and still should hand you over to the Witness Protection Program. All you're going to do is cause us trouble and potentially expose all that we've worked so hard for."

"I didn't ask for this, York," I spit out defensively. "Shit, what am I supposed to do with this information besides try to crack open memories locked inside my brain with a fucking deadbolt?"

"You should think about leaving," he says without missing a beat.

That sucks the wind right out of me. I turn on my heel and make my way down the stairs to the grass. I don't want to go back inside and face everyone. If this is what's going on, maybe he isn't the only one who feels I'm jeopardizing this place. I head for the boathouse with heavy feet. I feel off balance. I collapse on a chair, trying to fight off the nausea. Jesus, what did I eat? I open and close my eyes. Everything is shifting to the right. I move my hand in front of me, and it blurs in its path like a rainbow. I flop forward on all fours, heaving, my stomach wrenching. I lay my cheek to the cool wood, staring out at the water, and watch the curtain of rain traveling toward me. The raindrops bounce off my face, freeing me of my sweaty forehead and feeling very cool.

They don't know who The American is? Just that he'll be looking under every rock in the US until he finds me? Wow, I'm royally fucked. How, or rather why, is this happening to me? Oh, God, what if I ruin all this for the Logans? Three generations, and they've saved countless lives. I lean forward, emptying my stomach again. I feel miserable. I flop back down on the deck; I don't have the strength to do anything else. My clothes are drenched, but I don't notice anything but the violent pain in my stomach. Oh, no! I roll and continue the horrible act of emptying my stomach, though there can't be anything left in there. I close my eyes and promise myself I'll speak with Cole about leaving.

"Savannah?" I hear Keith call through the rain. "What are you doing?"

I don't move. I barely find my voice.

"Need a minute."

"Can I get you out of the rain—" He drops in front of me, the brim of his hat streaming with water. "Jesus, Savi, you look horrible." He reaches out to take my wrist and checks my pulse. I hear his rain jacket squeak as he mutters something into his radio. I can't make it out; things are going gray. "I need to get you inside."

I push away his hand, letting mine fall in front of him with a smack. I feel like I'm heavy as lead. There is no way he is going to move me. If he did, I think I might black out from the motion.

"No," I whisper, concentrating on a rock. I need something to focus on that isn't moving. He watches me for a moment, then stands. Oh, good, please leave me be.

Chapter Seven

Cole is sipping a brandy, listening to John tell a story about a flat tire he got while coming back into the US from a snatch and grab in Mexico, when Mark catches his attention. He waves him into the kitchen and follows, only to find him looking distraught.

"Keith needs to speak with you," Mark says, handing him his radio. Cole looks at him curiously. Mark is on duty tonight, but if Keith requested him, it must be important. "You need to take this."

"Logan to Delta Seven."

"Logan, you need to come to the boat house. I have a situation."

"Be right there." Mark is already handing him a rain coat, a worried expression on his face.

He jogs down the lawn over the sopping grass, his boots sinking in, making it slippery. Keith stops him a few yards from the boat house.

"It's Savannah." Cole's stomach sinks. "I found her lying on the deck of the boat house. She looks really sick, and her pulse is racing. She won't let me move her. I didn't want to force her." He gives Cole a look; they all know better than to force things with their "guests." Victims of kidnapping are to be handled with kid gloves. "I just thought she'd respond better to you." Keith grips his arm as he comes closer. "Cole, she doesn't look good."

"Take me to her." Cole follows him around the corner to where a drenched, lethargic Savannah lies on the deck floor. Delta Six is holding an umbrella over her head. Cole's heart sinks as he rushes to her side and drops to his knees, shocked at how pale she is. He checks her pulse; it is racing.

"Hey, Savi." He tries to remain calm and notices her eyes never shift from the horizon. "Why are you out here?"

"Tell Cole I'll leave," she barely whispers. Leave? He glances up at Keith, who gives a grim nod—she is clearly out of it. He bends down to get a good look at her pupils and finds them dilated.

He gives Keith the sign to call the doctor. "Code one, Keith."

Keith quickly calls it in.

She moans and holds her stomach.

"Savannah, why would you leave?" He tries to distract her as she retches again.

"The American—his name is connected with mine—he doesn't lose hostages."

What the hell? How does she know this? What she's saying is classified information.

"I need to leave before—" Her words are slurring and her eyes look heavy. "Tell Cole not to worry. I'll leave."

Over his dead body will this woman be leaving the safety of his house.

"I'm going to pick you up now, Savi."

"No," she whimpers, trying to push him away. "Sick." He ignores her protests and cradles her to him. She is so exhausted her body is like mush against his.

"Keith," he calls over his shoulder, "my entrance."

Keith runs ahead and opens a side door reserved for Cole only. It is a direct route to his room.

Once they are out of the rain and in the back hallway,

he turns to Keith. "Go get Abigail, and don't mention a word of this to anyone. Call in someone to replace you tonight, get dried off, and meet me back in my room."

Keith nods then glances at Savannah before he leaves.

Cole is happy it was Keith who found her and not one of the other guys. They might have moved her, thinking it was for the best.

He opens the door to his bedroom and places her on his bed. She grips his jacket, and he stills.

Her eyes are closed, and he knows she is barely hanging on. She moans and lets go of him and clutches her stomach, and he grabs a small garbage can.

Wow, she's really sick.

"Oh, my goodness, Savannah." Abigail comes rushing in his room with a homemade medical bag, then pulls out a thermometer and sticks it in Savannah's ear.

Savannah moans again and tucks her knees to her stomach, her breathing growing shallow.

"No fever. Cole, should we move her to her bedroom?"

"No, this situation stays here until we know what's making her sick."

"The doctor should be here any minute," Keith chimes in.

"Okay, boys, give me five minutes so I can get her into something dry, please."

Cole pulls out a black t-shirt and hands it to Abigail before walking into the private hallway with Keith.

"I want you to keep this whole thing quiet for now, Keith."

"Of course."

"Did she say anything to you?"

"She kept saying she needed to leave." He shakes his head. "She was talking to someone earlier, but I couldn't see from my post. It got heated with whoever it was—

she caught my attention when she shouted. I watched her leave the deck and walk down to the boat house. She stumbled as she reached the chair. I thought perhaps she had too much to drink, so I let her be. But then she fell forward and collapsed on the deck. By the time I got there, she was vomiting hard and was white as a ghost. I'm sorry I didn't move her, but—"

"No, you did the right thing." Cole thinks for a moment. "I want to know who she was talking to, and if you hear anything at all, I want to know about it immediately." Who would have opened their fucking mouth?

"Of course." Keith disappears down the hallway.

***

"When did the symptoms begin? Did anyone notice?" the doctor asks, his expression serious.

"She was fine when I brought her lunch at noon. She said she was just tired." Abigail looks pale.

"She seemed fine when she came to talk to me around eleven," Cole adds, wracking his brain, trying to remember if she seemed different. "At dinner, she seemed fine too. She ate a little."

"Anything to drink? Alcohol?"

"No, she's not a big drinker," Cole says, crossing his arms.

The doctor draws her blood then tucks it carefully into his bag.

"Do you think it's the flu?" Abigail asks impatiently.

"No, I don't think so. If I was to guess, I'd say she either has food poisoning or she ingested another type of poison." Abigail gasps as Cole balls his hands into fists and tucks them tightly against his sides.

"No one else is sick." Abigail looks horrified. "We all ate the same thing. I made dinner."

Cole squeezes her shoulders. He would never think anything but the best of Abigail.

"Then perhaps something she drank." The doctor slides the IV into the top of her wrist. "Someone could have slipped something in it."

Savannah moans quietly as the needle pokes her skin.

"It's all right, sweetheart. This will keep you hydrated." Cole fights the urge to comfort her.

The doctor looks up at Cole. "Do you have any bottled water that hasn't been opened?"

"Yes." He moves swiftly to his mini fridge and hands him one. He watches as the doctor measures out a tablespoon of charcoal into eight ounces of water.

"In," the doctor checks his watch, "fifteen minutes, the anti-emetic shot I gave her for vomiting should kick in. Get her to drink all of this." He stands and places the bottle on the table. "I'm going to get this blood to the lab. She's stable for now, but if she gets worse before I return, call me immediately."

"How long until the results come in, Dr. Rice?" Abigail moves to Savannah's side and rubs her arm gently.

"First priority, Doc." Cole gives him a look from across the room.

"Always, Logan. I should know in a few hours."

"Use my private cell." Cole doesn't want to risk anything being overheard. There are too many unanswered questions.

Abigail walks the doctor out the back way.

Cole sits in a chair and watches her sleep. She looks tiny in his king size bed. He tries in vain to push the awful thoughts of *'What if?'* aside. What if no one saw her down there? What if...

He's seen people in a lot worse shape, but with Savannah, it's different. Every part of him wants to lie down next to her, breathe her in, and hold her tight. He wants to bring her the comfort she deserves. He rubs his face, leaning back in the chair. He checks his watch and grabs the glass.

Sitting on the edge of the bed, he gently moves her hair out of her face. "Savannah," he says softly, making her stir. "Open your eyes for me."

She moans as she tries to open them.

"Here, drink this. It will help your stomach." Her mouth opens slightly. He slips the straw between her lips and talks her through drinking the whole thing. "Good job. Now you can sleep."

She doesn't move after that.

A knock at the back door brings Cole to his feet. He opens it to find Keith holding a bottle of brandy and two glasses.

"Thought you might need one." Keith shrugs as he steps into the room. "What did the doctor say?"

"Possibly poison. Results should be back soon."

Keith looks shocked and hands him a glass.

"What did you find out?"

"York spoke to her." Keith makes a face as Cole's expression hardens.

Cole takes a long sip, trying to control his anger.

"He was explaining to her that she needs to remember everything about The American. He's pissed at you—"

"He's pissed at me?" Cole shouts. They both glance at Savannah, who stirs.

"Yes, he says we shouldn't have taken her back here. That WPP is a better choice." Keith holds up his hand, stopping him from his rant about the WPP. "That's all I know. Either way, he was straight with me when I asked, giving me the information. He didn't seem to be hiding anything. I told him you wanted him to take my post tonight." Keith grins. "He wasn't pleased, but he went."

"I bet," Cole hisses, sipping his drink. They sit in

silence for a little while and listen to the rain beat against the window.

***

"Cole?" Abigail's voice comes from the doorway. Neither man heard the door open. "Dr. Rice is here."

Cole glances at his watch, stunned to see three hours have elapsed. "Hi, Doc. You didn't call my cell?"

Dr. Rice checks Savannah's vital signs, and everything seems to be all right. "I decided to come over and give you the news directly." He removes the IV.

Cole is quietly going mad while the doc checks her over again.

"It was tetrahydrozoline poisoning."

"What?" Abigail turns to Cole for clarification.

"Eye drops," Cole answers. "Every man carries a bottle. The elements are rough on the eyes. How much was in her system?"

"Enough," the doctor says.

Suddenly, a dark feeling comes over Cole, and he grips the back of his chair. "Dr. Rice," Cole's voice is low, "I need you to remove the test results from your database right now."

"Of course. I'll call the lab immediately." He slips out into the hall.

"What are you thinking?" Keith asks.

"I don't know, but I don't like this, and I think we should keep any details about what has happened under wraps." Cole downs his drink in one swallow.

"I don't understand, Cole." Abigail crosses her arms. "How could she possibly have been poisoned? None of our boys would do this."

"I don't want to go there either, but someone did do it. She wouldn't have done it to herself."

"Why erase it from the database?" Keith asks,

confused.

"If they run the lab and it goes into the database, it's a pretty unusual poisoning. It might stand out, and we don't need anyone taking an interest. I just hope the lab didn't enter it online yet."

"Oh, dear!" Both men look at Abigail. "She likes the lemonade I make. I made her a large batch yesterday morning, and it sat in the fridge all day. So, anyone could have spiked it at any time."

Cole lets out a long breath and turns to Keith.

"Check the video surveillance footage. Let's see what we come up with."

Keith squeezes Savannah's hand then leaves.

"Abigail, could you bring me some of that lemonade, please? I'd like to take it in for testing," Dr. Rice asks from behind them. "Cole, I'll be back tomorrow to check on her. She should recover just fine. We caught it early, and she didn't ingest enough to—" He pauses, seeing Cole's expression. "She just needs rest."

Cole plops down on his chair with a sigh. This whole situation seems surreal. The mere idea that one of his trusted men could betray him makes him sick. Loyalty is essential in this business. He'll have to fill his father in on all this immediately. He really needs the old man's advice.

He wonders how to deal with York. What in the hell was he thinking, opening his mouth to Savannah about anything? She doesn't need to know that her life is never going to be what it was, that she probably will never be able to go back, especially not with what he suspects is going on.

He downs another ounce of brandy, hoping to take the edge off, then leans back and glances at the clock. 3:50 a.m. He finally puts on dry clothes then collapses back into his chair, unwilling to leave Savannah in case she wakes. He is exhausted as well…

***

"No-no-please."

Her words make Cole's eyes pop open, and he lifts his head to see her twitching.

"No more! I'm sorry."

He jumps to his feet and moves to the bed. "Savannah," he whispers, "wake up."

"Nooo."

He shakes her softly until her eyes finally open.

She looks up, startled. Her chest is heaving, and tears trickle down her cheeks.

"You were dreaming," he says. "You're safe."

She shakes her head slowly as she falls back to sleep. "Don't leave," she mutters, moving her hand on top of his.

"I won't. I promise." He kicks off his boots, not caring about whether it's right, and climbs in next to her. He leans his back against the leather headboard and holds her hand as she sleeps. Yup, he is putty in her hands for sure. *Shit.*

"You smell like him," she murmurs, still mostly asleep.

"Smell like who?"

"Cole."

He feels his heart speed up then lets out a chuckle. He knows it's wrong, taking advantage of her in the state she is in, but who is he kidding?

"Is that a good thing?"

She sighs. "Very."

Okay, he's in. He's about to toss all his chips on the table. She needs to be his. Now that he has confirmation that she is interested in him, his guard drops. The overwhelming protective instinct he has been experiencing since she arrived crash down around him like a landslide. Yup, he has officially fallen head over heels for this woman, and it scares him half to death.

***

The smell of apples fills his senses. Its intoxicating warmth spreads down to his toes. He is thoroughly enjoying this half-awake, half-asleep time next to her—until he hears someone clear their throat. His eyes flutter open to a grinning Abigail.

"Morning." She beams, her eyes shifting from him to his side.

He rubs his eyes then looks down at Savannah tucked into him. He isn't sure exactly where to go with this and gives Abigail a silly grin. His brain takes a moment to remember all the details of the night before.

"I'll just leave your breakfast here." As she places the tray on the table, he notices there are two servings. "I'll be sure not to let anyone bother you this morning."

"Abby—" he mumbles, trying to make his brain function properly.

"No, no." She holds up her hands and walks backward toward the door. "Just stay put." She continues to grin widely.

Oh, thank God it was Abigail. He knows he can trust her to keep his confidence. Well, actually, who is he kidding? He shakes his head. No doubt she's calling his mother right now, filling her in on all the details.

Savannah shifts next to him. Her hand moves to his stomach, and her head falls on his chest.

He waits until her breathing is smooth and even, and then wraps his arm around her back, holding her a little closer to him. He loves the way she molds to him. He knows he should slip out of bed before she wakes—she'll probably freak out if she wakes in his arms—but he can't seem to move. His brain and heart are having a battle. Finally, he flips off his brain and basks in her warmth, falling back to sleep.

***

His vibrating cell phone brings him out of his groggy state. He starts to move but realizes Savannah is still draped over him. He snakes the phone free and checks the ID, seeing it's a text from Mark wondering where he is. He switches the cell to silent and places it quietly on the nightstand.

"Cole?" Savannah says softly.

"Yes." His stomach sinks. *Oh, God.*

She shifts and tries to sit up, but can't.

"It's all right, Savannah," he assures her. "It's not what you think."

"Why am I in this room, in bed with you?"

His brain mentally slaps him. *Ass!* He decides to go with the truth.

"Because you asked me to." *Because I can't leave you alone.*

She moves again, this time managing to lift herself onto her knees.

He experiences a loss at the sudden lack of body contact. He instantly misses her.

"What happened?" She looks down at the t-shirt she is wearing and gasps, quickly tucking it between her legs—not that she needs to. It is like a dress on her. "How did I get in this? And why is my head pounding?"

He sits up and leans against the headboard. "You're in my room because it's the safest room in the house. Plus, there are two ways to come and go. Do you remember anything from last night?"

She looks around and takes in her surroundings, her hand holding her stomach. No doubt she still feels awful. "I remember getting sick, and Keith."

"You were poisoned, Savannah. We think someone

may have spiked your lemonade."

Her expression changes, and all the color leaves her face. She's remembering. Tears pool in her beautiful dark eyes, breaking him in two. "What? Who would have poisoned me?" she cries as she tries to understand what happened. She wipes the back of her hand across her cheek, catching a tear. "I—I have to go." She moves to the other side of the bed.

Cole jumps to his feet and catches her as she loses her balance and tumbles forward.

"No, you're staying here." He scoops her up and places her back on the bed.

"No, you don't understand—" She fights him, but he pins her to the mattress with his body.

She tries to push him off, but she's too weak to fight for long.

"I do understand. I know York spoke to you."

Her gaze turns to meet his.

"I know he told you about The American, and that he doesn't lose his captives. And that he'll hunt you until he finds you. But, Savannah," tears are streaming down her cheeks now, "I promise you I will not let him find you."

Her lip quivers. She looks terrified.

"Please, stay and let me protect you." His face is inches from hers. He gently lifts the sheet and dries the corners of her eyes. "You have to trust me."

"I—I do," she whispers without hesitation.

He closes his eyes, letting out a sigh of relief.

"Cole." He opens his eyes at the sound of her soft voice. "Did you spend the whole night with me?"

He nods, not sure if he can speak. Her trust means more to him than he thought it would.

"Thank you." She lifts her head and gives him a soft peck on the cheek.

Her lips are like velvet against his stubble. Every nerve in his body stands at attention. This woman is waking up parts of him that he didn't know he had. He slowly peels his body off hers, knowing he can't hold her like this forever. He pulls her up with him, so they're both sitting up.

"Who do you think drugged me?" She shifts the t-shirt around her legs again.

He clears his throat. "I don't know. I have Keith reviewing the video." He watches as she rubs her head. "Are you feeling okay?"

She nods, but he can tell she is lying. "I need a shower and my toothbrush," she mutters with a tiny grimace, "and some Advil."

He opens the drawer next to the bed and hands her two Advils and a bottle of water.

She hesitates before taking it.

"It's all right. The water is from my fridge. No one comes in here without a security code, and only Abigail and I know it."

"I found something…yesterday, I found something. I need to show it to you."

"Okay, Savi, but let me get you to your room and have Abigail help you get showered. Then you can show me."

"All right."

Cole pulls off his shirt, opening his dresser to get into something clean. He catches her gaze reflected in the mirror.

She studies the tattoo on his shoulder. "What does *De Oppresso Liber* mean?"

He had gotten it after his first year. It depicted an eagle holding two arrows wrapped in the American flag with the words written in a horseshoe shape around it. It isn't particularly large, about the size of a hockey puck. A lot of the other guys got huge tattoos, wanting to make a statement, but he didn't do it for anyone else but himself.

"To free the oppressed," he answers as he slides a clean t-shirt over his head. "All right, up you go."

She lets him help her off the bed, and he waits until he knows her legs are steady. He wraps an arm around her waist, letting her lean her weight into him. God, she feels good against him.

***

"Where are we?" she asks, glancing around.

"The back passage through the house. It's a safety precaution if we ever come under attack." He feels her flinch as they move along the passageway.

"What's in there?"

He moves to the open door and lets her look inside the tiny room with its wall full of books and a floor filled with plush cushions.

"Oh, it's so cozy," she says delightedly.

"It's a room my mother designed when my father would work long hours and the house became too busy. She'd lock herself in here for hours, losing herself in her stories." He smiles, remembering curling up in a ball next to her as she read *Moby Dick* to him.

"Here we are." He opens a door and helps her through.

She looks baffled that part of her wall is actually a door.

"Can I access that passageway from in here?" she asks, eyeing the door as he shuts it behind them.

"Yes," is all he offers her, and she doesn't press for more information.

He sits her on the bed and calls for Abigail to come up. He feels her mood change as she looks around her room and her arms wrap around her stomach.

"What's wrong?" he asks as he kneels in front of her.

"I just feel—" Her dark eyes stare into his. "In your

116

room, I feel—" She stumbles again.

"Safe?" he asks, hoping he isn't wrong.

She nods and drops her head.

He brushes her hair behind one shoulder. "8986," he whispers.

She looks up at him, puzzled.

"You pull back the panel there where the door meets the wood. The code is 8986. 8987 is the code for my door, if you're feeling scared."

Her eyes soften, and she wraps her arms around his neck, pulling him to her.

His body doesn't think twice about wrapping his arms around her and burying his face in her neck. *Oh, God, she smells amazing.*

She rests her head on his shoulder. "Sorry." She smiles against him. "I must smell terrible."

"No." His voice is hoarse.

She pushes herself back with both hands on his shoulders to stabilize herself. He is still wedged between her legs, but she doesn't seem to care. Her eyes flicker down to his lips. He wants her to make the first move, not sure how fragile she might be with all that has happened to her.

God help him, he is losing his control. If he just moves forward a few inches, he'll be where he wants to be. He watches as her tongue licks her bottom lip, and he moans.

"Cole, I've never felt—"

"Here I am, Savannah!" Abigail bursts into the room and halts mid-step when she sees the two of them. "Oh, I'm so sorry."

Savannah drops her hands and shifts back on the bed. Cole closes his eyes, silently cursing their intruder.

"I'll see you in a bit, Savi, ahh…after you've had a chance to clean up and get a bit more rest."

"Thanks."

Chapter Eight

I feel more human after a two-hour nap and a shower. Dr. Rice comes by and checks on me, saying how lucky I am that Keith found me in time. I am also informed the lemonade was indeed spiked with Visine eye drops. Apparently, it can cause a lot of harm if ingested. If I had drunk a second glass, I would be a lot worse. There are some cases where people actually died. I appreciate the doctor's explanation, but it is upsetting, to say the least.

Poor Abigail is in fits, apologizing to me. She fusses over my pillow about six times and asks if she can get me anything. I assure her I'm fine. I just want to get up and stretch my legs. I get the green light from Abigail, but I have to promise to eat, and if I felt tired, to get rest and not fight it. I promise more for Abigail's sake than for me, and seeing her eyes light up on the way to the kitchen is well worth the promise.

"I'm thinking oatmeal with sliced almonds? It's healthy and will stick with you."

"Sounds good. Thanks," I say as I sit on a stool at the breakfast bar.

"Don't worry, dear. Cole gave orders that all food was to be tossed out and replaced, so everything should be fine."

My jaw drops. "All the food? Are you kidding me?

118

You had enough to feed an army!"

"We are the Army," Mark chimes in, ignoring my eye roll. He looks me over. "How bad was it?"

"Let's just say I felt like I was knocking on death's door." I shudder at the memory. "But I'm better now."

"Glad to hear it." He leans over and plucks a grape from the bowl then lowers his voice. "Cole, Keith, Mike, and I are the only ones who know what happened, and we want to keep it that way until we know what we're dealing with. Okay?"

"Okay, sure, but who's Mike?"

"Delta Six. Keith had him watch you while he filled Cole in on the details."

"Oh. Have I met him yet?" I try to remember.

"No, but you won't forget him after you do." He smirks. "Let's just say I'm glad you were out of it when he was watching you. He's one scary looking son of a—" *Whack!* A tea towel hits Mark in the face.

"Mouth, Marcus." Abigail scowls and points a wooden spoon at him. He laughs as she sets the bowl of oatmeal in front of me along with a glass of orange juice.

***

Cole doesn't show his face again for the rest of the evening. I'm disappointed because I still haven't shared what I found with him, but I realize it isn't that important in the general scheme of things. I'm feeling pretty beat and pass out around seven, not waking until eight the next morning.

I'm told Dr. Roberts needs to take some personal time off, and we'll pick up where we left off when he returns. In the meantime, there is someone on call if I need to speak with them. I don't.

I spend the next day lounging around my room under Abigail's watch. She won't let me do much. I know she is making sure I'm all right.

The next day, my body is more than ready to get back to my daily routine.

"Hey, Savi." Mark appears in the kitchen. "What are you up to today?"

"Oh, you know, got a meeting at eleven, client lunch at noon, presentation at two. Same old, same old."

"Bored, are we?"

"I just need to move." I bite into an apple.

"We're running drills up and down the mountain. We're dressed in blue, and we'll be firing paintballs, so don't go giving any of us black eyes again, all right?"

"No promises," I joke.

"Well, if you're in the mood, give it to the guys with the red armbands. I'm green." He winks.

***

I take the longer path up to see the horses. I enjoy this route. At one point, it gives you the most beautiful view of the lake. I wish I had a camera. I'll have to see if Abigail knows where I can get my hands on one. Perhaps there's a place in town.

I settle on the grass and soak up the cool mountain air. I lean back on the ground, closing my eyes. I love the way the wind blows and makes a soft, wispy sound, and how it grows louder as it gets closer.

"Savi." I squeeze my eyes shut. No, they will not break my happy Zen moment.

"Savannah." Mark hisses my name again.

"Can't hear you," I hiss back. I feel the vibration of him crawling up next to me.

"You know how to shoot?" My eyes snap open to see his blue helmet flipped up in the front. "You up for a bit of fun?"

"Hell, yeah."

***

Before I know it, I am pulling on John's dark blue camo outfit. Thankfully, I wore my dark hiking boots, but it doesn't matter because John's pants cover them almost completely. I can see why they picked John; he is the only one who is just slightly taller than I am. I notice the name tag reads Agent Black.

"Are you still training?" I ask as John shoves the gun in my hand. Holy hell, is it heavy.

"We're done. Now it's playtime. We need someone who can fit down in that gully and into the hole in the barn." He points at a building. I wouldn't call it a barn, exactly. "Once you're in there, you need to capture the flag and tuck it in here." He points to a pocket on the vest. "Then run like hell on wheels back to me so we can fly it first."

"Seriously, the US Army plays capture the flag for training?" I laugh.

"It's a great training tool. Trust me, you'll see." He holds the gun up to my eye. "See that right there? Line it up with your target then shoot." I line it up with the can and squeeze the trigger. *Pop! Pop!* I actually hit it! I jump up and down, giving myself my own high five. Mark smirks. "Great job. It's actually a little scary that you hit the target."

"I play a lot of video games." I shrug.

"If you get shot, you go to a room in the far corner of the building where you'll wait for five minutes then be released out a side door. Meet back here if that happens."

Oh, my, there is a lot to take in. "So, who else is on our team?" I ask, hoping for Keith.

"We're green. They won't shoot at you. Lean your head forward."

Yeah…that's the green team. What about the red? He

scoops up my hair and pulls on the helmet.

"Do they know I'm not John?" I start to feel uneasy.

Mark pulls my visor down. "No, it's better this way. Just stick with me." *Wait! What?* "Oh, and, Savi, don't get shot."

John gives me a thumbs-up and runs away.

Mark grabs my arm and pulls me low and down along a path. "Whatever you do, don't take your helmet off."

I nod, knowing there isn't a chance in hell that's going to happen.

He gives me quick instructions then points me at the hole in the building. "Heads up, and don't shoot green." He pats my back and eases me into the opening.

It's a little hard at first with all the clothing, but I manage to get in.

Holy shit! This is no barn. I just walked into a training room for the friggin' Green Berets. I drop down behind a metal shield. *Okay, Savannah, you can either chicken out or live a little. There are no paparazzi and no Daddy to disappoint. Perhaps you'll get a shot at York.* Oh, yes, that does the trick.

I move to my knees and take in my surroundings. I see the flag, but I also see a guy with an orange band shimmying down a pipe on the far wall. *Really? A pipe?* Good Lord, I'm in trouble, and Mark never mentioned a third team. I rest the gun on the top of the shield, awkwardly aiming at orange, and take the shot. *Shit!* I hit right above his shoulder.

He drops the last fifteen feet and rolls under a stack of crates.

I duck, hoping he didn't see me. Okay, think. I see some scrap metal and make a beeline for it. I hear shots being fired, but none hit me. *Keep moving, Savi.* I scan the debris and spot a long cement tube. I run to it and peek inside. I see a flash of an arm, and I wait, watching his reflection in an old hubcap. I see a blurry movement and make my move.

Hello, Red. I grin, raising my gun and popping two in his back.

He turns in disbelief and raises his gun in the air as he walks out of sight.

Hell, yeah! What a rush this is! My heart is pounding through my chest. *Okay, back in the game, Savi!* I crawl along the side wall, keeping my body low. A series of loud pops pierces my ears. Looking up, I see orange splatters. I freeze and hold my hands over my head. *Shit, shit, shit, shit!* Thankfully, the noise and my helmet muffled my scream. I open my eyes and discover a set of black boots in front of me. Oh, shit! The tip of a gun is staring at me. I have to fight the flashback that is coming on full force. Then a quick pop hits his shoulder, and he is out. I nearly burst out in glee. I give him a little wave as he walks away and notice he's on the red team.

He flips me the bird over his shoulder.

So, that makes two red down, and one orange that spread nine bullets at the wall. I keep moving. I finally look over and see I'm only a few feet from the flag. Screw it! I jump to my feet and sprint toward the flag. I leap, and my hand just brushes over it as I feel three pops to my lower stomach. *Noooo!* I fall to the ground, now thankful for all the gear. I feel the paintballs, but it doesn't hurt. I jump to my feet; I have to look like I do this all the time.

Oh, no. I'm supposed to know where to go. *Damn it!* I hear some laughter off to my left. *Thank God.* I walk in and see the guys with their visors up, cracking jokes about how they got shot. I take a seat against the wall and fight the urge to cross my legs. I look around and try to sit like them. I spread my legs and lean on an elbow. I feel ridiculous; this is not comfortable. Someone on the orange team comes and sits next to me, his arm and chest dripping green paint. I wonder if Mark shot him. He holds his fist out to me. *Oh, right. Fist bumps.* I bump him back and give a nod. I notice he doesn't remove his visor either. I wish I knew who he is, but his name tag is now covered in green. I glance up at the screen where the times are counting down for each guy. This place is seriously cool. Scary as hell—but frigging cool.

"You have fun last night, Black?" I feel an elbow to the ribs by Orange, who points at Keith.

I nod, hoping he won't ask me another question.

Keith looks at me strangely then shrugs as he stands.

"Heads up, guys. Lopez says he saw Savannah by the stables." I freeze. "So, stay clear of that area."

Everyone nods, and I find myself mimicking them. I feel a little loved that they are watching out for me.

"Is she wearing a dress or pants today? I want to know if I should be on high or low ground," York calls out, and I tense again.

"When will you learn, York? She's just not into you," Keith shoots back with a sigh. "Leave the poor woman alone."

I jump to my feet when I see my time is up. I race out of the room, not wanting to hear any more. Just as I'm crouching under a table, a loud siren goes off, and people start walking out of the building.

***

As soon as I'm outside, I see why the siren went off. No way! I see that the orange team is flying the flag. They are all cheering, holding beers in the air.

Everyone comes together and removes their helmets. I almost lose it when I see the orange teammate with the dripping green on his arm and chest sitting right next to me is Cole.

"Game's over, Black," York shouts. "Helmet." He knocks on my head.

Oh shit, oh shit, oh shit. Finally, Mark comes to my side with John. Everyone stops and looks at me, then John, then me some more…

"I recruited one more." Mark laughs and nudges me to remove the helmet. I unclip it and pull it off slowly, making my messy hair fall all around me. The looks on their faces are priceless.

"Hi." I beam at them.

"Wait," Keith holds up his finger at me, "was that you on the ground right before I got shot?"

I smile and repeat the wave.

"Oh, my God." He starts to laugh but stops when he sees Cole's face.

"That wasn't smart, Mark," Cole bites out. "We'll discuss this later."

Mark moves in front of me, blocking Cole's stare. "He has a job to do. Don't worry, he's not mad at you." He grins. "Well, fuck me sideways, how much fun was that?"

"It beats a day at the office." I laugh, high-fiving him. "I have to admit I was going to kill you when I saw the inside of the 'barn.' You sent me to war!"

"Pretty cool though, right?"

I burst out laughing again. "Yeah, it's something I'll never forget. Oh, wow. Thanks, Mark. I kind of needed that."

"Anytime. All right, I'm going to go take the heat." He hands me a beer, then leaves to face the music with Cole.

Keith comes to my side, and I ask, "How much trouble is Mark in?"

"Cole and Mark are tight. Normally, he'd get watch duty for a night, but now—" He stops himself. "He may get a little more."

"Why?" I fumble with the beer cap. Maybe it isn't a twist off. He takes out his wallet and removes a silver looking card. No, it's actually a bottle opener? Cool. He flips the lid off with a smile.

"Handy little thing," he says, tucking it away, but not before I notice the letter S engraved on it. I wonder if they all have one. He waits until it stops foaming and hands it back.

"Thanks."

"We're cracking down on the rules now." He gives me shrug.

"Ah, I see. Because I'm luring The American closer." His face flinches. "It's okay, Keith. I get that I'll be here for a while, and I'm on the top of 'The American's most wanted to re-kidnap' list." I sigh, taking a sip of the beer. "Any word about the poison?"

"Cole is the one you should be talking to about that. Sorry, Savannah, but we have rules."

***

The conversation around the dinner table is pretty interesting tonight. Cole has yet to join us.

Abigail is floored that I had participated in 'the battle,' as they call it.

"You think that was a wise idea, Mark?" She narrows her eyes at him.

"It was worth the punishment." He winks at me.

I love that Mark took one for me so I could have a little fun. I'll have to make it up to him somehow. I heard that he took all the heat, not wanting John to get in trouble as well.

"What you get, anyway?" Keith asks, chewing on a roll.

"Three nights at the Peak." He shrugs.

"Shitty," Keith responds.

"The Peak?" I ask, not following.

"It's the worst post to be assigned, and it's normally reserved for the rookies," Keith explains, "especially this time of year with the wind and rain. Makes my bones ache just thinking of it."

"Oh, Mark, I'm sorry."

"Don't be. The look on the guys' faces when you took off your helmet is worth every minute up there on that cold, cold hill." He holds his beer up. "To Agent Black, someone not to turn your back on." He eyes Paul, who I had hit two times in the back. Everyone raises their glasses to me as we all start laughing.

"So, when is the next battle?" I'm joking, but everyone grows quiet. "Come on, you said I could shoot."

Cole comes to the head of the table, looking less than impressed. "Sorry I'm late, Abigail. Dinner looks great." He glances around the table. "Please don't stop the conversation on my account."

"Tell me, Savi, how did you manage to pop me in the back?" Paul bravely asks.

"Hubcap. I could make out your movements in the reflection."

"Impressive." He chuckles.

"Paul," Cole wipes his mouth with his napkin, "tell Savannah how you hurt your neck."

Paul sighs loudly. I guess I won't like this. "Keith dropped from twenty feet above me, slipped a disc in my neck. Hurts like hell when it rains."

"Keith, tell Savannah about your knee." Cole turns to where Keith is sitting.

"I got plowed from the side by Mike. We both fell ten feet off a beam, and he landed on my knee."

Cole points to Mark. "Left shoulder."

Mark turns, pulling up his shirt and revealing a jagged scar across his shoulder.

I gasp and cover my mouth. It looks terrible.

"Fell on a metal peg, got dragged a few yards. Tore right through my gear."

Cole focuses back on me. "My point, Savannah, is all this happened during our training in paintball. We didn't know it was you in Black's uniform today. Any one of us could have seriously injured you. You will be involved in no more battles."

Chapter Nine

Cole watches everyone go their own way after dinner. No one seems up for socializing tonight. He is fine with that. He's still reeling from what happened at training.

John appears and drops his duffel bag at the door next to Cole's and signals he is ready.

Cole nods at him and heads for the stairs, knowing what he is about to say isn't going to be easy—at least not for him.

Savannah's door is open. He peeks in and sees her sitting in front of the fireplace, the glow of the flame casting shadows on her face. Her hair is in a messy bun held up with a pen. A few pieces have come loose, and she looks sexy as she leans over to study a photo.

"Savi," he says quietly so as not to scare her.

She glances up and gives him a sultry smile.

"May I come in?"

"Sure."

He walks in and notices papers and photos fanned out in front of her.

"Is this what you wanted to show me before?"

"Yes, I found something." She hands him the picture she was just studying. It's of her father at a charity event. "Look who he's toasting with." She points to the bracelet. "He knows the girl who took my picture in the pub."

Well, damn, she found something.

"This was taken four months after my kidnapping. They must be close, because my father doesn't smile like that with just anyone."

Huh—interesting.

She tucks a piece of hair behind her ear. "I tracked down the number of the charity event coordinator. I've met him before. I thought I could call him."

"No, Savi—"

"I won't give my name or anything, but I could get the guest list. I've been to these things enough times to know who's who, and I could start the process of elimination."

"I'll get you the list," he says a little harder than he intended to.

"Fine." She dismisses his tone.

"What's this?" He picks up an article about a woman who was kidnapped.

"Well, I've been researching *Los Sirvientes Del Diablos* and found a few stories of the victims who were returned unharmed. Shocking how few there were." She rubs her stomach. "Their ransoms were huge—like a couple million. One woman was only gone a month, and they got one-point-five for her." She sighs. "Cole, my ransom just doesn't make sense. Their pattern changed with me, but why? I'm wracking my brain. Why was The American involved in my case?"

"Okay, slow down. This is a great find," he says, holding up the picture and studying it. "I'll make the call and get the guest list. This is all one giant puzzle, and you'll go mad asking all the questions at once. You need to pick one and start there. If you hit a dead end, put it aside and pick up another. A path will soon show itself, then a picture will start to form. Have you had any more flashbacks?"

She bites her lip, debating telling him.

"I remember my first proof of life," she finally whispers, "when I met Maria." She looks really uncomfortable. She bends down, picking up a small piece of paper. "Here's the number for the charity." Her face is flushed, and her eyes are watery. "His name is Gary. He's really friendly."

"Hey, what's wrong?" he asks, stepping toward her.

She shakes her head and hands him the paper. "Some flashbacks are harder than others." She lets out a shaky breath.

Before he can ask any more questions, John sticks his head in the door. "Hey, Savi." He grins at her. "Logan, the chopper will be here in fifteen. We're good to go."

"You're leaving?" She looks up, clearly startled.

"We got a lead that needs to be followed in TJ."

She shakes her head and steps away from him. He doesn't like it when she does that.

"Who's all going?"

"John, Paul, Mark, and I."

"For how long?" She looks unhappy, almost nervous.

"Three to four days at the most."

Her eyes go wide as she processes his words.

"Savannah, it's—"

"I don't want you to go," she blurts out, and his lungs freeze. "I-I don't want you to go, Cole."

He reaches out and pulls her to him.

She comes willingly into his arms.

She trembles as her arms tighten around him, and he breathes in deeply, her apple shampoo making his heart ache.

"Don't go," she whispers.

"Ahh, Savi, I don't want to, but I have to," he murmurs into her hair.

"It's not safe. What if—"

"We don't use 'what-ifs.' We check in once in the

morning and again at night. I'll be back in a few days."

She pulls away slightly to look up at him. "Promise me you'll be back."

He knows he shouldn't. He never would have before, but looking into her eyes—feeling the way he does—he cannot stop the words.

"I promise."

She closes her eyes and leans her head on his chest.

He reaches up, removing the pen from her hair, and runs his fingers through it. "You have no idea how hard it is to walk away right now."

"Then don't."

Oh, God, she's killing him. His brain is firing off so many things, but he cares about only one.

She lifts her head, almost like she can hear him. "Cole."

"Yes."

"Kiss me."

He dives down and presses into her soft lips.

She wraps her arms around his neck, pushing her body into his. The first swipe of her tongue makes him dive deeper, and she moans as she becomes jelly in his arms.

He can't get enough of her. She tastes so sweet. One hand travels down to her waist. His fingers run along her velvet skin, and his knees go weak. She feels so tiny in his arms; he has to remember to be gentle. His hands slide around to her back, then down over her ass, giving it a firm squeeze.

She nibbles at his lower lip, and he grows painfully hard. "Cole." She leans back, and her hands travel down his stomach.

He shivers, pulling her back to his lips. He needs to taste her.

"Logan, choppers are here," John shouts from down the hall.

She doesn't stop the kiss, so he puts everything he has into it until he finally finds the strength to pull away, leaving her off balance.

"See you in a few days." He kisses her once more, quickly, unable to hang around any longer. He knows he has to get away from her. She is like a drug, sucking him backward.

"Be safe," he hears her whisper. Damn it. He turns, gives her a smile, then leaves.

You've crossed the forbidden line, asshole! He smiles a little, though, as he rushes down the staircase, her taste lingering on his tongue. His head is swimming as he squints, making his way toward the chopper, flinging his bag inside, and jumping into his seat.

Mark gives him a questioning eyebrow then joins his grin like he just figured out where he was.

Cole closes his eyes and lets himself have a moment to relish the past ten minutes.

***

I flop down on my bed, staring at the ceiling. I want to laugh, cry, and scream—my body is firing sparks all over. I have never been kissed like that before—or is it that I've never felt like this about a man before? Either way, it is amazing. Now he has four days to think about it. What if he realizes it's a mistake? I'm technically a client. *No, don't go there, Savi. Enjoy your high.* I cross my arms over my head, smelling him on my clothes as I close my eyes and drift off to sleep.

***

Autumn Ball, Manhattan, 2014. I hit enter, and my fingers strum the desk. I have decided my first task is to find out who the silver bracelet woman is, why she took my picture, and why she was following me. Everyone is a suspect, so I wonder if it was a coincidence that she was there the same the day I was taken. I decide to Google the events I know my father would normally attend. The Autumn Ball was a few days ago. I click on images, scrolling through six before I spot my father. He's shaking hands with some people in one photo, in another he is standing at a podium, and in a few pictures, he is with the chief of police, who is making a speech.

I keep clicking and clicking, and it becomes pretty tedious, but I decide to keep at it. Just as I am about to give up and try another tactic, something catches my eye. I lean in to get a better look. I click on the image to make it bigger, then click print and grab it from the tray the minute the machine lets go. Holding it under the light, I'm able to make out my father's table off to the right of the picture. He is sitting beside a woman. His body is blocking hers, but I can see her wrist, and there it is—that bracelet again. I rub my head, trying to take in what I'm seeing. Not only did this woman take a picture of me, but at two different events since I was kidnapped, she's been photographed with my father. What the hell?

I need a break to clear my head. I know something isn't right here, and I'm not really sure what to make of the whole thing. I need time to mull it over. I scribble down the number for the event coordinator and leave the room.

***

I find myself in the kitchen, measuring out ingredients for my mother's famous chocolate chip cookies. I tripled the batch because I know one would hardly be enough. I love baking. I love how my brain goes into idle mode and lets my hands do all the work.

"The guys mentioned they smelled something good, but I think I may have died and gone to heaven." Keith snatches a cookie off the cooling rack and shoves it in his mouth. "Mmmmm, warm cookies."

I laugh and pour him a glass of milk.

"Thanks." He takes a swig. "Damn, those are good, Savi." He takes another.

"Thanks. I love to bake."

"I love that you love to bake." He grins.

I transfer the last twelve cookies to the rack, not looking at him.

"Any word from the guys?" I ask casually.

He nods and sets his empty glass in the sink.

"Checked in this morning. They crossed the border and are heading to the location now."

"Cole said they check in twice." I want him to know Cole spoke to me about it.

"Yes, they'll check in again when they're back at the safe house." He pauses, watching me. I pretend not to notice, then he clears his throat. "Should be around seven, our time." He grabs a few more cookies. "I need to go get some stuff done. I'll see you later."

***

The dinner table has a few new faces. I'm assuming they step in when Cole's group is gone. I notice York takes over Cole's seat at the head of the table. He can't possibly be in charge while Cole's away, can he? The thought makes me ill.

"Savi," York greets me with a superior tone, "meet Two, Three, and Four." He waves at the new guys at the table.

Two rolls his eyes. "We also have names. I'm Adam, this is Dell, and that's Quinn. Nice to finally meet you. We've heard all good things."

"Yeah, like you rocked it at paintball," Quinn says, winking. "Heard Cole was livid though."

"It was fun." I grin, remembering the rush. "He was pretty upset, but he cooled off."

"You're not scared of him, are you?" Adam asks, amazed. I don't want to act like I know about Cole's background story. I know there is a lot more to him than that.

"Of Cole? No, why would I be?"

Adam sets his fork down. "I've watched him snap a man's neck as he strolled by like it was nothing." I close my eyes at the image. "He's not exactly warm and fuzzy."

"I spent seven months with men who made me beg for my next meal and beat me so I could hardly walk. So, no, Cole doesn't scare me at all. He's been nothing but nice to me."

"Point taken," Adam adds quickly. "If it counts, I really like your cookies."

I laugh, and York looks a little irritated. I ignore him.

"Thanks. So, what is it that you guys normally do?"

"We're normally traveling and aren't often at the house," Dell answers. "It's nice to have a break. We step in when Team Blackstone is called out."

Blackstone. "How often is Blackstone called out?" I ask, sipping my wine.

"Depends. They're the Alpha team here at Shadows. They handle the high-risk stuff, and they're called out, oh, maybe once or twice a month." Dell takes a swig of beer. "We're at a level five because of your case. Things are a bit tense along the border. *Los Sirvientes Del Diablos* are stirring up a lot of dust since you dropped off their radar."

"I still don't understand why I'm such a big deal to them. You'd think they'd cut their losses and move on. Christ, it's just fifty grand."

"No, Savannah, you're worth more to them than just fifty grand. I mean, they're blackmailing—"

"Dell!" York snaps.

I flinch and knock over my empty water glass. *What the hell?*

"Sorry, Quinn, ah…did you catch the game last night?" Dell tries lamely to change the topic.

"Oh, no," I hold my hand up to York, "you don't get to shut him up. This case involves me, and I get to hear all the details. Dell—out with it."

"Not a word, Dell," York warns.

"Stop, York," I hiss. "Who are they blackmailing? My father? Lynn? Why? With what?"

Dell shakes his head. "I'm really sorry, Savannah, I shouldn't have said anything—"

"Like hell you shouldn't."

"Savannah, enough." York stands and places his hands on the table, staring me down.

I stand also and meet his stare. My hands are vibrating with anger.

"Shut your mouth."

Abigail suddenly leaves the table.

"Pardon me?" The table grows silent. "Why are you angry? Because Dell didn't trap me on the patio to tell me this?"

His eyes narrow at me as he clenches his fists.

"Stop, or I'll make you shut up." He bites out each word.

I raise my chin, feeling my emotions change. I need to pull off a huge lie.

"You. Don't. Scare. Me," I say as I hold my gaze steady on his.

"I should." A few of the guys rise to their feet, ready to step in if need be.

I smile sweetly. "You'll never fill that chair the way he does." I toss my napkin on the table. "Excuse me, guys."

I make my way down the hallway. My high is quickly being replaced with the fear I said I didn't have. I look down at my wobbly legs and run smack into something hard. I snap back, but I get jolted forward into the arms of the biggest, scariest tattooed man I've ever laid eyes on. His arms are huge; he looks like he bathes in steroids. He is tatted up from his smoothly shaved head to, I'm guessing, his toes. Holy mother of shit.

"Umm," is all I can get out before I find my voice. "I really, really hope you're Mike."

He grins widely and helps me steady myself. "Yup. I got word York was at you again."

I roll my eyes. "That man hates me. I bet he'd buy me a plane ticket to The American himself if he could get away with it."

He laughs loudly. "You really get under his skin, and we all love it." His expression turns serious. "Did he threaten you?"

I look down. The last thing I need is this getting back to Cole.

"Look—we had words. He'll cool off, and tomorrow's another day." I can see him thinking.

"You know Cole can watch the security tapes of the house from where he's at, right?"

"Let's not give him a reason to lose focus on the job he's doing, okay?"

He nods, and it seems like he agrees with me.

"There's a radio in the kitchen by the intercom. If you change it to our numbers, you can get us directly. Seven is Keith and I'm Six. You need us, you call us. Deal?"

"Okay, deal. Thanks, Mike."

***

The next day, I avoid York as much as possible. I hear Cole's team finally checked in at eleven the night before. I can tell things aren't going exactly to plan by Keith's tone when I enter the kitchen this morning. He and Abigail both appear stressed, although they assure me everything is fine. I don't press it.

Abigail and I decide to have dinner in the entertainment room and watch some of our favorite movies.

"When does your sister arrive?" I ask, stabbing a piece of lettuce with my fork.

"In two days. She'll be here for Thanksgiving and stay for a few months. That's pretty normal for her. We're really close."

Lynn flashes in my memory. I quickly tuck that emotion aside.

"Cole's parents will be here too, and you'll get to meet his mother, Sue. She's lovely, warmhearted, and a pretty smart lady. She's quick and sees a lot."

"Living here, you would have to be," I joke. "How did you even start working here, Abigail? I mean, it's not like a position here would be listed in an employment ad in the local newspaper."

"No, definitely not," she laughs. "I started working for the Logans when Cole was six. As he got older and didn't need a nanny anymore, they moved me here. I love it. These boys are like the kids I never had."

"Mark's your favorite, isn't he?" I ask, knowing I'm right.

"I do have a weak spot for Mark, mainly because he and Cole have been best friends for about twenty-three years. Mark's mother wasn't around much, and his father left when he was born, so he always looked at me like a parent." She sets her plate on the couch and turns to me, grinning. "Can you keep a secret?"

"Of course." I'm excited for a little girl talk.

"Mark met a girl a little while ago. They've been talking. Her name is Melanie. She works in town, so one day I decided to check her out, you know, make sure she's good enough for my boy. Well, I found her working at the coffee shop. She's tall, slim, with red hair—sweet little thing, and I did something." She stops, her expression guilty.

"What did you do?" I can barely wait to find out.

"I introduced myself to her. We ended up talking for twenty minutes after her shift, and I invited her to Thanksgiving dinner." She cups her mouth. "He's going to kill me!"

"Oh, my God." I burst out laughing. "That's classic! Do you think she'll show?"

"I do." She wipes a tear away. "Oh, Lord, Savi, what do I do?"

"Maybe Mark will invite her, and you'll be off the hook."

"She did mention he was hinting around—"

"Wait! Back up a second." I shake my head. "I don't understand how you're able to invite someone to come here to the house for dinner."

"Oh, no, sorry. Daniel's best friend, Zack, has a restaurant and bar here in town. They have great food. Plus, it's a huge break for me."

"Oh, I see. Well, maybe we can blame John." We both burst out laughing. Poor John. He got in some shit over the paintball game too. Guess Mark didn't take all the blame.

"Perhaps." Her expression shifts. "These boys work really hard, and they do a lot of the things an average person can't. Holidays, no matter how big or small, I try to make sure they're celebrated because they deserve to have some downtime to just be themselves." She raises her eyebrow at me. "I think that's why I invited Melanie. I want Mark to find someone he can come home to someday. So, I'm just giving him a little push." She chuckles. "Isn't that what parents do?"

"I think it's sweet." I just love Abigail, and I can't wait to meet her sister June.

Chapter Ten

A pounding headache wakes me out of a dead sleep, and I crawl out of bed feeling lightheaded. I make my way to the kitchen where Abigail has a stash of Advil in her personal cabinet above the stove. I down three and drink two glasses of water then sink into a chair, propping my head on my hands. A movement to my left brings me fully alert.

"Well, if it isn't Savannah Miller, case number 22571," York mutters, leaning against the wall and holding a beer. I immediately get the impression it isn't his first.

I'm not in the mood for him, so I stand and move toward the hallway, but he slides over, forcing me to change route to the living room instead.

"You're pretty quiet now, aren't you, pretty lady?" He follows behind me then steps in my way. I stop trying to go around him and head for the stairs, going down two at a time.

I don't know where I am going; I just don't want to be alone with him. I slip into an office and shut the door behind me, but his shoe stops it from closing, and he slams it open. "Oh, Savi, you don't seem so brave now."

"Move, York," I order. I raise my chin and square my shoulders as he steps toward me, taking a sip of his beer.

"Or what? You weigh a buck fifty soaking wet. I

could blow and you'd fall over."

I hold up my hands as I feel the desk hit the back of my thighs.

"Not so brave when you don't have your knight here, huh?"

"I don't know what you're talking about," I whisper, feeling like an ass. What a stupid line that is.

"So, you're saying that you and Cole aren't fucking?"

I cringe at his tone.

"Well, that changes things, then." Before I know what is happening, he yanks me to him and crushes his lips to mine.

The mix of beer and his cologne nearly brings my dinner up. I push, pound, and kick, trying to get him off, but he has me pinned. His hands start to roam. *Oh shit.* I shove my knee up and drive it in his crotch as I bite down hard on his lower lip. He cries out as he falls backward. I leap over him and dash for the hallway, not getting three feet before his arm snags around my waist, and he slams me into the wall. Air rushes out of my lungs from the impact.

He grips my arms hard and lifts me off my feet, looking angrier than I've ever seen him. Blood drips from his lip. I got him pretty good.

"You're fair game, Savannah. There hasn't been a woman like you here before—young and real pretty. I rather like it." His grip tightens on my arms, and I can't help but cry out. It only makes him squeeze tighter. "I think I'm going to claim you as mine."

Oh, what? Seriously? We hate each other!

"Get your hands off me!" I cry.

He laughs as he drops me to my feet and presses his erection into my stomach.

"Screw off, York!" I hit his chest hard, but he reaches down and rips my shirt open as he traps my arms at my sides and slowly runs his gaze down my body. I am so thankful I wore a bra to bed tonight. He lets go with one hand to undo his belt.

"Stop it! No, York!" I start to cry when I realize he actually intends to follow through. "Please, York, no. Don't do this."

He is fumbling with the buckle, cursing at me to shut up.

I take the opportunity and knee him again, hard. This time he falls backward, tumbling into the wall. I run in a full sprint up the stairs, across the living room to the other set of stairs in the entryway. I wrap my ripped shirt around me. When I get close to the bedrooms, I hear Abigail's door open just as I reach my door. I slam the door and lock it behind me, sliding down to the floor, sobbing and out of breath. Unable to think straight, I don't know what to do. I haven't been that terrified since I was back in my prison room.

"No," I hiss, squeezing my eyes shut. *Not now. I can't go back there. Stay in the present!*

"Savannah," York whispers from outside my door.

My eyes pop open, and my heart pounds in my throat.

"Open the door." He rattles the doorknob. "I can hear you breathing." His voice is oddly calm, considering he has had two hard blows to the crotch. "You know I can pick this lock in a heartbeat." I scramble off the floor, hop to my feet, and frantically feel around the wooden panel for the key code. The knob rattles again. Finally, the panel flips down, and I punch in the code 8986 twice before I get it right. The door pops open, and I slip into the darkness.

My trembling fingers feel my way around the wall. There must be a light switch, but I don't want to chance anyone seeing me. I find the little library room that belongs to Cole's mother. When the door closes behind me, a tiny glow shines from a light in the corner, and I flop down on the pillows, curl into a ball, and cry myself to sleep.

***

"Ouch," I whimper as I roll onto my back. My eyes feel dry and puffy as they adjust to the soft glow. Gold lines make a beautiful Indian pattern along the ceiling. I gasp when I realize I'm not in my room, as the memories of last night come rushing back to me. I lift my hands to cover my face and feel the pain in my arms. Looking down at the pair of black and blue hand prints—one on each arm—I can't believe I escaped him. Shit! I scramble to stand on shaky legs. My head is fuzzy, and I retch as I wait for the dizziness pass. I sneak out of the library and stand outside my room. I put my ear to the door, listening to hear if anyone is in there. It sounds clear, so I punch in the code and slip inside.

Everything looks okay. Nothing has been moved, my unmade bed reminding me of what almost happened. My stomach drops when I see the time—ten thirty! Oh, God, I hope Abigail hasn't come up to check on me yet. I rush into the shower after grabbing a blue tank top with a grey sweater that ties in the front. I know there will be no blow drying my hair today because of my arms. It will have to dry wavy. I stand in front of my door, trying to convince myself to go downstairs and face everyone. I am beyond mortified that someone might see the security tapes. I need to figure something out.

"Good morning, Savannah." Dell smiles as he reaches for the OJ in the fridge. "Sorry about last night."

"You have nothing to be sorry for, Dell," I reassure him. "Where is everyone?"

"If you mean York, he's been in Cole's office all morning. I think he's nursing a hangover, because he's hurting today." He laughs. "Serves him right. He gets such a power trip whenever Cole's gone."

Good. I hope his balls are swollen to the size of grapefruits.

"Yeah, he sure does," I mutter. "Hey, do you have any pain medication that's stronger than Advil?"

He stops mid-bite.

"Why, did you hurt yourself?"

I look away, not wanting to lie, but my arms really ache.

"Isn't there any goddamn ice in this place?" York yells from down the hall.

My stomach turns as fear kicks in.

"You know what? Never mind." I head for the stairs and up to my room. Once my door is locked, I start to shake. How am I going to live in this house with him? I crawl onto my bed and concentrate on my breathing.

***

"Savi." Abigail shakes my arm.

"Ouch," I cry out, and my eyes open, seeing her puzzled face.

"Sorry, but it's time for dinner."

I roll back over, wincing in pain. "I'm not hungry."

"Savannah Miller," she whips out her mother tone, "I know for a fact that you haven't eaten a thing today. I don't know what's going on with you, but I will not leave this room unless you are with me."

I sigh and pull myself up quickly before she can touch me again.

"Care to share?" she asks as we walk down the hallway, her expression questioning.

"Not really." I pull my sweater tighter around me. "Sorry." I feel badly not being able to share what happened, but it's still too raw, and God knows what she would do.

We walk into the living room to find Dell and Quinn talking to Cole. My stomach jumps. They're back! Abigail winks as she walks by. Oh, man, she's good. But as my excitement rises, my nerves do too.

"Hey, you." Mark leans in, giving me a peck on the cheek as he hands me a martini. "You look like you could use something stronger than wine tonight."

I take a long sip of the heavenly drink.

"Guess I was right," he remarks.

"When did you guys get in?" I ask, watching Cole's back. He still hasn't spotted me.

"Thirty minutes ago." He shakes his head. "It was a rough trip. Glad we were able to come home early."

"Rough?"

"Honestly, you don't want to know."

I probably don't.

"Come on." He tugs on my arm, and I flinch as he walks me over to Dell, Quinn, and Cole. I scan the room for York.

Cole looks tired, but when he catches sight of me, the smile that runs across his face makes my stomach warm. "Hey." His eyes dance over me.

"Welcome back."

"As promised," he whispers so only I can hear him. I can't help the smile that sneaks out as I take a drink.

"You." Keith points at me, rushing up to our group. "You want to explain how you dropped off the radar this morning?"

Fuck! I shake my head and look around. Luckily, no one is paying attention. Abigail has turned some music on, and it drowns out his voice.

Cole looks at me then Keith.

"I-I got up early and went for a walk by the lake."

"You're a shitty liar, Savi."

"Look, can we not do this now?" My eyes plead with him to drop it. I feel my goddamn eyes starting to water.

Really, can someone throw me a fucking bone, here?

"Just be thankful Dell said he saw you, or there would have been a search party looking for your ass." He suddenly steps forward, giving me an unexpected hug.

"Don't do that again, or I'll put a tracking chip in your arm." I let out a long breath, and he pulls away, eyeing me, then huffs and walks off.

"Seems we missed some action while we were away," Mark chimes in.

I look up at Cole, who is watching me carefully.

"You don't even know the half of it," Quinn mutters. I shake my head at him. God, why won't people talk about something else?

"Hey, boys," Abigail calls out, "could you help me?"

Cole doesn't leave. Instead, he moves a little closer. He bends down, and his mouth hovers at my ear.

His hot breath makes me shiver.

"There wasn't a moment when I was gone that I didn't think of you, Savannah. You're like a goddamn drug that's making me weak in the knees." My breathing catches as my heart beats away, doing a happy strum. "It's taking every ounce of my self-control not to kiss you right now."

"I wouldn't stop you," I say before I can even think about it.

He steps away, shaking his head and smiling.

"Umm, Cole, I need to—"

"Heard you were MIA, Savi," York's voice makes my blood run cold. "You want to explain where you were?" My entire body is locked in place. All I can do is stare at my drink.

"What happened to you?" Cole asks, moving the attention off me.

"Tripped. Fucking cat."

Ha! I want to knee him again for blaming poor Scoot,

but my body betrays me and I stand immobile, listening to his lies.

"How'd everything go while we were away?"

"Same shit, different day, right, Savi?" He wraps his arm around me and tugs me painfully to his side, grinning. "We had one of our little spats, but we made up. Didn't we, pretty lady?" He makes my skin crawl.

"Well, good." Cole takes a drink of his brandy, but I see him look at York strangely. "Glad to hear it."

I try to move away, but York's fingers dig into my hip.

"Cole," Mike calls out, "a minute?"

"Be right back," Cole says and heads off to join Mike.

No! I don't want to be here. I want to go back to my little safe spot in the library.

York leans in. "You speak a word of what happened last night, and I'll personally hand you over to the Cartels myself." He kisses my temple and walks away.

I wrap my arms around my stomach after downing the rest of my drink.

Mark shows up and hands me another. He watches as I finish half of it in one swallow.

"Mark," I whisper, "do you have any idea when you're going away next?"

"Possibly next week, but it's not set in stone."

I feel the blood drain from my face.

"I don't think I can stay here."

Mark drops down to my eye level. "What? How can you say that? What are you talking about?" His eyes search mine, but I feel numb. I'm shutting down.

"Dinner is ready," Abigail announces.

I turn and walk toward the table.

***

Everyone is deep in conversation. Paul is talking about the men they encountered at a house they cleared out.

I, on the other hand, am very aware of York sitting directly across from me.

Cole finally joins us, sitting on my right. Abigail is on my left, as usual.

Mark replaces my empty glass with another.

My head is swimming; no food and two martinis cause quite the head trip.

"What number is that?" York asks, pointing to my martini glass.

I lick my dry lips, pick up my glass, and take a long sip, keeping my gaze on his as I give him a silent 'fuck you.'

Cole looks between the two of us, trying to understand what is going on. Cole's smart enough not to ask me in public.

"So, Abigail, what time does Aunt June arrive tomorrow?" Mark asks.

"Seven." Her face perks up. "You're picking her up at the bus stop, right?"

He nods.

I want to ask if I can go along, but I decide not to push my luck, considering later on that evening we'll be heading into town for Thanksgiving dinner anyway. I'm excited to see some of the town. Hell, I just want to see past the first set of gates.

"Aren't you feeling well?" Cole leans over when I look up. "You haven't touched your plate."

I glance down. "Just tired," I fib, picking up my fork and popping a green bean in my mouth.

After the table is cleared, everyone moves out to the living room. I spot Dell by himself, pouring a drink, and I want to make my move and corner him for more details about the possible blackmail comment he let slip, when

Mark steps in my path.

"You care to explain yourself?"

"Not really."

"Okay, what happened while we were gone?" He waits, but I can't find the words. I can't even think up a good lie. He grabs my arm and pulls me to Cole's office, closing the door behind us, then he stands and crosses his arms. "I've got all night."

Ouch! "I don't want to be here anymore," I blurt out.

"Bullshit," he tosses back.

"I don't feel safe."

"Yes, you do." His eyes narrow in on mine. "At least you did right up until we left. So, what happened while we were gone?"

I shake my head. I don't know what to do.

"Savannah, did someone hurt you?"

I let out a sob and put my hand over my mouth, wanting to spill everything but scared to.

He stands in front of me, holding my arms.

I flinch and look away.

"The men in this house are part of a tight group. We all have to be able to trust one another. If there is something we need to know, you have to tell us before we bring any more people to this safe house."

Oh, God. I start to cry harder.

"He told me he'd hand me to the Cartels if I tell anyone." The words are out before I can stop them.

"Do you think Cole would ever let that happen? He's my brother, and I can honestly say this is the first time I've seen him head over heels for a woman."

I feel myself blush.

"He is one scary guy and knows a lot of dangerous people. No one in their right mind would cross him."

I nod but can't help thinking, *York did.*

"Okay, so that being said—" His voice suddenly changes. "Who hurt you?"

I pull in a sharp breath. "I'll tell you, but you need to help me erase the tape. I don't want Cole to see it."

"No deal, Savi. I'd get fired for that."

My anger rises. "Then show me where they are, and I'll do it."

"I can't let you on his computer. Besides, Cole has the tightest security system you can buy, and he has a ridiculous number of passwords."

Well, that, I believe. "I don't want Cole to see me like that. He may not want me—" I stop myself, shaking my head.

"Savannah." He grips my arms.

This time I cry out.

He lets go as his eyes narrow. He quickly tugs at my sweater, but I step back. "Savannah," he says again and reaches over and yanks it off my shoulders.

I try to cover up the marks, but he bats my hands away.

"Holy fucking shit!" he snaps. He turns me to the side to get a better look at the perfect handprints, then steps back, running his hands through his hair and covering his mouth as he thinks. After a moment, he moves to Cole's computer and starts typing away.

"Please, Mark," I beg him, "don't." I pull my sweater back on as I race up to the front of the desk. I knew he knew the passwords. "Mark!" He isn't listening. "Please, please, please, stop." Then his face drops, and I watch in horror. It's like seeing a train heading for a car full of people who can't get out. I know when he gets to the part where York throws me up against the wall, because the color drains from his face. He slowly stands and walks toward the door. I throw myself in front of it.

"Mark, please, I promise I'll tell Cole. Just wait until after tomorrow."

"Savannah, please move." His tone is eerie.

I stare up at this 6'2" man who could easily pick me

up and move me aside in the blink of an eye, but he doesn't. He's asking me to move. I place my hands on his shoulders just as he did mine.

"Mark, Abigail is so excited to see her sister. This will ruin the mood in the house, and I'm so tired of the attention being on me. Please, do nothing until after Thanksgiving dinner. Do it for Abigail and the rest of the house. They deserve a break."

His eyes squeeze shut while he thinks.

I think he's going to say no, but his eyes flicker open, and I can tell he understands.

"You have until tomorrow night. If you don't tell him by then, I will."

Oh, thank God. I drop my head. "Okay, yes. Thank you."

"Are you hurt anywhere else? Anywhere at all?" He looks so upset that I want to hug him.

"No, I promise." I wipe my cheeks dry and try to reassure him. "It's just my arms. He was drunk."

"So, he didn't trip over Scoot and bite his lip," he mutters more to himself than to me.

"No. Do you believe he would hand me over to the Cartels?"

He runs his hand over the back of his neck. "Fifteen minutes ago, I would have said 'Hell, no,' but now, after seeing that tape, I don't know."

"Oh, God." I feel sick.

"York knows all the ins and outs of this job. He knows which lines you don't *ever* cross. I don't care if he was drunk. He wasn't too drunk to throw you against the wall or to form a complete sentence."

"Wait? Could you hear us?"

"There's no audio yet, but we all lip read. I could make out some of it."

I try to let all this sink in. "What's going to happen to him?"

Mark moves back to sit on the couch while I stand, not sure if I'm coming or going. Fuck, I'm so scattered!

"Well, if Cole doesn't kill him, which I suspect he will, he'll be sent back to Army headquarters for a psych check. They'll want to review the tape to see if you want to press charges."

A chill races up my spine. That is the last thing I want to do. I just want him gone.

"This is going to be a big blow to the house, although I always knew there was something wrong with that son of a bitch."

"I don't understand why he'd risk his career. He knows the cameras are all throughout the house."

"Cole has been upgrading the entire security system, and right before we left, they were working on the cameras downstairs. They were having trouble getting them to connect to the server, so they were offline for six hours. He probably thought they were still down. Fuck, I want to rip his head off right now."

There's a knock at the door, and we both jump. Keith pops his head in.

"Is there a party I don't know about?" When he sees my face, he comes in and shuts the door behind him. "Okay, what's going on?" I shoot a look at Mark, who is standing up.

"Nothing that can't wait for a day," he says, walking me to the door.

Keith doesn't buy it, but doesn't push it either, and the three of us walk back to the living room, where only a few people were left.

Cole's face relaxes into a smile when he sees us walking over to him. "Hey, where did you two run off to?"

"Just got chatting and lost track of time," Mark says, looking around the room. Oh, God, there's York a few feet away.

I can practically feel the rage building in Mark's body as he watches York. I begin to feel even more nervous when I notice Cole watching him too. I need to think fast.

"I'm really happy you're all back." And that's what I come up with? *Smooth, Savi.* Cole looks down at me and smiles. Well, that is worth the dorky line. My stomach flutters. "I bet you're all beat."

"Very." He downs the rest of his drink.

"Me too."

"Come on. I'll walk you upstairs." We say good night to everyone.

Mark gives me an extra-long, soft hug.

***

The walk up the stairs is quiet. It isn't until we are alone that he put his hand on my back. Such a simple act makes me feel so much better. He checks my room, like he always does, and turns on my fireplace. I close the door then join him at the fire, and he stares down at me with that smile that reminds me I'm a woman with needs.

"You're so beautiful," he whispers and tucks my hair behind my ear.

"Thank you for keeping your promise." I close my eyes, feeling his hand running up my neck.

He cups the back of my head and tilts it to the side so my neck is exposed. "If I get to come home to this," his hot lips kiss me just under my ear, "I'll promise you every time."

My body goes limp as his words sink in.

He presses his lips back down as his tongue twirls in circles, and he chuckles between his kisses. "You have a wild heartbeat."

"I can't imagine why," I breathe. My hands move

under his shirt to skim along his stomach. I no longer register the pain in my arms.

His breathing changes, giving me some much-needed courage.

I let my fingers explore. Jesus, this man has zero body fat. I run my fingernails around to his back, and he hisses.

"You're testing my self-control, here."

I grin, happy he's feeling as weak around me as I am around him.

He wraps his arms around my waist and draws me to him. "I don't want to screw this up with you. I've already crossed a line I should never have crossed. Call me weak, but I'm drawn to you, and I've never felt this way before."

I feel like I might burst, but for a good reason this time. "I haven't either," I whisper and pull back. "The way I felt when you left, and again when I saw you downstairs—it isn't something I've ever...I mean, I understand you're risking your reputation being here right now, and I respect, well, not going public with it."

"Problem is," he reaches down and lifts me into the air, pulling me against him as I wrap my legs around his waist, "I want everyone to know you're mine."

I grin and raise an eyebrow. "Am I, now?"

He nips at my neck playfully then leans in and gives me a long, deep kiss.

My legs tighten around him as my body coils with lust, then he pulls away, leaving me breathless.

"I want you to be." He looks up at me with his deep, dark eyes.

"I want to be too," I confess, feeling lightheaded. I lean my head back against the wall as he licks the length of my neck. I moan, tilting my head to the side and squeezing his erection harder between my legs.

He slams his hips into me and growls as he sucks

where my collar meets my shoulder.

"Fuck me, Savi." He groans as he slowly lowers me to the ground and draws my hand to his mouth, kissing it softly. "Get some sleep, baby."

My insides melt into a pool in my stomach. This man positively has me wrapped around that smile of his. God, am I really ready to start a relationship with someone? Maybe I just need to stop overthinking things and let myself live a little.

Chapter Eleven

I change, then begin to pace the room, suddenly feeling guilty for not telling Cole what happened with York. I just need one more day. God, I hope Mark keeps his word. I stop pacing when I hear footsteps outside my door, and I see a shadow on the floor. A soft knock makes me shiver. What if it's Cole? Maybe he can't sleep either. Am I ready for this? I slowly make my way over and open the door.

Two glossy eyes stare down at me. Shit! His gaze rakes over my nightgown.

"Evening," he purrs as I try to slam the door, but he puts his foot in to stop it.

"Move your foot, York!" I hiss, swallowing down a lump of fear. Footsteps coming up the stairs draw his attention, and I shove him backward, slamming the door and locking it. Screw this! I grab a blanket off my chair and slip into the back hallway.

***

Cole wakes to banging on his door, then it bursts open.

Abigail is madly running around his room, and he squints as he tries to catch up.

"Where is she? Tell me she's with you!" She's talking a mile a minute, racing into his bathroom.

"Who?"

"Savannah! She didn't sleep in her bed again last night, and I can't find her anywhere!"

That wakes him up. He jumps to his dresser, pulling on jeans and a black t-shirt.

They both hurry to her room to confirm it is empty. Hearing voices coming from downstairs, Cole bolts out the door. Abigail on his heels, he flies down the stairs and into the kitchen.

"Wow, where's the fire?" Paul holds up his coffee mug.

"Have you seen Savannah?" Abigail asks breathily.

"Yes, she's out on the patio." Dell points outside. "Everything okay?"

Cole doesn't answer. He moves through the dining room, his stomach in knots. There she is, dressed in a white sweater and light pink tight-fitting pants, sipping a cup of coffee. Her hair hangs in big curls around her shoulders. Christ, she takes his breath away. She must have sensed him watching because she turns to look at him. Her eyes light up then drop quickly after looking over his shoulder.

"That girl is getting a goddamn tracking device in her neck this time!" Keith shouts, storming into the dining room. "Cole, this is the second time she's done this," he complains.

"Calm down, Keith," Abigail says just as Savannah opens the door behind them. She is biting her lip, her eyes downcast.

"Why are we shouting?" Mark looks like he got two hours of sleep.

"Sweet boxers, man." Cole points to his Ironman underwear. Mark flips him the finger.

"Savannah, I warned you." Keith points a finger at

her.

Her eyes shift to Mark's. He catches the look and suddenly appears more alert.

"I'm so sorry. I fell asleep in the entertainment room. I couldn't sleep."

"Wrong answer, Savi. I watched the tape."

She runs her hands through her hair as Mark mirrors the action. Keith glances between them, confusion evident on his face.

"Keith, I'm here. I'm okay." She starts fidgeting again, her gaze turning nervously to the kitchen.

"That isn't how this house works."

"Keith," Mark whispers, "give her a free pass just one more time, okay?"

Keith shakes his head. "Last time, Savi, so help me God." He holds up his hands then turns and leaves, muttering into his radio.

"T-minus fourteen hours, pretty eyes," Mark mutters to Savannah.

"Anyone care to fill me in?" Cole asks, crossing his arms and sitting on the edge of the table. Both of them stare at the ground but say nothing. "Well, here's the problem. Mark, you don't make eye contact with me when you're hiding something. You've been doing that since you were a kid, and Savi—" She looks up at him, running her fingers through her hair. "You do that," he points to her hand, "when you're not being honest or you're scared." He sighs when they look at one another. "What happens in fourteen hours?"

"Cole," Savannah steps closer, holding up her hands, "you asked me a little while ago to have trust in you, and I do. Could you have a little in me when I ask you to just give me today? Please?" Her eyes hold his for a moment. God, he's falling hard for this woman, but this secret feels like it is going to end badly.

"This isn't going to be good, is it?" Her face flushes

160

as she looks at Mark. "Do I need to be worried about anyone's safety?" Savannah's face flinches.

"I've got this for now," Mark says. "Savannah has her reasons for keeping quiet, and though I don't quite agree, I respect her wish to wait until tonight to share it with you, or I will."

Okay, this sounds big. "Mark, can you give us a minute?" Cole waits until they are alone then angles his back to block the security camera, as she nervously plays with the candle on the table. "Baby," he whispers, "I won't push this issue. I feel like Mark's got it handled for right now, but you have to tell me where you go at night." She sets the candle down, turning it between her fingers. "What if something happens and I need to get to you? You almost killed Abigail with worry this morning."

She nods. "Your mother's library," she says quietly. "I feel safe there."

He lets out a sigh, a little surprised he was unsure for an instant. He didn't know what she was going to tell him. For just a moment, he thought it was another man's room, and immediately felt guilty for even going there in his head.

"I'm sorry for using that back passage, but I really feel safe in there," she repeats. "It's been a rough few days, and I overslept. I was hoping to slip in and out without anyone noticing. I really am sorry, Cole."

He reaches for her hand, settling his on top. "Don't be sorry. I'm just relieved it wasn't someone's room you were seeking out. It makes me happy you feel safe in there. Use it anytime."

"Truthfully," she moves a little closer, "I wanted to go to your room." He inhales sharply, and her eyes lock with his. "Lie in your bed, smell you all around me," she whispers as a corner of her mouth goes up, looking damn sexy.

As she stands in front of him, smiling, he shifts and feels his temperature rise. His fingers curl around the edge of the table. She is making him painfully hard.

Straddling one of his knees and leaning to the side, she reaches for her coffee cup and continues. "Sleep in nothing but one of your t-shirts."

Her breath against his neck has his hands in a death grip on the table.

She pulls away, chuckling into her mug. Oh, she is good; she knows he is about to burst.

"Savi," he growls, "left top drawer—my t-shirts."

She laughs as she heads into the kitchen. "Two can play this game, baby." She smirks over her shoulder with a sway in her step.

God damn, that ass.

***

He hears a scream from the entryway and hops to his feet and hurries out to the dining room.

"Ahh! I can't believe you're finally here!" Abigail shouts into her sister's shoulder.

Cole shakes his head, rubbing his chest. What is it with women and shouting when they greet each other?

"Coley!" Aunt June grabs his face and smacks a kiss right on his lips. "How's my handsome young man doing?"

He grimaces at her nickname for him. "Fine, thanks."

"So I've heard." She winks at him. "Oh, my!" She looks over his shoulder. "And you must be Savannah."

"I am. Nice to meet you."

June pulls Savannah in for a hug, making her twitch. She quickly recovers, but Cole still catches it.

June steps back to get a good look at her. "I bet you're a nice change of scenery for the guys, huh?" Savannah's face reddens.

162

"Oh, June, leave the poor girl alone. Come on, Savi. Let's find you something to wear tonight." Abigail links arms with Savannah and pulls her toward the stairs.

"Must be some girl to put a look on your face like that." June elbows him in the ribs.

Cole smiles. He has no intention of lying to her. It's not like he can, anyway, he thinks wryly.

"That, she is." Aunt June is always so observant.

***

Cole sits at his desk. He doesn't even get his email open before a knock at the door disturbs him. He glances at his second monitor and sees Keith.

"Come in."

"Look, we need to talk about this whole Savannah disappearing act—"

"She's been going to the private library," Cole interrupts while studying his computer screen.

"What? How does she know about that place?"

"She saw it when I was bringing her back to her room after she got poisoned."

"And you're okay with that?"

"Something happened while we were gone. She felt nervous and went to a place where she felt safe. She only knows the code to her own room." He leaves out the fact that she knows his too. "She can roam all the hallways in this place, but she can't access any room without the codes. You know that."

"What if she finds the door to the bottom floor?"

Cole leans back in his chair. He doesn't like being questioned so much. "Then she sees a door that looks like every other door in the hallway. No codes, no access."

Keith nods and takes a seat.

Cole sighs. This is going to be a long day. "What do

you know about what happened?"

"All I know is she and York got into it over dinner. She was talking to the new guys, and Dell slipped up, admitting that *Los Sirvientes* were blackmailing someone."

Cole's jaw clenches. He needs to have a word with Dell.

"I guess that got Savi upset, and she pressed for information, but York had a power trip moment, and the two of them got into it."

"How badly?"

"Bad enough that York actually threatened her."

Cole's anger instantly flares. *Christ, York needs to tame it down.*

"A few more words were exchanged, and she left. Abigail came and got Mike. He caught Savannah in the hallway—nearly scared the poor thing to death. She seems a bit rattled, but other than that, she was all right. So, I don't know if the blackmailing thing is playing on her, or if it was the dinner fight. She just seems different. She's been hiding away from us until you all came home." Keith rises. "Look, Dell felt terrible about what he said. Don't be too hard on him. It's York's power trip that needs to be brought down a few pegs. That man is a loose cannon, and I swear he has it out for Savi."

"Sounds that way."

"Anyway, it's all on the tapes, so you can see it for yourself."

Cole runs his hands over his face. "I can't do anything until I get this report finished and sent over."

"I'll leave you to it."

***

Cole fusses over his tie in the mirror. He prefers boots and camo gear over a suit and tie any day, but it's a long-standing tradition to go to Zack's restaurant in town for Thanksgiving.

Zack worked for Shadows many years ago. When he retired, he didn't like the idea of leaving the area, so he opened a restaurant and bar with his younger brother. Cole's father and Zack now live two doors down from one another, best friends attached at the hip since they were kids. Abigail teases him and Mark for having the same kind of friendship. She's right, he laughs to himself. He can't imagine not having Mark around.

Normally the "guests" who stay at the house are kept at arm's length. Forming a relationship like his with Savi simply doesn't happen. They certainly have never had one included at their own off-site holiday dinner. Zack doesn't shut down his restaurant completely for them, but with the number of agents going tonight, he isn't too worried about taking Savannah out in public. "Though you can never be too careful," he mutters to himself, tucking his gun into the holster on his hip.

He shrugs on his jacket and inspects himself. He wears a black suit with a red tie, and his hair is gelled down and slicked back. He shakes his head. "I look like a fucking attorney from Wall Street. Fuck!" He knows he can't handle the city life. He wonders if Savannah misses it. If they do end up together, will she want to go back to New York? The thought makes him uneasy, so he pushes it aside.

Cole heads downstairs to find Keith and Mike waiting for him. As they hurry outside, he notes the temperature has dropped dramatically. His cell phone shows it's twenty-six degrees out.

Paul opens the door for him to hop in the Escalade.

Savannah is in the back, and he makes his way directly toward her, purposely ignoring his two grinning aunts until he is beside her.

"Ladies, you look lovely this evening."

"Same to you, Logan." June winks.

His grin widens as he takes in Savannah's appearance. A long, white fur coat is wrapped around her small frame. Sparkly earrings peek through her curled hair, and that heavenly apple smell is lingering around her. "You look lovely, Ms. Miller."

"Why, thank you." She smiles, her eyes dancing. "You look quite handsome yourself."

"It's the tie," he grunts, tugging it away from his neck.

They drive in a convoy of four—two Escalades and two spotter cars. He doesn't like driving the mountain roads at night. There are too many high areas where a sniper could wait. Cole doesn't realize Savannah is picking up on his vibe until he sees her face. Reaching for her hand, he threads his fingers through hers, figuring since they're in the back, no one will notice. June is keeping the conversation going with Paul and Mark up front. She squeezes it, but he can see she's anxious. He points with his free hand.

"See over there, those lights—that's the city. Not much further."

"You're nervous," she whispers.

"Not nervous, just alert." He leans in until his lips brush over the shell of her ear. He breathes in her scent as her grip tightens. "I like having you tucked away on my mountain where I know you're safe."

She still seems worried, but before he can ask, his phone begins to vibrate.

"Logan."

"It's Keith. We're at the restaurant and in position. Place looks busy, but Zack is ready for us. Your parents are here, along with a few of their friends."

He glances at his watch. "Copy that, six minutes out." He snaps it shut and gives Paul a nod to let him know everything is a go.

"Savi, what do you say if someone you don't know approaches you?" Mark asks from the front seat.

"That my name is Nicole and I'm here with family on a ski vacation."

"Perfect. And if you feel uncomfortable or nervous in a situation tonight, what's your safe word for us to step in?"

"Blackstone."

Cole looks down at her and hears Mark turn around too.

"Okay, Blackstone." Mark glances at him, puzzled.

Cole hops out the side door, scanning the parking lot first then helping everyone out. He keeps close to Savannah as they walk into the restaurant. His parents sit at a very long table with Will, a guy he grew up with—it is great to see him—and as they all exchange greetings, his mother nudges him as she meets Savannah. Good Lord, is everyone aware he has feelings for this woman? Or was Abigail just on the horn again?

He gasps as he helps Savannah take off her jacket; her black dress is so tight it's like a second skin. The sleeves hit right above her elbows, the length a little lower than mid-thigh, and it has a deep V-neck. Scowling at Abigail, who is avoiding his stare, he realizes he's still clutching her coat. He smoothly tries to wrap it back around her.

"You should keep this on. You'll freeze."

"I'm all right, thanks." She waves a hand and takes her seat.

He grumbles as he hangs the coat on the rack. He sits next to her, watching the guys at the table take in her beauty—or her chest. York is gawking. He has to fight with himself to not wrap his arm around her chair and claim what's his.

Drinks are served, and Cole's father rises to deliver a familiar holiday toast to friends. After dinner arrives, everyone dives into various dishes and conversations.

"So, when are you guys heading back to TJ?" Kyle asks. He is one of Cole's childhood friends who joined the Army the same time Cole did.

"Possibly next week." He sighs, seeing Mark glance at Savannah. "But I—ah, I'm not sure if I'll be attending that trip." He wants to see who is listening to them.

"I've never known you to skip out on a chance to snap someone's neck," York comments, taking a bite of his turkey.

"York!" Cole's mother hisses. "That's totally inappropriate."

York shrugs, seemingly unfazed by her recriminations. "No secret you have more kills than any of us."

Cole can't believe he's hearing this. His mother pointedly looks at Savannah, who is downing the rest of her wine. He stabs his finger at York. "One more word like that, and you'll be finding your own way back." He doesn't shout, but his clipped tone says it all. The guys are all good buddies, but there is still rank in his house, and he will be damned if he's going to let York forget that.

Cole shakes his head, turning back to Kyle. "I have a lot to catch up on. Frank is breathing down my neck."

"Yeah, I get that." Kyle moves his attention over to Savannah. "So, tell me something about yourself."

She leans forward and rests her forearms on the table, her bracelets making a pretty noise as they clink together. She pulls her dark hair off one shoulder, showing off her slender neck that his tongue is begging to taste. "What do you wanna know?"

He shrugs. "Something that none of these guys knows yet."

Cole gives her a slight nod, letting her know she can be honest with these guys. They've all signed NDA contracts.

She presses her lips together, taking a moment to think. "I love the blues. Give me a local pub with bad food and live music, and I'm a happy girl." She smiles as she remembers. "My friend Lynn and I would spend every Friday night at this little hole-in-the-wall pub in Queens just to listen to a musician named Flat Street Tony. He played the cello and had a voice that would make your soul dance." She lets out a little laugh. "One night, Tony came over and gave us a signed copy of one of the first vinyls he ever recorded. I have it mounted—" she stops herself, "had it mounted in my living room." Her mouth twists as she looks down at her fingers. "No paparazzi, no Daddy to disappoint, no one cared who I was. It was my little slice of heaven." She looks up, seeing the entire table is listening to her story. "So, to answer your question, I like the blues." She runs her hands over her lap.

"A girl who likes a dive pub, bad food, and mellow music. Jesus, Savannah, you're like every man's dream." Kyle laughs into his beer bottle. "Don't let this one leave."

"Didn't you hear, Kyle?" Savannah leans toward him and lowers her voice. "I'm taking over Agent Black's job."

Cole turns to her, only to find her grinning ear to ear, her eyes sparkling. It takes some major self-control not to grab her, throw her up against the wall, and take her right then and there.

"Savi, are you trying to get me in more trou—" Mark laughs stopping mid-word. "Melanie?"

Savannah's head whips around to Abigail, who looks like she's just seen a ghost.

"Who is this?" Cole whispers and leans toward Savannah, suspecting she knows something.

She turns so their faces are almost touching. "The girl

Mark's been seeing."

Really? That might explain why Mark's been so eager to do the runs into town lately.

Melanie says to Abigail, "I was just grabbing something to eat and saw you. I thought I'd come by and say hello."

"Well, that's nice of you, dear. I'm Abigail. Please, won't you join us?"

June is already grabbing a seat and wedging it between Mark and Savannah.

Mark shoots Cole a look, mouthing he's going to kill Abigail.

Savannah has to squeeze against him. Luckily for him, most of the action is on her side, so now he has an excuse to wrap his arm around her chair. She seems to like this. As she settles in next to him, she runs her hand over his thigh. He lets out a puff of air, fighting off the nasty thoughts that are flashing through him.

"I don't want to intrude..." Melanie starts to say, but Abigail pushes her into the seat.

"Nonsense."

Cole catches his father's gaze. He's smiling at both him and Mark, and his mother is beaming too. Well, at least his father seems all right if something is going on with him and Savannah. He needs to speak to him about it though.

"Do you work here in town?" Savannah asks Melanie.

"Yes, at The Cliff. It's a coffee shop my parents own. I'm helping them out while I go to school. I'm getting my marketing degree."

"Oh, I have a degree in marketing. I used to work for—" She catches herself. "So how did you and Mark meet?"

Melanie doesn't seem to notice Savannah change the topic.

"Yes, how did you two meet?" Keith asks, clearly loving this situation.

"Agent Black's job?" Cole whispers over Savannah's shoulder, his lips brushing over her warm skin. She chuckles. He can tell she enjoys getting a rise out of him. "I hate your dress."

"No, you don't."

He can't help but smile. Damn woman is good, but he can play this game. He looks around, seeing most of the attention is on Mark and Melanie. The restaurant is loud and very busy.

"I want to run my hands up your thighs and find out what you're wearing under that ridiculously tight dress." She stiffens. Yes, at the moment, he has the power. "Push you up against the wall, bury my face in your neck, and show you just how fucking hard that dress is making me." He gently traces circles along her smooth inner thigh. "Find out if you're as ready for me as I am for you." She swallows hard as her cheeks flush. "I want to taste—"

"Savannah, come with me to the bar?" Abigail asks, pulling his attention away. He wants to scowl at her again, but she doesn't know what he was up to.

Savannah pushes back her chair and leans in, pretending to point to something in the far corner.

"Nothing," she whispers, "to answer your question. I'm wearing nothing underneath."

Poof! The power shifts back to her as his eyes widen, running down her body.

"Excuse me." She gives him a sexy smile.

"I don't know how you guys get any work done with that walking around the property," Kyle jokes.

"What do you all do?" Melanie asks Cole, who is trying to drag his eyes off Savi.

"Army."

"Really? I've always heard there's a group that trains

somewhere around here, but you never see them in their uniforms. Is that you guys?"

"Yes, we train all over the country."

"Well, it's kind of nice knowing there's more protection up here. Seven policemen are hardly enough to handle this whole town, especially with the number of tourists we get. They should bring more cops in."

Cole has to agree with her. The town is understaffed, but the police are well trained and work well with his company. No locals have ever stumbled upon their location because there are three separate armed gates spaced three miles apart, and you have to have a level five clearance to get through any of them. If anyone spots the house, the rumor they put out is the property belongs to a Kent Cuttingham, who made his millions in the green air industry. The Army and his father have every angle covered when it comes to the Shadows house. So far, there's never been a problem.

"Cole," Abigail places her hand on his shoulder, "either Savi has been recognized, or she has an admirer."

He turns to where she shifts her gaze. At a small table by the window sit three men and a woman.

"Navy sports coat, blond hair," she says through a smile as she notices Kyle watching them. "I didn't want to hurry her away from the bar since she and June are talking, but he's been watching her since we walked over. I notice he's been pointing to her, and he said something to his friend on his left. They were looking at their phone and nodding."

"Another round?" Cole asks the table as he stands cheerfully. "Mark, you want a scotch, neat?"

"Yeah, that sounds good." He nods. *Scotch, neat* is their code for possible threat.

"Melanie?"

"Nothing for me, please. I'm driving."

"Very well." He turns to Abigail. "Go have a seat. I'll

check it out."

Cole casually heads toward the bar while watching the table by the window out of the corner of his eye. He catches Zack's arm as he goes by.

"Table of three men and the woman, who are they?"

"Out of towners. Sounds like they're from Chicago."

"All right, can you do a sweep? Find out what they're talking about."

"Of course." He moves off toward the kitchen.

Cole makes his way over to Savannah and slips in behind her. "Nicole, can I get you another?" She flinches but quickly recovers.

"Please." She pushes her half empty wine glass aside. "Let's make it a martini this time." Cole orders while June finishes her story then leaves, saying she needs to go hound Melanie.

"Here," Cole slides the glass to her, "just act normal, baby."

"My legs are shaking." Her trembling hand moves for the glass, but she stops to shake it out.

"Hey, man," Cole says to the guy next to her, "would you mind shifting down one so the lady can have a seat?"

"Oh, yeah, sure." The man moves down a seat. Cole helps Savannah onto the tall bar stool.

"Thanks. I thought I might fall."

"I'd never let that happen."

She smiles, but he can tell she is nervous.

"How did you know who Melanie was?" He hopes to distract her while he watches the table of four.

"Abigail found out he was talking to her, so she introduced herself and ended up inviting her to dinner. You think Mark will be mad?"

"No," Cole laughs. "It's not surprising she's playing Cupid. It's not the first time she's tried this. Abigail wants grandbabies more than anything."

"Yes, I got that impression." His eyes shift to hers as she chuckles. "She asked if I was on the pill." His mouth drops open. "Even though she knows I am, it was one of the first things your physician spoke about to me. He said it's a smart move since I live in a house full of men." She laughs. "Yeah, that was fun to wrap my head around, but after my conversation with Abby, I think I may need to start hiding them."

Cole lets out a laugh of his own. Oh, that Abigail is a trip sometimes.

"Well, she should be flattered," Zack says. "They think she's Megan Fox. I think at most they'll ask her for an autograph. They were going to approach her until you showed up."

"Okay, thanks, Zack."

"Anytime." He looks over at Savannah. "I hope you enjoyed your dinner."

"I truly did. You have a wonderful restaurant, Zack. Thank you for having us."

He leans in so she can hear him. "You are welcome anytime. Get Cole to bring you to dinner some night. I'll reserve you the booth in the corner so no one will bother you. I'll cook you something special myself."

"Well, that's an offer I can't refuse." Cole nods. "We'll have to set that up soon." An evening alone with her sounds perfect.

"Wonderful!" He claps his hands together. "All right, I must go. Enjoy the rest of the night."

Cole watches Savannah sip her martini. She seems to be a little more comfortable now. She peers at him over the rim of her glass, her eyes holding his, making him gulp. "Have I been spotted?"

"No, they think you're Megan Fox."

She coughs on her drink, laughing. "Well, that, I'm all right with. Bring 'em on. I can talk about Optimus Prime and Autobot Drift."

Cole bursts out laughing. *God, she is funny.*

"Sorry, you're out of luck. They won't come over because I'm here."

She raises her eyebrow.

"Over my dead body, baby."

She gives him a playful smile.

As long as they don't snap a picture of her, he doesn't care what they think. Social media is a real bitch. "Let's go back to the table."

***

"We'll see you for breakfast, dear." Cole's mother kisses his cheek before she gets in their Land Rover.

"Drive safe," he says to his father, shutting her door.

When Cole reaches the SUV, he walks up to Abigail and June, laughing at Mark about the look on Mark's face when Melanie arrived.

"No, no, please, laugh away. I'm glad my stomach hitting the floor and rolling out the door was so entertaining to you." He scoffs from the front seat, only making them laugh harder.

Savannah looks out the window, off in her own little world.

He sits next to her, fixing the vent to blow warm air on her. "You see something?"

"No, just thinking."

She seems far away, so he leaves her be and signals for Paul to start their drive home.

"A little music, Paul?" June asks. He turns on some music, and the Beatles' *Hey Jude* fills the car.

Savannah's hand rests on his thigh.

She appears troubled. He wraps his arm around her and nestles her against his side.

She runs her hand along his waist, flinching when she feels his gun.

He kisses the top of her head and holds her tighter. He doesn't care if Paul sees him in the mirror; he wants to hold her. She has something big to tell him tonight, and it is obviously playing on her. He's been patient, but she's suffering, and it bothers him.

She tucks her head into his neck and relaxes a little.

His phone vibrates in his pocket. He reaches down, seeing it's a text from Keith.

Keith: Green Land Rover. Since Zack's. Branching off. See who he follows.

"Paul," Cole's voice is sharp through the music, "keep on course."

Paul nods, checking in the mirror.

Savannah sits up and looks out the rear window.

"Look forward, please, Savi."

She stares at him, sensing his mood change. "Is there someone following us?" Her voice is shaky, and she starts to rub her hands over her lap nervously. "Cole, say something, please."

"Besides the blues, what other kind of music do you like?"

"I'm not five, Cole. Your attempt at a distraction is a little insulting. Keep me in the loop, or the panic that's about to surface will be the least of your worries."

He has to fake a cough to stop from laughing. *She's so feisty.*

"Keith noticed a Land Rover following us."

"So, couldn't they just be going somewhere?"

"Not on this road."

"We have company," Paul announces.

Savannah reaches for his hand. He loves that she looks to him for comfort.

"How far are we away from the house?" she asks.

"Ten minutes to the first gate," Cole answers while

texting Keith back.

Just as they approach the turnoff for the first gate, the Land Rover slows then suddenly speeds around them.

Paul flashes his card to the first guard and is waved through.

Once the gates close behind them, Savannah puts her hands over her face. "I hate this." Her words are muffled.

"I know." Cole rubs her back, wishing he could make it better.

Savannah heads straight into the house before Cole gets a chance to see if she is all right.

"Give her a moment," Abigail says, looping her arm through her sister's. "This is a reality check for her tonight."

"We got the plate number. Let's go run it," Mark says as they walk to Cole's office.

Chapter Twelve

I flop on my bed after changing into a tank and yoga pants, and wrap my sweater around me, needing to feel safe. The drive home played on some buried emotions that are surfacing quickly. I close my eyes and fall asleep immediately.

"Savi." I stir. "Savannah," Abigail whispers loudly, "wake up, please!"

I pry my eyes open and see her frantic expression.

"What's wrong?"

"You need to go down to Cole's office before he kills him!"

I sit straight up, and it feels like the room is tilting to one side. "Oh, no!" I jump out of bed and run down the hallway, taking two steps at a time. My heart is pounding in my ears as I shove open the door to his office. Cole has York by the neck against the wall. Mark is shouting something.

"Cole! No!" I run over to him. "Please don't do this."

"How could you hurt her?" Cole yells at York, ignoring me.

York is struggling to breathe.

I reach up and touch Cole's arm; it's like steel.

"Cole, please look at me!" I beg.

"Savannah, get out of here!" Cole yells, barely hanging on to his temper.

Keith blows into the room. "What the fuck?"

"No, Cole," I cry, trying to get his attention. "Look at me. I'm fine. I'm not hurt."

"Mark!" Cole barks out, making me jump.

Mark comes over quickly and pulls my sweater off my shoulders.

"Mark!" I shriek. "What the hell?"

Cole's gaze flickers over at me, taking in the bruises on my arms. His eyes instantly grow dark and angry. He punches York in the gut, doubling him over.

York collapses, gasping for air and clutching his midsection.

I yank my sweater back up, tears streaming down my face. "I trusted you. I can't believe you told him!" I scream at Mark.

"He didn't." Cole's voice is like ice. He's standing perfectly still, staring down at York. "I watched the tapes."

"Savannah," Mark says, ignoring my last comment, "tell Cole what York threatened you with."

What is Mark doing? Is he trying to make the situation worse? "Mark, stop." I'm shaking, and my emotions are shot all over the wall. I just want this to end.

"Savannah." Cole doesn't sound like himself, and it's borderline scary.

I look at York, who is giving me the nastiest look I've ever seen. My mouth dry, I run my trembling fingers through my hair. I feel sick.

York pulls himself up to his feet and stands like he is getting ready to fight.

I step back as he shakes his head at me.

He moves his hand up to his lip, wiping off the blood. "Aww, Savi, we could have had something beautiful," he smarms. "You should've kept your fucking mouth shut. Bad move." He chuckles then starts coughing.

Mark moves in behind me.

As I stand frozen, he hooks an arm around my waist, holding me tightly. What the hell? "The sick son of a bitch threatened to hand her over to the Cartels himself if she said anything," he tells Cole.

Cole launches himself at York, sending him hard into the wall.

"No!" I try to get away, but Mark wraps his other arm around me. I thrash all around as the two of them fight. "Let me go! Keith, stop them!"

Keith shakes his head. It feels like I'm watching a movie and I have no control of the outcome. "Cole, stop! You'll kill him! He's not worth it!" Nothing is getting through to him. I'm shaking so violently that I start losing focus. Then it hits me.

"*Blackstone!*" I scream at the top of my lungs, making the entire room freeze.

Cole's fist is inches from York's bloody face, his breathing heavy and his look that of a madman. He drops York's limp body on the ground and steps away.

Mark's death grip on me loosens, freeing me, and I sink to the floor and sob.

"Get him out of here," Cole rasps.

Mark and Keith pick York off the floor. York starts laughing like he's delirious. "Watch your back, Savannah."

My hair is blocking my view of him, but I can feel his eyes on me.

Mark jabs him in the ribs, and he cries out.

"Go!" Cole orders. The three disappear through the back door.

I stand on my shaky legs, feeling like I might pass out. My head is swimming with everything that just happened. I try to open the office door, but it is pushed shut, his arm above me.

"Savannah," Cole's voice is bleak, "please stay."

My hand falls away from the handle.

He lets out a heavy breath, takes my hand, and leads me out of his office through the back door.

His room is just how I remembered, big and open. He doesn't speak a word as he strips off his bloody shirt and dress pants. He disappears for a few minutes in the bathroom.

I stand, completely unable to move. Suddenly, he's in front of me, pulling off my sweater. He inspects my arms as I look away, feeling raw.

He bends down and gently kisses the bruises on each arm. He drops to his knees in front of me and wraps his arms around my waist, pressing his head against my stomach.

"I'm sorry, baby. Please forgive me." His words nearly break me.

"Don't apologize. You didn't hurt me." I feel such sadness that he thinks I'm upset with him.

"If I had been here, I could have protected you."

"You told me you don't do what-ifs." I cover my face and start to cry. "I just want it to all go away, but he wouldn't leave me alone."

Cole is silent.

I wipe my cheeks dry and try to get hold of myself.

"I almost killed him. I wanted to," he confesses.

I drop my hands with a heavy thud. "Me too."

"Thank you for stopping me." He looks up and holds my gaze while he gets to his feet. "No one but you could have."

I sigh, exhausted. "Come on."

He pulls back the covers to let me crawl in. He wraps his arm around my stomach and draws me to him. His chest expands as he blows out a long breath. I know he's worried about what I witnessed tonight, so I lift his hand off my stomach and kiss his battered knuckles. He leans in, giving me a kiss on my neck.

"Who told you about 'Blackstone'?" he asks.

"Dell."

I hear him mutter something as he pushes a button on his side table, turning off the light.

"Thank you for protecting me," I say into the darkness.

"I always will." His words make my heart thump louder. I'm falling fast for this man, and it's more than a little scary.

***

I wake to a steel cage around me—we didn't move an inch last night. I wiggle, trying to stretch, and his grip loosens, so I slip off the bed and head to the bathroom.

"Holy…!" I exclaim with a smile when I walk into the world's biggest bathroom. Deep red and gray run throughout the whole room, right down to the tile in the four-person shower. It has eight jets and three showerheads. A large oval tub sits in the corner with a view of the mountains. It's gorgeous. I stop gawking long enough to use the restroom and steal Cole's toothbrush.

"Ew!" I hiss when I notice dried blood on my pants and on the hem of my shirt. It's probably Cole's, but the idea of it being York's has me tearing my clothes off and throwing them in his hamper. I spot double doors and decide I need something to wear.

Rows of t-shirts, uniform shirts, heavy knit sweaters, and pants line the walls. Clearly, this is his military closet. Everything is so perfectly placed I'm almost intimidated to touch anything. I realize I'm taking too long, so I grab the closest t-shirt and shrug it on. It's dark green and has ARMY written across the front and LOGAN on the back. It's huge and comes down to my knees. I roll one side up and tuck the knot under the shirt, keeping it in place so it isn't like a tent on me.

I open the door to find him propped up in bed, reading on his phone. He looks sexy with his messy hair and the sheet covering one leg. He glances up and does a double take. A lazy smile runs over his lips.

"Morning," he says, his voice raspy.

"Didn't mean to take so long. I took a wrong turn in there," I joke.

He chuckles as his eyes rake over me.

"Sorry." I look down at his shirt. "There was blood on my clothes."

"Don't be. I never thought that shirt could look sexy until now."

I smile, not sure what to do now. Last night was intense, and our emotions were high.

"Come here, baby." He holds out his hand. He pulls me onto his stomach, guiding me to straddle his waist. His fingers run through my hair as he watches my face. "What are you thinking?"

"Honestly?"

"Always."

"I'm nervous what happened yesterday might affect us."

"How so?"

"You're losing a man who's been with you for...how long? You guys have a great thing here. I don't want to be the reason something bad happens." I fumble with the hem of my shirt. "I begged Mark to erase that tape." I feel him flinch. "He told me he couldn't, that he could lose his job."

"Smart man," he mutters.

"I saw the look on his face when he watched it." I look up. "I didn't want to see that on yours."

He twirls a piece of my hair around his finger, thinking. "I'll be honest with you. It took me to a dark place I haven't been before. Mark walked in with York right as I finished watching it. I don't remember how I got my hands wrapped around his neck or how I got him against the wall." I swallow, remembering it. "I could tell York didn't give a damn about the consequences for doing what he did—it happens to some of us. We see things in our business that harden us. Some deal with it differently than others. The signs were there, though— all his comments to you, his lack of respect for rank. I'm just sorry I didn't see it until it was too late."

"Honestly, I'm fine."

"You weren't fine, Savi. You were being threatened in a place that's supposed to be safe. You had a man who you were supposed to be able to trust force himself on you, hurt you." He closes his eyes, struggling with his words. "Christ, he was going to—"

"Please," I place my hands on his bare concrete slab of a stomach, "I don't want to talk about this anymore. Other than being a little sore and frightened, I'm fine, and he's gone." I lean over, feeling like I need some more contact with him, and kiss his chest. "This is where I feel safe, whose hands I want on me, whose lips I want to taste…" He shivers at my distraction.

"Savannah," he moans.

"He may have hurt me, Cole, but you saved me."

He reaches down, grabs my hips, and flips me over, devouring my mouth. His nails run down my thighs and around my behind.

He yanks my hips off the bed and grinds into me. "Feel what you do to me?"

I do; it is digging into me hard. "I can help with that." I lean forward, pull off my shirt, and unhook my bra, then toss both aside. *My…I'm bold this morning.* I think I need to feel something, something that will push aside the fear that's weighing heavily at the back of my brain.

"Oh, baby," he moans, savoring the view. He runs his hands down my sides, then along my stomach, and finally over my breasts.

I bite my lip to stop from crying out. It has been too long since I've been touched.

"You're fucking beautiful, Savannah." He leaves hot trails with his tongue.

My fingers find his hair and grab on, making him kiss harder.

"Mmm, you taste so sweet." He slips one hand into my soaked panties and runs a finger between my folds.

I arch my back, wanting more. "Ohhhhh…"

He closes his eyes. "I love how responsive you are." Just as his finger is about to make a pleasurable dive, there's a knock at the door. We both jump.

"Go away," he calls out between kisses.

"Logan, your parents just arrived, and Dan is looking for you," Paul says, instantly sucking all the fun out of the room.

Cole squeezes his eyes shut, cursing. "Yeah, all right, thanks."

I sit up and push him back. I need to return to my room and have a cold shower. I grab the Army shirt and tug it over my head.

"I totally forgot they were coming." He sighs, hands on his hips.

I step up on my tiptoes and give him a playful kiss. "To be continued," I tease, smacking his butt and giving him a grin.

He hooks his arm around my waist to pull me back to him then turns me to face him. "Are you really all right?"

I run my hands over his shoulders. "I am."

He leans in and gives me a quick kiss.

***

I pull off a piece of muffin and pop it in my mouth

while listening to Cole's mother, Sue, discuss her Christmas plans.

"Savannah, you should see what the town does for the week of Christmas. All the businesses decorate their stores, and each night for five days one place holds a party," Sue explains, beaming.

"It's a really big deal if your store is selected to hold one of the parties," Abigail adds. "Of course, Zack's was picked. He is every year."

Mark appears at the patio door. "Savi, would you mind grabbing Cole for me? I would myself, but—" He points to his soaking wet boots. It has been raining all morning.

"Of course." I hop up from the table to find him.

"Yes, Mark, you stay right there. I just had the floors cleaned," Abigail warns as he pretends to move his foot inside, laughing.

I make my way down the hallway toward Cole's office and hear voices when I get closer.

"Where is he now?" Daniel shouts. I freeze outside the door.

"Downstairs," Cole answers. *York is still in the house! Where downstairs?* "He's not talking, just says he wants to talk to her." My stomach twists.

"No way. He's crossed a line he can never come back from." Daniel pauses. "Does Savannah have any idea about her father?"

I step closer to the door, not caring I'm eavesdropping.

"No, and there's no reason to say anything until we're absolutely positive we're right." I feel the hair on the back of my neck stand up.

Daniel clears his throat. "This is bad, Cole, not only for the reputation of this house, but he knows the details of her file. He could easily leak what—"

A chair scrapes on the floor and makes me miss what

Daniel says. Damn it!

"…plus the blackmail, and God forbid The American gets wind of her whereabouts. She'll be plucked out of thin air so quickly we won't have a chance in hell of getting her back—not this time. With his reputation, he'll send her back one limb at a time, using the local news station, just like the last one."

The walls start to shift as I process his words. Suddenly, the door opens and Daniel stares down at me, horrified. "Savannah!"

Cole appears behind him.

"Mark," I feel like I'm having an out-of-body experience, "is-is looking for Cole." My voice is barely above a whisper.

I turn on my heel and walk down the hallway, each step feeling heavier than the last, Daniel's words "one limb at a time" bouncing around my head. Then there was the comment about something being leaked. What was that? I sink into my chair at the table.

"You look like you've seen a ghost, dear." Sue reaches out and touches my hand. "You're freezing."

"Savannah." I turn at the sound of Cole's voice. He is visibly shaken. "Can we talk?"

Mark peeks his head in the door. "Hey, Logan, I need—"

"Savi, please," Cole cuts him off.

Everyone is staring at me. I need to get some space to process what I heard. I feel myself shutting down and my walls building up.

"Mark needs you right now," I say, finding it hard to look at him…or anyone at that moment.

"What if I need you?" he counters, as his mother turns her head back and forth between us. What is he doing? He's risking his career and his reputation right now.

"Son, deal with Mark." Daniel rests his hand on

Cole's shoulder. "Give her a minute."

Cole doesn't move right away, not until his father gives him a nudge toward the door. As soon as he is out of hearing range, Sue looks at me with an inquisitively arched eyebrow, to which I can merely shrug.

"Savannah," Daniel starts to say, but I stand. I need some space.

"Excuse me." I take off toward the door, grabbing a jacket on the way, and head out into the pouring rain.

I don't know where I'm going, but the forest looks inviting. I walk for a while, weaving in and out of the trees. The sound of the rain on the leaves soothes my aching head. I grow tired of the constant battle with the slippery ground—flats are not made for hiking. The rain starts to taper off as I come to a small clearing by a brook. I tuck my raincoat under me and sit to rest under a tree, finally allowing myself the freedom to cry as I let my brain go over what I heard.

***

Cole sits at his desk, watching the live feed into York's cell. He's sitting on his bed, strumming his fingers on his thighs. What happened to him? York's a known ass, but he'd never hurt anyone before. Fuck, what if he had succeeded in raping Savannah? The thought is crippling to him. Cole rubs his face, feeling drained.

"You're in love with her, aren't you?" his father says from the doorway.

Cole's hands drop away. "No." Was he? He cared for her a lot, but love?

His father grins and shuts the door behind him. "Son, I had that same look on my face when I first fell for your mother."

"I've only known Savi for what, a month?"

"Sometimes it only takes one look to fall in love."

"Yeah, well, I know we shouldn't even be talking about her like this."

His father sighs as he crosses the room to take a seat in front of him. "Normally, I'd say no, we shouldn't be, but I know you'd never step over the line for just anyone. I see the way she looks at you too. It's not a one-sided feeling. Christ, you could see her relax when you wrapped your arm around her chair at dinner last night."

Cole leans forward, resting his arms on his desk. "What am I supposed to do? I love the way I feel when we're together. Her smell lingers on my clothes, and it drives me mad all day. I love who I am with her. Her words were the only ones that got through to me last night. If she wasn't there, I think I would have killed York. She can bring me to my knees with one look, and her lips..." Cole stops when he notices his father's expression.

"Welcome to being in love, son," he chuckles. "Good fucking luck."

Cole shakes his head. *Oh, shit. I'm screwed.*

"Even if that's true, how am I supposed to be with her here in this house? The guys will lose respect for me if I get involved with one of our victims—I mean 'guests.' It's a huge violation."

"Yes, but if you truly are in love with her, you have to take the risk. Don't let your job stop you from living your life. But that's a decision only you can make. As for the guys, they'll see you're not in it for a quickie—never been your style—and we raised you better than that." He smiles. "You both have some huge obstacles to overcome when she finds out the truth. It could be a game changer. What if she wants to go back to New York? This—" he indicates, waving his hands, "isn't for everyone."

"I know." Cole tosses his pen aside. "For the first time, I'm totally lost on what I should do."

"Take some time and think about it. It isn't something you can decide right away. You've got a lot to deal with right now, and she's not going anywhere."

Cole nods and picks up his radio, changing the channel to seven. "You have visual?"

"Ten-four. She's two-point-four miles west of the house."

"She's a little wanderer," Daniel says with a chuckle.

"What's she doing?" Cole asks, wishing he could see her.

"Sitting by the brook. Been like that for the past thirty."

"All right, stay with her, but keep your distance."

"Copy that."

Daniel stands, tucking his hands in his pockets. "Come on, let's go find your mom. She needs her Cole fix."

Cole follows him out of his office. "So, tomorrow, Frank will be arriving with a few others to take statements. They believe York is tied in to the poisoning, but they don't have enough evidence yet to charge him."

"What time tomorrow?"

"Thirteen hundred."

"Maybe we can get your mother to take the ladies into town to help get Savannah through this."

"Yeah." Cole shudders at the idea of Savannah leaving the house again, but it would be good for her to have some girl time.

***

I close my eyes, feeling the thumping of my brain inside my skull.

Why was my father being blackmailed? Maybe he

was involved in buying weed? If so, big deal; who isn't? Christ, most of the people in politics have a hook-up.

The American's history is something I can't even process yet.

Then there's York. Where is he downstairs? I thought I had seen the bottom floor. Would he really sell me out? He couldn't hate me that much, could he? Maybe he was in it for money? Either way, I wish I could talk to him, find out what's going on in his crazy mind. Is he the one who poisoned me? I never did hear if they found the how or why of it. I feel myself going into shutdown mode. I want to stop thinking at all, but I can't help it. This is what I do when I suffer an emotional overload. I fight it, but it's no use, and I feel myself drifting off to sleep.

I awake, suddenly shaking. I'm frozen to the core. Snowflakes prick my cheeks like tiny needles, one by one, bringing me out of my fog. When my eyes adjust, I see it's getting late.

I have no idea how long I slept after mulling everything over. I'm still confused. I now realize there is way more to what happened to me than meets the eye. Problem is—I'm not sure I want to know all the details. Along with the truth come many lies, and I think it might be more than I can handle.

A rustle in the trees sounds to my left. I tense and then remember.

"Which one of you has he sent to babysit me today?" I call out, leaning my head back against the tree. Snapping twigs and heavy footsteps become louder as the tall, dark figure comes into view through the falling snow. "Ahh, are you here to slap a tracking device on me now?" I half joke, a little drunk off my emotions.

"Come on, Savi, it's starting to snow harder." Keith holds out a hand.

"I don't want to go back yet."

"You'll freeze."

"I'm not cold."

He raises his eyebrow, obviously not buying my protest. He then pulls out his radio. "Delta Seven to Logan." He waits with a smug look on his face.

I roll my eyes.

"Go ahead, Keith," Cole's voice comes over the radio.

I don't break my stare with Keith. I'm not scared of him.

"Ms. Miller is refusing to come back to the house, despite the fact she's soaking wet and it's starting to snow. Permission to use Code Forty-Five?"

Forty-Five? What the hell is that?

There's silence for a moment then it crackles. "Give her the radio." Keith hands it to me.

I sigh, taking it out of his hand. "Good afternoon, Cole," I say calmly.

"Savi, please go back with Keith before you freeze to death."

"I like it here. I was rather enjoying the silence before you sicced your watchdog on me," I tease and look up at Keith, grinning. "No offense." He bites back a smile.

"Savannah, you see Keith's left shoulder? Well, if you don't get your backside off that ground and start walking toward the house, you're going to be hoisted over it and carried out."

My jaw drops, my temper rising fast. I hand the radio back to Keith, wrap my arms around my knees, and stay perfectly still on the ground. Yeah, I can be one stubborn ass sometimes.

"Well?" Cole hisses impatiently.

"Permission to use Code Forty-Five?" Keith asks through a grin. He's loving this.

"Permission granted."

Everything gets blurry as Keith scoops me up, tosses

me over his shoulder, and starts marching through the woods. I try to protest, hitting his back and shifting around, but all this does is make his death grip tighter. After a few minutes, I am suddenly struck with how I must look. I begin to crack up, and before I know it, I'm in a full-blown laughing fit and struggling to breathe. When we get to the clearing, he drops me to my feet. I stumble backward and roll on the ground. I have to hold my sides, they hurt so badly.

Keith joins me in my laughing fit as he pulls me to my feet. "Was that fun for you?"

"Yes, it was, thanks."

He rolls his eyes as we start back to the house. "I'll deny this if you ever repeat it, but I really like how you are with Cole. No one else would ever dare talk to him the way you do."

"People have mentioned that before. Saying they're surprised I'm not scared of him. What is it I'm not seeing?"

"Cole is normally all business. That's what makes him so great at what he does. People have nothing but respect for the guy and his family. He's a great friend to have. He'll be the first to take a bullet for you. But I've seen what happens if you cross him, and it's not pretty."

I look up at him, slightly nervous about what he'll say next.

"Is that why you didn't step in last night with York?"

"Yes. York knows the consequences of betraying Cole and this house. York got off easy. If you weren't there to stop it, I have no doubt he would have left in a body bag."

I shake my head at that thought. I know he is right.

He sighs. "So, you overheard Dan and Cole talking?"

A knot in my neck begins to tighten. "There's a lot I don't know about my…ah…case. I feel like I won't be overly pleased with the outcome, will I?"

He pushes his lips together. "I'm thinking not," he says. "I'm really sorry about what York did. I wish you told me, but Mark explained to me why you didn't. It was really sweet of you to think about everyone else." We walk in silence for a bit, listening to the freshly fallen snow crunch under our feet.

"Keith." He looks down at me. "What if I don't want to go back to New York after this is all over?"

He pulls me against his side. "Then we'll make you our chef," he says with a grin. "Speaking of baking, Abigail just got a shipment of apples in. You think you could make another apple crisp for me? After all, I did have to babysit you all day."

I elbow him playfully. "Fine."

Chapter Thirteen

Cole taps his heel repeatedly on the floor, waiting "patiently" for Keith to return with Savannah. The snow is starting to pick up, leaving a thick layer on the ground. *Christ! What is taking so damn long?*

"I see them," Abigail calls from the window.

Cole hurries to the door and out onto the porch. His parents follow while Abigail and June stay at the window.

Savannah's arms are wrapped around her middle, and she has Keith's gloves on, looking like she's freezing. As he walks down to meet them, he sees her blue, shivering lips muttering something.

"Did you have to carry her?" Cole asks, glancing at Keith.

"Yeah," he replies with a chuckle. "She laughed the whole time, so it wasn't as effective as I hoped."

"Cold yet?" he asks her. "Go have a shower, before you freeze to death." He's feeling so many emotions; he knows he is coming across as angry.

No doubt confused by his tone, she shakes her head and leaves.

"I don't think that's a good idea, Savi—" Keith starts to say as Cole gets hit with a snowball in the back.

He spins around to find Savannah making another one. She stands back up and chucks it at his shoulder, sending pieces of snow down his front. Both his parents have their hands over their mouths, waiting to see what he'll do next.

"Don't be crabby with me, Cole Logan," she shouts through the snowflakes. "You see Keith's left shoulder? Well, if you don't get over your cranky mood, you're going to be hoisted over it and carried to the lake for a refresher." She crosses her arms as she throws his words back at him.

Keith bursts out laughing as she turns on her heel and heads for the stairs, mumbling something to his parents and making them laugh too.

"Oh, dear, I just love her," his mother calls out.

Yeah, he can see that. "All right, Keith," he says, fighting his smile. *Christ, she is something else.* He was not expecting her feistiness. "Thanks for bringing her back. You can go inside."

Keith twists his mouth, trying hard not to laugh again. "At the risk of stepping over the line, my friend, that girl is perfect for you." He slaps Cole on the shoulder as he runs inside.

***

I crawl onto the couch, burrowing under the blanket Abigail wrapped around me, and am handed a cup of coffee. Daniel is lost in thought, and Sue is sitting across from me, grinning.

"I'm sorry." She chuckles. "I just keep picturing Cole's face when you hit him with the snowball."

"It was pretty funny," June chimes in, holding a plate of brownies in front of me. "Try one."

I take one off the plate and bite into it. "Oh, wow." I savor the taste on my tongue. "June, these are delicious."

"Savannah, were you dating anyone before?" Sue blurts out.

"No."

"I'm surprised a beautiful woman like you isn't married with a possible child on the way."

"Let's just say I didn't meet Mr. Right back in my old life." I glance at June then stare down at the piece of brownie in my fingers. It is slowly melting.

"Perhaps you'll find him in this life," Sue says, smiling.

"Perhaps what?" Cole asks as he takes a seat. He drapes his arm around the back of the couch behind me. I see Sue beaming again.

"Girl talk, dear," his mother says quickly.

Cole looks at his father. "Sorry, Dad."

"Yeah," Daniel sighs.

I glance at Cole. "Do you still need me to enforce Code Forty-Five? Or are you out of your crabby mood?" I grin as he shakes his head, grabbing my hand with the brownie in it and nipping it out from between my fingers. "Hey!" I laugh.

"Mmm, warm brownie," he moans, rolling his eyes back.

"Perhaps she already has," Abigail whispers to Sue, but I catch it.

"Oh, I think I can hear Christina's heart breaking from here." June chuckles.

"Aunt June!" Cole's expression suddenly turns serious.

"Who's Christina?" I ask, wondering why she mentioned her.

"She's been in love with Cole since she moved here four years ago." Sue shrugs. "She's a bit on the crazy side."

"Please don't start, ladies," Cole warns.

"Why would her heart break?" As soon as the words come out of my mouth, I feel like an ass.

"Because I'm not interested in her," he answers

quickly. "One date, and she was practically making wedding plans and naming our babies."

"What was the name for the boy again?" Abigail laughs to her sister.

"Fritter." June slaps her hand over her mouth to hide the smile.

"As in apple fritter?" I ask, barely containing myself.

"Exactly!" Sue and Abigail chime at the same time.

I look up at Cole. "Fritter Logan. Sounds like a character from *Lord of the Rings*!"

Daniel bursts out laughing. "Oh, my God, it does!"

"Any time you're all finished." Cole flops his head back against the couch.

"Ohhh." I pat his leg. His hand falls on top of mine, holding it there for a moment.

"Obviously, if I had known she was that crazy, I wouldn't have agreed to the date in the first place. Last time I let Mark set me up on a blind date."

"Hey, man, she's hot," Mark says, sitting next to Abigail. I try to pull my hand away from Cole's, but his grip tightens. I wonder what he's thinking, but he doesn't look down at me. "I didn't know she was bat shit crazy!"

"Mouth." Abigail swats his arm.

"All I saw was a fine ass and a pretty face," Mark says, earning two swats. "Hey," he complains, "you're always telling me to be honest, so here I am, and what do I get?" He gives Abigail a kiss on her cheek. I can see how much he adores his adopted mother.

"I ran into Christina yesterday," Dell says, joining our conversation. "Cole, I guess you left your coat there Thursday."

Thursday? The day they arrived home from their trip? I feel a strange pang of jealousy, and what makes it worse is Cole flinches. This time I pull my hand out quickly enough that he can't stop it.

"What's with her keeping it so bloody hot in there? I swear she does it so she can wear those skimpy outfits. Don't get me wrong, I'm not complaining—"

"Dell," Sue holds out her glass, "could you get me a refill, please?"

"Oh, of course." He scoops up her glass. "Anyone else?"

"Scotch, neat," Cole blurts out.

Mark's grin grows a little wider, making me wonder if that means something.

"So, Savannah," Sue says brightly, "would you like to join the ladies and me in town tomorrow for a spa day?"

"Umm…" I fumble with my words, having mixed feelings about leaving the house, but it's not every day I get a chance to be pampered. "That sounds nice, thank you."

"Keith and Paul will join you," Cole informs his mother.

"Of course, son." She nods like she's used to him speaking this way. "We'll take good care of Savannah."

I sigh, wishing I didn't have to be treated like a child. Cole's fingers start rubbing my neck, and I'm confused by his public display of affection. I catch Daniel's eye, and he grins then looks away. *Maybe they're fine with it?* I wonder what was said between the two of them. I would love to have been a fly on the wall for that conversation.

Dell hands Cole his drink and perches on the arm of the couch next to me.

Mark checks his watch and smacks his hands together. "Puck drops in five minutes, guys!"

"Who's playing?" Sue asks.

"Kings and Blackhawks," I answer, not really thinking about it. Mark and Cole both stare at me. "What? I have male cousins. It's embedded in me to catch the highlights and knows who's playing." I shrug.

"Who's your favorite team?" Mark asks, quieting down the group. He shifts forward on the couch and looks very serious.

"Penguins," I say, feeling strong loyalty toward my favorite team.

Mark jumps in the air with a shout. He pulls me up, wrapping his arms around me.

"Listen up, everyone!" he calls with his arm over my shoulders. "Miller is a Penguins fan!"

The entire room breaks out in cheers. I laugh and shake my head. I have to admit it feels pretty damn good being in a room full of people who genuinely like me for me.

Dell grabs my hand before I can sit. "I think I just fell in love with you," he says, deadpan. "Marry me!"

"Well, with a proposal like that..." I joke. "Hell, yeah, sugar, I'll marry you."

"One condition." He points at me. "We get married in our jerseys."

"Oh, Dell," I fan my face, using a southern belle accent, "it all sounds so classy."

"I know." He winks.

It doesn't take much convincing for the boys to have me join them to watch the game. Nine of us sit in the entertainment room watching the seventy-inch TV. The announcer blares all around us—I count six surround sound speakers.

I'm in the back corner with Cole, feeling pretty beat after the day, sipping a stiff Dell-made drink called Tale of the Devil.

"Please know," Cole squeezes my hand under the blanket, "I just went to pick up a package at Christina's store. It was hot, and she made me wait, so I removed my jacket and forgot it there, nothing more."

"Cole, we weren't together then anyway," I whisper,

downing the last of the drink.

"I thought we were."

"Logan, phone call," John interrupts us from the doorway. "Line three."

"Shit." Cole rubs his face. "I have to take this. Be right back." He pats my hand then leaves.

"Another, Savi? It will help you sleep," Dell says with a wink.

I nod, loving the idea of sleep.

I remember seeing the score 2-0 Kings near the end of the third period. I stir to Mark trying to wake me. It isn't happening. "I'm fine here," I mutter.

"Come on, you." Mark scoops me up.

"You don't have to carry me," I mumble. "I can—I think…nope, I can't walk—thingsssss are blurry."

"You're slurring your words." He laughs. "You sound like a hissing cobra with those dark eyes of yours." That makes an image flash in front of me.

"Cobra, cobra," I pronounce the word carefully. "I've seen a gold cobra."

"Wow, you really don't drink much, do you?"

"Two cobras, after he hit my face."

Mark stops. "Who hit your face?"

"American man." My head flops to the side. I'm so tired. "I remember now. I've seen him before." Mark sits me down on the bottom of the stairs. He pulls out his cell and calls someone. I lean against the wall, watching the stairs blur together as another memory comes to me. "He has a ring that has—" I tip forward, but Mark grabs my shoulders, stopping me.

"What has she had?" Cole's voice booms in front of me.

"A tail," I answer, very matter-of-fact. "Wait, now, that's not right."

"She's had two Tale of the Devils." Mark moves over as Cole comes into view.

"And I saw two cobras," I remind Mark.

"Yes, Savi. Gold, right?"

"Mmmhmmm." I nod. "With black eyes."

"Where did you see this?" Cole asks.

"Right after he hit my face. It hurt a lot."

"The American," Mark adds. "She said she's seen him before, something about a ring."

"Yes, a ring," I squint at my fingers, trying recall which finger it was. Cole takes my hands in his.

"Where else have you seen him, Savi? The American."

Memories start flashing in front of me. They're all going by so fast.

"Baby, look at me."

I try to focus. I hate when these flashbacks come; it stirs so many emotions.

"It's okay, I'm here," he reassures me.

"Once at a restaurant with Lynn. He was at the bar, watching me," I say quietly, trying to concentrate. "And at the market." My head turns to one side as I remember something else. "His boots made a sound that was different, like nails tapping on tile." I lower my voice. "He came to my prison one night." I swallow, remembering. "He stood over my bed, staring down at me." I raise my hand to my lips. "He whispered something in Spanish and kissed his two fingers and pressed them to my forehead."

"Do you remember what he said?"

"Yeah, he said, '*Pronto serás mia, mi amor.*'"

Cole's eyes widen, and fear runs across his face.

"Are you sure that's what he said? Think, Savannah."

I nod a bunch of times. "Yes, I wanted to know what it meant so I could research it, but forgot about it until now." I push my hair out of my face. "I think I might be drunk. Wait-wait! What does it mean?"

"I'll tell you in the morning." He scoops me up and

carries me up the stairs.

My head is spinning like a Ferris wheel. "You don't have to carry me!"

I hear him laugh as I open my eyes and squint, focusing on his jawline. He has a five o'clock shadow that's begging my fingers to trace along the outline.

"You're very handsome, you know that?"

"And you're very beautiful."

"I'm engaged," I joke.

"Oh, baby, the only guy who will ever have a ring on that finger of yours is me."

My heart stops—did he just say that? I decide to see if he did.

"Mmm, Savannah Logan, I rather like the sound of that."

"Me too." He pulls back the blankets and sits me on his bed.

Huh, I guess he did. "You're very confident," I say with a grin.

"I'm confident when I know I'm right about something."

"Wait, you just walked me through the front door of your bedroom." I look around. "Someone will see!"

"I don't care. Arms up."

I do, falling forward. "I think I might be really drunk, which is bad, because drunk girls are not flattering."

He pulls off my top and replaces it with one of his t-shirts. "Well, I kind of like you like this." I smile at his words. He leans me back and starts undoing my pants.

I grin, lifting my hips off the bed.

"I know that look." He smiles back at me. "And trust me, baby, there's nothing I want to do more than to sink myself deep inside you. But I will not have our first time end with you passing out on me."

I moan. "I love that you're such a gentleman." He pulls my pants off and looks down at my panties.

"Yeah…it feels great right now," he says sarcastically, closing his eyes and taking a moment. "Come on, under the blankets you go," he says as he tucks me in.

"You're still dressed." I yawn.

"I am." He sighs. "I still have some work to do."

The room is spinning. I watch him shake two different pills into my hand.

"Take these." He supports me and helps me drink some water. Way too out of it to even ask what they are, I close my eyes and feel him stroke my hair.

"Will you come to me later?" I mumble as I drift off to sleep.

"I always will."

***

Cole pours himself a fourth cup of coffee. He is beyond beat. He only got two hours of sleep on his office couch while going over reports for York's case. Frank is arriving in twenty, and he needs to get his head in the game. Outside his window, he sees the guys heading up the mountain for their morning training, and he wishes he could join them and burn off some tension.

Checking the time to ensure he catches Savannah before she leaves for the spa, he hurries down the hallway and finds her pulling on her jacket in the entryway as she chats with his mother.

"Hey, I thought you were training with the guys." She smiles up at him.

"I wish," he mutters. "Can I speak with you for a moment?" She follows him into a room.

"What's wrong?" She runs her hand across his morning scruff. "Did you get any sleep last night?"

"I want you to stay in touch with me today," he replies, ignoring her question. "My mother has a phone, so send me a text when you get settled at the spa, okay?"

"Okay," she says. "But, Cole, you're kind of scaring me."

"I just don't like the idea of you driving through those mountains without me. I don't like you being away from me, period," he admits.

"Me either." She sighs, and he's happy to hear her say those words.

"However, that being said, I want you to have fun, but don't let the ladies pry too much. Mom adores you and will want to know everything."

She smiles, her eyes holding his. "I should go." She wraps her arms around his neck and kisses him deeply.

He squeezes her to his chest, reluctant to let go.

She pulls back. "Try to get some rest, baby."

He loves how she cares for him like they've known each other forever.

"Okay, you need to go or you'll never get out of here." He kisses her one last time.

***

I think I've died and gone to heaven as I sink further into the brown goo.

"Who would have thought mud would feel so heavenly?" June moans, sipping her champagne.

"Who would have thought I could stomach this," I hold up my glass, "after Dell's mad concoction last night?" I laugh, thinking about something. "Sue, is Dell York's replacement?"

"No, he's just filling in until they bring in someone else."

"Ladies," Carlos interrupts, "time to move on."

We spend the next three hours being pampered to the nines, everything buffed and polished. The girls encourage me to add some honey highlights to my hair, saying it will help brighten my mood, and I am stunned with how much I love the look with my huge curls draping down my back. We all decide on complete makeovers after that.

I feel amazing. As we take our seats for a late lunch at Zack's restaurant, I'm thankful the lunch rush is over. There are only two tables occupied besides ours.

"Ladies!" Zack calls out as he hurries over to our table. "You all look beautiful!" He turns to the male host, clucking his tongue. "Adam, you should sit them in the window. They would draw in more customers."

"I agree." Adam winks at me, and I smirk. I find his boldness funny.

"Please, let me make you something special." He snatches the menus and gives them back to Adam. "You all just sit back and let Zack take care of you. Wine." He nods at Adam.

"Thank you, Zack," Sue says as Zack leaves.

Abigail grins at me. "Looks like someone likes the way Savi glows today."

I smile, moving the attention over to Abigail. "Speaking of liking the way someone looks at someone, care to give the dirt on Dr. Roberts?"

June perks right up. "As in, the house psychologist?"

"Yes, June," I grin, "that one."

"I'm not sure what you're referring to." Abigail tries so hard not to smile, but it doesn't work with three people waiting to get the goods. "We kissed once," she says, picking at a piece of bread.

"What?" the three of us yell at the same time.

"Why do I not know this?" June snaps at her at sister.

"I didn't want you to say anything to him. Besides, it was a one-time thing in the summer. We haven't spoken about it since." She waves her hand. "It was nothing."

I shake my head. "I sit in front of that man for an hour a day," I say. "I see the way he looks at you. He likes you, Abigail."

She smiles back at me.

"Let's plan to have him over for dinner this week."

"Yes, let's!" June chimes in.

I beam at June then turn to see Abigail blush. "Don't let someone good slip through your fingers, Abigail. You deserve to be happy."

"Speaking of deserving to be happy," Sue sits back in her chair and looks at me, "what's going on with you and my son?"

Oh, shit. I lean over and pour myself some more wine, and Sue laughs.

"Ladies, *bon appetit*," Zack announces as he and Adam serve our lunch. "Chicken Souvlaki with roasted potatoes and grilled asparagus," he says with a flourish.

It smells amazing. Everything looks so perfectly placed on the plate I almost don't want to touch it.

Adam leans over my seat and whispers, "You must have come from the spa...you smell of vanilla."

I nod, fighting the blush I feel rising in my cheeks.

"Can I get you anything else?" I notice he isn't asking the rest of the table.

"No, thank you. I'm fine." I glance at Sue, who is chuckling.

We are all pretty quiet as we start eating. I'm hoping to God they don't bring up Cole again, but I know it's highly unlikely.

"What do you miss most from home, Savannah?" June throws me with her question.

"I-I'm not sure," I stammer. "I mean, I miss a lot of things, but my life was so different." I lean back to allow Adam to clear away my plate. "It wasn't exactly going the way I thought it would. I was becoming less and less connected to the outside world because of the paparazzi. I was trying so hard to be what my father wanted and so hard not to be what the press was convinced I was, that I lost who I actually was."

June nods. "So, who is the real Savannah, and what does she want out of this life?"

"Umm…" I hadn't really thought about it. "I guess I'm still figuring out who I am. As far as what I want out of life, it would be to find someone who loves me for me." I tilt my head, giving it some thought. "Someone to curl up with on a stormy night, holding me till it passes. Someone who, no matter what, kisses me hello and goodbye." I think of Cole. "Someone who can melt my heart with just one look, make my knees weak when they say my name. Make my breathing stop when they reach out to touch me." I look up to see three women staring at me with dreamy eyes like I'd been singing a love song. I cough, and we all sit up a little straighter. "I'm tired of putting my life on hold. I just want to be happy. I know I have a long road ahead of me and a lot more hurdles to get over, but the fact that I know I will be doing it with all of you makes it a little easier," I confess.

"That's a lovely thing to say, dear." Sue reaches for my hand and gives it a squeeze.

God, it feels nice opening up and letting them in, even if it's only baby steps. I smile to myself. Something else pops in my head and makes me happy.

"The piano, June." I glance at Abigail, who gives me a wink. It means so much that she's never spoken about me playing it when I first arrived. I know she understood it was a private moment for me. "I've only played twice since my mother passed, but I love to play the piano."

"There's one in the living room, dear," June says. "You'll have to play for us some time."

"We have a piano here!" Zack booms, coming toward the table.

How the hell did he hear us?

"You want to play?"

"No, no, I'm too rusty." I hold up my hands. "Perhaps another time."

"Okay, but I'm holding you to that," he says through a grin. "Ladies, I hope you enjoyed your lunch. We'll see you soon, right?"

"Of course." Sue stands and gives him a hug.

We say our goodbyes as Adam races ahead of us to open the door.

"Have a good afternoon," he says with a bow. "I hope to see you again real soon, Nicole."

"I'm sure you do," June jokes on the way over to the SUV.

Keith is on the phone with someone and watches me as I come toward the car. "She's fine. We're about to head home. Okay."

He smiles. "You got the boss in a knot because you didn't text."

"Oh, shoot!" I hit my forehead. "I forgot."

"No worries."

"Sorry."

Chapter Fourteen

Abigail and June sit in front of Sue and me. June is prattling on about Dr. Roberts, demanding to know all the juicy details. I notice Sue is quiet, like she is deep in thought. I decide I may as well give her something, since she's been so incredibly generous and loving toward me.

"I really care a lot about your son, Sue," I say quietly, so the guys up front don't hear. "I've never felt like this before. It's a little new to me, and a little scary." I drop my gaze to my hands, suddenly wondering if maybe I have too much baggage for her son. "We may not be the perfect fit, but he makes me feel alive when we're together."

"Savannah," she says, "you and Cole fit perfectly together. I can't tell you the last time I've seen my boy truly happy." Her eyes gloss over. "He cares for you deeply too, I can tell."

"Tell me you want children," Abigail hisses over her shoulder, and I throw my hands over my face.

"We want a little Fritter!" June laughs.

"Well, I don't know about 'Fritter,'" I say, "but yes, I've always wanted kids."

Abigail and June both turn to look at me.

"Don't toy with us, Savannah." Abigail raises a brow. "Our boys need to have babies. We've been waiting too damn long."

"Oh, my!" I laugh as Sue nods in agreement with them.

Later, as Abigail and I start dinner, I realize I haven't seen Cole since I left this morning. There seems to be some tension in the house, and I recognize Mark and John also seem a little on edge.

"How was your day?" I ask, trying to feel them out.

"I've had better." Mark grabs a beer from the fridge, popping the top off with one of those credit card openers with the S logo. "You may want to make extra. Looks like our company will be staying for dinner."

"Company?" I ask, surprised. "Who's here?"

"I just don't understand why they'd put oil and water together in the same house," John grumbles as Mark ignores my question, and tosses him a beer.

"Oh, no, they're not!" Abigail stops stirring the soup and shakes her head. "When's Dell leaving?"

"Already gone." Mark shrugs at me, seeing my face fall. "It's how it works here."

I feel badly I didn't get to say goodbye.

"I'll be damned if he joins Blackstone. I don't trust that man."

"I assure you, I have no interest in joining Blackstone," a tall guy with short brown hair says, coming into the kitchen. "The less of Logan I have to see, the better." He steps in front of me, blocking me from the salad I'm working on. "You must be Savannah Miller."

"I am." I wait for him to move; I don't like the way he spoke about Cole.

"I'm Derek Rent." He holds out his hand, so I give him a quick shake and move around him. "Looks like we'll be housemates."

"So I've been hearing." I try to sound friendly, but if Cole, John, and Mark don't like this guy, there must be a good reason. "Welcome."

"Don't listen to these guys," he says as he takes a seat at the island, stealing a chopped mushroom from my pile. "No one likes the new guy."

"New guy would imply we don't know anything about you, but unfortunately, that's not the case," Mark says as he downs his beer.

"Ah, Mark, are we still going to do the same old song and dance?"

"Where's Cole?" I ask, changing the subject. I wish he was here.

"He's talking to Frank in his office," Derek says with a long sigh. "Things got pretty heated earlier."

"Is everything all right?" I ask as I toss the mushrooms in the bowl.

"Not when I left the room."

The usual large crowd doesn't join us for dinner tonight, but Mark, Paul, John, and Derek are at the table. As I sit down, Keith slips in to my left and tells us that Cole, his father Daniel, and a man named Frank Brandon will be joining us shortly. Abigail, June, and Sue try to lift the tension.

"I still think it was priceless when Carlos tried to get Keith in for a seaweed wrap." June laughs. "The look on your face, Keith—"

"Was like confusion mixed with disgust," I finish for her, and the girls and I start laughing.

"Why would anyone wrap themselves in something you eat between two sticks or avoid in the ocean?" Keith shakes his head. "I'll never understand why women do the things they do."

"Amen." Mark raises his beer.

"Sorry we're late." Daniel leans over and gives Sue a kiss on the cheek.

"Savannah." Cole grabs my attention. "This is Frank Brandon."

I stand to shake hands with him. With his green

camouflage pants, black heavy knit sweater, and his hair in a crew cut over intense, dark eyes, he is the ultimate definition of an "Army guy."

"Nice to meet you." I smile at him, simultaneously noting that Cole and Daniel look exhausted.

"It's a pleasure to finally meet you, Ms. Miller." He moves around the table to sit directly across from me.

I slip back into my chair and watch Cole's face. Something seems off.

"So, Ms. Miller, how are you adjusting to the house?" Frank asks, digging into the scalloped potatoes.

"Please, call me Savannah. Just fine, thank you. I feel safe here, something I didn't think I'd ever feel again."

He nods while chewing. "That's nice to hear. Savannah—have you ever been to Washington?"

Cole stands, scraping his chair loudly on the floor, and disappears out of the room.

"Umm, yes, once when I was a child. I don't remember too much though," I reply as Cole returns with a glass of brandy, "so please don't quiz me."

He chuckles. "I won't." He looks over at the ladies. "How was your trip into town today?"

I think it's strange he knew we were out.

"It was very relaxing, nice to be pampered sometimes. Mix that with a little girl talk, and you have a great day," Sue answers.

"Your hair looks nice," Cole says.

I smile at him, happy that he noticed.

"Adam thought so too," Abigail says, laughing. "We went to lunch at Zack's, and that poor boy was tripping all over himself, making sure she was well taken care of."

"Oh, I bet," Cole mutters.

"Can you blame him?" Derek gives me a smile and a shrug.

"He was only doing his job," I protest, shooting a

look at Abigail. "It was nothing."

As the dinner dishes are cleared away, Frank asks if I will join him in the living room for drinks. I look over at Cole to make sure he's joining us as well. He nods at me and follows us, with Mark and Daniel right behind him. I notice Keith and Paul are hovering around as well; something's up.

Scoot pounces on my lap, demanding his normal belly rub. He wedges between Cole and me and presents himself rather shamelessly. I start rubbing while being handed a Mark special, which concerns me, considering he knows firsthand how drunk I was last night. The presence of the martini tells me I'm probably not going to like what I am about to hear.

"Savannah, I want to talk to you about your case." Frank leans forward in his chair, "but first I want you to tell me what happened between you and York."

And so it begins.

I fill him in on as many details as I can remember and answer a ton of his questions, including a few I wasn't comfortable with.

"So, you didn't give him any signals that would prompt him to come on to you?"

"No!" I snap angrily. "I told you we didn't get along since the moment we met."

"Can we get on with this?" Daniel asks, annoyed.

"Was York involved in my poisoning?" I ask.

"I can't really answer that." Frank shifts on the couch.

"Well, I guess I can't really answer any more of your questions." I fold my arms as my temper rises.

Scoot bats my hand, but Cole takes over the rub so I can focus.

Frank lets out a long sigh and presses his lips together while he thinks. "Yes, we believe he was."

I nod, letting that information sink in. "Why? I

haven't done anything to that man. Why would he try to kill me?"

"He wasn't trying to kill you—"

"Says you."

"He was trying to send a signal to The American as to where you are. If you went to a hospital, they would have entered your file online, and it would pop up to anyone who knows where to look for a case of poisoning by tetrahydrozoline. Thankfully, Logan was able to figure this out and stop the doctor before he entered it."

I turn to Cole. "I guess that's two times you've saved my life."

His expression is so troubled I want to ask him what is wrong, but I can't.

"Savannah, we have a problem," Frank says bluntly. "It was bad enough when we found out The American was involved in your abduction, but now to know he's in love with you, that's—"

"Wha—What?" I set my drink down heavily on the table. "What are you talking about?"

"*Pronto serás mia, mi amor.*"

I look at Mark, then Cole, remembering my conversation from last night.

"Soon you'll be mine, my love," he clarifies for me.

My blood pressure drops through the floor as I stand, suddenly chilled. I awkwardly sit on the stones next to the fire.

"I'm sorry, I thought you knew what it meant," he says, taking in my reaction.

"No." I shake my head in confusion.

"You were in no state to hear what it meant," Cole explains, his expression worried. "I couldn't risk you disappearing into the woods again."

"Savannah," Frank pulls my attention back to him, "we know York has connected with someone who has ties to The American. There's a chance he may have given up your location. I feel it's best you come with me to Washington until we get this cleared up."

So many things run through my head at once, and all I can do is hold on until my brain catches up.

"I know you're comfortable here, but if The American is on his way—"

"So, you don't know for sure," I manage to whisper.

"No. York won't talk to us." Mark steps toward me. "He'll only talk to you."

"Mark!" Cole snaps, and I jump.

"I'll do it."

"No!" Cole snaps again.

"Where is he, Mark?" I ask.

"Downstairs."

Cole springs to his feet and lunges at Mark, sending Scoot hissing under the couch.

Daniel jumps up and gets between them.

Downstairs! Where?

"Cole, sit!" Daniel pushes him backward.

"Even if we did allow you to speak to him, it wouldn't matter. We need to get you out of here," Frank says, standing.

I stand too, shaking my head. I head for Cole's office, where I know he keeps my file, having seen where he put it on the day I first met with him. I return with it a few moments later and hand the file to Frank. He looks puzzled but opens it.

"If you're saying I need to leave here, then you can toss out my agreement, and I'll go home."

"No! Savannah!" Cole shouts, coming toward me. I hold up my hand to stop him.

"If you're saying that me staying here is going to make it unsafe for these guys, and the location of this house might be compromised, then I want to go to New York."

"I don't think you understand how big this is," Frank

says, surprised by my reaction.

"You're right, I don't. I'd love some answers, if you're willing to provide them."

"Frank, give her some." Cole looks pale. "She needs to understand how serious this is."

Frank tosses the file down on the table as he sits. "Please, Savannah, take a seat."

Cole reaches out and grips my arm, pulling me down next to him.

Frank lets out a deep breath and leans his arms on his legs as he studies at me. "Someone contracted to have you kidnapped. We're not entirely sure who yet, but we have a few theories. One being your father's right-hand man, Luka."

I keep shaking my head. Luka has been like an uncle to me forever.

"The others?"

"I don't want to go there yet."

I feel like I was hit in the stomach by a hammer. My meal is threatening to shoot up my throat like one of those high strikers you find at the carnival to test your strength. "My father's one of them, isn't he?"

"Savannah, everyone is a suspect right now," Cole says quietly.

Frank sighs. "After you were taken by *Los Sirvientes Del Diablos,* they found out something and decided to turn the tables. They were ordered to kill you after the first day, and that's when we realized you weren't involved."

I jump to my feet. I'm pissed. "Pardon me?"

"There was the possibility that you and your father planned this. He's up for re-election, and it gave him a ton of attention with the press, but—"

"Are you fucking kidding me?" I hiss, turning to Cole. "Did you believe that too?"

Cole shakes his head. "Savi, your case just keeps

growing. Yes, before we got you, it was a possible thought. Once we had confirmation you were still alive and still under their watch, we realized there was something more going on." I feel sick. "We're sure they're blackmailing your father with something."

"Oh, my God," I whisper, fighting the spins.

Frank clears his throat. "We're not saying your father is involved with you being taken, but they have something they're using to blackmail him, threatening to expose it if he doesn't pay."

"Wait!" I pace the floor, trying to catch up. "When did they start blackmailing him?"

"Over a month ago."

"You mean right before I was rescued?"

"Yes."

"Why start then?"

"We don't know."

"Maybe York gave them the heads up on your plans to rescue me?"

"That's something we're considering." Frank nods. "Look, we don't know who set up the kidnapping in the first place. We don't know where *Los Sirvientes Del Diablos* or the rest of the Cartels are, but they have something they're using against your father. We don't know where The American is, but he's a damn smart man and always gets what he wants, and he wants you. If you go back to New York, you'll be taken."

I run my hand through my hair then grab Cole's drink off the table, downing the brandy in one swallow. *Holy Christ, that's strong!*

"I'll take my chances," I mutter, and both Cole and Mark jump to their feet.

"No. I won't let you." Cole grabs my hand and pulls me to my feet. He wraps his arm around my waist, holding me tightly. "Frank, she's just scared."

"Frank," Daniel says in a calm voice, "my father built

and created Shadows. As of two days ago, I signed my company over to my son. I believe if everyone who's employed in this house is behind having Savannah continue to stay here, then she should be able to stay, if that's what my son wishes."

"I do," Cole answers without missing a beat.

Frank ponders the idea. "If everyone is on board, then fine, we'll stand behind you. But think about what you're risking if they find her or this place."

"No, guys." I swallow the lump in my throat. "Daniel, that's incredibly kind of you, but I don't want them risking all this just for me." I fight back the tears that are threatening.

"Savannah, stop, please." Cole grips me harder.

"Call a house meeting," Frank says, watching the two of us.

Cole no longer cares who sees his affection for me?

"Frank, may I have a word with you in Cole's office?" I ask, and Cole flinches. "I'll be right back," I say. "*Please trust me*," I beg him with my eyes.

"Of course." Frank waves toward the hallway.

Chapter Fifteen

Cole feels such a loss when she leaves his side. Watching her walk away, he wonders what in the hell they're going to discuss.

Daniel calls over the radio to ask everyone to leave their post temporarily for a house meeting in the living room—ASAP.

Mark grips Cole's arm and pulls him off to the side. "I wanted Frank to tell her about the blackmail. It might trigger something for her. Plus, we don't want her going back to her father yet. Something still isn't adding up there. I'm sorry about the York comment. I thought maybe she'd stay if she could help with the York investigation."

Cole nods. He knows Mark is trying to help, but he hates the idea that Savannah might go looking for answers from York.

"You're up, son." Daniel nods at the crowd now gathered in the living room.

Cole moves to the fireplace, and everyone stops talking—waiting to find out what's going on.

"Thank you all for coming in so fast. Here's the situation. As of right now, we've discovered York may have been in communication with The American's people. We now know The American had other plans for Savannah." Cole swallows the bile in the back of his throat and continues. "It seems he was planning on taking her for himself and has stepped up the hunt for her. Frank Brandon is here and wants to take Savannah back to Washington for her own protection, but Savannah won't go. She wants to go back to New York rather than put Shadows at risk." A light roar sounds among the crowd.

"No! She'll be killed!" Abigail shrieks, holding her stomach.

"Here's my plan." Cole holds up his hand to get their attention again. "Frank will allow her to stay here as long as everyone is in agreement and understands the consequences that come with protecting her here at Shadows. This could get bad, so if you're not okay with it, please let me know, and I'll lay you off temporarily until this is over—no judgment passed. With a show of hands, who is not all right with Savannah staying here?" No hands are raised.

"I think I speak for all of us when I say Savi isn't going anywhere." Keith's voice booms throughout the room.

Cole gives him a nod, and relief spreads over him. Now he just needs to convince Savannah.

"If you don't mind," Mike tugs at his jacket, "I'm sweating in my gear, and I would like to get out there and watch for that sick son of a bitch."

"All right, go. Thanks, guys." Cole waits for the crowd to leave then leans his forehead on the mantel, taking a breather and wishing this would end.

"Oh, dear," Sue rubs his back, "your father just filled me in. I'm sure she's just scared and worried about all of you. Give her some time. You know this is a lot for her to process."

"I don't know what I'll do if she leaves," he whispers.

His mother steps around to face him.

"We had quite the talk in the car on the way home. She really cares about you, Cole."

"Mention the part about the fritters, Sue," June says as she eavesdrops while walking by.

Sue tries to hide a smile. "Yes, well, the aunts," she nods toward Abigail and June, "got confirmation that she does want kids."

Oh, Lord! Poor Savannah. He could only imagine the firing squad of questions that were thrown at her. Although the idea of having a little one running around wasn't as scary as he thought it would be. He shakes his head. *What the hell is happening to me? I've only known this woman for two months!*

"Son." Daniel nods toward the hallway where Savannah is shaking Frank's hand.

"I'll see you all tomorrow," Frank calls before he disappears out the door.

Savannah walks into the living room, and he can see she's been crying. He can't help but wonder what is going on in that pretty little head of hers, but knows he has to give her some space. He doesn't say anything.

"I have until tomorrow to decide," she says, not meeting his eyes.

"Come and sit, Savannah," his mother says as she puts her arm around Savi's shoulders and walks her to the couch, draping her favorite blanket around her. "Can I get you anything?"

"No. I'm all right, thanks."

"What did Frank say?" Daniel asks as Mark leaves the room to answer his cell phone.

"He just filled me in on the risks if I stay or leave. He answered a few more questions, and in turn, I answered a few for him. I will not go to Washington...the idea scares me more than going back to New York. Trusting people doesn't come easily for me anymore. I'm just really confused." She rubs her head. "I don't think of

New York as my home anymore, and after what I learned tonight, I feel like I can't trust anyone there." She starts to cry. "The worst part is I have mixed feelings toward my father. What does that say about me? I'm a horrible person. I'm sorry," she says, standing. "I really need some time to think this all through." She looks over at Cole. "I promise—no woods." With that, she turns and heads upstairs.

Cole jumps to his feet, pacing the room and ignoring the low hum of voices in the background. He knows he can't let her leave. Needing to prove how much he cares for her, he takes off toward her room with his mother's protests to give her more time ringing in his ears.

Marching down the hallway, he throws open her bedroom door then locks it behind him. The shower is running, so he strips off his clothes and heads toward the bathroom. He does not hesitate as he opens the shower door and steps in.

"Cole!" She jumps, letting her gaze travel down his body. "Oh!"

He grabs her around the waist and lifts her up against the wall.

She lets out a squeak as her legs wrap around him.

He likes her this way. She can't run, and he has full access to her long, slender neck. He leans in and kisses her below her ear, feeling her pulse quicken. "What is there to think about, Savi?" he whispers hoarsely.

She runs her hands through his wet hair and lets out a sigh. "Cole, I can't stay."

Oh, hell no. He positions himself at her opening and slams in.

She screams, gripping his shoulders.

He nearly doubles over, she is so tight and ready for him. "Does that feel good?"

"God, yes! Again!" She wiggles her hips. Her chest pushes into his face. Sweet Lord, she's beautiful! He pulls out and slams in again, nearly buckling. Christ, she feels amazing. He takes a minute to control himself—it's been a long time since he has been with a woman. He slams again, making her shoot up the wall.

"Yes!" she shouts and claws at his skin like she is starving for him.

He slows the pace, teasing them both with short little thrusts.

"Cole, please," she begs, wiggling to get more friction. "Please."

"If you leave, I'll never see you again. You told me you were mine." She starts to whimper as he thrusts up hard. "This is where you belong, baby, with me—nowhere else."

She leans forward and seals her lips over his, kissing him deeply.

Oh, this woman is going to kill him. He returns to his rough movements, giving her everything he has. He's completely lost in her…his mind is spinning with all her gasps and moans.

"Cole!" she calls out. He can tell she's close.

"Give it to me, baby. Give in."

She screams as her entire body shakes and squeezes him like a glove. His vision goes cloudy as he loses all control, emptying himself into her.

They are both panting as they come down from their high. She's like jelly in his arms, completely spent. He washes her, having to hold her up with one hand. He wraps her in a towel and puts her to bed. He quickly dries himself off, chucks the towel in the basket, then crawls in behind her, their naked bodies giving each other comfort.

It's pitch black, but he can tell she's still awake; her breathing is uneven. He kisses her shoulder, his lips lingering on her silky skin. "I'm not letting you go, Savannah," he whispers. She doesn't say anything, but she pushes herself tighter against him.

***

I tap my fingers on the railing, watching the numbers light up one by one. Fifteen more to go.

"Savannah!" Luka calls out as I step out of the elevator on the twenty-sixth floor of the Maxwell building. "What are you doing here?" He gives me a hug.

"I'm meeting Dad for lunch."

He looks at me oddly, and I know what's coming. "He must have forgotten. He left about ten minutes ago."

I curse inwardly.

"Third time in two weeks—a girl could get a complex," I joke, giving him the best smile I can muster. "I guess I'll head back across town."

Luka squeezes my arm. "Sorry, sweetheart. I'll let him know you were here."

"Thanks." I click the button a few times then decide I'd rather write my dad a Post-it and stick it to his monitor so he will see it when he gets back. I race off toward his office. Margo, his receptionist, is away from her desk, so I slip inside, grab a pen, and quickly write, 'You forgot again...you owe me three lunches- S'

I post it to the monitor and let myself out.

"Oh, hello," a woman with straight blonde hair cut in a bob greets me. "Savannah. right?"

"Ah, yes." I smile. "Where's Margo?"

"Her father is sick, so she had to go visit him in Philly."

Later on that evening, my father finally calls me.

"Hey, Dad," I say, rubbing my eyes.

"Savi, sorry I forgot about today." I hear a woman's voice in the background.

225

"Dad, do you have company?" I grin.

"Don't be ridiculous, Savi, it's just Margo. She came over to drop off a file."

"Right." I laugh, walking over to grab a blanket off the chair.

"We'll reschedule for another day. Got to go. Good night, Savannah."

"Have fun, Dad." I'm still laughing as I hang up. I stop suddenly when my eye is drawn to someone standing across the street. He seems to be looking directly at me. He is holding what appears to be a folded newspaper, and when he turns away, I note how the light reflects on his boots...they look odd, like they turn up at the tips. How strange.

My eyes open as my heart pounds out of my chest. I look at the time—four thirty. Cole is wrapped around me, so I gently try to move his arm, but it locks around me.

"Why is your heart racing?" he whispers against my neck. Crap.

"Bad dream. I'm sorry I woke you."

"You didn't." He rolls on his back and pulls me against his side so my head rests on his chest.

"You haven't slept?" I feel terrible.

"What were you dreaming about?"

I sigh as he dodges my question.

"I remember another time I saw The American. He was outside my condo, watching me."

Cole doesn't say anything, he just stares at the ceiling. What I wouldn't give to know what he is thinking. When I can't take the silence anymore, I roll on his stomach and straddle him. The only light is from the full moon, so it's hard to read his expression. I trace paths down his stomach with my fingertips, and it flexes when he folds his arms behind his head. I know he is upset with me, but I haven't had time to really think since I passed out after our shower encounter. I shiver when I remember the feeling of him inside me. I push my weight on my knees to get the angle right then sink down before he has a chance to stop me.

"Savannah!" He jolts forward and grabs my hips. "Fuuuuck."

I shift my body, adjusting to his size. He lies back down as I start a slow, lazy pace.

His hands press over his face as he sucks in a deep breath. "Christ, woman!" He grabs me, holding me still as he shoves his hips up and tries to get deeper, faster.

I push his hands away, smiling. I am in control this time.

He shakes his head and groans as I set the pace, again running my hands down his front, stopping in all the right places. Payback is going to be fun.

I pull him almost all the way out, but only take him back an inch.

He hisses out a puff of air.

I pull up again and slam down, knowing I can't take much more.

Suddenly, I am on my back and my legs are hiked up over his shoulders. He pushes into me, taking me hard. My eyes close and I smile—I love how dominating he is in bed. Ha! He's dominating outside the bedroom too. I do love how I got him to this point, knowing he would take over.

"Look at me, baby."

I open my eyes—he's inches above me, his eyes showing me how worried he is. "Right here is where you belong," he says as he slams hard, making his point and taking me over the edge.

I'm lost in a sea of colors as I scream out his name, my orgasms coming in waves.

He covers my mouth to muffle my screams as I feel

him quiver, finding his bliss right after mine. He flops down and rests his head on my stomach as I run my fingers through his damp hair. "I want to do that to you every morning," he says as he kisses me above my belly button right before he rolls off, pulling me back onto his chest. "Next time, I want to take it slow, make it last for hours."

I don't have any words for the way I feel. Instead I lean up, kissing him once under his chin.

I wake again at seven. This time, Cole doesn't budge when I slip out of bed. I pull the blankets over him, making sure he's warm before I jump in for a quick shower. I manage to get dressed without waking the poor guy.

"Good morning," Abigail says, handing me a cup of coffee. "You get any sleep?"

"A little." I sigh, feeling a bit sore. Two times with Cole, and I should be sitting on a donut ring. "Cole is still sleeping. He's really tired. Can you make sure no one wakes him?"

"Of course. And Frank arrived twenty minutes ago. He's outside with Daniel if you want to speak with him."

"Yes, I do. Thanks."

She comes around the island and gives me a hug. "Please don't leave us. We all love you." She sniffs, letting me go.

My eyes prickle. "I love you too, Abigail." And I do. Wow, I really do care a lot for this woman.

I pull on my coat and boots and head out. It's snowing lightly as I make my way over to Frank and Daniel at the stables.

"Good morning," I say, coming up behind them.

"Hello, Savannah," Frank says. "Have you made your decision?"

Daniel takes off his knit hat, slips it over my head, then grants me a Logan smile. "I'll see you indoors."

***

Cole opens his eyes, feeling like something is off. His hand quickly does a swipe of the bed, and he jumps when he notices she's gone. Shit! It is quarter to eight, and Frank was supposed to arrive at six thirty. He flips down the panel on the wall, enters the code, and races toward his bedroom. He needs to get some clothes.

Running down the stairs and into the kitchen, he finds his father and Abigail looking worried.

"Where is she?"

"Out by the stables," Abigail says. "They've been talking for over an hour."

Cole moves over to the window and spots them. Savannah has her back to the house, and Frank is nodding.

"Why didn't someone wake me?" he asks, trying to think clearly.

"Savi wanted you to sleep."

Of course, she did. He flops himself on a stool, thinking he can barely remember the last time he slept past seven a.m.

"There's nothing you can do but wait," Daniel says from behind him. "Looks like they'll be a while, so go have a shower. You look like hell."

After taking his Dad's advice and grabbing a brief shower, he joins them back at the kitchen table. His mother hands him a plate of bacon and eggs. He rubs his head. This waiting is killing him.

"How did she seem last night?" his mother asks, sitting across from him.

"Confused. I can tell she doesn't want to go."

"She doesn't," Keith states, joining them. "She told me when we were walking out of the woods. She asked, 'what if I don't want to leave, what happens then?'"

Cole sags into his seat.

"She's leaving because we're all in danger," Daniel says into his coffee mug. "She cares about us so much she's willing to risk her own life to make sure we're all right. She's a pretty amazing woman."

"We're always in danger," Keith huffs. "Never stopped us before."

The front door opens, and they all stop talking. Savannah comes around the corner first, shivering from the cold.

Cole quickly pours her a cup of coffee. "You didn't wake me."

"You needed to sleep," she says, reaching out and squeezing his arm. Her fingers are like ice. Just as she takes the mug, Frank enters the room.

"Well, your girl puts up one hell of a fight," he says, pulling off his hat and sitting at the table. "I'm mentally fried."

Cole leans back and holds onto the island as his stomach bottoms out again.

Frank makes a show of checking his watch. "I have to run into town. I'll be back this evening with my men to transfer Agent York back to Washington."

Savannah steps forward and shakes his hand. "Thank you."

Everyone is quiet. After they hear him leave, all eyes are on her.

"Well," she sighs, "I guess you're stuck with me."

Cole sags against the counter as everyone hurries to hug her. It feels like his feet are welded to the floor.

She turns and pushes up on her toes, whispering into his shoulder, "I didn't want to leave this house, these guys, or you."

The corners of his mouth lift as he leans down. "I wouldn't let you, even if you tried."

She turns toward him. They are so close he can feel her warm breath on his cheek. Cole glances around and sees everyone is busy. He leans in, giving her a light peck on her lips.

She tilts her head, surprised, but grants him a smile that reaches her eyes. He's fallen.

Chapter Sixteen

I push the cart slowly through the aisle.

"Okay, so, silver and gold?" Abigail asks as we enter the third Christmas store in a row.

Since I decided for a second time to stay at the house, I thought it was about time to decorate.

Abigail and June normally do a Christmas tree, but that's about it. Not this year. If I'm staying, we are decorating just like Lynn and I did back in New York. Winter wonderland.

"And red," I add as Abigail holds up a package of white, sparkly snowflakes. "Now, those are perfect. How many in a package?"

"Umm, twelve—oh, look, gold ones too."

"Perfect. Grab three of each."

She laughs and drops them into the cart.

"So, do you know how Melanie and Mark are doing?"

Abigail holds up some thick red ribbon. I nod while selecting boxes of ornaments and a red velvet tree skirt. "They're doing really well, actually." She beams. "He's even talking to me about her now. He wants to invite her to the light show in town when we all attend."

"Wow, kind of like meeting the family officially…again!" We break out laughing.

After three more stores, I am more than impressed

with what we got. Paul shakes his head each time we come out with a cart full from each place.

"I'll take you to Zack's once I know you're settled," he says. "I'll take off to the grocery store to save some time."

"Okay…" I hesitate before giving him my list.

"What?"

"Just don't substitute things."

He smirks at me; we've been down this road before.

"When it says—"

"I know." He snatches the list out of my hand. "When it says sharp cheese, don't get medium cheese. Oh, I remember." He chuckles and waves me into the SUV.

Zack is more than happy to see us. Our impromptu shopping trip didn't allow us to give him a heads up that we were coming, and he falls all over himself with glee. Adam, remembering last time, seats us by the fireplace.

"Ladies! What an unexpected pleasure," Zack says warmly. "Are you in town to do a little shopping?"

"Savannah wants to spread some Christmas cheer throughout the house, so we needed to buy some decorations." Abigail smiles as she removes her coat.

"I think we bought the town," I joke.

"Well, isn't that fun!" He snaps his fingers at Adam. "A bottle of my personal favorite." Adam rushes off toward the back. "You two sit back and let Zack take care of you."

I smile. That seems to be his line with us. I am more than willing—he always makes the best food.

"Can I ask you something personal?" Abigail takes a sip of her water.

"Sure."

"Who taught you how to play the piano?"

I clear my throat around the lump that comes whenever anyone mentions the subject. "My mother."

"I thought so."

"Why's that?

She thinks for a moment. "You have a lot of emotion when you play. Would you tell me about her?"

"She was wonderful." I shrug, then seeing she's really interested, continue. "She was the kind of mother who would drop anything and play with you. She taught me how to bake, how to ride a bike, how to sing." I can't help but let out a chuckle. "She was the singer in the family. I just play the piano."

"What about your—" she starts, turning red and fanning herself.

"Abby?" I look around the restaurant.

"No, look at me," she says. "We're just talking."

"Yes, that's what we're doing." I laugh, puzzled. Then I realize what's putting her into a state.

"Hello, Savannah, Abigail. You both look lovely today."

"Thanks, you too," I say. "What are you up to today, Dr. Roberts?" I eye Abby, whose face is finally starting to return to her normal shade.

"I had to pick up some packages then decided to have a bite of lunch."

"Please say you'll join us," I ask as Abigail's eyes widen.

"Thank you, that sounds nice."

Adam rushes a chair over for him. He must have been watching us.

"It can get lonely, eating every meal by yourself," he admits as he settles in and glances at Abigail, who has yet to say anything. "That's a lovely blouse, Abigail. It makes you shine."

"Thank you." She smiles coyly. "And I see you're wearing your red tie."

This time it is Doc Roberts who blushes. "Yes, well, it is my favorite."

My jaw nearly drops when I realize they must be referring to last summer's romance.

"So, Dr. Roberts, do you have any plans tomorrow night?" I feel badly that I'm breaking up their moment, but I am about to grant them another.

"I do believe I'm free."

"Wonderful. Please join us for dinner. It's Abigail's night off—" She looks at me, puzzled. "And I'm in charge of cooking. Her sister, June, is in town, and I understand you've never met."

"You have a night off?" He smiles at Abigail. "Well, how can I refuse?"

I have to press my lips together to hold back a yelp of joy. "Well, that's great! Be there at five?"

He nods, and I see Abigail trying not to smile.

"Can you excuse me a minute? I need to use the restroom." I decide these two can use a little private time.

I head for the restroom but get sidetracked by a newspaper sitting on the bar. I glance at the front page then begin reading the local news about the light festival.

I hear a chiming noise outside and look out the window, and I notice someone across the street. There is something familiar, but then he is gone. I freeze in place. Pushing the newspaper away from me, I squint, but it's bright out with the snow. The moment I think I see him, a trolley comes by and he hops on, turning so his back is to me.

I open the front door and step outside. My mind is racing...his blue coat, red hat, blue coat, red hat. Continuing down the narrow, snow-covered sidewalk, I round the corner and see the man getting off at a bakery. I hurry across the street so quickly a car has to slam on its brakes. The driver shouts at me, but nothing registers in my urgency to follow this man. I slip into the bakery and look around at all the faces, then I see a blue coat draped over a chair, but the guy isn't there.

"Umm, did you see the man who owns this jacket? Did you see what he looks like?" I ask the couple at the table next to the coat, but they both shrug, shaking their heads.

I turn to two women behind the cash register. "Where is the man who owns that jacket? Has he ordered yet? What does he look like?" I repeat urgently.

"Umm," one of the young women stumbles, "I-I'm not sure. I'm sorry."

"Don't be sorry, just think. Where is he?" I nearly shout at her. The whole place is looking at me when the bathroom door opens and a man comes out, checking his belt.

"That's him," the girl at the table calls out.

"It that your blue jacket?" I ask the man.

"Yes," he answers.

Oh, God. I rub my head. *What the hell was that, Savi?* Talk about freaking out. I shake my head, feeling stupid.

"I'm sorry, I thought you were someone else." I start toward the door but look back.

"Excuse me," I call out to him, "are you wearing a red hat today?"

"No, green." He holds it up.

My stomach drops when I look at his jacket again. It's different. It's a pea coat. The other guy's was a ski jacket. Shit.

I push the door open as someone steps in front of me. I hold the door for them, but they don't move. I look up and see Paul peering down at me. *Oh, shit...*

"What do you think you're doing?"

"I'm sorry, I thought—" I shake my head. I don't want to say I think I saw Jose Jorge. I'll sound crazy, and they'll probably add an extra hour to Dr. Roberts's sessions. "I'm sorry."

"You are damn lucky I found you when I did. Cole is—"

"You called Cole?" I snap. "I've been gone what, five minutes?"

"No, I called Keith, and you were gone fifteen."

"Keith!" I toss my hands in the air as I walk around him. "That's even worse!"

"How is that worse?" He hurries to catch up. "Look, you can't run off on me like that."

I stop and turn to him. "I didn't run off on you. I just thought—" I shake my head. "Look, it won't happen again. I'm sorry. Can we just forget about this?"

"Fine."

Lunch goes fairly well after I dodge twenty questions about what happened. Dr. Roberts isn't buying it, but at least he leaves it alone for now. He and Abigail appear much more relaxed with each other, and they both seem to be looking forward to tomorrow night's dinner. I slowly come off my adrenaline rush, but the image of blue coat, red hat guy is burned into my memory. Somewhere deep down inside there's a part of me that thinks it could be him.

Abigail fills me in on their conversation while I was away from the table. I guess he's wanted to see her for a while now, but wasn't sure if she felt the same way. Her face is positively glowing. I've never seen her so happy before. She hugs me as we walk to the car, thanking me for tomorrow night. The rest of the drive, she prattles on about this and that. I keep catching Paul watching me in the mirror.

Sinking into the couch while Abigail tells June about our day, I glance at all the bags, thinking I should probably get started with the decorating, but I don't get up. Instead, I close my eyes, needing a minute to think. I hear someone clear their throat, and open my eyes to find Keith looking down at me. His arms are crossed, and he has the look of death on his face.

I hold up my arm. "Go ahead. Chip me." He rolls his eyes.

"Oh, boy, would I love to," he snickers. "Are you insane?"

"Possibly." I sigh, covering my face with my arms. "Does Cole know?"

"Yes." *Of course...* "He was there when Paul called."

"And on a scale of one to ten?" I ask, peeking out.

"It was ten, but now I'd say an eight."

I sigh again. I seem to be doing that a lot these days.

"He's on a conference call, but I'm sure he'll want to see you afterward."

Oh, I bet.

* * *

Cole stares at the speakerphone. Frank is giving him the play-by-play on what happened after they left the house this afternoon. Reaching over for the crystal bottle of brandy, he pours himself a double. This shit is getting out of hand. He takes a drink, setting the glass down and flexing his hand—the hand that has been gripping his pen since Frank started his story.

"That's un-fucking-believable!"

"Yeah, well, it was pretty intense." Frank clears his throat. "I got to go. I'll be in touch."

"All right." He rubs his face, feeling exhausted, when Abigail's text comes up alerting him dinner is ready. He lets her know he won't be joining them. He needs to make some calls—the first one to his father.

Cole doesn't come out of his office until close to ten. Faint music reaches him as he walks down the hallway. He comes to an abrupt halt when he steps into the living room. *Holy shit...*

"Pretty amazing, hey?" June asks, handing him a rum

and eggnog. "She's been working on this all evening."

Savannah is up on a ladder, putting a star on top of the Christmas tree. It is decorated in silver and gold with thick red ribbon wrapped all around it. A red velvet tree skirt lies underneath. The fireplace has garland outlining it, with lights strung through, and more red ribbon. A huge, tastefully-lighted, matching wreath hangs above it. Silver and gold sparkly snowflakes are hung at different lengths in each window. Candles are placed throughout, tying the whole room together. June points to the banister going up the stairs, which is covered in garland to match the fireplace. A big vase sits on the entryway table, containing a huge poinsettia. She even gave it a light dusting of glitter to make it sparkle like the rest of the place.

"Wow," is all he can get out.

"Is everything all right, dear? You look stressed."

He shakes his head. Now isn't the time to get into things.

Savannah's smile makes him want to run to her. "What do you think?" she calls out.

"It's amazing." He winks, watching her grin widen.

Mark walks by holding a bag of trash and stops next to him. "What's going on?" he asks quietly.

Cole shakes his head as Savannah climbs back down the ladder. Derek is, of course, ready for her in case she falls.

"Don't fuck with me. Your face is telling me something big is up."

"Later." He glances at Mark, and his eyes narrow in on his chin. "Nice glitter."

"Oh, come on!" Mark hisses, rubbing his chin. "This shit doesn't come off." Cole tries to hide his smirk. "Oh, fuck off!" He storms off toward the bathroom.

After everything is put away, everyone comes together for drinks and sweets. Mark hovers by the table.

Every once in a while, Cole looks at him funny just to screw with him. He loves messing with him. He looks for Savannah, but she's disappeared, so he finds himself drifting back to his conversation with Frank, and his stomach twists as his thoughts go dark.

"You care to tell me what's going on now? Or do I need to call Dad?" Mark asks from beside him.

"Downstairs." He motions with his head.

He starts to tell his story but hears Savannah whispering with someone around the corner. He holds up his hand to Mark.

"That's the thing I don't know," her voice trails off.

"Well, that's the deal," Derek says.

What the hell? Cole steps into view, and Savannah jumps.

"Cole…" she starts, but he cuts her off.

"What the hell is going on?" He shakes his head, making eye contact with Derek. "Go upstairs, Rent," he orders.

Derek looks at Savi. "Will you be okay?" *Really?*

She nods, running her hand through her hair.

"Why are you here with him?" Cole nearly shouts at her. "Do you know how this looks?"

"What are—?"

"First you run off at Zack's, leaving Paul to hunt you down, leaving Abigail unprotected because, what, you wanted a fucking pastry? Then I find you down here with Derek whispering in the dark. What the fuck is going on?"

"No! It's not—"

"You know what, never mind. I don't want to fucking hear it, Savi. Start using your fucking head, and think about someone else for a change."

She flinches and her gaze drops to the floor. "Can I speak now?"

"No." His jaw twitches as he tries to hold back his

anger. "You should probably go upstairs now." He watches her turn on her heel and stomp up the stairs.

Mark comes around the corner. "Wow," he whispers.

"Shut up."

"That was harsh, Cole. She's one of the most selfless people I know."

"Fuck!" Cole rubs his face. Today's events have his emotions all over the place.

***

I head up through the dining room and out to the patio. I need some fresh air badly. As I pace the snowy deck, trying to catch my breath and soothe my hurt feelings, the last ten minutes loop over and over in my head until I'm breathing harder and start to see spots. My hands clutch at my stomach as I try to calm myself—shit, shit, shit!

"Savi?" Derek calls, slipping out the door. "You okay? What's happening?"

"I just need a minute." I hold my hand up. Between Cole's words and possibly seeing Jose today, I am about to toss my dinner. I squat down into a ball, covering my head with my arms as a vivid memory hits me.

"Eat, perra!" the fat man shouts at me, jamming a roll at my mouth. "Eat, or you'll get my fist again."

I shudder. Was that really him in town, or am I losing my mind?

Derek's footsteps echo as he comes closer. He doesn't speak but simply puts a hand on my shoulder, a friendly gesture to let me know I'm not alone.

I take the comfort and let my stomach settle. After a few moments, he goes back inside, and I stand, breathing through my nerves, and head for the door.

I find Keith talking to John.

"Keith," I say, "can I speak with you?"

"Sure thing," he replies, and we walk off to the side.

"Since Cole is too busy yelling at me to listen, will you let him know the reason I walked off today is because I thought I saw Jose Jorge?"

Keith's face falls. "Yeah, okay," he replies. As he shoots off toward his office, I make my way up to my room.

***

My eyes pop open at five. It takes me a moment to realize I'm not back in my prison. I shower and get dressed and head downstairs, where I light the fireplace and lie on the floor near Scoot. He curls into my stomach as I lie on my side, my head resting on my arm. He must have been up late, because I'm not getting hounded to scratch his tummy. Closing my eyes and listening to his soft purr relaxes me.

"What do we know so far?" I hear someone say as I drag myself from my sleepy state.

"Just that he was standing outside of Zack's." Cole is speaking from the kitchen.

"Okay, where is she now?"

"Her bedroom."

I awkwardly move to my feet, feeling a little sore from sleeping on the floor.

"Did she get a good look at his face?" I recognize Daniel's voice as I round the corner.

"Somewhat," I answer, making them both jump.

"Where were you?" Cole eyes my fur-covered shirt. I don't answer him; I'm still pissed. Instead, I reach for a mug and pour myself some coffee.

"You should have told someone," Daniel says, giving me a small smile.

I stop at the island and turn toward him, still ignoring Cole.

"I was going to," I mutter. "I need to change."

"When you're done, please find us in Cole's office."

"Sure." I nod and head upstairs.

***

As Daniel holds Cole's office door open for me and I take in the room, I note that Keith is sitting across from Cole and both look as tired as I feel.

"Come and sit down, Savannah." Daniel points to the open seat. Keith gives me a smile as I sink down next to him and everyone stares at me. I'm not sure if I'm supposed to talk.

Daniel is the first to speak. "So, tell us about yesterday."

I sigh, trying to hold back the emotion that is twisting inside me again.

"I went to use the restroom," I begin, "when I saw a newspaper on the bar and stopped to look at it. Then I glanced outside and saw a man looking my way. He looked so much like Jose Jorge, I was really shaken up. I couldn't believe it, so I started to follow him. I needed to be sure. Jose—" I stop myself.

"Jose what?" Cole asks, leaning forward in his seat.

Oh, God, I feel sick. "Jose was the one who used to whip me." I wipe a pesky tear away. I can almost hear the tension thicken. "If it was him, I needed to know. I couldn't lose sight of him. I wasn't thinking—"

"Yeah, you sure weren't," Cole hisses, and I turn to him.

"You don't need to remind me again, Cole! You got through to me last night," I toss at him, making him flinch.

"Then what?" he asks tersely.

"So, now you want the details?" I blurt. I can't help myself; he hurt me.

243

"Yes." His jaw flexes.

I look away. "I followed him to the cafe. I went inside, but he wasn't there. I lost him." I leave out the part where I harassed a poor employee and a customer.

"What was the man who you thought was Jose wearing?" Daniel asks.

"Blue jacket with a red hat and jeans."

"Why didn't you tell someone right away?" Cole asks.

"Because I felt stupid! I thought I saw a man I hate more than anything in the world, and I went off chasing him to...what? Confront him? He overpowered me for seven months, so I don't know what I was thinking. I was going to tell you, Cole. I just hadn't seen you all day other than when we were decorating, but you disappeared again." I gulp and continue my tirade. "When I went downstairs to grab some ice for Abigail, I ran into Derek. He saw I was upset and asked what was wrong, but I told him I wanted to talk to you about it first. That's when you came down and saw us. I wanted to tell you then, but you never gave me a chance. You just tore a strip off me and accused me of frigging around with Derek. I'd never do that to—" I stop myself, remembering we aren't alone.

I feel the need to apologize to Daniel. "I'm sorry for running off. I realize how dangerous it was, not just for me, but for Abigail too." I glance back to Cole. "It was selfish of me, and it won't happen again."

Cole shakes his head and stares down at his desk. Everyone is silent.

"Are we done here?" I ask.

"Yeah, Savi, you can go. Thanks," Daniel says, rising to his feet.

***

Cole leans back in his chair and watches her leave as his father takes her seat, rubbing his head.

"Am I missing something, or is Savi in a bad mood today?" John asks, coming into the room and making himself a cup of coffee. Realizing the tension in the room, he turns. "Ahh, did I just walk in on something?"

"Savannah thinks she saw Jose Jorge," Cole says.

"Do you think it was him?" John asks then glances around the room.

"I don't know, but she thought it was him enough to risk her safety. She followed him two blocks before Paul found her."

"Holy shit."

"Keith, I need you on this. Get the security tapes and find out what you can."

"Sure thing." Keith pulls out his phone.

Cole's e-mail alerts him to an incoming message, and he sees it's from Frank. "Shit!" He quickly opens the attachment and hits print.

"Trouble, son?" Daniel asks, seeing Cole's face.

Cole hands the paper to John, who takes one glance at it and lets his head drop. Keith snatches it out of his hand and reads it with Daniel over his shoulder.

"Shit, boys…this is huge." His father's words are haunting.

Chapter Seventeen

I need to burn off some serious tension. Prepping dinner just isn't cutting it. I head downstairs in my workout gear. My neon yellow-soled sneakers squeak as I hit the polished hallway leading to the gym. Abigail had done well buying the newest gym clothes. My black spandex capris have a matching yellow stripe up the side and pairs nicely with the black top that hits right about my belly button. I open the door and find Paul and Derek working with weights.

"Hey, Savi," Paul calls out between reps. "Come to sweat?"

"That's the plan." While I try to decide what I want to start on, my eyes catch a door on the back wall. Remembering that Keith mentioned there was a boxing ring here somewhere, I go over and peek in the window. An instructor is showing John some moves. I slip inside, curious to learn more.

I watch as John lays a series of punches into the man's glove.

He turns and does a kick in the air.

"Okay, good, but take five and try to get your mind clear. You seem off today." The instructor tosses him a towel.

John glances up and sees me. "Oh, hey, Savi."

"Hey. You don't sound happy to see me."

"Sorry. Interesting day. Has Cole found you?"

"Not since this morning. Why?"

"Just wondering," John says as he downs some water. "What are you doing here?"

"Just thought I'd check out the ring."

John's phone rings, and he steps out to answer it.

"I'm Mario," the instructor says, leaning on the ropes.

"Savannah."

His eyes narrow. "You've never boxed before?"

"Nope."

"You want to be able to say you have?"

"Sure." I smile and take his hand, and he pulls me up and holds the ropes apart for me.

"Put these on." He hands me a pair of red gloves. "First, you need to know the proper stance." He tells me to put my right heel and left toe on the centerline because I'm right handed. My weight should be even on both feet and my knees slightly bent. I'm told to keep my feet diagonal, more than a shoulder width apart, and raise my back heel slightly. Hands up, elbows down, eyes just above the tops of my gloves, keeping my chin tucked in.

"And breathe." He grins. "Okay, I won't go over the basic step drag right now because John will be back soon, but for now, let's see how you toss a punch. Have a little fun."

I smile at that. I shove my fist forward, meeting his glove.

"Good, but this time breathe out as you punch, and don't flex your fist and arm until you hit your target."

"Okay." I nod, trying to remember everything. I go back to my stance and try again, this time remembering to breathe.

"Nice!" He grins. "Again." After a few rounds of this, he starts doing it back, showing me a few blocking moves.

"What?" Derek says when he enters the room. "Mario got Savi in the ring?"

"Yup." I toss a punch at Mario's shoulder, but he blocks it at the last moment. "Better watch your back, Derek. I'm learning some mad skills over here." I laugh, trying to avoid a punch, but get hit in the arm instead.

"Really?" he jokes. "Thanks for the warning."

"Oh, no!" Paul whines loudly, moving Derek from the doorway. "Savi, really?"

"What?" I ask, seeing John coming back from his phone call.

Derek laughs on his way back out.

"You know what." Paul gives me a look.

"Savi, you're asking for trouble," John mutters, taking a seat as he pulls out a protein bar. He downs it in two bites.

"I'm a twenty-eight-year-old woman." I throw another punch harder than I thought I could. "If I want to learn how to box, then it's my right to do so." I send two quick punches at Mario. "So, if you all don't mind..."

John holds up his hands in surrender.

"Okay, so," Mario eyes everyone, "what am I not getting here?"

"Nothing," I mutter and throw another punch.

"You're sparring with the boss's girlfriend," Paul says.

"Paul!" I shout. "What the hell?"

"Seriously?" Mario's face drops.

"Seriously!" Cole says, standing inside the door. We all turn to face him.

Shit.

"Oh, sorry, Savi." Mario shakes his head and starts removing his gloves.

"Savi, out of the ring." Cole waves his hand at me.

"Why would I do that, exactly?" I ask, feeling my

temper rise yet again.

"Savi," he warns.

"It's not against house rules for clients to use the gym," I look around, "and I'm in the gym."

"Oh, boy," John mutters, grabbing his bag and moving toward Paul, who quickly follows him out. Mario steps out of the ring and runs to catch up. Great, now I'm alone with Cole.

Cole runs a frustrated hand through his hair as he walks toward me. "You're right, Savannah, clients are welcome to use the gym." He jumps up and ducks under the ropes. In two strides, he's in front of me. "But as my girlfriend, I don't want you sparring with anyone else in this house."

"Cole," I huff, removing my gloves and tossing them aside.

He hooks an arm around my waist and tugs me to him. I struggle with the fact that I long to be in his arms but am still hurt. "After last night—"

"I'm sorry, Savannah." He cuts me off. "I didn't give you a chance to explain yourself. I jumped to conclusions, and I'm sorry."

"Yeah, you did, but you also said some really hurtful things." I retreat from his hold. "Honestly, I think we need to step back and take a breather. My head—"

"I'm not letting you go, no matter how hard you push me away. We had a fight, but couples do that—"

"Couples also trust one another," I point out. "You obviously don't trust me."

He moves in front of me again. "I do. It's just that yesterday was pretty awful, along with you running off. Then I find you downstairs with Derek. I took my whole day out on you. It was wrong, and I'm sorry, baby." He leans forward to kiss my forehead. "Please say you forgive me."

I sigh, wrapping my arms around his waist as he rests

his cheek on my head. "I do." We stay like that for a few minutes, both needing one other. "Can I still play in the ring?"

"No."

"Why?"

"Because I don't like seeing someone hit you, even if it is just for fun."

"Fine." I mean, how can I argue with that response? It's sweet how much he cares for me.

"What are we doing about the Jose situation?"

"I'll be discussing that over dinner tonight."

Oh, no.

"Can you do it after dinner?"

He pulls back to look at me. "Why?"

"Because you'll dampen the mood. I need it to be light and fun tonight."

"Why?" He pulls me back to his chest.

"I'm giving Abby and Dr. Roberts a push toward each other."

I feel him shaking his head, and a slight chuckle follows. "Okay, but I have to talk about it afterward."

"Deal." He helps me climb out of the ring and through the gym. His eyes lower to my mid-section.

"I hate your top."

"No, you don't," I laugh.

***

June hands Abigail a large glass of white wine.

Abigail frowns. "You know I like red."

"Not tonight, Abby." June scowls. "You never drink red on the first date. Do you want your teeth turning dark?"

"No, you're right."

I hide my smile as I put the lid on the feta cheese salad and place it in the fridge, thinking about the list of things I need to do. Okay, salad is done, chickens are prepped, veggies are chopped and ready to go. Now for dessert.

"You look pretty, Abby, in your pink wrap-around dress," I say to help her with her nerves.

"It's June's," she replies, smoothing the fabric. It doesn't surprise me. June is the younger sister and has a taste for fashion. She looks at me. "Thanks, dear. You look lovely too."

I smile, looking down at my purple V-neck top and black leather leggings paired with heels.

"So, this weekend is the light festival in town. Are we all planning on going?" Mark asks as he comes into the room. He stops dead in his tracks when he sees Abigail's outfit. "What are you wearing?" He turns to me. "What's going on? Why are you three so dressed up?"

"Calm down, Mark," June says. "Dr. Roberts is coming for dinner."

"Oh, okay." He heads to the fridge but stops again. "Wait." He looks at Abigail. "But why are you so dressed up?"

"Oh, so close." June laughs into her glass.

"Are you...? Is this...?" He shakes his head. "Are you dating the doc?"

"No," she shoots back, "we're just talking." Poor Abigail can't hide her smile.

"Am I the only one who doesn't know?" He turns to me. "Does Cole know? Of course, he does." He tosses his hands up. "I don't know how I feel about this. I mean, I haven't had time to think this through." He sinks onto the stool, rubbing his head. "I mean, the doc's a good man, but is he good enough?" He's now talking to himself, and June rolls her eyes. The doorbell rings, and Mark quickly stands and fixes his shirt. "I'll get it."

"Be nice," Abigail warns while June and I are

holding onto the counter, laughing.

"That was quite possibly one of the funniest moments I've had yet," I say, dropping my hands to my knees, trying to catch my breath.

"He's so protective," June says as she wipes the tears away. "It's so sweet."

"It is." Abigail nods, downing her drink. "Okay." She stands and runs her hands over the skirt of her dress. "Come on, ladies."

"I need to finish up, so you go on. I'll be there shortly," I say, filling June's glass before they head off toward the living room.

I set the timer and pop the potatoes in. When I stand back up, I feel a pair of hands wrap around my waist. "Hi."

"Hi," Cole says, resting his chin on my shoulder. "You look nice, and you smell like dessert." I can tell he is stressed; he sounds tired.

"Are you okay?" I fold my arms over his, holding him closer to me.

"Not really," he admits, "but we'll get to all that later." He kisses my shoulder. "I needed this." He sighs and nuzzles my neck.

"Happy to help." I lean back and give him a peck on the lips. "Doc's here, and Mark is freaking out." I laugh. "It was really funny when he found out why he's here."

"Ha, I bet."

Cole grimaces when Derek's voice booms through the house.

"What happened between you guys?"

He groans. "About five years ago, he was trying to be a hero and didn't have my back when we were clearing a house. I nearly got my throat slashed by a Cartel member who had a knife tied to the end of his rifle."

I gasp and cover my mouth.

"It wasn't even what actually happened, it was how

he was afterward—like we look out for ourselves instead of as a unit. That's why he'll never be in Blackstone. I don't trust him."

"I understand."

Derek's voice is getting closer, so I start to move, but Cole doesn't let me go.

"Cole?"

"I'm not ready yet."

I smile. "How about you hold me tonight?"

I feel his chest rise and fall heavily, then he kisses my shoulder again and steps back.

"Hey ya, Savi," Derek says, entering the kitchen. "What's for dinner?"

I turn to the fridge and pull out the chicken breasts. "Chicken stuffed with feta and roasted red peppers."

"Mmm, sounds good." He leans over to take a look.

"I should get these on the barbecue." I reach for the dish, but Cole takes it and says he'll do it.

"He's in quite the mood," Derek comments as he takes a seat at the island.

"Well, I can't imagine you'd be happy having to deal with what he does in the course of a day." I go to pour myself some wine, but his hand grabs the bottle before mine does.

"Allow me." He smiles. "So, tell me something, Savi. Were you dating anyone before…" He pauses.

"No," I answer truthfully. I know where this is going.

He shifts a little closer. "Well, I was thinking you should let me take you out. You know, like a date."

And there it is…

"Oh, buddy, you're so blind." Keith laughs, stepping into the kitchen. Clearly, he heard my awkward moment.

Cole walks back in from outside and sets the dish on the counter. He looks at me, then Keith. I'm sure he's wondering why the air in the room is so charged.

"So, what do you say? Friday, six o'clock?" Derek

pushes on, not caring about our audience or the fact that it's against house rules. Keith leans against the fridge and grins back and forth between me and Cole, loving every minute of the show.

"What's going on?" Mark whispers as he joins Keith.

"Savi just got asked out on a date."

I glare at both of them.

"Oh!" Mark's face suddenly brightens. "Oh. Okay, continue." He waves his hand like this is a live performance.

"There you are, Savi," June says, coming to my side. "Come say hello to Dr. Roberts. You did, after all, invite him."

"Sure," I say, trying to smile. "Excuse me." I want to throw my arms around June and thank her for getting me out of there when she did. She winks at me, and I guess she must have overheard too. I mouth 'thank you' and head for the doctor.

Cole keeps his word over dinner and doesn't bring up work. He helps keep the topic light, even though I catch him and Mark exchanging looks. Dr. Roberts and Abigail are hitting it off nicely. June seems thrilled to see her older sister gushing over a man. Not that Abigail gushes, but she certainly is glowing.

"I can't believe you did all this," Dr. Roberts says, waving his hand around the room. "It's stunning. You certainly have an eye for decorating."

"Thank you." I smile. "Christmas is my favorite time of the year."

"I love that you love Christmas and it's your favorite time of the year." Keith laughs and picks up a cookie. "So good."

"Is that cheesecake?" Mark asks, bloody well knowing it is. He leans to the side and takes it off the table behind him.

"I swear, you sit there just so you can be close to the

desserts," I say.

"I do." Mark laughs and plops a huge piece of cheesecake on his plate.

The conversation picks up again, and we soon retire into the living room for drinks. Cole is speaking with Dr. Roberts and it looks serious, so I don't go over.

"You never answered my question," Derek says from behind me.

Shit. I turn and attempt to smile. "I'm actually seeing someone, but I'm flattered you asked me."

"Sure." He slips his hands in his pockets. "I'm sorry. I wouldn't have asked if I knew."

"It's okay."

"Can I have everyone's attention? I have some information to share with all of you," Cole calls out over the chatter. "Please gather around. I would like to get this over with."

As we move toward Cole, Keith tugs on my arm so I sit next to him and June.

"Are we late?" Daniel asks, coming into the living room with Sue.

"No, you're right on time." Cole nods as they take a seat.

I notice he doesn't give them his normal warm greeting. Sue seems a little off, but I pretend not to notice as we all gather, waiting for Cole to start.

"All right," he says, as he put his hands on his hips. "At approximately seventeen hundred yesterday, Frank, along with Agent Bridges, left to transport York to Washington. Thirty minutes into the flight, York got hold of Agent Bridges's gun, killing Bridges, and during the altercation, a stray bullet hit the pilot, wounding him." He pauses as everyone starts whispering, then continues. "In the ensuing struggle, Frank shot York and killed him. I won't share all the details, but the pilot was able to fly on to Washington. He's okay, just going to have to use one wing for a while." He seems to realize he almost made a joke and looks stricken.

"Poor Agent Bridges. Did he have a family?" Abigail asks quietly.

"A wife, but no children. She has been contacted," Cole chokes out.

"Why?" I ask, unable to make sense of it all.

"York admitted to Frank that he had been selling certain information to the Cartel." He looks directly down at me. "And to poisoning Savannah."

I shake my head in disbelief.

"He swore he didn't give up the location of the house, but he knew it was only a matter of time before they forced his hand, and he wanted out. Seems he got in over his head, thought he could be selective as to what he would tell them. He was wrong."

"Frank is all right?" Mike asks from behind me.

"Yes." Cole looks around the assembled group. "I've known York for ten years. I truly believe he didn't give up the location of Shadows. He got greedy, but even his moral compass wouldn't allow him to go that far."

A few people start to get up, but Cole clears his throat. "One more thing." He looks at me. "This morning, Blackstone got word that we are on standby."

My heartrate drops. I know this means when they get word, they will have to leave almost immediately.

"Frank has confirmation of The American's location. We have the green light to take him out, dead or alive."

Holy shit.

"Did Frank give you any indication of when you might leave?" his mother asks, holding onto his father's arm.

Cole takes a drink. "It could be any time. We're waiting to get a visual before we leave." His eyes flicker over to mine again, but I break our connection. I feel too raw.

"For now, we keep on doing what we're doing. I don't believe the house is in any immediate danger. That's all for now. I'll keep you updated as we know more."

It takes everyone a few moments to move. I, on the other hand, fly off the couch, needing some space. I make it to the kitchen before I hear him.

"Hey, hey, hey," Cole reaches for my arm, "don't run."

"I'm not." I close my eyes, hating that I just lied. "Okay, yeah, I was."

He moves closer and slides his hand down my arm to lace our fingers together. He brings our hands up to his mouth, giving mine a kiss.

"Everything is going to work out."

"How do you know that?"

"Because fate would not have brought you to me only to take you away." He smiles and kisses my lips. "And now that I have someone to come back to, I'll have to be extra careful." He kisses me again.

I try to clear my head, remembering he could be leaving at any point. "Can you promise me something?"

His jaw twitches, but he nods.

"Promise me that whenever you get the call, no matter where you are or what you're doing, you'll see me before you leave." A tear slips down my cheek; he catches it with his finger.

He runs his hand along the back of my neck and kisses me with such passion I forget to breathe. He backs away. "Oh, God, baby, I promise."

I nod as he reaches for a tissue for me. I dry my cheeks and take a deep breath.

"There you are," Derek says. "I wanted to see how you're doing."

"I'm fine." *Please go away.*

"You know what fine stands for, right?" he says with

a grin.

"Freaked out, insecure, neurotic, and emotional," I reply. "I'm an Edward Norton fan."

Derek throws his head back and laughs. "I heard you were funny, but you're quick too. I like you."

Cole, who is leaning against the island across from me, rubs his face with both hands. I know Derek is getting on his nerves with the flirting.

"So, who are you dating, anyway?" he asks boldly.

"Me," Cole says, lowering his hands. My jaw drops, but I quickly recover.

"You?" Derek's eyes widen. "You're dating Savannah?"

"Yes."

"Isn't there some house policy?"

Cole glares at him. "My house, my rules, remember?"

"How convenient for you." He snickers. "Nice that the boss is sticking his hand in the honey pot."

"Weren't you just trying to do the same, Derek?" I ask.

"Remember your rank, Agent Rent." Cole stands and points at him. "We might live together under one roof, but you will still treat me as your superior."

Derek shakes his head but clenches his jaw. "Yes, sir," he says smartly as he turns and leaves the room.

"Cole," I step close to him and grab his shirt, "take me to bed?"

He smiles down at me. "Sure, baby."

Cole still seems annoyed when we get to his room.

I sit in the chair in front of his window and watch the snow fall, hit the window, and slowly melt, trickling down the glass in a hundred different paths.

Crash into Me by Dave Matthews Band flows through the room as the light dims. Cole moves in front of me, and my gaze drags lazily up his body. His dress shirt is open, tie removed, sleeves rolled up, hands tucked in his pockets. I feel my lips turn upward; this man is pure perfection.

He squats in front of me and grips the back of my calf, sliding his hand downward until he hits my ankle, where he gently removes my shoe. He repeats this for the other one.

I watch his stomach muscles flex as he moves about.

His dark eyes lock with mine and blaze as he hooks his arms under my legs and behind my back.

I wrap my arms around his neck as I am lifted into the air.

As he looks down at me with hooded eyes, his expression unreadable, he hesitates.

"Cole?"

His grip tightens right before he lays me gently on his bed. Peeling his shirt off and tossing it on the floor, he climbs over me. His lips find mine, and he slowly and softly swipes his tongue along the inside of my mouth.

"Let me love you the way you deserve." He brushes my hair back from my face and tilts his head. "You are the most beautiful woman." He kisses along my jaw, up to my ear, then stops as a long moan escapes him. "It's like someone got inside my head, found my deepest desire, and created you."

"Cole," I whisper, feeling pure emotion take over, "no one has ever made me—"

His lips capture mine before I can finish. His hand travels down my side to unbuckle my pants. He pushes them down and chucks them over his shoulder.

I lean up and remove my sweater, desperate for his mouth back on me.

He whips his pants off in a flash, kissing my stomach. His hands travel up to my breasts, gently massaging them through my lace bra.

"You're so soft," he breathes between kisses, "so

perfect." His hot fingers release the clasp to expose my breasts to his hungry lips.

I drop my head back into the pillow as a shot of lust bursts through me.

Spreading my legs and settling in between them, he lines up and nudges forward. He flattens his chest to mine, his hand cupping my face, and stares down at me with such adoration. "It scares me how much I need you, Savannah."

I hold my breath as his words hit me.

"I physically hurt when you're not around to touch."

I run my fingers along his jaw as he leans into me, closing his eyes.

"I'm right here, yours to touch whenever you want," I reassure him.

He lets out a sweet breath as he slides his thick length into me, deliciously, painfully slowly. His eyes lock with mine, holding me captive until he's fully in.

I tune in to the sad voice of Sam Smith singing *Not in That Way*. My eyes close as my emotions play tug of war. My heart is incredibly invested in this man, tangled in a web of love that almost makes it difficult to breathe.

He is pouring out his feelings, opening his heart, and exposing his soul to me. All that is running through my mind is he'll be leaving soon.

"Don't, baby," he murmurs over my cheek as he moves at a gentle pace. "Don't go there now. I'll come home."

I press my lips together, letting a few tears leak out.

He kisses them away. "Stay with me, my sweet Savannah."

My eyes flutter open.

"Fall with me. I promise I won't let you go."

All I can do is nod as he kisses me breathlessly.

The slow pace is making my head spin. A ball of fire grows quickly in my stomach. My legs are restless, so I wrap them around his waist, feeling his back muscles twitch, and my hands grip the sheets as he whispers my name.

"Cole!" I beg, knowing I'm so close.

He starts kissing along my collarbone.

The mix between his hard breaths and his hot lips tips me over the edge. I freefall into fireworks, losing my ability to think. I can only feel. I'm tumbling, spinning, twisting inside. I'm vaguely aware that I'm screaming something incoherent. Cole's shaking and gripping my legs, driving deeper. It's all too much, but I don't want it to stop. Sweat bursts out along my skin, my hands hanging on for dear life as we reach the peak together, his body convulsing along with mine. I feel myself floating back to earth, like a feather taking its sweet time to land.

Sinking back into the mattress, I feel like I'll never move again. Cole wipes the hair out of my face as he smiles down at me. At the same time, he slides out, and I flinch at the loss of him.

He gets a warm facecloth to clean me, then after chucking the cloth in the general direction of the bathroom, he crawls back in, making the bed dip. He tugs my limp body into his chest and runs his fingers up and down my spine.

I close my eyes and give in to the utopia rushing through my veins. Being in Cole's arms has never felt more right. He owns every part of me. Just as I'm walking the thin line to blissful sleep, I feel Cole's chest vibrate against my cheek.

"You can always fall, Savannah, because I will be the one catching you."

Chapter Eighteen

"Savannah!" I feel my shoulder being shaken roughly. "Savannah, wake up!" Cole whispers urgently.

"Okay, I'm awake. What's wrong?"

Cole tosses clothes at me.

"Get dressed," he says, pulling on his pants. "Quickly, we don't have time!"

My mind scrambles as I tug at my clothes and slip on my boots.

"Here!" He hands me my jacket. "Follow me." He grabs my hand and opens the bedroom door, checking to see if it's clear. "Come on!" He hurries down the hall. Why aren't we using the back stairway?

"Where are we going?"

He doesn't answer, stopping as he unlocks Abigail's room. Abigail, June, and Sue are huddled on her bed, looking terrified.

"Stay here, no matter what. Don't open the door. I'm the only one with a key." Cole holds my shoulders as he bends down to eye level. "You'll be safe. Wait for me." He kisses me then instructs June to lock the door behind him.

"No, Cole, wait!"

"Savannah, stay!" he orders.

I look toward the women, feeling completely confused since I was woken out of a dead sleep. My mind is madly trying to come to terms with what is going on.

"Come here." Sue pats the mattress beside her. "Tell me, Savannah, when you guys were coming down the hallway, did you hear anything, see anything?"

"No." I shake my head. "I don't think so."

"Oh, God, this is bad," June cries. "I always knew this day would come, but now…" She reaches for her sister's hand and starts to pray.

"I don't understand. What's going on?" I ask.

"The Cartels," Abigail says in a strangled voice. "Mark said there are at least twelve of them."

"Oh, my God," I say, starting to shake, "this is all my fault."

"No, dear," is all June says.

There's a pounding on the door, and we all scream at once. Someone yells something in Spanish, then the door blasts open. Wood chips fly all around us, and we're momentarily stunned before Abigail starts screaming at the top of her lungs.

I see a black AK-47 rise out of the dust and flash three bright bursts of light followed by a thud.

June flies to her sister's side as two more flashes appear, and then June flops to the floor on top of Abigail. I feel Sue fling herself on top of me, pushing me back on the bed as her body gives four violent shakes, then goes limp. Her blood drains all around me, covering my face and hair as I struggle to get free. When she falls to the side, I see The American standing in the doorway, wiping his hands with a white handkerchief.

"Time to go," he says, like nothing has happened. Like he hasn't just killed three people I love! I ignore him and rush to Sue, holding her cooling body in my arms as I try to bring her back, but she's so pale.

"Please," I cry, choking on a sob, "wake up!" There is so much blood. The American grips my arm and pulls me toward the door.

"I said time to go!"

"No!" I scream. "Please!"

"Savannah! Savannah!"

My eyes open as I leap out of bed, still screaming for my friends. I run for the door when a strong pair of arms wrap around me. "How could you kill them?" I sob. "They're my family."

"Savannah, stop, it's okay. You were dreaming." Cole's chest vibrates against me. "It's okay, it's okay."

"Cole?" I whisper.

"Yes, baby, it's me."

"Cole." I turn in his arms, sobbing into his chest and collapsing as he lowers me to the floor with him. I hold on to him for dear life until the nightmare wears off and I'm left to deal with its hangover. After a while, I finally calm. As I rest my head on his leg, his fingertips run along my arm, back and forth.

"You want to talk about it?" he asks softly.

I shake my head. Even the question brings on more tears.

"Okay, when you're ready, then."

After some more time goes by, I decide to ask a question that's been bothering me. "If the house was to be attacked, is there a safe room?"

"Yes, there is," he replies gently.

I let out a long breath.

"Under the entertainment room, there's another level. It's where we kept York. There are four jail cells, and beyond that is the safe room. More like a safe floor. It's huge—the size of the kitchen, living room, and dining room combined. It's untouchable from the outside. If we ever were to get attacked, you would use the back hallway and follow whoever is taking you down to that room, where you will stay until it's safe."

I shift to look up at him. "Would you come with us?"

He plays with a piece of my hair between his fingers. "The captain doesn't jump on the lifeboat."

A few more tears slip down into my hair. "But what if he has a reason to?" I counter, grasping for straws.

"Baby, I know it's scary, but I'll protect you."

"I'm not worried about you protecting me, Cole. I worry about something happening to you." I move to sit up, my head clogged from crying so much. I wrap my arms around my drawn-up legs and rest my chin on my knees.

"This is my job, Savi, and I'm good at it. If it means anything, I'm not scared. It's what I do." His mouth twists as he looks at me. "What are you thinking?"

I shrug, feeling tired, but now I'm nervous about falling asleep. "Sometimes I feel like this is one big dream. I mean, this kind of thing doesn't happen every day. I feel like I'm stuck, helpless, and taking up the Army's time and resources. I know this isn't my fault, but it doesn't make me feel less of a burden to you all." I let out a long sigh. "I just want answers. I want to know who's behind this whole thing. I want my life back."

"I know you do." Cole pulls me to my feet and lays me back in bed. He wraps his arm around me, tucking me against his side. "You're not a burden, Savi. You're one of the best things that's ever happened to this house. Not just for me, but for everyone." He moves my hair out of his way and kisses the side of my forehead. "Try to get some sleep. You're not alone. I'm here."

I close my eyes, counting his heartbeats until I finally pass out.

***

Five Days Later...

We walk hand in hand down the decorated street,

strings of colored lights hanging in rows along both sides. Christmas trees stand outside every shop, beautifully trimmed with every imaginable ornament and decoration. Carolers dressed in historical costumes sing *Carol of the Bells* as they stand next to a hot chocolate booth. A horse-drawn carriage is pulling a family of four down the street, with sleigh bells ringing as they pass. Sue was not kidding. This town certainly is in love with Christmas. This is truly amazing. It looks like a scene right out of a Thomas Kinkade painting. I glance up at Cole, who's looking very classy in his black wool button up coat and gray scarf. I search his face, trying to see if he's here with us or thinking about what's ahead.

The tension in the house has calmed down some since Cole held a house meeting the other night after dinner.

Keith could not confirm if it was Jose Jorge or not the day I thought I saw him in town.

But like Cole said, there's nothing we can do but be prepared. He was wary about this outing, but Daniel convinced him that we have to keep on living as long as we take the proper precautions.

I had on a wig and glasses earlier, about to head out the door, when Cole stopped me.

"How do you feel?"

"Honestly, a bit funny." I held up a piece of the wig. "I never pictured myself as a blonde."

He smiled and pulled it off.

"I think if we're careful enough, you won't need this." He chuckled adorably. "Here." He tugged on a light pink knit hat. "That's better." He fingered one of my curls. "I like the sexy-librarian glasses though," he jokes.

I batted his arm but kept the thick rimmed glasses on. They really do change my appearance.

Spotting Mark and Melanie walking together up

ahead makes me smile when I notice she has linked arms with him, her fire red hair peeking out of her green hat. They look happy; it's refreshing to see everyone enjoying themselves. We really needed this.

I stop at a jewelry shop window—who could resist? I press my hands on the frame to get a better view. "Oh, it's beautiful," I whisper, the glass fogging briefly from my breath.

Cole leans over my shoulder to see what has caught my attention. It's a small crystal teardrop with a real snowflake preserved inside, hanging in the middle of a delicate chain. The way the crystal is set helps magnify the tiny flake.

"Really does make it one of a kind." He smiles as he says it.

I have to laugh, thinking how true that is. We continue walking to meet up with the group since we've fallen a bit behind.

Cole doesn't seem to be in a hurry. He suddenly flinches, then mutters something. He stops and leans down close to my ear. "Please go with what I say next." He shakes his head, then I hear what's making him uneasy.

"Well, well, Cole Logan," says a long-legged blonde with unbelievably white teeth.

"Hello, Christina," he replies through clenched teeth.

Oh, the bat-shit crazy ex!

She glances at me, then down at our joined hands.

"Who's this?" she asks him, not acknowledging me.

"This is my fiancée." He smiles at me, and I play my part well by stepping up on my tippy-toes and giving him a rather long kiss.

"You're engaged?" She looks like a trout with her mouth hanging open. "Well, that's a pity."

I roll my eyes.

"Yes, we are, and we have to meet up with the

family, so…ah, take care, Christina." He nods and steps around her.

"Happy holidays, Serena," I say sweetly.

"It's Christina," she huffs behind me.

We round a corner before Cole says anything. "Well…"

"She seems nice."

He laughs and pulls me into him, giving me a hug.

"So, your fiancée, huh?"

"It's not far from the truth, baby," he mutters into my hair, but before I can get him to clarify exactly what he means by that, he's tugging my hand in the direction of Zack's restaurant.

Dinner is just being placed in front of us when Cole's cell phone rings.

Mark looks worried as Cole excuses himself from the table and steps outside.

"Could be anything," Keith whispers in my ear.

Watching Cole through the window gives up nothing, as his back is turned to me, so I can't read his face. Twenty long minutes go by, and everyone at the table attempts to draw my attention away from Cole.

Finally, Sue comes and sits in Cole's chair and gets me to focus on her.

"Hey," she says, gently running her hand over my forehead. "Are you feeling all right? You look a little pale."

I shake my head and think about this morning. Actually, over the last few days I have been feeling a little strange, but it's to be expected with all that's been going on.

"I'm stressed, and my stomach's been a bit off."

Her eyes narrow, then she nods. "Have you been getting much sleep?"

"Surprisingly, yes," I reply. Minus the horrific nightmare at the beginning of the week, I have been getting lots of sleep. "I even took a few naps."

"Well, that's good." She smiles.

I think I've convinced her I'm all right, but it makes me wonder how bad I must look. I peer out the window, but Cole is gone. Looking around, I see he's not in the room. Just as I'm about to get up and search for him, he returns, putting an icy hand on my shoulder.

Mark looks at him, and I catch some kind of emotion run across his face, but nothing happens.

Sue gives him back his chair and heads over to her seat. She whispers something to Daniel, and his eyes flicker over to me.

Really, guys, I'm all right.

"Cole?" I say, turning my attention to him.

"Savi, you should eat. Your food is getting cold." He is studying my untouched plate.

Seriously? You want me to eat?

"Was that Frank?" Mark looks past me to Cole.

"Yes."

"Are we being shipped out?"

Cole glances around the table then shakes his head.

What does that mean?

"So, Mark, what are your plans for Christmas?" Melanie asks, breaking the tension.

Mark takes a long, deep breath before replying. "Umm, I'm leaving tonight, actually, for my cousin's cabin."

I stare at him, unmoving.

"Oh, yeah? When will you be back?" she asks.

"Not sure yet," he says with a smile plastered on his face, "but when I get back, we'll have to go on that ski trip we talked about." He fidgets uncomfortably.

I shove my plate away while Mark's words hit me like a blow to the head. "Excuse me." I rise from my seat.

Cole stands and signals his mother.

"Savi," he says, sounding worried.

"I just need the restroom," I say, not meeting his eyes.

Sue comes along, acting like she has to go too.

My head is spinning. I begin to feel a little dizzy, and Sue helps me to the leather couch in the powder area of the restroom.

"Here." She holds a cool towel to my face as she sits next to me.

"They got the call," I whisper. "They ship out tonight."

Sue takes my hand and puts her fingers over the inside of my wrist.

This is odd. "I'm all right. I just feel a little dizzy."

"Mmhmm," she hums, continuing to check my pulse.

"How do you deal with it?" I am desperate for some help.

She sighs and lets my arm go.

"It took a while to get used to it," she says quietly. "I just found things to keep me busy until he came home. Luckily for you, you have me, Abigail, and June, until she goes home, and the rest of the house."

"I'm scared," I admit.

"I know." She gives me a comforting hug. "So am I."

***

Cole is doing everything in his power to concentrate on the meal and the guests, but his conversation with Frank left him very uneasy. He nods to his father to meet him at the bar. They both excuse themselves and make their way over.

"Two brandies," Daniel orders as Cole runs his hand through his hair. "All right, son, what did Frank say?"

"Blackstone is shipping out tonight at twenty-three hundred."

His father hands him his drink. "Target destination?"

"Mexico City."

"That far south?"

"Yeah."

"Hmm," Daniel says, rubbing his neck. "Are you thinking—?"

"Yeah, I am."

"Should I make the call to Agent Joel?"

"Definitely."

"Cole," his father says, placing a hand on his shoulder, "we'll protect her. I'll bring in my guys and make sure it's Fort Knox up here. You need to focus on this trip and do whatever it takes to get your head in the game."

Cole looks up and sees Savannah is back at the table.

"I hear ya, Dad."

***

I watch as Mark says goodbye to Melanie. I feel torn, wondering which side I would like to be on. Maybe there's something to being kept in the dark about their work. But at the same time, not knowing would kill me. Oh, Christ, I'm my own worst enemy.

I feel Cole come up behind me, and he slips his arm around my waist and ushers me out into the cold air. Sue and Daniel decided to spend the night, and say goodbye to the guys before they leave.

When Cole broke the news to Paul and John, I was surprised by their reactions. They acted as if they were just given an updated weather report. I, on the other hand, am feeling tired—very tired. I lean into Cole, wrapping my arm around his waist.

"You cold?"

I shake my head. The Christmas thrill I had earlier is long gone now. I wish the holiday would pass so I don't have to think about the fact that our first Christmas together will now be spent apart.

We all walk quietly back to the cars. Cole's body language has changed. He seems like he's lost in thought. I want to ask him what's on his mind, but that seems silly considering they're shipping out in four hours.

The ride home is painfully quiet. Cole holds me close, stroking his thumb over my hand.

I can tell he's scanning the horizon. I wonder if he ever gets tired of being alert all the time.

Cole grabs my hand after I hop out of the truck. "Take a walk with me?"

"Sure."

He holds my hand and leads me to a path in the woods. We walk in silence, with only the sound of the snow crunching under our boots. Arriving at a clearing on the top of a hill, we look down at the lake. The moon is bright, and it casts a shimmering trail through the ripples in the water.

"Wow," I murmur, not wanting to break the mood. "It's so pretty."

"Savannah?" Cole says quietly.

I turn and find him staring at me.

"I want you to be extra careful when I'm gone. No trips to town, no running off into the woods. Please, keep someone with you at all times. Promise me?"

I nod; I understand how serious this is.

He steps toward me. "I need to be able to focus while I'm away. I need to keep a clear head."

"I promise, Cole. I do understand. Don't worry, I won't run off, I—"

"I'm in love with you, Savannah." *Oh.* "I couldn't go away this time without telling you. This is a first for me. I've never felt or said those words to any woman before."

My eyes brim with tears. "Cole." I clear my throat. "I hate that the first time I'm saying this to you, you're leaving me, but…I love you too."

He closes his eyes and breathes out a shaky sigh.

I cup his face with my hands. "It's a first for me too." I kiss him softly. "Promise me you'll come back to me."

He tightens his arms around me. "I promise, baby."

***

I wake with a start, my eyes feeling puffy. Reaching behind me, I remember he had indeed left me last night. It seems like only moments ago we were tangled in the sheets together, showing one another how much love we had to give. Glancing at the clock, I see it's nine thirty already. I jump out of bed and head to the shower. I can't believe I slept so long.

"Hi, Savi." Abigail hands me a cup of coffee as I take a seat at the island. She slides me a red box with a bow. "Cole left this." She smiles, waiting for me to open it.

I pull on the bow and slowly open the lid. My hand flies to my mouth as my eyes fill and overflow with tears.

"Well?"

I turn it around to show her the crystal teardrop with the fortified snowflake inside.

"Oh, Savannah it's beautiful," she exclaims, clutching her hands together over her chest in a moment of joy.

"I saw it last night in a shop while we were walking to Zack's. Cole must have slipped away after his phone call." I pull out a note stuck on the bottom as she helps me clasp it around my neck.

To remember the day we spoke

those special words,
Yours – C

I hold it to my chest as a lump builds in my throat. "Abby?" I sniff, then feel a huge wave of nausea. My head spins so hard I almost fall off the stool. "Whoo."

"Savannah?" I see Abigail call out, but I barely hear her. Sweat breaks out across my neck, and my stomach turns. Oh, my God, have I been poisoned again?

She shoves a bucket in my face just in time for me to loudly empty my stomach.

"Oh, my," Sue says from somewhere behind me. "Let's get her to bed."

Chapter Nineteen

I wake a few hours later.

Sue is sitting with someone at the table by the balcony door.

"Hi?" I say groggily.

"Savannah, this is Dr. Brown. She's an OB/GYN."

I move to sit up in the bed.

"Okay." I shake my head. "Why is—?" Then it hits me—no appetite, nauseated, emotional, tired— "Am I pregnant?"

Dr. Brown steps toward me. "I believe you are, Ms. Miller."

What? "But I'm on birth control!"

"No birth control is one hundred percent effective. Sometimes these things just happen. I'm assuming you know who the father is."

Really? I blush when I look at Sue. Oh, God, I know she wants grandbabies, but it's too soon! What if she thinks I'm trying to trap her son? Hell, we only *just* announced that we loved each other last night.

"Savannah." Sue smiles at me.

"Yes, I do. It's Cole." I lean my head back, wondering what the hell Cole is going to think.

"Well, that's good, then." Dr. Brown smiles down at me. "Do you remember when your last menstrual cycle was?"

I think back but am drawing a blank. "I honestly don't remember."

"All right, I will need you to come by my office in a few days. I don't have the equipment here, but I want to perform an ultrasound examination. We want to make sure the baby is off to a good start." She opens her bag. "For now, start taking these." She hands me a bottle of prenatal vitamins. "Have Sue contact me when you can make it in. Please get lots of rest and be sure to eat." She rises to leave.

"Thank you, Dr. Brown," Sue says, walking her to the door. "I'll be in touch."

Sue turns to me with the biggest smile on her face that I've ever seen. "Oh, Savannah!" She tosses her hands in the air. "I've never been happier!"

I feel like asking for a time out so I can process what the hell I've just been told.

She crawls on the bed next to me. "Are you all right?"

Not really.

"I don't know," I answer honestly, suddenly remembering her behavior at the restaurant. "You knew, didn't you?"

She smiles. "I had a feeling, but I was waiting to see if I was right. This morning confirmed it. That's why I called Dr. Brown. She's the best in town, and I've known her for years."

I nod, trying to keep my head on straight.

"He told me he loved me last night," I say, fingering my necklace. "I love him, Sue, I really do." She sniffs then reaches for my hand. "What do you think Cole will say?" I ask nervously.

She laughs, wiping her cheeks, "He's going to be so happy, Savannah!"

"You think?"

"I know."

"It's terrible timing. It wasn't planned."

"That may be, but everything will be fine."

"Sue," I look up at her, "can we please keep this between us?"

"Daniel knows."

"That's fine, but just the three of us, okay? I don't want Cole to be the last to know."

"Of course. No one but us three."

I let out a long sigh and try not to panic about what's growing in my stomach. Then I think of Cole, and the idea of a part of each of us in one little body makes me smile. I find myself rubbing my belly as I fall back to sleep.

***

Cole holds the satellite phone to his ear while he separates himself from everyone. They're all exhausted from the day. They had a run-in with a group of Cartels, and their camp was discovered. They had to grab what they could and haul ass to a new location. He glances at his watch—it is just past midnight.

"You guys good?" Keith asks.

"Yeah, just barely," he says as he briefs Keith on the day's events and current situation.

"All right, well, everything is quiet on our end."

"Good," Cole says, hesitating.

"Savi's got the flu," Keith says.

Cole hears the smile in his voice. "So, if you start feeling sick—good luck, because she's been in bed all day."

Poor Savannah. He had planned to call earlier and hoped she was close so he could speak to her. The fact that it was against his own house rules to use check-in time for anything personal was totally beside the point. Since Savannah came into his life, all his rules went out the window.

"You want me to wake her?"

Keith's question throws him; was he thinking out loud? "No, it's late. We're watching the house, early tomorrow, or rather today, so this is my check-in for…" he looks at his watch again, "last night and this morning."

"All right. Stay safe."

"Will do. Raven out."

***

"I see seven men on the east side," Mark whispers, "five on the west."

"Copy that," Cole replies, moving his binoculars to confirm. "Seven on the east and five on the west." He shifts and reaches for his radio when it crackles to life.

"Fox One to Raven One," Paul says over the radio.

"Go ahead Fox One."

"We have a green Hummer heading toward the house, approaching from the northeast."

Cole spots the truck and follows it. "Copy that, Fox One, I have a visual. I want to know who's in that vehicle."

"Ten-four."

The Hummer passes through the gate without any problem and stops in front of the mansion. Two armed guards open the door and pull out a man in a navy blue business suit and a cream-colored cloth bag over his head.

"Hum," Cole says, "interesting that his head is covered but his hands aren't tied."

"Yup." Mark nods.

"Seems our mystery guest might be doing business with The American."

"Guess they don't trust him to know the location."

Mark squints. "You think it could be the mayor?"

"No, this guy is taller and slimmer."

They watch as the suit and one of the armed guards disappear inside and the Hummer takes off back the way it came.

"Guess he'll be staying a while." Mark rolls onto his back and stretches out his neck, then checks his watch and pulls out a protein bar. Cole inches backward and leans against a rock out of view. He spits his gum out and opens his water.

Mark pulls at his vest. "Fuck, I miss the snow."

"Me too," Cole says, thinking of Savannah.

"I know that look."

"Yup, you have it too," he shoots back, making Mark grin. "All right." Cole puts the cap on his water then pats his side, looking for…

"Here." Mark tosses him a piece of gum. Ever since they joined the Army together, they've been chewing gum. When they are out on duty, it helps them relax. Cole pops it in his mouth while he studies the map.

"Ahhh, yuck, what the fuck is this?" Cole grimaces.

"Hubba Bubba."

"What are you, a twelve-year-old girl?"

"It makes for a better chew." Mark shrugs.

"It's disgusting."

"No, what's disgusting is your old man cinnamon gum."

"I can literally feel my teeth sticking together. What shit flavor is this?"

"Sweet and sassy cherry."

"I…I…" Cole shakes his head. "I don't even know what to say right now." He spits out the gum and replaces it with one of his own. They both lie on their stomachs and inch back to their post.

***

279

I sit on the living room couch, holding my purse on my lap, completely lost in a memory.

"I didn't even know you were seeing someone," I say, sitting next to Lynn on my father's couch. Lynn had arrived on Dad's doorstep looking like she'd just seen a ghost.

"I'm not seeing someone, Savi. I just hooked up with someone, and now I'm late."

"How many days late?"

"A week," she says, drying her eyes.

"So," I quickly do the math and my jaw drops, "was it someone from..." I inch closer, seeing my father in the kitchen, "from the charity event we went to last month?" She closes her eyes for a moment and takes a deep breath. "Oh, my God, was it Jones, that smokin' hot blond guy from Dad's office?"

"Luka's 'assistant'? No, not Jones!" She shakes her head in disgust. I ignore her bitchiness toward his title, as I know for a fact that Jones works his ass off for my father and everyone else in the office.

"Then who? And was he not wearing a condom? Not trying to sound holier-than-thou, but come on, Lynn, even I have a sta—"

"Have a what?" my father asks, giving me a stern warning not to finish my sentence. He hands Lynn a bottle of water and takes a seat across from us. "So, you're pregnant?"

Lynn's eyes widen. She looks to me for help, but I'm just as stunned that he heard us talking.

"Umm, I don't know," she says, turning three shades of red.

"Who's the father?" he asks, like he has a right to, but I don't stop him because I'm dying to know too.

"I'd rather not have this conversation until I know for sure."

My father slams his glass down on the table. "How could you be so stupid?"

"Dad," I shoot back. "Don't."

"Be quiet, Savi." He scowls at me and waves a finger in my face. "I swear if I ever find out you're pregnant before you're married, consider it aborted. You will not shame my name." He looks at Lynn. "You should consider the same thing or get a ring on that finger before the press finds out." He leans forward, narrowing his eyes at us. "Figure this situation out before I do." He stands and leaves the room, cursing under his breath.

I reach for Lynn's hand and give it a squeeze. My stomach turns. If my mother could hear him now, she'd be devastated. Thankfully, later on that night, the pregnancy test comes out negative. I've never seen Lynn so relieved, but I never did find out who the possible baby daddy was.

"Ready?" Keith asks, standing next to me.

I didn't even hear him come in the room.

"Yes."

Keith held his ground when Sue and I told him I needed to go into town, but once Sue said the letters OBG, he backed off, not asking any more questions. I'm sure he thinks I have some kind of infection. Normally, I'd be embarrassed, but today I find I'm too excited to care. I would love to share this with him, but I want to tell Cole first. Besides, Derek is in the SUV with us, and he's been a little distant ever since he found out Cole and I are dating.

"Hood up, hair tucked in, and glasses on, okay, Savi?" Keith instructs from the driver's seat. He glances at me in the mirror.

I nod, doing all the things he told me.

Mike is two cars behind us. He's the spotter for

today.

We pull up to the curb and wait for Keith to get out and open my door.

Derek opens the office door for me, and I see Sue standing in the waiting room.

She rushes over and wraps me in a hug. "Thanks, guys, I can take it from here," she says to Keith and Derek.

They both take a seat by the door, glancing around at all the women. They look very uncomfortable, which makes me smirk.

With Sue's arm still around me, she walks me to the back.

I'm guessing they know her pretty well, since they wave and let us go on through.

I change from the waist down and wrap a paper sheet over me, which rips twice as I try to get comfortable.

Lying back, I'm a little nervous as Dr. Brown explains what is about to happen. A very long, cold probe up is shoved up my "wuha," and I breathe out, staring upward and counting the flakes on the ceiling.

Sue gives a tiny gasp and places her hand on her chest.

"See that right there?" Dr. Brown taps her finger to the screen. "That little round circle is your baby."

I look back up to the ceiling, crossing my arms over my face, and start to cry.

"Oh, Savi," Sue says, coming to my side, "don't cry. Everything is going to be okay."

"I know." I sniff and try to catch my breath. "I just wish Cole was here for this."

"I know, dear," she whispers. "Me too."

I wipe my cheeks and look back over at my baby. My heart thumps loudly as I watch the little circle pulse along with mine. "Wow." My voice hitches, and my whole body floods with emotion.

"Heartbeat looks perfect," Dr. Brown says with a smile, clicking away on the keyboard. "And I'd say you're about five weeks."

I press my lips together, trying not to smile at my dirty thoughts of Cole and me in the shower, in his bed, my bed, my—

"Here you go." She hands me a picture.

"Can I get one more?" I ask.

"Of course." She prints another. "Get dressed, then we'll go over all the dos and don'ts."

She and Sue start to leave, but I call Sue back as I sit up.

"You need to share this with Grandpa." I hand her one of the ultrasound pictures.

"Thank you!" she cries, giving me a hug. "I can't wait to."

I tuck the goody bag the doctor gave me in my purse and meet Keith at the door. He sees my red eyes and gently reaches for my arm.

"I'm not sure if I want to know the answer to this question, but I promised Cole I'd watch over you like a hawk, so I need to know. Are you okay?"

"I am, actually." I grin. "I really am." My stupid eyes water again.

"So why are you crying?"

My heart plays tug of war with feeling unbelievably excited, but terrified for Cole. "I miss Cole," I admit. "I just wish I could speak with him myself, hear his voice—" I sigh, feeling sappy. "Sorry."

"Don't be." He gives me his famous Keith side hug. "When I spoke with him last night, I could tell you were on his mind." He leads me to the truck.

***

"Eggs or waffles?" Abigail asks, handing me a cup of

coffee.

I look down at the cup and remember I shouldn't drink it. *Oh, shit, I have to break up with coffee too!* I look down at my beloved drink and make a promise I'll return as soon as I can. Oh, this is going to be hard to hide.

"Just toast will be fine."

Abigail whirls around with a concerned look. "Savannah, what's wrong?"

Shit. "Nothing, I'm just not that hungry." And the idea of eating eggs or waffles makes me want to puke.

"What are you not telling me?"

Oh, Lord, I feel awful not letting her know there's a little fritter on the way.

"Savi?"

"I think I still have that flu."

Her eyes soften at my lie as she heads toward the toaster.

"Savi," Keith calls from the hallway, "can you come here, please?"

I follow him to Cole's office, and he points to the landline, smiling as he shuts the door behind him.

I sit in the massive, leather chair and pick up the receiver.

"Hello?"

"Hey, baby." His voice rasps over the phone, setting off about a million butterflies in my stomach all at once.

"Hi," I choke out, trying to keep my tears at bay. "Are you all right?"

"God, I miss your voice."

"I miss you too, Cole. When are you coming home?" I know I sound desperately needy, but dammit, I am.

"As soon as I can possibly get there, I will. Right now, we're doing surveillance, making sure we know as much as possible before we make our move." He pauses for a second then chuckles.

"What?"

"You called the house *home*."

I smile. He's right; I guess I did. "Yes, well, it is my home now."

"Hmmm," he hums into the phone, "it sure is."

I bite my lip and am about to tell him about our little creation when I hear him let out a long sigh.

"What's wrong?"

"It's a first for me to be struggling with being in the field. Normally, I do my job with no distractions, but knowing you're there without me…it's hard to concentrate."

Oh, God. I try to think quickly.

"Cole, listen to me. I am not leaving this house for any reason. I'm not running off, and I check in with Keith as often as possible. Please, please don't worry about me. I'm fine. I just want you to concentrate on what you're doing so you can come home to me safe and sound." I squeeze my eyes shut. The topic of our baby is on the tip of my tongue, but I can't do it. He'll stress out that much more. "You made a promise to me, Cole."

He clears his throat. "I did." I hear someone talking in the background. "Savi, I have to go." He pauses. "I love you."

"I love you too, Cole." I feel the tears spill over as the line goes dead. "…and I'm pregnant," I whisper to the dial tone.

"Savi?" Keith sticks his head in the door. I hang up the phone but don't get up. He moves into the room, watching me carefully.

"I need you to do something for me, Keith."

"Okay."

"Don't tell him about me going to town today."

"Savannah, he hasn't asked yet, but if he does, I can't lie."

"You can't tell him, Keith. He told me he can't

concentrate because he's worried about me. I told him I'm not leaving the house. If you tell him, it will only make things harder for him."

He shakes his head. "I can't. You're my friend, but he's my boss. I—"

I stand and pull the ultrasound picture from my pocket and hand it to him.

He takes one look then glances at my stomach.

"Five weeks." I smile, rubbing my belly.

"Oh, my God."

"Keith, if he finds out I went to town, he'll want to know why, and I can't—not while he's in danger out there."

"Okay, I agree with you." He comes around the desk and gives me a huge hug—picking me right off the ground. "I'm really happy for you guys. Wow."

"Thanks," I wheeze. "Can you put me back down?"

***

Cole folds his arm under his head and stares out the window of the abandoned house outside of town. His team has been holed up here all night since being forced to withdraw from their primary position. They are hunkered down to avoid detection, which leads to gaps in perimeter security. Through one such gap wanders the Cartel scout.

The boy is maybe ten years old and seems as surprised as Cole and his men when he comes upon the camp without warning.

Paul spots him first, but by the time Cole figures it out, the boy has already given the signal.

Three minutes later, the headlights of a Land Rover race toward them. Luckily, they are next to the river and manage to slip away unmolested.

Cole has never messed up like that before and is

angry with himself, but he couldn't seem to get his mind off Savannah. Dammit, he is worried something is going to happen to her. It's the first time he's really had a reason to get back, and God, does he want to go home. He misses so much about her, even the way she looks at him, like he's the only one she sees.

Ahhhh! Focus! He squeezes his eyes shut, trying to clear his head. Nothing is working. He looks over at Mark, who is passed out in the corner, taking advantage, as only an experienced combat soldier can, of any spare moment to grab some Zs.

Paul is propped up against the wall, using the handle of his weapon as a pillow. John is at the door, leaning on the window frame on first watch. Cole jumps out of bed and grabs his gun.

"John, I'll take the first shift. I'm wide awake, and there's no sense in neither of us getting any rest."

"Thanks, but if it's all the same, I'd rather not," he says, not leaving his post.

Cole nods his understanding, unable to shake off a bad feeling. These situations are high stress, and The American is someone they've been up against before; the man is ruthless. Cole rests his weapon on the wall next to him and sits on the ground, angling himself so he can see out the back window. They sit for a long time, tuning in to every single noise that finds them.

"How's your sister?" Cole whispers. John's sister was hit by a semi in an intersection four months ago. It was touch and go for a while with the swelling in her brain, but she somehow came out of it all right—well, somewhat all right. It was really hard on John, considering she's his twin and they are very close.

"Better, physically. They say she should be able to walk again," John says. "As for her mental state, she's still missing most of her childhood. She doesn't know anyone but Pops, so that's hard. At least they caught the driver. He was eighteen hours over his log book."

"Oh, man, I'm sorry."

"It is what it is," he mutters. They both go back to comfortable silence.

Later, Cole looks at his watch. It's seven thirty in the morning. He and John never left their posts, neither getting a wink of sleep. They often work on less in situations like this. Cole reaches for the satellite phone.

"Checking in at oh seven thirty-five," Cole says as the call connects and Keith answers.

"Roger, Raven One. What's the plan today?"

"We're going to hit the house. They had company yesterday, so we want to get in there and see who it is."

"All right, copy that. Going ahead with plans to move in on the house today." There's a pause. "Daniel and Sue decided to stay here at the house. Agent Joel and three others arrived this morning, so the extra backup is here. Sue has been keeping Savi busy, so—"

"Good, that's good." That makes him feel a whole lot better. "All right, I'll check back in with you tonight."

"Stay safe."

"Will do. Raven One out."

Cole tucks the phone into his vest pocket then downs a protein bar and a few chocolate covered coffee beans. He takes a deep breath, clearing all thoughts out of his head, and finally focuses on what's to come.

"Okay," he says as he walks into the room where the guys are packing their gear. "Let's go get 'em."

Chapter Twenty

I roll over when I hear a knock at the bedroom door. Keith stands there with his hands tucked in his pockets.

"Hi, Keith." I glance at the time. It's four in the afternoon. I've been hibernating in my room all day. I canceled my appointments with Dr. Roberts until Cole comes back. I'm not in the mood to talk about my feelings. I just want to feel the way I feel. I know this has everyone concerned, but for once, I'm being selfish and not caring.

"May I come in?"

"Of course." I move to sit up against the headboard as he sits on the side of my bed.

"This," he takes my ultrasound picture off my bedside table, "deserves to be in something nice." He pulls out a small silver frame with a swirly design and slips the picture inside. He sets it back down, angling it toward me. "There." He smiles.

My lip quivers and tears leak out and drip down my cheeks. I lean forward and give him a hug. "Thank you, Keith, for so much." When I pull away, I see his eyes are glossy, and we both pretend not to notice.

"Right, well, come on downstairs. Daniel and Sue are here with luggage, so I'm assuming they're staying for a while."

Smiling at him and loving that idea, I agree and hop

off the bed.

Abigail watches me all dinner long. I'm not eating, but it isn't because of the baby. I had caught a news clip about my father while I was getting out of the shower. The reporter asked if there was anything new about my disappearance, and my father said no, but he seemed different. I wonder what is going on there. I wonder if he paid the ransom and then realized he wasn't getting me back. Merely seeing his face brought all sorts of emotions to the surface.

"Savannah?" Sue's voice brings me back to the here and now.

I realize everyone has left the table.

She and Daniel are both standing and watching me. "Is everything all right?"

"Yes." I nod then look down at my barely touched plate. "Sorry, I'm just tired."

Daniel looks at Sue, and they both walk me into the living room and sit me on the couch. Sue makes me a cup of chamomile tea while Daniel hands me a light green gift bag.

"What's this?" I ask, setting it between my feet.

"Something for you now, and something for the little one later."

"Oh!" I pull out the white tissue paper and reach in. I feel the softest little nose, and a smile breaks out. I nearly cry when I sit the teddy bear on my lap. He's brown, with black eyes and a black nose. He has an Army hat with Army boots and a little jacket with Logan Jr. sewn in green thread, making my heart burst. "It's perfect, thank you," I whisper, rubbing its little ear.

Daniel leans forward and kisses my head. "No, Savannah, thank you." He smiles, sitting back down as Sue returns with a tray full of fruit and cheese, along with the wonderful-smelling tea. Taking a few sips, I soon find myself relaxing.

We chat about everything—my past life, my new life, and what names I like for the baby. By the time I head to bed, I'm mentally fried, but for the first time in ages, I'm feeling positive about my future. I reach down and rub my tummy. "'Night, little one."

***

Cole slams his body up against the wall and closes his eyes as he listens to the footsteps around him. Two upstairs and three coming toward him from the east. His radio clicks two times, Mark's signal to let him know he's still okay. Paul checked in moments ago, but John hasn't yet. He clicks his radio once, checking in himself. He catches a reflection in a picture, and he waits until the man steps into the bedroom. One…two…three…he counts, then reaches out and wraps his hands around the guy's neck and twists violently, snapping it. Lowering the former threat to the ground, Cole rolls him under the bed and waits for the other.

"Raven Two, what's your position?" he whispers into the radio.

"Two-three west," Mark replies.

Perfect. He's on the second floor, three doors from the stairs.

Cole sneaks a look out the door. "Ten-four, Raven Two. Raven One inbound."

"Copy."

Cole raises his gun and checks to ensure it's clear. He locates the two men upstairs and sees two across the hall. The lights are dim, and with his black gear, camouflage, and face paint, he should be hard to spot. He moves fast and makes it to Mark's room in a matter of seconds. Mark is crouched behind the door.

"Just a graze to the shoulder," Mark quickly informs him.

Cole checks it out. It's deep and bleeding, and he'll need a few stitches, but all things considered, Mark's okay. Cole makes fast work bandaging the wound, then hands Mark a few of the caffeine chocolates to help keep alert.

"John?" Cole asks, worried.

Mark shakes his head no.

"Okay. Paul?"

"First floor hall closet was where I saw him last."

Cole shakes his head bitterly. He doesn't want to use the radio unless he has to. He's not sure where John is or whether he's been captured or killed. Either way, there's a good chance they'd have found John's radio by now, and would be listening. Bad enough they possibly just gave out their own location.

"We need to move," Cole says, looking out the window. "Have you seen The American?"

"No, but he's here. The Hummer and Land Rover are still parked out front. No one has left."

"Okay, I'll head downstairs. I'll signal for you to come when it's clear." Cole moves in front of Mark. "You wait, understand?"

Mark's face is pale and drenched in sweat, but he nods.

"Remember our pact?" Cole grabs his brother's face so he'll look at him. "We joined together—"

"We retire together," Mark huffs out.

"Right. Stay with me, 'cause if anything happens, I'll tell Melanie you died skiing on the bunny hill." Cole grins.

"You would too."

"Right, so stay with me."

"Yeah, I'm here with you."

Cole gives him a nod and slips out the door into the darkness, moving down the staircase. A quick glance at his watch shows him they should all be checking in again in ten minutes. Where the fuck is John? His hand runs along the wall until he finds the handle to the closet door. "Green Fox One?"

The doorknob turns, and Cole sees Paul sitting on the floor, nursing a blood-soaked leg. *Shit*! He moves in to get a better look. He hastily unties the soaked bandage and feels how deep the wound is. He curses when he sees how much blood Paul's lost. His face is growing paler by the minute.

They need to abort the mission. "Stay here. I'm sending Mark for you, then both of you get out."

Paul starts to argue, but Cole shakes his head. "That's an order, Agent."

Cole peeks out the door and clicks his radio, signaling Mark to come down.

"Any sign of John?" Cole asks as he rewraps Paul's leg.

"No, the last time I saw him was in the dining room," he replies, huffing through the pain. "We got separated, and I got knifed and ended up here."

"Okay, set your watch for ten minutes. Start the clock after I leave. If I don't return with John, get out. That's a direct order."

"Yes, Colonel." Paul nods and wipes the sweat from his forehead.

Cole helps him to his feet and props him up against the wall then slowly opens the door. Seeing Mark coming down the stairs, he moves across the hall and signals all clear, then covers Mark until he's safely inside the room with Paul. Staying low, weapon raised, he moves carefully through the living room, then the dining room.

Something hits his shoulder. He turns and sees John crouched down between two lion sculptures. *Thank fuck.*

John points to his radio dangling in pieces around his chest.

Cole checks around and gives him the hand signal to get up and move to his position.

John nods and joins him at his side.

"We're aborting the mission. The others are hit. We need to get them out of here. GF One and R Two have both lost a lot of blood. If we get separated, meet back at our command post."

John nods, and they start toward the front entryway. A man comes into view on John's right.

Cole lunges forward, covering the man's mouth while wrapping his arms tightly around the startled target's neck, cutting off his airway. He orders John to move on.

The man elbows Cole in the stomach, but Cole squeezes harder until the man stops struggling and goes limp. Cole sees his men making for the door, then he spots another two men heading toward them from deeper within the residence.

Cole quickly pops a bullet in the first man's head and is about to do the same to the second when he takes a hard blow to the back of his head. He drops to his knees, a loud ringing sound taking over his brain right before his vision goes dark. His face hits the ground with a heavy thud.

***

I roam the property, soaking up the sun even though it's still freezing out. Derek stays close. We've managed to get past our awkward moment in the kitchen and have started to build a friendship. I am thankful for that, since living under one roof with so many people can take its toll.

He's still flirty, but I think it's all in good fun. We chat about music as we approach the front of the house.

"Other than blues, what else do you listen to?" he

asks, tucking his hands in his jacket pockets.

"Umm, Beck, Radiohead, Weezer, and I fell in love with this Canadian band called the Tragically Hip." I grin, remembering one of their songs called *Ahead by a Century*. I must have played it twenty times in a row one day. "They started in the early eighties. You should check 'em out. They're an alternative rock band."

"So, you like alternative rock?"

"I like all music, but yes, that would be my second favorite." I smile, then spot Keith watching us from the porch. A slow chill runs up my spine as he slowly starts to walk our way.

"Savannah, can you come join me inside?" Keith asks, looking white as a ghost. Panic forms and grows inside my stomach, making its way to my heart, which is now beating rapidly. I see Derek make eye contact with Keith.

A moment later, Derek takes me by the arm and walks me toward the front door. I don't want to be indoors.

I want to run far away from what they're about to tell me. I don't want to think the worst, but it's there, teeter-tottering between the good and the bad. One moment I'll be okay, then the next I'm looking for an exit.

Keith opens the door to Dr. Roberts's office.

I feel the tension in the room, and a rush of goose bumps breaks out, making me shiver.

Daniel's arm is wrapped around Sue. Her eyes are glossy and her hands are clenched into fists.

Oh, God. I look around at everyone's faces as a haunting prickle dances along the back of my neck.

June holds out her hand for me to sit next to her. I do, nearly falling over my shaky feet.

Abigail joins us a moment later, dabbing her eyes with a tissue. Dr. Roberts gives her shoulder a quick squeeze. Everyone is painfully quiet as Daniel gives

Keith a nod to begin.

"Fifty-four hours ago, Team Blackstone entered the house known to be The American's main residence." He clears his throat as mine closes. "Things didn't go according to plan. They had to abort the mission. While attempting to retreat, they came under fire. Everyone got out, except Cole."

Everything stops. Time. Movement. Brain waves. Breathing. Heartbeat—you name it, it just stops.

I barely hear his next words, but they eventually find me. "We do know he's alive."

"How?" Sue cries out, reaching for her husband, who grips her hand tightly.

"We've received confirmation from Washington that the satellite camera picked up an image of Cole being transported to an unknown location by The American and the Cartels."

My lungs beg me to take a deep breath. Finally, I do, letting out a horrible sob.

Abigail leans over, rubbing my back as I fall forward onto my thighs.

"We don't know all the details, but the guys are in pretty bad shape and have been ordered to return to the house once they've been checked out by the medic in Washington."

"They...they left him there?" I whisper, hot tears coursing down my cheeks.

Keith looks at me and presses his lips together.

"Frank is now in charge," Daniel says in an eerie voice, "since Cole isn't able—" He stops himself, taking a deep breath. "They're coming home, and that's an order from Frank. They don't have a choice, Savannah."

"Yes, they do!" I shout through my tears. "What about Cole? What if they—" My hand covers my mouth. Another loud sob escapes as I stand, feeling sick and light headed. "Please make them go back." I turn to

Keith, crying out every word. "Please, please, Keith, please, make them go back and find him. I want him back. He needs to come back!"

"I'm sorry, Savannah. It's out of my control." Keith's eyes plead with me to understand.

I back up toward the door. I feel claustrophobic—the walls closing in and the ceiling lowering. I need to get away. Everyone is watching me. Some stand and approach, but I hold up a hand, warning them off. I just want Cole back. I bump into Derek, who's now standing in my path. I hear Sue say to Daniel that I should calm down. How can I calm down when they are telling me that Cole is being held captive? Not when the father of our baby is being held against his will. No, I need to get out of here…*now*.

The look I give Derek makes him move aside. Dr. Roberts calls out for me, but I hear nothing but the door handle turning. I move without thinking up to my room, punch the keypad on the wall, and drop onto the pillows in Sue's private library. I curl up, passing out immediately. My thoughts quickly return to when I was held safe and sound in his arms. Yes, it's only a dream, but I'll take what I can get.

***

Sue finds me sometime later with Keith's help. She slowly lowers herself to the floor.

I'm awake, facing away from her. I ache too much to move.

She lies behind me and wraps her arm around my mid-section, holding my hand in hers.

I sob, desperately needing a mother, and she sobs, desperately needing a child to hold.

She holds on while we both go through a roller coaster of emotions. We fall asleep and wake several hours later, feeling drained and in need of some water.

We decide to go for a walk, neither wanting to be alone.

Keith and Daniel are working away in Cole's office. We don't want to disturb them, so we head outside for some fresh air. We don't talk about anything important, just mindless jabber when the pain becomes too much. I'm thankful for Sue needing me as much as I need her. She is fast becoming my rock. Thank God for her and Abigail. I don't know what I would do without them.

I flinch when she does. We hear it before we see it, and the noise of the rotor makes my heart pound. I turn to see the black helicopter flying low over the mountains behind us. As it descends, it kicks up snow to swirl around us. I squeeze her hand, knowing how hard this is going to be.

She tugs my arm, and we head back toward the house.

We're almost to the porch when the SUV stops next to us. Keith comes to my side.

The doors open, and Paul gets out first. He's struggling to stand up straight.

John is next. He goes to Paul's side, grabs his bag, then wraps his arm around Paul's waist to stabilize him.

Mark keeps his head down as he comes into view. His body language makes me uncomfortable. I notice not one of them has made eye contact with me.

Keith motions for us to come inside.

Sue never lets go of my hand as we slump down onto the couch, waiting for them to join us.

They drop their bags and carefully make their way in. Daniel helps John sit Paul on the couch. His leg is in a small brace, making it hard for him to move around.

Mark's arm is in a sling tied tightly to his chest, and he's like a robot making his way to his seat. He sits and stares at the floor. I'm not even sure if he knows we are all here with him.

"Here." Daniel sets Mark's drink on the table and stands by the fire. I notice Mark doesn't reach for it. We all wait while the guys gather themselves.

"Nothing went according to plan." Paul's voice is quiet. "The moment we entered the house, it all went to shit."

My stomach is in knots. I want to yell out "what the fuck happened? Where is Cole?" But I don't. Instead, I sit and stare at Mark, who still hasn't raised his head.

"A maid caught us as we moved through the kitchen. She dropped her tray, and one of their men saw us."

"There were so many of them," John says, clearing his throat. "My radio got busted when three of them jumped me. I managed to get away and went to our next location, but no one came, so I went back to the last spot I'd seen Paul in the dining room. I found a safe spot and tried to fix my radio, but it was done."

"After I got a knife to the leg, I found cover in a closet. Thirty minutes later, Cole found me," Paul says.

I break my gaze from Mark and look at Paul.

"He saw my leg and told me Mark had a bullet wound. He said we were to abort the mission. That's when he left, looking for John."

John rubs his head. "We got stopped on our way over to get them. Cole took one man down and sent me ahead to get the guys out. I met Paul and Mark in the hall, and we headed for the door. The last thing I heard was a gunshot and a Cartel falling down the stairs. I glanced back when we were running for our check-in point. I-I—" He shakes his head. "I couldn't see him."

My head starts to prickle, my eyes feel fuzzy, and my hands go cold as I listen.

"We waited for him." Paul takes over because John is barely holding it together. "We waited all night and into the morning. We fixed each other up as best we could and called in for support. By the time they came, the place was cleared out. We were ordered to return here until further notice."

My eyes shift around the room, trying to absorb what we're being told. I want so much to yell at them to go back, but I can see they're as raw as I am. They had to leave a man behind—their Colonel, their friend, and brother. I can't imagine.

Suddenly, I feel a horrible cramping pain in my stomach, one that matches the pain from the gaping hole in my heart. I wrap my arms around my mid-section as my face breaks out in sweat.

"Savi?" Keith kneels in front of me. "You need to calm down."

"Calm down? Calm down!" I repeat as the anger burns through me. I stand and feel the pain wrap around my middle.

"Yes, Savannah," Daniel warns, but I don't know what they're getting at.

I back away, running both hands through my hair, tears streaming down my face. My chest feels like it's going to explode. I raise my arms wide. "You want me to calm down while Cole is sitting in a prison somewhere, or six feet—" I stop, closing my eyes. I feel everyone staring at me. I drop my arms, hitting my legs with a thud. I turn on my heel and head for my room, where I curl up in a ball to ease the pain in my stomach and cry myself to sleep.

***

Cole gasps as one of the men sticks his finger in the large gash across his torso. Over the last two days, he has been tortured by some very imaginative assholes. The electric shocks, waterboarding, and whippings haven't broken him yet. The two rats in front of him seem to be growing bored. They leave him hanging by his wrists from a chain, his feet a foot off the ground. His shoulders have lost any feeling long ago. The pain he should be feeling is blocked by long hours training to turn that part of the brain off.

He watches as they walk down the hallway, forgetting to shut the door. He takes the opportunity to listen to all the sounds in the little house. He concentrates on trying to remember the steps from when he arrived. Eleven steps from the Land Rover, three steps past the doorway, fourteen to the bedroom. He hears a TV turn on, and the opening of twist-off beers. He closes his eyes and slips into meditation mode, taking this time to rest so he will be mentally strong enough when they decide to come at him again.

***

A bright light burns into his closed eyelids. Cole senses he's not alone.

A shadow moves in front of his face, and the sound of nails on tile sparks a memory. Savannah's description of The American's boots. Cole plays like he's passed out, hoping to gather something from him.

"So, this is the famous Colonel Cole Logan," The American says in perfect English.

"*Si señor*," a man's voice answers.

"How many men did his team kill?"

"*Veintiocho.*"

Yeah, motherfucker. Twenty-eight down, a billion more rats to go.

"And he's not talking?"

"No."

"I think I may know how to fix that."

Two footsteps later, he gets a hard punch to the stomach.

"Time to wake up, Colonel," The American says sharply.

Cole coughs and struggles to catch his breath, then leans forward, taking in what the man is wearing. His signature black and white suit, a cowboy hat, and his ridiculous cowboy boots with the gold-headed cobra sticking out at the tips.

"At last, we finally meet after all these years," he says.

Cole keeps silent and watches him, studying his movements. He has a slight limp in the right leg, and he keeps tilting his head to the left like his neck is hurting.

"So, I'm going to ask you a question, and you're going to answer it. Where is my Savannah?"

It takes everything in Cole's body not to react.

The American nods and fixes his left shirt cuff. "So, short term physical torture doesn't seem to bother you. I wish we had more time, but sadly, we don't." He taps his mouth with his finger. "I wonder how strong you are mentally." He smirks. "Mr. Donovan, would you please join us?"

Cole's gaze moves to the door when he hears footsteps.

It only takes a moment to realize who it is. A wheel of photos flicker through Cole's memory, the most recent from when they were doing surveillance on the house and this guy showed up. A navy blue suit on his wiry body, with a cream-colored cloth bag over his head is hard to forget.

"I take it you recognize me?" he asks, smirking.

"I do," Cole grunts.

"You see, Colonel, we have a problem. You screwed up a very important business deal for me." He moves closer. "This can be very easily fixed if you would just give me Ms. Miller."

Cole has an idea. He rotates his shoulder and flops

his head around like he's losing consciousness.

Mr. Donovan looks at The American. "Can you at least put him in a chair or something?" He points to Cole's stomach. "This is offensive to me. I don't need to see this all stretched and bloody."

The American shakes his head slowly, annoyed, but calls for the men to come. "Don't try anything," The American says, sticking a 40mm in Cole's face as the men release the pulley system and lower him into a wooden chair. They keep his hands and feet bound, but don't tie him to the chair. He notices one of them is wearing a longhorn belt buckle. The horns look more like a weapon than a decoration.

A dull ache runs through him as he starts to feel the beating his body took, but he relishes the fact that his plan worked and he was released from the ceiling. His mind slips back into survival mode as he sits, his body starting to build strength as the seconds tick by.

"Now," Mr. Donovan says as he takes a seat in front of him, "where's the girl?"

Cole moves his tongue around his mouth. Tasting tin, he spits to his side...yup, blood. He looks over at the man, taking his time answering. "Why the girl?"

"Do you know who I am?" He leans forward in his chair. "I mean, really know who I am?"

"Luka Donovan, the mayor's assistant."

"Correct. I've known the mayor's daughter for a long time," he says, smiling at Cole.

Cole smiles back, but for a very different—much more violent—reason.

"You see, the mayor is up for re-election. The numbers are good, but due to his daughter's constant fuck-ups, they're not great. So, a change was necessary." He leans back and shakes his head. "I never would have been able to pull it off if it wasn't for Lynn."

Cole always suspected Savannah's best friend, but

could never connect the dots.

"Savannah trusted her more than anyone," he continues conversationally. "So, when Lynn and I met for dinner and she agreed she could get a customer of hers to pose as a prospective client who could lure her 'friend' down to the parking lot at the right time, it was perfect."

"Joe Might?" Cole interrupts.

Luka nods with a shrug. "You see, Colonel, much like in your profession, I, too, meet a lot of shady people. You start to learn things. Like money doesn't always buy you what you want, but a pretty face and a smoking body like Savannah's can."

Before Cole even thinks about what he is doing, he lunges forward, plowing Luka off his chair and into the wall.

Luka grunts as the wind is knocked out of him.

Cole elbows him in the face and knees him in the stomach just as he feels a hard crack between his shoulder blades. He drops to the ground, and the butt of the gun collides with his temple. The pain doesn't register as he tries to get back up, but The American sticks the gun in his face, and he freezes.

"Make one more move, and I'll blow your head off," he hisses.

Cole closes his eyes, teeth grinding loudly, no doubt trying to calm himself.

"Get him out of here!"

Two men grab hold of Cole, and another keeps his gun in his face.

He sees Luka in a ball on the floor, moaning and holding his stomach. He tries to force himself to control his thoughts, as the deadly violence in them will probably get him killed if he doesn't. Handcuffing him to a water pipe in a small closet and slamming the door closed, they leave him alone in the dark. Cole shifts and leans his head against his hands, using pressure to stop the bleeding from his temple. He lets out a long sigh and thinks of all the ways he could escape. He just needs to get his hands on a weapon.

A small breeze of cool air next to where the pipe meets the wall draws his attention. He lines his eye up with the one-inch hole, and he can see outside. There are lights about twenty yards away. He must be in a small town. He turns back around when he hears footsteps, then muffled voices and a loud crack, followed by a thump. The light under his door goes dark as something is dragged outside the room. He shakes his head, not eager to know.

He pulls at the pipe to test its strength. He leans back, kicking at the base of it, but it's no use. "Fuck!" he whispers to himself, resting his head against the wall. He needs sleep. He closes his eyes, but all he can think about is Savannah. She must be beside herself right now. His chest hurts at the thought of her. He knows she will be devastated to find out Luka and Lynn are behind her kidnapping.

Chapter Twenty-One

"Wake up!" Luka kicks him in the ribs. "I said wake up!"

Cole opens his eyes, even though he's been awake most of the night. He dismisses the pain in his ribs and smirks when he sees Luka is sporting a black and blue goose egg over his eye.

Luka glares down at him. Closing the door, he pulls up a chair and sits, watching Cole. "I heard you were one tough Green Beret. Hell, you became a Colonel at thirty. You must really be something," he croons. "But, you see, Colonel, everyone has a weak spot." He leans back and crosses his legs. "And last night you showed me yours." He smirks. "She's beautiful, isn't she? Her long, silky hair, her tan skin, those dark eyes that seem to pull you in, that slender body with *just* the right amount of curves...mmm, so lovely." He shakes his head like he's remembering something. "I don't think there's a man in that office who didn't dream about screwing her."

Cole's jaw muscle twitches as the adrenaline rushes throughout his body.

"I can see you've fallen under her spell too, which explains why you won't give up her location. Don't waste your time." He laughs. "She has a pistol personality, a gatekeeper guarding her heart, and she doesn't open her legs for anyone."

The wave of emotion that hits Cole is unreal. He actually finds himself grinning on the inside and the corners of his mouth tugging on the outside. Yes, he found his way to Savannah's heart. Now he just needed to get back.

"Sounds like you're interested too?" Cole murmurs, hoping to get more detail about the kidnapping.

"Nah." He shakes his head. "I like my job too much to touch that, so I settled for the best friend."

Cole rolls his eyes; what a prick. "Tell me something, Luka." Cole shifts, resting his forearms on his bent knees. "How did you locate someone to kidnap Savannah?"

Luka chuckles. "You'd be surprised how easy it is to find someone willing to remove my little problem. A word here, a word there, and I had a few offers, but when *Los Sirvientes Del Diablos* approached me, we soon had a deal. She was nabbed and taken to Tijuana. She was supposed to be killed within a week, but then this guy," he points over his shoulder and out the door, indicating The American, "got in touch with them and made his own deal. He wanted Savannah for himself, but agreed to wait until the ransom money came through." He pauses, leaning forward. "There are rules, you know. You can't just come in and take her. He had to wait until it was a done deal."

Fuck, this guy is a talker and a real asshole. Cole is going to enjoy fucking up his face.

"But then *Los Sirvientes Del Diablos* got greedy. They got in contact with the mayor, saying they have his daughter, and that someone else was interested in her, so whoever pays the most gets the girl." Luka removes his glasses and rubs the bridge of his nose. "The mayor didn't react the way I thought he would. I swear he was relieved she was gone. His own daughter! His polls were climbing. He started dating a woman." His voice softens.

"Don't get me wrong, Colonel, he loves Savannah, but she just wouldn't climb aboard the campaign wagon, and a man has his priorities." He sighs loudly.

"Hey!" The American yells, bursting through the door. "What the fuck are you doing?"

"Just chatting," Luka says calmly.

"I didn't bring you here for a fucking meet and greet. Get out so I can get this done." The American slips a pair of brass knuckles over his fingers and makes a fist.

"Is that really necessary?" Luka asks, making a disgusted face as he stands. "May I have a word with you outside?" He touches The American's shoulder, but jumps back when the man turns on him, grabbing his arm and twisting it.

"Don't fucking touch me, ever!" The American snarls. "Outside!"

Luka nods as he rubs his arm and follows The American out the door. It slams behind them, leaving one man with a machine gun alone with Cole.

Cole tilts his head and stares at the man. He's so young, maybe early twenties. His face is sweaty and his body is shaking, making his fingers flex on the gun.

The kid tosses the strap over his head. "You move," he says in a thick accent. "I blow your head off."

Cole smiles at him and whispers something under his breath, waiting for him to come just a little closer. Sure enough, the kid takes two steps toward him. Cole suddenly grabs the side of the pipe as he kicks the barrel of the gun so it shoots up and slams the kid in the eye. He falls backward with a scream and scrambles to the other side of the wall away from Cole's reach.

The door flies open, and The American sees the kid on the floor, holding his head and groaning in pain. He looks at Cole, walks up to him, and punches him in the side of the head once with the brass knuckles.

***

It's dark again when Cole comes to, a tiny crack in the wall providing a cool breeze. His skull feels like he was hit by a Mack truck, probably fractured. It hurts like hell just to open his eyes, and he's thankful the light is off. The door opens as another wave of nausea hits hard. He leans over and vomits. *Fuck.*

A water bottle is dropped at his feet. He looks up to find Luka standing above him. *Oh, Christ, here comes good cop-bad cop again.* He moves his hands down the pipe, using his foot to slide the water bottle toward him. He opens it awkwardly and takes a drink, the cool water like liquid gold. His stomach immediately feels better. If only he could get some painkillers. He chuckles a bit at the thought.

"Something funny?" Luka asks, sitting on the floor across from him.

"Not really," Cole huffs as he drops the empty bottle on the floor.

"She hated the press, you know." He starts his story like they were never interrupted. "Savannah hated her father for choosing his job over her, so she'd get drunk and parade around town, disgracing herself."

Cole bends down and reaches for his throbbing head, feeling the blood trickle down his neck. Luka tosses his water bottle at him and hits his leg.

"You paying attention? 'Cause this is where it gets interesting."

Cole glares over at him, dropping his hands and straightening up.

"One night, I found the Mayor drinking in his office. He confessed that someone contacted him with proof of life for Savannah, but since he didn't pay right away, now they were blackmailing him, saying he'd set the whole thing up. I knew *Los Sirvientes Del Diablos* told him I was behind it all. I could tell by his look. I thought it was over, but instead, he asked for my help. I was shocked. After all, she is his daughter, but I dodged a major bullet. We both want to be at the top, and we'll do whatever is needed to get there."

He claps his hands, making Cole's head pound. "So, a new plan is hatched! We start to use the media as much as possible. No one could accuse us of not caring about our missing Savannah. We ignore the ransom demands and hope they'll dispose of her. Everything was running smoothly. There was no contact with them, everything was good. But then, a few months later, I'm at a bar, and boots, here," referring to The American, "approaches me, saying we better pay up, or they're going to release a recording they have with the mayor on the damn phone discussing the ransom deal. They were going to prove he did know his daughter was alive, and he didn't give a shit. So, we started low balling. We started with fifty grand, just to buy us some time to think, but before we got the chance, she vanishes into thin air."

Cole leans back, trying to get his aching head to absorb all the information Luka is throwing at him.

"Hang on." Cole stops his babbling. "You thought ignoring a group with ties to the Cartels was going to make them go away? Had you even heard of the Cartels before you got involved with them?" This guy is seriously stupid.

"They got paid for taking the girl. As far as I was concerned, our deal was finished. They were the ones who didn't fulfill their end of the bargain."

"You're playing stupid in the Devil's back yard," Cole says in disbelief, not caring if it pisses off Luka. "Hell, you made a deal with his God-damned self-proclaimed servants!"

Luka rubs the back of his neck. "Yes, I understand that now," he agrees, nodding sadly. "They accused us of taking her and started sending reminders that we owe them two million or they'd release the tape." He raises his voice. "They threatened my family, and Lynn, and they tried to set my car on fire. Boots, or 'The American,' as you call him, finally realized we had no idea where the hell she was or what was going on. After a lot of money and time, we found out the fucking US Army has her hidden away." He leans forward again, staring right into Cole's eyes. "You see, Colonel, I did make a deal with the Devil, and I have to see it through. So, this brings us to you. I need you to give the girl to The American, I need to pay the two million, and the mayor needs to win this election so we can all go and live our lives the way things were meant to be. It is a very easy fix."

Cole's mind is blown. So many lies, so many deceitful people. He can't believe her own father could give her up so easily. God, this will kill her, if nothing else does.

"How stupid do you think I am?" Cole asks. "You think with all you told me that you're going to let me go? Luka, I didn't become a colonel at thirty because of my fighting skills."

"I really don't like repeating myself, but considering all I told you, I'm sure your mind is spinning. So, where is she?" Luka sighs, ignoring Cole's comment.

Cole decides he needs some more information before he makes his move.

"Why would Lynn betray her?"

Luka seems to consider. "I'll answer you, and in return, you answer me." He straightens his tie. "Lynn and I became involved a few years back. She didn't seem to mind that I was eleven years older. We kept it quiet, and no one knew, especially Savannah. Lynn despised her. She was jealous, and she couldn't understand why Savannah didn't want to be a part of the campaign and involve herself in her father's life. Why couldn't she see that we would all benefit? We would be taken to the top with him." He shakes his head. "Lynn had a bad childhood. She resented Savannah for having had a good one, and now she was throwing away Lynn's chance at finally getting what she deserved."

"Watching your mother deteriorate over four months hardly makes for a happy childhood," Cole shoots back, feeling his anger bore through his veins.

"It really was for the best, although her mother was not a supporter of Doug going into politics." Luka shrugs and rolls his eyes. "Apparently, Savannah takes after her."

Cole starts to laugh. His patience with the man has run out, and his vision is clouding. "You're so fucked."

"That may be so," Luka says, getting to his feet, "but I'm not the one handcuffed to a water pipe in a house full of men who want me dead." He opens the door and signals for someone to come in. He turns to Cole. "Last chance."

The American walks in, looking pissed off and stressed. "Well?" he asks Luka.

"Fuck you," Cole says, making the two of them look at him.

"What?" The American scowls.

"I said...fuck you."

The American studies him for a moment then takes out a handkerchief, dabbing his brow as he considers. "Okay, Colonel, we're done here." He nods at two men to come in while he points his gun at Cole's head.

One of the guys is the kid from earlier, his eye swollen shut. The kid removes one of the handcuffs, freeing him from the pipe. He slaps it back on Cole's wrist and jerks him to his feet. Normally, he would make a move, but he is outnumbered and can hear more men in the other room. No, for now, he'll wait for the perfect moment before he strikes.

"We could still get it out of him," Luka protests, but The American shakes his head.

"He won't talk. He has too much pride. Don't you, Captain America?" He laughs. "I know you care for the girl in the same way I do. We both love her. I can see it in your face when I mention her name."

Cole's face hardens.

"I can't wait to feel her under me, Colonel. I can't wait to hear her whimper and beg when I—"

Cole shoots forward, head-butting The American and sending him backward. The guard with two working eyes knocks Cole in the head with the stock of his rifle, bringing him to his knees.

He cries out as his ears ring, pain exploding in every direction throughout his head.

The American's boots clink on the floor as he comes closer. "Take him to the tub. I think the colonel needs a little reminder who's in charge here." He looks at Longhorn. "I need to make a trip into town. Give him ten, then cuff him back to the pipe."

"*Si, señor.*"

Cole hears the American leave the room, the door shut behind him, and the roar of an engine.

"Change of plans," Longhorn says to One Eye. "Get the back room ready, *esé*." He smirks down at Cole. "Time for some fun, Colonel."

***

I've been a mess for the past three days. I just lie in bed and watch the time tick by, wondering where Cole is. I catch myself slipping, thinking the worst, but then I feel guilty for giving up hope. I cry a lot and barely eat. June and Abigail take shifts watching me. Sue has been curled up on my bed most of the time. She needs comforting as much as I do. We take turns being strong for each other while Daniel and Keith work frantically with Frank, trying to use their contacts in Mexico to track down Cole. Mark, John, and Paul try to help, but they are all ordered to stand down. It's now personal for them, and two of them are still recovering from their wounds.

Derek is in charge of the new men Daniel brought in. Everyone seems to be busy doing something but me. I feel stuck between moving forward and wanting to stay in the past, when Cole was with me. I hum quietly to my stomach. I find it soothes me, and I hope it soothes the little one too.

Needing a change of scenery, I head downstairs. When I hear shouting from the entertainment room, I head that way. I peek around the corner to see what is happening. Everyone in the room seems to be waiting for a video to start.

"All it says is that it's a message for Team Blackstone," Daniel says, looking pale.

The video comes into focus, and I reach for the wall for support. Cole is on his knees, beaten, shirtless, and sweaty, a nasty cut running along his torso. Blood drips in trails over his face from a gash on his head. His mouth is gagged, and his wrists are cuffed in front of him. He looks up into the camera, making my heart stand still. Everyone gasps and cries out. Mark stands and moves closer to the TV.

A man stands next to Cole; his hands are crossed in front. Then I see it. He's holding a large machete. I freeze, unable to breathe. My brain begs me to look away, but I can't.

"All you had to do was return her," the man says as the camera moves up to his face. "Blackstone killed twenty-eight of our men. Now I will kill one of yours, and will continue killing until you give us what we want." The camera zooms in on his face then slowly moves down his body to the knife held over Cole's neck.

Cole is breathing hard, beads of sweat obvious in the close-up zoom.

Suddenly, the machete flashes. The force of the cut sends Cole's body in a twist, and he slumps to the ground. Blood sprays everywhere, including onto the camera lens.

Everything goes silent. People are moving in slow motion around me. I lock eyes with Mark, who has heard me gasp and discovers me watching them.

He is horrified and frozen, staring at me, until everyone turns to see me standing there.

Daniel cups his mouth in horror while Paul and John gasp, rising to their feet. A sharp cramp in my lower abdomen makes me cry out, and I fall forward as pain grips me in a vise.

Mike is standing nearest, and he leaps toward me, cradling my head before I hit the floor.

The physical pain is overwhelming. I gasp, trying to catch my breath. My fingers claw at my stomach. *What the hell is happening?*

"Call the doctor!" Keith shouts as he flies to my side.

I see the horror in his face when his eyes flicker to my stomach.

Daniel pushes Mike out of the way and bends down.

"Shh, sweetheart," he whispers through a sob. "Just breathe." He strokes my hair, murmuring something to Keith.

Everything goes black.

***

"Her HCG levels are low," a nurse says as I stare at the wall, expressionless, everything numb. "Twenty-six forty. I'll go check the results of her urine test." She nods to the doctor as she leaves the room.

"Savannah, do you feel any discomfort?" I feel so much pain, the idea of pinpointing a single one seems impossible.

Daniel touches my hand, tears streaming down his face as he bends down to my eye level.

"Savannah?" he whispers.

I close my eyes and nod once.

I feel the unwanted pressure as the probe is inserted, and the odd noise like you're standing too close to a speaker while holding a microphone fills the room. A tear rolls down my face as I see Cole standing in front of me. It's only for a moment—then he's gone. A sob hits me. I want to curl into a ball, but I can't. I have to wait until they find out if the only tiny piece of Cole I have left is still alive inside me. I close my eyes. This is all too much.

Chapter Twenty-Two

The Next Night

I feel Sue slip off the bed. Her steps are quiet as she shuts the door behind her. She only leaves when she thinks I'm asleep. I open my eyes and discover it's still dark out. My head is pounding, but I don't care. I don't want to be alone, but I don't want anyone with me except Cole. Keith has permanently taken up residence on the couch in Cole's room, saying he won't leave until I do.

I roll over, hugging Cole's pillow and breathing in his scent. I sob, not just because I lost the one person I love more than anything, but because I will never hold our baby. My only comfort is that Cole will. I never believed in heaven or hell, but right now I just want to picture them together, happy, and waiting for me to join them. I imagine Cole holding our little one. Telling him how much I love him, kissing his soft, deep-brown hair, and looking into his sweet, dark eyes—so much like his father's. I reach for the Army teddy bear and bring it to my chest. I feel so empty, so lost. I've felt pain before, but that was nothing compared to this. How am I supposed to move forward when everything in my body is telling me I can't? I'm over this life; I want a redo.

I focus my eyes on something taped to the back of Cole's nightstand. I shift, pretending to pull the cover over me. I see what it is and feel like fate is finally on my side. Taking a deep breath and closing my eyes, I make a silent promise to myself for the second time in my life that I will make it back to my family. There's a difference between living and surviving, but this, right here, is neither. I lean up slowly to look at Keith; he's fast asleep. I reach for the handle, slipping it out of the holster, my hand slick with tears. Still clutching the teddy bear in one hand, I raise the pistol to my temple with the other. For the first time in a long time, I finally feel like I'm at peace.

***

Mark sits at Cole's desk, sipping his brother's brandy. He's finally gotten his hands on the DVD the Cartels sent. He had to convince Frank to let him have it before he left in the morning. He feels strongly they are missing something—he just doesn't know what.

He presses play and watches the tape again and again, until something finally catches his eye. He backs up the tape and watches frame by frame. "What?" Mark whispers in disbelief, setting his drink down so sharply it splashes over his hand. He shifts forward and watches the last scene before Cole slumps to the floor.

"Holy fucking shit!"

The End

"I'm sorry for what happened to you,
but I'll never be sorry for tracking you
down and falling in love with you."
~ Cole Logan

shattered

BROKEN TRILOGY
BOOK TWO

J.L. DRAKE

Prologue

There's a difference between living and surviving, and this was neither. My life was never going forward. It had always been on hold while I dealt with everyone else—my mother, my father, my keepers. I was finally gifted a few months in which I fell in love with a man who made me feel more alive than I ever thought possible. Now, because of me, he's been ripped from my life, murdered in the worst way possible for all of us to witness, and I lost our unplanned baby. There is nothing of me left to pick up the pieces; I don't even want to. So here I am, gun to my head, waiting to join my little family on the other side.

Chapter One

Somewhere in México

Cole

"You did what, Raul?" The American hisses at the man who wears the ridiculous longhorn belt buckle.

"No-no, *señor*, he's alive, see?" He steps out of The American's view to show that, yes, Cole is indeed alive. "No harm done."

"No harm?" The American pulls out a knife, grabs Raul's hand, slams it against the wall, and within a blink the man's pointer finger is rolling on the floor.

"Ahhh!" Raul yells.

"He's our only leverage! And now they think he's dead. Fuck!" The American punches the blood-splattered wall. He turns to face Raul, whose white face is staring at his missing digit. "If you weren't married to my cousin, I swear I'd behead you myself."

"*Sí,*" the man responds weakly.

Luka wipes his mouth with a rag. The smell of blood must be getting to him. He glances at Cole, who's watching them. The corners of his mouth tug upward. He likes seeing Luka's weaknesses.

***

Savannah

I stare forward, hands shaking, tears streaming down my face. I'm so close to them. If only...

The ring of Keith's phone rips through the silence, making my finger freeze, trembling on the trigger. I squeeze my eyes shut and try to focus.

"What?" Keith's raspy voice answers. "Wait, back up. What?" My eyes slowly open, and I see Keith's head turn toward me. His face falls as he notices what's in my hand. "Wait!" He drops his phone, and it bounces off the floor as he jumps to his feet. "Savannah?"

"Stop," I cry, shaking my head and keeping the gun tight to my temple. He stops at the end of the bed, his hands raised to show he won't move.

"Please, Savi, give me the gun. Mark just called with—"

"Stop," I cry out again through a sob. I'm so close. "Just leave me."

"No." He doesn't elaborate.

"I don't want to hurt anymore. I have so much pain. I don't want to live without him. I don't want to live without our baby." I drop my head and pull up my knees. Keith can see I'm moments from ending it all. *Just squeeze the trigger, Savannah!* I keep a firm grip on the gun that's imprinting my temple. "At what point did fate decide I don't deserve to be happy?" I scream as memories pour out of me. "I've served my time. I watched my mother die. I watched my father pull away and stop loving me. I was kidnapped, and I had a birthday trapped in a twenty-four by twenty-four room! Now I lose my lover and our baby! I don't want to know what's next, Keith—I just can't!" The gun bounces around on my head as my sobs become louder. "Everyone I love leaves me. I just want it to end!"

"I know, Savannah." He kneels on the bed and shifts

322

toward me. "But this is isn't the way." He moves up next to me and runs a steady, slow hand up my arm and over my hand. Wrapping his fingers around mine, he whispers, "Give it to me, sweetheart, please."

Suddenly the weight of my pain is too much. It makes my hand relax enough that he slips the gun from my grip. He grabs my shoulders and pulls me into him. I feel him start to shake.

"I miss him too," he barely whispers.

This is my undoing; I completely break down.

I am a coward.

***

Mark

Mark races up the stairs and down the long hallway toward Cole's room. He flies into the bedroom and sees Savannah, curled up in a ball sobbing, and Keith looking terrified.

"What? What's going on?"

Keith shakes his head as he holds up the gun. Mark feels the blood rush from his face when he realizes what could have happened. He grips his hair as he tries to think clearly. He needs to speak with Keith and Daniel *now.*

"Keith," he says quietly, feeling ill, "Cole's office, five minutes." Keith nods.

He turns and runs out of the room and into Abigail's, which she has been sharing with her sister June.

"Abby!" Mark hisses as he snaps on the light. "I need your help."

"Huh?" June squints at the sudden brightness.

Abigail reaches for her robe. "Mark, dear, what's wrong?"

"I need..." He pauses to control to his jumbled

thoughts. "Where's Sue?"

"With Savannah. Why?"

Mark shakes his head. "I need you to go in Cole's room and wait with Savi. Something happened, and I don't want her to be alone. I—"

Abigail pulls on her slippers. "What happened? Where's Keith?"

"I need a meeting. I-I think I found something." He starts to leave, but turns. "Abby, you know better than anyone where Cole might have weapons stashed around his room. Please get rid of them."

She looks at June, baffled, then nods at Mark.

Mark bangs on the spare bedroom door, yelling out Daniel's name. Sue answers first, looking exhausted.

"Sue! You need to go see Savi." Her face drops as she pushes by him and runs down the hall. Mark moves into the room and sees Daniel pulling on a T-shirt. "I need to speak with you now." Shrieks from Cole's room make Mark squeeze his eyes shut.

Holy shit, this is out of control.

***

Mark is busy pulling up the file, while everyone plays catch-up.

"Jesus Christ!" Daniel rubs his head, listening to Keith's story.

"If Mark hadn't called…" Keith's hands drop heavily to his sides. "I-I thought she was all right. She's been so quiet, I thought she was dealing with all this in her own way. I had no idea she'd go this far."

"Guys," Mark interrupts, pointing to the flat screen, "tell me what you see." He presses play on the DVD from The American. Daniel shoots Mark a nasty look. "I know, believe me, I know, but just watch, please."

Daniel takes a deep breath and watches his son's

murder all over again, but this time he steps a little closer.

"Wait," Mark says, and Keith moves next to Daniel.

"Oh my god!" Daniel's head jerks toward Mark. "There's no tattoo!"

"Exactly." Mark nods, freezing the video with the man's shoulder in view. "That man isn't Cole."

Daniel picks up the phone and makes a quick call before returning to the stunned group. "Frank will be here in an hour. Get the guys up. We need to have a meeting."

"What do you think we should do?" Keith asks.

Daniel folds his arms. "Get the guys prepared. We move out tonight."

"I'm coming." Mark's tone is stern as he removes his sling.

"Yeah, you are." Daniel nods and looks at John. "Paul can't come. Have Derek take his place."

Mark stops mid-step, hating how much his team despises Derek. "Not Keith or Mike?"

Daniel turns to Keith. "Savannah or Cole?"

Keith runs his hand over his forehead. Mark knows he's close with Savannah, and she trusts him more than anyone in the house, but the idea of bringing back Cole is tempting. "Cole."

"Okay," Daniel agrees. "Living room meeting at zero two hundred hours."

Half an hour later Mark waits while zoned out, trying to sort his thoughts and mentally prepare for what's to come. What if they're too late? What if Cole tried to escape after that video and they had to kill him? Mike sits bouncing his knee and watching Mark pace the living room. Derek sits next to Mike, half asleep. He yawns loudly, making Mike glare at him.

"Show some respect, Derek."

"I was out cold, Mike. It's just a natural reaction

when one gets awakened the way John woke me."

"Stop talking—"

"Guys," Mark whispers, shaking his head. Now is not the time for a pissing match. Emotions are too high.

John walks behind Paul, who is limping along on a crutch from his recent knife wound to the leg. Daniel appears with his wife, Sue. He sits her down on a chair. She looks confused but keeps glancing back at the stairs. No doubt she would rather be with Savannah than here with everyone else.

"I'm here," Frank announces, bursting through the front door. He doesn't bother taking his boots off as he sits down on the couch.

"All right," Daniel addresses the room. "I'm making this short and sweet. The man who was killed on that tape wasn't Cole." The room is so quiet you'd think someone pressed a pause button. "When the body twists in the video, the man doesn't have a tattoo on his shoulder, and we all know Cole has his Special Forces one."

"Yeah, that's right," Paul chimes in. "So—"

"How confident are you it's not him?" Frank moves his attention over to Daniel.

"I've watched it two more times, and I'm one hundred percent confident the man on that tape is not my son."

Frank stands and pulls out his cell phone. "Good enough for me. Give me a minute." He heads for the kitchen.

"Dan?" Sue whispers from her chair. "I don't think we should say anything to Savannah until we know what we're dealing with. I don't think she can handle it." A tear slips down her cheek, and Mark's stomach twists tighter. "I don't think I could handle seeing her shatter the last piece that's holding her together."

Daniel walks across the room, taking his wife's hand

in his. "I agree, dear."

"You will go too." She stands stiffly, wrapping her sweater around her hunched body. She looks like she's barely holding on to her emotions.

"Yes."

She nods. "Go bring our son home." He reaches over and gives her a kiss on the cheek, then watches her move toward the stairs, the shock of the evening's events making her move like a zombie. Daniel sighs then turns to look at everyone just as Frank returns.

"All right, we have a possible location. We have two scouts watching the house. It's in a small town right outside Tijuana."

Dan steps forward, wiping his sweaty palms across his weathered face. "Since Paul is out, Keith will take his place and Mike will be in charge of the house." Derek begins to argue, but Daniel shakes his head, stopping him. "The team needs absolute trust, Derek. You've shown that you don't work well in a unit. Until you prove yourself, you're staying here." Derek leans back, muttering under his breath.

"I'll give you access to anything you need," Frank informs them. "I need this to be a quick extraction. Get him out of there before we start an even bigger goddamn war with those assholes, though I'm not opposed to lighting the whole place up on your way out." Frank rubs his face roughly. "Chopper will be here in thirty."

"Okay, men, let's move it," Daniel orders as everyone quickly scatters. "Frank, I need to see the blueprints for the house."

Abigail clears her throat. "What if—"

"No," Daniel whispers, looking grim, "no what if's."

She nods and gives Mark a quick hug. "Be careful, my boy." She kisses his cheek. "We're having prime rib."

Mark grins a little. "Well, in that case…" He stops

himself as the painful lump rises.

"I know, sweetie." She runs her hand along his cheek. "He's going to be okay."

"Yeah," he sighs, hoping to anyone who is listening to make his best friend be alive.

***

Savannah

I sit in Cole's tub and stare out the window. I can hear June and Sue whispering about something when Abigail comes into the bathroom. She shuts the door, then comes to sit in the leather chair across from me. It's two in the morning, and since my pathetic attempt at suicide failed I have everyone in the house awake.

"Are we going to have to put you in a padded room, Savi?" she asks, making my heart squeeze. "I know you're hurting; we all are, but don't bring more hurt to this family by ending your life." I pull my knees up to my chest and wrap my arms around them. She sighs then clears her throat. "I'm so sorry, Savannah, about the baby."

"Please," I swallow around a sob lodged in my throat, "don't."

She moves behind me and starts pouring warm water over my hair. We don't speak again as she washes my hair, dries me off, and then walks me down to the kitchen. I'm very aware of the atmosphere in the house, and I'm sure it's due to what I have done. The level of anxiety is like an elephant in the room.

We pass a couple of guys who quickly stop talking as we approach. They don't look at me. Daniel comes into the room looking like he's on a mission. I look away, but he wraps his arms around my shoulders, pulling me into him much like his son used to do. I fight like hell to stop my tears, but it's no use. They are always ready to break the dam that is made of frigging toothpicks.

"Some of us have been called out for an assignment," he says, pulling away to look at me. "Mike is in charge since Keith is filling in for Paul." He looks over at Abigail. "We shouldn't be any longer than forty-eight hours." He steps back and walks out of the room. I want to ask why he's going, but I concentrate on trying to stop my annoying crying instead. I cried like crazy over my mother's death, but this is a different kind of loss. My heart is shattered forever, and I know that even though I did not end my life today I have no desire to go on.

"Savannah," Keith says as he slips onto the stool next to me, "will you be all right while I'm gone?" I nod, feeling very tired. He takes my chin in his hand "Savi, Mike is easy to talk to, and Derek will be hovering around more than normal. None of your disappearing acts, you hear me? Right now with The American—"

"I won't," I cut him off, pushing up from my stool. "Be safe," I whisper as I walk out into the living room and sit down in my favorite place in front of the fire. Scoot, the little shit housecat, comes immediately to me and rolls onto his back, flops his legs open, and purrs until I give him some attention. I let my mind wander, remembering sitting on the floor scratching Scoot when Cole first joined me. Cole rubbed his belly with the warmest smile. I wipe my cheeks. Lowering my head to the floor, I tune in to the crackle of the fire.

"Merry Christmas," I whisper as I kiss Scoot's furry head and slowly drift off to sleep.

***

Cole

Cole presses his mouth to the small hole in the wall,

attempting to suck in some fresh night air to clear his head. His wrists are handcuffed to the water pipe. They're rubbed raw and blistering. His ankles are bound by ropes, and he's freezing because he is wearing only his army pants. They took his shoes and shirt right before the beating started.

His head flops back, resting on the cement wall. Savannah's sweet voice finds him, and he gets lost in his thoughts.

"Promise me you'll come back to me." Her dark eyes *are flooded with tears. It's against all Army and personal rules, but if this is what it takes to make the look go away, then he'll promise her the world.*

"I promise, baby." He wraps his arms around her. "I want to hold you." She nods as he takes her hand, walking down the path.

"It's so pretty through here," she whispers, trying to break the sadness of the situation. "The forest just goes for miles and miles. It's an endless path to who knows where." She clears her throat. "So much freedom." He squeezes her hand. "Have you ever just wanted to follow the moonlight?"

He glances over to see the moon is casting a trail deep into the forest. "I have thought of that, many times, actually." They both walk, deep in thought.

Suddenly she stops dead in her tracks. "Run away with me."

His lips curl up as he brings their joined hands to his mouth and kisses her fingers. "I'd love nothing more than to run away with you, Savannah. But running won't make what I do for a living go away. It's a part of me." He wipes a stray tear off her trembling chin, soaking up this moment with her. "I'm nothing without you." He leans down, catching her lips and kissing her softly. "And you, baby, are the best part of me."

Drawing her lip in between her teeth, she nods. Letting out a long breath, she turns to gather herself.

"You want to head back?" She slowly shakes her head. "What do you want to do?"

She steps over to the edge of the cliff, looking down at the house. She spreads her arms out as wide as they can go.

"I want to fly," she whispers.

Cole pulls out his radio, watching her head tilt to look up at the sky. "Mark, you there?"

"Roger." Mark laughs over the radio.

"I need you to get Mike to bring me something."

Several minutes later Mike appears off to the side. "Have fun." He winks before he runs back down the path.

Cole grins as he walks over to Savannah, who is still lost in thought.

"Your wish is granted." Her eyes open then drop to what Cole is holding. "You said you wanted to fly."

The smile that runs across her lips is the sweetest thing. He takes a minute to let it etch into his memory.

He points the wooden toboggan down a clear path and tugs Savannah between his legs.

"You ready?"

She wraps his arms around her waist. "Ready."

He pushes off, and they start to move and pick up speed. Savannah's laugh echoes off the mountains, making him laugh. She jumps up and offers him a hand. He takes it, pulling her back down on his lap.

Something runs across her face and a tiny smile appears. "I didn't think it was possible."

"What?" he asks, confused.

"Possible to love you even more than I do right now."

"Move!" Someone shouts, making Cole jump. Savannah seems unfazed by the man yelling. Her lips are

moving, but he can't hear her.

"Savannah?" he asks, nearly panicked. "What's going on?"

"Up!" the voice says again.

One minute he's with her, the next he's back in his room...

Men are shouting outside his door. He wipes the bead of sweat from his neck. A dream, a memory, a fantasy, whatever you want to call it, it's his and only his. They can't take that from him.

A voice makes his skin crawl as he turns and rests his back on the wall. Wincing from the cold, he slips back into another memory.

Everything changes once the video is made.

He is dragged into the room where a camera is pointing at a Mexican flag on the wall. He is positioned on his knees while the guy with the longhorn belt buckle, the one they call Raul, orders one of the men to leave. Moments later the man returns with a white guy in a Hawaiian print shirt and khakis. He drops him on the floor and nods at Raul. The guy looks either half dead or drugged.

Cole is trying to catch up when he sees Raul reaching for a machete. He can feel the blood drain from his face and swallows hard. A man comes over and inspects his neck, then does the same to the guy on the floor.

"Same," the man says to Raul.

"Good."

Than it hits Cole this is all being filmed, but why? He sees the red light go on, and they instruct Cole to stare into the camera. They turn on a bright light and aim it at him. He watches as Raul stands to his side and starts a speech. The camera travels down, and he sees the little red light go off. Someone grabs Cole and pulls him aside, shoving a pistol in his face. He watches in horror as they rip off the other man's shirt and hold him up.

"Not a word," the man warns, shaking the pistol at Cole.

The camera travels up Raul's waist then moves over to the man's neck, not showing any of his face. A moment later his throat is sliced open. Blood flies everywhere, including on Cole's arms and chest. The man turns and flops to the ground. The realization hits that this video is going to be seen by his family, but before he can even form another thought he's being dragged back into the closet and again handcuffed to the pipe.

He had heard The American come back, raging mad after hearing Raul made the video and sent it off without his knowledge. Clearly The American and Luka Donavan had nothing to do with the tape. In the days that followed, Cole had been driving himself crazy imagining all sorts of horrific scenarios of his family seeing what they thought was his beheading. He feels sick thinking of Savannah and her reaction to such a thing, let alone his parents.

Jerking awake after another terrible nightmare, Cole desperately runs his hands along the pipe to the ground and picks up the jug of water they threw at him the night before. He has been carefully sipping it, making sure he doesn't get sick by drinking it too fast. He winces as he moves, feeling the large open gash on his stomach. He knows it's probably getting infected in his filthy living conditions. Thankfully, they have been taking him outside to relieve himself. One time they didn't secure the blindfold properly, and Cole got a good look at his surroundings. He's been out enough times now to know what direction to head when he finally makes his move.

The door opens and The American steps inside the

room, turning on the overhead light. He chucks a protein bar at Cole, and as he fumbles with numb fingers to pick it up, he sees it's one from the vest he was wearing the night they raided the house. Cole's stomach sinks as he realizes they went through his gear.

"So," The American says, smiling. "I'm gathering it just clicked for you that we found this," he holds up the picture, "tucked in the lining of your vest. Isn't there some rule that you're not supposed to carry anything that can lead us to your loved ones?" Cole jaw tightens as he glances at the picture of Savannah. "So Luka was right," he nods, "you're in love with the girl too." He smirks, glancing at the photo as his thumb brushes over her face. "What an interesting turn of events." He checks his watch then stands, studying Cole for a moment, then turns off the light and leaves.

Fuck me.

***

"Up!" a man yells at Cole, thinking he's asleep. In fact, he was listening to the background sounds to see if other men are around. All is quiet.

Perfect.

The man kicks him in the leg. "I said up!" Cole's eyes slowly open.

The guy leans over and fumbles with the key to unlock the cuffs. His eyes are dilated and he looks strung out on something. Cole waits patiently while the man releases him. He needs to see if anyone is in the house. The man is so out of it he forgets to blindfold him, and Cole watches where he puts the cuff key after he links his other wrist. "Out." The man nudges him between his shoulder blades with his rifle.

He keeps his head down but notices two guys just as high nearly passed out on the couch, along with a tray

334

lined with cocaine in front of them. One man looks over at them and grunts something about how it isn't the time to let the *gringo* out yet, but the man just urges Cole to keep moving. Cole peeks at the time on the wall and learns it's just past midnight. Lots of darkness left to use to his advantage.

"Tree." The guy points to the nearest tree. "Hurry."

Cole nods then glances over the man's shoulder like he sees something. The guard turns quickly, and Cole wraps his arms around the man's neck and holds on tightly. Cole hooks his leg around the man's; holding him closer to his body he flexes with all his might finally feeling the pop he is waiting for. The guard goes limp and falls to the ground, slipping from his grasp. Cole quickly plucks the key from the guard's pocket, frees himself from the cuffs and tosses them into the shadows. He snags the gun and rolls the man into the brush, all the while watching the door for the two other men. They don't show. Just as he pushes off the man's body, he feels something square in his pocket. He pulls out a phone.

Perfect.

With the gun flung over his shoulder and the phone secure in his pocket, Cole runs into the thin wooded area and heads north toward the mountain where he can find high ground and good cover. He runs and runs and runs, letting the stars guide him. Breathing is everything; you need to control your breathing to keep your heart rate steady so you can run longer. Luckily for Cole, he has long legs which allow him to sprint through the brush. After about forty minutes of flat-out running, he slows, feeling pain deep inside his gut. He stops and holds onto a tree. His hands reach down and feel blood soaking the top of his pants. *Mind over matter.* What he needs is some clean water and a piece of clothing to wrap his midsection.

Something catches his attention off to his left, and he drops to the ground, swinging his gun in front of him and scanning the tree trunks. It's dark, and the woods are thick in some areas, but Cole can spot a panther stalking its prey before it can spot him.

A familiar whistle breaks through the silent night. It takes Cole a few moments to recognize the tone. He squints when he hears it again.

"Raven One," a male voice calls out in perfect English, "I'm a scout for Eagle Eye One."

Holy shit, he's a fucking scout for Frank!

"Name?" Cole calls out, still keeping his gun raised.

"Staff Sergeant Mills, Colonel."

"Show yourself." There's a rustling sound, then a man dressed in dark clothes appears, holding his hands up. Cole grips the gun tightly but lowers it as soon as he sees the man lift his shirt, showing a U.S. Army tattoo confirming which unit he's in. He's definitely part of Frank's team. "You alone, Mills?" Cole asks, allowing himself to sag against the tree.

"No, sir. Sergeant Hahn is on high ground while I came down here to find you."

"You were watching the house?"

"Yes, sir." Mills nods and comes closer as he checks the time.

"You expecting someone?"

"Yes, sir. Blackstone is on their way."

"Wait," Cole says, shifting his weight. "Blackstone is on their way here?" Mills nods. "When?"

"Should be arriving in twenty."

Well, fuck me sideways.

"Let me see your radio, Mills." Mills hands it to him, saying they're on channel six. Cole holds it to his mouth and clicks the button. "Blackstone One to Blackstone Two; do you copy?" Seven long seconds go by before he hears him.

"Blackstone Two to Blackstone One; your voice never sounded so sweet, brother." Cole grins at Mark's comment. "Meet at Eagle Eye Three's lookout point."

"Copy that, Blackstone Two, meeting at Eagle Eye Three's lookout point." He hands his radio to Mills and nods toward the trees. "Lead the way."

"Yes, sir." Mills hesitates then reaches into his pants pocket, handing Cole a small pill in a plastic wrap. Cole shakes his head, not needing anything to cloud his judgment until he's back on U.S. soil. They head toward the mountains until halfway up Cole pulls Mills to the ground. A spotlight swipes the edge of the mountain; Cole spots it coming from a Land Rover about two miles from them. He signals for Mills to hand him his radio and clicks the button several times until he hears clicking back. He slips the radio in his pocket and cautions Mills to stay low but keep moving. They reach the top just as he hears the chopper blades off in the distance and his radio clicking Morse code at him. It's Mark wondering if they still have company. He clicks back confirming they're several hundred yards behind them and to be prepared.

Mills slides between two rocks and into a small hole which offers a panoramic view of where Cole had been held captive. He removes a small box of rations, water, a blanket, and his duffel bag.

Eying up Mill's duffel, Cole looks at him. "How long have you been here, Mills?"

"A week, sir. We got word someone was being held down there, so Frank had us watching the house. Hahn and I thought it was you, but given the video, we figured it must be someone else. We didn't say anything. We had to be sure it was you before we could report to Eagle Eye One." Mills cocks his machine gun, getting ready to fire. "The day they took you outside without your shirt, we were able to confirm it was you." Mills nods to

Cole's tattoo. "Your ink was a dead giveaway." He hands Cole another gun, then motions to head back out into the open.

The chopper is just landing as they come to the clearing. Mills moves over the edge and signals the Cartels are close. Cole nods to the chopper when Mills is suddenly flung backward from the force of two bullets to the side of his torso. Cole leaps forward, grabbing Mills by his arms and pulling him back toward the chopper as it lands. Mark suddenly appears at his side.

"We have to go!" Mark shouts, clutching Mill's other arm and helping Cole pull him inside the chopper.

"We need to pick up the other scout!" Cole yells as they signal the chopper to leave.

"It's too risky!"

"The other scout!" Cole commands, catching a glimpse of his father. They exchange a look.

"The other scout," Daniel calls out to the pilot. He gives Cole a tight smile, then drops his gaze to Cole's bloody midsection. "You all right, son?"

"Yeah." Cole reaches out and grabs his father's shoulder, giving it a light squeeze. The pilot radios to Frank and gets Hahn's coordinates. In minutes they are landing to pick up Hahn. He hops in and immediately leans over Mills, who is holding his hand over one of the wounds. He looks at Keith and gives him a slight nod, thanking him for looking after his partner till he got there.

"Hit it!" Cole's voice rings through the chopper and makes everyone jump to positions. Immediately three small bombs hit the house where Cole had been held.

Cole leans back into the seat, finally letting the pain sink in. Mark crawls over and has a look at Cole's cut.

"This is a bad one, Cole." He sees Mark glance at his father. He nods, knowing he'll need staples and some seriously strong antibiotics. His eyelids feel heavy and he slowly drifts off.

Cole barely remembers being lifted out of the chopper. He has only a vague recall of the doctor telling him what needed to be done and of getting the staples across his torso. He was told he had a cracked skull and therefore a concussion. He welcomed sleep when it came, bringing with it dreams of holding Savannah.

I kept my promise, baby.

Chapter Two

Cole swings his feet so they dangle over the edge of the bed and attempts to get up. He's been in this private hospital room in North Dakota for two days, and it's been long enough. His torso still burns like hell and his head feels like someone is in there enjoying themselves by smashing his skull relentlessly with a sledgehammer, but he knows he needs to get up and get moving.

"Whoa...!" The spunky little redheaded nurse holds up her hands, coming into the room. "Where do you think you're going, big boy?" He's known Molly for a few years now; this is where the guys come if they need medical attention when they're injured. They have to get clearance to go back to the house. She may be a sweet woman, but she has a will of iron, so he knows he has to tread lightly.

"I need to go, Molly. I've been here long enough and I feel a lot better." He reaches for his shirt, slipping it over his head with a grunt.

Her hands go to her hips. "I haven't cleared you yet."

"So clear me."

"Cole, you know I can't do that. We're still worried about your head."

"Head's fine."

"Cole," she scolds him.

Frustrated, Cole argues. "Molly, you can either clear me or make my day shitty by having me fill out more paperwork than I already have, but either way I'm leaving."

She sighs and studies him then smiles tightly. "Give me ten minutes."

The door swings open and Cole's father walks in holding two coffees.

"Maybe you can convince him to stay," Molly grumbles as she leaves the room.

Cole shakes his head. "Don't even start, Dad. I need to get home."

Daniel hands Cole his coffee and sits in a chair watching him struggle to pull on his pants. "I agree we should get you home."

Something in his voice causes Cole to stop his attempt to button his fly, and he looks at his father. "What happened? Is Savannah all right? Is she hurt?"

Daniel takes a deep breath and runs his finger along the rim of his cup before turning back with a tired look. "We thought she was asleep in her room, but she came down when we were looking at the tape."

"Fuck." Cole rubs his aching head as he slowly sits down, letting that piece of knowledge sink in along with the memory of the poor guy who was unlucky enough to be his double in the video.

"Yeah, it was, ahhhh…" Daniel clears his throat. "A lot has happened since you've been gone. If you're feeling well enough, I think we should get you back. Damage control is going to take some time. She has been through a terrible shock."

Cole sighs then winces from the pain. "Does she know I'm all right?"

"We thought it was best not to say anything until we physically got you home. We didn't want to add any more ups and downs to the emotional rollercoaster she's already on."

"I feel like you're not telling me everything, Dad. You've never lied to me before, so please don't start now."

Daniel leans forward and rests his elbows on his knees. "No, son, I'm not lying. There are just some things that aren't my place to discuss with you."

Cole watches his father for a moment, seeing something like pain flash over his face. It doesn't take much to figure out that something is up, and it isn't good. It has his stomach in a knot. "Just tell me, is she all right?"

"Yes, she's all right," his father says, standing up, "but there are so many questions that need answers, Cole. First we need to get you out of here. While we're waiting for Molly to get your clearance, you need to call your mother." He hands a cell phone to Cole.

"Yeah," Cole takes the phone, "of course."

"I'll be right outside."

Cole dials and tries to think about what to say.

"Daniel?" His mother's worried voice rings through the phone.

Tears threaten Cole's eyes as he takes in a deep breath and speaks. "Mom?" There is the longest pause, then a quiet sob on the other end.

"Oh, honey," she manages to get out.

"I'm okay, Mom, truly. A few bangs and scrapes, but all things considered, I'm fine. Dad is here with me and we're heading out shortly. We should be home by late tonight."

"All right, son, I…" Her voice shakes.

"Mom, please don't tell Savi that I'm coming. Dad's right to keep it quiet…just until I make it back. Some things happened while I was gone and—"

"Of course, honey, I agree. She has been through so much…" She starts crying again. "Get Dad to call me later to give me a better idea of your arrival time. I love you, Cole, so very much."

"I love you too, Mom. I'll see you soon." He wants to talk to Savannah, to tell her he's alive and okay, but something tells him that he should have her in his arms first, just in case. He feels torn, but with the way his parents are acting, he knows things aren't right.

"Well, you look like shit." Mark grins, bursting into the room in typical Mark style. *God, he missed him.* "You ready to go, or are you going to fake your injury some more? Molly's a hot little number, hey?"

"Really?" Cole rolls his eyes while Mark tosses him a piece of gum. He doesn't think before popping it in his mouth until his tongue is invaded with a nasty taste. "Oh shit!"

"What?" Mark shrugs, looking positively delighted that he got Cole to eat it. "It's called Cool Cola." Cole makes a face and spits it into the trash. "You now owe me two pieces of Hubba Bubba, dude."

"Yech." He reaches for his water, swirling it around his mouth trying to relieve his taste buds.

Mark laughs. "Come on, the chopper is waiting. It will take us to the mountains, then we'll drive the rest of the way. Changing it up, just in case."

"Good plan."

***

Savannah

I notice Sue's mood has changed from this morning. She has actually eaten a whole meal, seems to be interacting with people, and her usual demeanor of looking like she's off in space is replaced by someone more like she used to be. *Lucky her.* I, on the other hand, feel like an empty shell. I try hard to act somewhat

343

normal just so people will stop hovering over me. I feel like I did when I first arrived at the house—completely out of place, full of pain and not sure where I belong. I pick up my untouched plate and place it on the counter. I can feel Abigail and June watching me. I turn toward the hallway and make my way to the front door, shrugging into my coat and boots and heading outside.

It's lightly snowing and everything is silent. As expected, the front door opens and closes and I hear footsteps behind me.

Please, go away.

"I just need a minute, Derek,"

I'm so tired.

"First, don't ever refer to me as *that* selfish ass," Mike says, approaching me. "And second, I just wanted to go for some fresh air too." I roll my eyes, but I find his company welcome. Mike has been busy the last two days hiding away in Cole's—his office. Oh god, even thinking his name makes me shake and want to curse at the sky. I really am losing it.

"He's not that bad, you know," I whisper as we make our way through the fluffy snow.

"Who, Derek?"

"Yes." I nod. "Derek has been friendly and respectful."

"Well, that's good," Mike says with mild sarcasm. I let it go, too tired to take it on.

"Let's go this way." He points toward my favorite spot up in the mountains.

"Sure." I follow mindlessly, my boots crunching in the snow. It used to be one of my favorite sounds, but now, not so much.

"I know it's late, and it's the last thing you ever want to talk about, but I'm sorry about your baby, Savi."

I feel like I've just taken a punch to my stomach, but I manage to hold it together. "Thanks, Mike," I whisper, truly knowing he's a good friend. I let my mind wander as we reach the top and look over the beautiful landscape. I let out a long, shaky breath. "Our baby was the only little bit I had left of Cole." I swallow around the lump in my throat. "It's all my fault it didn't live." Mike's arm wraps around my shoulder. "It was the only thing I had left, Mike." I start to cry quietly as he holds me. He removes his arm, checking the time on his watch.

"No, it's not," he whispers.

I wiggle his arm off me. "I don't want to hear about having faith and God does things for a reason. God does mean, cruel things sometimes—" I feel my anger rise and am about to take my hurt out on my friend when I hear an engine and see a pair of headlights coming our way. The guys must be back from their latest mission.

"Sorry, Savannah, you won't get a speech from me. I don't believe in God." Mike smiles. "I believe in karma and the big bang."

"Good," I respond, but his growing grin is making me uneasy. The SUV pulls up and Mike starts walking toward it.

"Come on, Savi, let's greet the guys. I'm sure they've had a tough trip."

"Yeah, just give me a minute." I wipe my cold face free of tears. God, I am sick of crying! I stick my icy hands in my jacket pockets and try to get my head clear. The last thing the guys need to see is 'fragile Savannah' right now. I turn on my heel take a step forward and stop dead in my tracks.

What?

Cole is standing a few feet from me wearing a black jacket, a hat, and army pants. I shake my head in disbelief, reminding myself to breathe. It can't be…

"Savannah," he whispers, giving me a half smile. I look over at the guys, who are all grinning like fools.

Cole starts toward me. I notice he has a small limp, I see his face, his unsure smile—it feels surreal. I can't move.

"But I watched you die," I whisper as he reaches out and cups my face. His hands feel so warm. "I'm dreaming." I start to sob. "This is a fucking dream, this is cruel." I start to panic, as I've experienced moments over the last few days where I could almost believe none of it had happened, only to realize with dread that it had.

"No, baby," he leans in, "this is fucking real." He smashes his lips to mine, making me feel him. I reach around his neck and deepen the kiss, just wanting to feel something, even if only for a moment. His thumb brushes away my tears as he slowly pulls back, and I see tears in his eyes as well. "Hi, baby." My hands move through his hair, over his face, down to his shoulders. I let out a giddy laugh, but it gets caught in my throat. I shake my head, not sure what to say as the shock begins taper slightly, so I go with the obvious.

"Hi," I say back. "How?"

He shakes his head, staring deep into my eyes as if *I'm* not real.

"Let's get inside and I'll tell you everything, okay?" He winces when he lowers his arms.

"Are you all right?" I step back, inspecting him. He is obviously in pain, but he looks intact.

"I am now." He takes my hand, threading his fingers through mine. He raises them to his mouth, kissing our joined hands. Tears stream down my face as I take in that he's actually standing right here in front of me. My Cole, my love, my reason for living is back.

We walk in silence, and the guys follow behind us. His hand continues to squeeze mine. I have no idea what to say or what to think, but I can feel my heart thawing just a little.

Sue flies out the door. I let go of his hand as she wraps her arms around her son. She is crying happy tears. Abigail and June do the same, all taking their turn to ensure he's alive and well. I step back a few steps, feeling so confused. I bump into Daniel, who smiles down at me as he gives me a side hug.

"It's just shock, honey. You'll come around soon. Give yourself a moment to let it sink in."

I turn away from everyone as I gather myself for like the eighth time today. Lord, what I wouldn't do to have a handle on my emotions. I feel his hand find mine again, and I turn and see him looking down at me with a questioning expression.

"Don't let go again, okay?" He gives me a tug toward him, kissing my forehead as he leads me into the house.

We all gather together in the living room to celebrate his return, everyone laughing and talking. I can't seem to pull myself out of the shock and sadness that still has a firm hold on me. What's wrong with me? I should be ecstatic, but instead I'm swimming with a hundred different emotions. I try to interact with everyone. Mark hands me his special Marcus Martini. I take it and thank him, but I just stare at it.

"Okay, honey, let's hear the story," Sue says after everyone has quieted down. "I need to know, as I'm sure everyone else does."

Cole nods then takes a long sip of his beloved brandy and squeezes my hand. "Let's see, the last thing I can remember is keeping watch as the guys left the house. We needed to get out of there. Mark and Paul needed a medic. I must have been hit on the back of the head. I woke to someone taking an electric—" He stops himself and looks at me. "They roughed me up a bit, wanting to get the location of the house. They kept me handcuffed to a pipe in a small room, fed me just enough to hold on. This went on for a while until The American showed up. We had some words, and finally he got tired of me not answering his questions. The days kind of mesh together, but mostly they just pumped me for information. One night The American left the house, and that's when the video was made by a man named Raul."

I start to shake. I feel it start in my legs then travel up my spine through my arms and hands, and my teeth start to chatter. I sit my untouched drink down since it's spilling over my hand. Keith catches my eye, but I pretend not to notice.

"So if that wasn't you on the tape," Paul says, squinting like he's not really sure he wants to know, "who was it?"

I feel Cole's grip tighten. "They had a guy already drugged. His build was similar to mine. I don't know who the poor bastard was, but we need to find out to let his family know. They obviously didn't plan it well, as they didn't catch my tattoo." Cole bends his head down, breathing deeply. "It's an understatement to say that was a pretty bad day."

"Yeah, it was." Mark looks over at me. I quickly wipe a tear away, shaking my head at him.

Cole looks down at me, then at everyone in the room. "Look, everyone, thanks. I'll fill you in more tomorrow, but right now I need some time with Savannah, and we all need sleep." He stands and pulls me up with him.

When we reach the bedroom, he takes in the couch that's made up like a bed against the wall and looks at me.

"Keith," I whisper, moving to the bathroom and attempting to tuck my feelings away. Once I'm washed and ready for bed, I head back out and see Cole sitting on the edge of the bed, staring at me. He holds out his hand, reaching for mine. He pulls me between his legs and looks up into my eyes. My heart squeezes when I think about how I almost ended my life, thinking he was gone forever.

"I know this is really confusing, and it kills me to

realize you saw that tape, but I'm here, and I'm fine." I swallow hard, needing to be strong. I run my hands through his hair.

"You kept your promise," I say through a tight throat.

His mouth curls up and his eyes crinkle. "A promise is a promise." He frowns when he studies my face. "What happened while I was gone?" I try, I really do, to get the words off my tongue, but I stay silent. Instead I reach for the hem of his shirt until his hands stop mine. "Savannah, please." I shake my head no, and he doesn't push...yet.

I hear him flinch as he raises his arms over his head, and a moment later I see why. My hands fly over my mouth as I gasp. A huge bandage is wrapped around his mid-section.

"You're hurt!"

"I'm all right," he hisses. "I'm just exhausted."

"No, you're not all right." I carefully stand him up. Undoing his pants, I help him lie back on the bed and crawl up by his head. I lean against the massive headboard as he shifts to rest his head on my legs.

"What was it like?" I ask, wanting to compare what he went through with what I had.

He sighs and closes his eyes. "Frustrating not being able to defend myself physically. It was all mental, but thankfully I had something to focus on." His hand slides over my thigh. "I think the hardest part was knowing I was alive but you all didn't."

"Yeah," is all I can say. The lump in my throat has returned.

I run my fingers through his silky hair methodically until I hear his breathing become even. My mind is running a marathon, but I cannot make sense of any of it yet. I'm still off on the sidelines of it all, too exhausted to even try. I glance at the clock and see it's two in the morning. Unable to settle yet, I slip Cole gently off my lap, slide off the bed, and head downstairs.

I lean back on the cool bricks after lighting the fireplace in the living room, set a large glass of brandy in front of me and try to take a sip, but my stomach rejects the liquor. Everything becomes a blur as my eyes fill and tears spill over my cheeks. I rest the tiny teddy on my lap like one would do with a child and cling to the little silver frame wishing with all my heart I had listened when people told me to calm down. How could I be so blind? So selfish? I killed our baby.

"It's not your fault."

My head snaps up, and I find Keith watching me from the kitchen. He comes over and takes a seat next to me. I shift so he has some room.

"Yes, it is." I sniff, swimming in a sea of emotions. "All of this is my fault, but the fact that I lost—" I shake my head and try to clear the terrible images flickering in front of me. "To top it off, I had a—" I can't say the word so I skip over it, "to my head and almost—"

"You had what to your head?" Both Keith and I jump at the sound of Cole's husky voice. I slowly look over, seeing him standing there in his sweat pants, bare feet, and nothing else. His face looks angry and confused as he takes a few steps toward us. "Someone better tell me what the hell happened while I was gone."

Keith reaches over and squeezes my shoulder as he stands up, nodding at Cole. Cole takes his seat and watches me closely. I take a deep breath through my nose, knowing this is the moment when I have to break his heart, as mine is broken, to tell him what we had and then lost—our child.

"What's that?" He points at the teddy his father gave me. I hand it to him and watch his eyes roll over the little name stitched into its army jacket. His gaze flicks up to me, making my lip tremble. I slowly turn the small frame around and show him the ultrasound picture. "Are you…?" He looks at my stomach.

"Was," I correct him through streaming hot tears. "I was five weeks till the day the video arrived." His eyes widen then drop slowly and he shakes his head. He then covers his mouth with one hand.

I want to scream, sob, and run away from all of this pain. I can see I'm about to break him, by chipping away a piece of an already battered soul. It's just not right. *So much of me is shattered.*

"I'm so sorry, Cole."

His red glossy eyes shoot up to mine. "No, no." He kneels down in front of me, holding my hands. "No, baby, *I'm* so sorry you went through all of this without me. I-I…" His voice catches. "I can't believe you were pregnant with our baby."

Here it goes.

I pull back to look at him. "I don't know how you feel about this, but I was going to keep it."

"No," he wipes my cheeks dry and moves to sit next to me, "*we* were going to keep it." My heart swells as I fill him in on all the details, like how Sue and Daniel were the only ones to know, then Keith because I wanted him to keep my secret until he returned safely. I take him through the moments when I miscarried, sobbing quietly as I share the details with him. The whole time he holds me tightly, giving my head light kisses. Then we sit in silence for a while, grieving together. His sobs are hard to hear, but he needs to let it out. It's hard seeing someone who is normally so strong crumble in front of you.

Suddenly he stops moving. "What did you have held to your head?" I try to move, but his grip won't let me.

"I—I found your gun behind your night table." His entire body starts to vibrate, and I spit out the words in fear I won't be able to finish. "I lost you, I lost our baby, and I still don't know who's behind my kidnapping. I

351

had no reason to live. I just wanted to be with my family." The words are falling out of my mouth with no filter. "Then Keith's cell phone rang, and I hesitated, and he saw me. He...he talked to me, helped me off the ledge." I just keep talking as Cole's eyes bore into me. "It was a pretty dark time, Cole, the darkest I've ever been." I shift to look up at him. His eyes are squeezed shut now, and I move to kiss his jaw. "I won't say I'm sorry about it, Cole, because I didn't know you were alive, and if I am to be honest with myself, I think I would have tried again. But now you're here, but the baby isn't, and I'm trying to tell myself it wasn't meant to be, but it still hurts." The painful lump grows larger. "It hurts so damn bad, but having you back makes me see we can get through this if we—"

He suddenly leans forward, capturing my mouth with his. I know the drive behind the kiss is fear, so I follow, letting him take the lead. He needs to feel in control, and I'm willing to hand over the reins. I am too emotionally exhausted to be strong right now.

"Come back to bed," he whispers. "I need to hold you."

He leads us upstairs and we climb into bed. I shift carefully so as not to hurt his staples, and wrap my arm over his chest and my leg over his waist. I burrow my face in his neck, and it starts to sink in that he is really back. I feel his chest rise and fall, and with a deep sigh his fingers find mine, entwining them.

"Do you hurt?" he asks in a tight voice.

"Not in the way you're thinking."

Just my heart.

I hear him swallow loudly and clear his throat. I know it is all hitting him now. We lie tangled, letting each be strong for the other while we take turns to grieve.

"I love you, Savannah," he whispers.

"I love you too, Cole."

Chapter Three

Cole

Cole wakes to an empty bed, noticing Savannah laid out his painkillers and a bottle of water for him. He downs the two pills and heads for a much-needed shower. It takes him longer than normal to get dressed, which is annoying as he also has to change the dressing on his staples. The cut is healing well and the infection is gone; he just has to wait a week before he can get the staples pulled. He makes his way downstairs and into the kitchen where Abigail is baking something and talking quietly to his mother.

"How'd you sleep, dear?" his mother asks him, giving him a kiss on the cheek. She looks him over silently, probably to satisfy herself that he is really here and in one piece.

"Fine." He yawns and reaches for the coffee.

Keith enters the kitchen and comes up next to Cole, looking out the window.

"Thanks, Keith," Cole says quietly, "for taking care of her when I couldn't and for stopping her—"

"Don't thank me. Savi is like a sister. I'm just glad you're back."

Speaking of her... "Do you know where she is?"

"Dr. Roberts."

"Really?" Abigail and Sue both say at the same time.

"Yeah, I know." Keith turns to them.

Cole looks around the room, seeing their faces. "Why are we surprised?"

Sue shakes her head. "She stopped the sessions after we found out you were...gone. I guess she just needed some time to sort things out on her own."

Cole leans back against the island, feeling beat even though he just got up. He checks the time, as he has a meeting with the guys in his office in fifteen. His stomach flutters when he hears her voice down the hallway.

"It's therapeutic, Savannah," he hears Dr. Roberts say. "Sometimes things that used to bring you comfort can still help you heal new wounds and old wounds too."

"Maybe," she sniffs. "It's just it makes me think of him, and it's hard to know where to place those feelings right now."

"I understand and that makes perfect sense. Try to pull from the old happy memories. You need to find a release, and this sounds like a perfect way to do it."

"I prefer Mark's way better," she huffs, rounding the corner.

"You'll get the poor guy fired, if Logan finds out." Dr. Roberts smiles when he sees everyone staring at them as they enter the kitchen. "Hi, Cole, it's great to see you looking well." He extends his hand for a shake. Before Cole leans back, he reaches for Savannah and guides her to his side, needing her to ground him. She nuzzles and molds herself to him.

"How was the session?" Cole asks.

"Good." Dr. Roberts smiles at Savannah. "But I'm sorry, I must get going."

"I'll walk you out." Abigail jumps to her feet.

Cole leans down and kisses Savannah on her head. "I

have a video conference, but will you come see me afterward?"

"Sure." She gives him a smile, but he can see she is raw from her session. She leans up and gives him a kiss.

"Oh, Savannah," Abigail holds up a spoon full of cookie dough, "can you taste this? Something's missing."

Savannah's face goes funny as she moves to Abigail's side. She runs her fingers delicately over the top of the red Mixmaster.

"Something wrong, dear?"

"My mother," she whispers through a tiny smile, "she used to have one just like this. Cherry red." Her eyes light up. "I haven't seen one in years."

Abigail kisses her cheek, making Savannah notice everyone is staring at her. She takes the spoon and tastes the dough. "A pinch of cocoa powder."

"That's it!" Abigail shouts, giving her a hug. "Maybe I should leave the baking to you."

Cole smiles at the interaction between Savannah and Abigail, and leaves the kitchen to head to the conference room.

"How's the…?" Mark points to his side as he takes a seat at a large table in a conference room downstairs.

"Annoying," Cole grunts out, feeling the burn from within his deep cut.

"I bet it is." He winks. Classic Mark, he's always thinking about food or getting laid.

Guess that's not such a bad obsession.

Daniel, Keith, Paul, and John take their seats around the table while Cole fires up his laptop and gets Frank on the conference call. His face flashes on the large screen on the wall, and Cole centers the microphone between them.

"Logan, good to have you back." Frank nods as he rustles some papers on his desk.

"Good to be back. How is Mills doing?"

"All things considered, he'll be just fine. Has a long road to recovery, though."

Cole spends the next hour going over every detail of what happened. Meanwhile, Frank is emailing his snapshots of the two main men were who were helping The American, and one recent one of Luka Donavan, still in Mexico.

"Strange that he's still there," Cole says, leaning back in his seat. "I would have thought he'd be hightailing it back to New York to warn the mayor I'm gone. They know they screwed up by telling their dirty little secret." All the men look at Cole, clearly wondering what he's referring to. "Luka and Lynn," he explains, "her best friend and family friend, are the two who are behind this whole shit storm."

"What?" Mark nearly chokes on his coffee. "You mean to tell me that Savannah's only real family, the woman she talks about all the time, is behind her kidnapping?"

"Yes." Cole nods. "Not only was she behind it, but she hired a guy to pose as a potential client for the company to take Savannah out and to get her home at the right time for those savages to take her."

"What about her father?" Frank asks, fishing for a lead. "Anything there?"

"According to Donavan, when her father got word she had been kidnapped and Luka was behind it, he decided his little pistol was better off staying with *Los Sirvientes Del Diablo* than to be there with him getting in his way." Cole makes a face. "He is up for reelection, and with his daughter being kidnapped his votes skyrocketed. He knew she was eventually going to be killed, and dear old Dad did nothing about it. He completely wrote her off."

"This is insane," Keith mutters, getting up from his

chair. "How do you tell her something like this?"

"You don't," Frank says, moving toward the camera. "Until we have proof of this, Savannah is not going to hear about it. She's been through enough already."

Cole glances at his father, who is watching him. His father shakes his head, agreeing with Frank's decision.

Shit.

Cole drops his gaze, knowing it's best right now to keep quiet. She's been through too much.

Mark turns to Frank. "Okay, so what now?"

"Now, we start to dig."

***

Savannah

I lie down on the floor and shimmy myself under the branches of the Christmas tree. It was something I always did as a child, looking up at the lights and enjoying how they lit up the needles and made it look so pretty. It is a peaceful thing I haven't done in a long time.

Scoot finds me in a matter of seconds and jams up next to my side, purring for affection. His big brown eyes close as I rub his belly.

I take a deep breath through my nose and let the smell take me away to a childhood memory where my mother and I chopped off a few branches to make a door to the snow fort we had worked on all afternoon. Dad came out with a tray of hot chocolates with marshmallows, and we all crammed into the fort and enjoyed our snack.

I hear a click and bend my head to see who it is. I find Keith holding a camera and grinning at me. He kneels down and turns the camera around so I can see the picture. I laugh when I see Scoot's and my legs sticking out from the bottom of the tree.

"Now that's funny." He offers me a hand to stand. "Cole asked if I could find you to see if you'd join him for lunch. He's just finishing up some paperwork in his office."

"The man never stops, does he?"

"Nope."

Hearing my heels click on the wooden floor makes me shake my head. I didn't think I would be happy walking back to his office again. The door is already open, so I poke my head around and see him, arms crossed, standing in front of his huge floor to ceiling window. He looks powerful and strong, making me grin as I step further into the room. He's still here with me.

He must have heard me because he slowly turns and graces me with a smile that hits me right in the center of my heart. "I was beginning to think you stood me up," he teases.

"I was just admiring the view." I make my way over to him and tuck myself into his side. "What were you just thinking about?"

His grip tightens on my hip but he doesn't say anything for a moment then kisses my head and asks if I am hungry.

"I am." I give him a wink.

"First..." He laughs, heading over to his desk and pulling out a square, flat box. He comes back and hands it to me. "Merry Christmas."

I slide it out of his hands and pull at the bow. I peel back the top and my breathing nearly stops. "How did you get this?"

"I have my ways." He leans in and grants me a soft kiss on the cheek. I swallow hard as my fingers stroke the record signed by Flat Street Tony. The very record that used to hang on my living room wall. But even more surprising is what is under it. My chin begins quiver.

"Oh," I whisper.

"I hope it's okay that I—"

"*Yes*," I laugh through a sob, "this one was my favorites of us." My heart lodges in my throat as I hold the 8x10 photograph of my mother and me, when I was ten, at a carnival. "Thank you Cole, truly it means the world to me." I smile up at him, feeling my love for this man growing more and more. "I can't believe you were able to get these for me!"

"I'll do anything to put that smile on your face, baby."

"That I don't doubt."

We settle in on the couch and eat our lunch and make small talk, but I can sense he has something to tell me.

"I have to leave in three days," he finally blurts out.

My heart jumps out of my chest. I know it would run right out the door if it could, just to avoid any more pain. He must sense this, because his hands grab mine quickly.

"It's not what you think. Team Blackstone is going to help with a special training exercise for the Green Berets." I feel my body go slack, allowing my heart to slowly recover. "Normally we'd be heading to North Carolina to Camp Mackall, but due to the sheer volume of candidates this year, we're doing the training at Camp Green Water here in Montana."

"I didn't know you guys helped out with the training."

"We don't have to, but we volunteer our time. Plus I'm looking for a new recruit. Derek won't be staying on for much longer, and nothing is better than a fresh soldier I can mold."

"Derek is leaving?" I feel kind of sad. We have become friends over these last few weeks.

"No, not really." His eyes darken. "Frank has another position for him. He's a good solider, but he doesn't fit if he isn't trusted."

I want to argue but I decide against it. Cole makes logical decisions, so if Derek is to leave, it's for a good reason. "How long will you be gone?"

"Two weeks."

"Oh." My stomach twists.

He squeezes my hand. "I'm only going to be thirty minutes from here."

My eyebrows shoot up. "Really?"

"Yes, will you come visit me?"

"Can I?"

"Yes." He grins. "I don't want to go very long without seeing you, Savi."

I swallow hard, trying to sort out my nerves. "Me either."

***

"Six! Five! Four! Three! Two! One! *Happy New Year!*" everyone shouts, raising champagne flutes in the air.

I glance over and see Dr. Roberts sneak a quick kiss from Abigail. Mark sees it too. He rolls his eyes and looks away, muttering something about "that better be all he's expecting tonight."

I turn my attention to Cole, who has a wicked grin on his face. "Psssst," I whisper as I sit my glass down on the mantel and flick my finger in his direction. "This is the part where you kiss me."

He steps closer. "Then a kiss, Ms. Miller, you shall receive." He quickly grabs my head with one hand and the other runs up the length of my spine. With one fluid motion he dips and kisses me until I am breathless. My world tilts as his lips work magic, waking up every single nerve in my body. When he pulls away I realize everyone is clapping for us. I am thankful it is dark, because I feel my face turns at least three shades of red at that moment.

Cole chuckles as he pulls me to my feet.

"I didn't realize you were such a romantic, Colonel." That is a lie, but I can't think of anything else to say. I run my hand through my hair, taking a moment to calm myself. I pick up my glass and peer down into the empty flute. "Cole?"

"Yes?"

"Do you think you could help me with something?"

"Of course, what's up?"

"Can we speak in your office?" I start to walk.

He reaches for my hand and we head for his office. He punches in the code and lets me enter first.

"You want something from the bar?" he asks, walking over to pour himself a brandy.

"No." I pause by his desk and slip my dress off my shoulders, letting it fall to the floor. I step out and hop onto his desk, wearing a black and red lace bra, matching cheeky panties, and my black heels. "I had something else in mind."

"Oh, yeah, what's that?" he asks as he turns to look at me. His jaw drops as his eyes rake down me and a shameless grin spreads across his lips.

"You on top of me on your desk." I pat the surface then lean back and rest on my arms. "Come bang in the New Year, baby." I grin, feeling oddly bold, but that's what Cole does to me, and I love it.

In three strides he's in front of me with his shirt off, both hands on my knees, gazing down at me.

"How did I ever get so lucky?" he whispers. "Will I hurt you?"

I reach for his hand and pull him down so he is close to me. "Cole, I'm fine. You won't hurt me. Nothing was damaged there." I arch my breasts into his chest, reach for his belt buckle, and yank it open. "I need to feel you."

Cole stands up, pulling his pants down and kicking them out of the way. He reaches under my knees and pulls my butt to the end of the desk. He leans down and kisses my stomach up to my bra and stops at my neck.

"I will never tire of feeling your silky skin," he says between kisses. "I love the way you smell."

"Cole," I whisper as I run my hands across his strong back. My heartbeat is a hammer in my chest.

"The way you say my name is like it is made solely for your sweet lips."

I hear a ripping sound, and my panties sail over my head. I can feel him resting outside my opening; it is a maddening feeling.

"Co—"

He pushes gently into me, and the slow friction makes my head flop back and my back arch high.

"My sweet Savannah," his husky voice flows out across my chest, "you're like a dream I never want to wake up from."

He shifts so he is in deep, staring down at me. His eyes are incredibly dark and possessive. His lips brush over mine, muttering something I can't make out.

He leans back to stand, gripping my hips, and makes slow and sweet love to me, and the entire time his eyes stay locked with mine.

Chapter Four

Cole

Cole stands fully dressed in his gear, watching over sixty-three men low crawl through a sea of mud. It's cold inside the warehouse, but it doesn't matter. These men need to be able to handle anything thrown at them.

"There's been talk you're looking for a recruit."

"Major Anderson," Cole nods, "nice to see you again."

"You too, Colonel." He crosses his arms as he stands next to Cole. "Any men caught your attention?"

Cole smirks, not wanting it to be known that he is indeed looking. It's been five days of hell for these men. They've gotten maybe twenty-eight hours of sleep total.

"I have three if you're interested," Anderson says quietly. Cole doesn't bite; he continues to watch his own prospect. "Forty-three, eleven, and fifty-nine."

Cole scans the men's arms and finds the three Anderson pointed out. Fifty-nine is already on his radar. His name is Captain Terrance Roth, from Texas. He's thirty and one tough son of a bitch. He'd be perfect to work under Mike, since Cole wants Keith to join Blackstone. Keith has proven time and time again that he should be on Cole's team, but Cole never moved him because he always liked the way Keith ran the outside unit. But with the way he has taken care of Savannah since she came to the house, Keith is now guaranteed the spot. Cole just hopes he'll take it.

"On your backs," Cole orders. "Sit ups—go."

"Yes, Colonel," the men shout in unison.

Cole glances at Mark, who is on his phone. He is smiling, then quickly hangs up. After a hundred sit ups, Cole orders the men to stand in rows and pick up a long, thick log.

"You lift the log over your head, to your other shoulder and repeat this till I say otherwise," Cole instructs. "Do not move your head. Go."

Cole walks through the rows of men, making sure none of them is slacking on lifting their part of the weight. He stops in front of number thirty-four, who slumps to his knees.

"What's you problem, candidate?" Cole barks.

"Legs aren't working, sir."

"You need to see a medic?"

"No, sir."

"Then get back up and lift that log!" he demands. "You think it's fair for the rest of your team to carry the weight while you take a rest?"

"No, sir."

"Then move!"

The man squeezes his eyes as he tries to stand. He's finished; Cole can see it. "I can't."

"Are you VW?"

"Yes, sir."

"I need to hear you say it."

"I voluntary withdraw."

"Okay, thirty-four, head that way and give your name to Major Paul." He orders the rest of the men to lay the logs down.

Cole moves along the rows. "Drop and roll,

365

candidates." The men drop to the ground and roll all the way to one end of the pit, then roll back. Over and over again. He notices another man slowing down, holding the other men up.

He strolls over to his line. "If seven-eight can't keep up, roll over him," he shouts to the men who are enjoying the holdup. "Seven-eight, are you getting dizzy?"

"No, sir."

"Seven-eight, are you getting tired?"

"No, sir."

"Then why are you holding up your line?"

"Sorry, sir." He picks up his pace just a little. Cole nods to a medic to watch this one for vertigo.

Cole continues down the line of men. "This isn't for the weak, candidates. If you can't make it here, what makes you think you can make it out there?" His voice booms throughout the building. "You're part of a team, and if you forget you are a part of a team, then we will send you home. If you can't follow orders, we will send you home. If you don't pull your own weight, we will send you home. It's all mental, do you understand me?"

"Yes, Colonel!" they all yell out.

"Now on your feet. You have five minutes to get your gear and check the information outside."

"Colonel Logan," Major Paul yells, catching his attention from the men. "You have a visitor." Paul's face gives nothing away but he can probably see a ping of excitement spread through Cole. He nods, signaling for Mark Lopez to take over.

Cole briskly walks over to the main building. The cold air wipes his face, making his eyes sting. His stomach is in his throat as he opens the double doors and heads to the front desk.

"Hi, Colonel," the receptionist greets him. He nods outside with a little wink.

The moment he steps outside his eyes lock on to hers, and everything in his body comes alive. God, he loves this woman. A sexy smile runs across her lips then she breaks out in a full sprint, jumping into his arms and wrapping her legs around his waist.

"Hi, baby." She grins, her eyes sparkling with need.

"Hi." His voice is husky as he grips her body tighter around him. She wiggles, feeling how turned on he is. He's been deprived of her for five days, and he's been hard since he left her that night. He sees Keith grinning behind him before he waves goodbye.

"Is this allowed?" she asks suddenly, looking around at where they are. She tries to free herself from his grip, but he grabs her head, slamming her lips to his, just needing to taste her. She squeaks but gives in, running her hands through his hair and giving it a hard pull. "Cole," she pants, "your room now."

He drops her to the ground, takes her bag in one hand and her hand in the other, and beelines it to his room. Her laughter only makes him pick up the pace.

"Hey, Savi." Mark grins from the stairway, blocking his path to his release.

"Move," Cole grunts. *I need this woman under me now.*

Mark's eyes light up. He fucking knows what he's doing. "So, Savi, how has it been—?"

"Move, Mark." Savannah laughs, shoving him out of the way and leading Cole to his bedroom.

Cole turns over his shoulder. "Cover my next shift."

"Yeah." He chuckles and goes to leave, but not before he calls out, "Don't break any furniture."

"No promises," Savi whispers, stopping at the top of the stairs. She looks up at him and licks her lips. "It's been like a hundred and twenty-three hours since I've seen you. I almost forget what you feel like."

"In that case, let me remind you." Cole unlocks the

door and barely has it shut when he grabs her and pushes her up against the wall. His knee is between her legs, holding her in place as he yanks off his shirt and unbuckles his belt. She manages to remove her shirt in record time too. He removes her pants and panties just as she grips his shoulders and jumps up wrapping her legs around his waist.

"I've missed you." She giggles as his grin grows wider.

"Let me show you how much I have. Shower with me?" he asks as she nods, running her hands through his hair and giving it a small tug. He growls as he walks them into the bathroom.

She yelps as he places her on the cold counter. "Sorry." He laughs as he tugs his pants off and starts the water.

Her gaze drops to his erection and she lets out a hungry moan. "You can make it up to me."

"I intend to, a few times." He grips the back of her knees and tugs her forward, and his fingers slip inside her easily. "Mmm, you were ready for me." He groans as he pushes his fingers in further, feeling her velvet insides squeeze around him.

"I'm always ready when it comes to you, Cole." She flops her head against his chest. "Please, I need you."

He pulls his hand away and lines himself up with her. He nudges the tip inside, relishing how tight she is.

"Oh, baby," he whispers as he slowly makes his way into her. Yes, this is his Atlantis. He feels her breath blow out across his skin; everything feels so intense when they are like this. So raw and primal.

"Remind me." She wraps her legs around his waist, pulling him deeper. Her hands reach for his dog tags and guide him to her lips.

Cole clutches her waist and lifts her off the counter and steps into the shower. He pulls out and turns her around, pressing her into the wet tile. He grabs his solid erection and spreads her legs to make room for him. He slides back in, pressing his front into her back. He raises her arms above her head, entwining their fingers together. He thrusts forward hard, making her shoot up the tile, and her scream only fuels him further. His hips continue to thrust as he spreads kisses down her neck and shoulders.

"Cole," she moans, leaning her head back on his shoulder. "Yes."

"Who do you belong to, baby?"

"You," she replies without missing a beat. "I belong to you."

"Hell, yeah, you do," he pants as he plows into her. His hands are everywhere; he needs to touch every inch of her. Her little sounds lead him in a path that she desires. "I love you so damn much." This pushes her over the edge. She screams and shakes in his arms, and he comes right afterward, pumping her full of five days' worth of pent-up stress.

She turns to face him and reaches for his neck, her eyes sparkling. "I love you too, Cole, so much it hurts sometimes."

He kisses the tip of her nose before he washes her off and wraps her in a towel then does the same to himself. They lie naked in bed watching the sun slowly set.

"You hungry?" he asks, fingering her damp hair. "Dinner will be served in twenty."

She pushes at his chest, forcing him to lie back, and crawls up on his lap. "That should be enough time for what I have in mind."

Thirty-five minutes later they walk out of his room and down to the dining hall.

***

Savannah

I smile up at him as we walk down the stairs, feeling very satisfied. "I have to admit this uniform is incredibly sexy."

"The green makes my eyes pop," he jokes, making me laugh.

"Are you going to be all scary when you're with the men?"

"Not unless they step out of line." He peers down at me. "This is the last hurdle for making the cut for Green Berets, Savannah. We're here to see if they have what it takes. We yell, but it's nothing they can't handle. A lot of these men have been in the Army for a long time, and those who haven't will learn quickly enough."

"I guess." I sigh, thinking the Army would be no place for me. "So have you found anyone you like yet?"

"A few, but there's one in particular I've been watching."

"Who?"

"Fifty-nine."

"Does he not have a name?"

"Not here, he doesn't. They're all assigned a number so they're all equal."

"Oh." *Makes sense.*

"Ready?" he asks as we approach the door.

"Wait, what if they ask me questions?"

"No one will be asking you questions. You'll be sitting with Blackstone and my father."

"Daniel is here?" I suddenly feel happy. I love Daniel like he is my own father.

"Yes."

"Wait." I grab his hand. "I don't want to be disrespectful in there, so what do I call you?"

He laughs as he opens the door. "Come on, baby." He places his hand on my lower back and walks me through the door.

I swear the entire place goes silent and all eyes are on me. "You're not in uniform, that's why everyone is staring." *Yeah, that's why*...or maybe it's because the big bad Colonel has a civilian female in the dining hall.

Daniel rises to his feet and wraps me in his usual bear hug. "Good to see you, sweetheart."

"You too." I beam as I take a seat next to Cole.

"You've made quite the stir here." John laughs as the dining hall grows noisy again. "Everyone wants to know who the civilian is with the Colonel."

"I trust you set them right," Cole notes, rather than asks.

"Nah, I figured this way would be more fun," John smirks as he hops to his feet. "Come on, we're up." He nods to the cafeteria line.

"Colonel?" a guy wearing number sixty-one says, standing behind us. "May I have a word with you?"

Cole sighs as he stands. "Savi, go ahead with John and get something to eat. I'll meet you back here."

"All righty, you ready for a five star meal? We have chicken or chicken or chicken." John laughs as he digs in, taking a huge portion of hunter chicken. I take a small amount and pair it with a roll and veggies. "Here." He hands me a bottle of water. "Grab a knife and fork from there," he points to a tray, "and we're done."

"Hang on," a guy, says handing me a napkin. "There you go."

"Thanks." I go to move, but he shifts in front of me.

"Here, let me." He takes my tray out of my grip and starts walking back to the table. It's a nice gesture; if only half the place wasn't watching us. I notice his number is nine, and I think I spot his table because they are the ones who seem most interested. Then it clicks, making me chuckle.

"So what do you win by carrying my tray to the

table?" I ask as I come up next to him. He attempts to hide his smile but it doesn't work.

"To be team captain on whichever assignment I choose." He blushes slightly. "When you show leadership, you stick out more. I need to gain as many points here as possible."

I see Cole watching us out of the corner of my eye, and I see our table watching me too. "Tell me something, nine, what's your name?"

He stands a little straighter. "Corporal Davie."

"Do you know who I am?"

"No, miss, I don't."

"Pretty risky for you to take on that bet."

"I like to take risks, but I figured being a gentleman wasn't causing any harm," he shrugs innocently.

"Are you being a gentleman?" I question his motives.

"Yes, miss, I was raised right. My mamma always says you respect a lady and they'll respect you."

I reach for the tray just as Cole does. "Cole," I glance up at him, "Corporal Davie here was kind enough to carry my tray for me. Wasn't that nice?"

Cole studies my face and nods. "Yes, it was. Come on, baby, let's go eat."

I see Davie's eyes pop open when he realizes he just carried the Colonel's girlfriend's tray.

"Thanks again, Davie," I call over my shoulder as I follow Cole back to the seat.

I watch as Davie sits at his table and no one speaks a word. "Cole," I begin, and he turns to look at me. "Has nine been doing well?"

Cole shrugs. "Not overly. He's weak in the water."

"Do you think he'll make the cut?"

"No not unless he gets past his fear of drowning."

I'm confused. "Isn't that a normal fear?"

"Green Berets can't be scared of anything."

I scrunch my face up, trying to follow. "So you're

telling me you're scared of nothing."

He wipes his napkin over his mouth then stares down at me with a look that almost frightens me. "Just you."

"Me?"

He leans in a little closer, resting his arm on the back of my chair. "I'm scared to death of losing you." I want to make a comment, but I don't. It wasn't Cole's fault he was taken from me before. Sometimes I have to remind myself of that; a part of me finds it easier to lash out than to accept what really happened.

"You won't lose me, Cole. I love and trust you more than anyone." I see a pained look run across his face. He picks up my left hand and rubs my wedding ring finger. I think he's going to say something, but he doesn't. I reach up and quickly run my hand over his five o'clock shadow. "I wish I knew what this face means." He takes my hand and gives it a quick kiss, then turns his attention back to his dinner.

"Savi," Daniel calls out, "how long you staying at camp?"

"Umm, just until tomorrow afternoon," I answer. "I have a date in the evening."

"Oh?" Cole raises an eyebrow.

"Yes, dinner and a hike." I feel Cole stiffen at the word hike.

"Who's the lucky fellow?" Mark asks through a mouthful of chicken.

"Make that plural. It's with Abby, June, and Sue," I laugh. "There's a meteor shower."

"And?" Cole asks, making me roll my eyes.

"Keith and Mike, possibly Derek, but he was muttering about it being cold when we were out last night. Such a baby," I chuckle until I see Cole's jaw flex. Oops. "We were just walking along the water's edge. The house can be busy sometimes."

"I see." Cole leans back and pushes his plate away.

"And where was Keith?"

"Umm…he was dealing with Frank." I notice Cole glances at Mark and then his father. The tension starts to build the more we sit in silence. "So," I look at everyone, "can I get a tour?"

After the grand tour of the grounds, I can feel Cole stewing about something. He has been off since dinner, and I would bet money on it being that I mentioned spending time alone with Derek. It's quite cold out as we walk back to the main building. I see some of the men heading toward their bunks.

"Are they heated?" I ask.

"Yes, but just enough so they don't get hypothermia."

"Yikes," I whisper.

"Don't have heaters in the mountains, just what's on your back."

"That sucks."

"It always sucks."

"Then why do it?"

He stops at a whiteboard and starts scribbling something.

'03:00 60km Barrel run'

Yikes.

"Personally, I couldn't imagine doing anything else." Cole tilts his head up toward the sky.

I tuck my freezing hands into my jacket. "Even after what…happened?"

His gaze drops to the ground. "I know it's hard to understand, but yes."

A few of the guys are hanging around a large fire pit. We make our way toward them. I wish so much I could hear what's running through Cole's head right now. Something is definitely off.

"Evening, Colonel." One of the candidates nods politely at Cole. "Miss," he says as he addresses me.

So this is fifty-nine, the one Cole has been watching.

"Roth," Cole says. I notice he doesn't address him as his number. Maybe it's because they're not training at the moment. Another man comes up to join us. He is much shorter than Cole and Roth, almost eye level with me.

"Colonel Logan, it's nice to meet you," the man says. "I'm Captain James. I was happy to hear our half of the group got to train here at Camp Green." He looks at me. "So this is the lady who's got the camp buzzing." He extends a hand. "Captain James."

"Nice to meet you, Captain." I shake his hand then quickly shove mine back in my jacket. Cole puts his hand on my waist, moving me in front of him so I am closer to the fire.

Cole and Roth start talking about Roth's time over in Afghanistan. I tune them out, leaning my weight into Cole. His hands are stroking methodically up and down my arms. It feels nice as I watch the fire crackle and pop.

"Lovely girl you got there," I hear Roth say. "Well, I should hit the sack. I see we're going to be up shortly."

"Good night, Roth." Cole leans down, whispering in my ear, "You seem quiet."

"I'm comfy," I answer, still in my trance from the fire. He chuckles as he wraps his arms around me.

"I want to take you to bed."

"And I want you to." I sigh, loving the way I feel in his arms.

***

"MOVE, MOVE, MOVE!" Cole shouts at the men as each one carries his teammate across a field three feet deep in snow.

I see Roth carrying James like he was weightless, taking long strides well ahead of the rest of them.

"If they fall," Daniel says, handing me a coffee, "they have to go back to the start and do it all over again."

"Really?" I ask in disbelief as he takes a seat next to me on the bench.

"Yes, they have to know they can't fail. Most of these men can do it. It's all mental."

We watch as two men fall and don't get back up. Cole goes over and starts yelling at them. I can't make out what he's saying, but it doesn't sound nice. I cringe, feeling bad for the guys.

"He'll ask them what's wrong," Daniel says, noticing I'm shifting uneasily. "See?" He points. "See how Cole nods at someone? That's the medic. He's letting them know that the men are all right, but to keep an eye on them. He'll ask the men if they are VW, voluntary withdrawing. If they are, they will be asked to leave right away." Daniel looks at me. "We are not here to break the men. We are here to make sure we let in America's best. These are all great soldiers. They're just not all great Green Berets."

I watch Cole reach in his pocket and take out his cell phone. He glances over at us and answers the call. After a few minutes he motions for another man to take his place. He signals something to his father, who then excuses himself to follow Cole into the main building.

"Excuse me," I ask one of the men working a stopwatch a while later. "Could you tell me the time?"

"Sure, it's fifteen hundred."

"Three p.m.?"

"Yes." He smiles.

Cole and Daniel have been gone for over an hour and a half, and Keith will be here to pick me up shortly. I decide to go over to the main building, where I run into Davie from the dining hall.

"Hello again," he says, coming up to me sporting a broken nose.

"Oh, ouch!"

"It's fine. At least I got a breather." He shrugs.

"Have you seen Colonel Logan?"

"I did, he's in the main office," he points down the hallway, "second door on your right."

"Thanks, and good luck to you."

"Thanks, I'm gonna need it."

I hear some shouting as I get closer, and I pause outside the door, not sure what I should do. I decide to take a seat next to the door. Ten minutes later the door opens and out walks a woman holding a bunch of files. She's turned away from me and doesn't shut the door all the way as she hurries off in the opposite direction.

"I don't like that idea, son," I hear Daniel say. "I see what you're saying, but it's suicide."

"I know, but if I can get back in under The American's hold, if I can get them to think they've got me—"

What?

"Logan, if they find that wire, they'll kill you on the spot," Mark hisses.

"They won't," Cole argues. "We need that information. We are so close. If we don't do this, Savannah will never be free. Her father knows so much. We can get these fuckers!"

Cole's words echo in my head, as everything else around me goes quiet. I don't even realize I am moving until I'm back up in his room gathering my bag, and I hear Keith's voice.

I slip out of the room and head down the stairs where Cole is quietly chatting with Keith in the corner. He stops and plasters on a smile when he sees me coming. *I'm tired of all this whispering.*

"Hey, baby, sorry about leaving you right before you have to go."

"Is everything all right?" My voice sounds off, and I

know he hears it too. His eyes narrow as he studies my face.

"Yes, of course." He leans in and gives me a kiss. I try to respond, but I am in too much shock with what I just heard to act normal. This is not the time to talk about it with him, though. "Hey, are *you* all right?"

"Mmmhmm." I glance at Keith, seeing his face is stressed. "I'll see you in a few days, right?"

"Yes, of course." He leans down once more and kisses me. I want to ask him to promise me, but I know he'd ask start asking more questions. "I love you."

"I love you too."

The trip home is uneventful, and after everything is unpacked, I head for the kitchen where I run into Derek, who is in a foul mood.

"Savi, could you ask Mike to meet me in the garage? He's in Cole's office."

"Sure, Derek." I smile, not wanting to know what is pissing him off right now.

I knock on the door and see Mike on the phone. "Derek needs you in the garage."

"Okay, thanks." He rushes past me. "Shit, could you give that file on the desk to Keith?"

"Sure, no problem."

"Thanks!"

I move over to Cole's desk and pick up the file. As I do, some papers fall out and land on the other side of the desk. I start picking them up, when I glance at the computer and see a forwarded email to Cole from Frank with my father's name as the subject.

I have never invaded someone's privacy before, but this e-mail involves me, and I'm tired of not knowing anything.

I strain to listen for any voices, but all is quiet. I shift and click on the email but stay on my knees, hidden in case anyone comes in. I don't want to run the risk having anyone catch me, so I press print and wait till the two pages came out. I fold and tuck the papers into my back pocket. I collect the file for Keith and click out of the e-mail back to the inbox.

Once I finally get a moment alone in my room, I pull out the papers. I take a deep breath and scan the email.

Logan, how would you like us to deal with this?

Holy shit!

My father is reaching out to Frank about knowing I am alive and being protected by the U.S. Army in a safe house somewhere in the States. He's not angry they've had me for so long without telling him. He just wants to see me. *Wants to hold his daughter he thought was dead.* Tears slip down my face as I read. My father pours his heart out to Frank, begging him to let him see me.

I read Cole's reply.

Frank, I just did. See below.

My eyes scan his words back to my father. I'm confused. Why is Cole telling him that he doesn't deserve to see me? There are answers to be had before he will *ever* let him see me.

My back hits the wall then my butt sinks to the ground, hard. Things don't make sense. Why would my father reach out to Frank? How did he find out I was here? Why hasn't Cole told me about the email? And why would Cole want to risk his life to get answers from The American?

After a long time on the floor, I finally stand. I know what I need to do.

Later, I try to act normal with everyone up on the hill, but I can feel Keith watching me. I know he knows something is bothering me. He tried to pry it out of me on the drive home, but I was too blown away by Cole's idea about letting himself be taken by The American again to let him get it out of me.

Derek is my target tonight. He has a weak spot for

me, and I intend to use it. I wait for the meteor shower to start, then slowly make my way over to where Derek is standing.

"Pretty neat, huh?" Derek whispers, as little bursts of light travel across the sky. "Amazing to think they're two million years old."

Here it goes.

"Derek, I have a problem." His gaze drops to mine. "And I think only you can help me."

"Oh?"

"Can we speak privately?"

He studies my face, seeing I am indeed struggling with something, then glances over at Keith. "Savi needs to go back to the house."

"I can take her," Keith says, rising out of his chair.

"It's cool. I'll take her. I need to use the bathroom anyway." Keith's eyes narrow on me again, so I muster up a smile and shrug.

Derek leads the way down the path as I follow behind, sorting what I want to ask in my mind. I stop him at the stairs, not wanting to go inside. I don't trust anyone overhearing, and knowing the guys can lip read off the cameras, I am even more cautious.

Derek leans against the railing and tucks his gloved hands into his coat pockets. "What's going on, Savannah?"

I rub my mitts together more out of nerves than the cold. "I know you and Cole have a stressful past, but I also know that when it comes down to it you would be there to help him out, right?"

He shrugs. "Yeah, I guess."

"What if I told you I know something bad is going to happen to Cole, and only I could stop it? Would you help me?"

He rubs his chin, sensing he's not going to like what I have to say. "I'm listening."

"I came across something that wasn't intended for my eyes, but…whatever, I read it."

"Ah, shit," he sighs, "what was it?"

"An email from my father to Frank. He wants to see me." Derek stops moving. "Cole emailed him back, saying that the only way he'd let my father see me again is if he got some answers." I pause and glance up at him. "Derek, I can get these answers. I think my father is being blackmailed by the people who kidnapped me. I need to see him and help him. We haven't always had the greatest relationship, but he's still my father. I need you to fly me to New York and get me to him."

Derek's face is unreadable. His gaze drops to the ground then he leans back, rests against the railing, and lets out a long breath. I hold my breath and wait, but he takes too long. So I decide to try my other concern, *one* thing Agent York and I did agree on. "I'm scared that if we don't fix this soon, they might come after the house. Cole is planning on getting himself taken by The American again." I step closer to Derek. "You of all people saw what happened to me while he was gone. I can't let that happen again. So you either help me, or I'll figure it out my way."

He shakes his head. "Why haven't you gone to Cole about this?"

"Seriously?" I roll my eyes. "Have you met Cole?"

A tiny smirk graces his face. "Point taken. I'm sure if he could wrap you in bubble wrap, he would."

"I'm thinking more a foam padded room."

Derek starts to pace in front of me. I can picture the wheels turning in his head.

"You know he will have me fired for helping you."

"I won't let that happen, you have my word." I try to hide my smile. "Are you saying you'll help me?"

"You haven't left me a choice, have you? I say yes and get you there and back safely, or I say no and you leave and get yourself in a shit load of trouble. Either way, I'm fucked."

I sag with relief. "Thank you, truly, Derek."

"Fuck," he hisses under his breath, "why couldn't you have asked Keith?"

"He would have said no, and tied me to the chair till Cole comes home."

"Smart man." He starts walking down the porch stairs. "Come on, we should get back. I'll make some calls tonight. Be ready to leave for 'town' tomorrow morning. Leave your bag packed inside your bedroom. I'll grab it on my way downstairs, and we'll head out from there."

"All right," I nod. "Thank you again, Derek. I knew I could count on you," I say, feeling my stomach twist into a painful knot. I don't want to lie to Cole, and I certainly don't want to leave him, but I will not stand by while he gives himself over to The American. This ends now.

***

I fold the letter and place it on Cole's pillow, knowing I'll get a few days' head start before he sees it. Hopefully Keith will not want to tag along today. Poor Keith. I know he'll be upset, but hopefully in time he'll understand too.

I fling my purse over my arm and head downstairs.

"Good morning," Abigail says, handing me a cup of coffee. "I never got to ask you, how was your visit with Cole at Camp Green?"

I slide onto the stool, wondering where Derek is. "It was really nice to see him. After seeing what he does there, you can bet I'll never cut it as a Green Beret."

"Ha! Me either, dear." She laughs, cracking two eggs into the frying pan.

She starts talking as I hear a hissing sound off to my left and see Derek, waving for me to follow.

He mouths, "Time to go."

I feel uneasy as I get to my feet. I would be lying if I said I wasn't terrified about leaving the grounds…leaving this town without Cole. Wrapping my arms around Abigail from behind, I give her a big hug.

"I love you, Abigail."

"Oh, sweetie," she coos, covering my hands with hers, "I love you too."

I don't let go, and hold on an extra minute. "Please know I wouldn't be who and where I am today if it wasn't for you."

She turns to look at me, but I back away, ducking my head. "I'll be back later."

I think she thinks I don't want her to see I'm emotional, because she lets me leave without another word.

I'm almost to the door before Keith calls out my name. *Damn, almost made it!* I suck in a sharp breath and turn to look up at him as he trots up to me.

"Hey, I was wondering if you'd like to come with me to pick up Cole later on in the week. He'd love it."

I feel my friggin' eyes betray me as they go glossy. "Yeah, sure…that sounds, um, like a good plan."

"Hey." He comes closer, tilting his head to the side. I feel his eyes penetrating my defenses. This guy is good. "Everything all right?"

"Oh, yeah." I hate to use this, and I'm sure as shit going to go to hell for saying it. "Just having a down day." I shrug, alluding to my miscarriage, but to be truthful there hasn't been a day I don't think about our little something who could have been. *Ahh…not now, Savannah!*

Keith's face drops as he studies my face carefully. "Cole warned me, but I truly didn't see it until now."

"What? What are you talking about?" I'm thrown by his comment.

His lips press together as he once again studies my face long and hard. I can almost feel his eyes burning into my brain, probing the part that's holding my lie at bay.

"Anything you want to tell me, Savannah?" His voice is low.

I swallow hard, feeling my forehead break out in a line of sweat. "No."

Yeah, that was convincing...

Feeling terribly guilty, I slowly walk away from him, but I stop and turn to look back, chewing on the inside of my lip while my brain struggles to find the right words.

"Keith?"

"Yes?"

"Thank you."

"For what?"

I shrug attempting to play it cool. "Just—for everything."

He takes a step toward me as I take one back. "Savannah—"

"Savi, you ready?" Derek asks, coming into the entryway. "I need to be at Christine's in an hour, so I gotta go." He nods at Keith. "Hey, man, we're heading to town. You need anything?"

"No," he shakes his head, his eyes still on me. "I'm good."

"Talk to you later, Keith," I mumble.

"I hope so," I hear him say as I close the door.

Chapter Five

The drive to town is painful. My hands are twisted on my lap as we come to the town's outer limits. My legs are jittery, my heart's trying to escape the growing anxiety, and all the while I'm blinking away tears for Cole.

"We'll park and transfer into Agent Stall's car. He'll drive us to the airport," Derek announces while we wait at a stoplight. He glances at me. "Now is the time if you're having second thoughts, Savannah."

"No," I squeeze out, and watch as the stoplight turns to green. Little snowflakes dust the windshield, making me shiver. I hope I'm doing the right thing. I'm past changing my mind now, as I know I must prevent Cole from putting himself in danger in order to help me again.

Agent Stall is not overly friendly. He barely says two words the whole three-hour drive to the airport. I am handed an ID with the name Nicole Johnson and a printout of my airline ticket. We quickly board, taking our seats toward the front of the plane. It isn't first class, but executive...not bad. I notice Derek needs the extra leg space. He stretches out, then pushes the call button and asks the flight attendant for an orange juice. He seems relaxed.

I, on the other hand, am having an internal anxiety

attack. So many things are blowing through my brain. I'm terrified of the answers I'm headed toward.

Once we are up in the air and the seat belt sign is turned off, I hop up, nearly plowing over Derek to get to the bathroom. Inside the tiny room I lean over the sink and splash cold water over my face. "*I can do this. I can do this. I can do this.*" I close the lid to the toilet, take a seat, and run my hands through my hair. "Calm down, Savi." I try to remember Dr. Roberts and his relaxing techniques…in through the nose, out through the mouth, count to thirty, breathe slowly again…then rubbing my sweaty hands over my jeans, I take a moment to think.

A loud knock makes me jump to my feet. Opening the door, I'm faced with an annoyed woman who eyes me with obvious hostility.

"Only two bathrooms for sixty passengers," she mumbles as she shoves her son in ahead of her.

"Sorry," I whisper, although I'm not. I'm sure she'd prefer me to freak out in the bathroom than in front of everyone, including her child. Rude woman.

"You okay?" Derek asks once I return to my seat and fumble with the belt.

"Sure." I lean my head back and close my eyes.

Luckily, the layover in Salt Lake City is only thirty minutes, just enough time to find our gate and grab a coffee.

Four hours into the flight, I feel the plane start its descent. I clench the arm rests until my fingers turn white. Derek takes pity on me and attempts to distract me.

"Okay, so once we land, a friend of mine will meet us at baggage. From there we'll go right to your father's office. I have eyes on him currently, so if he leaves we will find where he is and change route."

"We're going there today?" The words fall off my tongue.

Derek turns in his seat to look at me straight on. "Savannah, we have a flight to catch tomorrow night. You have this one chance to get your information. I'm already putting you in danger by taking you off the Shadow grounds." He rubs his face. "I'm seriously going to be stripped of my job for this."

"Then why are you helping me?" I ask, needing to know.

He turns to face forward again, downing his juice and crushing the cup under his hand. "I have my reasons."

"Which are?" I ask, being nosy, but I need the distraction, and honestly I want to know.

He clears his throat and shoves the crushed cup into the pouch hanging off the wall. "I fucked up when I was on the team. I was young and dumb." He shrugs, but I can see what he did weighs on him. "So maybe this will show them I can be trusted, that I can get you back safely, and with answers." He lets out a laugh. "Or maybe not, since this is insane."

The captain's voice blares over the speakers, announcing our arrival. Jeez, I hadn't noticed we landed.

"If it means anything, Derek, thank you."

"Yeah, sure thing." He looks out the window, and I know our heart to heart is over.

***

Cole

Cole goes over his checklist, finding what time fifty-nine is scheduled to complete the blind navigation course in the woods. The candidates have to navigate through the woods with only a map. If they're caught using their head lamp, they get a point taken off. It's no surprise fifty-nine, Adam Roth, is at the head of the pack.

Since he is so close to finishing, Cole decides to meet Roth at the last checkpoint to talk to him about the possibility of joining the house. He's on his way when he spots Keith pulling up to the main house. It's dark, but he can see there's something wrong when the other man jumps quickly from the car.

"Keith?" Cole shouts. Keith stops, then turns and begins to head in his direction.

Cole sees his father coming out of the main building to join them. Obviously his father knows something isn't right either.

"What are you doing here?" Cole asks, once he's close enough.

Keith points at the main office. "Let's talk inside."

Mark joins them as well. Keith clears his throat, looking pale and sweaty.

"Where are John and Paul?" he asks, seeming to gather himself.

"They're still out in the field. What's going on?" Cole asks between clenched teeth.

"I don't have all the details yet, but Derek took Savannah to town this morning and they haven't returned."

Cole's stomach drops as his head tries to process what was just said.

"What do you mean?" Daniel asks, crossing his arms. "Did you trace the SUV? They all have trackers, you know that."

"I did, and it was parked outside Christina's store. We checked, of course, and she said they didn't come in but figured they were planning to after they did some errands. She didn't think about it till later, as she got busy. She did remember seeing a black truck drive by a couple of times. I got the plate number, and it's registered to an Agent Michael Stall."

"Did you get hold of Stall?" Mark asks, shaking his

head.

Cole's hands ball into fists at his sides—something's off. Derek is an ass, but he wouldn't hurt Savi.

"Yes, and after some threatening, it turns out Derek paid him to drive him and Savannah to the airport."

"Airport?" Mark hisses, glancing at Cole. "Why the fucking airport?"

Keith glances at Cole and lets out a long breath. "I have a theory." All eyes turn to Keith as he continues. "This morning Savannah was acting really strange. Abigail said Savannah was acting almost like she was saying goodbye. She did the same to me. I could tell she was lying about something. She's a bad liar." He pulls out a piece of paper from his back pocket. "I found this in her wastebasket in her room." He hands it to Cole.

Cole quickly unfolds it and scans the words. *Fuck!*

"What is it?" Mark moves to his side, trying to read the paper.

"She found the email from her father to Frank, and my reply." Cole's words are quiet. "Dad," he looks to Daniel and feels all the blood rush from his face, "she's walking into a trap."

Cole,

I came to this house stripped of everything, and you built me into something. I have never felt whole, never felt a sense of belonging, never felt true love until I met you.

My leaving is to give you something you gave me—peace. There are so many lies that surround me. They need to be dealt with, and only I can find the answers. I'm tired of being broken. I'm ready to fix this. I will not let you hurt for me again. I know I can do this and I'll soon be back in your arms.

You will forever be my knight who stormed the castle wall and saved me from all the evil that held me prisoner.

I love you, Cole Logan.
Forever yours,
Savannah x

Cole sits on the edge of the bed, his hands shaking as he re-reads her letter for the tenth time, fighting back the nausea that's pooling in the back of his throat.

"Oh, baby, you just walked into the lion's den," he mutters as he picks up his duffel bag.

"Ready when you are," Mark calls out softly from the doorway.

***

Savannah

I watch the familiar scenery fly by. As we ride in the tinted Ford Explorer to my father's office, my mind wanders. Well, I've wanted to know what this would feel like ever since I was taken to my own personal hell almost ten months ago. It doesn't feel like home anymore; it feels cold and crowded. I suddenly miss the wide open space of the Montana mountains, my friends, and yes, my family. New York City isn't right for me anymore. I have found peace and happiness—I've moved on.

The weight in my belly that's been forming since I stepped on the plane is getting heavier as we drive closer to the office. My fingers catch and run along the chain to the tiny snowflake that hasn't left my neck since Cole gave it to me. I'm so nervous my leg is bouncing wildly, making a thumping noise on the floor.

Derek's phone rings, and I flinch. I watch his face when he reads the caller ID. He swallows hard as he answers the call.

"Logan."

I hold my breath and watch Derek's eyes squeeze shut.

"Yeah, one second." He looks at me and holds out the phone. I don't want to take it, I can't, but…

"Cole?" My voice gives away how much I miss him.

"Savannah," the worry is thick in his voice, "what the hell are you doing?"

"Ending this."

"It's not the way!" he nearly shouts.

My anger surfaces. "Right, and you getting taken by The American again is?"

Silence.

"I heard you talking at the camp, Cole. I can't go through that again. It's time I finish this. I love you more than anyone or anything, so it's time I get the answers. I deserve it, but without anyone else putting themselves in danger for me." He attempts to say something, but I cut him off. "I'll be all right. I'm just going to figure out who's blackmailing my father so I can find out who is actually behind my kidnapping."

"No, Savannah, you don't—"

"I'll be home tomorrow night. I love you Cole." I quickly hang up, turn off the phone, and hand it back to Derek, who is wide-eyed.

"Problem?" I ask, feeling a new sense of strength. I

knew I could do this. I have to do this, for Cole and me to move on with our lives.

"Not at all." Derek smirks briefly and goes back to looking out the window.

***

"Here." Derek gives me a tiny cell phone that fits inside a small pocket in my dress. It looks like a remote I had for the Apple TV back in my old life. "Just in case we get separated, speed dial one is me, and two is Cole. You don't have to look, just feel where the buttons are."

I nod and feel for the little buttons until I am familiar with how to press them. I'm still not sure what the hell I'm going to say when I see my father.

We are in a café across the road from my father's office building. I've changed into a black Ponte sheath dress with heels and stockings. I have to look like I belong in the corporate world so Derek and I can walk in and not stand out. Derek's connections got us in contact with a woman on the tenth floor. She's going to meet us downstairs and walk us in so we don't have to give a name to the front desk, and then we can bypass security. We don't want anyone knowing I'm here.

"Put these on." Derek hands me a pair of thick-rimmed glasses. I do, as Derek shrugs on a trench coat over his dark blue suit and then he helps me into mine.

"Ready?" he asks.

"Yeah...yes, I am." I try to produce a brave a smile, but I'm a mixture of fear and, strangely, excitement.

We step outside, letting the freezing New York air swirl around us. Derek links arms with me and helps keep me from slipping on the black ice as we cross the street.

A woman with a friendly smile greets us at the door and speaks to us like we were old friends. Security eyes us but says nothing as the woman puts on a good show for them. I keep my head down, and my scarf wraps around most of my face. As soon as we step into the elevators, Derek thanks the woman and hands her an envelope. Hush money.

People shuffle in and out as we rise through the building. Finally we reach the tenth floor and she turns and leans up to my ear. I stiffen at her closeness and notice Derek reaches for something, but then stops when he sees she's just whispering.

"October TMZ, top left corner. You're not the only one making it in the media." She gives my arm a small squeeze and disappears out the elevator doors.

I'm confused by her comment, but I memorize what she said so I can deal with it later. Derek looks at me, puzzled, and I shake my head, needing to prepare myself for what is ahead. Besides, we don't have time to talk, as the doors soon open to the twenty-sixth floor.

Oh shit.

As much as I'm bundled up, I am cold, and I feel the hairs rise on my arms. Derek and I stop to see if Luka is in his office. His door is closed, so my guess is he is in a meeting. We move on, and before I can think, Derek opens my father's office door.

"Mayor Fox?" Derek says in a direct voice.

My father's grey eyes look up and lock with mine.

Holy...

Chapter Six

Dad.

He blinks a few times before he stands, rounds his desk, and stops a few feet from us. I hear rather than see Derek shift my way.

"Savannah?" my father whispers in disbelief. His face is white as a sheet. "Is that really you?"

"Hi, Dad." I feel the words catch in my throat.

His hands outstretched, he makes his way toward me but hesitates as he comes in for a hug. As soon as his arms are around me I feel…uncomfortable? Weird? Strange? I don't know, but I don't like it.

"I can't believe you're alive." He pulls back and grasps my shoulders. "Look at you."

"Dad, we need to talk, and I don't have much time."

He looks over at the door. "Did anyone see you? Do you think you were followed?"

"No, it's okay. I have some questions that need answers, Dad. Like who's blackmailing you? Do you know why I was taken? Why was my ransom so low?"

"Whoa, slow down, dear." He smiles at me, still with his hand on my shoulder. He thinks for a moment, then says, "Tell you what, we need a proper place to talk about all this. Meet me for an early dinner this evening." He smiles at Derek. "Both of you. Come to the house so we can talk without worrying that the media or anyone else will see you. I'll answer your questions then, but not here. It's not safe. You really should go." He suddenly looks uneasy and makes a show about looking over his shoulder.

I glance at Derek, who doesn't like the idea and is obvious about it, but he takes his cue from me and agrees unhappily. "Umm, yeah, okay."

"Great, four sound all right?" Dad asks, as I check the time. It's a little after one. "I'll call ahead and have dinner ready for us."

"All right, we'll meet you there."

My father turns to Derek. "Thank you for bringing her here." He extends his hand for a shake. Derek takes it quickly and moves toward the door.

"Savi." Derek flicks his head for me to follow.

"See you at four, Dad."

"All right, dear." He kisses my forehead. "Be careful. I love you, sweetheart." He sounds so sincere my earlier uneasy feelings evaporate. Wow...it's been a long time since my father uttered those words to me and meant them. There's no media here to make a show for.

"Me too."

"Are you out of your mind?" Derek explodes as soon as we make our way across the street. "That guy is as fake as a three dollar bill, Savi. What are we doing letting him call the shots here? Why—"

I cut him off. "Derek, it's okay. We have no choice. My father was right; his office in broad daylight isn't the right time." Giving him a look, I walk away from him, my own thoughts in a jumble. It was such a shock seeing him again. I need time to process all this myself, and Derek doesn't know my father and how complicated it is being in his position in the Mayor's office.

Derek starts making calls out on the patio as soon as we arrive at our hotel. Derek chose this hotel because it is so close to my father's home. I stare out the window, seeing his penthouse condo across the street with its dark gray curtains. I always thought they were so heavy and dreary for the room, but he insisted on keeping them.

I shower and change into pants and a cream colored blouse. I curl my hair and add earrings and a few bangles to my outfit. I may have been gone for some time, but I know my father will still expect me to dress appropriately, and I will not disappoint.

"Yes, honey, I'll see you soon. I love you too." Derek speaks quietly with his back to me.

I pick up my purse and slip the tiny phone into my bra. I didn't know Derek was seeing someone. He must have noticed the look on my face, because he smiles and rolls his eyes.

"She's the prettiest brown-eyed girl I've ever met." He laughs. "And now she's begging me to bring her home a souvenir from New York."

"Oh, really?" I grin. "You should stop by Draped in Lace. They have—"

His hands fly over his ears, cringing. "That's not something I want to buy my six year old niece!"

"Oh!" I laugh. "In that case, the gift shop downstairs may have something."

"That's where we're headed. I need your help."

After twenty minutes of looking at every knick-knack the gift shop owns, Derek finally decides on a snow globe of the Rockefeller Center ice skating rink at Christmas. It makes a beautiful gift any six year old girl would love. I know because I have…had one.

Convincing him to stop for coffee, we take a seat near the back and enjoy a few minutes before we have to leave. My nose scrunches at Derek's strong black coffee as I blow the steam off the top of mine, adding a little more cream and sugar.

"My parents brought me to New York when I was

eleven," he says, breaking our silence. "My sister and I were so excited to see the Rangers play the Kings. That's when Gretsky was playing for them. My parents planned this whole day of fun for us, batting cages in the morning, lunch at Times Square, then the game and ice cream afterward." He smiles, remembering. "Man that was a good trip."

"I bet." I sip my coffee, happy we're talking about anything else but the real reason we're here. "Where are you from originally?"

"Washington, born and raised," he says proudly.

"Are your parents still there?"

His face falls a little. "My old man died a few years back, heart attack. My mom is there, though, with my sister and my niece. My sister left her husband around the same time Dad died, so she moved in with Mom." He pauses. "I try to step up when I can, so my niece has at least some sort of male figure in her life." He glances at me. "Sounds like Frank is moving me back to Washington, which is good because I was planning on transferring anyway. Shadows and me," he shakes his head, "well, let's just say we *ain't* a good mix."

I feel sad, as I do like Derek. He's been a friend, but it's obvious for whatever reason the guys don't like him, and I understand that. Trust goes hand in hand with everything in their line of work.

"Oh, Derek, I hope you'll be happy there." I didn't say Cole had already told me.

He grants me a smile. "I'll miss a few things." He winks.

"Mmm." I chuckle, finishing off my coffee.

"Let's go back up to the room," Derek mumbles, as he checks his phone for the hundredth time. I know he'll be glad to get this over with.

It takes him two times to open the hotel door with the key card. I pretend not to notice, but I can see he's jumpy.

"You all right?" I ask as he pulls down the handle to open the door.

"Yes *I* am," he mutters, letting me walk in first.

Two steps past the threshold, I'm met with a set of intense dark eyes that steals every last ounce of air from my body.

Oh...

We stand two feet apart staring at one another. My heart pounds loudly as he flexes his jaw dramatically for me to see. Instead of feeling nervous, I feel the inner pull that he brings out in me. My tongue darts out and does a swipe along my lower lip. His eyes narrow and I see that familiar flicker. He feels it too, I can tell, but I need to stay strong if I am going to do this. I draw in a deep breath.

"Cole." My voice comes out raspy.

"Savannah." He says each syllable slowly.

"And...I'm gonna leave now," Derek whispers backing out of the hotel room. Neither of us talks until we hear the door close.

"When did you get here?" I ask, turning my back to him and calmly placing my purse on the bar top.

Suddenly both of his arms trap me and his mouth is at my ear. "I'm so angry at you right now...!" *He is actually vibrating.*

"Cole—" He bites at my neck, giving my nerves another jolt.

"Do you have any idea how scared I've been these last twelve hours?" he hisses as runs his hand along my stomach. "I want to handcuff you to me right now and drag your ass back to Montana." His other hand grabs my ass, squeezing it and making my hand drop back against his shoulder. "Why didn't you tell me?"

I close my eyes as his hand slides in the front of my pants, running just shy of where I want him to be.

"Because you would have said no."

He whips me around, grabs my waist, and hoists me onto the bar top. He moves between my legs and clutches my lower back, hauling me into him. "Damn right, I would have. You're mine, and I protect what's mine." He reaches over, clasping my chin, and gives me a rough but sensual kiss. By the time he pulls away I'm nearly panting with built-up lust. "Christ, Savannah, are you out of your mind? What if something happened to you? Then what?"

My mind scrambles to think clearly. "Cole, I'm fine. I'm meeting my father to get some answers."

I feel his hands pull away from me, and he runs them roughly through his hair. He closes his eyes, muttering something to himself I can't make out.

"Logan, we have eyes on the building, and we're not the only ones." Mark stands in the doorway. "Hi, Savi." He smiles, raising one eyebrow, but his cheeky smile fades fast when he takes in Cole's expression. *Of course Mark is here.*

"Which building? And who else is here?" I ask, looking from Mark to Cole.

"How many?" Cole's voice is all business.

"Three."

"Will someone answer me?" I try again. "Cole?"

Cole sighs as he thinks. "All right, double our men on theirs and have the snipers ready on my command."

"Snipers?" I nearly shout. "What the hell is going on?" I can tell I'm not going to get anywhere with these two, so I quickly shift off the bar before Cole knows what I'm doing. I grab my purse and head for the front door.

"Where are you going?" Cole calls out to me, signaling for Mark to block the doorway.

I turn on my heel and find him right in front of me. "I'm sick and tired of people not answering me, Cole.

Ask your *man* to move! I'm going to talk with Derek. At least *he* acknowledges me when I speak." I eye up where Mark's foot is, ready to stamp on it.

Yeah, I can tell he doesn't like that comment, but right now I don't care. I feel like I am treading water with no end in sight. Everyone knows things but me, and it's infuriating. I spent seven months with no control over my life, not knowing from one minute to the next what would happen to me, and I will not live like that again. I turn and stare Cole down, because at this moment I am friggin' angry, and I want answers.

Cole looks at me for a moment, his expression tight. "All right, Savi, hold on. As much as I'm against this— you meeting your father this evening—Frank felt it was about time we got some answers, and maybe this is the way to do it." His jaw twitches. *Oh boy, he is mad.* "So, you and *Derek* will attend your father's dinner, but with a wire and plenty of backup." It's not lost on me the way he says Derek's name like it's acid on his tongue.

"Wire?" I swallow. "Isn't that a bit extreme?"

"Extreme?" he shouts, his hands flying to his hips. "Extreme is you running off to New York with *Derek Rent* to confront your father with the Cartel hot on your trail! Extreme is you not seeing what's going on here!"

"The Cartel knows I'm here?"

"When will you get it, Savannah? They have eyes everywhere!"

"Christ, Cole, fill me in, then!" I shout, taking a step toward him. "Please, for once in my goddamn life, will someone tell me something? I'm tired of living in the shadows, only seeing the grey and black!" I take another step until I am right in front of him. "Don't I deserve that much?"

"You deserve the world, Savi." His whisper catches me off guard. I shake my head and try to remain on track.

"Don't be sweet right now, Cole." I pause. "Please," I lower my voice, "don't try to steer me off course. My father did all the time."

"I wasn't trying to." His hands slip around my waist, pulling me in. "It just came out. It's how I feel, and when all of this is over I intend to give it to you." His voice is low but still harsh. I can hear his frustration. "Look, baby, there *are* some things you need to know that are going to—"

"Logan," Mark says. I forgot he's still here. "We need to prep Savannah." He opens the door further, and in walks Keith.

Oh, fuck me!

"How mad is he?" I whisper to Cole.

"Let's just say not as mad as me."

"I am sorry, Cole."

"Let's just get through this." He kisses the top of my head and turns me around to face Keith.

Keith is holding a small box. He stops in front of me and speaks quickly, not looking directly at my face. "This is your tracking device." He opens the box and reveals a silver bracelet with a white stone in the middle. "It's undetectable." He quickly snaps it around my wrist. "Don't," his eyes finally meet mine, and they are cold, "take it off."

"I won't."

"This is the wire." He opens a second box from his pocket and shows me a matching necklace. "This will help—"

My stomach sinks. "I don't want to wear that." My voice caught in my throat.

"You have to," Keith states firmly, but as he looks at me, I can see he has conflicting expressions playing over his face.

I clasp my snowflake pendant. "No, Keith, I haven't taken this off since—" My eyes sting. It represents more than just Cole; it's a little reminder of our baby too.

"Savi," Cole whispers in my ear behind me, "just for the evening. I'll hold on to it and keep it safe." I hold myself very still for a moment then nod, not wanting to speak in fear I'd cry. Cole moves my hair aside. I feel his warm hands move over my skin as he unclasps it. He reaches for the necklace Keith is holding and secures it in place. It feels heavy. I don't like it.

"Testing, testing, one-two-three." Keith says in a quiet voice. John pops his head in the door giving a thumbs up.

Is Paul here too?

"No mention of the house, no mention of any of the guys being here, no mention what you've been up to. Most importantly, don't let them separate you from Derek." Keith warns, "If anything happens and you need us, your safe word is what?"

"Blackstone," I answer without missing a beat.

"Right."

"Guys. I'm going to be all right. It's my father who's in trouble now." I notice Keith glance at Cole. "Now what?"

"We leave in two minutes," Keith says as he turns around.

"Keith," I call out, making him stop. "I didn't run. I took someone with me and left a note. I was only trying to do the right thing, and I knew you and the rest of the house would never have let me come. Derek was my only chance to make things right."

He turns fully to study me. "I know you were doing what you thought was right. I know you found out what Cole planned to do, so the fact that you wanted to protect him and all of us makes me understand why you did what you did." He pauses. "But that doesn't mean I'm not furious with you, and it doesn't mean I'm not sticking a tracking device on your goddamn ass when we get home." I see his eyes crinkle slightly.

"Deal." I walk over and give him a hard hug. "I love you, Keith. You're family. Thank you for understanding."

"Yeah, well, don't get used to it. I'm not normally, so take what you can get." He gives me a little shove and nods at Cole. "I'll meet you outside the door."

I let out a long breath and try to absorb this situation.

"You ready?" Cole moves in front of me.

"Cole, is there anything I should know before I go in there? Please don't lie to me."

He rubs his chin, thinking. "Know I love you and will do anything to protect you, and when this is all over I intend to make you smile for the rest of your life."

I roll my eyes. "That would have been incredibly romantic if you didn't say it like I was going to war."

"In some ways you are."

"What does that even—?"

He grips the sides of my face and kisses me with so much lust I nearly forget what I was about to do. I put my hands on his shoulders as I press myself into his solid body. As quickly as he came in for the kiss, he pulls away and takes my hand.

"I love you." He pulls me toward the door.

"I love you too."

***

Cole

Cole pulls her into the adjoining room where Paul is at the table testing out the pin camera.

"Hey, Savi." Paul gives a tight smile and holds up the pin that is shaped like the New York state flag. "This will be our eyes."

Cole takes the small pin from Paul's fingers and pins

403

it to Savannah's blouse and waves his hand in front of it.

"All good," Paul states.

"Ummm," Savannah is biting her lip. "This is all a bit much."

"No," Cole answers simply, "it's frankly not enough."

"Okay, Savi." Derek enters from the hallway. "You ready to go?"

Cole's eyes narrow in on him. He is still furious at Derek and knows they will be having plenty of words after this is over. His instincts were right when it came to Derek Rent. He still doesn't trust him, and he hates that he still has to use him at all.

"You keep her safe, Rent," he says, pushing his finger hard into his chest, "or I'll personally take you out."

"Cole," Savannah hisses, squeezing her body in the space between them. "Please, let's just go before they decide to put any more devices on me." She turns to look at Cole, trying to act brave, but he can see she's scared. He wants nothing more than to take her home and lock her away in his bedroom and keep her safe from everything. "I'll see you soon." She kisses him on the lips softly, but he swipes his tongue inward, tasting as much of her as he can. She squeaks, making him kiss her harder. Finally he pulls away and lets her catch her breath. "Cole?"

"Yeah?"

"You're going to have to let go." She glances down at his cast-iron grip on her hips.

"Right." He steps back, watching Derek walk her out and unknowingly into the lion's den.

"I don't get it," Keith says, appearing at his side. "I know *we* are under orders not to tell her anything, but are *you* really going to let her go in blind?"

"I know Savannah, Keith. If she goes in knowing

who is behind all this, she'll charge them like a pissed off bull. It's safer for her to be her normal innocent self. They'll be less apt to harm her if she truly doesn't know anything."

Keith huffs. "I sure saw it before she left. I should've gone with my gut and followed her."

"No," Cole shakes his head, "you did the right thing and we were able to catch up with them."

"Perhaps, but she's sure as shit not known for her lying skills."

"Certainly not, and I love that about her," Cole admits.

"Me too."

Suddenly they both feel their conversation is getting awkward, and they start moving about. "Right, well, let's get this over with." Cole sits down at the table, watching the computer monitor.

"Well, fuck me," Mark hisses from the window, staring down at the street a pair of binoculars glued to his eyes. "Logan, you'll never guess who's here."

***

Savannah

I walk nervously down the sidewalk, my arm looped through Derek's, on the way to meet my father. It is starting to snow. I try to act normal, I really do, but after being surprised by Cole and the guys and being lit up like a Christmas tree with trackers, mics, and video equipment, I feel a nervous dance going on in my stomach.

"Maddison, my niece," Derek starts, "she reminds me so much of my sister. She has these big brown eyes like the cat from Puss in Boots." He laughs. "All that little girl has to do is look up at me and I turn all mushy. I'm visiting her after we get back home, and I'm going to take her to Disney World. She loves Sleep In Beauty. I've ordered her that princess dress from the movie. I'm soon to be her favorite uncle."

I can't thank him enough for chatting. I know he is doing it for me. I even forgive him for messing up the Disney character's name and manage to smile at him. I really need something to focus on because I do feel like I want to puke. The love he has for his niece is obvious. "That's really sweet of you, Derek. I wish I had an uncle like you growing up."

"Well, my sister and I were really close growing up. She practically raised me, as my parents worked a lot. I want to be a good uncle to her daughter. Besides, I doubt I'll ever have a kid, so Maddison is about as close to a daughter as I'll get."

"Why would you say that?"

He shrugs. "I love my job too much to give enough time to a woman."

"Oh, please, you just haven't found the right one yet. When you do, things will change."

He lets out a long breath. "You may have a point. I thought Logan was going to be a lone wolf up on his mountain until you came along."

"I'm happy," I smile up at him, "and you will be too someday."

"All right, enough *chick chat*. It's show time." He holds the door open for me. "No matter what happens up there, Savannah, I'm right there with you."

"Thanks, Derek." I squeeze his arm, happy to have him with me, and extremely happy now that Blackstone is watching and listening.

We ride the elevator up to the penthouse. The doors open, and there is my father wearing his usual black suit with a glass of scotch in his hand.

Chapter Seven

"Hello, dear. Come in, come in." He gives me an awkward hug then takes my jacket. I see his hand run along the pockets.

"Father." I nod, glancing around and noting that everything looks the same.

"Captain Rent, thank you for joining us this evening." My father shakes his hand.

I try not to let it bother me that my father knows Derek's rank. I'm guessing he did his homework before we came over this evening.

After my father makes us a drink along with his small talk, the doorbell rings, making my stomach drop into my lap.

"Are you expecting someone?" Derek asks, standing at my side.

My father rises and gives us a warm smile. "Actually, yes."

I stand, glancing at Derek, who looks as worried as I am. I thought this was a private dinner.

"Savannah?" I hear her voice and I nearly drop my drink. "Is that really you?"

"Lynn?" I can barely speak as she runs over and wraps her arms around me, embracing me in that familiar hug I missed dearly. She still looks amazing.

Everything matches, nothing out of place. I start to wonder about my own appearance. I quickly stop myself.

Don't go there, Savi.

"Oh my god, I thought you were dead! When your father called me to come over, I thought it was just for dinner, but when he told me you—" She pulls away and looks at me with tears in her eyes. "You look amazing!"

"Thanks, so do you." I point to Derek. "This is my friend Derek. Derek, this is my longtime friend Lynn."

"Pleased to meet you." Derek's voice is laced with discomfort. I don't blame him; I wasn't ready for this either.

"Well, well, well, look at you, spitfire." Luka holds open his arms, coming into the room and granting me a large hug. "Never thought we'd see you again."

"Luka!" I smile at him. "If you told me I would be standing here with you guys a few months ago, I wouldn't have believed it." I turn to Derek and make the introductions. Poor Derek, he does not like this.

"Okay, now, enough hovering, everyone." My father beams. "We are all excited to have her safely home. Let's get some food, and then Savannah can tell us everything that's happened."

Oh, lovely, a trip down memory lane.

Derek sits next to me, facing Lynn and Luka, and my father sits to my left at the head of the table. After the entree is served, the questions begin.

"So you were held captive for nearly seven months, and we understand you were rescued a while ago, but why are we only seeing you now?" Lynn asks, confused. "Where were you between then and now?"

Wow, jump right in, guys.

I see Derek shift ever so slightly. I'm not sure how to answer her, but I don't need to because my father does for me.

"She was in a safe house." My mouth drops open.

"Where?" Lynn asks over the rim of her wine glass.

"I can't say," I reply, looking at my father.

"Why?"

"Rules," I answer truthfully.

"Really?" She takes a bite of her salad. "So are you and Derek dating?"

"No," Derek answers quickly.

"No, she's dating a colonel," my father says calmly. "Colonel Cole Logan, correct?"

What the hell?

I'm shocked, dumbstruck, just staring at him. "Dad, how do you know that information?" I am completely blown away by his calm comments and knowledge of my situation.

"I'm a powerful man who knows a lot of things, Savannah. I know, for instance, that your boyfriend isn't who he says he is." My father's eyes shift over to Derek's. "Just like you, Captain Rent, isn't that right?"

"I'm not following," Derek says, dropping his napkin on the table.

"Oh, well, allow me to explain then. Luka." Luka stands and hands my father a file. He flips it open and hands me a photo.

My hands shake as I look at the photo. I then look up at my father and to Luka in disbelief as I try to process what I am seeing. Cole is shaking hands with my Devil, Jose Jorge. My mouth goes dry as I look over to Derek, who is shaking his head.

"Then there's this." My father slides another picture over top of the one I'm holding. It's Derek in a coffee shop, ordering at the counter. "Note who's waiting for him in line off to his right," he says to me.

"Oh…" I whisper in shock. There is my captor, Rodrigo Heredia, the bastard, the man who ordered— and enjoyed watching—Jose beat the shit out of me to the point where I wanted to die.

"Interesting suit you have on in that picture, Derek," my father adds, taking a sip of his scotch. "Looks familiar, don't you think, Savannah?"

Holy shit, this picture is from today? My hand flies to my stomach as Derek leans into me.

"Savannah, he's setting us up."

"Pictures don't lie, Derek," my father hisses like a cat about to attack.

I shake my head, feeling faint as my blood doesn't seem to be reaching my brain. "Derek, please explain. How can this be? Tell me you didn't know he was there." I feel my eyes water as I hold up Cole's picture. "Explain this, please. This isn't making sense. How could he?"

Derek's eyes are full of panic. "No, Savannah. You know Cole, he would never hurt you, he loves—"

Pop! Pop!

Crimson liquid sprays across my body. My ears are the ringing, and everything seems to move in slow motion. I turn my eyes to my father, who is holding a gun, then to Lynn and Luka, who are staring at the table. My gaze travels over to Derek, who is slumped in his chair, head flopped backward with a huge, gaping hole in the center of his forehead. Blood drains over his open eyes, down his nose, along his neck, and into his shirt.

The entire room is silent except for the ringing in my head. I try to focus on what is happening. My brain fights to process this moment.

"Savannah!" my father orders. "Look at me."

I unglue my eyes from Derek and somehow do as I'm told.

"Are you being tracked?"

I can feel panic start in my feet and travel through me like the bullet that is now nuzzled into Derek's skull.

"Are. You. Being. Tracked?" I can hear him, but I'm

not registering his words.

Derek's blood is in my steak.

Derek's brain is everywhere.

Derek was just speaking to me, and now he's not.

Derek is dead.

My father shot Derek.

My father just shot Derek Rent.

My father pointed a gun and shot my friend.

Derek is dead.

My brain keeps looping. I'm on a merry-go-round that I can't get off.

Someone's hands feel all along my sides, sliding over my arms and down my legs. My shoes are being removed and checked and placed back on. It's Lynn. What is she doing?

"I don't feel any wires, Doug," Lynn says from her knees. "She's clean."

"I doubt that," Luka mutters, coming to my side. "They wouldn't let her come here unprotected."

"Savannah," my father snaps at me, making me look over, "Derek and Cole were in negotiations with the men who took you. They were going to hand you over for a price. The American wants you. His men are the ones who kidnapped you. He came after me…us," he points to Lynn and Luka, "saying we needed to pay for what was taken from him. They were blackmailing me for the money. I tried to pay, but it was never enough. They nearly sucked me dry. All I wanted was to get you back, but I couldn't find you. No one could." He leans toward my frozen body. "I will not let them take you away from me again. Derek wouldn't have let you stay without a fight."

This doesn't make sense. I can't get my brain to work. I need to snap out of the fog.

My hands fly to my chain but it doesn't feel right. It doesn't give me the comfort I need.

"The necklace," Lynn says reaching over and tearing it from my neck. She drops it on the floor and smashes it with her heel of her shoe.

What the hell?

Lynn bends over and picks it up. "Yup, wires." She chucks it in the corner of the room and moves in front of me, looking into my eyes. "Savi, we need to leave. They know you're here, don't they?"

I don't move a muscle, then lean to the side and vomit next to her. She jumps back, gasping in disgust.

"Shock," I hear Luka say through a full mouthful of bloody meat.

I nearly vomit again.

Lynn's shiny shoes step toward me. "No shit, Luka. You're as helpful as ever."

She hands me a napkin, and that's when I see it.

Oh my god!

The silver bracelet with the heart dangling from the center. I quickly snatch the napkin and wipe my mouth in fear I'll lunge at her. I can't believe she's the mystery woman with the heart bracelet! What does this mean? Is Lynn somehow behind this? Why would she take a picture of me the same night I was taken? Why was she even there?

"We've got to move," my father orders as he pulls me to my feet, my head spinning. He eyes my pin then roughly removes it, ripping my shirt in the process. He drops it in his water glass and yanks on my limp arm to follow.

"We've got company," Luka says as we follow him into my father's personal office. "They're in the elevator."

"Let's go." Lynn wraps her arm around my waist then stops. *Shit.* She looks over at me as she unclasps the bracelet, my last tracking device, breaking it in two. Grabbing my wrist again, she leads us through a door that I've never seen before. It reminds me of the one in the safe house leading to Cole's bedroom. I force Cole out of my head. I've got to pull myself together, but I'm still reeling from the memory of Derek's lifeless body in the dining room.

After a several flights of stairs, we are in the parking lot where my father's limo is waiting.

"Savannah!" Everyone turns to see Paul holding a pistol pointed at us. "Let her go."

"You've done enough damage, Agent Paul," my father yells back.

Paul looks directly at me. "Savannah, walk toward me."

I'm so confused, and physically nothing is working. I just stand there, not sure if I am up or down, left or right. I wish I could snap out of this fog.

"More are coming," Luka whispers with his phone to his ear.

"Savannah, walk toward me," Paul repeats.

I feel my father shift as if shielding me with his body, and I hear that godforsaken *pop* noise and see Paul plummet to the ground.

"No!" I scream and try to rush over to Paul, but my father hooks his arm around my waist and pulls me to the car. "No! Paul!" He shoves me in and jumps in after me.

"Ahhhh!" I scream, trying to get out the helpless feeling that has a tight grip on me. "Why?" No one answers me.

Lynn and Luka follow, and before I know it, we're speeding out of the parking structure and down into an alleyway where we quickly switch cars.

I'm tumbling back into darkness, once again held in its teeth. Lost, alone, and once more nothing makes sense. I've served my time in hell. Why am I back here? What did I do to deserve a second round? One thing I know for sure, I fought my way out before, and I'll sure as hell do it again!

Squealing tires snap me out of my thoughts as Luka checks to see who it is.

"She must have another tracker on her," he yells.

Lynn's hands once again run along my body. I bat her hand away. I hate that she is touching me. I hate that she makes me seethe with anger because her fucking bracelet makes a noise every time she moves her arm. It makes me want to rip it off and jam it down her throat. I need to get out of here! None of this makes sense!

"Savi," she whispers, "I'm only trying to protect you."

"Don't touch me, Lynn," I hiss under my breath.

"What's wrong with you?"

"I said don't touch me." I shift to the corner of the limo, curling up in a ball.

"Savannah," Luka shouts, "I won't ask you again. Do you have a tracker on you?"

I shake my head as Luka's anger toward me brings me to see things more clearly. "It's the U.S. Army, Luka. This is what they're trained to do. You should know; you hired them."

"Hired them?" Lynn looks confused. Her eyes snap to Luka's. "Why would we hire—"

"Lynn!" Luka snaps at her.

My chest starts to rise and fall as more shit is tossed at me. "Wait…you didn't hire them? Why did they come for me then? How did they…?" My head goes light. "Oh my god…everything…everything is a friggin' lie." I start to cry and hyperventilate at the same time. Cole lied to me! "Pull over, I'm going to be sick…*pull over!*"

"No! We can't," my father shouts, grabbing a bag and shoving it on my lap.

I snatch it up, holding it tightly. "Please, will someone tell me the truth for once in my life? I demand to know the truth."

Suddenly the car stops in an alleyway and I am being pulled out and shoved into a trunk.

"Be a good girl, Savannah," my father warns.

The last thing I see is Luka's face as he slams the trunk lid down.

"Oh my god. Oh my god." My panic escalates as the car begins to move. I can hear Dr. Roberts's voice in my head. "Breathe in through your nose and out through your mouth. Panicking won't solve the problem. Stop and look at your surroundings. See what you can do to help your situation. There's always something you can do." Holy shit…my phone!

I cover the ear part when I pushed the number two and send.

"Savannah!" His voice makes me happy but it's quickly masked with confusion and hurt. "Are you there, baby?"

"Yes," I whisper, feeling so many things.

"Oh my god! Are you all right?"

"No." I start to sob. "I'm not."

"Where are you, baby? Something is blocking our transmission."

"I'm in a trunk."

"A trunk?" he nearly shouts. "Okay, did you see anything when they were putting you in there? Your surroundings? Make and model of the vehicle?"

"No." I sniff trying to hold it together.

"It's okay, baby, hang in there. John is tracking your phone now. It won't be long until we have you."

"Cole," my voice quivers, "Paul?"

"He's all right. Bullet hit his vest, just stunned him a little."

"Derek is—"

"Yeah, we saw." There's a pause. "I can explain that picture, baby, it—"

"Don't," I interrupt. "I can't handle any more lies. I'm barely holding it together."

"Savannah, no—"

I pull my guard up. "Promise me that if Blackstone finds me alive, you'll let me go. I deserve a few years of happiness." My words are rushed in case they are my last. "I love you, Cole, and that's what hurts the most."

"He's feeding you lies, Savannah. I'm coming for you, and when I get there I'll prove I'm still your knight." My chest clenches as his words tug on my heart.

"We stopped! Cole, the car stopped!" My breathing picks up again. "Oh god, I don't want to die."

"You're not going to die, Savannah. I see where you are. I'm roughly twenty minutes behind you."

Oh shit.

"I hear footsteps."

"Hide your phone, but don't hang up."

I quickly shove it into my bra just as the trunk opens. A man I've never seen before stares in at me.

"Savanna Miller?" he asks in a thick Hispanic accent. I'm frozen, paralyzed in fear. He grabs me and slaps me across the face. "I asked you a question. Is your name Savannah Miller?"

"Y-yes," I cry out.

He glances at a picture then pulls out a needle.

"No! No, no, no, no, please! Don't!" I scream. "pleaseeeee!" It doesn't make a lick of difference. He shoves the needle into my arm anyway.

A moment later I'm staring at a dim light peeking through a crack as I quickly drift off, knowing it's a one way ticket to hell.

Chapter Eight

Cole

Cole listens as her sobs slow and finally go quiet. Thankfully, Keith is driving, because Cole is finding it impossible to focus on anything but Savannah.

"I will take down her father and everyone with him," Cole curses as he flexes his hands on his lap.

John is clicking away on a computer in the back seat while Mark is making phone calls to Border Patrol, trying to find out if The American is in the United States or Mexico.

Seconds. Minutes. Hours. There is still no sound from Savannah. Cole nearly loses it a few times, wondering if she is alive or not. Mark has to talk him down several times. They can't call in local PD or the FBI in case someone is listening or watching. The risks are too high.

Cole finally leans back and closes his eyes, trying to remember every single part of Savannah. The one thing that comes to his mind above all else is how those deep, dark eyes of hers seem to find him even in a sea of people. God, he loves her eyes. They are hypnotic and they are his. He slips off, remembering her…

"Good morning, Colonel," Savannah's low voice makes his eyes filter open. He grins when he sees she is dressed in his army hat and button up uniform shirt, which is conveniently left undone, showing off the sides of her perfect breasts. "Time to do your morning workout."

He shakes his head as he goes to grab her. She leans back, holding up a finger.

"No, no, Colonel," her lips spread into a sexy smile, "drop and give me twenty."

His hands rush to her hips, lifting her in the air sitting her down on his growing erection. "You look damn fine in this." He fingers the shirt. "With what I have planned for you, I'm never going to wash it."

She leans down, her hair falling all around them. "Now, that, Colonel, sounds like a damn fine plan." She lifts her hips, slipping him inside her. His eyes roll back as she feeds him all the way in. She's more than ready, making everything heighten. Her body starts to move in a sexy weave and he peeks at the mirror facing them. Fuck him, it's one incredible sight. The way she arches her back makes him grow even harder. Her hands go to his hair, clutching a handful while biting her lip with a moan. One hand moves to her hip, helping her rock, the other to her breast, giving it a little squeeze. She's a fucking perfect wet dream. "Cole…"

"Logan," John whispers from the back seat, pulling him from his dream and filling him with emptiness that comes with his reality.

Cole's eyes pop open. He glances at the clock and sees he's been out for nearly three hours. "Yeah, John."

"They stopped at a hotel."

Cole sits up straighter. "Which one?"

"The Hilton, fourth floor." John reads off the address and Keith immediately heads in that direction.

When they arrive, they pull up into the driveway and do a sweep of the cars. Nothing seems out of the ordinary. The four of them head into the lobby. Cole and Keith approach the front desk.

"Hi, and welcome to The Hilton West Virginia. How can I help you this evening?"

Cole sees the young woman look him up and down as he approaches her. "Perfect," he mutters to himself. "A friend of ours checked in about thirty minutes ago. I forget his room number, but I was wondering if you could help me out?" After flirting for an endless ten minutes, he finally gets the room number.

They pile into the elevator and make their way down the hallway on the fourth floor. A man dressed in a room service uniform comes out of a room. Cole grabs his arm and whispers in his ear that they need his help and flashes his military badge.

"Yeah o-okay," the guy stutters.

"Knock," Cole orders when they stop in front of room 402.

The guy knocks and announces room service. Nothing. He knocks again, and still nothing.

"Excuse me? Can I help you?" a man dressed in a suit asks them as he approaches. "I'm the night manager. Are you gentlemen guests here?"

"No," Cole answers quickly, "but we have reason to believe a woman is being held against her will in this room."

"Are you the police?"

"No, sir. We're with U.S. Army Special Forces," Mark chimes in, knowing that normally gets people's attention. "We need to see inside that room."

"Well, I need to see some proof—"

"Agent John," Cole snaps out, "perhaps Channel Five News would like to hear about how The Hilton is allowing a man to rape a young woman with the

419

manager's knowledge. What's your name, sir?"

"No, no, that won't be necessary." He pulls out a master key and opens the door. Cole barges through first, weapon drawn. His stomach sinks when he sees the bed.

"Oh, shit, shit, shit!" Cole hisses, turning to Mark and feeling helpless.

Mark picks up the note resting on Savannah's cell phone.

I expected more from the U.S. Army.

The girl has been bought and paid for.

She's long gone.

"They just gained an hour and twenty on us," John says quietly behind them. "After talking with the manager, I got a description. It was a Hispanic man who rented the room alone. He did say he was in and out in a matter of minutes. He's sending me the surveillance footage as we speak."

"All right." Keith nods at him, then looks at Cole. "Let's focus on the fact that they need Savannah alive."

They make their way back to their truck and head south on the interstate. Cole's stomach is a ball of fire in his gut. This is a far cry from when he rescued Savannah the first time, as his heart wasn't *as* invested. Yes, the moment he saw her picture in that file he was drawn to her...but now, she is his life, the air he breathes, the reason to come home from a mission. Life isn't worth living if she isn't in it.

John speaks up. "I have a location on their vehicle. Fuck, they're at a private airport."

"I'm on it," Mark says, pulling out his cell phone.

***

Savannah

I feel something warm caress my face, drawing me up and away from the darkness that is consuming me. My head hurts and my mouth is dry. I start to moan. Everything feels terrible, like I was out drinking the night before, but I know that isn't true. My eyes flutter open and I focus on a green wall in front of me.

"Huh?" I mutter. "Wh-where am I?"

"Shhhh, Savannah, you're right where you should be." Her voice rings through my ears.

Lynn.

The last god-knows-how-many hours come flooding back to me. I try to move away, but her hands keep me on the bed.

"It's okay, sweetie, take a few moments to let the drug wear off."

It takes all my effort, but I pull away and roll off the bed, hitting the floor like a wet rag. Ouch! With every passing second I can feel the drug leaving my system. I tug my heavy body off the floor and shift to lean against the opposite wall.

We sit staring at one another for a long time. I finally clear my throat, wanting some fucking answers.

"Your bracelet." I point and watch her quickly cover it with her free hand. "Is that new?"

"Sort of." She forces a smile. She's lying or avoiding the truth.

I pull my leaden legs up to my chest. "Lynn, I've known you forever. You wouldn't have bought that for yourself. So who bought it for you?" I watch as her face goes from friendly to angry.

"A friend."

I shake my head, feeling tears pool in my eyes. "I

know you took my picture the night I was taken, Lynn. But I want to know why."

Her face hardens. "I did it for proof."

"Proof of what?"

She leans forward. "Proof that you were out drinking again, and proof that you were with Joe Might."

I skip the comment about the drinking and focus in on what really confuses me. "Joe Might? The new client?"

"Yes."

"What does he have to do with anything?"

She pushes off from the bed and stands by the window. "I hired him to take you out and have you returned at home at a certain time."

I think back to that night. I remember Joe asked me to go to dinner. We had both skipped out on a very boring meeting. I drop my head to my knees, trying to accept what she is telling me.

"I-I don't understand, Lynn. Why on earth would you do that?"

Lynn sighs, acting like she's annoyed that I can't keep up. "Fuck, Savannah, you had the perfect life, damn it! You had a father who made a ton of money, you got a crap load of attention, and all you had to do was stand there and look pretty. All he ever asked of you was to help a bit with his campaign, but no, you had to whine and bitch about it to me!" She makes a face. "Oh, Lynn, I hate being in the media. Oh, Lynn, I hate all the attention. Oh, Lynn, they think I'm a drunk, blah, blah, blah." She stomps her foot like a child. "You had it so good, but were you happy? No! You couldn't see past your own nose. It was always about poor Savannah. Christ, it made me so pissed!"

As everything comes pouring out of her, all I can do is stare at my best friend. I considered her like a sister for years, and to hear the poison in her voice is shocking.

To hear someone you love speak to you like this with such obvious hatred is hard to grasp. How she despises me. Yet again, lies are being told; it is incredibly heartbreaking.

"If I was such a terrible friend, Lynn, why did you stick with me for so long?"

"Fame." She shrugs like I should have connected the dots. "You were going to take me places, and I knew I could benefit, until you started fucking up in the media. That's when everything changed, that's when I knew a decision needed to be made."

The perfect storm is starting to brew inside me, tilting my world off its axis. "Decision?"

"Yes, Savannah, you were bringing everyone down with all your failures, so I stepped up to the plate. I knew someone who knew someone who was involved in human trafficking. Small world, hey?" She chuckles to herself. "So I made some calls, and lo and behold, seems the Mayor of New York's daughter was a sweet little prize to get. So I hired Joe Might, a friend of mine, to pose as a potential buyer and make sure you arrived at your condo at the right time. I knew you would go get the files. You were always on top of things. You were always so OCD when it came to your job." She rolls her eyes in disgust. "Then poof, you were gone." She laughs. "Like a magic trick, now you see her, now you don't."

That storm finally breaks, and I jump up and grab her by the hair, the two of us falling on the floor as I punch and kick and hit her, feeling the anger fueling my muscles. I'm sick of the lies, sick of being a victim. She certainly wasn't expecting it, and I get quite a few good ones in before something cracks me in the head and everything goes black.

"*Perra.*" His voice jolts me from my sleep. "Oh, sweet *perra*, you came back."

I quickly sit up and take in my surroundings. I'm in an attractive room with Spanish décor. Sunlight is streaming in through a large window. It's hot. I'm sweating. I wipe my forehead and smell something funny. I realize I'm not alone in my bed. I scramble to my feet, seeing the blood. Oh my god, there's so much blood! I'm covered in it. My hair, my hands, my arms, my legs. My fingers shake as I tug the corner of the sheet that's closest to me. I need to know who it is. Dark hair peeks out. He is turned away from me. I see his shoulders, back, and waist. I drop the sheet and round the bed. I don't have to see his face to know who it is. My hands cover my mouth as vomit spews out of me.

"No!" I heave and wail at the same time. This can't be happening! The door opens quickly, and I see The American dressed in shorts and a t-shirt staring at me.

"You did this, you know." He points with his chin toward the jelly-like body. "If you had just given yourself over to me in the first place, Agent Mark Lopez would still be alive."

"Fuck you," I hiss, wiping my mouth free of vomit. "Fuck all of you."

He walks toward me as I raise my chin to meet his stare. His shoulder rises and he punches me square in the face. I feel myself falling, but I never hit the ground. I just keep falling...

I jolt straight up, trying to make sense of what's going on. I feel around the bed, empty. I see a window, but it looks different than the one I saw before, and it is night. What? So was I dreaming before? Is Mark alive?

Pushing the covers away, I see I'm still in my own clothes. They're dirty, but at least they are mine.

"Oh, good, you're awake," a voice says, coming out of what looks like a bathroom. Luka approaches, holding out a bag. "Here." He sits the Nordstrom bag in front of me. "We need to meet downstairs in twenty. That should be enough time for you to shower, change, and be ready for the exchange."

"Exchange?" I blurt out, looking around the room.

Luka nods as he sits a cup of coffee on the table next to the window. "Yes, Savannah. You've been bought and paid for. We just need to make sure all the little details are properly checked out before we hand over our, for want of a better word, ace."

My head is shaking back and forth. It seems nothing in my life can be trusted. In disbelief, I listen to someone else I considered a good friend—an uncle, even—talk about selling me like I'm nothing to him at all but a piece of merchandise. The memory of the truck flickers. "Why the trunk? If I'm still your so-called ace, why did you hand me over to that man? Why risk it?"

He taps his head. "We had to risk it. Your boyfriend's team was hot on our trail. We needed to throw them off, so we hired a friend to take you for a joy ride." He shakes his head and smiles. "It wasn't until he heard you talking on that cell phone that he decided to do the hotel trick. He dropped you off to us before he went to the hotel and left a little note for Logan to find. It worked like a charm. Meanwhile, we hopped the first plane to TJ, and you are now lost in a sea of a million people."

Tijuana? Mexico...The blood drains to my toes. I promised myself I'd never step over the Mexican border again as long as I lived. I've experienced enough hell here for a lifetime, but here I am being handed over to The American in the one place I hate beyond all else. I can't do this. Not again. I just can't. I have to do something.

"Okay," Luka slaps his hands together, making me jump, "let's go." He stares at me as I sit like a stone. "You need some help with that?" He smirks and points to my blouse. My eyes shoot to his, more shocked than ever. Luka has never said anything sexual to me before.

Never even hinted at it. He really was like an uncle to me. It must show on my face, because he shrugs. "Not like I haven't thought about it before, Savannah. I'm only human. Can't blame a man for trying." I want to be sick again...or was I sick before? I can't tell if that was a dream.

I grab the bag and hurry to the restroom, slamming the door behind me. I turn on the water and peel my clothes off and toss them on the floor. I'm not sure when I'll have a chance to shower again, so I take my time. I find a razor, body wash, shampoo, and conditioner, and with my brain on overdrive I put them to good use.

I look at myself in the mirror, my hair almost dry from the heat blasting in through the tiny window. A light pink dress hits slightly above my knees, and I'm wearing cream color heels. I wonder if Luka was the one who bought the panties and matching bra. The thought makes me want to throw something at the mirror. My eyes focus on the razor beside the soap dish. I examine it, then take the thin comb and snap the skinny blades out. They drop into my hand in one small unit. I shrug out of the top of the dress, taking the sharp blade and cutting into the first layer of lace on the bra. Just large enough to tuck the blade inside so it's undetectable. I certainly won't be able to defend myself with it, but I am desperate enough to take anything useful, and I have other ideas if there is any possibility I'm going to be held in another cell. I set the handle of the razor back down so it looks normal and peek out the miniscule window.

All I can see are rows and rows of tin roofs. But I do spot a plane landing off in the distance. I must be close to the airport. Two streets down, I see a convenience store with a payphone outside. I need to get out of here! I nearly sob when I hear Luka's voice through the door telling me it's time to go. I push on the glass, not that I could ever fit through it, and scream, hoping someone can hear me. A pair of hands grab my wrists, pulling them down roughly.

"Not this time, Savannah. This time you play by our rules." He yanks me to follow, and somehow I do. He shoves me into the elevator and slams his hand over the L button. "Christ, woman, I wish you would just do as you're told!"

I stare at the side of his face, wanting so badly to kick him in the stomach. "Oh, I'm sorry, Luka. Should I just nod and smile as you hand me over to The American like I'm some piece of meat?"

"Shut up, Savannah," he grits out.

"Fuck you, Luka!" I snap back without thinking.

Suddenly he's wrapping his hands around my throat, slamming me back into the elevator wall. Hard. My head snaps forward from the impact. I cry out, but his lips smash into mine as his grip around my neck tightens. My hands claw at his shirt, but he doesn't stop. He thrusts his tongue forward as I try to wiggle free. He's too strong. Oh god, this is disgusting. Finally my brain kicks into action and I jam my knee with all the force I have into his tiny testicles. Immediately he lets go, falling backward. I gasp heavily, trying to get a full breath of air into my screaming lungs, and drop to my knees.

"Fucking bitch!" He groans above me as he drives his fist into my cheek. My teeth clench at the impact, and pain shoots everywhere. This is way too much like my last 'trip to Mexico.' My brain snaps to full alert. I need to be able to fight, I need to stay focused. The door opens and I see a blurry figure standing in front of me.

"What the fuck!" my father yells out. I feel his hands on me, lifting me to my feet. I have a small moment where I think my father might actually take pity on me, take me home and protect me from these monsters. "Are you insane? She needs to be in mint condition. If he

427

thinks we've hurt her in any way, he may back out of the deal." So much for 'daddy dearest.' *I'm a fool.*

"What the shit is taking so long?" Lynn shouts from behind us. "We have four minutes before he shows up. Let's move." I feel her cast-iron grip on my arm, tugging me toward the restaurant. I notice the staff won't make eye contact with me, and I think I may be the only guest.

Lynn drops me into a wooden seat as the other three sit around the table. I stare at the yellow flower floating on top of the water in a square clear jar.

"Savannah?" Lynn hisses at me. I look over as she opens her purse and shows me her handgun. Weapons don't really scare me anymore, so I don't react. "You try and run, I'll shoot you. I have excellent aim."

"Good for you, Lynn," I whisper with a sigh. I'm tired of her now. I look back at the flower, thinking about how much it reminds me of myself at the moment, just floating in a world I have no control over, and helpless to whatever fate comes my way. We're both screwed.

Mark, John, Paul, Keith, Abigail, June, Sue, Daniel, Scoot, Mike, Frank, Derek...Cole. I keep reciting their names over and over, trying to keep my brain sharp. I will not get lost again, I will not get lost in my mind. I need to stay in the present. Mark, John, Paul, Keith...My head turns to my father.

"How, Dad?" I shake my head. "Please just tell me how you can do this to your own daughter. Do I really mean nothing to you?" I hate that my voice cracks at the end.

He sips his coffee, glancing at Luka, then to me. "It's just business, Savannah. Please don't get all emotional right now. I need you to be on your best behavior."

It's not a good feeling when your heart breaks in two, but the anger fuses it back together in a matter of seconds. I bite the inside of my cheek to hold back the words, but it doesn't work. My eyes narrow in on his, and I let fly. "I hope you rot in hell, you pathetic excuse for a father! Mom was right, you were never much of a man." This isn't true, but I know it will hurt his pride.

He quickly stands and makes his way over to me and slaps me across the face. I fall out of the chair, hitting the floor and laughing hysterically. This time Lynn comes over, and I think she's going to help me to my feet, but she kicks my side hard. I cry out, coughing and trying to catch my breath. Well, if my plan was to get them all to hit me, it worked. I hope if I look like shit there'll be some hell to pay from The American.

I roll to my side, tucking my legs up to my stomach. "Mark, John, Paul, Keith." I start my chant but freeze when two cobra heads stop inches from my face. Fear dances around my stomach, replacing the pain of my possibly fractured ribs. He bends down and wipes the hair out of my face. Tears are streaming from my eyes now, big hot tears. My family is selling me, The American bought me, the love of my life may have betrayed me, and Derek is dead because of me! All I want is to do is disappear, have something swallow me up, because *anything* is better than the outcome of this.

"Who did this?" The American asks in a booming voice, looking at me, but I just shake. He reaches out and lifts me carefully and places me on the chair. This action scares me, as it feels almost tender, and for some reason that makes me even more frightened of him. I tense and sit awkwardly in the chair with my eyes glued to the floor.

"Ms. Miller." I look up and see a white man, who looks like a lighter version of Mike, black and white tattoos from head to toe, and big and beefy. I'm taking it he's the muscle for The American. He gives me a tight smile then glares at the rest of the group. He continues to stand by my side as Luka decides to start the conversation off.

"So, here she is. We held up our end of the bargain, and now it's time for you to do the same." Luka yanks at his tie, clearly uncomfortable in The American's stare.

Lynn tosses out her best smile. "So why don't you just make the call to Rodrigo, and we can all be home in time for tea?"

I shake my head, thinking I've never seen Lynn drink a cup of friggin' tea in her life. The table is painfully quiet. All I can hear is the pounding in my head, and I feel my cheek pulsing to my rapid heartbeat. I move without thinking, making everyone look at me. I hesitate but slowly reach into my glass of water and start piling up ice cubes into my cloth napkin, then hold my makeshift icepack to my cheek and eye, tensing in pain. Christ, it hurts.

Finally, The American, who is now watching me closely, turns to look at the rest of them. "Who hit her eye?" His words are spoken with such tightly controlled anger it makes me suck in my breath. "Three, two..."

"Luka!" Lynn blurts out, pointing to him across the table. You can actually see the blood drain from Luka's face and it twists with her betrayal.

The American pulls out a pistol, points it at Luka's skull, and pulls the trigger. His body flies backward to the floor. Lynn is screaming, my father is frozen, and I'm numb, beyond caring. The American and his muscle just sit there acting like nothing has happened, exactly how my father, Lynn, and Luka were when Derek was shot. *Karma.*

The American tucks his gun away. "When we are clear, I will call Rodrigo and tell them the deal is done." He stands and buttons up his suit jacket. "But I warn you, if you so much as step in my way, I will not hesitate to kill you like I did your friend." He takes my hand, pulling me up to my feet. "Is there anything you would like to say, Savannah?"

I stare up at him. "To which group of animals are you referring?"

He smiles gently like he's in love with me. "Less sass, my love. I can be good to you, and you do not want to anger me." His smile may be gentle, but his eyes have a glint of steel. "I can be very, very bad when I am angry, my sweet, but it is your call."

I nearly laugh at that. "I'm not your love, nor am I sweet, and you can do anything you want to me because, frankly, I don't care. It's all been done before."

My father stands and holds up his hands. "Savi, just do as you're told, please."

I shake my head in utter disbelief. "Really, *Douglas*, you want to play the concerned father now? Save it." I turn to Lynn. "So help me God, I hope this all comes crashing down on top of you both. I hope you burn in hell, you evil pieces of shit." I turn on my heel and exit the room with the muscle coming up behind me quickly.

"Ms. Miller," he calls out. I stop, knowing there's no point. I've been bought and paid for. The American comes up to me, gripping a firm hand around the back of my neck.

"You will never turn your back to me again," he whispers for only the three of us to hear. "Now, I have some work to do. Tim here will make sure you get home safely, where you will wait for me in our room, with nothing on. Oh, and, love, I like you to be smooth down south." His eyes drop to my crotch. He leans in, grips my head, and kisses me hard. I try to fight it, but he digs his thumb into my shoulder, making me cry and go limp. Once he's finished, he pushes me into Tim's grip. "I'll be home tonight. Make sure she's ready for me."

"Yes, sir." Tim nods and wraps his huge hand around my wrist.

I spit on the ground once he's gone. Tim says nothing

as he pushes me into the elevator and we go down to the parking level. He opens the door of a black town car and helps me in. I notice once the door is closed, it locks. Tim slips into the driver's seat, starts the car, and pulls into traffic.

That's when I shatter into a million pieces. A horrible sob bursts from my throat and I start to shut down. Mark, John, Paul, Keith, Abigail, June, Sue, Daniel, Scoot, Mike, Frank, Derek, Cole…but it doesn't work. I can feel myself slipping away.

I barely feel the car stop. I only blink a few times when Tim climbs into the back seat with me. He holds up his hands, showing me he won't hurt me. "Here." He opens a little black bag and shows me the label Extra Strength Tylenol. I look at him, confused. There has to be a catch. "Take three, miss, you'll need it. Are your ribs all right?" I shake my head no, because honestly they aren't. He nods then hands me a bottle of water, removing the lid.

"Why do you work for him?" I'm not really sure why I ask, but I want to know and I feel like I need to say something.

He tucks the Tylenol away, avoiding eye contact. "It wasn't a choice."

Chapter Nine

Cole

Cole raises his gloved hand up into the air, waiting for Mario to get into position. Paul and John are sprawled out on the couches, beyond beat from sparring with him earlier.

"Logan, you've been at this for over three hours." Mario shakes his head. "Your body needs a break, and god knows we do too."

"Again," Cole grunts out, still reeling with the decision to come home. It was the hardest decision, but they need to regroup and find what resources they can use.

Mario sighs and they continue to box for the next fifty minutes until he finally calls it quits. Cole, still with energy to burn, hits the free weights until he's physically exhausted.

After a cold shower, he finally heads to his office and pours himself a double. He tries hard to pretend Savannah is in his bedroom waiting for him to join her, her eyes wild with excitement as she peels off his clothes like it's the first time. The thought nearly brings him to his knees. God, he loves her...and now...He shakes his head trying to clear it. Then he lets out a long stream of air and makes a call.

"I wondered when I was going to hear from you." Frank's voice is quieter than normal.

Cole sips his brandy. "Anything?"

"Luka Donavan didn't return with the Mayor or Lynn." He sighs. "We had a tail on them, but he only caught up with them at the airport. The Mayor told the press that he and Lynn were on a much-needed vacation from the media. They were at the TJ airport."

"So you have nothing?"

There's a pause.

"She's been handed over, Logan. She was bought and paid for and, we believe, delivered to The American." Frank clears his throat. "Whatever you need."

"Blackstone will be shipping out at twenty hundred. I want your team, Frank. I want Eagle Eye."

"Consider it done."

"I need to make a trip to Texas too."

"Cindy?"

"Yeah, she knows a lot. I'll do what I have to."

"I agree."

Cole slams back the rest of his drink and sends out a text telling Blackstone they're leaving in sixty minutes. He closes his eyes and shifts into survival mode.

The house is quiet; everyone seems to be busy. He finds his mother in the kitchen stirring her tea and staring out the window. She turns when she hears his footsteps, and tears leak out of the corners of her eyes. Batting them away, she tries to be strong.

"She's a fighter, Cole."

"That she is." He slumps onto the stool, feeling the weight of the world falling all around him.

His mother slides a comforting hand over his shoulder. "She thought she was doing the right thing. You can't blame her for loving you too much."

"I don't."

"It's easy to walk into the lion's den when you don't know the lion is there."

"Trust me, Mother, she's well aware he's home now."

"Logan." Mark's voice makes his head snap up. Mark's puffy eyes give more away than he'd probably like to let on. "Umm, can I get you to look over the map with me?" Cole nods and stands as he forces a smile at his mom and goes to walk by Mark. Mark grabs his arm and wraps him in a hug, throwing Cole off. "I'm sorry," Mark whispers in a sob, holding him tightly, "I'm so sorry, Cole." Cole clings to his best friend, his brother, and finally lets out a little cry of his own.

***

Savannah

I keep my eyes closed, trying to hold the panic at bay. I start with Cole's shaggy, silky hair just long enough that I can get the perfect grip to haul him to my mouth. His dark eyes, his perfect nose, his lips, his smile that...I jolt forward as the car comes to a stop. I peer out the window and see we're in the middle of nowhere, sitting in front of two huge cast-iron gates. I memorize the make of the security system and carefully watch Tim punch 55725 into the key pad. The gates swing open and we start to roll forward down a long, dusty driveway.

The house strikes me as odd, though, as it looks like a home straight out of Louisiana. It has two stories and is painted white with green shutters. There are six pillars in the front, and two wrap-around balconies, one on top and one on the bottom. Lord, this place is massive.

Then it dawns on me this is my new prison. Sure, it's a step up from the last one, but nonetheless, it's still a prison.

There are men with rifles scattered across the yard, and security cameras pointing in every direction. German shepherds on leads are sniffing the ground. One catches my scent and starts to growl as Tim holds the door open, watching me crumble, falling apart all over again. He moves to help me out carefully. He's oddly gentle for such a big man.

He opens the door for me and nods at the butler and wait staff. They quickly scurry out of sight. Tim leads me upstairs to a bedroom immediately to the left. He tells me it's my room and that anything I need will be in the bathroom. I think back to what The American said. *Make sure she's ready for me.* I freeze, stuck mid-step.

"I can't do this, Tim." I start to shake. "Please, please get me out of here!" I turn to him with pleading eyes. "I don't belong here. I don't want to be here. I don't want that man touching me…" Tim reaches for my elbow, pulling me across the room and into the bathroom. He closes the door and holds a finger up to his mouth, urging me to be quiet.

He leans in close, making me stiffen. "Cry," he whispers, pulling back to look into my eyes with a strange expression. "When he goes to touch you, cry and say no. He won't be able to do it. Denton is one evil fucker, but the one thing he won't do is touch a woman against her will."

I blink a few times and try to absorb what he just said. Denton? So The American's name is Denton. "Why?" I struggle to get my thoughts in order. "Why in the hell would he bring me here? Does he really think I would let him sleep with me?"

Tim shakes his head slowly then checks his watch. "Denton's smart." He taps his head. "Very, very smart. That's why all these years no one's been able to touch him. He'll use mind games to control you, and before you know it he'll get you into his bed. Denton can convince a priest to kill; he's that good at manipulation."

"Why does it sound like I'm not the first woman he's had here?"

"You're the fifth."

"Fifth!" I hiss, only to have Tim's huge hand wrap around my mouth.

He closes his eyes like he's regretting telling me anything. "Yes, so you won't be alone here in this house." *Wait! The girls are here?* "You can't trust them, Savannah, they're all brainwashed, and whatever you say to them they will tell Denton, and you'll be punished." He drops his hand. "Punished in worse ways than when you were with Rodrigo."

My eyes flicker with fear as I scan the bathroom. "Tim, please tell me how to get out of here. I won't last. I'll end it now."

Stepping away from me and turning on the shower, letting hot steam fill the room, he motions for me to move away from the door and into a walk-in closet at the back of the bathroom. He closes the doors behind us and turns on the tiny light. I don't know why, but I don't feel nervous with Tim, maybe because he reminds of the guys back at the house. Big, but kind.

"Look, Savannah, I'm not a bad person. I never asked to work for the Cartel. I was just born into this life. My father was a runner for cocaine when he met my mother and got her pregnant. Trouble was, when she found out who my father really was, she tried to leave him. They only let her live until I was born." His eyes shift downward for a moment. "I found out later my father was the one who killed my mother. I'll spare you the details." *Thanks.* "After that, my father gained the trust of the higher-ups and soon ran a few groups smuggling weapons and people in and out. If I wanted to live, I had to keep my head down and my mouth shut. They started me out small, but once they realized I could slip through the border with no problem, I was transferred to work with my father, and from there to here. Denton has known me for a few years, and a year ago told me I was going to be working for him. You don't say no to Denton. I hate it here, I hate those women. Two of them I'm convinced played Denton, because they were evil from day one, and the other three are way past trying to live."

"I'm really sorry for your mother, Tim."

"Thank you, as I am for your mother."

This throws me. "You know my mother is dead?"

"I know all about you, Savannah, down to your shoe size."

"Well, that's not incredibly creepy," I mutter sarcastically.

"It's my job, just like it is for Logan's company."

My breath gets caught in my throat. Cole's name being uttered from Tim's lips is unnerving. "You know about Logan?"

"I know he's Special Forces. I know what he specializes in. I know that as soon as he slips back into the States, he drops off the radar just like Denton does. Denton has been trying to track Logan's group for years, but he hasn't succeeded. When Denton found out Logan had you, well, let's just say my job's been pretty miserable."

I sink onto a small chair, as my legs can no longer hold my weight. I'm just going to say it. "Tim, you must know, Logan is a good man."

"I do," he interrupts, making me pause and stare for a moment.

"Okay." I nod. "Well, you say you can slip across the border without being seen. Can you help me get out of here and back home?" I'm careful not to say where home is.

"You want to go home?" His eyebrow rises. "Back to

your father? Back to that bitch Lynn?"

"No." I stand. "I want to go back to the States where I can live a real life that's mine." He smiles slightly. I'm guessing that's the answer he was looking for.

"You'll never get that while Denton is alive."

I feel bold. "Then let's deal with that problem." His eyes pop open. "Look, Tim, I've been through some real shit before. I've never killed anyone, but I know good trumps evil. You said it yourself, Denton is pure evil. Let's try and make this world just a little bit better by taking him out of it."

He stands there towering over me, studying me, thinking for a few long moments. I feel myself start to second guess if I can trust this guy. Oh shit, maybe this is a test!

"It can't happen right away," he finally says, putting his hands on his hips. "It'll be too obvious."

"How long are you thinking?"

"A few months."

"Two weeks max is all I can do."

He makes a face. "A month."

"Two weeks."

"Three."

I let out a long, shaky breath, mulling over my options. I could try and escape, but if he punishes like Tim says he does, I know I'll break. "Okay, under one condition." *Oh god, what am I agreeing to?*

"What's that?"

***

Cole

Cole clicks his radio, signaling to Blackstone that they are close to the drop-off spot. They're five minutes out when a call comes through on the satellite phone. He glances at his father, who shakes his head. No one should be calling unless something's happened. Everyone is silent; only the rev of the Land Rover engine can be heard.

"Mike?" Cole answers quietly.

"You're not going to believe this, Logan, but...go ahead."

"Cole?" Her voice smacks his stomach into a somersault and lodges it right into his throat.

"Savannah? Where are you?" He has a ton of questions but he stops himself.

"Hi." He can tell she's fighting tears.

"Hi, baby," he gets out. "Where are you?"

"I'm somewhere in TJ. Some farm with a Louisiana-looking home. Cole, his name is Denton."

"The American's?" he asks, still shocked to hear her voice.

"Yes. Luka's dead. The American killed him. I don't know where Douglas and Lynn are. I'm here at The American's house, and there are other girls here. Five others." She races on, "The American brainwashes them. He says he wants to sleep with me tonight, but..." Cole clenches his jaw so hard he's sure he cracked a tooth. "Tim is his muscle, and he's going to help me."

"Hold on." Cole is trying to take in her words, but she's talking a mile a minute. "Who's Tim?"

"The American's bodyguard. He said he doesn't want to help Denton anymore. Cole, he's going to help me get rid of him. It will take three weeks, then Tim will help me get back home."

Cole glances at his father and shakes his head. "Savi, I need you to listen to me. Are you near a window?"

"There's nothing for miles, Cole. Umm, Depex...the-the security key code to get through the driveway gates is, ahh, 55725. "

Cole scribbles her information on his arm. "Okay,

calm down, slow down. How long did you drive for?"

"I don't know. Tim gave me Tylenol for the pain, so I slept most of the way."

Cole lets out a long breath. "Baby, that wasn't Tylenol. He drugged you so you didn't know where he was taking you."

"No, Cole, Tim is going to help me."

"Why did you have to take Tylenol?" Cole asks, ignoring her last comment. *Silence.* "Savannah?"

"My family all turned on me; that's why The American killed Luka. I think my ribs are fractured. Physically I'm okay, but until Tim offered to help me I think I was mentally slipping."

Cole closes his eyes, wanting to take her pain away. "We're about to cross the border. I'm coming for you, baby. I will make sure of it." He hears her starting to cry and jams his fist into the dashboard, cracking it. John pulls the Land Rover over, getting out with the others and giving him a moment alone with her.

"I have this tiny," she hiccups, trying to find her voice, "razor blade tucked into my bra. I thought about using it."

Cole's heart misses a beat. Leaning forward and catching himself, he pleads with her. "Please, Savannah, hold on for me, I need you. If you can take anything away from this phone call, take this. I'm coming for you. I'm in love with you, you know that! We're going to be okay. I just need you to hang on. You need to make me another Fritter."

"Yes, Colonel." Her voice suddenly changes; someone must have come into the room.

"Is there someone there?"

"Yes."

"Tim?"

"Yes."

"Just stay put, I'm coming for you. I need you to

repeat after me. *"Nos encontramos mañana enfrente de la marketa con la puerta roja a las tres de la tarde."* She does, making it sound like she speaks Spanish fluently. "Perfect job. Okay, don't say a word about any of us."

"All right," she sniffs, making him want to cry himself. "Colonel?"

"Yes, baby?"

"The snowflake…that's what I'm holding onto." The line goes dead.

"You got a hit, Mike?" he asks, knowing Mike is still listening and taking down all the information Savannah rambled off.

"Burner phone. I've already started the search on the security system. I'll be in touch."

Cole drops the phone on his lap, needing a moment to comprehend everything that just happened. His heart aches thinking about her last words. The night he bought the snowflake necklace for her was the night they both declared their love for one another. It's good to know that even after all she has been through, especially after seeing that photo, she still loves him.

His father is the first to get into the Land Rover. "Tell me, is our girl all right?"

Cole wipes his eyes. He hadn't even realized they were watering while he talked to her. "We'll see." Daniel reaches over and gives his son's shoulder a tight squeeze. The rest of the guys pile in, and as John starts the engine, Cole says, "Change in plans, boys."

***

Savannah

I watch Tim slip the burner phone into his pocket. He nods toward the bathroom.

"He'll be expecting you to be clean." He makes a

sorry face. "We can't have him wondering why I didn't do my job."

I look down, feeling a wave of nausea run through me. Can I really trust this man? I wonder what Cole made me repeat. I know better than to ask questions when we are not alone. Tim picks out a short dress and leaves, saying I need to be downstairs in one hour for The American's arrival.

I quickly shower, taking every so often to control my meltdowns, dress in the ridiculously short red dress, slip on what can only be described as stripper stilettos, and head downstairs. Every step makes my stomach knot tighter, makes me want to run out the front door and across the border to freedom at any cost.

A little old man, a staff member, gives me a small nod and points to where I'm supposed to go. I wonder if he knows I'm being held here against my will. I'm sure he does.

I step into a massive dining area and find myself stared down by five very scary girls who look like they're out for blood. I have no doubt that I just stepped into a new rendition of The Hunger Games. I take the open seat next to a blonde girl who snickers when I settle in.

The redhead with the bad dye job across from me makes a show of looking me over. Her drawn-on eyebrows are raised as she shoots daggers at me. Not knowing what to do with myself, I reach for my napkin and place it on my lap.

"*Esta gringa* thinks she has manners," Eyebrows snickers, making the rest of the girls laugh except the blonde girl next to me.

"Her name is Savannah," The American—Denton—says, his voice sucking every ounce of strength I have left out of me. "You can learn something from her, Tracy." He leans in and runs the back of his fingers down my cheek. I freeze, paralyzed in fear.

Tracy, a.k.a. Eyebrows, points her fork at me. "Shit, Denton, she doesn't even want you." She looks over at him, flashing a toothy smile. "You want me to show you how much I want you?" She opens her mouth and flicks her tongue. *Yuck.*

"Enough, Tracy, or I'll send you upstairs again." Tracy's face drops at The American's words.

Dinner is served, and they all start to eat. I stare at the plate, feeling like I want to vomit.

"Every girl has to eat, Savannah." The American rests his hand on mine. I quickly pull it out from under his, not wanting any kind of contact with him. "Are you going to fight me every step of the way, my love?"

"I'm not your love."

"In time you will be," he says, sounding very matter of fact.

"You can't love a monster," I hiss under my breath, hearing the girls gasp.

The American closes his eyes and takes a deep breath. "You will treat me with respect, Savannah."

"Like you have with me?" I counter, fearing my not-so-silver tongue is going to get the best of me here soon.

"Leave us," he commands the rest of the girls. They quickly grab their plates and scurry out of the room. Eyebrows mutters something about the attic as she leaves, making the hair on my neck stand at attention.

I notice Tim giving me a tiny shake of the head. I don't care; I won't be here for much longer. One way or another I will be leaving this house.

A serving guy snatches my plate from in front of me as someone else removes my fork and knife.

Denton chucks his napkin on his empty plate with a deep sigh. "I don't tolerate name calling. I demand respect from you." *My god, this man has some nerve.* "So what do you have to say to me?"

444

Don't do it, don't do it, don't do it!

"You're insane if you think you'll get me to break like the rest of your puppets." I get to my feet, making the chair scrape along the floor. My voice is oddly steady. "You're forgetting, *Denton*, I was held captive for seven months. They didn't break me, they only made me stronger." That's a lie, but he doesn't need to know that. I tap my head and lean toward him. "Mentally and physically. So what I have to say to you, *Denton the monster*, is fuck you." I say the last two words slowly and accurately.

He runs his tongue slowly along his teeth, and I can see him vibrating. Oh, I hit a nerve. But then a smile appears, and I know I won't like what's coming next.

"I think it might be time to show you that your life isn't what you think it is." He nods to Tim, who quickly exits, returning with a laptop and a file.

Okay...

Denton opens the laptop, clicks a few buttons, and then turns it to face me.

I lean forward then freeze, seeing it's the TMZ article the woman in the elevator mentioned. My eyes trickle down to the two people kissing and I almost lose it.

Chapter Ten

My father's arm is wrapped around Lynn's waist, and his tongue is stuck down her throat. He clicks a few images, showing me different angles. No matter how many times I look away and look back, I feel betrayed. He was like a father to her! She was his other daughter! How many times have I heard him say that? I wonder if Luka knew.

"Luka was involved too," he says as if I had asked out loud. "It is said they took turns sometimes, or perhaps at the same time. Lynn was their entertainment, but it is she who is the true mastermind of this whole situation." The American swings the computer to face him and starts typing away. "You see, Savannah, your own family wanted nothing to do with you. This threesome has been going on for years. Lynn was barely of legal age when your father approached her. Lynn has ambition; she is determined to make something of herself, so she went along."

This is insane... I sink back into my chair.

"How-how could you know all of this?"

"I'll get to that right after...this." He turns the laptop around again, and I feel my feistiness fade away, leaving raw, gritty pain. "Yes, Savannah, the Colonel has been a busy man since you've been gone."

446

"It's…" I take a moment gathering myself, "just a picture." *Another one to add to the pile.* Deep down I know there has to be an explanation, but he hits the arrow button, showing me another one, and the knife twists a little deeper.

"I know you and the Colonel have a relationship. I saw his face when Luka mentioned your name. We tortured him for hours and got nothing, but," he raises a finger, "when Luka mentioned you sexually, he reacted. It was a telltale sign that we found his weak spot." He shrugs. "But now you're gone, and men have needs." He hits another button, showing me more. The pictures are all with the same girl. They look to be in Texas. She a beautiful blonde, with long legs, huge boobs, and she is sporting the skimpiest outfits. In every picture he's touching her in some way. The one that hurts the most is where he's tucking her hair behind her ear, gazing at her the same way he looks at me.

"How did you get these? These could be from years ago, before I met him."

The American points to a digital sign that's off in the background. Shit, two days ago.

"How?"

The American closes the computer and leans back in his chair. "Remember, Savannah, everyone has a price. Anyone can be bought." His eyes flicker with amusement at his little comment. "It's all about finding what they want. I'm a wealthy man, Savannah. I can make things happen." I shake my head. My brain is spinning, desperately looking for answers. "I got to one of the Colonel's men. He was willing to do anything for me once I knew he had three kids in University. When I handed him a wad of cash, he practically wept."

"Who?" The word was like acid on my tongue. Everyone's face from the house flickered in front of me. "York?"

"Oh, please, don't be insulting, Savannah. York was an asshole pervert who couldn't even finish the job I ordered him to do."

"He almost killed me!" I slam my hand down on the table.

The American waves a hand at me. "But he didn't, just like he didn't get the results of your blood tests online like he was supposed to. He could have done it. He was fine with hurting you, and he was fine with handing you over to me, but he was never going to give up the location of their base. So I moved on, found someone younger, someone I can trust to do some digging. I sent the word out that York was done, and he offed himself before I could get to him. One less worry to deal with."

"So who is it?"

"Who do you think?" His eyes challenge me to answer, but I'm smart enough to keep my mouth shut.

"You're bluffing."

"Am I?" He opens a file and tosses a stack of pictures at me. They slide around the table, some falling to the floor. They're all of Cole and the blonde woman. However, some are at different times of the day and she's in different outfits. Clearly she and Cole had been spending time together and recently. "Nice to know when you are in trouble you can count on him, hey?" He pats my arm. "Well, the Colonel is clearly getting his own needs taken care of." He pauses for a moment. "Your life has been a lie. Nothing is what it seems, but *this,* my love," he leans forward and gives me a hungry gaze, "this can be something real."

My head drops. I feel so tired I just want it all to end. Everything hurts. I wish I could slip away somewhere, anywhere, even if it means I have to create a false happiness. At least I can blissfully pretend life is good.

"Now, let me take you to bed. I can make you feel so

448

much better."

That does it. I come abruptly out of my stupor and glare at him. "You touch me and I'll cut your dick off when you're sleeping. I will never sleep with you, so you wasted your money buying me. You can take your sick little twisted fantasy and shove it up your ass!"

"Oh, such a mouth. This is not like you, Savannah. You need to calm down. You have no one but me now to love you. The proof is in your past. The proof is in those pictures. Are you sure you want to threaten the person who saved you from all that? The one person who's asking you to give him a chance? I want you to be mine."

I stand. I'm done. This man is mad.

"I can never love a monster. How can you expect me to love you? You may think you can buy my body, but you can't buy my soul."

I see a flash of anger in his eyes, then he grabs my arm and drags me up the stairs to a small room in the attic, tossing me to the floor. Tim follows us and picks me up, muttering something about never speaking to The American like that. He apologizes for having to handcuff me to the wall, saying he hopes I'll only be left here for a few hours then leaves me alone with my thoughts. I can hear his footsteps as he heavily descends the steps. I lose all self-control, tucking myself into a ball, and pour my pain out through my tears.

I. Am. Done.

***

Cole

Cole shimmies himself to the edge of the roof, raising the binoculars and trying to get a visual on his target. The Red Door market is busy, so it's perfect for his men to blend in with the rest of the locals. Frank's Eagle Eye team of four is on the ground, while Blackstone is established on the rooftops. John and Paul have the entrance. Keith and Daniel have the exit, and Cole and Mark have the center.

He slides a fresh piece of cinnamon gum in his mouth as he scans the crowds. It isn't easy looking for someone they've never met before. Mike worked his magic with his contacts, and they finally came up with a name, Tim Powers. His father is heavily involved with the Cartel. *Of course.* There was even some talk that *Tim* killed his own wife after his son was born. Nice…not exactly the boy next door type. Cole glances down at the picture, studying Tim's tattoos. Most of them represent prison gangs. He has an angel on his neck and three sixes along his collarbone.

"Blackbird One to Raven One," his father's voice cracks over the radio.

"Go ahead, Blackbird." Cole raises his binoculars and scans the crowd.

"I have a visual on our subject entering from the west gate and heading toward you. Cream shirt, black hat, black pants."

"Copy that, Blackbird."

"Eagle Eye Two to Raven One. I also confirm visual on our subject. He's heading my way," one of Frank's team members adds to the radio waves.

Cole clicks his radio. "Copy that, stay in position. We follow him from here." After everyone confirms their visual on the target, they hold tight and watch his every movement, studying his mannerisms and surveying the crowd to see if he's alone.

They soon discover Tim travels in a group of four. They each carry two weapons in plain sight in the waist of their pants. Definitely not professionals, all smoking like chimneys, and one even polished off several beers and is now showing signs of being tired. Two of the four men look to be brothers and are more interested in playing on their phones than anything else. After three long hours of watching them, something finally seems to be happening. Tim Powers' back is to Cole, and he seems to be angry.

"Raven Two, are you getting this?" Cole asks Mark.

"Affirmative, the drunk is angry, saying the girl set them up and it's a waste having her handcuffed to a wall when she should be spread out..." Mark's voice trails off for a moment, making Cole blink back the idea of popping a bullet into the fucker's skull. Where the hell was she handcuffed? "Subject is yelling back, saying go get the car."

"Be ready to move. Fox One and Two, let's go." He orders Paul and John down to the SUV so they can be ready when the time comes.

Rushing to get to the car before the men get there, Daniel signals at Cole to cover him as he drops to the ground and slips a tiny tracking device to the 1993 Honda Civic that Tim arrived in. Moments later they're following the low-riding car down a busy street. Mark is in the back seat, tracking the car to make sure they have a good signal in case they lose them.

They settle into what becomes a long drive. An older couple who seems to be on a Sunday drive, as well as two other cars, are between them and the Honda, so it's an easy job to tail them without being obvious. Finally, after about two hours, the Honda pulls into a small driveway of a rundown home.

"*Mijo!*" An elderly lady comes hurrying out, kissing one of the brothers on the cheek and slapping the other upside his head.

John parks far enough away so they won't be detected, and they quickly set up their equipment in order to hear exactly what's being said.

"Tim, what's Denton's new girlfriend like?" a younger woman asks from inside the kitchen. Cole hands his father a pair of earphones as he shifts his into a better position.

"Why you want to know, Gigi?" Tim laughs. "He's not interested in you."

"Screw off," she hisses. "I just want know if she's a *gringa* like you."

The young girl shouts as someone smacks her.

"*Sí*, she's a *gringa*. Pretty little thing. Denton fought hard to get this one, but she's already in the attic. She has a mouth on her." He laughs again. "She called him a monster and said to go fuck himself." They all laugh.

The old lady makes a tisking sound as she clanks some dishes. Cole and his men flinch at how loud it is over the earphones.

"Ha! You can laugh, but I know I can give Denton what he wants. Why would he want a *gringa*? I can see myself in that grand house, just like the one from Skeleton Key. I would be wearing pretty clothes and..."

The men cut her off, laughing and teasing the woman, saying she should go there and kill the girl so Denton could see that she is the one he should be with.

Cole looks at Mark, who is the movie buff, waiting to see if he knows what the girl meant by the house from Skeleton Key. Mark clicks away on the laptop then turns it around to show him.

A Louisiana style home? Here in TJ? That's different and should be easy to find. Mark nods and gets to work, and Cole mentally kicks himself as he remembers Savannah mentioning it looked like that.

In the house a chair scrapes the floor as the girl asks, "So did the GI Joe crew show up?"

Someone snickers something Cole can't make out, then a cough. "No one showed. I think the girl was fucking with me, seeing if she could trust me. Too bad for her." He snorted. "She'll get hers. Denton will take his time breaking her and will enjoy himself the whole time. Denton is a sick fucker."

Mark makes a face at Cole, knowing he isn't the only one itching to get a moment alone with this guy.

As night rolls around, Cole and Mark take the first shift, and the rest pass out in a matter of minutes. One thing about being in the Army, you can fall asleep anywhere, and when you're told to sleep, you don't think twice. You find a spot and you're out. Mark trades places with John later in case Tim decides to leave in the middle of the night.

They're silent for a few hours, Cole's mind spinning with thoughts of Savi. Wondering if she's hurt, if she's wondering where he is, wondering what she ever did to deserve this life.

"I didn't think we'd be back here with Savi again," Mark whispers as he takes a bite of his power bar. "She'll forgive you, Cole." He turns to look at him. "Once you explain that photo with Rodrigo, she'll understand and forgive you." Cole shakes his head, knowing how bad that picture looks, but it had to be done. "She loves you," Mark shrugs, "so don't worry."

Cole rests his head back against his seat, staring up at the sky full of stars. He hopes to hell Tim isn't one for sleeping in, because come seven a.m. they are raiding the motherfucking house.

***

Savannah

I move my head side to side, tuning in and out of someone speaking.

"Do you think it was wise to mention Roth to her?" Tim's voice seems far away.

A ticking sound makes my stomach turn. I know he's here; his damn boots give him away.

"Are you questioning my motives?" His voice makes my blood freeze in place. "She needs to know that her life is over, that she can be reborn again with me. I never gave his name, never said how close he's getting to—" I can't hold on. I feel myself slipping back into a place that makes me feel no pain, only love.

Three hours later I am in agony. I cry out as the American slaps me and then punches me in the stomach for the second time. My mouth is getting me in trouble again. I know it would be better for me if I kept quiet, but I'd rather make him angry and be hit than be forced to sleep with this man.

"You will bend to my ways, Savannah," he barks down at me as his stupid cobra boots tap along the wooden floor. For the last hour he has been questioning me, trying to gain some information on where Tim went. He had heard from one of the girls that Tim had spent some time in my room when I arrived. I wasn't about to out the one person who may be helping me. "Did you sleep with him, Savannah? I should have known you were a little slut. You probably spread your legs for the whole damn Army." I smirk at him, thinking that if he suspects I slept with his muscle that maybe he won't touch me. "You think this is funny?"

"No." I slowly shake my head, feeling lightheaded with pain. "I think it's hysterical. You wanted me so badly that you hunted me down for so long, and five minutes with Tim and he's got me against the wall doing the one thing you've been fantasizing about for all that time?" Well, that was it. I found The American's weak spot. His eyes widen as red hot anger flickers across them. I see him lose all sense of control. Oh, shit.

I curl up in a ball, my knees protecting my stomach and my arms covering my head, and hold on. This beating takes me to the edge, and I know it could be the end. I force my thoughts to turn inward, ignoring the punishment my body is taking.

I'm twelve, sitting on my bed and clipping pictures from a magazine. My mother comes in my room holding two cups of lemonade. She's so weak she can barely hold their weight, so I hop up and take them from her, then clear a spot on my bed for her to sit. She leans over to see what I'm doing. I return to gluing the pictures on the Bristol board, telling her it's my art project for family studies. We have to show what our perfect apartment would look like.

"I love the colors." She smiles, pointing at the red couch and matching red appliances. I try not to stare at her for too long. She gets uncomfortable with how much weight she has lost. She has commented on her own reflection and old she looks. She has taken to wearing silk scarves around her neck in pretty colors. I think she still looks beautiful, even when she's just wearing her head scarf and not her wig. My mother could walk around bald and still be the most gorgeous woman in the room. "You know, when I was eighteen, my best friend Jessi and I got a place together. It wasn't much, but we had been saving for two summers and we went out and bought everything new. I remember I bought a red Mixmaster. It cost me a lot, but it was the absolute favorite of all that I got that day. I loved that mixer. I had so much fun experimenting with recipes. It's how I started making those chocolate chip cookies you love so much."

"Oh, so that's the story of how your famous cookies came about. Well, in that case…" I reach behind me and hold up a red Mixmaster picture and glue it on my counter. "Now my apartment is perfect."

She reaches out and runs her soft hand along my

cheek. "Promise me someday when you get your own place you'll live for both of us." I want to burst into tears. I hate when my mom talks like this, but it's the truth, it's our reality, and my mother who I love more than anything is dying a slow, painful death. And every day she is here trying to be strong for me and my father, a father who is rarely home anymore. "All I ask from you, Savi, is to live it to the fullest and be happy. Do it for me, if not for yourself."

"I promise," I whisper, fighting the tears.

"You can cry, honey. I cry too." She lets go and starts to tear up along with me. "It's okay not to be strong. Part of living is feeling, and part of feeling is hurting." I move to crawl up next to her. "As long as you don't let the hurt consume you. Sometimes we all just need time to work it out."

"I don't want you to leave me, Mom." I sob into her t-shirt. "I don't know what to do without you."

She holds me as tight as she can. "Just because you can't see me, doesn't mean I'm not here, Savannah, and you're half of me, so therefore I'm never really gone."

A sharp kick to my battered ribs jolts me back to reality. I'm flooded with incredible pain and everything goes black as I pass out again. This time my mom is nowhere to be found, only darkness and pain and loss. Once again I am alone.

"Up." His voice breaks my lovely dream.

My mother starts to fade, and the last thing I hear her say is, *"Fight, my sweet Savannah, fight for your life."* Sunlight burns through the holes in the roof, making me squint. I see The American is wearing nothing but a pair of satin PJ pants.

Oh no.

He reaches down and undoes my handcuffs, scooping me in his arms and holding me close to his chest. His lips make contact with my hair and I force my tongue back. "How badly did I hurt you?"

Are you fucking kidding me? Is this a joke?

He walks me out of the attic, down the stairs, and through a hallway I don't recognize. The lights are dim, the smell of flowers fills my nose, and faint music can be heard as we approach an open door. I catch the blonde girl from dinner peek out the door at me. Her eyes fill with tears as she steps back in the darkness.

"I want to make you feel better, Savannah." His voice is low and in control, not like earlier. "This is my room," he says as he steps across the threshold.

Oh my hell.

A king-size bed sits in the middle of a large room. Brown curtains with gold patterns hang heavy throughout the space. A fireplace is lit, and a record player is playing an old Louisiana tune. Candles hang off the wall on dungeon-looking holders. I do spot another pair of handcuffs dangling from the headboard.

I thought I was past feeling fear, thought I'd seen it all.

He places me on the bed. "Now, my love, time to use your mouth in the way it's intended. Lean back and open up."

No. I was wrong. This is my deepest, darkest fear.

***

Cole

Cole checks his watch once again. Every minute that ticks by makes him grow more and more angry. All he can think of is that while this fat fucker sleeps in a warm bed, Savannah is chained to a wall. He senses Mark's mood is the same. All it takes is one look at him and they both slip out of the SUV with their weapons raised.

"I was wondering how much longer," Keith smirks as the rest exit the SUV.

It's nearly four thirty in the morning, and darkness surrounds the house. The team moves as if they are part of the night. Cole takes a quick inventory of how many are in the house, and they confirm six. Tim Powers, his three men, the mother, and younger woman.

Daniel moves smoothly as he picks the lock and opens the door for John and Paul to move in. The two brothers are passed out on the couch. Cole and Mark move into the bedroom Tim and the younger woman are in. Cole nods to Mark as he points a gun at the woman's head. Cole wraps his gloved hand over Tim's mouth and nudges his rifle hard into his side. Tim's eyes pop open. He starts to move but stops when he realizes what's happening. Cole tells him to keep quiet and points to the girl with a gun to her head. Tim nods that he understands.

"Good. Now get up and walk outside. Our men have everyone in this place covered. We have plenty of firepower, so keep your mouth shut. You try anything, and they all die."

"Yeah," Tim shakes his head, then Cole pulls him to his feet and shoves him out the door. Tim moves through the living room, taking in the fact that Paul and John have guns pointed at his friends. Once outside, they hurry him to the SUV. They cuff him, pat him down, and then push him into the truck. A steel divider separates the back from the rest of the vehicle, so Daniel keeps a gun pointed on Tim as they speed away from the house. Within minutes they're on the road heading to an open field they saw earlier.

Pulling off the road, Mark hops out and opens the back of the truck, grabbing Tim and slamming him to the ground. The men point their weapons at his face. Green lasers bounce around on his chest. Cole pulls out his flashlight and shines it in his face, making him look away.

"I take it you're here for the girl?" Tim grunts, shifting his body in obvious discomfort on the rocky soil. "I was waiting for you."

"So here we are; now where's the girl?" Cole asks calmly.

"The American has her," he answers, pissing off Cole. He wants a damn location, not the name of the shit he already knows.

Cole grabs his shirt and sends a powerful punch into his face, breaking his nose. *Fuck that feels good.* Tim shouts and slumps forward, hitting his head on the ground. Mark pulls him back to a kneeling position.

"I repeat, where is the girl?"

Tim spits blood on the ground, breathing hard. "I was helping her, man, I was going to get her back to you."

"Bullshit." Cole pulls his arm back and glances at Mark. "Kill the brothers." Mark starts to turn, but Tim shouts for him to stop.

"Please! Don't!" He curses and squeezes his eyes shut for a moment. "Denton has her at his place." Cole slowly lowers his hand, waiting for him to go on. "Denton, The American, he has her. *Mierda*! I'm not lying. He has her, he has many girls in the house. I can take you to him. She is in the attic, her mouth got her in trouble, so..." Tim lifts his shoulders in an exaggerated shrug. "I can show you where, but don't hurt my family. My brothers may be *hombres estupidos*, but they're all I've got."

"Girl first." Cole nods to John, who shoves Tim into the middle row of the SUV. Cole calls Mike back at Shadows and fills him in on everything, including The American's proper name. Mike has arranged for a chopper to be standing by, ready for the pickup. Mike tells Cole that he has established contact with a few

Mexican police, friends of a friend, willing to provide support with the mission and to take out The American if need be. Nothing would please Cole more than to kill The American, but they need him alive. They have questions on so many other kidnappings that only he can answer.

They drive for forty minutes down a long desert road, and Cole knows the sun will be up in an hour. Time is running out. Normally they'd wait until that night, but there's no way he's making Savannah stay in that place for any longer than she has to. Cole speaks to the team in French, letting them know how the attack will play out.

"See that light up there?" Tim points to it with his chin since his hands are cuffed behind him. "That's the house. Denton will either be in the attic with your girlfriend or in his bedroom in the back."

Cole leans forward to get a better view of the grounds as they get closer. John pulls off to the side of the road, pulling on his night vision goggles, as do the rest of the men. John starts asking Tim about the security system and any triggers around the property. Tim fills them in, but they all take it with a grain of salt.

Finally, after sending the coordinates to Mike, they head on foot toward the house.

Cole signals to his father and Keith to take the west, and to Paul and John to take the north side of the property with Tim. Mark nods to Cole as they sneak up behind one man and his dog. Mark tosses a rock in the opposite direction, throwing the dog off while he wraps a rag around the animal's mouth, making him fall fast asleep. Cole's arm slips around the man's neck, snapping it without hesitation. Mark lowers the dog carefully to the ground and gives him a quick pat.

Moving on, they encounter three more men, killing them instantly. Before they hear the panting, they see the flash of color leap in the air and grab Mark's arm, sinking its teeth into his flesh. Mark jams his gun in between its jaws, breaking its hold. The dog whimpers as he runs off toward the house.

"You good?" Cole asks, scanning for their next victim.

"The bitch bites me, and *he* has the nerve to cry. What the fuck?" Mark hisses, wrapping his wound. "Why can't people have cats? Really, all they do is sit there and plot your death…is that so bad?"

Cole chuckles as he shifts positions, happy to hear Mark is indeed all right. "Remember that the next time you're cursing Scoot for getting your pants full of fur."

"Love the furry prick," Mark huffs.

A snap from behind them has Cole pointing his laser beam at his father's head. "The west side is a no go." Daniel nods to Keith coming up next to him. "I say we enter through the north door, keep a low profile, grab Savi, and get the fuck out."

They quickly hatch a new plan, fill Paul and John in on it, and hurry to make their move before the sun starts to rise.

"Watch your step." Keith points out two triggers that will set the house alarm off if you step on them. "They're scattered throughout the property." Cole nods, taking note. It makes him wonder how many of The American's men set off the alarm in the past.

"Those triggers are the least of your worries," Tim butts in, getting a hit to the gut with a rifle by Keith. "I'm just saying there are too many men for you all to take out."

"We'll see," Cole grunts.

Weaving in and out of the triggers, the men keep on high alert.

When they're about five yards away from the door, a click echoes through the morning air. Everyone freezes. Cole slowly turns to see John's scrunched-up face.

"Fuck me," John growls and glances down at his right shoe, which is holding down the trigger.

"Don't move," Cole whispers, waiting for the attack. But nothing happens.

"If you lift your foot," Daniel says calmly, "it will trip the alarm."

"Go." John flicks his head. "Let me know when you're on your way out, and I'll book it back to the car."

"No—" Paul cuts him off, looking over at Cole. "You guys got this?"

Cole nods, knowing he'd never leave Mark unprotected either. "I'll let you know. Stay low."

Daniel makes it to the porch first, scanning the wood for triggers. He signals all is safe. "Set your watches. We're in and out in ten minutes."

"Where's the bedroom from here?" Keith shoves Tim to the stairs, making sure he knows who's in charge. "Speak."

"Stairs will be right there." Tim flexes his shoulders like the handcuffs are too tight, trying to point to the entryway. "At the end of the hall there's a set of double doors, that's Denton's room. More than likely she's there."

"You better be right." Keith looks over at Cole, who is ticking with anger.

Cole glances over his shoulder one last time at his guys before they disappear into the house.

One of the female servants freezes as she watches the men enter the house.

"The new girl?" Cole hisses in a whisper. The woman mouths master bedroom in Spanish. Cole's stomach drops. "Not a word," he whispers back.

She nods then holds up a hand. "The others, please," she pushes her hands together like she's praying, "let them go." Daniel nods from Cole's left.

"Move." Cole jams the gun a little harder into Tim's

back.

"Hey!" someone yells from another room. Keith is quick, popping two bullets into his forehead. The woman who just helped them cups her mouth to stop her scream. Suddenly she points behind them just as another guy tries to stab Daniel. Cole kicks his knee, forcing it to snap in the wrong direction. He takes the butt of the gun and rams it into the man's temple.

"Move." Cole can tell things are escalating quickly.

They slowly move up the stairs. The first room to the left is open...strange when every other door is closed, so Daniel does a quick sweep then signals the all clear.

"It's your girl's room," Tim whispers to Cole, before moving forward down the hallway. Cole watches the bottom of each door in case any lights turn on; they need to stay invisible. "The master is at the end of the hall with the double doors. I knock twice so he knows it's me."

Cole leads the pack. He looks at the men as they approach. Tension is high, to say the least. He nods at Tim, who lifts his sweaty fist and knocks twice.

"Tim, that fucking better be you!" The American shouts, his voice a high pitched squeal. "You better have done what I asked!"

Tim opens the door and moves inside, smiling. "Yeah, Denton, not only did I get the Colonel, I got his whole fucking ar—"

Trap...it's a fucking trap! So many things are happening in front of Cole, but nothing matters when he knocks Tim to the floor and catches sight of why The American is so panicky.

No...

Chapter Eleven

The American is straddling Savannah's lifeless body, giving her CPR. One look at the guns drawn and he jumps back, raising his hands.

Daniel is the first to move. He races forward, hitting The American with the butt of his gun. Shrieks become louder as two females burst out of the bathroom and attack Keith and Mark.

Cole leaps forward, climbing on top of Savannah. Two fingers check her pulse while his other hand checks her pupils. "Please, baby," he whispers. Shutting out the war around him, he concentrates on trying to bring life back to her body. Nothing. He shoots up, lacing his fingers on top of one another pumping her chest, desperately wishing he could reach inside her and hold her heart in his hands. One, two, three…he counts, his lips meet with hers and fill her lungs with his own breath. Focusing all his energy on her, he's hoping for a miracle. She looks so small and fragile, her beautiful eyes once so lit with fire are cold and dim. "Don't you dare leave me, Savannah. I swear to god I will give you the world if you come back to me."

Mark suddenly appears at his side, his hands moving all around as he tries to assess the scene. "Mark." Cole's voice breaks as he looks at his brother in pain.

"Come on, Savi." Mark starts rubbing her limp arm. "We need you."

"Please, no!" Cole begs. His *everything* is slipping away, the only woman he's ever loved, the mother of his unborn baby, leaving him, but not by choice. Damn it, it's not fair! He pounds on her tiny chest, feeling the world has committed the worst crime...there is no good on this earth ...only evil.

Suddenly, Savannah gasps and starts coughing, twisting to her side under him. "Savi!" Cole shouts, grabbing her head and pulling her to him. She starts sobbing, and a horrible shaking takes her, her breath ragged. He carefully strokes her back and watches her blue-tinged face slowly turn to a waxy white. As soon as she takes him in, she whispers his name. He wraps her in his arms gently, allowing himself a moment to breathe.

"Cole." Mark's voice gets through to him.

Snapping out of it and back into Army mode, Cole realizes they don't have much time before company arrives. He pushes the fear of the last several minutes away to deal with later, knowing right now he needs to get them all out of here alive. Keith informs them that one of the girls tripped the alarm. Paul and John are now guarding the door, waiting for them to arrive. The redhead in question is looking at them with a nasty expression on her face. Damn, it won't be long. They have to get out now. Cole looks at the girls and tells them if they want their freedom they better get the hell out now. The blonde girl eyes Savannah's trembling body then bolts down the hallway, but the rest stand in fear or, God knows, they might be suffering from a type of Stockholm syndrome or something. Either way, he figures he isn't going to worry about them; they aren't his problem. "Let's move!" he directs his men. Daniel and Mark force a handcuffed Tim and The American to their feet and head down the hallway.

"Raven One to Fox Two," John's voice flows over the radio, "we've got company in five minutes." Gunshots ring over their earpieces. "You guys need to move now!"

"Ten-four," Mark answers. "Get the SUV ready, we're transferring two hostages."

"Copy that, Fox Two."

John and Paul spray bullets at the men as they try and close in on them. They take out more than half of The American's army. The rest seem to pull back when they get sight of Blackstone's hostages.

Daniel has the two men blindfolded and piles them in the truck, handcuffing them to a metal bar. Tim is pleading with Daniel to let him go, that it was all a misunderstanding, while The American remains silent.

Cole feels Savannah's grip tighten as he gets closer to the vehicle. He wishes he planned this better as he jumps inside, keeping her on his lap tight against his chest. Mark, Daniel, and Keith squeeze in beside them, while Paul takes the front with John.

"Call it in," Cole orders Paul once they are on the road. Headlights are coming up quickly behind them.

Savannah doesn't speak. She barely even moves. He has to keep shifting to make sure she is all right. Her eyes are glued to Daniel's watch, and she hardly blinks. It takes everything Cole has not to turn around and kill the man who tried to take everything from him. Wanting answers on what the fuck happened back at the house is eating away at his mind.

Ten, fifteen, twenty minutes go by. Cole keeps checking the side mirror, watching the same headlights follow them along the dark road. No shots have been fired yet.

"I can smell you, my love," The American whispers into the silence, making Savannah tense as she hears his voice, snapping her out of her trance. Daniel shakes his

466

head at Cole, making sure he doesn't react. "I can still feel your soft lips, your smooth skin, and the taste of your tongue." Savannah turns her face into Cole's chest, silently sobbing.

"He's trying to get to you, baby, just tune him out," Cole whispers in her ear. He kisses her softly, wanting to calm her.

The American chuckles and leans his head back against the window. "When my hands felt that last tiny gasp of air pass through your lungs, I knew I should've stopped, but your eyes were hypnotic. You held me in the moment."

Cole reaches forward and grabs Paul's stun gun from his hip. He shifts Savannah so she is sitting upright, turns, and forces the tip of the gun through the bars and stuns The American in the neck before anyone has time to react. The American screams out, his body jolting upward. "One more word and I'll kill you." Cole doesn't even recognize his own voice he's so fucking livid. Yanking the wires from the gun, he presses Savannah back down to his chest and hands the gun to his father while the asshole tries to control his breathing.

"House to Blackstone," Mike's voice breaks through.

Cole presses the button on his neck to activate his earpiece. "Go ahead."

"Chopper is standing by, backup arriving in five, Frank and Eagle Eye will meet you on the other side of the border. We see you on satellite and are monitoring behind you, will communicate if they show signs of making a move. So far they're only watching."

"Copy that."

***

Savannah

I squeeze my eyes shut, concentrating on Cole's smell, sweat mixed with soap. It's just what I need to ground me. So much has happened it's hard to stay focused. I'm tired, sore, my neck and throat feel like they're on fire, and my head is pounding. It's terrifying to know The American, Denton, or whatever his name is, is sitting a foot away from me. He tried to kill me and almost succeeded. My mind goes to Tim. He was using me; thank god that backfired. But am I really safe? This will never really be over until The American is dead. I don't even realize what I am doing until I feel Cole's hand slip on top of mine, stopping me from taking his gun from his leg holster. Instead of saying anything, he laces his fingers through mine, ever so calmly bringing them to rest on my leg. His lips kiss my hair for a long minute, breathing in deeply and helping me drift off to an unpleasant sleep.

Suddenly all hell breaks loose and I'm being hoisted out of the car. I'm in Mark's arms now, not Cole's, and there is a lot of shouting, gunshots, and a chopper whose rotor is madly cutting into the early morning air. My brain fights to catch up with this madness.

"Move, move, move!" someone shouts at Mark. Paul is shooting off to our left. I can see the concentration on his face and the puffs of dust as bullets ping around him. It all comes at me as if in slow motion. I see John inside the chopper with his hand extended, reaching out for me. His mouth is moving as though he is yelling something. I can feel the jolt of each step Mark takes as he runs toward John. I feel no pain now; it's all so surreal. When we are close enough, I'm tossed into John's arms and he lifts me into the chopper. He places me on a seat across from The American, who is still bound and blindfolded. I scan about the massive chopper and can't find Cole.

468

The pilot is shouting for the guys to get in, and John is barking out orders to Paul, who is still firing off his weapon. Mark suddenly flies inside with Daniel, who looks to be bleeding from his arm. The chopper blades are kicking up a huge dust storm, making it hard to see and hear the fight outside. I feel the chopper start to shift. *What's going on?* Cole and Keith jump on at the last moment before we rise into the sky, and my body sags with relief.

I can't keep my eyes away from The American. It's odd seeing him looking so vulnerable. With his handcuffs and blindfold, he certainly doesn't frighten me anymore. He's not wearing his stupid cobra boots. He's barefoot, wearing only a pair of jeans and a shirt. Memories flood through me of him on top of me in the bedroom, of the lies Tim told me that if I cried he'd stay away, knowing now that only made him more intrigued. I feel sick as I think of it. The harder I sobbed, the harder he squeezed the life out of me. I stopped fighting him. I would rather be dead than give in to that man and let him have me.

I reach into the top of my dress and slowly ease out the tiny blade from my bra. Looking around, I see that everyone looks exhausted. Cole is wrapping Daniel's arm, and the others' attention is on that. As much as my body hurts, as much as I'm mentally finished and just want to close my eyes again, I know this might be my only chance.

I shift silently onto my knees and crawl forward. I catch Keith's face as my movement draws his gaze, but he doesn't stop me. He's just watching. He puts a hand on Mark when he turns my way. It's not easy moving around on the chopper, but I make the five foot distance and sit on my knees next to The American. Leaning in and letting my hair brush his shoulder, he senses my presence and his face turns up with a smile. My lips are close to his ear as I whisper so only he can hear me.

"Anyone can be bought, Denton. It's all about finding their weakness. Yours was me. Problem is I already belong to someone else, and that someone else always gets what's his. You never had me, and you never will. So while you sit in your six by twelve jail cell I want you to picture the Colonel with his hands on my body, touching me, and my moans of ecstasy that are his alone."

His neck muscles flex as he clamps down on his jaw. "This will never end, my love." He suddenly leans into me. Even through his blindfold I can feel his eyes burning into mine. "I always win." His mouth is still smiling at me.

He's right. I'll never be free if I don't end this now. My eyes drop down to his long throat, and the blade in my hand becomes hot as fire. As I raise my arm, I see my future flash in front of me. If this doesn't end, I'll forever be afraid. All my anger boils to the surface as I throw my body weight forward, aiming for his neck. A large hand wraps around my wrist while the other hooks my waist and pulls me to the other side of the chopper.

"It's what he wants, Savi," Cole huffs in my ear. "He wants you to kill him. His hell is being caught. Let him live so he can suffer." He pries the blade from my fingers and hands it to Keith, who is shaking his head with a smirk like I never stop surprising him. "It's over, Savannah, I promise it's over."

***

We make two stops before we finally land back in Montana at the safe house. The American, whose name I now know is Denton, is handed off to Frank and a team of his men who arrived back from TJ just hours earlier. Daniel had to be dropped off at a private hospital in

North Dakota to have his wound treated. When I ask what happened to Tim, The American's muscle, Keith tells me he got shot in the head. I nod, not wanting to know which team did the deed, since I now know Tim's loyalty lay with Denton all along. He used me to try and trap Cole into coming to the market. Thank god Cole was smart enough to see through it. I hate that I didn't.

Stepping down on solid ground and taking in the scenery feels pretty amazing, but seeing Abigail and June run up and wrap me in a bear hug is even better. Thinking back, I know there was a point I didn't think I was going to be here again. I thought I was going to live the rest of my crazy, messed up life with Denton or until I made it end. As they fuss over me, I feel a bubble of warmth start to rise from my stomach to my heart.

"Come on, dear, you must be freezing!" I tug Cole's jacket around me a little tighter as she looks at my bare legs in the army boots, smiling. "Let's get you inside." I glance back at Cole, seeing him smile and nod at me. I return the smile, but it fades when I start to walk, as the soreness in my body reminds me of what The American did to me physically.

Sitting in my room on the edge of my bed, I'm still huddled under Cole's jacket, wanting to shake off an odd feeling that has a grip on me. I know I'm terribly tired and I want a shower, but I can't bring myself to move. I wonder where my father and Lynn are. I wonder what they're doing right now and if they've heard that I'm free again. I feel my face prickle all over like I want to cry, but I don't. I just sit and stare at the floor.

I may have fallen asleep for a few minutes, because I find myself slumped on the bed uncomfortably. I finally force myself up and get showered, dressed, and back downstairs to find everyone doing what they do best whenever they come from back from a job. Drinks in the living room. It feels wonderful to be back here, and I find myself thinking of Derek, realizing I'll never see him again. I want to mourn for him, knowing that it is my fault he's not with us, my fault he's being buried, and why his little niece won't be getting her New York snow globe. I got him killed; that death is on me, and me alone.

"One Marcus Martini for you." Mark grins as his eyes fall to my neck where I know from checking myself out in the bathroom mirror I have a purple and blue necklace of bruises. I gladly take the drink and pluck an olive off the stick. "Cole should be down soon, he's just making his report. Look, Savi, I know you've been through a lot. I hope you know how much we all care about you. Is there anything you want to talk about? Are you okay?"

"That's a big question," I answer honestly.

Mark nods, looking at the room full of all our friends smiling and talking. "This is a big day, not only because we brought you back home, Savi, but we took down The American. It's been a long seven-year hunt for that bastard. He's been a real thorn in our side, and every one of these guys has reason to celebrate."

I tuck my feelings aside and click Mark's beer. "You're right, Mark. You know I love you guys and couldn't be more thankful for what you've all done for me. Now let's go celebrate."

Later that night, I lie back on my pillow and think about the evening. Cole wasn't able to come celebrate at all in the end, as he had a video conference with Frank and some other important people about the capture of The American. I am too tired to last more than a few hours and really just want to sleep and turn off for a while. *Thinking is overrated.*

It is about three a.m. when I feel Cole slip into bed with me. Something cold touches my skin, and I feel him placing my snowflake chain back on, fastening it around my neck. I squeeze my eyes shut, realizing how much I missed its comfort. His arm slides over me and pulls my back flush against his front. He sighs and breathes me in deeply then tucks his face into my neck, lacing my fingers with his, and we both fall into a deep sleep.

***

The week goes by in an odd blur. Everyone seems to be doing their thing, whereas I just float around unable to focus on anything. Cole is extremely busy. I've seen him twice for dinner, but he doesn't talk much and seems preoccupied. His apologetic comment that he is mentally fried was given with a quick hug in the hallway. Abigail and June are helping Derek's sister with his funeral arrangements but don't talk to me about it. I'm sure they are only being kind, but leaving me out of it makes me feel isolated and guilty instead. Keith, John, and Paul are hardly around, and Mike only will talk to me if I stray too far off the grounds.

I start to feel strange in this house, a little lost and, frankly, a little hurt. No, to be honest, I'm really hurting. Feeling my mood sink even lower, my heart weighs heavily in my chest. I find myself drawn down to the entertainment room. Sliding down onto the smooth wooden bench, my fingers lift the cover, exposing the soothing ivory keys.

My eyes close and my heart swells as I feel her sit down next to me. Letting out a long, slow breath, my fingers touch the keys softly.

"Let's play our song, but add a little of your flavor to it," Mom suggests, grinning at me with a bump to the shoulder. "Come on, sweetie, let whatever is bothering you flow out through your fingers." I take in a another deep breath and let the pain flow from my soul.

The first line to *These Arms of Mine* by Otis Redding

slips past my lips, and the notes start to form the song's beautiful melody.

***

Cole

Cole moves about the kitchen looking for something quick to eat, but nothing looks appetizing. Abigail joins him, holding a newspaper which she drops on the counter in front of him. Cole leans forward and reads the headlines, seeing the news about The American has made the front page. "One of America's most wanted fugitives captured."

"The question is will her father be next?" Abigail sets a sandwich down in front of him. "You need to eat more than an apple. I can make myself another one. Where's Savi? I haven't seen much of her lately."

"You don't hear that?" Mark says as he snatches the sandwich off the plate and takes three big bites. Cole steps out into the living room, hearing the piano and Savannah's deep, soulful voice. He turns to look at Mark in disbelief. "Yeah, for like ten minutes now. Girl has some mad talent."

Before he gets a chance to hear much more, the song ends. The sound of the piano cover closing has Cole and Abigail slipping back into the kitchen, pretending to be busy as Savannah climbs the stairs and enters the room. She blushes slightly as she sees them. He can tell she thought she was alone in this part of the house.

"Hey, Savi," Abigail says, standing in front of the fridge. "You thirsty? I just made some lemonade."

She nods and comes over to the island, standing next to Cole. He leans over and gives her a kiss on the cheek, but her body turns slightly, almost as though she doesn't want it. "Are you all right?" Her body language screams no, but she nods.

"Really, Savi?" Mark says through a mouthful of cookie. "You're gonna lie to Logan?" he sputters, sending crumbs into the air. "You seem to forget what we do for a living. Besides, the way you played and sang that song nearly brought me to my knees in tears."

"Mark!" Abigail scowls, making Savannah gasp. "Filter, my son," she scolds him.

"What?" He shrugs. "It was a compliment."

***

Savannah

I shift while watching him scribble on his tablet. Snow is falling outside the window behind him, brightening up all the scruffy areas, softening the landscape in a winter wonderland again. "Tell me, Savannah, how does it feel to be back?" Dr. Roberts asks, as we sip our coffee in our usual meeting room next to Cole's office. I was the one who asked him to come this morning. Something feels off, and I want to get to the bottom of it.

"It feels great…good, I mean. It's a relief to be back, of course."

"But…" He pulls his glasses down on his nose, knowing there's more.

I shrug, not sure how to put it. "I don't know. I mean, I've been back here for a week now. I'm happy. I'm safe. I'm so grateful to the guys…I just thought it would feel a little different."

"How different?"

I shift again and tuck my dress a little tighter around my legs, feeling nervous about answering this question, knowing that once I say it out loud, it makes it true. "It feels like it's not quite where I need to be."

He nods like he understands me instead of displaying the confusion I expected from him. "Savannah, you were left to look after your mother for the four years she was ill. Weren't you fourteen when she passed?" I nod miserably. "So, that would have made you ten when you took on a very adult emotional task, correct?" I nod, agreeing. "Okay, so then after your mother died, your father began his political climb to the mayor's office, thrusting you into his world. Suddenly the press is hounding you, your life is turned upside down, and you start to run into problems, so you put your life on hold once again for your parents. A few years later you are kidnapped and held for seven terrible months." I clear my throat uncomfortably and start to say something, but he holds up his hand and continues. "Finally, you are rescued and brought here. Then," he pauses with his finger in the air, "a few months later you are taken once again, then rescued *and* brought back here again." He looks at me with one eyebrow raised, waiting for a response.

"Okay…" is all I can muster.

"What I'm saying, Savannah, is you need to give yourself some time for you. You need to process all that has happened. You haven't had a chance to live your *own* life yet. You're twenty-nine years old and—"

"…Still feel like I'm going in circles with no direction and no end in sight," I answer, feeling like he has just hit the source of my problem. "I don't really know who I am and what I want, and now that all my major life-altering problems seem to be ending, I find myself lost." A horrible feeling hits my stomach when I suddenly think of Cole.

"Finding yourself doesn't mean you have to give up anything. It just means you need a little time to be alone."

"Space," I whisper, closing my eyes. "I think I just

need some space that's mine."

***

Cole

Cole hangs up the phone after a long three-hour conversation with Frank. Turns out they have enough evidence to convict Lynn, thanks to Joe Might, who is willing to throw her under the bus to get a lesser sentence for himself. However, the Mayor is pinning it all on Luka Donavan. It's easier to blame the dead than the living who have a voice.

He pours himself a cup of coffee and leans against the window, watching the snow fall. A storm is coming. They're supposed to be getting forty-five inches of snow. He's thankful his father arrived home safely last night. A bullet grazed his shoulder, and now he and Mark are joking that they actually planned their new matching scars.

"Cole?" Savannah whispers behind him. He turns, feeling the strange vibe that seems to be there whenever they are together lately. He knows he really needs to address the Derek issue, as she still must have raw feelings about it. She's been acting different since she got back, and it's not like her to keep him at arm's length. It's killing him. "Cole," she repeats when he doesn't answer right away, "do you have a moment?"

He nods and rubs his face. God, he is tired. He sits down on the couch while she takes a seat across from him.

"Why?" he asks without thinking.

"Why what?"

"Why are you over there and not over here next to me?"

"Because I don't think clearly when I'm that close to

477

you."

"Well, I don't like it," he admits.

She stares at him for a moment then comes over and sits next to him. His hand reaches for her automatically, tugging her closer, but she stops him. She slides to the other end of the couch, looking uncomfortable.

"Okay, I'm listening," he says, raising his hand to show her he won't grab for her again.

It takes her a few minutes, but she finally clears her throat. "I saw some pictures."

He doesn't hesitate. "Savannah, we met Jose four months ago. He thought we were looking for work with The Cartels. The guy is a bit of an idiot, and we quickly gained intel on your whereabouts. We met up with him a few times at that café, and apparently so did The American. That's how we found you—"

"No," she interrupts, her face growing pale, "not that picture."

Cole turns, pulling a leg up so he can look at her better. "Then which?"

"The one with the blonde." His stomach rolls. *Oh fuck*, how the hell? "The one where you were holding her in your arms like you hold me. The one where you are staring at her with the same look you have for me. The one where you are kissing her with the same lips you use on me." She pauses, nearly in tears. "I thought..." She shakes her head, standing and putting more distance between them. "I'm sure there's some reason why you were doing that with her, but..."

"There is," he chimes in.

She holds up her hand to stop him. "But regardless, those little things mean something to me. I thought they were *only* for me."

"They are." He stands and goes to her, but she steps back. He hates not being able to touch her when he wants to. He shouldn't, but he shares, "She's an

478

informant for Shadows. She's the one who helps us gain info on the Cartel. Her brother runs tight with them. She's had a crush on me forever, and when you were taken, I knew I had to…I played dirty to get anything I could on your whereabouts. But, Savannah, she means nothing to me. I did it all for you, for us." He can feel her pull away mentally, her big beautiful eyes filling with tears again. "I love you, Savannah, I always have. Please don't pull away from me. My heart can't take losing you again."

She steps forward, then stops as big, silent tears roll down her cheeks. With each one that falls, a piece of his own heart falls along with it. "I promised Keith I'd help him with something."

"Savannah, please." Cole catches her by the hand, but she shakes her head, making him release her immediately.

As she reaches the door, she turns, keeping her head down. "I love you, Cole, but put yourself in my shoes. Think about how much that would hurt seeing me with another man, looking at him like that, even if it *was* for a good reason."

"It would destroy me," he admits, feeling sick.

She nods once, then slowly closes the door behind her.

Cole grabs for one of his brandy glasses and sends it across the room, feeling all kinds of fucked up emotions. It shatters into a million pieces right along with his heart.

Chapter Twelve

Savannah

Walking, walking, and more walking around half of the lake, I'm just trying to make sense of everything. By the time I make it back to the house, I'm more mixed up than I was when I started. It's late, the sun is setting, and the snow is coming down harder. After a quick trip to my room, I go to the kitchen, grab a bottle of wine, a glass, and an opener, and head downstairs. Luckily, most of the guys have been busy with the wind-up of The American case, so everyone seems to be keeping to themselves.

I step out into the freezing air in a pair of flips flops. Climbing up onto a chair, I cover the camera pointing in my direction with a t-shirt. I rip off my top and chuck my shorts to the side. I toss my hair into a messy bun as I sink into the deliciously hot water. It feels divine. I instantly feel the tension slip away from my body. In the winter they keep the hot tub covered with a tent that opens at the sides. I open only one flap, so I have a private view of the lake.

My second glass in, and I feel pretty damn relaxed. I can't believe I haven't come here sooner. Closing my eyes, leaning my head back, I listen to how quiet the snow makes everything. It makes for a perfect moment.

"See, Savi, this is the perfect place for a vacation." Lynn *grins with a lime green straw wedged between her lips. She's on her fourth margarita since we hit the beach an hour ago. She surprised me with a trip to Fiji for my birthday. We're staying in a little bungalow on Castaway Island. No one knows me, allowing me to blend in perfectly.*

I slip my sunglasses on, plucking the melon from the rim of my mojito and popping it in my mouth. The cold juice is refreshing. "Yes." A grin tugs at my lips, as our morning yoga trainer, Diogo, grabs a paddle board and heads for the crisp blue ocean. "I think this is one of the best presents you've ever given me."

She laughs, clinking her drink to mine. He might be married, but nothing matters with an ass like that.

"I wonder where his tan line ends." I give her a devilish grin.

She shakes her head. "I have goggles, wanna go find out?"

"Yup!"

A shadow casts over Lynn, making me squint to see who's interrupting our fun.

"Hello, ladies, my name is Jerry. I teach a scuba class with the resort." Jerry grins with a large set of pearly whites and shows us his hotel ID. "Our first class starts in ten. Would you like to join?"

I glance at Lynn, who is downing her drink with a dirty grin.

"Yes, Jerry, that sounds like a great plan."

Poor Diogo.

I didn't even know I was grinning until my reality comes crashing around me, making my eyes pop open. I rub a spot over my heart, which hurts like hell when I think of our happy *fake* memories. I wonder if my father planned the whole trip, just to get me out of the media.

"I hate my past," I bitch, shaking Lynn's face from my thoughts.

"I'm glad I didn't send Dell out here to check on the camera," Cole says, standing in front of the open side and making me jump. His hands are tucked into his pockets as snowflakes hit then disappear when they meet the heat of his body through his sweater. He's very sexy in his black sweater and jeans. "Is that even considered a bikini?" I think about my suit rather than look at it. I guess its white strings may be a little skimpy, but I wasn't planning on having company. "You want to be left alone?" I shake my head and take a slow sip of my wine, watching him intently. He yanks off his sweater, giving me a moment to gawk at his strong arms, chest, and back. I try to hide my body's natural reaction to him, but it's impossible. Pure lust rises to the surface whenever he's around. His pants come off next and are set down carefully by his boots, his inner Army ways coming out. He settles in the water across from me, his legs stretched out on either side. Our eyes wander over one another, both knowing we've been physically attracted to each other from day one, so neither of us even pretends to look away.

I tip my glass of wine in his direction as if to ask if he wants some. He nods, holding out a hand for me to come to him, but first I lean back and pour more wine into my glass. Keeping low in the water, my eyes on his, I move toward him, stopping just in front of him but not quite touching. He suddenly leans forward and grasps my hips, lifting me to straddle his lap. I squeak when the wine spills over my arms and down my chest, the cold liquid making me shiver. He bends down and drags his hot tongue across my skin, licking the wine from between my breasts, then along my collarbone and up to my earlobe where he nibbles lightly. I try not to react, try to keep a clear head, but instead I let out a sharp breath as my senses take a dive. Cole takes the glass from me, downing half of it while keeping those gorgeous dark eyes on mine. Then he comes in for a kiss, and that does it. I turn my head to the side; suddenly all I can picture is those lips on the blonde's. He downs the rest of the wine and sets the glass aside.

The wind picks up, blowing snow in on us. I shift down and back, and so does he, so we're both better protected from the storm, which is now becoming a blizzard. Cole pulls me back onto his lap where I meet a rather intense look. His fingers walk up my back, undoing the ties on the back of the suit. It springs forward as he lifts it over my head. My bottoms are removed just as fast, then he shifts and removes his.

He moves so his erection is between my aching thighs, with me just barely touching him, and waits, wanting me make the first move. I hesitate while I battle it out with myself, and in the end my lust wins and I slowly slide down over top of him, making us both drop our heads back, sighing. He wraps an arm around my waist and the other grips my shoulder as I start to move very slowly. I can see his muscles flexing, trying hard to give me control. His jaw is set perfectly still as my breasts bounce in front of his mouth, his stubble teasing them as they brush by. The contrast of the cold air and the hot water is an intense sensation. Cole comes in for another kiss, but I turn my face away and continue at the same pace. He growls and grits his teeth, bucking his hips to get me to move faster, but I don't. In fact, I move slower. Yes, I'm punishing him, but it's hurting me too. I hate hurting, I hate even more that he's the one who hurt me. I swallow past the growing lump, trying desperately to shove the feelings away.

"Enough of this shit." He pulls me up, flips me over the side of the tub, and thrusts back in. He lies his front over my back, holding me down. "Stop punishing me," he growls. "I only did what I had to do to get you back. I only kissed her, nothing more. I hated it, but I'd do it again if it means saving your life." He pulls out, then slams back in. "I know you're dealing with a lot, but you better let me in. If you have something to say, then say it, but don't," he slams in again, making me cry out, "ever deny me your lips, Savannah." He pounds in again, sending water spilling over the edge. He pulls out, making me whimper. "They are mine, just like this," he palms my ass, "and this," his fingers slip inside me, driving me wild. I grind my hips into him, wanting more. His other hand slips over my chest, making a point to stop over my heart. "All of it is mine, just like all of me is yours." He leans back and grasps my hips with both hands, and nudges just the tip of him inside. "Will you kiss me when I'm done fucking you?" I don't answer. I'm so pent up I'm about to jump out and roll in the snow for some kind of relief. "Savannah!"

"Yes!" I cry out as he plows back in over and over. I don't want it to end. He's the only man who has ever made me feel every possible feeling at once, but at the same time feel each individually as well. It's intoxicating. It's erotic. It's…it's…it's…I scream as every muscle clenches, sending me off toward the snowy night. He shouts and grips my shoulders, his whole body shaking on top of mine. He pulls out, flips me over, and attacks my lips. He's like a hungry animal and I'm his first meal in months. Within minutes he's entering me again, but this time he has me straddling his lap, facing him. He does all the work since I've become like jelly, but it doesn't take long for my senses to kick back in to match his rhythm.

"Cole," I moan as he bites my neck and massages my breast. "I hate that you hurt me," I confess, wanting to get it off my chest. "I hate that it was *you* who hurt me."

My rocking has picked up pace; I'm close now. I'm panting, and I can feel him struggling with having to stop to talk, wanting to keep going, so I grab his face and kiss him. I'm torn too, but right now I need this closeness. I love him. This sets him off and he stands, holding me with him and sitting me on the highest seat, nearly out of the water, and hooks my legs over his shoulders. He hangs on to the side of the tub, getting in as deep as he possibly can. I clench around him, feeling full as he hits all the right places. My eyes roll up to the roof of the tent, seeing many colors dance around as I fall into a sea of passion. I couldn't be happier. Only he can make me feel this way.

"No one else," he grunts as he fills me with another hot burst of him.

We're both completely spent by the time we finish. I sit wrapped in his arms, watching the white curtain, the snowflakes dancing in a beam of light from the house. You can barely see three feet in front of us now. Cole slowly kisses my neck like he can't stop.

"Cole?" I whisper, not wanting to break this moment, but I need to, sadly. That nagging feeling is still there.

"Mmmm." His chest vibrates.

"I-ah, umm," *Fuck.*

"Tell me. It's nothing we can't handle."

*Shit, I can't. Ahhh...*I chicken out, so I go with something else that has been on my mind. "What's going to happen to my father?"

Cole sighs and holds me tighter. "It will take time, but he'll make a mistake somewhere and we'll nail him." He pauses. "Do you want your father to go to jail?"

"Yes," I say simply, because any father who can willingly hand over his daughter to someone the way he did, and kill Derek and shoot Paul...this man is not my father. He is someone else. "I'm struggling with Derek's death."

Cole turns my face around with his finger, and his look is serious. "You need to understand something, Savannah. What Derek did was wrong. That was his mistake, taking you there with no backup. It went totally against all he should have learned in his training. Whether or not he thought it was a good idea, it wasn't. That's why Derek would never have made it on the Blackstone team. He makes dangerous choices. His death is not on you." His hands cup my face so I look into his eyes. "Believe me, what happened is on him. No one blames you."

I nod in fear of saying anything. I hurt like hell on this topic. What Cole is saying makes sense. I just need time...time...I try to open my mouth and say the words to him, but I can't.

"Who hired you to come find me? I know my father didn't."

Cole cups some water, warming my shoulders. He doesn't answer right away. I know he's thinking about my question and his answer. "Sometimes when cases get as big as yours and are splashed all over the newspapers, we look into it ourselves without being asked to by the family. It didn't take us long to see there was something fishy about your case. The more we looked into it, the more things weren't adding up. So I put my men on it and we tracked you down."

"Wow," I whisper, picturing the guys chasing leads.

"When I saw your picture," he pauses, making me look up at him, "I couldn't stop staring at it. You drew me. You are so beautiful, Savannah. We pulled every string, asked every favor, sneaked in places off the grid, just to find a clue that would lead us to you. And I may have done a few things I'm ashamed of, but I don't care."

His finger hooks my chin and tilts it up, his eyes dark as night. "Baby, I'd play dirty for you any day."

I smile and give him a soft kiss under his jaw. Threading his fingers through mine, I sag back into his lap, resting his hand over my stomach. Sometimes I feel like the baby can feel him.

"I had no idea that you and I would have ended up here." He squeezes me a little tighter, then leans down, brushing his lips over the shell of my ear. "I'm sorry for what happened to you, but I'll never be sorry for tracking you down and falling in love with you."

***

"You're awfully quiet." Keith peers at me from the driver's seat. I made a lunch date with Sue today. I miss her and have only seen her once since I've been back. Keith had to go into town to pick up something from Christina's store, so he offered to drive me.

"Just thinking."

"About?"

"About…stuff."

"What kind of stuff?" he tries again.

I shake my head. Nosy bugger. "I'm just need to process some things."

"I'm a great listener." He grins. Keith has taken on the role of an older brother.

I don't want to raise any red flags with Keith since he can read me like an open book, so I go another route. "Is Dell back to replace—?

"Rent?"

"Yes, to replace Derek?" He nods, peering over at me. "I thought so."

"Dell has been waiting to work at Shadows for a long time. This will be his chance to see if he has what it takes. Plus, Logan is still looking into recruiting one of the men from the training session earlier in the month."

Something nags at the back of my brain when he

mentions the recruit but quickly fades away. I can't quite bring it into focus. Keith parks the SUV in front of the UPS store, motioning for me to follow. "It's okay, I'm fine staying here," I say, smiling to reassure him.

Keith steps out and comes around to my side and opens the door. "Just because The American is in custody doesn't mean all the danger is gone." He helps me out. "Besides, I haven't put my tracking chip in you yet."

"Oh, yeah, you're funny." I follow him into the store, really not wanting to see Christina again. He holds the door open with a mischievous expression.

"Who says I'm kidding?"

Holy hell, this place is hot! It must be a hundred and ten in here. I yank open my jacket and start to laugh. Keith eyes me funny, then gets it.

"Yeah, now you know why we leave our jackets behind." He rolls his eyes and points to the counter. "And now you'll see who Victoria's Secret's biggest fan is." Then I notice her, Christina, wearing one of the skimpiest dresses I've ever seen. She might as well be wearing a child's shirt. Wow, I don't think that could be classified as a dress. Getting a little closer, nope, that's a silk nightgown. Her hair is cut in a pin-straight bob, a different style since I saw her last. She reminds me of a pinup girl with her red lips and heavy eye makeup.

She bats her eyes at Keith but scowls when she sees me. I don't even bother to plaster a smile on my face. I'm not in the mood to play nice.

"Hello, Keith," she coos, leaning her breasts over the counter. "I believe I have a package for you and the boys. I'll go grab it." Her hips sway as she heads out back.

"Yikes," I whisper, making Keith crack up. She returns a moment later with three large boxes. I have to give her credit, I'm really not sure how she manages to walk in her stiletto heels. She looks positively ridiculous, especially considering we are in the back mountains of Montana, and in a UPS shop at that.

"Tell me, Keith, I thought Cole was coming by today." *And there it is.* "Not that I don't like seeing your handsome face." She eyes me up. "I just need to speak with him." Her freakishly red lips mold into a pout. Keith lifts the boxes and nods toward me, indicating the door, but I don't move.

"He's busy," I answer, staring at her, "but I'll let him know you said hello."

She turns, crossing her arms and pumping up her fake breasts. "Actually, if you could tell him to stop by, that would be better."

"Or I could relay the message to him," I counter, trying to control my claws that are itching to pop those fake tits.

Her smile grows just a little as she reaches under the counter and pulls out an envelope. "Oh, okay, well, be a doll and give him this. I didn't get a chance to when we were out at dinner the other night."

I don't move. I stay completely still. I've mastered this reaction as I've been blindsided enough times. Taking a step forward and reaching for the white envelope, I avoid touching her devil-red nails.

"Tell him thanks," she bats her eyelashes at me, "and I'll return his shirt to him just as soon as it gets back from the dry cleaners."

"Claressia, right?" Hot anger is starting to surface and I fight like hell to bury it.

"Saaavi...?" Keith calls out in a warning. "We're going to be late."

My nails are digging into my palms as I turn and walk out. Taking a deep calming breath of cool air helps to ground me. I slip into auto pilot and hop in the SUV. Keith is watching my face as he turns over the engine, adjusting the hot air to blast at me, but I turn it off, not wanting to thaw the icy barrier I'm building.

"You know it's nothing. Christina is a bitch, she's just—"

"Sue is waiting," I remind him, fastening my seatbelt. He shuts up, thankfully, and we head down the icy road to Zack's restaurant.

Brown is the color of the dirt. Ivory is like an elephant tusk. Taupe is the color of the stone in my ring. Cream is like the color of the seats, hunter green like the guys' army camo. "B-I-T-C-H!" I say in my head. It's something Dr. Roberts told me to do when I get upset. Take the word that best fits the scenario, break it down into something else and make it a better word. Let me tell you, it's *not* working.

Sue greets me with a massive hug, even granting me a kiss on the cheek. God, I love this woman; she's so warm and loving. Sometimes I swear I see a little bit of my mother in her.

"Are you sleeping all right?" she asks, mistaking my hurt for lack of sleep. I nod and slip into the seat across from her and pluck up the menu. This is a big red flag for her that something is up with me, considering we've never ordered off the menu once since coming to Zack's. He always insists we try the meal of the day, and we always do.

She waits until Keith gets settled at the bar before she turns her attention fully on me. Zack greets us with a glass of Pinot Grigio and informs us that they have Dijon salmon already in the skillet for us.

"Okay, spill it, Savi." Sue stares me down, daring me to lie. I don't, I can't, not about this. I need her help.

"Under one condition."

"What's that?" She leans closer as I begin to let her inside my head and the madness that's been eating me up inside, desperately needing release.

***

Cole

Cole pulls into Camp Green Water, where team Blackstone spent two weeks volunteering their services, and also where he is scouting out a new recruit for the house. He makes his way over to the third big warehouse where the recruits are back for more training. These are the men who made the first cut. His boots squeak across the tile floor as he nods to the captain who's blowing a whistle for the men to walk on the bottom of the pool with a brick in their hands. He blows it once, and the men drop to the bottom. Two staff sergeants are in the water with masks, ready to help if need be, and two follow up on top for a bird's eye view.

"Colonel Logan." Captain Miles shakes his hand. "So you're here to take one of my men, are you?"

Cole smirks, knowing every man would love a chance to come play at Shadows. Their reputation excites anyone who's a thrill junkie...so, most men. "I have a few in mind, but I only need one."

Miles watches as the men resurface at the opposite end. He blows the whistle again, getting them to return the same way they left. "I have three more rounds, then they're all yours."

"Sounds good." Cole observes, keeping a close eye on the number that interests him, but then his attention is tugged to a different recruit. He moves down to the edge of the pool and watches the situation. One of the staff sergeants begins to makes a move, but Cole holds up a hand, wanting to see what will happen.

One of the men has stopped to help his teammate who got caught up in his rope. They're both struggling, needing air, but this recruit isn't giving up. He even goes so far as to pull his buddy along with him as they finish the drill. By the time they finish, the recruit is barely coherent, and his buddy is passed out but comes to quickly.

Cole takes note of his number and smiles. Savannah will be happy.

"Number nine," Cole calls out once the man is standing upright. "A word, please."

The man is wide-eyed as he takes in Cole's presence. "Colonel," he huffs, out of breath.

"Corporal Davie, nice work down there."

"Thank you, sir."

Cole rubs his face. He wasn't expecting this turn of events. "I was under the impression you had an issue with water, but what I just witnessed makes me think you've gotten over your fear."

Davie takes a long breath, looking back at his buddy. "Well, sir, you never leave a man behind. If he didn't finish, then we all don't finish." He laughs a little. "I'll be frank, I have no desire to do that again, but I will if I have to." He turns and looks at his buddy. "Pipes is a good swimmer, sir, he just got disoriented."

Cole nods, liking his answer. He couldn't have asked for a better one. "Get dried off, pick up your things, and meet me in the main office in thirty."

"Ah-yes, sir." He looks confused but does as he's told.

Exactly thirty minutes later, Davie takes a seat, dropping his bag at his feet. He looks around the office, apparently taking in the severe lack of décor in the old warehouse. Cole closes the file and glances at his cell phone, waiting for an update from Keith. He and Savi should be back at the house by now, but he knows he doesn't have time to call.

"Davie, I have to be honest. I had another recruit in mind for a position at Shadows, but after what I just saw, I think I may have to change my mind."

"Oh?" Davie can't hide his interest. He rubs his blond crew cut like he's used to it being a little longer.

"Would you be interested in a spot at Shadows?"

"Yes, I would, very much so."

Cole leans over the desk, putting emphasis on his next words to make sure he is very clear. "You understand what you will be giving up by joining the house? Relationships are next to impossible, secrets are your life, twelve to fourteen hour shifts are not unusual, and in rough elements. The house and team will become your family. I treat my men well. I haven't had a complaint yet."

Davie sits up a little straighter. "I understand, sir. I've always been interested in Shadows. I know what I will be sacrificing, but I don't have much to lose. My only family was my father, and he just passed two months ago. I have no ties. I'm basically a shadow already."

Cole knows about Davie's father and how he drowned off their fishing boat, but never once does Davie bring it up or use it as an excuse, and that's a damn good quality in a man. He's tough and can control his emotions. Davie is clearly a perfect match for Shadows.

"Pack your bags, Davie, we leave in an hour."

The smile that appears on Davie's face is enough to lighten anyone's mood. He grabs his bag and jumps up, holding out his hand for a shake. "Thank you, Colonel, I won't let you down."

"I know you won't."

Davie leaves just as Roth, number fifty-nine, is about to knock on the door. Cole tells him to take a seat as he opens his file and looks over the paperwork. Cole knows he is a true candidate across the board. He is the one Cole has had his eye on from day one. Roth is made for Shadows, but there is still something that niggles at Cole. "Roth, I'm sure you got wind that I've been looking to recruit a man for my house."

"I have." He leans back in his chair, looking pretty confident, which irks Cole a little. York was cocky.

"But there has to be trust." Cole watches as tiny beads of sweat break out across his upper lip. "Do you feel you are trustworthy?"

"I-I do," he stumbles. "You've seen my chart. I've passed everything with flying colors. I haven't failed one test you've thrown at me."

"I'm not questioning your physical strength or your ability. That we know. I'm talking about trust. If there's no trust, then there's no team. No team means there's no job."

"You *can* trust me." The words come out, leaving Cole uneasy. Something feels off. He's been around long enough to go with his gut, and right now it's screaming at him to cut Roth loose.

"Then why did you swim by Corporal Davie, while he helped Pipes finish the drill? He's not nearly the swimmer you are."

He leans back in his seat and crosses his arms. "You get don't stats like that," he points to his file, "picking up the weak."

Cole clamps down on his tongue, thanking his gut and letting a few quiet seconds go by as he studies Roth's face. "Well, thanks for being honest, Roth. Now it's my turn. I don't think you're the right fit for Shadows." Roth's face falls; clearly this is not what he is expecting.

"Colonel, can you give me a chance? I'll do anything, just let me come to the house and I'll prove it." Roth looks almost panicky. Cole runs Roth's words over in his head.

"I'm sorry, Roth, but I'm staying firm on my decision. Now," Cole stands and collects his things, "I have to go. Take care, Roth. You're a good soldier.

You'll do well."

Davie is standing by the front door, bags packed, with an excited grin on his face. A few of his buddies are congratulating him. When he sees Cole, he stands a little straighter and holds the door for him. Respectful, oh yeah, Cole knows he has made the right decision.

They drive directly to Zack's, unable to take him to the house until all the documents have been signed. Frank has to go over the contracts, have Davie sign the NDA, and be sure he fully understands what is expected of him. Davie is clearly book smart and asks all the right questions. The longer Cole spends time with him, the more he feels good about his choice.

"Can I get you anything else?" The host, Adam comes over holding a pitcher of water and refilling their glasses.

"No, thanks." Frank covers his glass with his hand, indicating he doesn't want any more. "Just let Zack know we're leaving, please."

"Sure, he should be done with Nicole's paperwork by now."

Cole's head snaps up at the use of Savannah's cover name. "What?"

Adam nods and picks up a plate, balancing it in his hand. "Yeah, he spent a good hour with her earlier this afternoon. I'm not sure why, but you know Zack. He's like a vault. Anyway, she and your mother left about two hours ago, saying they needed to meet someone." A smile breaks along his lips. "So pretty and sweet with just the right mixture of sexy...man, what a combo." He whistles as he leaves the table, missing Cole's death look.

"I hope he was talking about Nicole." Frank snorts, making Davie crack up. Even Cole smiles, but only for a moment. He is confused. *What the hell is going on*?

Chapter Thirteen

Savannah

I check the clock. It's a little after six when we arrive back at the house. Sue has decided to join us for dinner. I know why, and I appreciate it. Daniel greets us as we enter the foyer. His arm still looks sore, but he refuses to use the sling. *Men.* He gives Sue a kiss and wraps me in a typical Logan bear hug while asking us how our day went. Sue speaks to him as I slip out of my coat and boots and head upstairs to change into a dress. I got wind from Abigail we are having some company when she suggested I choose something from the left-hand side of the closet. I change into a little black dress, thinking it's a safe bet, as it matches my dark eyes. I have to smile at myself in the mirror as I realize I resemble my mother more than my father. Feeling more than a little pleased and with a quick touch-up in the makeup department, I head downstairs.

"Well, well, well, if it isn't my soon-to-be wife," Dell jokes, giving me a playful smile and a small hug. "Don't you look lovely?"

"So do you, Dell. I heard you were back, glad to see it's true." I spot Cole across the room talking to Frank and someone else, his back is to me.

"Can I get you something to drink?" He wiggles his eyebrows. "Tale of the Devil?"

I laugh and hit his arm. "No, thanks! Two of those had Mark carrying me to bed last time."

"It was kinda fun," Mark jokes, wrapping an arm around my shoulder. "You were an open book of info that evening."

"Mmmmm." I roll my eyes, remembering how drunk I was.

"Can I steal you for a moment?" Mark asks, excusing us from Dell.

Mark keeps his arm around my shoulders as he walks me over to Cole. "What did you and Sue do today, Savannah?"

I look up at him, trying to see if he knows. Keith promised to keep quiet, and Keith keeps his promises. "Why?" is all I manage to get out before he interrupts.

"Melanie told me you stopped by, and you had some questions." Shit, I forgot to tell her to keep it to herself. "Are you really looking for a job in town?" Oh, he thinks I'm looking for a job. Okay, I'll let him run with that, until I speak with Cole.

"Something like that," I mutter because I hate lying.

Cole studies my face as I come up to his side.

"There she is." Frank nods. "Savannah, please meet—"

"Corporal Davie!" I reach out to shake his hand, smiling and pleasantly surprised. "How are you?"

Frank looks at both of us, confused. "I wasn't aware you two knew one another."

Davie shakes my hand. "We met when Savannah came to the camp a few weeks back. It's nice to see you again."

Keith appears as I tell Davie it's good to see him again, giving me a nod toward Cole, wondering if I spoke with him yet. I quickly shake my head no.

"Good, Keith, you're here." Cole grins. "I wanted to ask you, would you be interested in joining Blackstone?"

Keith face lights up before he tucks it behind his mask.

"I'd be honored."

"Happy to hear that. You'll be active as soon as Savannah's," he pauses and lowers his voice, "case gets cleared up."

I roll my eyes, hating all this.

"Wouldn't want it any other way." Keith glances over at me. "You're up, buttercup."

Pressing my lips together, I shake my head.

"Could you excuse us, please?" Cole leads me away from the group with his hand on my back, directing me to his office. Once inside away from the noise, he asks me if I'd like a drink.

"Yes, whatever you're having," I answer, making him stop and turn. I never ask for a brandy.

He studies me while he starts fixing our drinks, leaning against his desk while I sip my brandy a few feet away. I'm a bundle of nerves. This could go south if I'm not careful.

"Anytime you're ready," he prompts me. "I've got all night, baby."

I sigh, taking a rather large swig of the brown liquid and feeling it burn on its descent. Sue and I discussed this at length, but I feel like I'm about to break his heart...and possibly mine.

"Now that The American is caught, Luka is dead, Lynn is in custody, my father will be soon, and the truth is finally out," I begin, "I see my life has pretty much been a messy lie. My life has been shattered, and it's time I pick up the pieces. Since coming back this time, I've been feeling all kinds of different emotions." His face tightens a little. I can tell this is going to completely blindside him. "I need to make a change." He downs his drink, setting it aside, and folds his arms, which flex like he's holding back a reaction. I close my eyes, deciding to rip the Band-Aid off. "I need to move out." Silence. My eyes flutter open to find him staring at the floor. "Cole, I need to find out who I am before I can move forward. I just need some time." He slowly nods.

"It's not completely safe yet. Your father—" He doesn't look at me.

"Is being watched by the NYPD, so if he ever heads this way, they'll let you know. I'm only moving in town, just down the street from your parents. It's a cute little place, one bedroom, a sweet little kit—"

He suddenly stiffens. "You already found a place?"

I only nod, realizing how bad this must look. "I got a job at Zack's. I have your parents nearby in case I get into trouble, and Melanie is my neighbor. I know this is a shock, but I really need to do this, Cole. Please understand."

He shakes his head and looks anywhere but at me. "And where does this leave us?"

I want to make sure I use the right words. He needs to know I don't want to break up; I love him. I just want some separate space so I can live a little, be Savannah Miller, the girl who has a dark past but is ready to face the light on her own two feet, not have someone looking after her. This house is amazing. It's my home, but the guys are too protective. Now that the threat is pretty much gone, I'm ready to take back my life, but before I get a chance to tell him all this, he tilts my world a little more. "You know what, maybe some time apart is a good thing. I have a trip coming up, and I don't want to have to worry about you while I'm gone."

"Don't want to have to worry about me?" I repeat his words, feeling the sting. "You want to break up?" I barely whisper, feeling my entire body tingle as the blood drains to my feet. His words slice me open. I know he worries about me, but I didn't know how much he minded it.

He scoops up his glass and moves swiftly across the room, pouring himself another drink. "You seem to have everything figured out. Seems this goes hand in hand with your plan. Besides, we knew this would have to come to an end sometime. You're a city girl, I'm a country guy. It's not a movie, Savannah. This shit doesn't work out. It's not always a happy ending. You don't belong here anymore. You don't need our protection now."

I stare at his back in utter shock. I'm moving to Redstone! It's like fifteen or twenty minutes from here, not New York! I can't even form a thought. So instead I place my glass down on a coaster and pull out the paper from my dress pocket, feeling like it is burning my hand. "Christina asked me to give you this. She said thanks for dinner." He quickly turns as I rest the envelope against my glass. I leave before he can say another word, but I don't miss his 'deer caught in headlights' look before I go. I don't want to break up, but I'm also not going to be the woman who stands by while another woman has time with him.

The day passes in a haze, and that night at dinner the table is buzzing with news about the house's newest recruit, Davie. He and Dell seem to be hitting it off pretty well. I wait until dessert before I share my news with the house. Keith is watching me. I think he's worried about me leaving, but I'll be all right. Cole is to my left, not eating, just nursing his drink. I won't let the hurt in—yet—not until I'm behind closed doors by myself. If I show weakness now, they'll never be okay with me leaving.

I stand, feeling slightly lightheaded, and clear my throat as the hum around the table dies and all eyes fall on me.

"What's up, Savi?" Mike asks, cocking his head to the left.

I force a smile and start, "Umm, I just want to say thank you for everything you've done for me. I've been through a lot, and if it wasn't for all of you, I wouldn't have made it. But, like they say, all good things must come to an end. You caught the bad guys, and now I'm free." I try to make a joke, but instead my eyes water. "So, I got myself a little place in town, near Daniel and Sue's, so you will be officially Savannah-free shortly." It's hard to watch their faces drop and see their eyes flicking from Cole and back to me. He is staring intently at his drink.

Dell is the first to speak, breaking the painful silence. "But is it safe?"

"If she stays in Redstone, she should be fine," Daniel says softly. "We'll keep an eye on her. Zack will too."

Mark shakes his head, looking pissed off. "You don't have to go, Savannah. None of us want you to leave."

"That's very sweet, Mark," I say, feeling the pain ooze through the cracks in my armor, and this makes me angry. "But I'm a city girl, remember. I don't belong here."

"Cole," Mark pleads to him, "say something."

"He's said enough," I interrupt, just wanting to go upstairs. "Look, everyone, you are the family I never had. I'm only in town. You'll still see me all the time; you just don't have to worry about me anymore. You can go back to being the heroes and knights for some other person in the world."

Keith shakes his head at Dell, who is about to make a comment. I decide to end on a light note before I make my exit. "Just watch your back, because you never know when Agent Black will come back."

John laughs, breaking the tension at the table. Mark smiles, but I can tell he's not happy.

***

A glance at the clock shows it's two a.m. Sleep just doesn't seem to be happening for me. My bags are packed with everything Abigail got for me when I arrived at the house, and they are already loaded in the SUV. I'm not supposed to leave until tomorrow afternoon, but I need to get out now. Cole won't speak or even look at me, and the pain is becoming too much to bear. I just want to leave now. Yes, I'm running, but this time I can't help it. Dressing quickly and making the bed, I take one last look my room, remembering the first day I arrived here. How scared I was, how lonely I felt. I didn't think I was going to make it. I remember the first time Cole touched me, kissed me, and made love to me in the shower. A small smile comes to my lips saying goodbye, because if I don't smile I'll cry, and I'm not ready to yet.

My boots seem loud as I walk down the hallway, I grab a pair of car keys out of John's jacket, but quickly tuck them back in when I see headlights light up the entryway. I step outside just as the passenger window rolls down. I know who it is; he must have been waiting. I climb in the front seat, giving Keith a guilty smile.

"I knew you'd leave in the night." He turns the heated seats up and heads for the first gate. I watch as the massive cabin that was once my safe house grows smaller in the mirror. A part of my heart wants to run back…but it wants Cole, not the house. But he doesn't want me. I force my eyes to look forward. I must move forward and not look back.

***

Cole

Cole sits on the edge of the bed, gripping the unopened letter from Christina. He knows what it says, what they always say. She wants him back, they are perfect for one another, and she can't live without him. The fact that she gave it to Savannah makes him uneasy. He doesn't trust Christina, and her behavior is becoming more aggressive. No doubt she was hoping Savannah would read the letter. She'd fed her a fake dinner story as it was. He wants to toss it in the fire and watch those memories of her burn away, but something stops him, and he decides to keep it along with all the others as evidence in case she tries to pull something later.

"Knock, knock," his mother whispers at his open door. She is wearing her night robe. "May I?"

"Sure." He watches her as she makes her way across the room and takes a seat in his leather chair next to the fire, warming her hands with a little sigh.

"Please don't be upset with me for helping Savannah find an apartment."

Cole tosses the letter on his nightstand and leans back against his headboard. "I'm not angry. I'm just hurt that she wants to leave me. We worked so hard to stay together, and the first moment she gets a chance to leave, she takes it."

"You think that's what happened?" she asks, shaking her head. "Dear, she didn't *want* to leave, she *had* to leave." Cole makes a face, not following. "We had a long talk over lunch today. She loves you more than anything, Cole. She left because she was feeling lost within herself. She left so she could make herself stronger so both of you could work as a couple. Don't be selfish with her, Cole. She needs this time to find out who she is."

Cole closes his eyes; he's such an asshole. This is the

second time he's let his emotions get the better of him, and he lashed out at her. "I thought she was breaking up with me earlier, so I did it first," he whispers, covering his face in shame. *Fuck.*

"Well, that explains it. Oh, dear, you have so much to learn about women." She whistles and leans back in the seat.

Cole swings his legs off the bed. "Explains what?"

"Why she left in the middle of the night."

"What?" he neatly shouts. "She's gone?"

His mother moves to sit next to him. "Keith took her." She places her hand on his knee, stopping him before he interrupts. "Give her a few days, Cole. Let her settle in, then go make it up to her. She's not going anywhere. Remember, we have eyes and ears all over that town. She'll be all right."

Cole stares at the fire, listening to his mother and knowing she is right, but his gut is telling him to run to her, wanting to hold her tight and keep her safe. She gently rubs his back like she used to do when he was a boy. They sit for a long time, listening to the fire pop as he slowly relaxes and lets the realization settle that Savannah needs space from the house, from the guys, from him.

"She's my everything," he finally says with a catch in his voice. "I love her, Mom."

"I know you do, son." She kisses his cheek softly. "And you'll get her back."

"Yeah, I will."

The End

"Your eyes are so beautiful it's as if someone removed a star and made you from all it's beauty."
~ Cole Logan

mended

BROKEN TRILOGY
BOOK THREE

J.L. DRAKE

Prologue

They say time heals all wounds, but they fail to mention it's a bitch of a journey.

I'm twenty-nine years old and feel I haven't really lived yet. My life up to now has been filled with lies, loss, death, betrayal, and heartache. After several months of hell, I'm finally over the worst of it, and now I'm starting to mend, slowly pulling my life together and picking up the pieces.

It's time to live…my way…

Chapter One

Savannah

I close the door behind Keith, and watch him disappear down the hallway. I lock the two deadbolts, chain, and latch, and breathe a sigh of relief. Keith installed them all the night I arrived, while I pretended to act like I was fine without them. *Not true*. He spoke with the man at the front desk about keeping an eye on me, and also put sensors on all my windows...I live on the fifth floor.

After I grab a quick bite to eat, I head over to the mirror, checking my outfit and smoothing my hands over my hair. *I can do this*. I pick up my keys after a little mental pep talk and head out, pushing myself to move forward. The painfully slow elevator calls me, but I opt for the stairs instead. It's been a week since I left the safe house and moved here, a week since I've seen Cole. Keith keeps finding odd jobs around my one-bedroom apartment that he can only do during the night, since he has to work through the day. I know he's nervous to leave me alone, and frankly, I like having him on my couch. Of course I keep telling him to leave and stop babying me, but that's just another lie I add to the already long list.

Secretly, I'm worried my friends back at the safe house are growing tired of me, so I'm trying to act as independent as possible. That's why I'm walking three blocks to Zack's restaurant, knowing that Keith is sitting in the coffee shop across the street, watching me to make sure I get there all right. I smile to myself and pull out my sunglasses. Who knew scary old Keith would end up being a protective older brother?

I grin, thinking about the other day.

My apartment is quiet, something I don't enjoy anymore. Melanie is out with friends and wanted me to join them, but all I want to do is watch old reruns of Lie to Me. Maybe I'll learn something. Resting my glass of wine on my leg, I pull the covers over me more. It's cold, and I'm too stubborn to turn up the heat. I don't want my electric bill to be too much. Daniel is trying to pay my bills, but I'm determined not to have that happen. I'll be making enough when I start my new job in a few days. I don't need much.

I'm not sure what time it is when a light knocking wakes me. Oh, wow, I must have dozed off. I pull my lazy ass off the couch and trudge to the door, looking through the peephole to find Keith staring back at me.

After I unlock all five locks, I open the door. He is holding a plastic bag.

"I got you a fish."

What?

He holds up the bag, showing me a purple rainbow fish staring back at me through the plastic.

Ewww.

"Why?"

I hate fish.

He smiles, seeing my discomfort. "'Cause you're lonely and could use someone you can't push away." He steps past me, but turns when I go to close the door.

"Wait."

"I don't push people away." I fold my arms as I look down the hallway and wonder who else is coming.

"Right." He chuckles as he runs water into a glass bowl he took from another bag. *"You'd be surprised how attached you can become to* Aloof, *here."*

I shake my head. *"Aloof?"*

He nods as he slips the fish into its new home. *"Seems suitable for how you've been lately."*

I close my eyes, feeling his words hit me like a blow to the gut. *"I'm sorry, Keith. I'm not trying to push anyone away. Especially not you. I-I...don't know what I am."*

He sits the bowl on my counter, rubbing his finger along the glass and getting the fish's attention.

"I know things have been rough lately. Just don't shut us all out." I nod miserably. The cookies are on top of the fridge. I reach up and grab them and sit them in front of him.

"Truce?"

"I was never mad at you. I just miss the old Savannah sometimes." He takes my hand and drags me into a side hug, while he snags two cookies at once. *"Do you need anything?"*

I shrug, knowing he needs this. *"Actually, the tap in the bathroom has been dripping."*

His face lights up. *"I'll go get my tools."*

"Wait, Keith, who is comin—"

"Why does your elevator take nine years to get to the fifth floor?" June jokes, setting a large box on my kitchen table. I nearly jump into her arms. I'm so thankful to see family here in my own place.

June nods at Abigail, who is holding a bag full of homemade food.

"Thought you might like something different to eat." She opens my fridge and sees my jar of peanut butter

and bottled water. "Well, I thought you might be hungry."

"Thanks!" I peer over her shoulder and see a container of her lentil soup. Yum.

June pours herself a glass of wine, then wanders over to the couch and retrieves mine from the side table. "This is a lovely place, dear."

"Thank you." I sit at the counter and watch Abigail.

"Here," Abigail says, pushing a large wrapped present toward me. "This is to keep Keith happy."

I grin, wondering what the heck it can be. I pluck the silver bow off and rip the paper down the sides. My hands stop mid-tear when I see what it is. "Oh my."

"I hope it's the right color."

"It is." I open the box and carefully pull it free from all the packaging. My fingers run along the red paint, down the neck, and around the shiny metal bowl. "It's just like her Mixmaster." Pressing my lips together, I rein in my emotions. How did I ever get so lucky to have these two amazing women in my life? "Thank you so much!"

"You're more than welcome, dear." They both give me a hug.

It looks perfect next to my coffee maker. I turn to see June and Abigail looking at my living room. Leaning against the counter, I feel happy they're here. This is nice. I really have to try harder.

***

"This is your locker, aprons are here, bathrooms are over there, and this is where you punch in and out." Zack takes the time card and slips it into the slot where we hear it stamp the long yellow form. "There, you're officially on the clock." He motions for me to follow him through a short hall to the bar which is alongside his restaurant. "Since you've bartended before, this shouldn't be too hard for you. Jake will show you the ropes."

"All right." Butterflies dance in my stomach. I'm nervous about being around such a large crowd; it's been a while.

He hands me my nametag. "Here's the deal, Savi. You have any problems with the customers, talk to Jake. He's great, and he'll have your back no matter what. We don't have much trouble here, but there are always a few...well, you know what I mean. But if *Savannah* needs help," he gives me a look to make sure I understand that I go to him if something comes up with my case, "you come find me. I should always be working the same shift as you, but if for some reason I'm not, Keith or Daniel won't be far away. Any questions?" I shake my head, taking it all in. "Jake," he calls out, "meet your new sidekick."

A tall, well-built guy about my age flashes me a set of pearly whites. "Well, aren't I just the lucky one? Hey there, I'm Jake."

"Savi." We shake hands, but before I pull away, he spins me around, studying me.

"Okay, first, this isn't going to work." He shakes his head and reaches under the bar and hands me a t-shirt. "Go put this on." He smiles and points to a small door. I quickly change into a black V-neck t-shirt that has a bit more cleavage showing than something I would have picked out. The shirt hangs just below my belly button, showing half an inch of skin above my pants. Jake rubs his fingers over his lips when he sees me. "Good, but..." he pulls my ponytail free and lets my hair fall around my shoulders, "this is better." He nods approval. "Sex sells, and in the afternoon and night this place is buzzing with tired men looking for a drink. With that body and face, Savi, we'll have this place packed to the max, and that means…tips!"

Just after seven, the place is slammed. Thankfully, Jake is patient, and my memory hasn't given up on me. I've never made four apple martinis at once, but I'll tell you what, I can now. I learn quickly that the girls who come to the bar are rich and impatient, and most of the men are into some kind of extreme sport or other. I barely have time to think about breathing before the next order is being barked at me, but I'm soon into the swing of it and am getting the job done.

"You have a gentleman caller," Jake says over my shoulder as I enter the order into the computer.

I glance over and see Mark grinning as he snags an empty seat in the middle of the bar. I finish up and head over, wiping my hands on a rag.

"Well, hello, stranger," I lean over and give him a hug. "It's good to see your face."

He eyes my shirt. "He's not going to like this." That painful knot in my stomach tightens, but I shrug his comment off. "How are you, Savi?"

I laugh and lean over the counter to make my point. "Really, how am I?" *Like you all don't get a play by play update from Keith.* He smirks, nodding at the Stella on tap. I grab a glass and pour him one. "I'm all right, but I'd be lying if I said I didn't miss you guys. How are things at the house? How's Abby? Is June still here?"

"You can come home, you know." He peers at me over his glass, but when he sees my shrug he changes the topic. "June is still here. She's talking about moving in permanently. She hates being away from her sister. You know how she and Abby are," he smiles.

I slap my rag against the counter. "Really? It will be so great to have her around!"

"Yeah, it will be." He turns his attention to a customer who's calling out for me. I hold up a finger and rush over to the guy.

"Hi, what can I get you?" I ask.

The man pushes up his sleeves as he takes a seat. "You, for starters." I sigh inwardly and keep my expression the same.

"How 'bout a drink?" I counter, but this makes him smile.

"Scotch, neat, keep them coming, and if by the end of the night you do a good job, I'll do the same for you." He slips me his credit card and hotel key. I stare at them both in shock. This man doesn't waste any time. I pluck the credit card and, ignoring his key, make his drink. When I hand him the drink, he wraps his fingers around mine. "I'm Don." He reaches over with his free hand and fingers my nametag. "Savi, that's a pretty name."

"Thanks," I say, pulling my hand away. "Excuse me." I head back over to Mark, who is watching me like a hawk. I slap on a smile and ask if he wants another.

"Really, Savi, you want to work here? With *these* guys?" Mark twists his beer in his hand as he points with his head at the Don guy. "Cole isn't going to like this."

Shaking my head, hands on my hips, I raise an eyebrow at him. "Were you sent here to spy, Mark, or did you come by as a friend seeing a friend?"

He glares right back. "First, I'm seeing family, not just a friend. You don't think I'll be hounded when he calls in tonight? Please spare me the look. I have to report something to the poor guy."

I reach for a towel and wipe down a nonexistent water ring. "Where is he this time?"

"Washington. He testified against The American yesterday." My throat suddenly goes dry. "It went well. He should be home tonight or tomorrow." He makes a face, and I know what he's going to say.

"When do I have to go?" The blood drains from my face when I think about having to see those people again.

Mark downs his beer. "Cole is trying to get you out

of it. We're hoping you can do it from here using video chat, but it would be more effective if you were there in person."

"I'll do it," I say, tossing the towel aside. "Tell Frank I'll come to Washington."

"You don't have to, Sav—"

"I should get back to my customers. It was really nice seeing you, Mark. Please say hello to everyone for me." I start to walk away, but Mark hooks my arm and stops me.

"Come by the house tomorrow night and have dinner with us."

I shake my head. "Sorry, I'm working."

"Then during the day?"

"I'll see," I pat his arm and leave to tend to the rest of the customers.

"You did great tonight," Jake says a few hours later as he tugs the strap of his bag over his head. "Can I walk you out?"

"Sure." We step out into the freezing air, and tiny snowflakes wander down from the sky. I wrap my scarf around my neck. "How long have you been working for Zack?"

Jake starts walking in my direction. "For about three years. I don't have any family here, so he's taken me under his wing. I see he's done the same with you." I nod, feeling very at ease with Jake. He's very kind and soft spoken. "Actually, you seem to have a lot of people keeping an eye on you," he says quietly. "That guy who came by tonight, is he your boyfriend?"

"Just a close friend," I smile, thinking if Mark came off as my boyfriend, maybe Don will lay off the next time he comes in for a drink.

"That's good, because I know he's dating Mel." I glance up at him. "She's a friend too. So what's the deal, Savi? You have Mark, Zack, and that huge, tall guy who's like your shadow."

"Keith," I say with a laugh. "He's like an older brother."

"Okay, so what's with the army of men? You, like, in some kind of trouble?" I nearly trip on flat ground with his guess.

"You're pretty observant for only knowing me for, what, nine hours?"

He pulls the collar of his jacket up higher to keep the chill off his neck. "It's sorta something I do. I love to people watch." He stops and turns to face me. "I'm just offering an ear if you need it." He points with his head. "This is me." I smile when I see we are standing in front of my building.

"What floor?"

His face drops. "Oh—ah…I didn't mean…"

I grin when I realize how that just sounded. "I meant what floor, because I live on the fifth."

He tosses his head back, laughing. "I'm in 5G."

"5H." I extend a hand. "Nice to meet you, neighbor."

We take the stairs, bitching about the elevator, and saying goodbye outside our doors. Once inside, I check my phone, which is on the counter where I left it. I keep forgetting I own one now. Two missed calls from Keith and a text letting me know he won't be spending the night.

My stomach twists when I realize I'll be on my own for the first time since moving here. My finger taps the counter as I re-read the message. I guess I'm going to have to get used to this. It is what I wanted. I text him back saying I'm home and no problem.

After a long shower, I still can't seem to unwind, even though the water felt wonderful. I pull on yoga pants and a tank top and lie in bed, pulling the covers to my chin. I find myself staring at the ceiling, wishing I could stop jumping at everything that goes bump in the night.

Tears leak out as I think of Cole. I wonder if he's thinking of me. Probably not in the way I'd want. I want to call him so badly to find out if he really meant those words, but I can't. I can't show weakness; I have to stay strong. I stroke absently along the spot next to me, feeling the coldness of the sheets there, and jerk my hand back. I curl into a ball and let my armor flake away. Oh, I miss him so much. I would do anything to smell him right now. Then I remember something, and my feet hit the cold wood floor, hurrying my steps. Yanking open the top right drawer, I see it tucked neatly inside. I remove my tank top and pull on Cole's camo t-shirt. His name, Logan, wraps around my back almost like it's his arm. Looking around my room, I decide this just won't do, so I grab my comforter and pillow. Instead of going back to bed, I head out to the living room where I click on the TV and make myself comfy on the couch facing the door. I spend the next four hours watching reruns of Fresh Prince of Bel-Air.

At nine in the morning, I hear a knock at the door. Keith always texts when he's in the building. Standing on my tiptoes, I peek through the peephole and laugh, opening the door to Jake standing in a pair of fleece PJ pants holding an empty mug, his blond hair pointing every which way.

"I smell coffee," he moans like he's still asleep.

Opening the door wider, I let him in. "Are you sleepwalking?" I joke as I lock all five locks behind him.

His eyes are still slits, but I see him take in my bed on the couch and Cole's shirt. "If I am, will you still share that delicious smelling coffee?"

"Come on," I laugh, waving him toward the kitchen. Jake plunks down on a bar stool as I move about, fixing us each a cup. "Cheers." I clink my mug to his, and he grins as he sips the brew.

"Sweet Lucifer down in hell, what is this?" At first I think he's being insulting, but his face says otherwise.

I lean my hip into the counter and give him a look. "I add a little something to the coffee."

"Savi, I hope you realize what you did," he says with a smirk. "From now on you are now my morning date."

I smile. *See, Savi, progress.* Jake and I spend the rest of the day camped out under the warmth of my comforter. I'm totally at ease with him. He's never once made me feel uncomfortable, and I figure if Zack trusts him, I can. We order pizza and watch a marathon of Louie CK standups until an hour before our shift starts. Keith texts a few times, and I assure him I'm fine, because I am…at the moment. I've made a friend.

"Savi, can I ask you something?" Jake says, taking a wet napkin to his greasy fingers. "Who's Logan?" I'm thrown by his question until he points to the back of my shirt. *Oh.* "Looks like a legit army shirt, and I'm guessing you're not in the force."

"He's—was my boyfriend," I stumble, feeling that knife to the heart.

Jake nods and shifts so he faces me. "Was it serious?" I nod. "Is he still around?"

"Yeah, it just ended recently, so it's still raw." My voice is barely a whisper.

He smiles, leaning his chin on his hand. "You love him, don't you?"

"I do."

"It sucks to love someone but not be with them." He sighs.

I feel like he may be referring to something in his life, but I don't pry. "Yeah, it does."

"Why do I feel like you have quite the history, Savannah…?" He waits for my last name, but I hesitate. He watches me for a moment. I can see him thinking, then his whole face brightens. "All right, no more prying today. We have to get to work. I'll be waiting for you outside your door in forty-five. For the love of god, do something with that hair of yours!" He laughs and snags another piece of pizza as he heads out the door.

We make it to work on time and the day passes quickly.

"You two look great!" Zack shouts, slapping his hands together. Jake and I are practicing our bar flare, and find we make a pretty good team. "Oh, Jake, your father called again." As Jake's face goes white, Zack quickly adds, "I told him you don't work here anymore."

"Okay," is all Jake says in reply. *So, Jake has a story too.*

The phone buzzes in my pocket, but I don't take time to look at it because I have a whole snowboard team taking up a table near the window. I grab the iPad and hurry over for the order. Thankfully, they all want the same thing, six pitchers of Bud Light. Once they are looked after, I head back to the counter where Don from last night is downing a scotch, neat.

Jake gives me an annoyed expression and hands me the guy's receipt. "The creep wants *you*. He was pissed I made his first drink, because apparently you can fuck up pouring scotch into a glass…jackass."

I roll my eyes, agreeing, but it's all part of the business.

"Don," I say with zero emotion, "would you like another?"

He licks his lips as he stares at my breasts. "Yes, I sure would." He holds out his glass, and when I reach for it, he runs his free hand up my arm. "Such a pretty woman."

Stepping away and getting a new glass from the bar, I turn my back while I pour. A strange feeling prickles up my spine. I look around, then freeze as I see Cole standing by the door watching. He's in a dark dress shirt and pants, his suit jacket hanging off his arm. Slowly approaching the bar top, he leans on the counter. All the while his eyes burn through me.

"You gonna drink that, or am I?" Don's arrogant voice breaks through the pull Cole has on me. I sit his drink in front of him and reach out to the bar top for support.

Cole pulls at his tie, undoing it, and tosses it on the counter near my hand. I resist the urge to hold it up to my nose and draw in his intoxicating scent. Instead I just pour him a brandy from the top shelf and sit it in front of him as I slowly raise my eyes to meet his stare.

"Thank you." He nods and takes a long sip from the glass.

I muster up all my strength and try to act like his presence isn't affecting my body. "Were you away?" I pick up the rag and dry a non-existent spill.

"I just came back from Washington," he sighs, rubbing his head.

"Have you been home yet?" The words fall from my mouth.

"No, I haven't been *home* yet." His eyes met mine, holding me captive, his mouth wet from the brandy.

"You just needed a drink?"

He shakes his head. "Old habits die hard." His eyes drop to my lips, and everything in my body begs me to lean forward. My tongue darts out as my lips scream for moisture. If we were alone right now, I know I'd give in.

"Sweetie, could I order some food?" Don asks, obviously irritated he's not getting any attention. I close my eyes and try to snap out of this bubble. I turn to find Don waving a menu at me. "I'll take a medium rare steak, with fries and a side of slaw."

"Anything else?"

He reaches in his back pocket, pulls out something, and leans forward, tucking his hotel room key in my cleavage. I toss it on the counter as I turn away, only to hear him chuckle. "You'll give in to me soon, sweetheart."

The mirror in front of me catches Cole's murderous expression, but he stays in his chair.

Throughout the evening, Cole never leaves his stool, barely speaking to me, just observing. Don is extra flirty, which is extremely annoying. Jake is busy but asks if I want Zack to escort Don out. I say no because he's already dropped at least two hundred in the last two nights. I can handle myself.

"Thirty minutes," Jake calls out to me, which means bed in sixty-five. "Are you going to get any sleep tonight?"

"What?" I spin around on my heel.

"Come on, Savi, sleeping on your couch and your eyes puffy from crying. Don't lie to me, girl, I know lack of sleep when I see it." I sneak a glance at Cole, who is, of course, still watching and listening to us.

"Logan," a voice calls out, and Keith takes a seat next to Cole.

Jake catches my eye, looks with one eyebrow raised at Cole, points a finger at him, then slowly moves it to me. "Ohhh, seriously?" I pull on his arm to get him to stop, pleading with him to shut up. He grins in a boyish way and gives me a slow wink. "I'll go punch out for us."

"Thanks," I mutter, trying to tone down the blush I know must be there. I turn to wipe down the bar and see Zack approaching us, smiling at the guys as he gets closer.

"Savi, you're doing great! Everyone loves you here." Zack comes around the bar, high-fiving me. "I heard one of the customers is being a bit of a handful."

"Nothing I can't handle," I assure him.

"Who?" Keith asks Zack, ignoring me.

Zack leans against the bar. "He's a monthly, works for a sports magazine. Bit of a jerk, but nothing to worry about. Besides Jake is watching over her, so she'll be fine."

Cole gets up and walks behind the counter to wash out his glass only inches from me. I can feel his warmth, and I sneak in a quick breath as I give in to the addiction of his scent. As soon as the smell attacks my senses, I have to walk away. It's like a kick straight to the gut. I head out back to my locker to grab my coat and change from my flats to my boots. I sink down onto the bench, feeling just how tired I am. The three-block walk home seems like ten.

"I don't like you working here." Cole's body fills the doorway. He looks concerned as he leans his weight into the wall.

I stand and fling my bag over my shoulder. "I'll be fine."

I hear him sigh. "Savi—"

I don't want to talk about us right now; I'm too tired. "Do I have to testify in Washington?"

He pushes off the wall and takes a few steps toward me. I grip the strap on my bag to stop myself from reaching out to touch him. "Yes." My stomach sinks at that three letter word, and I press my teeth into my lower lip as my chin begins to tremble.

"When?" I ask and stare at the floor.

"Not sure yet, but Frank wants you there two days before so he can prep you." His shoes come into view. He's so close, and I can't think when he's this near.

"You'll be testifying against Lynn too." This time my eyes flick up to his. I wasn't ready for this. I still haven't dealt with the fact my best friend is the mastermind behind my kidnapping, the one who had a threesome with my father and a man I considered an uncle. My hand flies to my stomach as the room starts to tilt, and he reaches out to stabilize me. I step back, just needing a minute. "Let me touch you," he whispers.

"I can't."

"Why?"

"I'll fall." I move around him and make my way back into the bar where Zack is talking with Keith, but I do catch his hiss.

"We've talked about that before."

"Savi, why didn't you come by the house today? I waited for your call. I could have come and got you." Keith pulls on his jacket. "I almost came to get you anyway when I got your one-word text."

"Laundry," I answer, then grab my tips from the bar and shove them in my pocket. It's a lousy lie, but I'm too tired to think of anything more to say. "I'll see you tomorrow, Zack," I wave and head for the door.

Jake is waiting outside the door with a strange expression on his face, but as he sees how tired I am, he throws on a smile. His eyes move up over my shoulder before I hear Cole call out for me.

"Let me drive you back," Cole says, coming up behind me and buttoning up his jacket. "It's freezing."

It is freezing, and my hands are already ice, but I have to be strong. Other people who left Shadows don't have the Army driving them home after their night shift. "No, thanks. I find it helps me wind down." *Another lie.* "Besides, Jake is waiting." I point over my shoulder.

Cole glances at Jake, then at me. I can tell he's not happy but not fighting me on it...that's interesting. He steps forward and pulls off his scarf, wrapping it around my bare neck. I struggle not to immediately bury my nose and soak up the scent as he tucks a lose piece of hair behind my ear.

"Text Keith or me when you get home," he whispers, then steps away as I slowly turn to face Jake, who is looking off, trying to give us some privacy.

I pull out the key and open the door to my brightly lit apartment. I've been leaving a light on so it feels like I'm coming home to someone. Once all the doors are locked, I toss my keys in a bowl and head for the shower, then change into Cole's t-shirt and slip into an already made bed on the couch, facing the door. I'm so tired my eyes close immediately, but I only manage to get twenty minutes of sleep before something creaks in my bedroom, making my eyes pop open. I grab my cell from my bag and text Keith that I am home. I find myself writing a text to Cole too.

Savi: Home.

It pings a moment later.

Cole: Did you just get home?

Savi: No, I fell asleep.

Cole: Why aren't you asleep now?

I hesitate, then go with the truth.

Savi: Heard something, it was nothing.

Cole: Something like what?

Savi: Just a noise, but it was nothing.

Cole: Are you able to get back to sleep?

Savi: Yes.

Cole: Text me if you can't.

I pause, my thumb hovering over the send button.

Savi: *I miss you.*

I slowly delete each letter one by one.

Savi: *Thanks, goodnight.*

I want to text him to come over, but I don't. Instead I stare at the ceiling until I can't take it anymore. Turning on the TV for company, I decide I might get a cat just so I have something to cuddle up to. Aloof isn't really cutting it. I look over at the fish floating perfectly still and staring at me.

I muster up the courage and creep into my bedroom and grab the little army bear Daniel and Sue bought me for my baby. Suddenly feeling an overwhelming sadness, I cling to it as I watch Friends until the sun comes up.

Chapter Two

My eyelids feel like lead as I force my aching body up off the couch to let in Jake, who is knocking at my door. It's nine a.m. Giving me a once-over, he slips into my apartment holding a laptop with his "just be happy I'm not a twin" coffee cup balanced on top. I find it kind of cute that he always brings his own mug.

"I'd ask how you slept, but it's pretty obvious you're on night two of no sleep." Jake settles onto *his* stool in my kitchen. I pour him a cup and one for myself. I can't wait for the creamy liquid to hit my tongue. Lord, I love coffee. "I want to ask you something, Savi, but I don't want you getting mad at me."

"Okay," I mumble, cracking four eggs into a frying pan. I pull out some fresh chopped peppers, onion, ham, and cilantro and sprinkle them into the pan, adding a little grated cheese and spice. I glance over my shoulder when he doesn't continue and see him typing away on his laptop, so I decide to wait him out. When the omelets are finished, I divide them onto two plates and set them on the counter. They might not be fancy, but they look pretty good. Besides, I need protein badly; caffeine just won't cut it.

"Is this you?" he says suddenly, turning the laptop around, showing a news article with a picture of my father and me with a dramatic crack down the middle and the headline "Rumor Mayor Fox Hired Cartel to Kidnap Own Daughter." I want to vomit, but instead I pick up my fork and cut into the egg. As soon as my tongue touches the Jell-O-like substance it rejects it, and I spit it out, very unladylike, on my plate. Hopping to my feet and shoving my dish in the sink, I lean on the counter with my back to him.

"So I'll take that as a yes," he whispers, closing his laptop.

Tears! Stupid tears are flowing down my cheeks. I blame part of it on lack of sleep. I stand staring at the counter and hear him come up behind me.

"Savi." He reaches for my shoulder and turns me so I'll face him. He smiles at me, holding both my hands. "I didn't mean to upset you. I just knew you looked familiar, and when I heard your name and saw the SWAT type guys watching over you, well, I went with my hunch."

"I-I can't talk about it," I admit, shocking myself with my honesty.

He closes his eyes and presses his lips together, taking a moment to think, then stares down at me. "When I was sixteen, my father came home early from work to find me and his boss's kid having sex on the couch."

"Okay," I murmur, thinking that would be embarrassing.

"It was the first time he ever laid a hand on me, and he beat me until I stopped moving. He threatened my life if I ever saw *Eddy* again." My heart breaks at that moment. His father is an asshole too; he didn't love him for who he was. All the vibes I have about Jake make sense now. He never hit on me because he is gay. "I play the single hottie from L.A. because it works for me. The women pay good money to see this ass in jeans." He laughs darkly and points at his butt. "But if they knew the truth, Zack would lose a lot of regulars, and I'd never do that to him. Zack's too important to me. He's the only one who knows the real me, and now you do too." He sighs and gives me a wink. "A secret for a secret."

I smile through my tears. "Thank you, for being a friend when I really need one." I lean forward, giving him a hug.

Jake and I decide to head to the mall for some decorations to brighten my place up a little. We take his Prius, since it has started snowing again, small flakes, which I know means we're in for a lot of accumulation. The mall is quiet and looks like Cupid threw up all over it. I hate Valentine's Day. I forgot malls decorate weeks before the actual event. After Jake drags me to every candle, picture, pillow, and kitchen store, we walk out of the mall with four huge bags of goodies.

Jake opens the trunk and tosses the bags inside, and I stop breathing.

***

Cole

Cole pours himself a cup of coffee and takes a seat next to Mark in the entertainment room. They'd decided to play poker earlier in the evening, since Dell and Davie are starting on the night shift and wanted to join in on the fun.

"Coffee?" Mark asks, pointing a finger at Cole's mug.

Cole rubs his fingers through his hair. "No sleep for me. I have to work after this."

"You work too much," Paul says, puffing on a cigar. "You should be joining in the fun."

Mark holds up two fingers to John as he ditches two

cards and picks up the new ones. "He used to have fun." Mark gives a laugh. "Seems to me the house has been pretty quiet since a little firecracker isn't around to get into trouble anymore."

"Yeah, like playing paintball or sparring in the ring," Paul adds, glancing at Cole. "Feel free to bring her back, Logan. It's getting a little dull here."

Cole rolls his eyes with a smirk. "Have you met that woman?"

"Yes," his father says, entering the room, "and we want her back."

Mark leans over the table. "Even if you can see her whenever you want, you shouldn't say that. We miss her, and what's with that bar? Have you met that creep? Mr. Scotch Neat? The man is an ass!"

"All right, boys." Abigail sets a bowl of chips and hot wings on the table. Everyone stops talking immediately as they dive in.

"Fold." Dell chucks his cards in front of him. It's their third round, and Mark has won twice, and now he's gloating.

"John, I see you and raise you five." Mark grins and turns his attention to Daniel, who looks like he's thinking.

Cole's pocket starts to vibrate. He pulls out his cell and glances at the screen, then quickly answers it. "Savi?"

"Ahh, hi. This is Jake, actually. I work with Savi at the bar." Cole looks at Mark, who's watching him. The table grows quiet. "I'm sorry for calling you, but I think she's having a panic attack or something. Any suggestions on what I should do?"

"Hold the phone up to her ear." Cole quickly walks out of the room and up the stairs, grabbing his jacket and keys.

"Okay…ahh…here she is."

Her erratic breathing fills the phone. "Savannah, it's Cole. Can you tell me what's going on?"

"I-don't—" She pauses, trying to catch a breath. "I-can't…"

"It's all right. Where are you?" he says calmly.

"M-mall." She starts to cry, her sounds muffled by the phone, then Jake is back on.

"We're at the mall parking lot, section 3C. Are you coming?"

"Yes, I'll be there in twenty."

Cole pulls into the parking lot fifteen minutes later, easily spotting Jake. Savannah is on the ground in a ball, leaning against a light pole. It's just getting dark and the temperature has dropped drastically in a very short time. He hops out and leaves the car running.

"She won't get in the car!" Jake calls out as he gets closer. "She won't come near it. I don't know what happened. One minute we were having a great time, the next she's freaking out."

Cole bends down close to Savannah. "Hey, baby, I'm going to pick you up and put you in my car now. I'll take you back to your place." She lifts her head and peers up at him through blood-shot eyes, tears streaking her face, shaking uncontrollably. She leans forward and wraps her arms around his neck.

"Cole," she whispers, sounding relieved.

He lifts her up and carries her to the car, telling Jake to follow them back home.

A few minutes later, Jake opens the door to her apartment. "I'll get changed and come back to check on her."

"It's all right, I'm going to spend the night," Cole says as he places Savannah on the couch and removes her jacket. "I called Zack. Both of your shifts are covered tonight." He stands, sighing. "Thanks for calling me, Jake. I...we...both appreciate it."

Jake hesitates, then glances at Savi, who seems to be slowly coming around. "Are you all right?"

Cole knows Jake is just looking out for her, and he respects that, but he needs to leave now. "I've got it."

"It's okay, Jake, thank you." She stands, wavering a bit. She sends him a small smile to reassure him. "I'll call you tomorrow."

Jake nods, closing the door behind him. Cole removes his wet boots and jacket, taking in Savannah's new place. He doesn't miss the makeshift bed on the couch or the box of tissues next to it. He bends down and picks up the little army bear that had fallen on the floor, tucking it under the covers and feeling his stomach twist a little. Following the sound of the water running in the bathroom, he pushes open the door to find Savannah scrunched down in the steaming tub. Her hair is pulled up into a messy bun with a few pieces framing her face. Eyes tightly closed, she leans her head back and takes a shaky breath. Cole leans against the counter, legs and arms crossed, and watches her pale face slowly returning to its normal color.

"So what happened, Savi?" His voice is low.

She keeps her eyes closed as she speaks. "Thank you for coming and bringing me home, Cole, but you don't have to stay."

"I want to stay. Now what happened back at the mall?"

Her chin starts to quiver, and he can't help moving to her side, needing to touch her. He bends down behind her head and starts gently massaging her shoulders. The moment his hands slide over her smooth skin, he feels the mood shift. Leaning forward so his lips hover above her ear, he whispers again, "Savi, tell me what happened back there. Please talk to me, baby." He wants so much to tell her how he really feels and what he would like to do to her right now, but is afraid of her pulling back from him even more. He doesn't want her to think it's all sex between them; he loves her so much more than that. How can he explain to her that she means more to him than anything on earth? He can feel her heart beating under his hands and realizes she is holding her breath.

Suddenly she moves forward, reaching for the plug, then steps out and wraps a towel around herself. He follows her out to the living room where she hands him his jacket, not making eye contact.

"Are you kicking me out?" he asks, not taking his jacket.

"Like I said, thank you for helping me, but you can go now. I'm sure you have lots to do." She reaches to unlock the door, but he stops her. "Cole, please."

"Please what?" His hand slides down the door, meeting hers. Her hand shoots to her towel, holding it tighter around her front. "Please leave so you can crawl onto the couch and not sleep another night? Have you slept at all since Keith got switched to night duty?" She sneaks a glance at her couch. "I hate that you won't look at me." Her eyes slowly travel up his body, leaving a hot trail until they meet his. "Don't shut me out. I won't let you."

"I'm not!" she snaps, suddenly fuming with anger.

"Don't lie to me, Savi!" he snaps back.

"I'm n—"

He takes a step toward her and wraps both hands around her face. He slams his lips into hers, not caring about holding back. She pushes him away but squeaks when one hand moves the towel open and slides down her stomach and between her legs. Just as he suspected, she's ready. No matter what's going on between them, they can never deny their sexual attraction for one another.

Her hands fly out, undoing his belt and tugging down his pants, and all the while his tongue is showing her what he wants to be doing. He backs her into the kitchen as he kicks away his pants and loses his shirt. She stiffens when he lowers her down on the cold countertop and slips two fingers into her. She grabs for his erection and runs her small hands around, matching what his fingers are doing to her.

"I need to be in you," he whispers into her lips, not caring how desperate it sounds. It's the truth. She spreads her legs further as she guides him in. He sucks in a sharp breath as he tries to remember to stand. Once he's fully in, he still holds her around her waist with one hand while running his other fingertips along her slender neck, tipping her up to look at him. He leans down and brushes his lips over hers. They both have so much to say, but can't seem to find the words.

"Lean back," he orders. She complies, holding his gaze as she does so. He grips her thighs and brings her closer to the edge of the counter. His eyes rake over her body, seeing just how perfect it is. The color of her skin looks like honey, her dark hair swirling around her sexy face. The best part of this angle is her eyes. They drag him into the hot, dark pools that seem to deepen in color when he's near. He flicks forward and he rotates his hips, and her lips part as she lets out a mute moan. He starts out slowly, watching her shoot up the counter as her full breasts bounce. She arches her back to get him deeper, and he changes his grip from her thighs to her hips, rocking a little harder. His eyes shut as she squeezes him from the inside. "Damn, Savi," he groans, getting lost in the feeling. Her leg muscles tighten, and her stomach flexes as her grip on his wrists becomes rough. She's close, and so is he, but he intends to make this last for as long as he can.

He pulls out, ignoring her curses as he hauls her off the counter and over to the couch where he bends her over the arm and takes her from behind. He covers her body with his, wanting every inch of her against him. Burying her head into the covers letting out a wild scream, she orgasms under him. He didn't want to, but the intensity of her orgasm makes him go off too.

Fucking perfect.

Once he can see straight, he pulls out and scoops her up and carries her limp body into the bedroom, not bothering to turn on any lights. The moon is enough. His erection still obvious in the dim light, she spreads her legs for him, and he settles between them, pressing in gently. Those gorgeous eyes roll back in her head as he slowly slides around in the slippery mixture. Nothing in the world feels as good as being inside this woman. They spend the next few hours making love, both giving in to their desires.

They are both hot and sticky when they finally pry apart long enough to make it to the shower. By one a.m. she is curled into his chest in the bed with his fingers running up and down the length of her arm. They're totally relaxed in the blankets he had grabbed from the couch while she was drying off. They haven't spoken much, but he needs to know what happened today.

"Savi?" he whispers, seeing if she's awake.

She shifts and moves her head slightly. "It was the trunk, in the parking lot, and," her voice is low, "it just brought me back to that day. I don't know why or what came over me, but—" He leans down and kisses her head. "Cole?"

"Mmm?"

She clears her throat, swallowing loudly. "Spend the night with me."

He smiles and turns her on her side, spooning her from behind. "Sleep, baby, I've got you."

Reaching for his hand and giving it a light kiss, she allows herself to fall asleep.

***

Savannah

I wake to Cole's arms wrapped around me tightly. I want to stay like this forever, but my bladder has a mind of its own. I wiggle out of his warm hold and move quickly to do my business, but return to find him getting dressed. I try not to show my disappointment. Now that the sun has risen, I know we're going to have to talk, so I slip on a robe and head to the kitchen, turning on the coffee maker and pulling out the cream. I turn to see Cole coming out of my room. I realize that although it feels weird seeing him here at my place, I like it. It's a step forward.

"I'm sorry, I have to get going. I have a meeting with Frank." He moves in front of me and kisses my lips gently, then pulls away with his eyes squeezed shut like he's got something to say. "Come home with me, Savi. You don't need to prove anything to anyone."

My head snaps back and I see red instantly. "Prove anything? Cole, this isn't about anyone else. This is about me."

"If you were home, I could protect you better."

"I don't need you to protect me, I—"

"Oh, really?" His hands fly in the air. "What was that last night?"

My mouth drops open. I can't believe he's is throwing that in my face. "I didn't call you, Cole. Jake did!"

"Thank Christ he did! You were huddled in a ball in the middle of a freezing parking lot, and you wouldn't get in the car. I had to come all the way from the house to get there!" He's almost shouting. "Just come home and make it easier on everybody. You're not ready."

My blood is boiling! Why can't he see the progress

I'm making? "So sorry, Cole, that I interrupted your evening. I didn't know Jake called you until he handed me the phone." I reach for my bag and pull out my phone, scrolling through my contacts until I find Sue's number and scribble it on a Post-it.

"What are you doing?" His voice is a low rumble.

I walk to the door and hold it open. "You should go." He grabs his jacket and steps out in the hallway. "Please thank your mother for the phone, but I will not be needing Shadows to care for me anymore." His face drops as I shove the cell in his hand. "I apologize for the inconvenience I caused you yesterday. Rest assured, it won't happen again." I don't wait for his response as I close the door in his face. He says something I can't make out, but I wait until I hear footsteps before I sneak a peek through the peephole. I watch as he leaves through the stairwell. My heart hurts, but I push aside the pain. I will not let my emotions run me, even if I did just let the love of my life walk out the door. *No, Savi, you kicked your love in the ass out the damn door. Fuck.*

***

I toss the rag I was using aside and jump up on the bar top. My feet are killing me. My bed is screaming— no, my couch is screaming my name. It's been nine days since I've heard from Cole. I won't lie, it hurts like hell, but I won't back down on living my life. It's painful, but I know I need this time for me. I need to be whole. Keith has even backed off. With my new phone, I texted Sue my number. I couldn't possibly freeze everyone out, especially Sue. She was there for me when I lost our baby, and I love her like my own mother. She was concerned about me, but she didn't pry.

"Can I ask you a huge favor?" Jake breaks into my thoughts, giving me the sweetest look and batting his lashes like a pro.

Oh no...

"Depends," I counter, taking the glass of wine he just poured for me. Zack lets us drink on the house, most likely because he knows we aren't big drinkers.

"This guy I'm seeing is coming to town. It's been two months since I've seen him, and we want to go out...but his buddy is traveling with him, and he doesn't want to ditch him. Problem is—"

"He's straight, I'm straight, and I'm the only one who knows we have a—"

"Secret for a secret." He grins, knowing he's got me.

I roll my eyes and wish the internet didn't exist yet. Then my past wouldn't have come back to bite me in the ass. "When and where?"

"Yay!" He claps then looks around quickly as he realizes we are still at work.

"Okay, Jake, as long as he knows he's not getting laid and there's zero chance of a second date."

"Of course." He jumps off the counter. "Thursday, drinks at Chaps."

"What the hell is Chaps?" I call out.

He turns and gives me a devilish grin. "We live in Montana, sweetheart."

I close my eyes, thinking a shopping trip may be in order...cowgirl boots are something I don't own.

***

Cole

Cole types a quick message.

Cole: Where?

Keith: Still at work, having a drink with Jake.

Cole: Let her know.

Keith: Will do.

Cole makes his way into the living room where Abigail is nursing a cup of tea. She's been battling a nasty cold and hasn't been able to sleep very well.

She gives him a warm smile. "Come sit with me, honey." She pats the seat next to her, and he does without a second thought. "You look stressed. Tell Aunt Abby what's going on in that handsome head of yours."

He smiles at the words she has used for as long as he can remember. "I think I may have pushed when I shouldn't have," he admits, letting out a long sigh. "We spent the night together, and in the morning, I pushed too hard, saying she should come back." He shrugs, feeling lost. "I know I made it seem like it would be easier for everyone if she did, and I wasn't thinking about how much she's accomplished since she left. Savi kicked me out, Abigail, and gave me back the phone with all of our contacts in it."

"Well, that explains the radio silence." Abigail sips her tea.

He runs his hand along his neck. "She's so stubborn, and I love that, but..." He can't finish the sentence.

"What if she moves on to someone else?" she asks, finishing his question. He nods, as a shot to his stomach has him in discomfort. "Cole, you know Savannah only has eyes for you, but she needs some time to breathe without someone dictating her every move. Let her walk a little on her own, then she'll run back to you. I promise."

"How do you know?"

She sits her tea cup on her saucer and takes his hand in hers. "Because I've been on this earth a lot longer than you, and I know true love when I see it. You're lucky enough to have found it this early in life. Most of us wait a lifetime or never find it. Give her space, honey. She loves you. Never doubt that."

"All right." He leans back and lets out a long sigh and watches the fire, trying to convince himself that Abby knows best. She usually does.

***

Savannah

I open my door to find Keith sitting on my couch and staring at his phone, and it makes the hair stand up on the back of my neck. He stands, and I know something isn't right.

"Sit, Savi." He nods to the chair, and I do. "You leave tomorrow morning for Washington. Pack enough for three days, and I'll pick you up at seven a.m." He heads for the door. "I'll see you then."

"Umm, okay," I whisper, feeling the layer of ice that has formed over our friendship.

He starts to leave, but stops. "How are you doing?"

"I'm fine," I lie, reluctant to draw on my earlier fight with Cole. He closes the door behind him, leaving me reeling with the thought of seeing The American again.

Sleep doesn't happen, if it ever even was a possibility. I'm running on thirty minutes per night. Once Jake spent the night after drinking too much, and I managed to get in a solid four hours. It's just not the same as being wrapped in Cole's safety net.

At six I'm packed and out the door, tired of staring at the living room wall. Yes, my place seems homier since Jake helped me decorate, but one could go crazy with how much I'm staring at it. I slip a note under Jake's door letting him know I'll be gone for a few days and to help himself to my coffee. We exchanged keys a few days ago.

I take the elevator because I have time and find myself a chair in the lobby. The man behind the desk gives me a nod before going back to playing something on his phone. I count how many times the heater kicks in, how many tiles are on the floor and ceiling, and how many times the man at the desk glances my way. After sitting for forty-five minutes, I can't take any more. Needing to do something, I open my phone to the only two numbers saved, Jake and Sue, and press call on the second name.

"Savannah?" Sue asks, puzzled. She has a right to be. I haven't spoken to her in over a week, and no doubt she's heard about my blow-up with Cole. I'm not trying to be distant with her; I just find it easier to pull away from everyone at the house altogether.

"Hi, Sue. Did I wake you?"

She gives a little laugh. "No, I've been up for some time. You know how I love the mornings." She pauses. "Is everything all right, dear?"

No. "Yes, I'm…" *Lost, tired, scared about my trip.* "I just wanted to see how you are."

"I'm fine. I've just been battling the snow like everyone this winter. How are you holding up?"

"Fine," I answer too quickly.

I hear her seat creak. "Okay, so we played the pleasant, do you want to tell me why you're really calling?"

"I'm scared," I confess.

"About? Your trip?"

I close my eyes. Of course she knows about Washington. "Yes, and then some."

"The trip, I understand. I would be too. That's perfectly normal." She pauses. "What else are you afraid of, Savannah?"

I reach for my necklace and clasp the snowflake

pendant. My throat tightens with thoughts of Cole, but no words come out because I don't even know where to start.

"Savi, when you get back, I want you to come to Shadows and spend Saturday afternoon and evening with us. It's been too long since you've been home, and everyone misses you. I understand you need your space, but it's not healthy for you to isolate yourself from everyone who loves you." *Home.* The word drips with emotion. I miss everyone terribly. How can I say no to Sue?

"All right," I whisper in fear my voice will break. I look up and see Keith speaking with the security guard. He's eyeing me as I say goodbye to Sue.

Chapter Three

"You ready?" Keith asks, reaching for the handle of my suitcase. I follow him out into the morning frost. It's still dark, making everything seem that much colder. The SUV is still warm, and we drive in silence all the way to the airport. It saddens me that Keith is pulling away, but can I blame him? It's what I told Cole I needed. Isn't it what I want, the chance to find myself? I can't do it if I have Keith taking care of me every day. So I keep my mouth shut, face forward, and try to push back the sneaking fear that's dancing along my spine.

The airport is quiet, with hardly anyone around. Keith hands me my ticket as someone approaches us. I watch as Keith holds out his hand and gives the man a firm handshake.

"Savannah, this is Agent Hahn. He's on Frank's detail. He'll be traveling with you to Washington and making sure you are well briefed before the testimony." I nearly fall over right there. Keith isn't coming; he won't be my rock as I go through all of this. "You'll be fine, and I'll be here to pick you up when you return." My heart slams into my stomach, looking for a way out.

I'm mute. All I can do is give a slight nod and follow Agent Hahn to the gate, where we walk out to the tiny plane and board. The plane that will drop me off at the feet of my worst nightmare.

As soon as we are in the air, I mentally check out.

***

Cole

Cole listens to his father brief him and his team about a target who needs to be extracted from Mexico City. They are possibly holding a child for ransom, and the parents happen to be the owner of the Garrisons' Casinos, one of the biggest casino companies worldwide and known to have a shady side. They've been asked to check it out and see what they can come up with.

Keith knocks and steps inside the door, halting the conversation. "Savi is on the plane. She should be there within the hour."

Mark's jaw drops as he shifts in his seat. "You didn't go with her?" Keith shakes his head, and Mark turns to look at Cole. "Why didn't he go?"

"We have to work," Cole mutters, picking up a file, but apparently Mark has more to say.

"Ummm, what?" Mark pushes himself out of his chair and stares at them. "You mean Savi is on that plane by herself?"

"Let it go," Daniel warns.

"No! Someone should be with her. She's facing The American and Lynn! Cole, you should be there, not hiding behind your desk."

Cole drops the thick folder, making John jump. "You don't think I want to be there, Mark? You don't think it's turning me inside out that my girl is a state away and only an arm's length from the people who tried to kill her? I was *ordered* to stay behind and do my job. I was *ordered* to leave for Mexico when all I want to do is be in that courtroom with her. I'm not hiding. I'm following orders since I didn't last time. I *have* to, for the sake of everyone, especially for the sake of Shadows' reputation." His anger is seeping out of him as he looks at Mark, who has backed off and is nodding. He gets it now.

Paul's phone rings, taking some of the tension from the room. "We have a hit. We should get moving."

***

Savannah

I shake the entire drive to the Washington base. Agent Hahn is friendly, but I just want to stay in my zone, turned off, not answering questions about the weather. We really have nothing in common. I think of Sue, wondering if I should call her just to hear her voice…but that's not the voice I really want to hear.

"Hello again, Savannah." Frank smiles as he greets me at the car. "Please come inside." He hands me a visitor badge and leads me into a large gray building where everything is muted, from the color of the walls to the people's clothing and even their voices. "This is my office. Can I get you anything?"

"Coffee would be great, thanks," I say in a quiet voice to fit the surroundings, then take a seat across from his dull metal desk littered with papers. On the wall are a few pictures of a younger version of Frank starting out in the Army, and two others with President Obama and former President Bush. Medals hang in wooden boxes, and an old-fashioned rifle sits in the corner as though waiting to be mounted. He probably never got around to doing it. He hands me a coffee before he takes a seat. "Thank you."

Flipping open a file, he gets right to it. "So you were first taken from your condo in New York by a Raul

Paru."

"Please jump right in," I mutter, taken aback. "I don't know who Raul Paru even is." Frank hands me a picture, and it takes me a minute, but then I see it, and the memory comes flooding back. My cut leg, the cold, thick substance which later I found out was blood, and the smell in the van. "The painters? These guys were painting my condo the week I was taken. I remember his belt buckle," I say as I press my finger against the buckle in the photo. I'll never forget that longhorn Texas belt buckle.

"Yes, they were scoping out the place, watching you, learning your habits."

I hand the picture back and remember Lynn making a comment about how you can buy those belt buckles on any street corner. I feel the wind being sucked out of me. That bitch! I can't believe she knew what they were doing because she fucking hired them! I wonder how many other times I ran into people she had hired to help take me out.

Frank and I go over all the details of my file, and I am pretty much fried by the time I am taken back to my hotel by Agent Hahn, who is staying with me. I am thankful for the two bedroom suite. He offers to order dinner for both of us, but I decline, just wanting to get some sleep. Tomorrow Frank has me meeting some lawyers, and I want to be able to stay awake for all the legal talk that's to come.

***

The day is a blur much like the first. I am taken into a conference room and questioned for about four hours on practically the same things, only worded differently. They give me so much advice I almost forget my own name. I'm not sure if I am coming or going. Finally, after

I am about to throw in the towel, they inform me that I am to wear a simple black dress with heels, and wear my hair down with no jewelry. I reach for my chain and hold it tightly, and one of the women agrees it is fine, but nothing more. They don't want me looking too flashy. I don't understand why, but I'm beyond caring. I just need to get through tomorrow, and then I can get back to my mountain.

"You want something to eat?" Agent Hahn asks as we walk back to the hotel. I shake my head. "How about a drink?" I look up to see him smiling. "I could really use a drink after that."

"That sounds really good, actually." I smile back and follow him to a small Mexican restaurant.

"Umm," I point to the sign, "not to be a pain, but can we get anything else but Mexican food?"

Agent Hahn chuckles a little, then points across the street to an Italian joint. "Is that better?"

"Much, thanks." I follow him to the crosswalk. We take a seat in the corner of the restaurant and are soon sipping a glass of merlot.

"How are you holding up?" he asks, picking up a piece of bread, dipping it in some oil and vinegar, and popping in it his mouth.

I shrug because I really don't know. "Ask me tomorrow."

He chuckles but grows quiet, thinking. "Do you know who I am?"

My fingers twist the stem of the glass, making the wine run up the sides then bleed back down, leaving heavy lines. "No, but if you're about to tell me you work for The American or the Cartels at least give me a five minute head start."

"Ha!" He tosses his head back. "No, hell no. I was the one who found Logan the day he escaped."

"Oh," I whisper, instantly feeling indebted to this

guy.

"I was also there when you were found at The American's house," he adds.

I smile at him. I'm starting to get used to the fact that so many people have met me at some point, even if I don't remember them. I feel the need to explain my behavior. "I'm sorry I've been so standoffish. I'm just trying to get through this so I can figure out what I want to do with what's left of my life."

"Sounds exhausting."

"It is!" I laugh, thinking it's nice to still be able to.

Our food comes, and we pick away, talking about little things. It isn't until he brings up the training for the Green Berets that something nags at me from the edge of my memory *again.*

"What?" he asks, seeing my face.

"Ever have this feeling you're forgetting something important?" I close my eyes and try to think. "I think it's got something to do with Davie...the newest recruit at the house." I see Agent Hahn studying me. "I'm sorry, it's nothing."

"It's okay. Yes, I have, and it's annoying."

"Very," I agree. "It's like seeing the end of a rope, but it's just out of reach, I feel like if I could only grab it and tug, the memory would come to me." I laugh and shake my head. "Oh well, tomorrow is going to be exhausting. I guess we should get back."

"Yeah," he grabs his coat, "let's get back."

"Agent Hahn?"

"Yes?" He turns to look at me.

"Thanks for taking me out for dinner and the talk. It helped a bit."

He hands me my hat. "Happy to hear that, Savannah."

Later, lying in bed with a slight buzz on, just enough to keep the shakes away, but not enough to make my head stop spinning thinking about tomorrow, my cellphone goes off beside me. A flutter of hope that maybe it's Cole goes through me, but it's not.

Jake: Coffee doesn't taste right.

I smirk and roll onto my side.

Savi: Yes it does.

Jake: It does, but I'm bored without you.

I miss my friend too.

Savi: Sorry. I'm coming home Thursday morning.

Jake: Good! You still on for our double date?

Shit.

Savi: It's not a date, but yes.

Jake: You want some dirt? I have good and bad.

I think for a moment…

Savi: Maybe…bad first?

There's a small pause, and I wonder if the news is about work. I wonder if someone got fired. Yikes, I hope not.

Jake: I saw Logan in town yesterday…with the town bitch Christina. She had her claws all over him. Just thought you should know.

My stomach sinks…oh…

Jake: Now for the good news! Zack hired some new staff…we're talking yummy staff! I think one may play for my team. One can dream.

I flop on my back and feel my heart squeeze to the point of pain.

Savi: Thanks for letting me know, and I hope so for your sake.

Jake: You all right?

Not at all.

Savi: I hope after tomorrow. I should go…night.

Jake: Call me if you need to chat. Night, Savi. xo

***

"You look…"

"I know." I snag the coffee Hahn got me and take a few long sips. "I didn't get much sleep."

"Did you get any?" he asks, slipping into his suit jacket and taking in the dark circles under my eyes.

"Would you?"

"No, probably not." He checks the time. "We should go."

Frank works wonders with this case, keeping the media at bay. The only ones who know I am going to be in court today are the lawyers and the judge.

I am told to sit on a bench and wait for my name to be called. Agent Hahn and Frank are busy talking to the lawyers down the hall, far enough away that I can't hear what they're saying.

My nerves are shot. I can feel a slight trembling starting in my legs. To say I'm scared would be putting it mildly. I am freaking out, full throttle. Every breath I take gets harder, like there is a weight on my chest. My phone goes off, making my purse vibrate. I was supposed to turn it off, but I forgot. Not thinking, I answer it.

"Hello?"

"Savannah?" Cole's voice washes over me. "Are you all right? Are you at the court?"

"I-I don't think I can do this." The words slip past my lips. "I don't want to do this."

"Hey, baby, you can. Think about how much your testimony will count. How long he will go away for. I know this is scary, but you are strong, and you can do this."

I hold on to his words, wishing so much he was here with me. Just hearing his voice helps to steady me.

"Savannah Miller," a clerk calls out. Agent Hahn and Frank come toward me, and I feel panic setting in.

"Cole! I…I have to go."

"Savi—"

"Thanks for the call." I hang up and turn my phone off. I can't listen to what he has to say. It might break the last straw holding me up.

The clerk holds open the door as I step into the massive courtroom. Surprisingly, there aren't that many people inside. My head stays straight as I walk past the table of lawyers whose eyes seem to be burning holes in me. My heart pounds three beats for every one step I take. I stand in front of the chair and behind the table while the officer asks me to raise my right hand and place the other on the Bible. I swallow hard, my throat dry. I'm hot. *Why is it so damn hot in here?*

I nervously take a seat as the prosecutor approaches

549

to ask me a series of questions. Things seem to move slowly at first. I have to recall the day I was taken, then describe the events of my seven months in captivity, and finally about when I was rescued. I'm so tired, but I'm here, so I can't stop now even if I want to. I keep my gaze fixed on Frank, who nods to let me know he's with me. Then the questions start to pick up, coming at me faster and faster and not giving me a chance to think.

"You say you saw my client? But yet you said you couldn't see his face? That doesn't make any sense, Ms. Miller."

"It was him, I know—"

"How do you know? How do you know it wasn't someone else?"

"Because I know—"

The lawyer smirks at me. "You need evidence, Ms. Miller. You can't just go on a hunch." I start to speak, but he cuts me off *again*. "Now, you said my client allegedly killed Luka Donovan. Are you sure, or is this just another hunch?"

"I saw him pull the trigger," I say, and can't hold back a snicker. I see Frank shake his head, warning me to calm down.

The lawyer picks up a small remote and points it at a screen. "Ms. Miller, you have a reputation for getting the attention of the media, yes?" My blood boils, but he doesn't wait for me to answer before a picture of me comes up on the screen. I gasp at the intoxicated picture of me published in US Weekly. He flips through several, and some I hadn't even seen before. "I'd say the camera loves you." His voice positively drips with sarcasm. "You never liked that your father was in politics, did you? And you obviously intended to make it a rough climb for him."

"Objection, Your Honor, badgering the witness."

"Sustained. Mr. Wilson, please get on with it."

The lawyer holds a hand over his chest. "Of course, Your Honor." He turns back to me. "You got yourself into trouble with the media quite a bit, yes?"

"No, that's not what—"

"So you used the media as your outlet, smearing the papers with the fact that he has a drunk for a daughter."

"Objection!" my lawyer calls out.

"Withdrawn, Your Honor." The sleazy lawyer puts his hands in the air.

What the hell?

Withdrawn or not, the twelve jurors still heard that lie. He faces me again. "You have to admit the media was only too willing to jump at a chance to print pictures of you."

He turns to the jurors and points a finger in my direction. "I think Ms. Miller was looking for a way to get back at her father for going into politics when he should have been at home helping her care for her sick mother. So she made a plan with Deputy Mayor Luka Donovan," my mouth drops open at this ridiculously untrue comment, "a plan that she would be kidnapped with the help of her best friend Lynn, who has had a small taste of political life and wants more. So much more that she seeks help from an old friend who happens to be Raul Paru, a known drug carrier for the Mexican Cartel. Ms. Miller gets 'taken' and stays in Cabo for several months until the U.S. Army gets involved and things get messy. So Raul Paru gets spooked and decides to set up his brother-in-law." The lawyer points to his client, who I can't look at. "My client, Denton Barlow." The jury looks at me, confused, like they're trying to piece this new information together. "Ms. Miller seduced, used, and manipulated my client into thinking she loved him. She even went so far as to sleep with him. She used him for sex, information, money—"

That's it! I hit my breaking point. I can't take these

lies any longer!

I jump to my feet with tears streaming down my face. "I was taken from my home in the middle of the night!" I scream, making everyone jump. "I was treated like a filthy animal, fed scraps, dirty water, bug infested bread. Beaten till I couldn't feel the pain anymore, for seven goddamn months!" I point at The American, looking him straight in the eye for the first time. "You bought me like a piece of meat. You said you loved me, and I despised you. I wasn't like the other women who believed your words. I am strong enough to see you for what you are, weak!" The judge is yelling something, but I'm not listening. As far as I'm concerned, it is just me and The American in this courtroom, and for once he can't touch me. "I know the truth, Denton, no matter what happens here today. I know you're a coward, that you buy women because they can't love the real you, they *can't stand* the real you. Rot in hell, you sick son of a bitch." My arm is being tugged as an officer hauls me out of the courtroom. I'm pressed into Frank's hold and taken into a small room.

"Jesus Christ, Savannah!" Frank says, running a hand over his buzz cut.

I lean over the table, suddenly exhausted. "I want to go home," I whisper.

"Savannah, you still need to testify against Lynn."

I can't. I won't. I'm finished. "No." I stand straight and my head spins. "I'm done, Frank." I open the door and walk out.

***

Cole

Cole holds the little boy's body close to his chest as they step off the chopper and head toward the safe house. Poor little guy passed out during the rescue operation. The kidnappers had Ryder for six days, tied to a bed in an old warehouse. All things considered, he's all right. Abigail comes rushing up and takes Ryder from Cole, whisking him inside to a warm bed. His aunt is cleared to take him into a witness protection program tomorrow. For now, the little guy just needs rest.

During Cole's much-anticipated hot shower, he hears his phone ringing next to the sink. He clears the glass on the door and sees it's Frank. He reaches out and answers it.

"Frank, what's going on?"

"Oh, fuck, they were rough on her." Frank's voice is bone tired "They called her every name in the book, saying she was the mastermind, that she seduced Denton. It was nasty."

Shit.

"How is she?"

There's a pause. "She lost it at one point and yelled at Denton, until she got kicked out."

"Fuck." Cole leans his head against the wet glass.

"Yeah, well, she left saying she was done. We lost her, her phone is off, and the hotel room is empty. So I'm guessing she's heading home."

Cole turns the water off. "All right, I'll figure it out. Just deal with the shit on your end."

By the time Cole starts downstairs, Keith is heading up. "She arrived at the airport. She's in a cab heading back to her place. I'd have offered to go get her, but she didn't call me. She called your mother."

Cole nods and pulls out his phone, but Keith stops him. "I don't care if she needs space, I'm not staying away. She's family, and if she's hurting—"

"I know, and I agree." Cole sighs and brings the phone to his ear. His mother answers.

"Cole, she's all right," his mother says calmly. "I just

left her place, and Jake said he'll take her out to get something to eat. She's upset, but she's holding it together for now."

"All right. Thanks, Mom."

"Anytime, honey."

After getting absolutely nothing productive done at work, Cole decides to check in on Ryder, who is still fast asleep in Savannah's old room. "Looks so small," he says softly to Abigail, who is sitting quietly beside the bed.

"It's truly sad that anyone should be kidnapped, but a five year old child?" Abigail presses a hand against her chest. "Poor little angel must have been so scared."

"Savages," Cole mutters and checks the time. Seven thirty. "I need to go out. Call me if he wakes."

"Of course." She smiles slightly. "Tell Savannah I say hello."

A short time later, Cole knocks on Savannah's apartment door, but there's no answer, and no answer at Jake's either, so he heads down to speak with the security guard.

"She left about an hour and a half ago looking mighty pretty. She was with her neighbor. Think they said something about Chaps bar."

Why would she go to Chaps to eat?

"Thanks."

Cole heads back out into the cold air, wondering what the hell is going on. Is that why she didn't want Keith coming to get her, because she had plans to go to a bar tonight? This doesn't sound like Savi.

Chaps is loud and crowded. Every type of cowboy boot and hat known to man is in this bar tonight. He feels very out of place; this is *not* his scene. Nor did he think it was Savannah's. He uses his weight to move through the sea of bodies, pulling down his black baseball cap to shade his eyes from the blinding lights as he scans the faces. He soon spots Jake and heads over.

"Where is she?" Cole shouts over *Big and Rich.*

Jake sighs, shaking his head at his friend. "Look, Logan, she's out on a date. She's had a horrible day and needs a night off."

Feeling like he just got sucker punched in the gut, Cole sees red. "Where is she, Jake?"

Jake rubs his face, then decides to make the right choice.

"Bruno's Cheesecake. Please let her enjoy her evening. She's in rough shape." Cole doesn't respond as he charges back outside.

Watching her through the cafe window, Cole sees she's in a tight pair of skinny jeans and a black lace tank top, wearing red cowboy boots. Her hair is in big curls tumbling down her back, and silver earrings sparkle as she shakes her head, smiling at the man across the table from her, who looks very interested in *his* Savannah.

He lets out a heavy puff of air and leans back so she doesn't see him. He takes out his phone and allows his thumb to rub over the screen. His hand twitches with the need to call her. A movement draws his attention back to her. Her date is standing, says something, then walks off, probably to order a drink. Turning her face toward the window, he sees her expression fall like she is about to cry. She pulls out her cell phone, checks the screen, and looks disappointed. *Maybe*? A tap on his back makes him jump and almost drop his phone. "What the hell!" Mark is standing behind him with a huge grin on his face.

"Whatcha doin'?"

Cole can't help but grin back; they are both spying on her. "How's her night going?"

Mark leans to peek in the window. "She started out at Chaps, but she didn't hang in there for long. She wasn't diggin' it. On the walk back, buddy tried to hold her hand, but she wouldn't let him. They've been here for about an hour. He's interested but respectful, so we'll see how the rest of the night goes." Cole glances over at her and sees her smile, but it's not touching her eyes. "She seems sad tonight. I heard the lawyer did a number on her." Mark clears his throat. "I think it would be good if she saw you tonight, Cole. Seriously, she's hurting."

"I don't know," Cole sighs, not knowing what to do.

"Fine, I'll make the decision for you. I could be out here freezing my ass off, or I could be in bed with Mel." He shrugs. "So, goodnight!" With that, he jogs away, laughing.

Fuck.

After climbing back into his SUV, he turns the heat up and hunkers down for a long night. Twenty-five minutes later, they're up and leaving Bruno's and heading down toward her apartment. He starts the engine and creeps down the street, parking a few spots away. She stops at the door and says goodbye, and the guy smiles and reaches for her hips, pulling her into him. She shakes her head as he goes in for a kiss, but he's too quick and misses her signals, planting a kiss on her lips. Fire burns through Cole's veins and his hand flies to the door handle, but he quickly stops himself as he takes in her reaction. She raises her hands and pushes him away, saying no. The guy steps back immediately, obviously apologizing, and hands her something that looks like a card. She takes it, waving him goodbye, then waits for him to walk away before she disappears inside, leaving Cole more than a little relieved, but also feeling pretty shitty for spying.

Chapter Four

Savannah

I work my shift like a robot, not speaking any more than I have to. Jake is the polar opposite, and is chatting on and on, excited about Graham, the new member of the wait staff. Graham resembles Taylor Lautner, no joke. I keep waiting for him to bust into a werewolf. My mind is spinning with thoughts of going to the safe house tomorrow. I truly hope no one wants to talk about what happened in Washington. Frank called this morning and informed me I'm being ordered back to testify against Lynn. It's out of his control, and he felt terrible for what happened with Denton's lawyer.

Jake suddenly grabs my hands and shakes me. "Why are you so distant? I need my wingman!"

I push all my crap aside and try to be a better friend. "How do you even know he's gay?"

"That's what I need you for." I raise an eyebrow, not sure I'm going to like this plan. "When he comes over here next time, lean over the bar to grab his order slip, then pretend to drop it and give him an ass view."

Oh Lord.

"What if he doesn't look, gets distracted or something?"

He gives me a don't-be-stupid look. "If he's straight, he won't be looking anywhere else."

Seeing someone snag a seat, I turn to focus on him, and realizing who it is, I smile and bend down to take his order.

Davie leans over so I can hear him over the crowd. "I heard you were working here. We have the night off, and I thought we should stop in and say hello."

"Well, thanks. What can I get you and…?"

"Two Fat Tires, and it's Dell. The rest of the guys are at some place down the street."

I pour his drinks, take a few more orders, and wait for the dinner rush to slow down a little. We normally have a slow dip at seven. Dell joins Davie, drinking a few beers. I try to engage them as best as I can, but Don, the woman repeller, is back, and apparently it's his last night before he returns to wherever the hell the devil spat him out from.

"Savi!" Jake whispers, nodding his head toward Graham, who is heading our way. "You're up!"

I roll my eyes and do as I was asked. I smile, lean in, grab the slip, drop it, and bend over. I make his order and fill my tray.

"Thanks, Savi." Graham smiles.

"Sure thing, Taylor," I joke back, but burst out laughing when he lets out a howl. Okay, so he's been called that before.

"Heard it all before." His gaze goes from joking to smirking as Jake appears at my side. "Nice performance, Savi, but I play for both teams." He winks and walks away, and my jaw drops as Jake puts his head to my shoulder in a fit of laughter.

"Oh my god!" I hit Jake's arm. "You're welcome."

"Does anyone actually work here?" I hear her call out from the other side of the bar. Jake mutters something as he approaches Christina, the evil bitch. "No," she flicks her finger, dismissing Jake, "her."

*Oh hell, speaking of the Devil's shit...*I make my way over, not missing the way Dell is scowling at her. "Three margaritas, one Stella, one glass of pino, and two shots of tequila," she barks at me. "You think you can handle that, or should I write it down?" I bite my tongue just as her friend comes up. "I was with him again last night," she says loudly enough for me to hear.

"Who?" I decide to play the game.

"Logan." She glances at me, making sure I can hear her as she turns her attention elsewhere. "He came out to the bar, then we went back to my place." She looks at her friend. "I love running my hands over his tattoo." I tune her out, mainly because Cole said he never slept with her. I hate that she can even get a rise out of me. A small niggle of doubt nestles inside me, right by my heart. I place her drinks in front of her and tell her the total. She flicks her credit card at me, hitting my arm.

Don't hit her, don't hit her.

After she signs the slip with no tip, she leans over but talks nice and loud. "If you know what's good for you, sweetheart, you'll stay away from him. He's mine, and I have ways of making people like you disappear."

I have a great comeback, I really do. I can be feisty, but the word *disappear* sends me three steps back. So instead, I change course. I wait for her to leave and pretend not to see the concern written all over Dell's face. I turn to Don and make my move. Leaning over, I whisper in his ear. He smiles and checks my cleavage once more before he grabs his drink and heads over to her table.

Davie is shaking his head when I return to watch the show. "What did you say to him?"

"Just that if he wants a farewell fuck, he's guaranteed to find it over there, because after three drinks she'll be pouring herself into his bed." I smirk and head off to take some more orders.

"It's dead," Zack announces by eleven. "Chaps is having some BOGO special, so why don't you guys go home early?" Jake and I don't move. It's sad we don't have Friday night plans. "All right, let's do one better," Zack says, shaking his head at both of us as he drops three shot glasses on the bar. He slips two straws over the hole, pouring the tequila in three different streams, filling all the glasses at once. *Impressive.* "Cheers."

I slide my butt onto the bar top and take the drink, chasing it with a lime. Graham drops off his tray on the bar and asks Jake if he knows of a place to go for a late meal. Jake smiles at me knowingly as he grabs his tips. I laugh and wave them both off.

"So, Savannah, how are you liking living in town?" Zack asks as he pours me another.

I drink it quickly. "It's nice."

Zack hops up on the other side of the bar top and turns to face me. "I know this is none of my business and a little late, but I am sorry about what happened in your life."

"Thanks." I shrug, taking a moment to think. "I think the worst part of it all is feeling like I don't really belong anywhere. I can't go back to New York for so many reasons. I have no family or friends there. I left Shadows because I felt like I needed to find myself, like they were worrying about me when they should be focusing on their open cases." I glance over at him, realizing I'm complaining. "Sorry, didn't mean to toss you into my pity party."

He shakes his head. "No, it sounds exactly like someone should in your situation. The only difference is their hearts aren't invested in someone tall, dark, and handsome." I smile and throw a sigh. He's right. "When I retired from Shadows, I couldn't leave. My family is here. What's that saying? Home is where the heart is.

This is where my heart wants to be, and I lucked out that my brother came and joined me." He pours me one more, but stops me when I go to drink it. "You may not think you've settled or put down any roots, Savannah, but you have a house full of people who care about you up on that mountain, and you have two in this restaurant. Stop worrying about what you *should* be feeling and just feel. Life is too short to float, so sink a little and start living." He holds up his glass. "To you."

"To me." I raise my drink and drop it back, letting his words absorb. "Now," I clap my hands together, needing to change the subject, "I want some juicy stories on Cole and Mark when they were younger."

***

Cole

Cole hangs up the phone with Frank feeling *off* with their conversation about Ryder's parents. They owe a lot of money and are more concerned about their casino than where their child might be. Abigail said the boy isn't coming out of his room, which seems normal, but they only had one child here before, and she was a little older. This is new for everyone. He was glad Dr. Roberts would arrive around twelve to evaluate him, then Frank could take him into town where is aunt is waiting.

His phone alerts him he has a text.

Mark: Living room.

Cole makes his way down the hallway, hearing all kinds of voices. The smile on Abigail's face makes his stomach twist, then he sees her hugging June. It's been three weeks, but she's really here in his living room. Savannah sees him and gives him a little smile, one that makes him want to grab her toss her over his shoulder and take her upstairs.

"Hi." Her eyes are deep and dark. "Can we talk when you have a moment?"

"Sure," he nods as her eyes drop to his lips momentarily. At least he sees she's still drawn to him, and his pants tighten as he breathes her in. He needs to be alone with her now. "You want to talk in my office?"

"No!" June squeals. "She just got here. You can talk about whatever later, but right now I want to hear all about what she's been up to." She grabs Savi's hand and starts pulling her to the couch. *Damn you, June...*

They talk and talk...you would think Savi has been gone for months. The only thing keeping him going is listening to her voice. God, he missed her voice, her laugh, the way she sneaks a peek at him every once in a while. Just letting him know she's thinking of him.

After some time, he heads back into his office. He has some emails to send before he can take the evening off. Now that Savannah is here, he wants to wrap this up faster.

"Cole," June whispers from his doorway. "Cole, you've got to come see this." He groans when he loses his train of thought. "It's Savi." He looks up and sees her smile now that she's got his attention. "You have to see this." He follows her out the door. "After everyone started doing their own thing and the place quieted down, Keith asked Savi to make him his favorite cookies, and," she pauses, "just look..."

He peeks around the corner, seeing Savannah in an apron, hair pulled up and speaking quietly.

"You want to crack the egg?" she asks Ryder, who is sitting on the island helping Savannah make the cookies. He turns back to June, who's beaming.

"He came into the kitchen and took her hand. She sat on the floor and started talking to him, then asked if he wanted to make cookies, and he said yes. She even lifted him up on there. He doesn't like being touched, Cole. He doesn't really take to any of us, but he likes her." June signals her sister to come see what they're looking at.

Savannah picks up a spoon and dips it into the jar of peanut butter from when she made Ryder's sandwich earlier. "You know what I love to do when no one's looking?" Ryder shakes his head and giggles when she scoops a spoonful of peanut butter and pops the spoon in her mouth. "You want to try?" She picks up another spoon and hands it to him. He hesitates, but she encourages him to do it, and he shoves a huge glob of peanut butter into his little mouth. "Great job!" She high-fives him.

"Natural born mother." Abigail peeks up at Cole.

"What are we looking at?" Dr. Roberts whispers, making the three of them jump.

"Ryder likes Savannah," Abigail answers.

Dr. Roberts takes a peek, then steps into view. Cole moves into the kitchen too, but stays back. Ryder spots the doctor and grabs Savannah's arm. "Good afternoon, Savannah. What are you making?"

"Hello, Doc. Ryder and I are making Keith's favorite oatmeal chocolate chip cookies."

"They smell good," he says, staying a few away. He watches as Ryder buries his head into her shoulder. Her hand runs along his back, soothing him. "I was wondering if Ryder would come and draw me a picture." Ryder doesn't move, but Savi bends down to his eye level.

"You know what, Ryder? My favorite color is purple. Would you draw me a picture so I can hang it on the fridge? The boys in this house never draw any pictures." She gives a loud sigh and smiles at him lovingly as he looks from the doctor to her again. He finally nods his little brown head and reaches out so she'll help him down.

"Let's go to the dining room, it's just right there, and draw Savannah a picture." Doc Roberts leads the way, leaving the two of them in the kitchen. Savannah goes back to making the cookies.

"That was pretty impressive," Cole says, coming to stand by the island where she's working.

She rolls some dough into a ball, dropping it on the tray. "He's a sweet little boy."

"You got him to eat. He hasn't eaten in two days."

"I know that feeling," she whispers, turning to stick the tray into the oven.

"How are things working out at Zack's?" he asks, trying to feel her out.

Davie comes in and scoops some of the cookie dough out with a spoon. "Other than the threats, I'd say she's doing pretty good," he says. Savannah glares at him, but he's too busy eating to notice.

Cole stiffens. "Threats?"

"It's nothing," she says over her shoulder.

"Nothing! That bitch has it out for you, Savi. I'd watch my back. You should have heard what her and her friends were say—"

"Davie," Savannah interrupts, "could you tell Keith the first batch is in the oven?"

"Sure." He takes another spoonful of cookie dough before he leaves.

"Who?" Cole's voice is harsh. "Don't lie, Savi."

She drops her head and sighs. "Christina." *Fuck me.* "I handled it, but if you could tell her not to threaten me at work, that would help. I don't need to hear about you two hooking up with all the customers around."

"Hooking up?" Cole moves off the stool and comes around to her side. "She said we were hooking up?"

"Yes, last night and a few other times. Whatever, just tell her to back off." She won't look at him.

"Savi, I wasn't with her last night."

"Okay," she mutters, brushing him off.

Fuck... "I was watching you, on your date." Her face snaps up. "I watched you at Bruno's, and later when he kissed you outside your apartment."

"You were spying on me?"

He shakes his head. "I was protecting what's mine."

"Oh my god!" She drops the wooden spoon she was using. "You broke up with *me,* remember, Cole. I wanted space, but I never wanted it from you." She reaches for the oven as the timer goes off. He waits until she's finished before pinning her in the corner of the counter.

"How did it feel when his lips touched yours?" He needs to know what she's really feeling right now, in this moment. His thumb runs along her bottom lip, making her mouth part. "Did you like it? Did you like the way he tastes?" She barely shakes her head as he leans in and runs his tongue along her lower lip. She sags into him as he starts kissing her, reminding her who owns this mouth.

"Cole," she says, pulling away as he kisses her jaw, "why didn't you come to Washington? I needed you." He stops and moves to look her in the eye.

"I had orders to get Ryder from Mexico City. I crossed the line falling for you, so when they tell me to do a job, I have to do it." He cups her cheek. "I wanted to be with you so badly, I used the satellite phone to call you, and that's a big no." She closes her eyes and leans forward, resting her head against his chest. His hands rub small circles across her back. "I'll be there when you testify against Lynn."

She pulls away. "I don't want to."

"You have to, Savi."

"I..."

"Ohh, so close," Keith says to Mark behind them

565

like they are watching a movie.

Mark scrunches his face. "Yeah, I thought Cole had her this time." He laughs with Keith, then looks at Cole and Savannah. "What? We're bored." He shrugs, not caring at all that they're intruding on a personal moment.

Savannah laughs unexpectedly, moving Cole aside and placing a plate of warm cookies on the island. "If you're bored," she glances back at Cole, "I have an idea."

***

Savannah

I dive into a snow bank as three bullets whiz by my feet. Mark pulls me closer to the fallen tree trunk.

"Oh, great, you've got Logan's attention. I thought we lost him back at the driveway."

I check my paintballs and see I have ten left. Plenty.

"No worries, Mark. I have a plan." He looks at me, waiting for me to explain. "Let's just say it involves June and one of our flags." His eyes light up, and his mouth spreads wide.

"You wanna join Blackstone? We could use a member like you."

"Let me be the one who gets Cole and I'll consider it," I joke, rolling on my back, looking up at the window and giving a thumbs up. Mark signals for Davie and Dell to move to the next spot, which is a huge mistake because Cole and Keith change positions and nail them the moment they start running.

"Two down, two to go!" Cole yells out to us. I see June and Mike round the corner looking just like Mark and me. *Perfect*. They make a move toward the wood pile, but Cole is quick and pops both of them in the legs and arms. He turns to Keith, fist bumping, and that's when we move. It's an epic moment. I hope I can replay the cameras and make a copy for myself. Mark swings off to the side and pops Keith in the back of his helmet. I stay low, and just as Cole goes to pop Mark, I nail him in the back three times.

Boom!

Everyone freezes as Cole looks from June to me, wondering what is going on. Then it clicks. He points his finger at me and chucks his helmet to the ground. His smile is dangerous, but all play. I remove my helmet, laughing and feeling very pleased that my plan worked out. Mark fist bumps me, calling out that we won.

"You, come here!" Cole shouts, storming toward me.

"Run, Savi!" Mark calls out. "Run very fast!" I turn and run, but my laughing isn't helping. My boots sink into the deep snow, but I manage to make it to the training barn. I glance over my shoulder to see he's a few yards away.

Once inside, I take in my surroundings and decide an old striped truck in the back corner is where I'll hide. I climb through where the windshield would be and head to the back seat. I hunker down and wait.

I wait and wait and wait…I'm starting to think maybe he had to go inside. Maybe he got a call or Dr. Roberts needed him. Crap…I unfold myself and crawl out the side window. Just as I'm at the front of the truck, he drops down from a rafter, grabs my hips, and tosses me on top of the hood.

I scream out, laughing. "You may have played me, but you forgot one important rule." He undoes my pants and yanks my bottoms, pulling my boots off with them. "You must always be willing to wait out your prey." He unzips his pants, exposing his massive erection. "And you, my love, are my prey." His fingers touch my opening, feeling how turned on I am for him. Just his voice alone sends a flood to the gates. I push all thoughts aside and relax. "So deliciously warm and ready," he whispers as he pulls out his fingers and gently feeds himself inside. My back bows over the hood, my head tips back, and my lips form an O as he fills me to maximum capacity. One hand sneaks up my shirt and palms a breast. "I rather like you like this, Savannah. I'm thinking we should try new places more often."

"I thought we christened my new apartment rather well," I pant as he rolls his hips, hitting every angle he can. I close my eyes, relishing how deep he is, and my tongue darts out, moistening my lips.

"Mmm, that's true." His hands grip my hips as he pushes in harder. I yell out, only fueling his fire. "You have no idea what your sounds do to me." I'm delirious, my vision is going as he keeps up the steady pace. "The way your eyes darken the more turned on you get makes me so hard it hurts." I claw at his arms, just as he yanks me off the roof.

He remains inside of me as he briskly moves us past the holding area and into an office where it's much warmer. I remove my jacket as he sits down on a leather chair with me straddling his lap. He helps me strip down so I'm completely naked. Taking one of my nipples in his mouth, he starts to suck. His other hand roams my feverish skin. I start to rock to build myself back up to where I was. He leans back and swivels me around so my back is to him. "Grip the desk, baby." I lean forward, doing what he says as he stays sitting. "So beautiful." His fingertips run along the length of my spine. He bucks his hips, and my grip slips. "Hold on," he orders while he stands and kicks the chair away from him.

His pace quickens again, each thrust hitting the end of me. His fingers dig into my shoulders and one hand fists my hair.

"Cole!" I cry, not sure how long I'll last.

"I don't care how much," pound, pound, "you try and

push me away," pound, pound, "you'll always be mine." Pound, pound. "No more dates, Savannah. No more kissing other men." Pound, pound. "You need something, you come to me."

"It wasn't a date!" I yell out, needing him to understand, but my thoughts get lost as I jump from the ledge. Stars shoot off, sound leaves, and I fall back down to heavenly earth. When I come to my senses, I'm on my back on top of the desk while Cole slips my shirt over my head. I lift my boneless body to help.

"Cole." I stop him as he goes to grab my clothes from the truck. "I didn't go on a date with him. I was doing it as a favor for a friend."

He looks confused. "Friend?" I nod. "Who?"

I sit up, but my bones are like jelly. "I can't say, but I promise you I made it clear that nothing was going to happen. I didn't know he was going to kiss me, and when he did, I felt wrong. Not just because you didn't know, but because it wasn't you."

"It hurt seeing it," he mumbles.

"And it hurt that you broke up with me without hearing me out," I counter, raising my chin. "Makes me think that if the going gets rough, you'll leave me without hesitation."

He steps closer and lowers his face to mine. "I'm sorry for what I said and the way I acted. It just scares me that you're there in that apartment by yourself, working at that bar with all those men wanting a piece of you. I know I panicked, and in turn it pushed you further away. I want a future with you, Savannah, but not until you're ready. I'm going to back off..." he raises a brow, "*to a degree,* and let you come to me when you decide you're ready for us." His stare is overpowering. "But, Savannah, when you tell me you are ready, be prepared for what's to come." I nod because I can't find my voice. He captures my lips and shows me how true his words are.

The walk back to the house is quiet, with just the sound of our boots. I start to grin, remembering that just an hour ago I pulled one over on him.

"What's with the grin?" he asks, peering down at me.

"I was just wondering how long it will take until the green will wash off your back." I beam up at him. "You know...when I tricked you and won the game." He goes to grab me, but I jump out of the way, laughing. "You know, the game you *forbid* me to ever play again." His smile changes into a devilish one. "Oh, yes, Colonel, I went there." I walk backward, keeping a distance between us.

"You're in such trouble," he says with an evil laugh. "You're in for it now."

I walk up the stairs with a little extra swing in my hips, turning to see him staring at me from the ground. "That's the plan."

Frank and Ryder step out as I reach for the handle.

"Good, Logan, his aunt just arrived at Zack's," Frank calls down to him.

Poor little Ryder looks so scared. "I hope to see you again soon, Ryder," I say, bending down to his eye level. "Don't be nervous of Frank. He just looks scary, but he's a close friend of mine, so you're in good hands." I notice Frank gives Cole a small smile. "Have a fun trip with your aunt." He leans in and wraps his tiny arms around my neck. I can't help but give him a kiss on the side of his head when he pulls away with watery eyes. "Bye, Ryder."

Frank takes Ryder's hand and walks him to the truck, with Cole trailing behind. I wipe away a few stray tears, feeling that maternal need to protect the little fella. I know he'll be fine. I just know he'll be scared from all this, and that's something you can never shake.

"I hate when we get kids," Abigail says from behind

me. I nod. She puts her hand on mine. "I know, dear, it *sucks*."

"It does." I laugh at her choice of words. "I've known this little boy all of six hours, but it still hurts seeing him leave."

Dinner is great and just what I needed, an Abigail-cooked meal. Keith stuffs his mouth with my cookies while everyone else eats cheesecake. Soon we retire into the living room while John and Paul set up the poker table downstairs. I take my favorite spot in front of the fire, where Scoot finds me, meowing dramatically and making sure I see how put out he has been since I've been gone. I work hard to make it up to him as his eyes roll back and his legs flop open. *He really has no shame.*

***

Cole

Cole watches as Savannah gives Scoot a good rubdown, and smiles at how he basks in her presence. Everyone is in good spirits, and in no time most are downstairs playing poker while Abigail and June head to bed.

"Savi," Cole whispers. He flicks his head toward the stairs. "Come take a walk with me."

"Where?" she asks, rising to her feet.

"Just downstairs."

He sits her down at the piano, a place where she's comfortable, and moves to stand by the window to watch the snow fall. It always seems to be snowing. He lets out a puff of air, reluctant to have this conversation with her. They were having a good day.

"Ryder seemed to like you."

"He's sweet."

"Are you all right?"

"About Ryder leaving?"

"Yeah."

Her eyes soften. "I've known the kid for six hours. It's sad what happened to him, but we didn't form a bond. Were you worried that I was upset because I lost our baby?"

He nods, wanting to be honest. "Yeah, I was."

"Thank you for caring, but I'm fine."

Cole shakes his head with a smile. He needs to stop underestimating her strength. He heads to the mini bar and fixes himself a drink, making her a martini just the way Mark does. He sits it on top of the piano and slides in next to her, lifting the lid to expose the keys. "Will you play me something?"

She reaches for the drink and takes a long sip. He wonders if she'll do this for him. It doesn't go unnoticed that she rubs her hands over her lap. She's nervous. "What would you like to hear?"

He brushes her hair away from her face and leans over to give her a kiss behind the ear. "Anything you want."

"Can you sit behind me?" She glances up. "I haven't played in front of anyone in a long time."

"As you wish." He takes his drink and sinks into the large leather seat behind her, angling it so he can study her profile. His stomach is in a knot for both of them. He pulls an ankle to rest over his leg and settles in for a glimpse into this part of her heart.

She closes her eyes and whispers, "Mom." He can almost picture her mother sitting there, encouraging her to play. Telling her how much she loves her. Slowly, a faint smile tugs at her cheeks before she extends her hands and presses down.

Her fingers dance along the keys, making it look effortless. He doesn't recognize the song. It's different at first, but then a note triggers his memory, and he soon realizes she's playing *Yesterday* by The Beatles. She's twisting the melody, adding a little bluesy touch. He likes it, likes it a lot, actually. But what stops his heart mid-beat is when she starts to sing the chorus. Her voice is low but strong. His brandy gets stuck in his throat around the knot lodged there. Setting his drink down, he leans forward and rests his forearms on his thighs, drinking in the intoxicating feeling. It's such a raw and powerful moment.

One finger rests against his temple as he closes his eyes, getting lost in the lyrics. A noise off to his side snaps his eyes open. He slowly turns and he sees his mother cupping her mouth. Her cheeks are wet, the same as his. Savannah, right here, right now, is making progress. She's trusting him with a talent she doesn't share with anyone. He smiles at his mother, who blows him a kiss before she disappears up the stairs.

Moving his attention back to her, he watches in awe as her body moves to the music, and he knows she's born to feel it. He never knew she could play like this. It makes him realize how much he still has to learn about her. Which gives him an idea.

Her shoulders rise at the high notes. Her hair slides off to the side, exposing her slender neck, while her eyes close, pouring her heart into every single word. It's easy to see this is her outlet and passion. He makes a note to look into converting one of the offices into a play room for her. So she can escape and play in private.

When the song ends, she doesn't turn to look at him. She just sits staring at the keys. Breathing in deeply, he clears his throat and moves to her side, seeing her teary eyes. "She was with me," she sniffs, "all the time I was in my prison. I could see her and feel her touch sometimes." A tear slips down, but he catches it before it falls. He doesn't have to ask her to go on. He's heard her tapes with Doc Roberts and how she decided to kill herself at the end, when she lost all hope. "Now she's only with me when I play." She ducks her head down so her hair hides her face. "I'm scared I'm going to lose my memories of her."

"Share them with me, so you won't." He lifts her chin, showing her his eyes, letting her see his sincerity. "Thank you for that, Savannah." He slowly leans down and drops a kiss to her lips, letting them linger a few moments before he says, "You have a lovely voice."

"Thank you." She sighs, closes the lid, and takes a sip of her martini.

He tucks her hair behind her ear, wanting nothing more than to make her feel better.

He offers a hand after he stands. "Come to bed with me?"

Her smile touches the corners of her eyes as she stands, threading her fingers through his. He pulls her in and buries his face in her hair.

"I need to hold you."

Her grip tightens as she turns into him. "Please do."

Chapter Five

"Cole," she whispers, her hand running across his stomach. "Cole, wake up."

"Mmm," he mumbles, pulling her closer and keeping his tired eyes shut. It must be two a.m.

The bed moves as she climbs on top of him. Her hair falls all around as she kisses his chest, his shoulders, his neck, and stopping at his ear. "I need you." His eyes open to her hungry gaze. "To dominate me." A flash of excitement spreads over her face as a wicked smile appears. She sits back on her knees, holding her arms above her head and letting a scarf drop from her fingertips. Oh sweet Lord, this better not be a dream!

He grips her hips, sending her to the side so she's flat on her back. He snatches the scarf and binds her wrists together. "You want me to be rough, baby?" She bites her lip as she gives a nod. "You haven't had enough from last night?" Her legs drop open to show how wet she is. Her eyes drag away from his, and lead a hot trail down to his straining erection.

"Make me scream, Cole," she says, her voice husky. "Make me leave here with a reminder of you."

Leave. That word stings a bit.

He hovers over her and rests his weight on one arm, while the other skims the back of his fingers down along her skin until they meet with the moisture dripping out of her. "You're full of me." He grins down at her. "I love that."

She pulls against the restraints, flicking her hips up so he'll touch her there. He loves how she gives up all control. He needs this just as she does. His fingers push inside, scissoring as they go.

"More," she begs. "Cole, I need more."

He leans down and nips her nipple, making it taut, then blows a stream of air over the top, and she gasps. She's hungry, and he loves it, but he also knows it grounds her when she's feeling lost. The idea of teasing her right now is tempting, but no, he'll give her what she wants. He moves to position at her opening and ever so gently nudges forward.

"Cole!" she nearly shouts, lifting her hips off the mattress.

He steadies his balance and thrusts forward, slamming into her with almost all his strength.

"Yes!" she cries in relief, dropping back in the mattress.

He grabs her legs, hooks them over his shoulders, and pulls her to the edge of the bed so he can stand. He nearly folds her in half as he leans over, getting as deep as possible before he starts thrusting at a maddening rate. Her breasts bounce around in his face, making him even harder. Her bound hands fly forward and run through his hair. He shifts his angle and gets what he's been waiting for, her scream. The scream that makes him pick up speed. She's close, so he pulls out and hauls her up and against the wall. Her hair is wild and sexy, and she pants and cries as he reenters her. He drops her down onto him and uses her body weight to slam down.

"Oh god, baby, I'm gonna come so fucking hard," he growls, biting her neck.

That does it. She bucks, screams, and fists him from

the inside. She gives in, tossing her head back. He follows, getting himself as deep inside of her as possible.

He presses his forehead to hers as they both pant and try to catch their breath. Her eyes go from wild with need to satisfied, and it's one sexy look.

"Shower?" he asks, peeling her away from the wall. She shakes her head and he laughs.

He frees her wrists and wraps his sweaty body into hers and kisses her shoulder.

***

Savannah

I head into the kitchen on a search for that heavenly smell I missed so much—Abigail's cinnamon rolls.

"Well, fuck me sideways," Mark says through a bite of toast. "Look who spent the night."

"Morning, Mark," I mumble as I pour myself a large cup of coffee and help myself to a warm roll.

He grins and brushes the crumbs off his fingers. "That it is!"

"Why are you so damn chipper?"

"Because, my sweet Savannah, Cole is winning you back, therefore we all do."

I can't hide my smile as I sip my coffee. Cole strolls into the kitchen, pulling on a t-shirt. I sneak a quick peek at his stomach and remember it flexing when he held me up against the wall, plowing into me like his life depended on it.

"Morning." He flashes me a dirty smile, then grabs my face and kisses me.

"Awww," Mark cues from behind us. "Hey, Keith, you owe me twenty!"

"What?" Keith mutters, coming into the kitchen. "Oh, come on!" He curses. "Really, guys, you couldn't have held out to Valentine's Day?"

"Pay up, dude." Mark holds out his hand as Keith shoves a twenty at him.

"You made a bet on us?" I laugh, realizing how much I miss this place.

Mark jumps up on the counter and bites an apple. The guy never stops eating; it's amazing. "Yup, as to when you'd all get back together." He snaps the twenty in the air.

"I'm getting that money back," Keith informs him as he heads out of the room.

"Whatever, dude!" Mark calls out, then looks back over at us. "Well, I'm out. See ya later, Savi."

***

"You look happy," Jake says as he pours a beer from the tap. Our shift is going by fast. We barely have a moment to think, it's been so busy. It's eleven, and only now is it dying down enough that we can talk in a normal voice. "Does this have anything to do with a sexy Army man?"

"Perhaps." I bump his hip with mine to move him over. "And Graham?"

"Oh, it's all good." He winks. "He's one dirty bird."

I laugh, but stop when I see his face light up when he looks at someone over my shoulder. I turn to find Cole making his way through the crowd.

It's been four days since I left the house. He whispers something in a girl's ear. She looks at me, then nods as she gets up and frees him an open seat. He removes his jacket and places it over the back, then undoes a few buttons on his dress shirt. Poor guy hates dress shirts. I feel his discomfort. He really is an army pants and t-shirt kinda guy.

I finish with my customer and head over. "Welcome

to Zack's," I joke. "What can I get you this evening?"

He smirks. "Brandy, neat."

I nod, then look over at the guy next to him. "And you?"

"Mmm…" he glances at the menu, "Fat Tire."

I place Cole's drink in front of him while Jake grabs the beer for me. "You from around here?" I play with Cole, who grants me one of his sexy smiles.

"You could say that." He takes a sip of his drink. "You have plans later on tonight?"

The guy next to him snickers. "Good luck, dude. No one has gotten into her pants. Believe me, my buddy has tried many times."

Cole actually laughs, which totally throws me for a loop. Jake looks at me, confused. I just shake my head. "Well, that's good to know." Cole takes another sip of his brandy. "I wouldn't want to have to kill someone."

I chuck my rag at Cole, knowing he isn't joking. He catches it and holds it out at each end. "This reminds me of last weekend."

I grin and shake my head. He's so playful right now, and it's fun. "Where were you?" I ask, tugging at my shirt and nodding at him.

"Meeting," he answers, finishing off his drink. I reach down to make another, and when I look up, the bottle nearly slips out of my hand.

"You!" *she* screams, pointing a finger at me. "I'm going to kill you!"

"What?" I gasp, trying to play catch-up with the crazy charging my way. "What are you talking about?"

She picks up a salt shaker and chucks it at me. I manage to move, and it flies past me. Cole is on his feet, holding a hand up to her.

"Don't act innocent, you bitch." She glances at Cole. "Your whore gave out my apartment number to Don, and he showed up on my doorstep, handing me a stack of cash and wanting me to screw him."

I move to Cole's side. "Christina, I never gave your address to Don! I don't even know where you live."

Jake bursts out laughing. "Maybe he knew your address because you screw every customer we get, Chris."

"Fuck you, Jake."

"No, thanks," he chuckles.

She suddenly charges me, but Cole blocks her path. Grabbing her arms, he waits until she cries out because of his grip. "You ever touch Savannah, and I'll make sure it's someone looking to do more than have a shitty fuck with you at your door, Christina. Leave my family alone. This is your only warning."

Christina is still heaving with anger when he lets her go, tossing her forward. She spits at my feet, and then Zack appears out of nowhere and kicks her out the door.

Cole ducks down so he's eye level with me. "Are you all right?"

"Yeah." I look around at a few stragglers, embarrassed, though I shouldn't be. She was the one who looked like a fool. "Can you drive me back to my place?"

"Of course." He takes my bag from Jake and offers him a ride, but he has plans with Graham.

Cole parks the car and walks me to my apartment, but stops in the doorway. "I can't stay, baby. I have an early meeting." I feel my disappointment hit hard but push it aside. It was my choice to live here in town. "Hey," he brushes my hair out of my face, "you okay?"

"Yeah, I'm fine."

He leans in, stopping right before he hits my lips. "I love you."

"I love you too, Cole." He gives me a long kiss before turning away.

***

My eyes glaze over as I dip my fry in the ranch dressing, twirling it around then popping it in my mouth. Jake has been talking a mile a minute about Graham and what they've been up to. I love Jake, but he doesn't have a filter when it comes to his sex life.

"Hey, you don't like your burger?" He points his fork at my untouched bacon cheeseburger. I shrug, feeling off. I think I'm just tired. Cole had to fly to Washington to deal with some things in person for four days, so sleeping has been a little hard again. "You're not going to freak out on me again, are you?"

I chuck the rest of my fry at him. "You're an ass." I hand my plate to a waiter who is going by and slip behind the bar, fastening my apron around my waist. "I think I'm just tired—"

A guy comes busting through the door, cupping his mouth. "Honey, I'm here!" I look at Jake, who is very obviously checking him out. *Shameless.* Graham appears from out back.

"No way!" He slams his tray down on the bar and heads over.

"I told you I'd come visit. Now spin," the guy orders, making Graham do a sexy little turn. "Damn, your ass looks fucking fab in those jeans." I see Jake stand, but he doesn't go over. The guy notices, tilting his head at Jake. "Well, looky here, is this…?"

Graham blushes and rolls his eyes. "Be good," he warns.

The guy makes a hungry face at Jake. "That's like telling the spider to let the fly go, my dear."

A very pretty blonde walks in behind him, chatting quietly on the phone. "Don't worry, I'm fine. Okay, I'll call you later. Yes, I promise. I love you."

Graham grabs the guy's arm and walks him over to

us. "Jake, this is my cousin, Pete Jones. He's from L.A."

Jake's face lights up, and he holds out his hand for a shake. "Nice to meet you. This is my friend, Savi."

"Well, smack my ass, Graham, you have some hotties here." The girl tucks her phone away, smiling and joining Pete's side. "This little love is my best friend, Emily." He waves his hand around dramatically. "You wouldn't believe the hell I went through to convince her boy toy to let her come up here."

"Pete." She shakes her head, extending her hand to me. "It's nice to meet you all."

"Can I get you a drink?" I ask, seeing Jake visibly relax now that he knows Graham doesn't have a secret boyfriend.

"Dirty martini with three olives for me, please." Emily checks her phone again as she takes a seat at the bar. "My theatrical friend will have a vodka cranberry."

I laugh as I make their drinks. Pete is something else; even his hand movements are loud. Emily smiles at her phone. I know that look. That's the look of some dirty texting, right there. "What are you guys doing up here? Vacation? Skiing?"

She takes a long sip of her drink. "Yeah, something like that." She laughs more to herself than me. "I had a hard last few months, and I just needed to get away. When I heard Pete was coming up here to see Graham, I thought it sounded perfect. The mountains can be so quiet, and I really needed to get out of the city."

I nod, knowing exactly what she means. "I get that."

Her phone buzzes. "Sorry." She turns the ringer off. "My boyfriend's a bit over protective."

I hear Jake laugh behind me. "I think you and Savi have a lot in common, Emily."

"Are you from here? I hear a bit of an accent," Emily asks, fiddling with toothpick.

I shake my head. "Born and raised in New York.

Living here for just under a year."

"That's a big move. Do you miss it?"

Do I?

"Honestly, I don't. I think I was meant for the mountains. It just took something big to get me here."

"A man?" She grins.

I lean my hip into the counter. "Yeah, something like that."

"An Army guy," Jake chimes in.

"Oh," Emily eyes go dark, "gotta love a man in a uniform."

I clink my water glass to hers. "Yes, you do."

Pete and Emily stick around most of the night, while I start to feel worse as the night drags on. I barely make it to the locker room when I throw up in a garbage can.

"Oh, sweetheart, are you all right?" Zack asks, rushing to my side. He pulls out a napkin then calls out to one of the staff to bring me some water. "Do you have the flu? It's been going around."

"Not sure," I croak, feeling like I could puke again.

Zack helps me to sit down on the bench. "I'm going to get my keys. I'll drive you home."

"No." I shake my head. "I'm all right, really."

Zack opens my locker and gathers my things "If you're sick, sweetie, I don't want you here."

The idea of going back to my lonely apartment makes me feel even worse. "Do you think you could take me to Sue's?"

He bundles me up and loads me in the car, and we head off to Sue's.

Zack holds on to me as we shuffle up the icy walkway. I'm so damn tired I just want to be in a comfortable atmosphere so I can sleep. Sue meets us at the door, looking worried.

"Come here, honey," Sue whispers, taking me inside and thanking Zack for bringing me here. "Are you hungry?" I shake my head. "You're awfully pale. How about some tea?"

"Okay," I whisper as she sits me down on the couch in front of the fire and removes my shoes. Wrapping a blanket around my shoulders, she helps me lean back so I can lie lengthwise on the couch.

I stare into the fire thinking about how I went from feeling crummy to shitty in a matter of a few hours. It brings me back to York and the poison. My stomach rolls at the thought.

"Here." Sue hands me a cup of chamomile tea and takes a seat across from me. "Thank you for coming here." She bats a pesky tear away. "It means a lot."

"You remind me of her," I murmur, still staring at the fire. "My mother, she was like a cozy blanket. The moment she was around, you felt wrapped in her comfort and warmth." I turn to see her glossy eyes reflecting the fire. "As much as I hate my past, it brought me to all of you. I'm incredibly lucky for that." She smiles at me, but her quivering chin gives away the emotion she's keeping at bay. "Umm, Sue?"

"Yes?"

I hold my mouth and bolt to the closest bathroom.

***

Cole

Cole walks through the bar, scanning every table for her. Maybe she's on break. He takes a seat next to a guy who's telling Jake a story about how he and his friend next to him did karaoke at Chaps last night. The girl seems to be a feisty little thing and keeps her friend in check as he tells the story like it's a performance.

He waits until the guy takes a breath before he waves Jake over.

"Oh, hey, Cole." Jake comes over with a glass, holding it up seeing if he wants one. "Savi call ya?"

"No," he looks around, "why?"

"Look, love, he's like sex on a stick," the guy next to Cole whispers loudly. "Screw L.A., I'm stayin' right the hell here." He leans over to Jake. "Is this where all the hotties live?"

"You have no shame!" The girl swats his arm. "I'm sorry, don't mind him. He's a fifteen year old perv stuck in a twenty-three year old's body."

Jake shakes his head, ignoring the guy's comment. "She went home sick, think she's got the flu. Zack took her to your parents'. Guess she didn't want to be home."

"It's not her home," he mutters, pulling out his phone and calling his mother.

"Hey, honey," his mother whispers. "I was going to call you once she fell asleep."

Cole waves to Jake as he leaves the bar. "I'm at Zack's. I'll come over. It's just the flu, right?" His thoughts shoot back to York.

"I think so. She's just tired and has an upset stomach. She's gotten sick a few times. You might get sick, honey, you sure—"

"I'm in my car."

"All right," he can hear her smile, "drive safely."

His mother is in the kitchen stirring a pot of chicken soup when he arrives. He gives her a kiss on the cheek and attempts to steal a roll from the baking sheet.

"She's on the couch." She nods as he looks over.

He gazes down at her tiny body tucked under a huge blanket, her hair framing her pale face with her hands folded beneath her head. She's the most beautiful woman he's ever seen, and she's his...well, almost his. He leans over to kiss her forehead.

"Cole?" she whispers, not opening her eyes.

"Yes, baby, I'm here. Get some rest." Within seconds

she passes out cold again.

"You hungry?" Sue asks from the doorway.

"Yeah." He follows her into the kitchen and takes a seat at the oak table. She sets a hot bowl of soup in front of him with a basket of homemade rolls. She sits across the table from him, trying hard not to show her grin. She's terrible at hiding her excitement. "Out with it, Mom," he says, buttering his roll.

"She came here when she needed someone." Her finger bobs the tea bag in and out of the mug.

"Yeah," he replies, "she did."

"She said I remind her of her mother," Sue beams, but he can see how much that means. His mother always wanted a daughter. His parents tried, but she couldn't get pregnant again. So for Savannah to take to Sue this way means the world. "So…" She clears her throat.

Cole shakes his head, fighting the grin that tugs at his lips. "So what?"

"Oh, Cole!" She bats his arm. "When are you going to ask her to marry you?"

Wiping his mouth, he leans back in his seat. "If it were up to me, she'd have been my wife a long time ago." His mother's hand flies to her chest, swooning in the moment. "But I won't push her into something she isn't ready for. She's well aware I'm going to marry her. I told her to let me know when she's ready, and I'll ask."

"Oh, honey." She laughs a little, hitting her forehead. "Where's the romance in that?"

"Mom, I'm not going to ask and have her say no." He stands to grab the pepper off the island.

"She won't say no."

"She might." He sighs. "Not really sure I can take that rejection."

His mother comes over and places both hands on his shoulders. "That girl came to our house because she is sick, and she was looking for family. She knew you

586

weren't here, Cole, and she still came. The way she looks at you, it's obvious she loves you more than anything else in the world." She pauses to catch her breath. "I watched that woman completely crumble when she thought you were gone. You're her world, so be hers. Don't wait for her to come to you. She's ready, she's just scared. So," she steps back, grinning, "plan something romantic and ask her."

Maybe.

"Yeah, Mom, I hear you,"

"Good." She leans in and gives him a kiss on the cheek. "I love you, honey bear."

"Excuse me," Savannah says faintly, and they both turn to see her slumped into the doorframe, looking exhausted. Cole goes over and feels her head. She doesn't have a fever. "May I get some water, Sue?" She looks over at him. "I'm okay." She tries to smile at him, but he can see she feels awful. "Zack said the flu is going around."

"Here, honey." Sue hands her a glass of water. "You want to try to eat something?"

Her hand goes to her stomach. "No, I just want to go back to sleep."

Cole slips his arm around her waist. "You want me to take you back to your apartment?"

"No," she shakes her head, making him smile inside, "I don't think I can stomach the car ride." She turns to his mother. "Do you mind if I stay here?"

"I thought that was the plan." She beams.

"Come on, let's go to bed." She sags into him as they walk up the stairs and into his old bedroom. She shuts her eyes the moment she hits the pillow. He removes her jeans and curls himself around her. Breathing in her addicting scent, he falls asleep with the idea of her being his forever.

***

Savannah

I try to be quiet as I bring up the little bit of water I drank earlier. I flush the toilet, wash my face, and brush my teeth, feeling mildly better as long as my stomach is completely empty. I find Cole and Daniel in the kitchen sipping coffee. Sue is making pancakes, which smell pretty good, surprisingly.

"Hey." Cole hops up and pulls out a chair for me. I sit and feel him give me a kiss on the head. I love how affectionate he is with me. I lean into him, seeking his warmth. He feels just right. "How's the stomach?"

"Not entirely sure yet," I mumble, trying to feel it out. Christ, Sue's pancakes smell good.

Cole sees me eyeing them and stacks two on a plate for me. "Eat, it will make you feel better."

Once they hit my tongue I can't stop. I don't even wait for the syrup. The fluffy white cake slides down my throat, hitting my stomach and landing with a hollow boom. Oh my god, I am so hungry! I don't think, just chew. Cole wastes no time refilling my plate, chuckling. I nod a thanks and polish off two more before I feel satisfied.

"I'm going on a hunch here and say your stomach is better?" Daniel teases, putting aside the sports section of the newspaper. I take a few sips of orange juice and feel my energy returning.

"I guess—" I stop when something catches my attention. Part of the entertainment section of the newspaper is flipped over, and one of my most favorite actors, Tim Roth, is up for a new role. Roth. Roth. There's that nagging feeling again.

Cole places his hand on my thigh. "What?"

My head is turning, determined not to lose my trail.

"Do you know anyone name Roth?"

He looks a little puzzled. "The only Roth I know is from training up at Camp Green."

I move two steps ahead in my memory, on the right path. "Umm, did I meet him?"

Daniel leans toward us, a little interested in where I'm going with this. "Yes, at the campfire outside. He was one of the recruits I had my eye on, remember, number fifty-nine," Cole says, glancing at his father.

The pieces of the puzzle are all starting to fall into place. "A recruit for the house, right? He would have come to the house and worked?"

"Yes," both he and Daniel answer at the same time, seeing I'm on to something.

There it is, the light turns on in my brain. I'm on top of the fucking memory, and the puzzle is complete! "Holy shit!" Cole squeezes my thigh, coaxing me to go on. "You remember I told you I saw those pictures of you and that blonde woman?" He flinches, but I reach out and cup his cheek. "I'm not digging up this memory to be cruel." I turn to Daniel. "When I was in The American's house, he showed me some photos to prove Cole isn't who I thought he is. He showed me pictures of him and an informant. My point in all this is that The American said he had one of Cole's men take the picture...well, actually, a lot of them." I feel Cole's shoulder twitch.

"You think it was Roth?" Cole asks, bringing my attention back to him.

"Yes, I heard him say his name when I was semi-conscious. One less than sixty," I mutter in disbelief. "The American tried to get me to guess who it was. He said one less than sixty. He also mentioned that he needed him to do well so he would be able to get the location of the house. " Cole's eyes flick over to his father's.

589

"I think we need to make some calls, son," Daniel's voice is calm but laced with anger.

"Savi," Cole leans in closer, brushing my hair back off my shoulder, "are you feeling better?" I nod, knowing where he's going with this. "Then I need to go. I'll call you later."

"Okay." He leans in and kisses me, then he and Daniel disappear, leaving Sue and me and a stack of pancakes.

Chapter Six

Cole: You at work?

Savi: I am, it's slow.

Cole: How are you feeling?

Savi: Tired.

There's a long pause.

Savi: I'm fine. Did you deal with Roth?

Nothing.

Savi: Cole?

Cole: Will you go on a date with me?

Huh? Where the hell did that come from?

Savi: Sure?

Cole: I've never taken you out on a date. I want to. Tomorrow, be ready at five.

I can't hide my grin. I'm suddenly feeling very excited about my day off. I hoe into my rare steak, licking my lips as I enjoy every bite. Yummy.

"Whatcha gonna wear?" Jake asks over my shoulder, reading my messages as I eat.

"Jake!" I scowl, but it doesn't work when I laugh after. I can't help it. I feel so happy. He snatches my phone and runs to the other side of the bar and starts madly typing.

"What are you doing?" I run after him, dropping my fork, but he's too quick.

He grins as his fingers tap away. Almost immediately there's a ring signaling a message has come in. Jake makes a huff and hands it back.

I glance down and laugh.

Savi: Panties are optional right? I won't if you don't.

Cole: Hi, Jake.

"He knows I wouldn't wear any," I say over my shoulder, heading for the kitchen to return my plate.

Savi: Will I see you tonight?

One step through the door and it hits me like a brick wall. I turn and heave my yummy steak right into the trash can.

"You're still not better?" Zack asks, popping his head out from behind a fryer. His normally crisp white chef's apron is all dirty because one of the cooks called in sick. He's busy—I can see it on his face—and he's stressed. Zack's is a very busy restaurant. "Savannah, you've been vomiting for four days now. You sure it's just the flu?"

I wipe my mouth with a spare napkin. I feel a little dizzy but stand and give him a smile. "I had the flu, but I'm over it now. I'm actually feeling a lot better, but I ate sushi from the supermarket and it didn't go over so well." I sure wasn't going to admit it was a steak from Zack's. His face twists, thinking about that damn sushi. I knew he'd gotten sick off it once before too. "Once it's out of my system I'll be fine," I assure him.

"Go home, honey, and don't come back till you're better." I start to argue, but he holds up a hand. "You're only going to run yourself down, make yourself worse. One of the deals I made with Cole was to look out for you, and if he knew you were sick and still working..."

"Okay." I hold my stomach, just wanting to get away from the smell. "I'll go."

I let Jake know I'm leaving. "I didn't know you were still sick." I shrug on my coat and pull on my knitted pink hat Abigail made me and lean into the counter, feeling worn out.

"I think I ate sushi too soon," I lie, not wanting to tell anyone I'm still sick with this on again, off again flu.

Jake makes a gagging sound as he hands me my tips. "Let me know if you want me to bring you home anything."

I step up and give him a hug. "Thanks."

Heading into the night, the breeze feels good across my sweaty face. The nausea is passing, but I'm left completely drained. My stomach has been on a roller coaster of binge eating. My feet are moving, but my mind is dreaming about my pillow. My pocket vibrates and brings me out of my dreamy daze. I remove my mitten and yank it out.

"Hello?" I say without even looking at the number.

"Hey, baby, I was just going to leave you a message," Cole's voice washes over me, warming me momentarily. I stop to look into a toy store that has a red and pink display in the window.

"Hey, where are you tonight?"

I hear him shift in his chair. "I'm just wrapping a few things up. Been a long day." He pauses. "I'm hard."

I stop mid-step with a grin that makes all the tired feeling leave in a puff. "Oh, yeah?"

"Yeah." His voice is deep and dripping with need. "I'm thinking about that little scrap of material you call a work shirt. The way your smooth skin looks against the color. The way your breasts pop out the top, begging for my tongue to run along them. I hate that shirt."

"No, you don't." I laugh a little as I run my finger along the window, tracing around a train that a tiny teddy bear is sitting on.

"Mmm," he chuckles, "I wish you were here. I hate that whenever my office door opens, I have a moment of hope it might be you, but it isn't." My hand drops as I lean against the cold brick wall and wish he was here too.

"Sometimes…" I whisper, wanting to tell him I think it was a mistake to leave the house, that as much as I need to find myself, sometimes I wish I was back inside the comfort of its walls. I miss everything right down to the way it smells. A horn honks at a car waiting at a green light.

"Where are you?" His voice has lost its husky undertone.

I rub my head, the weariness creeping back in. "I'm walking home."

"Why? Alone? Why now?"

"It's nothing." I sigh and push off the wall, starting my short walk home. "Zack overreacted. I ate something bad and got sick, so he sent me home—"

"So you are alone?" I hear a door close and pull the phone away from my ear, squinting to concentrate on the sound. "Give me ten. I'll be right there."

I stop at a crosswalk. "By the time you get in the car, Cole, I'll be walking into my apartment. I can see it now."

"You should have called me, Savi." His voice is quiet.

I yawn and my eyes water. "Cole, you need to stop worrying about me. Believe it or not, I did keep myself alive for twenty-six years."

I hear ice, then a slow pour of liquid, no doubt brandy. "Sorry," he mumbles. "I know you're perfectly capable of walking a few blocks. But I'll never stop worrying about you, baby. I've lost you too many times to allow it to happen again. Where are you now?"

I chuckle quietly. "Truthfully?" I glance at the stairs. "I'm waiting for the world's slowest elevator because I'm too damn tried to walk up five flights of stairs."

"You want me to come?"

"Always," I respond without missing a beat, "but no, you enjoy your evening. Truly, I'm just going to shower and head to bed. Zack told me not to come back until I feel up to it, so I'm going to sleep in, and I'll see you tomorrow at five for our date."

"Well, don't hang up with me until I know you're inside, okay?"

"Okay." I shove my key into the hole and unlock all the locks. When the door opens, I almost want to cry, I'm so happy.

"Hey, baby," Cole says, sitting on *my* chair and holding a glass of brandy in *my* damn living room.

"How?" I ask, not really caring. I just want to be wrapped in his warm arms.

"Zack called me and said you weren't well. I was already in town, and I was going to come by, but he said you had already left. I thought I'd surprise you." He stands as I come over and rest my frozen cheek on his chest. His arms wrap me up, and I let out a sigh and a long yawn. "Why don't you go get changed, and I'll make you something to eat?"

"Okay." I nod and peel myself away from him.

My shower lasts three minutes. I dry and slip into Cole's army shirt that I love, and then crawl onto the couch where my makeshift bed is made. Cole sets a cup of soup on the table along with some crackers. He sits beside me and encourages me to eat, but instead I lay my head on his lap, pull the covers over me, and drift off to sleep with his hand combing my hair. It's perfect.

"It had been a busy day." His words pull me out from my fog. "We'd just returned home. We had found someone who'd been missing for six months. He needed to be hospitalized, so he didn't stay at Shadows. I was in the middle of playing catch-up with my emails when John brought the file to me. It took me two days before I had a chance to open it." He twists a piece of my hair around his finger. I'm so tired, I can't open my eyes, so I just listen to his story.

"It was the middle of night, pouring rain, when I decided to move to the couch to be closer to the fire." He stops, chuckling a little. "This was back when Scoot wouldn't leave *my* side. The moment I opened that file, your eyes held me captive." His finger gently glides along my jawbone and trails up toward my temple. He makes my skin tingle, heightening my senses. "I think I stared at it for hours. Wondering what your voice sounded like, what your touch felt like, what your lips tasted like. I was completely consumed with your case after that. I turned down two assignments because I got a break on yours, and I couldn't let go." He stops talking, but his hand keeps moving. I almost drift off but fight it as I am enjoying his sudden openness. He seems a million miles away. "When I saw you lying in that bed, so small, and scared...I think a piece of my heart shifted out of place. I didn't realize how strong my feelings ran for you…" He leans down, brushing his lips over my ear. "I'm scared." His whisper nearly breaks me. "I've fallen for you, Savannah. Please catch me."

I start to move—I want to hold him—when I hear him clear his throat. I decide to leave him alone, let him have this moment as I try to control my own emotions trying to surface.

I love this man.

I wake to bright sun blasting through my window, and it takes me a few moments to realize I'm in bed. But what's odd is the sun is in a different place. I stretch my sniff neck to see the time and nearly gasp. Three thirty-two in the afternoon! What the hell? My hand runs along the opposite side, but it's cold. I wonder when Cole left and how he's feeling. My stomach grumbles, forcing me up and out of bed. I really wish it would decide whether it's feeling better or not.

The bathroom still has his scent. I pull back the shower curtain to find his body wash resting on the shelf next to mine, holding my breath at the sight. It's funny how something so small makes me grin like a fool. Why? Because to put it simply, it's just…normal. I grab my phone off the night stand and snap a picture. I attach it to a text message.

Savi: Thank you for giving me a normal moment. I love you.

The kitchen is spotless. He must have done my dishes from last night, and my temporary bed has been tidied and returned to my bedroom. I grab a banana and notice a note stuck to my coffee maker. I laugh, thinking he would know I'd never miss it here.

Good morning, my Savannah, there's

nothing better than waking up next to you. I won't lie, I will be late for work this morning. I watched you sleep for about an hour. Have I ever told you you're beautiful? See you tonight.

Yours ~ C

My grin makes my cheeks ache while I stick the note to my fridge so I won't lose it. My stomach rolls, only this time the thought of eating seems pretty damn good. I open my fridge and grab everything I can.

***

"Why am I nervous?" I ask, chucking a sweater out my closet door. I've been through at least six outfits, and nothing is working.

"I think it's sweet," Jake says, coming in behind me and rifling through my clothes. "Here." He holds up a red dress with long sleeves and a crisscross front. "Wear this with your knee high boots." I study the outfit, thinking it's actually good. "Always trust a closet gay. We know best."

I laugh and snatch the clothes from his hand, turning around as I take my t-shirt off to slip on the dress. "What time is it?"

"Four fifty-five. Is Cole normally on—" The doorbell rings. "The man has a key but rings the bell. A gentleman after my own heart." He bats his eyes at me.

"I'll have you know Keith gave him a key." I laugh, threading an earring through my lobe.

He points. "You want me to get that?"

"Please." I go back to some last minute prepping. I

hear Jake make a joke about the flowers Cole must be holding. I take a deep breath and look in the mirror. "Okay."

Cole is standing by the door, while Jake is prattling on about the weather. Cole is dressed in pants and a dress shirt. I know how much he hates to wear them, but damn, he looks sexy in business attire. His gaze finds mine, drops over my cleavage, and tumbles to the floor. A lazy smile appears and my heart skips a few beats.

"Hey, baby." He slips his fingers across his chin, circling under it, with the other hand stuck in his pocket. He slowly moves toward me like a panther hunting its prey, eyes dark and intense. His arms hook around my waist as he drops his lips to mine softly.

"Have her home by eleven. Lucky broad," Jake mutters then shuts the door behind him.

Cole holds my hand to his lips. "I need to tell you something." I look up at him and wait. "I got confirmation that Rodrigo is dead."

"Oh, that's—that's, wow."

I'm...I don't know what I am.

Cole nods. "One down, one to go."

"Three," I correct him, thinking my father needs to be taken out. I grab my jacket and purse.

Cole wraps his arm around my waist, walking me to the door. "Okay, no more talk about that shit. Tonight is about you and me." I lean up and kiss him on the jaw, one of my favorite places.

"Okay."

***

"I can't believe it!" Zack claps his hands together as we walk into the restaurant. "Finally, you two are on a real date! Please come, I've saved the best table." Cole helps me remove my jacket, running his hand down my back and swiping over the curve of my backside.

"This is going to be hard," he growls in my ear. I smile and turn around, conveniently grinding my bottom into his stone-hard erection. I look over my shoulder.

"It already is, baby." I bite my lip, fighting back the lust that's battling with my rational side. We *are* in public. He sucks in a breath as I take my seat. He lets it out as he slips across from me in the booth.

"Hi, Savi." Adam grins and fills my water glass first. "Red's a stunning color for you. Really makes your dark eyes pop." I blush slightly and glance at Cole's face. He's finding it funny.

Ass.

"Thanks, Adam."

"Are you feeling better? Or am I going to need to buy you your own trash can so you can carry it around with you?" he jokes.

"It was nothing," I say before I glance at Cole, who is studying my face. He can I see I'm lying. "Bad food too soon after the flu."

"2005 *St. Frances*, one of my favorites." Zack holds up the bottle to show us the label. Cole thanks him as he starts to pour the wine. "Adam, stop flirting. Table seven needs water."

"Bye." Adam grins as he walks away.

Zack laughs and shakes his head. "I feel for ya, Logan. You're going to be fighting men off this one left and right your whole life."

"Then I guess we are even," I cut in, and Cole rolls his eyes.

"Dinner will be ready in twenty. I promise, no fish, Savannah." Zack winks and heads over to check in on another table.

Cole holds up his wine glass to me. "To troubled times that only make us stronger. To unexpected love that only makes us fall harder."

600

"Well said." I clink his glass and take a sip, swirling it around and over my tongue. "It's delicious." I lick my bottom lip, only to get a growl out of Cole. I look over and see his hungry eyes.

"Please don't do that, baby."

I look down to see what he's talking about. "What?"

"That look and the way you lick your lips nearly has me ripping your clothes off right here."

This right here is one of the main reasons I can't get enough of Cole. He's so *animal*. I love the fact that he'll take me whenever, wherever. Not only that, but he tells me what he's thinking without hesitation. This. Is. Incredibly. Sexy.

I twist the wine glass between my fingers. "How would you have me?" I ask so casually people around us would think we were chatting about the food.

"I'd flick up that dress and find you bare and lay you flat on the table. I'd spread your legs and dive in for a taste first. Then grip your shoulders and slip in verrrry slowly." I can feel my chest rising and falling heavily.

"You like taking me from behind," I remind him, encouraging him to go on.

"I do." He takes a drink of his wine while his eyes swipe the crowded restaurant. "It's my favorite position with you."

"Why?"

His grin has devilish written all over it. "It's the sounds you make. They're different, they're more animalistic. It's sexy grabbing your hair and waist watching myself burying full tilt into your tight little opening. Your back curves, your head dips back, and your ass shakes when you want it harder." He closes his eyes in an effort to get control, his jaw ticks, then he looks me straight in the eye. "It's indescribable how much I need it." I find myself panting right there across the table from him at Zack's. In my workplace, no less!

601

I clear my throat and try to sort my thoughts as Zack and Adam serve our dinner.

"Filet mignon, with sautéed mushrooms and crumbled blue cheese, a side of roasted baby potatoes and fiddleheads." My mouth is watering by the time he's finished explaining. "Enjoy." He nods before backing away and directing Adam toward another table.

The meat is so tender that my fork glides straight to the plate. I moan in delight at the first bite. The flavors swarm my taste buds, begging me to pair it with the wine. I don't even notice Cole watching me until I tip my glass back and see his gorgeous smile.

"Aren't you going to try it?"

"I'm glad you like it." He picks up his fork and knife, taking a piece of the steak and placing it in his mouth. Cole might be a big guy, but he eats very politely. His parents have raised him well.

We go back to eating and making small talk about the town and its history. We're acting like a normal couple. I love it.

"How're Abigail and Doc?" I ask after our plates have been cleared. Poor Cole tugs at the collar of his shirt, and finally he just unbuttons it. "Feel better?" I grin.

"Yes." He laughs and leans back against the seat.

"Why didn't you just wear what you are comfortable in?" I reach over and take his hand in mine. I trace circles over his fingers, noticing how small mine look in comparison.

"I need to make a good first impression," he whispers, leaning over the table and kissing the back of my hand. "I need to show you I can be more than just a country boy." I slide my hand away and his head flips up. I shake my head slowly, seeing something I haven't before. *Huh.* "What?"

"Cole, I'm not interested in going back to New York.

That part of me has died. The very thought of returning there makes me scared as hell." He sighs and gives me a quick nod. I reach for his hand, grabbing his attention. "Honestly, Cole, my heart is with you. Ever since I met you, you've had it. You keep comparing yourself to something you think I am. If that's truly how you see us, then you really don't know me at all."

He looks around to see if the staff is within hearing. "How do I know one day you're not going to wake up and want to go back to the city life? That's not me. I can't do it. I need my mountain."

"And how do I know that one day you're not going to wake and fall out of love with me?" I counter.

"You can't stop loving a piece of yourself, Savannah. You are here." He points to his chest, making my heart want to leap over the table and join his. "Come on." He stands and offers me a hand. He helps me with my coat and leads us out of the restaurant.

His fingers thread through mine as we walk along the sidewalk that's now dusted lightly with fresh snow. Though it's not Christmas, the street is still lined with white twinkle lights, making the town sparkle. He stops us at a window. "You remember this place?"

"Yes." I point to a box now showing a cross necklace. "It was right there. I wear it every day." I pat my chest where it rests against my skin. I turn and point down and across the street. "And right there is where I first met Christina, and you told her we were engaged. I'm not going to lie, that was pretty damn fun."

"Yes, it was."

I pull him down so his lips meet mine and feel him tug me closer. He's warm and tastes like wine. I moan when his tongue massages mine. Snow starts to fall harder, pricking my face and making me shiver.

He clears his throat and wraps an arm around my waist, encouraging me to walk with him. I tuck myself in close, thinking how happy I am when we are together. Things seem to make sense, and so much of my worry floats away when I'm wrapped in Cole's arms.

"Want to get a coffee?" he asks, nuzzling my head with his cold nose. He nods toward a tiny coffee shop across the street. I spot his SUV and reach in his pocket and pull out his keys.

"I actually think I'd like to get back to my apartment," I say, dangling the keys. His eyes darken as he snatches them from my fingers. I laugh as he hurries me over and into the shelter of his truck.

The short drive to my place has me nearly crawling out of my skin. I feel like if his hands aren't on me in the matter of seconds, I'm going to lose it. He pulls into the parking lot toward the back, but when he goes to open the door, I stop him.

"What?" He scans the lot, wondering what he's missing.

The snow quickly covers the windows, hiding us from peeping eyes. I peel off my coat and crawl on to his lap. "Wow, Savannah, here?" I hold his face and swoop down to catch his bottom lip, giving it a nibble. His hands glide to my thighs, pushing my dress up. He growls when he feels I'm once again commando. "Jesus, baby," he mutters as he swipes his fingers between my folds, discovering how completely soaked I am.

I feel almost feverish with lust. I don't know what's wrong with me, but I can't help my hands that are nearly clawing at his belt. He must sense my need, because he lifts up and pushes down his pants and stands up his erection for me. I slide down, tossing my head back with a throaty moan.

He shifts his seat back to give us some more room. I grab the seat, raising myself a little off him, and start moving my hips in a slow, sexy roll. He grabs my ass, feeling the movement.

"Holy Christ, baby," he pants, kissing my neck. "That feels so damn good." I feel my wild side begging to come out. I try to keep it back, but it's taking hold of me. My need for hard, animal sex is surfacing. I squeeze him hard as I flick forward. He grasps my hips and hauls me down. Then I see it. Dominating Cole is starting to show...*perfect!* I squeeze one more time and muster all my will and slow my pace. It's not easy when my head is screaming for me to go on. "Oh hell no," he grunts, shifting me so I'm under him. He flattens the seat as he pulls out. "Up on your knees," he commands. I do, though the space is small and he is so big. I manage and feel his hands grip my hips. He thrusts back in and props one foot up and kneels on the other. He slams me backward...over...and over...and over. I'm so lost in my build-up I couldn't care less if anyone sees the car moving. I *need* this!

"Harder!" I scream. He reaches around and circles the perfect spot, and I go off, screaming his name into the chilly night fogging the glass all around us.

"Fuck, baby," Cole grunts from behind me, "you make me wild. Sometimes I'm scared I'm going to hurt you."

I swallow and try to moisten my dry mouth. "You won't." I shift and pull my dress back down. I scramble to the back seat so he has some room to get his pants on.

We skip the stairs and use the elevator instead. I sink into his side, feeling very relaxed and satisfied.

It isn't until we are in bed, naked and wrapped into each other's arms, that I ask a question. "Cole?"

"Mmm?" he says sleepily.

"Was The American telling the truth about Roth? Was he the one taking the photos?"

Cole pulls me a little closer. "Yeah, he was being paid pretty good to do it too."

"I'm sorry."

He yawns. "When I went to tell him he made it, my gut told me something was off. I'm glad I followed it, I'm even happier you remembered so he could be confronted."

I turn to see him over my shoulder. "So he confessed?"

"Not at first, but when we told him The American outed him, he cooperated. He'll go to jail for a few years, but most of all, the Army is kicking him out."

"Good."

He doesn't deserve to fight.

Chapter Seven

I wake to beads of sweat across my forehead and a strong urge to vomit last night's dinner. I roll out of bed and rush to the restroom. I barely make it before I'm cupping my mouth. I heave and retch for what seems like fifteen minutes. By the time I'm done, I am miserable. Somehow I make it back to my empty bed and sleep for another few hours. The nausea doesn't subside even during my restless sleep. By the time I give in and dry heave, I decide I need to make a doctor's appointment today. I call, and am relieved they're able to see me right away.

The waiting room is quiet, only me and another woman who looks like she's as sick as I am. Shit! I hope I don't have some crazy flu. She glances over and smiles a little, then ruffles inside her purse and pulls something out. She leans over and hands it to me. It's a roll of Arrowroot cookies.

"Try one, I promise it'll help." She nods.

I slip one out and nibble on the end. "Thanks." I try and force the cookie, but it takes a lot of willpower. My stomach is dead set against me feeling better.

"Your first?" she asks, tossing down her magazine.

I roll my head to look at her. I'm so friggin' tired I really don't want to chat right now. "First what?"

She points to my stomach. "Baby."

My eyes widen, snapping me awake. "Oh, I'm not—" I stop when it hits me. "Oh. My. God," I whisper, doing some quick math in my head. I can't believe I am so stupid.

"Congratulations." She stands after her name is called. "Maybe I'll be seeing you around."

"Maybe," I answer, completely shocked by this possibility. I try so hard to stop myself from getting excited, but a smile tugs at my lips.

I pee in a cup and wait with a thumping knee for the doctor to return. So many things are running through my head, one being...what now? A few weeks ago I would have been confused, but today, right now, I know what my heart wants. I want a home with Cole up on the mountain, full of our family. Suddenly, a haunting feeling creeps in when I think I still have two very stressful situations I need to get through—Lynn's court case, and what's going to happen with my father.

The door opening snaps me out of the thoughts screaming in my head.

"All righty, Savannah," Dr. Brown says, adjusting her blouse as she sits across from me. "How have you been since the miscarriage?"

I swallow hard and try to be brave. "I'm doing better, thanks."

"I'm happy to hear that." She opens my file while I cling onto the seat for fear of falling. "Given the details of your missed menstrual cycle and your urine results, I would say..." She turns a little wheel, concentrating as she goes. "Congratulations, Savannah, you are roughly seven and a half weeks pregnant."

A smile bursts across my face, instantly lifting my mood. "Wow, wow, all right."

"I take it this is something that was planned?"

I nod, thinking we never talked about 'trying,' but

we've been trying. No condoms and lots of sex means we were trying. "Yes, we have been. I just didn't recognize the symptoms until today. My work had a flu going around, so I just thought…" I stop and place my hand on my belly, confirming it to myself with touch.

"Where are you working?"

"Zack's, at the bar."

"Hum…" She nods and writes in my file. "Are you still living at the house?"

"Umm, no, I'm living in town," I answer, not sure where she's going with this. Or is this protocol?

She takes off her glasses and leans back in her chair. "Well, since you have had a miscarriage due to high stress, I need to know if there is anything I should be aware of that might endanger this pregnancy." She watches as the bliss drains from my face. "Savannah, I need you to be honest with me, if only for the safety of your baby. You got pregnant very quickly after your last one, and there are risks." She removes her glasses and leans her elbows on her desk. "Remember, everything here is strictly confidential."

"There is." I spend the next forty minutes filling her in on my life up until now, and what obstacles I'll be facing.

"Well, considering all that, I really would like to see you twice a month, and if you feel any discomfort of any sort, you come right in or call me." She hands me her card with her personal contact information. "I really need you to avoid as much stress as possible, though I know that will be hard with what's coming. Maybe you should think about not working?"

"Do I have to?"

"No, I'm just saying if it becomes overwhelming, take some time off. It's just not worth it." She hands me a ton of paperwork and research to go over. "So for now, here are some prenatal pills with some folic acid, you remember the drill. Do you have any questions?"

"Any advice how to fight the nausea?"

"Are you actually bringing up food?"

"Yes, a lot," I admit, remembering this morning.

She scribbles on a pad of paper. "Try eating a piece of chicken or turkey when you wake up. The protein will help take it away. But if it doesn't, take one of these three times a day, and it will do the trick. It will not harm the baby."

I go to leave, but she stops me. "Savannah, I want you to come back in soon so I can get a look at that little peanut. I want to check the heartbeat, make sure this pregnancy is strong from the very beginning."

"I will, but not without Cole."

She nods her understanding.

The walk down the long office hallway leaves me holding onto the wall for support. I've wanted a baby for so long, and here I am pregnant again. I fumble with my purse to pull out my cell phone. I stare at it once I'm outside. I'm not sure what to do first. I start to call Cole, but stop myself as a dark cloud moves in on my celebration. What if something happens again? Do I want to put him through this? Do I wait and tell him after the three month mark? Or do tell him now? My mind is spinning. I block everything else out and let my mind wander as I walk to work.

I'm still lost in my own little world when Jake decides to tell me about his date with Graham. His mouth is moving, but I'm not listening. In fact, I somehow lip read most of my orders. When I don't respond, I get a tap to the arm. Jake is staring at me like I was supposed to have a reaction to his story.

"That's great, Jake." I smile and toss out an empty bottle, replacing it with a new one.

He leans his hip into the bar and crosses his arms. "Is it, now? I wouldn't think Graham almost getting into a car accident is great."

"Wait, what?" I shake my head, trying to recall his words.

"No, I'm lying, but see, you're not listening!" He grabs my shoulders and gives me a little jolt. "What is going on? You're like Night of the Living Dead."

"Sorry." I say with a weak laugh. "I just have a lot going on." I wave my hand at my head.

He makes a face. "Anything I can do to help?"

I serve my client and take the credit card, swiping it down the machine. "I wish, but no. I just have to make a decision that I'm not sure how to make."

Jake gives me a hug, rubbing my back. "If you need me, you know where I am."

"Thanks, you really have no idea how much I needed to hear that."

***

Three days go by, and I'm still stuck in my routine, not sure what to do. Cole has been busy, so we've only been texting. He hasn't noticed my mood change since I saw him last. I go through ups and downs of being extremely happy, to scared to death, to just plan denial that my body would allow me to get pregnant again so fast.

I work my shift in another blur. Poor Jake must think I'm on something. My customers don't seem to mind so much that I'm not as chatty, which is good because I barely remember my left from my right.

I zip my jacket up and step into the chilly air, and before I know what I'm doing, I'm calling a cab. A short while later, I dial again.

"Keith?" I say once he answers. I can tell he's playing poker because his voice is muffled from his cigar.

"What's up with you? Everything all right?" I hear Dell hooting in the background about his poker hand.

"Can you do me a favor?"

"Of course."

"Tell the *Rambo wanna-be* at the gate to let me pass."

"Wait, you're here? Hang on." A moment later the guy's radio cracks and he waves me into his little heated booth. "What the hell, Savannah? I'll come get you. Stay right there!"

"Yes, sir," I joke, but he doesn't find it funny and hangs up on me.

Headlights blind the booth as he appears moments later. He hops out to open the passenger door, and I rush in, seeking the warmth. He turns the car around and glares at me. We pass through the other two gates before he even speaks to me.

"Do I even wanna know how you got here?"

I close my eyes, whispering the answer.

"A cab? A flipping cab!" he yells at me for breaching the house rules, but I stop him.

"I got him to drop me off a mile and a half away. He wasn't happy about it, but whatever. I hiked in the rest of the way."

He stops the car in front of the house. His hands grip the steering wheel, and the leather stretches under the force. "You hiked in the middle of the night, in the back mountains, where god knows what is out there just to come and visit? Why the hell didn't you call me or Mark?"

I grab my bag and walk toward the door with him close behind me. I know it was the world's stupidest move. I'm reckless for no reason, and I don't know why. Maybe it's because I've been before. "Yes, it sounds stupid, but honestly, the walk felt nice. I needed to clear my head."

"Stupid is not the word I'd use, Savannah," he grits

out.

I turn, feeling tired. "Where's Cole?"

He studies my face while moving past me to open the door. "Should I even ask what's going on?"

"No," I sigh, "not yet." I admit feeling like I owe him that.

"Office was the last place I saw him."

"Thanks, Keith." I drop my bag, remove my coat and boots, and replace them with my flats and hurry that way.

I knock and wait. "Yeah." His voice sounds tired. I open the door and find my Cole hunched over his laptop typing away in a black t-shirt and jeans. Just the way I love him. "What in God's name does anyone want from me at one a.m.?" he mutters without looking up.

"I didn't want to sleep alone tonight," I say softly, and his head snaps up. His face goes from stressed to relieved.

"Hey" his smile draws me toward him. I crawl on his lap and get him to wrap his arms around me. "How did you get here?"

"You seem stressed, Cole, what's wrong?"

"Work. Sometimes I think I need to pass some of it off, but I don't. I'm my own worst enemy." I rub my fingers over the stubble along his jaw, stealing his body heat. "You smell good." He takes a deep breath, then lets out a long sigh. "You have no idea how much I needed this." I lean up to kiss his neck, letting him know I do. "Answer me, Savannah." I know he won't let it go.

"Cab, then hiked it in the rest of the way." His body turns to stone. "I feel by now I should at least be on the guest list. Rambo out there, who has seen me at least a dozen times, wouldn't let me pass. Pointed his big old gun at me until I finally called Keith to get me through. Honestly, Cole, I need some kind of special pass."

"You took a cab and hiked it here?" I don't have to

look at him to know how pissed he is. The vibrating hand on my back is enough to alert me. "Just tell me why."

I shift off his lap and stand in front of his desk, sorting out what I should say. I go to open my mouth to tell him everything, but I can't. My nerves get the best of me. He's watching every movement I make, calculating it, trying to read me. I drop my head and hold back my pesky tears.

***

Cole

Cole can see something's bothering her, but he decides not to push. He's not sure if Frank has called her yet, and if not, he won't be the one to bring it up. The idea of her walking along the dark mountain road makes him want to punch a hole in the cabby's face. Who the hell leaves a woman on the side of the road in the middle of nowhere? He's not sure why Savannah does what she does. Sometimes he thinks she may not have any regard for her own safety, which scares the hell out of him.

"I just wanted to see you," she nearly sobs, twisting his heart. "I didn't want to bother someone to come and get me. It was my choice to move there. You've been so busy, and I've been feeling a little..." She rubs her stomach. If she's still sick, he's going to call Dr. Rice. If there's something going on, he needs to know now. York's face creeps into his mind and makes him uneasy. "I didn't really know what I was doing until I was at the gate. I know it was stupid, but..." Tears start to flow, but she doesn't try to hide them. She looks so tired and small as she breaks down.

"Hey," he stands in front of her, "it's okay, baby. You're here and safe, that's all that matters." He kisses her head as she sags into him. "Why don't you go have a hot bath, and I'll join you in a few? I just need to send off a few emails and I'll be done." She nods as she steps away, looking paler than normal. "Can I get you anything?"

"No." She tries a smile. "I just wanted to sleep here tonight with you."

He loves her words. She has no idea what that means to him, that she feels safe in his home. "Okay, I'll be up soon."

After thirty minutes of writing endless emails that he could quite possibly do right into the morning, he finally turns off the screen. He can't concentrate knowing she's here. He closes up his office and heads for the stairs. He hears the guys laughing downstairs; the poker game must be going well. He's sure Mark is wiping them clean. Tonight they play for money, so Mark's wallet will be that much thicker tomorrow.

He finds Savannah tucked into a little ball on his side of the bed. Her body is curled around his pillow. Her hair is pulled up with a pin stuck through the bun, and the loose pieces are still damp on the ends. He strips and joins her from the other side, forming his body to curve to hers. Her skin is warm and smells of his soap. He kisses her shoulder and along her neck, then his hand travels down her side and slips between her legs, where he finds her ready. She stirs with a little moan. Hell, even when she's asleep, she wants him. He parts her legs and nudges himself up and glides in with ease.

"Mmm, Cole," she whispers, still half out of it. She tries to turn, but he stops her.

"Sleep, baby, I just need to be in you." He squeezes his eyes shut, trying to control himself. She's so warm. The moment he's inside of her, nothing matters but her and him. He lies back down, positing himself so he can stay inside of her as he drifts off.

Something soft brings him out of a dead sleep. Holy shit, it's hot, wet...it feels amazing. A moan fills the room. His eyes are so heavy he can't open them, so instead he reaches out and grabs a fistful of her hair. Her hum vibrating down her tongue makes him buck his hips, pushing deeper. She sucks long and hard, then swirls around him like a cyclone. Three repetitions of that and he's jetting down the back of her throat. She doesn't pull away, just continues until he's finished.

Still trying to catch his breath, she climbs up next to him and tucks herself into his side.

"What was that?"

"Shh," she whispers, "go back to sleep."

He grins, still euphoric from what she just did. "You're never leaving this bed, you know that, right?"

"Okay," she yawns, falling back to sleep.

The next time he opens his eyes, the bed is empty and there's no head between his legs. No, in fact, his bathroom door is shut and he can hear her getting sick. The toilet flushes as he scrambles out of bed and across the cold wooden floor. He raises a hand to knock when he hears a bunch of pills hit the tile.

"Shoot," she mutters.

He knocks gently. "You all right, baby?"

There's a pause. "Yeah I'll be right out."

The door opens after a minute. She's pale, and her eyes are bloodshot.

Cole shakes his head and reaches for his cell phone. "I'm going to call Dr. Rice. You need to get looked at."

"I saw my doctor three days ago," she says as he reads a text from his phone. "Cole, umm..."

"Shit!" he curses as his phone vibrates in his hand, seeing Frank is coming to the house this morning. "I gotta get going." He turns to look at her. "Savannah, promise me, call Dr. Rice." His head's spinning. He doesn't want Frank to do this this morning.

Her face drops a little but quickly recovers. "Yeah, all right." She smiles and reaches for her bag.

"I'm sorry." He rubs his face and gives her a quick kiss on the lips. "I just worry about you."

Savannah drops her eyes to his chest. "It's fine, don't worry. I will call. I'm going to go say hi to everyone, then I need to head back into town. I work tonight."

"Don't leave without saying goodbye. I don't care if I'm busy. Interrupt, all right?" She nods but still won't look at him, and he glances at the clock. "I need to get ready."

***

Savannah

I watch him head into the bathroom then quickly dress, as doubt creeps up on me. I can't say anything; it would only bring him more stress.

Abigail is in the kitchen feeding Mark's bottomless pit of a stomach. I slip onto the stool next to him and feel my pill kick in. The last thing I want is Abigail or Sue noticing my behavior is off and guess at the pregnancy.

"Hey, Savs." Mark grins, holding a fork full of waffle. "Hungry?"

"Muh." I reach for his wrist and steal the waffle off his fork. "So good." I grin, and he glares at me.

"You dare come between me and my food?" He laughs, spearing another bunch and drenching it in syrup.

My mouth drops as I look over his shoulder. "Umm." He turns to see what has my attention, and I snag his fork, jamming another mouthful of his waffle in my mouth.

"You just went dick deep with that move, Savi. You just asked for it!" He pushes away from the island and

617

wipes his mouth. "I'm going to give you a five second start be—"

I don't wait for the rest of the sentence. I take off and head toward the living room, but see Cole coming down the stairs. "Cole!" I shriek, running over to him and laughing so hard I can barely breathe. "Help!" I wrap myself in his arms as Mark comes running over.

"Give her up, Logan." Mark holds out his hand then rubs his forehead with a dramatic sigh, but I see the amusement in his eyes. "She stole my food, man."

"You made it so easy." I laugh, holding Cole tighter.

Cole's laugh makes me want to hear it again; it's so playful and fun. "What do you plan to do to her?"

"The snow bank is looking mighty fine." He grins.

"You wouldn't!" I turn to look up at Cole and give him the best bedroom eyes I can muster. "How much time do you have before Frank arrives?"

"Oh, you play dirty." Mark lets out a loud *ha* and holds up his hands. "You owe me a cheesecake for this little stunt."

"Deal." I look up at Cole, who's shaking his head at me. "What? You were going to hand me over."

"Never." He smacks my ass just as the doorbell rings. "I gotta go."

"What does Frank want, anyway?" I ask, heading to the door with him.

He doesn't answer as he opens the door and lets Frank inside.

"He's close," Frank says, then stops when he sees me. "Hello, Savannah."

"He? So, who's close?" This may not be my business, but the look on Cole's face is telling me it is.

Frank glances at Cole for help. "Let me talk to Frank, and once I know all the details, we'll let you know what's going on." He steps forward and kisses me on the head. "Please, baby." I nod, reluctant to step over anyone just because of who I'm dating. I know Cole is walking a thin line with having me in his life the way I am. But something doesn't feel right.

I watch them walk off before I hear his voice from the living room. "Chocolate with a strawberry glaze." Mark grins and tosses an apron at me. "And I'll know if you made it with love or not."

I roll my eyes and head to the kitchen.

Keith emerges just as the cheesecake is put in the fridge. He pinches the bridge of his nose. I'm guessing he's tired from his late night of playing poker.

"Is Frank still here?" I ask, hoping he's gone by now.

"Yes, still in the office."

"Any idea what's going on?"

"No."

"And if you did?"

"Then I would know." He smirks down at me, trying to be intimidating, but it doesn't really work anymore. "You work tonight?"

"I do. May I borrow a car to get back to my apartment?"

He laughs. "I'll drive you home."

I pull out my cell phone. "You know I am perfectly capable of driving myself back to town." I send a quick text, and moments later Cole comes into the kitchen.

"You leaving?" he asks, nodding to Keith.

Keith leans against the counter with a devious grin "She wants to borrow a car to drive herself home."

Cole puffs out some air. "Sorry, baby, that wasn't in the agreement." I start to argue, but see him rub the back of his neck roughly, and decide it's best not to.

"Fine," I sigh, stepping up on my toes to give him a kiss goodbye. "Anything you wish to share?"

"Not yet," he says, resting his chin on my head and holding me close. "I'll call you later. I'll stop by if I can."

"I love you." I'm teary eyed. *Sweet Jesus, Savi, grow a pair.*

"Hey," he says, pulling back to stare down at me, "what is going on with you?"

Keith leaves the kitchen, saying he's going to get the car ready.

Frank walks into the kitchen with a phone to his ear. "Logan, round up Blackstone. Jose's trying to get into Guatemala. Be ready in thirty."

Jose! Everything around me starts to look funny. I step backward, feeling like I'm falling. Sounds are mixing together. I can't separate them. I don't feel Cole pull me to him, I just know he has me around the wrists, trying to get me to look at him. Mark appears, but his voice is funny, and black spots mar my vision. Then suddenly everything comes rushing at me. I start to panic, my breathing erratic. This is my biggest fear. Cole going to fight. That's why I got in the way with his plans to get recaptured last time! I wasn't prepared for Jose to reappear.

"Savannah! Look at me." Cole's voice cuts through my panic. "It's an easy trip, I promise. He's alone, and we're just going to pick him up and drop him off in Washington. It's—"

"No." I grip his sweater like he's trying to get away from me. "Please, Cole, send someone else! Don't leave me!" I'm crying now, and he goes blurry as my tears spill over. His eyes pop open with the fact I went from zero to ten in a matter of seconds. "If it's such an easy trip, send someone else."

"Baby, it's going to be fine." He lowers his voice to calm me, but it doesn't work. I wiggle free, holding onto the counter. "Mark, please!" I turn to him for help. He looks so sad but doesn't say anything.

"Ready!" John yells from the other room.

I want to puke, I want to scream, I want to crawl out

of my own skin, I'm so frigging scared right now. A loud sob escapes me, and I grab my mouth in an attempt to contain the rest.

I'm losing it.

Mark holds up a hand to Paul, who is coming in the kitchen.

"Savi, you need to hear me. Everything is going to be fine."

"Like last time! When you left and—" I hold my rolling stomach.

Cole takes a step closer. "I've been doing this a long time. What happened last time was—"

"Our baby needs a father, Cole!" I blurt out. He freezes as his eyes drop to my hand holding my stomach. "You're…"

"Just over seven weeks," I whisper, seeing his eyes crinkle in the corners, then a huge smile appears. He leaps forward and wraps me in his arms.

"Oh my god!" he whispers into my neck. "I love you, Savannah, I love you so damn much!" *Oh my god, did I just admit that I'm pregnant?*

"Don't leave me, Cole, I won't be able to handle it, not now, not again!" I shake, unable to calm myself. I need to hear him say it.

"I'll talk to Frank, see what I can do." He pulls back, drying my cheeks with his thumbs.

We both turn when we hear Mark shuffling around, doing some kind of dance. Keith comes in, and his brows are squeezed together in confusion. "Fuck me sideways, brother! Hand it over. Fifty big ones! Damn! I have one hell of a horseshoe stuck up my ass."

Keith's mouth drops when he sees Cole's hand on my stomach. "Really?" He beams. "I'm going to be an uncle?" He hugs me with a laugh. Then he turns to Mark. "The missus is pregnant, you know what that means?"

"Bubble wrap and a helmet," Mark jokes, and Cole laughs.

"Means more trouble for all of us. You imagine if they have a girl? Another Savannah?"

Mark's face drops. "Shit, we're all screwed."

I roll my eyes. "Right, so be nice, or I'll sic our little one after you."

Mark comes over and gives me a huge hug. "Congrats, Savi!"

"Thanks, Mark." I sigh and try to get a handle on what I just spilled. "Let's keep this between us right now."

"Do I wanna be Uncle Mark? Or Uncle M?" Mark thinks aloud as he leans against the counter.

Frank returns, and Cole leads him into the living room. I take a seat on the stool as my head spins. What if Frank doesn't agree to let him stay behind?

"Either way," Mark says, setting a glass of water next to me, "we won't be gone for more than fifteen hours."

I sip the water and think this is how it's going to be whenever he leaves. I'm always going to wonder if he'll return to me and our baby.

"Frank's team is going to step in and help out Blackstone," Cole says, addressing Mark and Keith, then he looks at me, "since I'll be staying behind this trip."

I drop my head to the cool counter as the weight of the world rolls off my back momentarily. The men quickly leave, and the house becomes quiet. Cole walks them to the chopper pad, giving instructions. I stay behind. Taking a seat on the large sofa, I curl up under a blanket when I feel my ear being nuzzled by a little pink nose.

"Hey, big guy." I reach up and pull Scoot onto my lap. He snuggles down into the fleece blanket with me and purrs a soothing rhythm. My eyes soon grow heavy, and I drift off.

Chapter Eight

Cole

Cole slips his phone into his pocket and heads into the living room where Savannah is lying on the couch. He lifts her legs and rests them on his lap, then places his hand on her belly. "You awake?" he whispers.

"Mmmhmm." She opens her heavy eyes. Scoot is not liking his nap being interrupted, and he shoots Cole a rather rude look.

"I spoke to your doctor," he says, gently rubbing circles. "You've known for about four days?" She bites her lip and her chest falls heavy. "Okay," he sighs. "She tells me you need to be careful with stress. So what happened earlier is that going to be an issue every time I need to go away?"

She sits up, lowering Scoot to the ground, and pulls her knees up to her chest. He recognizes it as her defensive move, so clearly they have a bump in the road here. "Baby, I have to be able to do my job, but I have to know when I leave you're going to be okay with it too. Maybe you need to talk to the doc about this, maybe—"

"Oh my god, Cole, no more doctors!" She stands and moves over to the fireplace, picking up a model car from the mantel. "I'm so tired of talking to people. Bottom line is you have no idea what it was like for me when you were taken."

"Don't I?" He leans forward and rests his arms on his legs. "If I recall, you pranced off to New York to find answers, only to get yourself taken. Seems to me I'd have an idea of what you went through."

She puts down the car and whirls around to face him. "Really? Did you see me held hostage, kneeling on the floor while a machete sliced through my neck? No. You were at most a day away from me, working on the actual hunt to get me back. I had to stay put and wait while everyone tiptoed around me, not wanting to stress me out." Her voice drops a bit, and he sees a painful flinch flash across her face. "Not that it helped any."

He sighs, knowing she's still hurting from that day; they both are. "So where does that leave us? I can't not travel, Savannah. Blackstone is my life." As soon as the words leave his mouth, he regrets them, and he sees her withdrawing. "I mean, it's all I've had for so long, I've built my life around it. I can't give up a family business just so you won't worry. I could drive to town and be hit by a semi."

She runs her hands through her hair and lets out a long breath. "I have to get to work."

He stands and raises his hands. "Seriously?"

"Cole, it's a little different, me working at a bar and you doing some crazy G.I. Joe manhunt for a guy who beats women within an inch of their lives and has killed men for looking at him the wrong way."

"I don't like you working when you're pregnant, Savi."

"Well, then, I guess we both don't like each other working, but neither of us is going to stop, right?"

"Savannah…" His voice has an edge to it.

She grabs her bag, then turns to look at him. Her face is so different. "I don't want to fight with you, Cole.

This is not how I saw this moment going. I think we both need space to think."

He hurries to block her path. "Think about what, exactly?"

She drops her head and lets her hair make a curtain around her face. She takes a moment to gather herself, then looks up at him with red eyes. "Everything."

"Ready?" Mike asks from the entryway.

"Yeah." She waves. "I'll talk to you later."

"Savi," he barks, grabbing her hand and hauling her back to him, "don't you dare find some reason to pull away from me. You can't tell me you're pregnant and then withdraw. I don't know what's going on with you, but you better start talking soon. I'll see you later on tonight, so be prepared to talk then." He grabs her face and kisses her. She fights it for a moment, then gives in. He gives her belly a little pat before he lets her go.

"Mike, call me the moment you drop her off at home, and wait and drive her to work. I don't want her walking in the snow," he warns as she shakes her head toward the door.

"No problem, Logan, I will." Mike smiles at her and offers to take her bag.

He watches them leave, then pulls out his phone to call Frank when June appears from the kitchen. Her smile tells him she knows about the baby. Good thing about June, she can keep a secret, even from Abigail, if need be. She comes to his side at the window and gives him a pat on the back.

"She's scared, honey," she says quietly, not looking at him. "It was truly horrific what she went through here. That poor woman shut down and wouldn't let anyone in, but it's how she survives. When she saw that video and then lost the baby all in a matter of minutes, oh Lord, it was…" She puts her hand over her mouth and shakes her head. "It was a nightmare. It scarred her. She still isn't right. I can see it in her eyes."

Cole nods, knowing she's right. "I can too. But I can't not work, June. I just can't, it's what I do."

"I know, Cole, and she does too, but I think this job is especially painful because it has to do with her. It'll take some time, but she'll come around. I bet you anything when you see her tonight she'll be better."

He rubs his aching head, wishing he could just pack up her shit and move her back home. "Let's hope."

"Congratulations, by the way." She smiles. "I promise I won't breathe a word."

"Thanks." He lets himself think about the little one growing in her belly. "You think you could help me with something?"

"Anything."

***

Savannah

I am tired and just want to hibernate in my little apartment. All afternoon I've felt like crap over my conversation with Cole. Never once did I plan to tell him I was pregnant and then get into an argument. Of course I'd never ask him to leave the Blackstone team. It's just with Jose, if anything happened to him, it would be my fault again. I feel like crying, but Jake bumps me in the hip, making me move so he can ring in his order.

"Thirty minutes left and the place is still packed," he groans. "I'm so flippin' beat, and all I can think about is passing out in Graham's goose down duvet. I swear I'm only with that man for his blanket. Well..." he gives me a smirk, "that and one other thing."

"I miss my neighbor," I pout, fighting down a surge of emotion. Seriously, this whole jacked up hormones thing is getting a little old.

His hands fly to his hips. "You think I don't lust over your coffee? Or your chocolate chip cookies? Oh!" He smacks my arm. "That reminds me. Keith was in here snackin' on one earlier. What the hell, woman?"

I chuckle, rolling my eyes. "He had some frozen from a while ago. Trust me, I've heard all about it from Mark."

"Mark doesn't count. He could eat an entire cow and have room for seconds. He doesn't love treats like I do, and I have no one making me any..." He gives me sad eyes and sticks out his cute little lip.

"Fine, the can on top of my fridge."

"Hang on," his eyes narrow on me, "you have some cookies in your apartment, like, right now?"

I open a beer and hand it to a woman. "I need them to bribe Keith with." I shrug, feeling no shame. I turn to my next customer and want to sigh, but I hold it together. "Hello, Don. Scotch, neat?"

"You know I come to this place just to see you make my drink." He smiles and places his credit card and his hotel key side by side in front of me. "I love how you wait on me."

I hold back my rolling stomach as I take the credit card, leaving the key behind. When I turn back around to hand him his drink, I jump when I see Cole sitting right next to him.

Don slides the key at me. "You know you want to take it, sweetie." I rub my face as my tolerance for this man drains out of me.

"Are you going to want another? We close in fifteen," I say rather rudely. Of course he doesn't notice. He's too busy staring at my chest.

I turn to Cole, whose jaw is ticking. I know he could punch Don once and kill the man. "Brandy?" I pull out a glass.

"Please." He nods, rubbing his face. He seems as

irritated as I am. "How are you?"

I pour him a double, slip a napkin under it, and slide it over. "Tired." I shrug.

"I can fix that, doll," Don cuts in, waving his room key at me.

Cole goes to speak, but I place my hand on his. "Trust me, Don, you're not going to want anything to do with me in nine months."

He makes a disgusted face. "Fuck off, seriously?"

"Seriously," Cole warns. "Show some respect."

Don takes a moment, not listening to him, then shrugs. "I'm into kinky shit."

Cole turns to look at him, and my blood runs cold. I actually fear for Don's life right now.

"Cole," I reach for his arm, "please." He squeezes his eyes shut, calming himself.

"We're done! Thank fuck!" Jake cheers behind me. "Here." He slips my tips into my pocket, then reads the situation. "Umm, I'll punch you out and get your things."

I take my apron off and wipe down the bar. All the while Cole and Don sit side by side, both watching me. Don has some balls or he has a death wish, or maybe he's just clueless, but he doesn't move away from Cole.

"Great job tonight, Savi," Zack says, coming in through the dining room area. "Hey, Logan, so the rumor is true." I know they're referring to the fact that Cole didn't go with the Blackstone team.

"It's the first time in twelve years." He glances at me. "Had a good reason to stay behind, though."

I give a small smile, letting the good feeling spread through me.

Don flicks his head at me. "Last chance, doll." He flicks his room key at me, hitting me in the chest.

Zack manages to get between Cole and Don in a flash. "Easy, Logan," he says calmly, then turns to Don.

"I'm going to give you exactly one minute to leave this bar, before the Green Beret behind me bends you small enough to fit inside your scotch glass." Don looks up at Cole. "I've heard you've been making trouble for my staff, and I've let it go because they've been handling it, but what you just did there was crossing the line. Get out, and don't show your face in here again."

"Are you kidding me? Do you have any idea how much money I spend here?" Don grumbles, grabbing his jacket. I hand him his card and his bill to sign.

"I don't care, don't need your money," Zack says, pointing to the door. "Leave."

Don looks over at me and grabs his crotch, making a total ass out of himself. "Your loss, doll. Could've been epic."

Cole starts to move, but Zack grabs Don by the jacket, yanking him toward the door.

"Always exciting since you started working here, Savi." Jake laughs, trying to bring the tension level down a little. "Here." He sets my things down on the bar top. "Graham is waiting for me. I'll call you tomorrow." He gives me a quick hug, says bye to Cole, and heads out front.

"You done?" Cole asks, shrugging on his jacket. I can feel the anger pouring off him. I want to kick Don's ass for putting him in this mood. I switch my shoes, tug on my jacket, and grab my bag, coming around to meet him on the other side of the bar. "Come here." He pulls me over, wrapping his arms around me. "I love you." He kisses my head and lets out a long sigh. "More than anything."

"I love you too," I whisper.

Back at my apartment, I snuggle further under my blanket on the couch. Cole is next to me while we watch *Zero Dark Thirty*. I ask a few questions about how real certain parts are. Kind of neat asking someone who really knows the truth. "Are you upset you're not there?" I ask guiltily.

He shifts from behind me. "A little, yes. I get a high from the hunt." His hand slides over my stomach. "But I'd be craving to be right here the whole time, and that would endanger the team." My hand covers his. "I know you're scared, baby, and we have some things that need to be dealt with before we can move forward, but we'll do it together, all right?"

I turn, loving his words. I reach up and run my fingers over his stubble. "All right."

"All right?" he asks, as if he'd been waiting for a fight. I nod with a smile.

"I won't lie, I am scared, but if I know I have you with me, then I'll be all right."

He leans down, capturing my lips and giving me one hell of a kiss. I have to push him away when my phone goes off and won't stop ringing.

"Hello?"

"Hey, honey." I mouth 'it's your mother' to Cole. He nods and looks back at the movie. "Sorry for calling so late. I was wondering if you are you free tomorrow. I was hoping we could all have dinner at the house. What with you working then having the flu, I thought that now since you're feeling better we could all get together."

"Sure, I'd love that. I could trade shifts with someone. I could do the morning instead—"

"Actually…" She pauses, then there's a strange noise.

"You have the night off, Savi," Zack says into the phone. "Go spend time with your family." I laugh and glance up at Cole, who looks at me funny.

"Thanks, Zack, I appreciate it."

"Sure thing."

"Hope that was all right?" Sue asks, feeling me out. "Daniel and I just ran into him."

I smile. "Of course. I'm looking forward to tomorrow."

"Wonderful, me too. Either Mike or I will come pick you up whenever you're ready."

"Okay, thanks. Bye, Sue."

I slide my phone on the table and snuggle back into my warm spot. My apartment can be so cold sometimes. Cole's hand immediately lands on my belly. I sigh, thinking how lovely it feels.

"What did my mother want?"

I tuck the edges of the blanket around me tighter, feeling a draft from somewhere. "She wants to have a family dinner tomorrow night. She even got me out of work tomorrow."

"Mmmm, you back at the house?" He nuzzles my hair, breathing in. "I love my mother even more right now."

I tip my head back and look into his dark eyes. His smile reaches the corners, making them crease along the edges. His stubble is the perfect length, and my fingers twitch as I reach up to steal a quick feel. He leans in, kissing my hand. He shifts so we're lying down, his body flat along the back cushions, with me staring up at him. His hand sneaks up my shirt and runs along my side.

"Hard to believe there's a little something inside this tiny belly of yours." He stares at my stomach, fascinated. "Did you get to see Sim when you had your appointment?"

"I'm sorry, what?" I laugh. "Sim?"

"Yes, she and him, therefore, 'Sim,'" he says, deadpan, circling my belly button with his finger. I hiccup, trying to contain my giggle fit. "Hey, now, stop. You're going to make Sim sick with all that shaking."

"Oh, Cole." I full out laugh and bring up my legs to stop the hurt. "Stop, I can't breathe." I roll onto my side and take slow breaths.

"Finished?" He pokes at me. "Well?"

I roll back over, and he resumes his circles. "No, I haven't. I've just had the urine test so far. I have an appointment in a week."

"First, *we* have an appointment. And how do they know? You may not be."

"Oh, trust me, baby, that stick had two neon strips that could light these mountains right up."

He grins, making me confused. "You called me 'baby.'"

"Is that bad?"

"No, I liked it."

"Baby," I joke, biting my lip playfully.

He swoops down and nips at my lip, freeing it momentarily before he draws it into his mouth and sucks softly. He pulls back, eyes dark as night, and checks the time on the phone. "What if I called Dr. Brown tomorrow and ask her to do an ultrasound?"

"You can't just call—" The look on his face tells me otherwise. "If you can make it happen, Sim and I are on board."

His face breaks out in his 'she gave in without a fight' smile. I yawn, turning into his chest, and he pulls the covers over us and holds me close.

"What do you think we're having?" I ask, as sleep begins to creep over me. Cole tucks me under his chin.

"Girl," he says in a matter of fact tone. "The world really needs two of you."

My heart swells to the point of pain. I move to give him a kiss on his chest. This man has made me feel more love in just a few months than I've ever felt from another man in my whole life.

***

Cole looks completely at ease in the sea of pregnant

women. He worked his magic and got us an early afternoon appointment at the hospital with Dr. Brown. How he did it is beyond me, but I don't care. I just want to see our little baby.

"Here," Cole pulls out a bottle of water from my bag, "you should drink this."

"I'm all right," I say, scanning a magazine on breast feeding verses formula. He takes off the cap and nudges it in my hand.

"You need to drink more water. You should be on your second one of these by now."

I chuckle and take the water and finish off the bottle. "Someone's been doing their homework," I tease, loving that he has been.

His hand falls on my thigh and gives it a light pat. "I want to know everything so I can take care of you two."

"Ms. Miller," the nurse calls out, glancing around the room. Cole mumbles something as he takes my hand and leads me into the hallway.

"Hi, Savannah, my name is Tracy. I'll be helping you today. First, I need you to give a urine sample, then you can meet me and…" She looks at Cole.

"Cole, the father." Cole rubs my belly from behind.

"We'll meet you in room four, okay?"

After I fill my cup, then get my blood pressure and weight taken, I find the door to the room where Dr. Brown is already waiting and deep in conversation with Cole, who is firing questions.

Of course, I smirk. He's so cute.

"Hello again, Savannah," she says as Cole pulls out a chair for me. "You look a lot better than the last time I saw you."

I shift, remembering how sick I was then. "Yes, the pills are helping a lot."

"All right, so let's get you undressed from the waist down and see how the little one looks."

Cole nearly doubles over when he sees the probe that's about a foot long slide inside of me. He's three shades of white until the little pulsing ring appears on the ultrasound machine. He suddenly grabs my hand and holds it tightly, but his eyes stay stuck to the screen.

"Strong heartbeat," Dr. Brown says, clicking a few buttons, "and I would say you are right around eight weeks, a little further along than I thought. Which will make your due date about early August. Congratulations, you two, you have a healthy looking baby. Let's keep it that way."

"You gave the doc a run for her degree," I joke in the car after our appointment, digging in a bag of trail mix to steal the chocolate chips before he notices. He scoops his free hand in, pouring a handful into his mouth while keeping his eyes on the windy road.

"I had questions," he says with a shrug. "And I don't wanna see you with a cup of coffee."

"Cole, she said a small cup is fine." I roll my eyes. These next seven months are going to be interesting.

"You need to eat more meat too." He gives me a sideways glance. "She said your iron is low, and that's one of the reasons why you're so tired."

"Cole—"

"Speaking of being tired, you should think of cutting back your shifts—"

I snap the lid on the trail mix and toss it down by my feet. "Please don't start, Cole. I love my job."

He sighs. Running a hand through his hair, he reaches for my hand and brings it to his mouth, kissing the back of it. "Sorry, I'm trying really, *really* hard not to let my controlling side take over. But when you toss in our baby, it's even more of a struggle. I just want you to get as much rest as possible, and this pregnancy to go smoothly."

"Look, I'll make you a deal. When I feel work is too

much for me, I'll stop."

"No offense, baby, but you're incredibly stubborn." I see him fight a smile, and he uses my hand to hide it.

I want to be truthful, for him to see I'm taking all this seriously. "I learned my lesson the first time, Cole." His smile fades. "I promise when it gets too much, I'll tell you."

"All right, but if I see you're fading, I *will* say something." He rolls his window down to speak with the guard at the gate.

***

The baked apple smell hits my nose when we walk in, and my stomach forgets all about the snack on the way up. I grin when I see June's green scarf hung over top of her black pea coat, and Abigail's boots next to one of Scoot's many beds. Keith's snow pants and mitts are by the door. Everything is as it should be, just as normal should be. I close my eyes, savoring the comfort that is this house. *It's perfect.*

"You coming?" Cole asks. I hold up a finger, asking for one more moment. "You all right?"

I open my eyes, seeing his puzzled expression. "I'm just thinking."

"About?" he asks, taking my hand in his.

"Things." I lean up to kiss his cheek. "Happy things."

"Hi, honey!" Sue beams with delight as we round the corner and see everyone in the living room enjoying some afternoon drinks before dinner. She stops in front of me, studying me for a moment, then leans in and gives me a hug. "Are you feeling better?"

"I am, thanks." I hug Daniel after he comes up behind her.

"See, nothing to it!" Mark hands me a martini with a wink. "Thought you could use this, just until you're ready to tell."

"Does this mean…?" I look at Cole, who grins.

Mark tosses his hand in the air in excitement. "Yes, as of six fifteen this morning, Jose Jorge is on U.S. soil, behind bars, with a shit load of charges against him. He'll be spending his next three lives as someone's prison bitch."

"Well, that's something to celebrate!" I cheer ecstatically.

"We have lots to celebrate," he says over his shoulder, heading for the kitchen.

Cole keeps me close to his side. Every so often his hand slips over my belly, letting me know he's thinking about little Sim.

"Hey, guys." Keith joins us, checking his phone. "I hate to ask this, but can I steal Logan for a moment?"

Cole leans in to give me a quick kiss. "I'll be back." I nod and watch the two hurry off to his office.

I mingle with everyone, sipping my water. Davie and Dell are telling a story from a few nights ago when they were in town at Chaps. I pretend to listen, but I'm more interested in where Mark is hurrying off to. I scan the crowd and see Daniel is gone too.

Where the hell is everyone? Oh no…is something happening? My father?

"Savannah?" Mike calls from the entryway. I whirl around. "Can I steal you for a moment?" A strange feeling creeps over me as I sit my drink down and hurry over to him. "Let's take a walk." He waits as I get ready, growing more nervous with every moment.

He opens the door to let me go first. It's dark and the temperature has dropped, so I wrap my scarf around my neck and wait for him to lead the way.

"How have you been?" He guides me across the driveway toward the woods.

"Cut the crap, Mike. You didn't ask me out here to

see how I'm doing."

He smiles and shakes his head. "Yeah, you're right." His face changes, softening a little. He points to a glow in the woods. "Follow the light, Savannah." He nods for me to head in that direction.

Puzzled, I start to walk. After several steps I hear Mike whisper something. I turn and look back, but he's walking away from me. What's going on?

I stop at the tree line and take in all the glass lanterns marking the pathway. Drawn by their light into the woods, I follow them, thinking how strange it is I'm not with anyone. I take comfort in knowing someone will be watching me. The further along I go, and the more I see the lanterns ahead. They are so pretty. Their warm twinkle leads me deeper into the woods, and the soft snow falling from the trees is soothing. Flames flicker with the tiny breeze, making the forest look magical. If I were to write a fairytale, it would be just like this. Heavy snow weighing down the branches, little hues of light with a glow just bright enough to look warm, an untouched forest just waiting to spill its secrets. The only thing missing is…I turn a bend to a clearing and see him…*oh!*

Chapter Nine

Cole stands by an open fire, and the orange glow makes it easy to see his smile when his eyes lock onto mine. Dozens of candles are nestled into the snow banks, creating a magical scene. He holds out his hand as I get closer.

"Hi." I grin, loving how just one look from this man makes my insides melt. "It's so beautiful, Cole. What's going on?"

He looks down at me. "Do you remember what happened here a few months ago?"

"Of course, it's where we said we loved each other," I say, thinking I might have figured out what's happening.

"Savannah, I've been in love with you from the first moment I saw your picture. It just took me a while to realize what that feeling was." His free hand runs down my temple. "Your eyes are so beautiful, it's as if someone removed a star and made you from all its beauty." My breath catches as my eyes water. "There has never been anyone I've ever wanted more in my life until I met you. You've opened my eyes, made me see that my life at the house doesn't mean I can't fall in love and be happy." His hand moves to my belly. "Baby or no baby, you've always been mine." He bends down on

638

one knee, pulling out a light blue box. "Savannah Miller, I swear under a thousand stars that I love you, and will fight to the end to make you happy." He kisses my left hand. "Will you marry me?" He slowly opens the box, revealing a sparkling princess cut diamond.

"Yes! Yes!" I cry, laughing, as my heart pounds a tattoo inside my chest. He slips it on my finger, then jumps up, lifting me off the ground spinning me around.

"I love you," he sighs, pressing me tightly against his chest, his voice muffled by my hair. He pulls back, looking down at me. His eyes are glossy, making mine water even more.

"I love you too, Cole." I take in my surroundings and see all he did to make this moment perfect. "I can't believe you did this."

"I'd do anything for you." He steps up, grabbing my face and kissing me with such passion it takes my breath away.

"Well?" Mark's voice chirps out of Cole's pocket. I laugh at how normal it is that he'd have a radio in his pocket.

"Raven One to Raven Two," Cole winks, "she said yes."

The roar that erupts from the house can be heard all the way up to where we are standing.

"You ready to tell the family about our baby?" He holds my hand as we walk along the snowy path down to the house.

I take a deep, slow breath through my nose, drawing the scent of the forest in deeply, letting this amazing feeling rush through me and around me. "I am. I can't wait."

Everyone hugs, kisses, and cheers when we return to the house. It isn't until dinner is finished and Mark digs into the dessert that Cole stands, taking my hand and helping me out of my seat.

"Can I have everyone's attention, please?" Cole clears his throat, and the noise dies down. "First, I want to say thank you to everyone who made my proposal happen. Second, Savannah and I have something we'd like to share with you." He waits for me to say it, but I can't. I'm next to tears with happiness. So Cole slips his hand over my belly, and everyone's eyes drop.

"Oh my goodness," Sue says, grabbing onto Daniel, who is already tearing up. "Really?"

"Really," I choke out. "Just over eight weeks."

Mark turns to Keith. "You still owe me, dude."

The whole table starts to laugh, and anyone's thoughts about the tension around the last time I was pregnant quickly fades, and Abigail and June attack me with hugs, saying they can't wait for their little fritter.

Sue finds me after dinner. Dabbing her red eyes, she takes my hand and leads me over to the stairs away from everyone. She tucks my hair behind my ear. Now I know where her son gets it. "Thank you," she sniffs, struggling to hold herself together. "Thank you for coming into our lives, for loving us the way you do, and for making my son and the rest of us incredibly happy." She loses her grip and starts to cry as I reach for her hand, giving her a little squeeze. She takes a moment, getting a grip on herself. "I can't believe you're pregnant again."

I press my lips together, trying to hold myself together too. "I know. I'll be okay, Sue. Things are different this time around."

"I know, honey." She hugs me and wipes her cheeks. She walks me back into the living room, where Daniel wraps an arm around me, kissing my head.

"What's going on?" I ask, seeing Mark standing in front of a whiteboard he brought up from the office downstairs.

"Okay!" Mark calls, writing out the guys' names. "Who wants the first week in August?"

"I want the eleventh!" I announce, and Mark points his marker at me.

"Yes! Now we're talking. The baby mamma is on board!" He scribbles my name down. "What about the father?"

"The fourteenth," Cole calls out from behind me, wrapping his arms around my mid-section, "and I bet it's a girl."

"Ohhhh, this just got interesting!" Mark shouts. "Who's next?"

***

My fingers drum on the bar top. My phone is burning a hole in my pocket. It's been three and half months since Cole proposed to me, and two weeks since he left on his trip to Mexico. The trip is running smoothly. They've been gathering information on a client who's gone missing for the second time in the past three years. Washington has been using all their manpower trying to locate the man. They're not allowed to tell me who it is, and I'm not sure I want to know. However, it's been over five days since they were scheduled to return. I should know better than to worry, as they've been checking in twice a day, but something feels off.

I rub my stomach as Jake places my dinner in front of me. We didn't get a chance to eat this evening, as it was so busy, and we're both starving. We decide to eat at the bar since the evening is now slowing down.

The burger is delicious. I love how our cook knows about my love for mushrooms, as I've got lots piled under the bun. I load up part of my plate with mustard and ketchup, swirling it around to make the perfect combination. This baby likes some odd things.

"That's disgusting." Jake nearly gags on a fry.

I shrug and dip the mushroom burger into the blend,

then biting off too big of a piece. "So good." I roll my eyes back, loving the tangy taste.

"Oh sweet Lord, that's..." Jake chucks his burger down on his plate, wiping his fingers clean. "I don't think we should eat together anymore." I laugh with a mouth full of food. "You're such a vision right now, Savi."

"Thanks." I down a glass of water to push the meat down faster. This baby is hungry!

Someone sits down, but I can't make out who it is, nor do I care. The burger is all I can focus on right now. Jake hands his plate to a server before he heads over to the customer.

"Hey, what can I get you tonight?"

"Actually, I need to see her." The voice makes me ill. His being here only means two things. He stands in front of me, while Jake comes to my side. "Could we have a moment alone, son?" He nods at Jake, who doesn't move.

"Jake stays." I push my plate away despite my stomach's protest. "What are you doing here, Frank?"

Frank shakes his head, not liking the extra set of ears, but he treads carefully. "I need you to come to Washington tomorrow. Lynn's case is up, and we need your testimony."

"And if I say no?" I counter, handing Gabe my plate as he stops to see who our guest is. "I'm not supposed to be put in stressful situations. If I got a doctor's note, would that help?"

Frank rubs his head. "Believe me, Savannah, I've tried to move mountains to get you out of this, but the court will subpoena you. You can either do it now, or later after the baby is born. My advice is get it over with now, so when that little tot comes, you can start fresh with all this behind you."

I pull out my phone and check for a possible missed

call. "Does Cole know?" I want to cry out 'but he *promised,*' but I know I'm stronger than that. Frank shakes his head. I drop onto the lower counter, suddenly exhausted. "Who will be coming with me?"

"Who do you want?"

I want Keith, but he's out with the team. "Mike?"

His face shows me he'd prefer Mike to stay running the house. "What about Sue?"

"Really?" I'm surprised by this.

"All right, I'll call Sue and let her know you agree." Frank stands, zipping his coat up. "Tomorrow, oh nine hundred hours, plan to be away for four days. And, Savannah, please don't run off this time." His eyes are not smiling.

I don't say anything; my nerves are already crawling to the surface.

Later that night as I crawl into my bed on the couch, I stare up at the ceiling and wonder what my father is doing right now. Is he with Lynn? Or is he staying away from her so as not to draw attention to their sick relationship? How on earth did I not know that the two of them were screwing behind my back? Am I that flipping naive? I let the events of the past run through my mind. I've been trying too hard to put this behind me, but it's not finished. I know it needs to be played out so I can be done with it once and for all. It doesn't make it any easier. I flop to the side, staring blankly at the TV that's playing the mini-series, The Hatfields and McCoys, on mute. The old movie makes so much sense. It's so cut and dry; you just take a gun and end the problem. Although if that were the case, I'd be dead long ago.

I chuck the blankets off and head to the bathroom for the fifth pee in the past thirty minutes. I haul my shirt up and look at my tummy in the mirror. I'm five and a half months and have a nice round bump forming. I think about how these last few months have gone. Cole has been wonderful, but his over-protectiveness is growing right along with the baby. It nearly killed him having to leave on this trip. I know he's been traveling a lot more lately to tie up as many cases as possible before little Sim comes.

The sound of the latch being unlocked on my door sends me to the living room, pressed against the wall in the shadow across from the door. My heart is pounding, but I know there are only three people who have a key. Jake, Keith, and Cole. A bag is tossed in first, followed by heavy footsteps. My fists clench as the dark figure is revealed, slumped with exhaustion, but the moment he spots me, his face lights up.

"I didn't mean to scare you." Cole closes the door behind him.

"It's okay," I whisper, staying where I am. He looks sexy in his army pants and jacket. His navy blue sweater peeks out the top of his scarf, making his eyes darker than normal, or he's just as excited to see me as I am him. He kicks off his boots and sheds his jacket.

"Come here," he commands with a dirty little twinkle in his eye. I step out from the wall and walk slowly toward him. His eyes drop to my favorite shirt. "Damn, baby, I love you in my clothes." His reaches out, touching my belly. "How's my little one behaving?"

"The little mite has an appetite." I place my hand over his. "Can't seem to get enough food."

"Can I get you anything?"

"Yes, but not food." I step back, pulling his shirt over my head and tossing it to the couch. He runs his hand over his five o'clock shadow while he thinks about his next move. "Do you normally hesitate this much when you're in the field, Colonel?" I smirk, waiting for him to strike.

He smirks back at me. "This is different. I want to

toss you up against the wall and hold you still while I work out the last two weeks of frustration on that tight little hole of yours, but," my chest falls heavily as my legs clench together, "I don't want to hurt you."

I roll my eyes as my sexual drive takes over. "Fine, I can find other ways that don't involve an over-protective fiancée. I have a showerhead with a multitude of settings." I turn on my heel but don't get three feet before he's behind me, bending me carefully over the kitchen table.

"Can your showerhead make you scream?" I hear his zipper, and his pants drop. I smile into the table, needing this so badly it hurts. His fingers explore how turned on I am, and they push in easily, pulling a moan from my chest. He bends his body over mine, kissing his way up my spine. "Spread your legs, baby." I do, and feel him brush my lust. He doesn't remove his fingers; he twists them around as I flex tightly onto him. "I needed you so badly I came right from North Dakota." His fingers slide out of me, and in slips his erection. "Oh god," he hisses. Starting a gentle flick of the hips, he rotates side to side, moving in all directions, raising my desire, my need, escalating my lust. His hands slide from my hips up to my shoulders. Once he has a firm grip, he presses me back into him. I scream his name, followed by a silent curse. "Don't ever question my need for you, Savannah." He grunts between each gentle but firm thrust. "I could snap you in two with the feelings that come over me when you're near." He pulls me up so I'm flat against his chest. His hands massage my breasts as he nips my neck. "Now I want you to come for me." His voice is a soft growl. "I need to feel you come, feel how much you missed me." He gently pushes me back over the table, lifts one of my legs so it's bent, and starts slowly thrusting hard and deep. His uncharacteristically measured, firm movements send me higher.

I claw, scream, and bite down as an orgasm rips through me. I can't see and can barely hear as I come back to myself. Cole carries my limp body to the bed, pulling the covers up.

"I need a shower." He kisses me roughly and disappears into the hallway.

His lazy smile remains imprinted on my brain as I drift off to a deep sleep.

***

Cole

Cole wraps the towel around his mid-section and peeks in on Savannah, who's passed out in the middle of the bed, her belly peeking out of the side of the blanket.

Her fridge is nearly empty, and her cabinets are pretty bare. What the hell has she been living on? Then he finds her stash. He grabs a spoon, and leaning against the counter, he scoops a huge ball of peanut butter into his mouth as his phone goes off in his coat pocket. He lunges for it, pressing the button before it can wake Savannah.

Frank: You made it there all right?

Cole: Yes, thanks for the heads up, Frank. I'll see you in Washington.

He thinks for a moment, then types.

Cole: What has she been eating these past two weeks?

Not even a moment later, he feels a vibration.

Jake: You don't even wanna know.

Cole: Try me.

Jake: You asked. Mustard-ketchup combo, mustard and potato chips, ketchup and potato chips. Oh! And her favorite right now is mustard, chips, and pickles all combined together. Your baby likes some f'd up foods, dude. I'm actually gagging right now.

Cole: Thanks for the visual. Appreciate it.

He changes quickly and heads outside.

***

"Savi," Cole whispers in her ear, but she doesn't move. "Baby, you need to get up." He kisses her cheek. "I have something you might like," he whispers, but still nothing. "I went to the market and got pickles and mustard." One of her eyes opens, and he grins. "I got all kinds of nasty food for you and Fritter."

"So we're back to Fritter?"

"Yes, it sounds cuter." She gives him an adorable smile. "Now, get up. There's a pile of pickles with your name on it."

"Really? Are you playing me?" She raises an eyebrow.

"No, I promise."

"How?"

"Jake." He squeezes her tight little bottom, enjoying the resulting moan.

"God, love a bestie who never sleeps." She stretches and rolls over, letting the sheet fall behind her. Her hand runs along her bare leg and up her side while she stares at him through those long lashes.

He tosses her a shirt. "As much as I want to roll around with you in this bed all day, you have a flight to catch in," he looks at her clock, "two hours."

Her face drops and she pulls the covers over her body again, not hiding from him, but from the idea of what's to come. He climbs in next to her, tucking her into his side.

"I know you're scared, but I'll be there with you every step of the way." She nods then slides off the bed, grabbing her robe and heading for the shower. She stops at the last minute, her hand holding onto the doorframe for a beat, before she turns to look over her shoulder.

"I love you, Cole." She leaves before he can say anything.

***

On the drive to the airport and through the flight, Savannah is very quiet. Her fingers flip the pages to her book, *The Beach House* by James Patterson, but she's yet to open it. Cole understands her need for quiet and just keeps a firm grip on her thigh to comfort her. When they touch down in Washington, Frank is there to greet them at the gate, and he drives them directly to the base.

Frank's glance flickers to Savi's in the rear view mirror. "We're going to be briefing you on the case so you're up to speed on everything." He clears his throat when she doesn't respond, continuing to watch the countryside fly by. Cole reaches for her hand, but she doesn't turn. She tilts her head and traces a fallen raindrop on the glass. "So," Frank moves on, "after that, we'll have dinner and—"

"I want to speak to Lynn," she says softly, cutting him off. Cole feels the hairs on his neck raise. "Alone."

Frank's eyes jump to his. "Savannah, that's not something I can—"

"If you want me to testify," she turns for the first time to look directly at Frank, "you'll make it happen."

"Savannah…" Cole lowers his voice.

"Cole," she counters, and he realizes she's in a feisty mood right now. He reluctantly bites his tongue, pressing his back into the cool leather seat. She is closing herself off from them, he knows. She's most likely experiencing all the anger and hurt she has after so many years of loving this woman like a sister. He feels sick putting himself in her shoes. If Mark ever betrayed him like that, he'd be broken by it too. His hand finds its way to their baby, surprising hers, which is already there. He covers her hand, and she uses the other to wipe a tear. His body twitches to comfort her, but he knows she's on the brink of losing it.

Chapter Ten

Savannah

I feel like stone by the time I sit in an old chair with metal armrests across the table from four tired-looking lawyers. An older style clock ticks directly above the door, and my heart times its beat to its rhythm. Rain pelts at murky windows that look like they haven't been replaced since the early sixties. My nose tries to push the musty smell away, but it doesn't work, and it makes my stomach roll even more. My attention is pulled to one of the male lawyers. My gaze drops to a coffee stain on his tie, and I silently describe his appearance to try to help ground myself. He looks just like the man with the red stapler in the Office Space movie. I can tell he's hungry, as he keeps eyeing his partner's Snickers bar.

"Miss Miller," Morgan, the lead lawyer, says, pulling my attention to the present. She fusses with the paperwork in front of her. I remember this woman from the last time I was here. She's a perfectionist, and I want to lean over and mess up her meticulously lined up files and her pen sitting parallel. "I need you to understand that we can't have a repeat of what happened the last time you were in the court." She peers disapprovingly over the ridge of her glasses. My tongue presses to the roof of my mouth, trying like hell not to lash out at her. I hear Cole shift his body. I'm so tuned in to him, I know he wants to say something, but he won't...yet. "I understand it was hard for you, but—"

"Don't," I hiss in a small voice, but it's enough to shut her up for a moment.

"Miss Miller, if you want this testimony to count, you need to keep yourself calm. The judge will not tolerate an outburst. All it shows to the jury is that you're a loose cannon.'"

"Is that why he got a double life sentence with no chance of parole?" I ask, cocking my head to the side. "Seems to me my outburst *and* the evidence proved to the jury that Denton is a monster, and he got what he deserved, so let's try this again, Miss Morgan." Her thumb starts clicking the top of her expensive pen. "I want five minutes alone with Lynn, before I testify against her tomorrow."

"That's not possible," she states.

I stand and grab my bag. Cole jumps to his feet. I expect him to try and stop me, but he doesn't.

"Wait," Morgan calls out, rubbing her head, "just sit for a moment."

I see Cole's mouth turn up, but when he turns around he's straight-faced again. God, he's good.

"It will take some time." One of the other lawyers starts to argue, but she raises her bitchy hand, and he backs off.

"Morgan," the lawyer closest to Cole says, "they'll never go for it."

"Humphrey, when I want your input, I'll ask for it," Morgan snaps, rubbing her head harder. Humphrey flushes up his neck. *Poor guy.*

"Look," she closes her eyes, "give me an hour, and I'll see what I can do."

"Fine." I start to turn, but stop and lean back over the

table, snatching the Snickers bar and placing it in front of her. "Just saying."

I see Humphrey cover his mouth, clearly getting my joke about the commercial. *'You're not yourself when you're hungry.'* Cole reaches for my arm and nearly pulls me out of the room. Once the door is closed, he bursts out laughing.

"I can't believe you did that," he croaks out. "Oh god, I wish Mark was here. He would have loved that." I smile, wishing he was too. His comic relief would be welcome right now. "Come on, let's get something to eat."

Two hours later, Humphrey is sent to find us in the cafeteria. He tells me after pulling in many favors, the judge still will not allow it, as Lynn has been violent since she's been in jail. I'm disappointed, but I get over it. I'll see her tomorrow, and I'll get to say my piece then, with or without the judge's help.

We head back up to that horrible room and spend the next several hours getting briefed. I must say Morgan is a little nicer this time around. Guess the Snickers bar worked.

The briefing lasts till evening, and we go down to the restaurant.

I stay lost in my thoughts throughout dinner. The guys try to engage me, but I am off in childhood memories with Lynn.

"Merry Christmas, Lynnie." I hold out a little white box and grin.

She snatches it out of my hand, ripping the bow in two. "Aww." She pulls out a chain with a half of a jagged heart dangling from the center. Lynn loves hearts.

"See?" I pull the other half out from under my shirt. "Not just friends—"

"But sisters too," she finishes, admiring the necklace

in the mirror. "Love you, Savi."

"Love you too, Lynnie."

I keep trying to pinpoint the spot when she turned on me. It's a deep ache that burns in my stomach when I think about her. How can someone imprint so strongly on your life one moment, and the next hire someone to kill you? I feel like I'm in a movie. Did our time together mean nothing to her? Surely there's got to be a time when she loved me like the sister I felt she was, the way I did her.

I can't eat, and I don't touch my water. I'm so lost I hardly feel Cole help me out of my chair and walk us upstairs to our hotel room. He lets me know he and Frank have some more to discuss, so he'll be in the other room, and suggests I take a bath.

"Then get some sleep, baby." He leans in, kissing my lips and giving my belly a rub. I nod, sitting on the couch staring at a black screen that stares back at me.

***

"Do you solemnly affirm that you will tell the truth, the whole truth, and nothing but the truth?" The clerk stares with piercing gray eyes, and a chill runs up my spine.

"I do," I say weakly, feeling my voice run like hell in the opposite direction. I felt more confident when I testified against Denton, but Lynn…I sit a little straighter and glance at the jury. Nine men, three women, one wearing a horrendous cat sweater she must have made herself, because no one in their right mind would try and market it.

Cole catches my eye and gives me a little wink, letting me know he's only fifteen steps away. I nod, swallow hard, and try to keep myself together. Cole's words repeat over and over in my head. "Just one more day, baby, then we can go home and put all this behind us." A door opens and a light roar of whispers erupts. I keep my eyes locked on Cole's, suddenly terrified to look over and face my reality. He mouths, "I love you." I barely nod and tune in to the judge, who is handing the floor over to Lynn's lawyer.

I'm shaking. I'm not ready. I'm so scared.

I force my eyes over to face my once best friend, my sister, and now my enemy who might get life…if she's lucky.

Lynn's face is paler than normal, and she's dressed to play the part of the young, innocent woman. She's wearing a cream colored skirt that hits right above the knee, white blouse, and a baby pink sweater, something Lynn would *never* wear. Hell, even her hair is down and pinned straight, and she hates her hair that way. I don't fall for it, of course. I know her, and I see it's still her in there. I do recognize her body language, right down to how she shifts in that cotton blouse. She hates cotton; Lynn always wears silk. Seeing her obvious attempt to hide her real self lights a small spark deep inside me. Though I do see her wrist is in a brace, and there's some dark color around an eye. I guess she has been fighting.

Her head lifts up and her eyes lock onto mine. A series of emotions run through me, but suddenly the strongest is pity. Not the kind of pity where I wish she weren't sitting there waiting for her fate to be determined, but the kind where I know she'll never have a life to call her own. *Karma.*

I think she misreads my look and gives me a tiny smile and mouths, "Hi, honey."

I sink my teeth into my cheek to the point of pain, but I let go when the lawyer clears his throat.

"Shall I repeat my question?"

I nod and give him my attention. "How long have you and Lynn been friends?"

"Since..." I cough, begging my voice to return. "Since we were tiny."

"Would you say she's like a sister?" My lawyer interrupts, but the judge waves him off.

"Yes."

"You two did everything together?"

"Yes."

"Family trips?"

"Yes." I shrug.

"Family dinners—"

His voice trails off into nothing when my mind recalls one particular family dinner. I'm sucked into a flashback and the courtroom fades...

...to my father's penthouse, where I'm showing up early because traffic was light, as so many people are out of the city for Thanksgiving. I open the door to see the place looks empty, but the smell of turkey makes my stomach jump to attention. Chucking my purse down next to another one, at the time I don't notice, but now I see it's hers. The cook is busy in the kitchen, so I leave him be.

"Dad?" I call out, removing my shoes from my aching feet. "You here yet?"

I scramble up the twisty stairs to the second floor, and come face to face with my flushed father. "Hey, Dad." I grin, but it fades when I see the panicked look on his face. "Everything all right?"

He pulls my arm and pushes me in front of him, hurrying me down the stairs toward the front door. "Can we re-schedule, dear? Something has come up. I'm sorry, but it can't be helped."

"What?" I pull my arm free, only to have him snatch it up again. "But it's Thanksgiving. What about dinner?"

"Savannah, you're twenty-two years old. Don't you think it's about time you find someone else to spend it

with?"

My face snaps back. "Wow! You know, some fathers would kill to have their daughter spend special occasions with them."

He opens the door and shoves my purse in my hands. "I'll call you later." And with that, the door is slammed in my face.

"What the hell was that?" I curse, pulling out my phone as I hurry to the elevator. Once I'm outside, I call Lynn, planning to warn her not to head to Dad's, since he's being an ass again. It goes straight to voice mail. I try again, knowing she'll pick up if I call right after.

"Hello?" Lynn's muffled voice comes over the line.

"Hey, Lynn. Shit, Dad's in another damn mood, so I'd suggest—" "Shhh, it's Savi," I hear her whisper to someone.

I grin. "Lynn, you're not alone? Where are you?"

"I-I'm at home. I-I was just about to leave, so I'm glad you called." I plug one ear as a firetruck goes by.

"Shit, Savi, ahh...my landlady is here again, so you know what that means."

"Yeah, have fun with that."

The vision fades away, and I'm back in the courtroom. The lawyer is prattling on about something, but I ignore him. I look back over at Lynn. The room feels as if the air is slowly being sucked out through a straw, causing my lungs to shrivel up and turn to dust. I realize what an idiot I was not noticing her purse, and now realizing I could hear that firetruck through her phone in the distance.

"You bitch," I snarl at her. She tilts her head, trying to understand where I'm coming from.

"What was that, Miss Miller?" her lawyer asks, raising a thick eyebrow at me.

"Yes, Lynn attended almost all family events, even some she and my father made up together." I watch her face fall and the color drain from it.

"How close would you say she was with your father?"

I shake my head while staring at her. She looks panicky, and I realize this is something that hasn't come out yet. "Is sleeping with my father at twenty-two close enough?" Her face lowers forward into her hands, drawing the jurors' attention to her. The courtroom suddenly grows loud, and the judge bangs his gavel repeatedly. Once the room settles, the lawyer starts in on me again but never touches on that topic.

***

I've been in the witness seat now for an hour and a half, and I'm growing tired. I know I'm stressed, because I think I'm getting small Braxton Hicks contractions. Dr. Brown warned me this could happen, so I'm not too concerned. Our lawyer has asked for a recess, seeing my discomfort, but I refused. I just want this to be finished. When I walk out those doors, I'm not coming back in.

Cole is watching me like a hawk. I can see he's worried; he keeps rubbing his face and twitching. I try to nod and let him know I'm fine, but really I'm growing more and more finished with rehashing my life to complete strangers who are judging my every word.

"Miss Miller," the lawyer mutters, heading back to his table and making a dramatic effect as he thinks, "do you love your father?" I start to answer, but he cuts me off.

"Remember, you are under oath."

I think about my words to be sure they're the right ones. "Yes, I love my father, but when he got into politics…"

"So now you don't?" he snaps quickly

"Would you?" I snap back, hurt.

"I'm not on the witness stand." I swear he smirks momentarily.

"My father doesn't want me, and I don't want him. It's simple, and I've come to terms with it." I rub my aching tummy.

He nods, pacing in front of me. "So you get 'rescued,' stay in a safe house, fall in love, get pregnant, all in a very short time? No offense, Miss Miller, but that doesn't make you look like you're a grieving victim." I lock my jaw, but my tongue is battling to be let loose. "What I see," he turns to address the jurors, "is a rich, bored little girl who hatched this plan and didn't care who she took down. Should we be looking into the Colonel to see if he was involved too?" I know he's trying to get me to break and let fly at him. I won't lie, I'm frigging close. I grab my stomach and blink wildly. "Just tell me why. Why hatch such a lie to take down everyone in your family, and especially this woman who was like a sister to you?" I run my sweaty hand over my mouth. "What has she ever done to you?"

I need to get out of here.

"Please," I whisper, but he keeps talking. "Please." I heave forward.

"Stop!" Lynn calls out and the whole room stops. "Savi?"

I think I'm going to be sick because she's trying to show concern for me. I shake my head at her. "Don't you dare!" I'm nearly in tears now. "You sat across from me in a room while I was being held hostage and didn't shed a tear for me when I begged you to let me go." I point my finger at her face. "You *sat* across the table from me while my father shot my friend in the face! Don't you dare try to pretend you care now!"

"The jury will disregard that last comment," the judge orders. Every member on that jury is staring at me with concern and interest.

"You screwed your way up the political ladder," I continue firmly but loudly, "and for what, Lynn? A cell block, a roommate, and shitty food?" The judge is yelling, but I don't care, raising my voice louder. "You may have taken my life from me, but I found a hell of a lot better one. You're pathetic. I feel nothing but pity for you!"

"Order! Recess!" The judge bangs his gavel loudly. The clerk helps me up and I hold the bottom of my stomach. Cole rushes to my side, wrapping a protective arm around my waist and yelling at Morgan that I'm done, no more. They got what they needed from me.

Once we round the corner and are away from the rush of people, Cole turns to check me over. His hands are everywhere. "Are you all right? What can I do? Should I call the doctor?" His words are frantic until he sees my face. "Why are you smiling?"

"Just call me a good actor." I shrug.

"You're not hurting?" He looks a little pissed.

"No, I am, but I knew we'd have to break soon, and there's no way I'm going back into that room. So I did what I had to, to make sure I got to tell Lynn what I wanted to say."

"Which was?"

"Which is no matter what, I'm still coming out of this on top." I pull him into me, resting my head on his shoulder. "I didn't mean to scare you, but I needed this to be over."

His hand wraps around my hair and tugs my head backward to look at him. "I couldn't handle sitting there for too much longer anyway." He kisses my lips and takes my hand. "Come on, let's see if we can get an early flight back home."

*****

659

Frank shakes his head at me and smiles. "I guess it could have been worse." He holds the car door open for me. "Thanks for not getting held in contempt this time."

"No problem," I joke, settling into my seat and feeling a mixture of things. I know it will take some time to work things out, but now this chapter can be closed, at least for me.

Cole settles in next to me, placing his warm hand on my leg. Suddenly, my hormones kick in full throttle. I casually slip my hand on his thigh, dipping low and feeling him immediately spring to attention. He shakes his head, laughing under his breath.

"You're killing me, baby." He leans down and gives me a quick kiss, pulling back slightly with his mouth hovering near my lips. "Oh, the things I'd do to you if we were alone."

My body hums with excitement. "Oh, the things I'd let you do to me if we were alone." I bite my bottom lip playfully.

"Frank, get out," he jokes as we pull into traffic. Poor Frank just shakes his head and turns up the radio.

"I love you, Cole," I whisper, nuzzling into his neck and seeking his comfort.

"Is that so?"

I kiss my favorite spot along his jawline. "It is." I doze off, and savor the fact that I'm finished with my part of the court proceedings.

I manage to get a little sleep on the plane as Cole rubs soothing circles over our little Fritter, relaxing my sore muscles as I think about my mother and what she'd think about this entire situation. The only upside to her not being here is she can't be affected by any of this. I only hope she can see I love someone who loves me as much I do him.

I wiggle my fingers, moving the heavy diamond and relishing its feeling and what it represents. Cole lifts my

Mended

hand to his mouth and kisses the ring; he is so tuned to my thoughts.

"Cole?" I turn to look up at him. "I want to go home."

"That's where we're headed." He brushes my hair off my face.

"No," I shake my head, "I want to come home."

His eyes sparkle as his finger traces along my brow, down my cheekbone, and stops at my lips. "Yeah, baby, let's go home." He leans down, sealing his mouth over mine and our words into a promise. I doze off, comforted by the warmth of his hand on my thigh.

The North Dakota airport is quiet. There are very few people around, as it's the middle of the night. I'm not looking forward to the long drive home, but I know I won't have to return to Washington for a very long time. If ever.

As we step outside into the fresh air, my fingers slip on the strap and I drop my bag, tripping over it and nearly falling flat on my face. Cole catches me in time and tugs me close to him. He checks me over, hands everywhere. I bat them away and tell him to stop fussing. I laugh when he starts in harder, clearly making fun of the situation. He suddenly pulls me in for a kiss, chuckling while his tongue plays with mine. A gust of wind whips my hair wildly around my face.

We both freeze as we hear *his* voice.

Chapter Eleven

"Savannah." A chill rips through me, tearing a hole in my armor and turning me into a quivering mass. My senses lock onto the .40 caliber pointed directly at me.

Though his face is shaded by a hat, I see sweat dripping from his brow. A drop lands on his lip then is blown away by his rapid breathing. At first glance, he looks all business. One wouldn't think he'd be carrying a weapon into an airport. I now know his look, and this will end in one of two ways. *Either one, I lose.*

Everything grows quiet, even though chaos whirls on around us. Time seems to stand still. I can only hear the mad beating of my own heart. I should have known better than to think I could ever be truly free. In slow motion, I look to Cole and say a silent goodbye. I want to cry, but I can't seem to find the emotion. It's lost like the rest of my life. "I love you," I mouth.

The gun is steady. He has complete control, and his eyes have never left my face.

Suddenly, Keith and Mark both appear out of nowhere, weapons drawn.

"No," Cole whispers. His grip tightens around my fingers.

The gun lowers to my stomach before he speaks. "The one woman I truly loved, you took from me. You have always been in the way. Enough is enough, Savannah." His bitter words cut through me.

Mark shifts closer to my side, muttering something to Cole, but I can't understand them.

"Dad?" I try to sound in control. I pull my hand out of Cole's death grip. I have no idea what to say, so I go with the first thing that comes to mind. "Can I ask you one thing, please?" I take a shaky step forward. The hot, heavy tears pooling in my eyes blur my vision. I hear the sound of guns shifting in the hands of those who are now surrounding us. "Do you remember the year we went up to northern Canada for Christmas? The year before Mom found out she was sick?" He nods, clearly annoyed by this trip down memory lane. "It was around eight at night when the power went out."

"Six," he corrects me, flipping the gun for me to hurry up.

"The temperature dropped, and we all huddled by the fire, not caring because we had our tree, the heat, and hot chocolate."

He rubs his head and mutters, "What's your point?"

I swallow hard, forcing my emotions back and taking another step closer. Where this bravery is coming from, I don't know. Maybe my mother is here, or maybe I'm just losing it.

"Savannah, stop," Cole warns behind me, but I hear him tell the other men to stand back too.

The gun is closer now. I can smell the steel. "Did you love me then?" I hold his gaze and see a tiny flicker in his eyes. His gun wavers a bit, then he points it directly in my face and pulls the trigger.

No.

Pop! Pop! Pop! I'm blinded and falling hard. The breath is knocked out of me as I'm covered with heavy bodies.

***

I wake to semi-darkness. It takes me a moment to see I'm in Cole's bed, and he's standing in front of the fireplace watching the flames and sipping brandy. He's only in a pair of pajama pants, his bare chest reflecting orange from the fire. He looks so tall and powerful the way his muscles flex, casting shadows. His head presses into his hand gripping the mantel.

I slip out of bed, move behind him, and run my hands along his warm back, feeling him jump then immediately relax. "Hey," I whisper against his skin, giving him a little kiss, "everything all right?"

"No," he mutters, downing the rest of his brandy. He puts the glass on the mantel and turns in one swift movement to face me, holding my head in his hands. His eyes are dark; I can see he's fighting to hold himself together. One hand moves to my hair, entangling his fingers and getting a good grip, while he leans forward and rests his forehead to mine, squeezing his eyes shut. "I can't do this again. I can't have you leave me. I need you, Savannah. I need you to be mine." His words seem painful.

"I am yours," I whisper.

His eyes suddenly pop open.

"Marry me now."

"Now? Cole, it's the middle of the night."

"Then tomorrow." He sounds frantic. "I promise I'll give you a fancy wedding later, just marry me."

I lean forward and press my hands over his chest. "Cole, I love you more than the earth needs the sun, but nothing in my life has ever been in my control. *Ever.* I want to stress about the food, the flowers, and the music, all that ridiculous wedding stuff. Because it will be normal—*my normal*—and I need normal." I walk my fingers up his chest. "Please understand how much I need this, how much I want it."

I can see his internal battle flickering though his eyes. His tongue runs over his bottom lip, the moisture on them catching the flicker of the flames.

"If stressing over food, flowers, and music makes you get your normal, then I'll wait," he says quietly. I'm pleased he hears me, but I can see something is still weighing on him.

I start to say more, but he picks me up, laying me back down on the bed. I think he's going to kiss me, but instead he lies down next to me, resting his head on my chest, his hand on my tummy. We stay like that for a long time, my fingers combing through his dark, silky hair. The only noise is the soothing sound of the fire. Just as I'm about to fall asleep, he speaks in a quiet, raspy voice.

"Tonight did things to me, Savannah." He draws a small square pattern along my belly. "Even though we got him, he did pull the trigger." He clears his throat. "Images flash before my eyes." Blinking away tears, I still can't believe my father pulled a gun on me, let alone actually pulled the trigger. I know why he did it, I know why the gun wasn't loaded. He was too much of a coward to kill himself, so he made others do it. If he had really wanted to kill me, he'd never do it at an airport with so much security around. My father is—was—a selfish, dangerous man who never thought of anyone but himself. "I've always been in control of my life," Cole continues. "Since I've met you, though, I've been tested. I need it to feel right again, so bear with me, because I'm going to be an over-protective husband and father. Give me time to work through these issues, all right?"

I lean down, kissing his hair like he always does mine. "I understand."

He kisses my belly then shifts so he's up on his pillow. "I need to hold you." I roll into him, tucking my head under his neck. I can feel his body battling with itself to work through what he witnessed tonight.

"Cole?"

"Mmm," he answers like he's a million miles away.

"How did my father find us at the airport?"

He waits a beat. "Mark checked with the airline. Looks like he followed us from the courthouse. He was on the same plane."

"How did he get a gun through security?"

Cole shakes his head. "They have footage of him retrieving it from a locker. He paid someone to leave it there. Mark found the man. He's just some lowlife looking to make a quick buck. He's been arrested, and he'll get a little time."

"Oh." I shudder, pushing the thought out of my head. He's gone, and that's all that matters now.

"You're safe now, baby." He pulls me tighter, lowering his voice and lacing it with a dark undertone. "No one will ever hurt you again. I promise you that."

I don't doubt his words, and for once I allow myself to believe I'm going to be okay. I keep quiet after that, falling asleep to the even sounds of his heartbeat.

Chapter Twelve

Cole

Cole tries to hold back a smile. "Steak or chicken?" she asks, holding up both packages. Her tanned belly is peeking out the bottom of her tank top. Her eyes narrow in on him. *Shit*. "Don't even, Cole."

He holds up his hands, but a smile breaks through. She's so damn sweet. Before he can blink, she's tossing a bag of chips at him. He laughs, catching them mid-toss.

"I'm sorry." He heads toward her and snags her around the waist. "You're the prettiest pregnant woman in here." He nuzzles her neck and breathes in her scent. Everything comes alive when that smell hits him, sending messages to the part she owns deep within him, the very middle of his heart.

She flinches suddenly, and his training kicks in. His eyes snap up, quickly tuning in to their surroundings.

"Cole," she whispers, her body stiff as a board. "Ummm."

He pulls back and sees her face growing pale, but her eyes are telling a different story. They are soft and growing excited.

"Cole, my water broke!"

He drops his eyes to the tiny line of water trickling down her leg, pooling by her pink toes. He quickly pulls out his cell phone. "Mark, it's time." She grins when she hears Mark hoot in the phone. Her teeth pull in her bottom lip; she's nervous. "Okay, baby." He takes her hand to help her step around her little puddle. "Let's get you to the car."

"Okay." She rubs her stomach and closes her eyes briefly, no doubt calming herself.

He hooks his arm around her back and under her knees, lifting her into the SUV. She suddenly holds her stomach, squeezing her eyes shut.

"Oh, oww," she cries, taking short breaths.

Cole pulls out his cell, starting the stopwatch. After buckling her in, he runs to the driver's seat and starts the car, turning the fan up to blow cool air on her damp skin.

By the time they reach the hospital, her contractions are ten minutes apart. They get her registered and in a room before Cole allows himself to relax a little, though he'd never let Savannah know he's nervous. Good Lord, what if something goes wrong? He scrubs his hands over his face as he lets out a long, bottom-of-the-lung sigh.

"Twenty bucks for your thoughts?" Mark walks up the hall toward Cole. Cole shrugs off his jitters and nods at the man he will always consider his brother. "How is she holding up?"

"Good." He takes the coffee Mark hands him. "They need to do another exam. I just wanted to give her some privacy." He shakes his head, chasing away the images from his head. "There's a lot of people...down there." He makes an action with his hands. "I thought I might murder someone." He rubs his hand over his scalp. "I just want her, *them*, to be okay."

Mark's hand lands heavily on his shoulder, giving it a tight squeeze, "Savi's a fighter, and it stands to reason that little spitfire in there will be a fighter too, just like

Mama." He grins, making Cole feel like he's got a whole extra set of balls right now. "Besides, you think any of those doctors would piss off the Green Beret in the delivery room?"

Cole laughs, letting the tension go.

"Excuse me, Daddy?" A nurse peeks her head out the door. She looks like a pixie. "It's time."

"Go make me an uncle." Mark smacks his shoulder. "Seriously, give Savi a kiss for me."

"Yeah." Cole finds himself grinning. *Holy shit*, I'm gonna to be a dad.

The clock reads seven, and they've been at this for five hours. Savannah's exhausted, Cole is beyond beat, which is odd because he can usually be up for sixty some-odd hours and still have no problem functioning. But this...this is different, this is his love and his child. His mind slips away momentarily.

Mark glances at Cole through the garage window. The corner of his right eye is bleeding, his lip is cracked, and his arm hangs loose. Cole watches as Mark's mother grabs a chair and lifts it above her head. He lunges forward, kicking in the window, but by the time his eyes adjust, he sees Mark unconscious on the floor. His mother smashed a chair over her own son. A mother. It's disgusting. Cole pushes her out of the way and drops to his knees, feeling around Mark's body. Please be okay!

"Cole, Cole?" Savannah's voice pulls him from the memory. "Could you hand me some ice water?"

He nods, promising himself that his child will never go through anything like what Mark had to endure.

"Okay, Savannah, I know this has been exhausting for you, but we need to do a C-section. You can't pass her shoulders, and she is lodged in there pretty tight." Dr. Brown looks over at Cole, and he feels the blood drain from his face. "It's routine, and it's actually less stress on the baby."

Savi reaches for his hand and gives it a hard squeeze. He pushes aside all his own fear as he looks down at her scared eyes.

"Less stress for the baby and no more pushing sounds like a good plan to me." He leans down, kissing her lips. "I'll be right there with you the whole time, my love."

"Okay," she sighs, her voice so weak with exhaustion that she barely gets the single word out. "Let's do this."

Dr. Brown nods at Cole. "Okay, Dad, you go with the nurse and put on some scrubs. Savannah, we need to get you all set up for the anesthesiologist."

After thirty agonizing minutes of pacing outside the room, Dr. Brown calls Cole to come in. Savannah is lying on a table, arms strapped down, and a sheet is blocking her view of what is happening.

"Hi, baby." He moves into her view, grinning behind his mask.

"I feel funny." She grins, but he notices her whole body is shaking. He looks over at a doctor sitting next to her head.

"All normal. Some people get the shakes, some people get the shivers." The doctor extends his hand. "Dr. Melnik. I'm the anesthesiologist and an OBG as well. She's in great hands here."

"Cole Logan, the father. That's great to hear."

"Savannah?" Dr. Brown says over the sheet divider. "Tell me if you can feel this." Cole peeks over and sees the doctor poke the bottom of her belly.

"No." Her voice is shaky.

"Perfect." Dr. Brown grins at Cole but doesn't warn him when she makes the first cut.

Oh Lord! His knees buckle, but he senses Savannah is watching him, so he pulls it together…somewhat. Her eyes lock onto his, showing terror and excitement all at once.

"You will feel some pressure," Dr. Brown announces, and suddenly Savannah is being moved about, but she doesn't seem to notice too much.

Something tells him to look, and before his brain can catch up, he glances over and sees his daughter as she is pulled from her mother's womb.

Air, movement, chatter, heartbeat, everything stops when his eyes land on his little girl.

"Oh my god!" he whispers in awe.

"No matter what," Savannah makes him look down at her, "you don't leave her side. Promise me, Cole."

"I promise."

Savannah's chin starts to quiver, and she bursts into tears when she hears their baby cry for the first time. Cole has to agree, it's the best sound in the entire world.

He kisses her hand. "I'll be right back." He steps up next to the nurse, who is cleaning the baby's skin and clearing her lungs. She's crying hard, and his hands itch to scoop her up. He bites his cheek. He wants to yell at the nurse to be careful. Lord, she's only seconds old! *Let me hold her, damn it!* His blood pressure is through the roof, and he's sweating from the damn full body outfit they have him in. All he wants is...

"Here you go, Daddy." The nurse turns, holding his daughter bundled up like a burrito. "Seven pounds, one ounce, and she has a great set of lungs on her." She places her in his arms.

As soon as she's nuzzled up next to his chest, she immediately stops crying. Her little black eyes open and stare at him. Tiny pink lips just like her mother's latch onto her fist, and she starts to suck.

She's perfect.

"Hi," he whispers, feeling tears slip out of his eyes. "I'm your daddy." He raises her to his face and breathes in her smell, embedding it in her memory. "Let's go see Mommy."

Savannah cries again when he holds her out close to her chest. Her arms are still strapped down, so he lifts her up to her face, letting her have skin to skin contact.

"Hi, baby girl." Savi smiles. "Oh! She has your eyes, Cole."

Cole grins, thinking everything about their baby is Savannah. That's why she's perfect.

After a rather rough bath, *so Cole thought*, finger and footprints are done, and everything that can be measured and poked is complete, and he *finally* gets to hold her again. He's told to hang out in the room in a rocking chair to wait until Savannah is moved to her room.

The wooden rocking chair has a soothing creak to it, and soon he finds a rhythm she enjoys and they both settle in.

Her little hands are free, and one is jammed in her mouth, making the cutest sucking noise. The other rubs his shirt back and forth. He sticks his finger into her palm, and she quickly latches on, making an adorable coo sound. This breaks the dam, and he starts to cry. He's emotionally exhausted, something that never happened until Savannah came into his life.

"You have some guests." The nurse points to a viewing window.

Cole carefully stands and brings her over to the window where his mother, Abigail, and June are pressed against the glass. He laughs as they all melt over her.

"Oh, sweet one, you are going to be so loved," he whispers into her tiny ear. "Mostly by your mother and me." Her dark eyes peek up at him, almost like she understands. "Daddy's little girl, aren't ya?" She makes a tiny squeak, making his heart squeeze.

Savannah is staring out the window when he returns to her room. She looks beat, but when she spots them coming in, her face lights up.

"How is she?" she whispers, holding out her arms.

"Perfect, of course." Cole waits for the nurse to park the rolling cot next to Savi, then places her in her eager arms.

"Oh," she sniffs, "hello, my little girl."

Cole sits so he's next to them, wrapping his arm around her back. He holds out his finger to the baby, pressing it back into her grasp and loving the bond they already have.

Savannah looks up at him, showing him her beautiful face. "We did it, Cole. We made it to the other side. We're going to be okay now."

Cole kisses her shoulder and looks at his little family. "Yeah, baby, we're going to be just fine."

She beams, relaxing against him.

"Savi?" he whispers, "I think I have the perfect name for her."

"Oh?"

He leans in and whispers. She suddenly turns into his shoulder and breaks into another sob. He knows they are happy tears. It's the perfect name for her...the perfect name to remember.

***

Savannah

I head to the kitchen to retrieve a bottle of water. The morning walks Abigail and I have been taking make my body feel like it's mine again.

I tap the counter, debating do it, or don't? It's just sitting there taunting me, calling me to use it. I never have before, but it's the only way to find him on this massive property. My fingers twitch then retract. Come on, Savi, do it. *Fine*! I pick up the radio, turning it to channel seven.

"Keith?"

"Savannah?" His voice is confused. "Are you all right?"

"Yes, umm…can I see you?"

"Yeah, I'm outside by the stables."

The sun is hot, *finally*, making my face flush as I walk down the pebble path. My long skirt hugs my legs as a breeze swirls around me. My hair blinds me momentarily, as my nose detects a heavenly scent. I love the mountains. Everything feels so fresh and natural. No city smog to ruin the crisp air. No car horns or buses, just nature.

I find Keith fixing the gate, but stop to laugh when I see one of the horses nuzzling his pocket. He keeps grumbling at her to move it along. Finally, he gives up and turns to pat her nose. "You're needy today, Winnie. I don't have time to play." I rest my arms over the rail and watch. The black pony, Winnie, nips at his pocket again. "Really?" He sighs. "Fine, but don't tell anyone." He pulls out a half-eaten peanut bar and holds it to her mouth.

"I saw that." I grin and duck under the rail, heading toward them.

"She wouldn't leave me alone." He shrugs, acting like it was nothing.

"Whatever, softy, your secret is safe with me."

He rolls eyes and grabs a hammer. "So, what's up?" I dig my sandal into the dirt and think about how to start this conversation. Keith and I are close, but this is a big deal. He turns to look at me, since I haven't said anything for the past fifteen seconds. "What's the problem?"

"The wedding is in, ah…two weeks." I stumble over my words. "I, umm, I've been thinking."

He closes his eyes. "You don't have cold feet, do you?"

"No!" I laugh. "God, no." I sigh and move closer to

674

him. "I don't have any family left—from, you know—my side. You are the one I'm closest too, the one I consider my big brother." He sets the hammer down and turns his attention on me. *Screw it.* "Keith, will you walk me down the aisle?"

His face changes as my words sink in, and his eyes soften then gloss over. "It would be my honor, Savannah." I leap into his arms, and he gasps at the force. "Thank you, Keith, so, so much." He hugs me hard before he clears his throat and steps back.

"Right, well, you tell me when and where, and I'll show up." I shake my head at his comment. *Men.*

I step back but smirk. "You better."

"Wouldn't miss it for the world." He grabs his hammer and heads back to the gate. I turn on my heel, feeling so pleased at our conversation.

"Savannah?"

"Yeah?"

"Thank you."

***

"Wow," I whisper in the mirror. I hardly recognize myself. "Molly, you did an amazing job." My makeup is flawless, and my hair hangs in long curls with one side pinned up.

"Here we are." Abigail beams, holding my garment bag. She hooks it behind the privacy divider. "Would you like anything?"

"Mark wanted you to have this." June hands me a martini. "It will help with the nerves."

Oh, I love Mark.

"Hand it over," I say, then take a long sip. I'm not nervous about getting married, just the thought of standing in front of everyone gives me the jitters. Thankfully, we kept it to a small number, not that a hundred and fifty is small.

Sue gasps when I step out to show them my dress.

"Holy…" I jump at the sound of John's voice from the doorway. "Sorry, but you look great, Savannah."

I look down at the form-fitting white dress that hugs my curves. A slit stops at mid-thigh. The beading starts at the right hip, spreading up and across to my left shoulder and scattering up the halter strap. It's the only piece of New York I would allow on this day. Sue called in a favor from a friend when she got word about the dress I wanted. Four weeks later, I found it hanging in my old closet with a note.

Your mother would have gotten it for you. I just helped her.
~ Sue

Needless to say, I sobbed.

"Sue," John motions with his head, "Zack is here with his crew to set up the food. Would you show him where to go?"

"Yes, of course." She turns to me. "It's perfect, honey." I lean in and give her a kiss on the cheek.

"Thank you, Sue."

June appears from somewhere with a secret little smile. "Here." She opens a velvet bag and pulls out a deep red garter outlined with black lace. "A little something for later."

I laugh as she pushes my dress back, slipping the garter over my shoe and up my leg, just above where the slit in my skirt stops.

"I love it." I wrap my arms around her, thinking this day couldn't get any better.

"Okay," June starts to fan her eyes, "I need to grab my camera. I'll see you down there."

I move toward to the mirror, taking one last look at

myself. I start to feel a little emotional. I would sell my soul to have my mother here with me today. The more I look, the more I see her in me.

"All right, ladies, the show is about—" Keith stops at the door. I catch his reflection in the mirror. His mouth drops open. "You look very pretty, Savannah." I smile and press my lips together. He stands a little straighter then steps forward, offering me an arm. "Miss Miller, it is time."

I thread my arm through his and take a deep breath. "Don't let me trip."

"Never." He grins down at me. "Come on, your future waits downstairs."

This is our day, our moment, our time. I beam up at Keith, feeling complete.

"Okay, I'm ready."

Chapter Thirteen

Sue and Daniel have outdone themselves with decorating the entire house and grounds for our outdoor wedding. Yellow roses line the walkway leading outside to the rows and rows of chairs full of eager people patiently waiting for my arrival.

I hear Abigail scold Mark for dipping into the appetizers. I chuckle and think that only Mark would hold things up at our wedding because he's sneaking food. Bottomless pit.

I hear her behind me, and the warmth that spreads right down to my toes is worth the possible spit-up that comes along with that sound. I whirl around and see her dark eyes peeking out from her tiny white hat. "Hellooo, my little love." I lift my daughter out of Sue's arms, cradling her in mine, breathing in her scent. She warms my heart from the inside out. "Are you going to behave for Mommy and Daddy today?"

"Fat chance." Mark grins and gives me a kiss on the cheek. "She is, after all, half you," he jokes, then steps back to take in my dress. "Oh, Cole is gonna love this."

"Mark!" Abigail hisses from the doorway. "Go."

"I am, I am," he mutters, heading outside. "Relax!"

"Come here, Olivia." Sue holds out her hands, taking her from me. I feel my heart squeeze when I hear her name. My mother's name. "Come on, Grandpa," Sue calls. "You and I need to help this little thing throw some flower petals. Let's make a mess!" She throws some in the air, laughing and hugging Olivia to her. It's hard to believe she's already six weeks old. "Let's not make Daddy anxious by keeping him waiting, or he'll get Uncle Keith to stick a tracking device on you." Sue laughs at Keith, who gives a nod with a deadpan expression.

"Savannah," Daniel grasps my elbow and leans down to whisper in my ear. "I wanted to give you my gift now. Lynn got life without parole."

I lean back to look at him. "Really?"

"Yes," his face lights up as his news sinks in. The fact that I'm not overly saddened by this makes me see I've made progress. My past is behind me. I give a little smile and know I'll be all right.

"Now," he gives me a kiss on the cheek, "it's your turn to live." I wrap my arms around his waist and mutter a heartfelt thank you.

"Have no fear, your Male of Honor is here." Jake comes strolling in, looking like he jumped out of a tuxedo ad. "I'm ready when you are."

"You're late." I raise an eyebrow.

"Sorry." He blushes, and I don't even want to know. Graham slips through the door, not making eye contact. I smack Jake's arm and roll my eyes.

"Really?"

"He surprised me with a trip to L.A." He shrugs, but I see his excitement just below the surface. "We're going to be staying with his cousin, Pete. It's getting serrriiious." I give him a hug. I know how important Graham is to him.

"I'm so happy for you, Jake, I am."

Suddenly, the music starts, which brings on the butterflies. *This is it.* Keith hooks my arm and nudges me forward.

"You're up, sweetheart." He smiles down at me. Jake walks behind Sue and Olivia, with Daniel beaming beside them. Talk about excited grandparents; I can't help but grin. Then the aisle clears and my heart stops.

Cole is in his full dress military uniform. He stands strong and tall, hands at his sides. His dark eyes lock with mine, his mouth parts, and his gaze slides down my front stopping at the leg-revealing slit. A devilish grin appears, and my feet move a little faster. Keith pats my hand, giving it a gentle squeeze.

My face hurts from smiling when we finally reach the altar. Keith shakes Cole's hand, giving a little bow to me. I grab his hand and step up on my tiptoes to give him a peck on the cheek. "Thank you," I whisper, and he blinks a few times before he turns and takes his seat.

Cole holds my hand and latches his eyes onto mine. I barely hear the minister speak; I'm so fascinated with this amazing man. He turns my life right side up, and everything makes sense when he's near. He's my life, and now it's going to be official.

Cole flinches, pulling me out of my thoughts. He gives a guilty grin, forcing the minister to repeat his commands. *I can only imagine what he was thinking.* Oh, right, the vows. *Focus, Savannah.*

Cole lets out a puff of air, outing the fact that he's had a brandy. I wonder if he's nervous too. I hear his words.

"I had this recurring dream, where I meet the love of my life, and we spend eternity together. Every day together we would fall deeper and deeper in love. Problem is, as many times as I've dreamed of her, she never had a face." He pauses to collect himself. "Until one night, when I opened a file and found her. I worked like hell to get you, and I'll work like *hell* to keep you. I love you and I always will, Savannah."

Jake hands me a tissue, and I dry my cheeks. I shake my head and try to sort my thoughts. Then I find my voice.

"I always wanted to be Cinderella." I smile shyly. "I wanted to blend in with the colors around me, not be noticed. I certainly never thought I needed a prince. I lost control of my life, I lost hope. Then one day a prince came and took me to his castle. I fell passionately in love. Not only did I *become* Cinderella, but my prince saved me not once, but three times." I step closer and let my lips graze over his smooth jawbone. "I love you, Cole Logan, with all my heart...Fall, Cole, because I *promise* I'll be there to catch you." He reaches out and pulls my head to him, smashing his lips to mine. Everyone breaks into laughter and cheers as he holds me tightly. He reaches deep down in my soul, and any damage left in my heart is finally mended.

***

"Mrs. Logan." Cole's extends a hand and leads me out onto the dance floor, spinning me once and waiting for the music to start. He asked to pick the song for our slow dance. So I'm very eager to hear the song he's chosen. He tugs me closer when the first note is played. My eyes shoot up to his when I hear it. Ed Sheeran's *Thinking Out Loud*. It's perfect. We start moving, and everyone blurs, and I almost forget we are not alone. He looks down and mouths a line from the chorus. I laugh thinking how unique our tale is. *Maybe I should write my story.* He slows the pace toward the end. His hold relaxes, and his chin rests on my head. Figures become bigger and smaller around us. No one matters but us right now.

"I hate your dress," he whispers as I feel him smile into my hair.

"No, you don't."

His laughs, dipping me backward. "Yeah, I don't. You're stunning, Mrs. Logan."

"Mrs. Logan," I repeat. "I like the sound of that."

His eyes light up, remembering the first time I said that.

Jake has me laughing as he dances around me to *Stolen Dance* by Milky Chance. Mark scoops me into his arms and twirls me around in circles. I laugh at his playful face.

"Where's Melanie?" I shout over the music. He sighs and flinches.

"She has decided to head to Chicago for school." Oh no. "So, we broke it off."

"I'm sorry."

He shrugs. "She's a great person, but we got to the 'question part' of our relationship. Where do I live, why do I leave for days on end …you know the drill." His eyes soften and show me his true emotion. "You and Cole are very lucky. Sometimes I think the only way I'll find love is if I change my profession." He smirks a little, pulling his mask back down. "And we all know that won't happen." He clears his throat. "Anyway, it's for the best. I've had someone return to my life that I'm not ready for yet. So until that gets cleared up, I need to stay focused."

"Anything bad?" He nods but doesn't go further, so I leave it be. I think for a moment; I want to choose my words carefully. "This may not count for much, but I know you'll find someone. Maybe not in this town, but she's out there waiting for you to find her."

He leans down and kisses me on the cheek, but before he pulls back his gaze flicks over my shoulder. "Well, that's interesting." He turns me around, and my mouth drops open.

I gasp. "Who is that with Keith?"

"I'm not sure, but I would like to know if she has a sister," Mark mutters, fixing his jacket. I roll my eyes at him, then do a quick scan to find Cole.

My heart nearly bursts when I find him dancing with Olivia off to the side. She looks so tiny in his huge arms. He's singing her the words to *Love* by Matt White. Her little fingers are over his mouth, and he kisses each one, beaming down at her with so much love. His face lifts, almost as though he can feel me watching. He grins and mouths, "Hi, baby." I wave at them and put a hand on my chest, feeling incredibly complete.

I point over my shoulder to Keith. Cole shakes his head, just as surprised as I am.

"He's free. Keith has secrets. I've seen one once before." Mark shifts to move in front of me, before I can ask what he meant. "Quick, if he's going to spill to anyone, it's you." He pushes me in Keith's direction. I laugh, wondering why Mark cares so much.

"Hey." I tap Keith on the shoulder, and he turns and gives me a look. "Can I have a dance?"

"Mmm hmm," he murmurs quietly. I know he's on to me. Keith's hold is very tense. I can't tell if he's uncomfortable, or if he just doesn't like to dance. "Spit it out, Savi."

I fight my grin, but I really am bad at hiding my emotions. "Who's the pretty woman?"

He drops his eyes to mine. "A date."

"A date?"

"Yes."

"I didn't know you were dating anyone."

"You never asked."

"Okay." I nod, thinking that's fair. I haven't, but Keith isn't someone you talk to about feelings. "What's her name?"

"Annie."

"How did you meet?"

He sighs a little. "She runs the bakery on Mulberry Lane."

I think for a moment. "Is it serious?"

He actually smiles. "No, Savannah, we're just having fun."

"Fun?" I sound like I disapprove, when really I simply find myself feeling protective. I don't want anyone to hurt Keith.

"Yes." He nods and takes a step backward, pulling me along with him. "She's just a friend."

"Okay."

His eyebrow raises as he peers down at me. "Okay?"

"Yes. As long as she's good to you, then I'm happy for you."

"Thanks." He laughs, but I can see that comment hit him deep. He knows I love him.

Daniel interrupts, asking to cut in.

After an hour of dancing, I take a break. The moon is bright, illuminating the thin fabric of the canopy draped above us. Twinkle lights sparkle from the trees, and the lanterns from Cole's proposal hang throughout the forest. The stars are out in the cloudless sky, scattered around the mountains. I step off the wooden dance floor Daniel made, removing my shoes and walking to the edge of the lawn. The grass is cool, and I shiver slightly. They have a spectacular view of the valley. Dipping my head back, I stare up and try to feel her. I recall all the things I love about her...her smile, the sound of her laugh, the way she loved to sing. "I'm happy," I whisper, "really, *really* happy, Mom." I take a deep breath and gather myself. Taking one last view, I turn on my heel to find him watching me a few feet away. His jaw flexes with a twitch of his lips.

"Come home with me?"

The house is surprisingly quiet. Cole takes my hand and leads me downstairs.

"Where are we going?"

He takes our joined hands and gives my diamond wedding band a kiss. "I want to give you my gift." He walks to the last room on the left. I've been in these offices before. He turns to look at me. "This is your room. No one will bother you. It's so you'll never forget." He opens the door and steps out of the way. I grab the doorframe to stabilize myself as I take in the room. "I picked the colors, but June did the rest. If you don't—"

"No," I huff, feeling my voice run off. "It's perfect." I cup my mouth as I step forward. The red soundproof room is huge, with a wall full of books, a seating area filled with gold pillows, and a fireplace. Gracing the center is a beautiful black grand piano.

He pushes off the wall and strolls up to me with a swagger. "I told you I'd give you the world if you came back to me." I want to ask what he means by that, but his hand reaches around my neck while the other slides down my leg, stopping at the garter. "What do we have here?" He drops to his knees to get a better look. He begins to slide his finger under it, but I move his hand to the side.

"Ah, ah, baby, with your teeth."

His eyes turn dark as night. "God, I love you."

My name is Savannah Miller,
and this is my happily ever after.

The End

Want to read the spin off from the Broken Trilogy?

Honor

Blackstone Series

By J.L. Drake

About the Author

J. L. Drake was born and raised in Nova Scotia, Canada, later moving to Southern California where she now lives with her husband and two children.

When she is not writing she loves to spend time with her family, travelling or just enjoying a night at home. One thing you might notice in her books is her love of the four seasons. Growing up on the east coast of Canada, the change in the seasons is in her blood and is often mentioned in her writing.

An avid reader of James Patterson, J.L. Drake has often found herself inspired by his many stories of mystery and intrigue. She hopes you will enjoy her books as much as she has enjoyed writing them.

Website:
http://www.authorjldrake.com/

Facebook:
https://www.facebook.com/JLDrakeauthor

Twitter:
https://twitter.com/jodildrake_j

Goodreads
http://www.goodreads.com/author/show/8300313.J_L_D
rake

Instagram:
@j.l.drake

Pinterest:
JLDrakeAuthor

TSU:
@JLDrake